B20502564 $4

KIRITH KIRIN

BY

JIM GRIMSLEY

Meisha Merlin Publishing, Inc
Atlanta, GA

This is a work of fiction. All the characters and events portrayed in this book are fictitious. Any resemblance to real people or events is purely coincidental.

With thanks to Henry Camp, consultant to the Wise.

KIRITH KIRIN

An MM Publishing Book
Published by Meisha Merlin Publishing, Inc.
PO Box 7
Decatur, GA   30031

Editing & interior layout by Stephen Pagel
Copyediting & proofreading by Teddi Stransky
ISBN: 1-892065-16-9

http://www.MeishaMerlin.com

First MM Publishing edition: May 2000

Printed in the United States of America
0 9 8 7 6 5 4 3 2 1

Library of Congress Cataloging-in Publication Data

Grimsley, Jim, 1955-
Kirith Kirin / by Jim Grimsley.
p. cm.
ISBN 1-892065-16-9 (alk. paper)
I. Title.
PS3557.R4949 K57 2000
813'.54—dc21

00-009018

Table of Contents

Maps	10
1. Kinth's Farm	15
2. Arthen	39
3. Camp	63
4. Kyyvi	81
5. Illyn Water	95
6. Wyyvisar	109
7. Aediamysaar	143
8. Suvrin Sirhe	167
9. Nevyssan's Point	191
10. Fort Gnemorra	217
11. Jiiviisn Field	225
12. Thanaarc	241
13. Inniscaudra	263
14. Kehan Kehan	283
15. Shenesoeniis	319
16. Laeredon	345
17. Telkyii Tars	253
18. Chaenhalii	375
19. Narvosdilimur	391
20. Charnos	409
21. Kleeiom	423
22. Aerfax	433
23. Senecaur	441
24. Ivyssa	451
25. Chalianthrothe	473

26. Montajhena   487

27. Seumren   493

28. Thenduril Hall   495

Afterword: Aneseveroth   499

Appendix 1: Glossary   507

Appendix 2: Jisraegen History   532

Appendix 3: Jisraegen Calendar   541

Appendix 4: High Places

          at the Time of the 34th Change   543

Appendix 5: Magic   547

Appendix 6: Translator's Note   553

Author's Bio   555

For Corey, Sarah, and Kathryn

KIRITH KIRIN

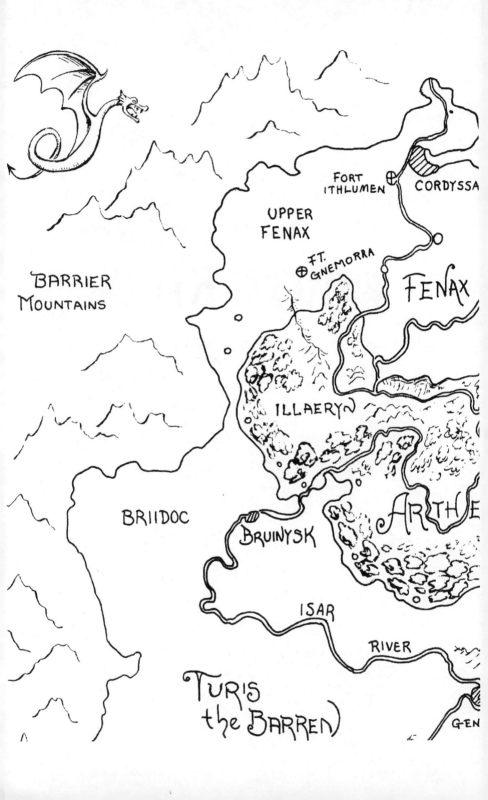

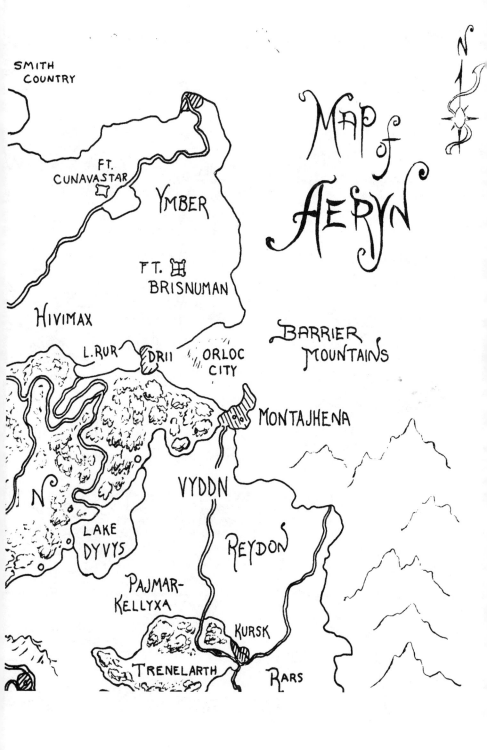

TURIS
the BARREN
ARROTH
L. MUR
CUNEVADRIM
L. ASHMYR
TELIAR
OSAR
RIVER
KARNS
CHAR
BLACK
SPUR
MOUNTAINS
BAY
OF

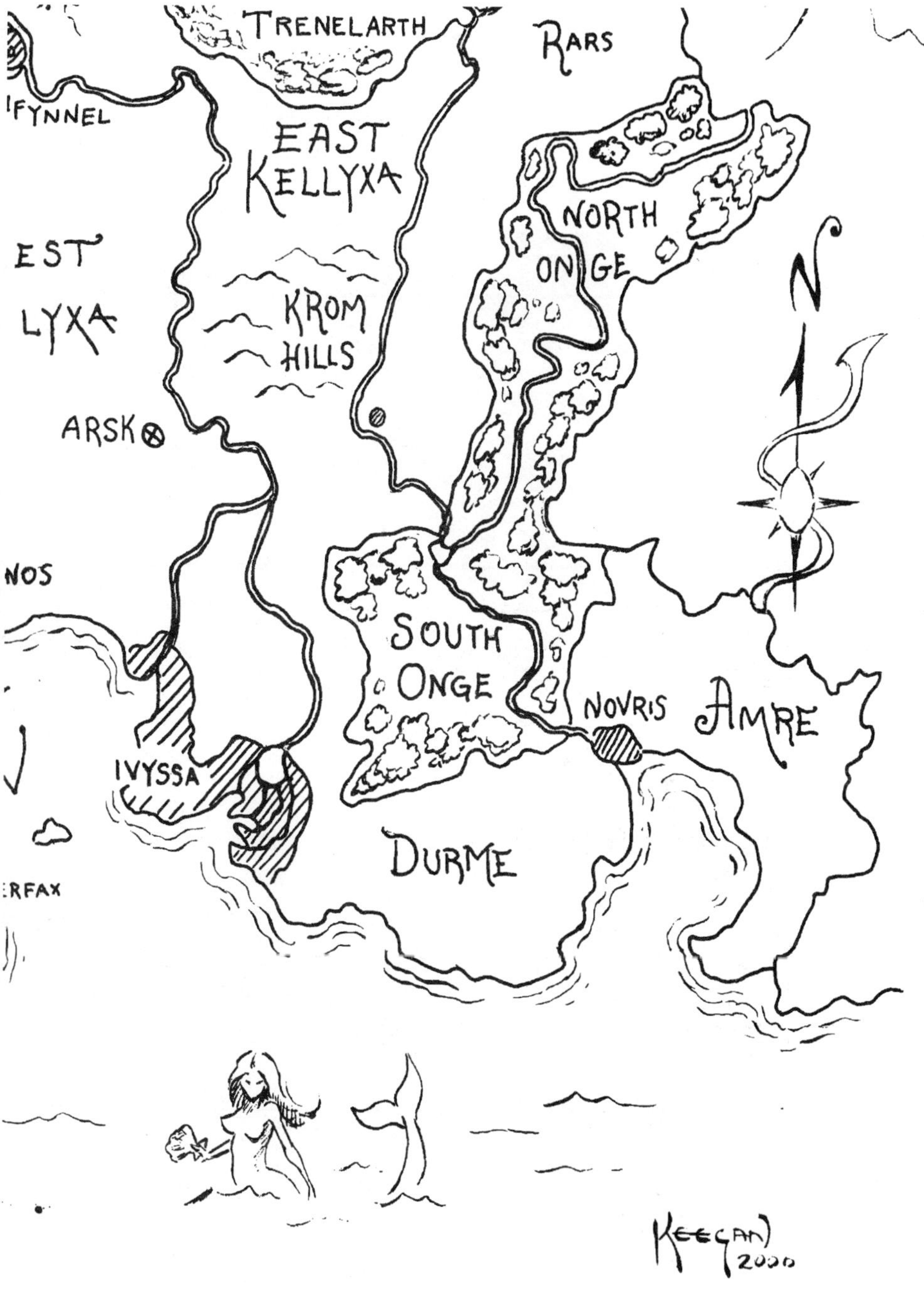
TRENELARTH
RARS
IFYNNEL
EAST KELLYXA
NORTH ONGE
EST LYXA
KROM HILLS
ARSK
NOS
SOUTH ONGE
NOVRIS
AMRE
IVYSSA
DURME
RFAX
N
KEEGAN 2000

CHAPTER ONE
KINTH'S FARM

1

In my country many lies are told about me now that I have become rich and famous, and a traveler in the northern part of the world is apt to hear every sort of fabrication about my birth and childhood. Looking back from so long after, I can hardly credit even my own memories, but I know that most of what is written could not be true. There were no storms blowing up out of nowhere, or fires on the eastern mountains, nor did trumpets sound in the under-land at the gates of the dead. No one had any visions about me, or foresaw any future for me, and no signs appeared in the sky.

As far as I was ever able to learn, the evening of my birth was balmy, the spring planting having begun on my father's farm when in the afternoon my mother Sybil felt birthing pains begin. She took to her bed and her mother, Fysyyn, helped with the delivery. This was a few days after Vithilonyi in the three hundred ninth year of the reign of Queen Athryn Ardfalla XXXIV. That evening my father, Kinth son of Daegerle, got supper for himself and my soon-to-be siblings. Fysyyn warned Mother that I looked to be headed for a hard time right from the start. Sybil lost a lot of blood but after a short intense labor gave birth to a healthy infant. Grandmother cleaned her up and changed her bedding and Mother held me and fell asleep.

I was born near enough to midwatch to make the event some what remarkable; the village scrivener argued over which day to write on my birth record. I was my mother's seventh child and her last; her fourth child by my father Kinth. One other of Kinth's children was born dead. This fulfilled a minor prophecy, since a fortuneteller had foretold she would bear seven living children, the last a sturdy boy who would be first to leave her. She named me Jessex, after my father's uncle.

My grandmother was Fysyyn, a Wise Woman of the Aerenoth Clan who got children from the famous hunter Veneth but never married him. This is a notable fact, for the Queen's magistrate hanged Veneth when he refused to obey the ban on entering Arthen Wood, and the lack of wedding beads was what saved Fysyyn from a similar fate. My mother was only a girl when her father died and she grieved him all her life. After his death, Fysyyn moved with her two children to Mikinoos, a village on the Chali Road north of the Forest. She had enough gold to buy a house and raised her children there, renting rooms to travelers. Mama told pleasant stories of the boarding house but Grandmother hardly ever spoke about it. Those years were marred by the disappearance of her son, Sivisal, again into Arthen, where many folks had vanished in bygone days, if stories were true. He went out hunting and never returned. His abrupt departure shocked my mother and she retreated into silence that lasted for years. Until one day she met my father in the Mykinoos market.

Kinth was a late child of a father with many children, and had it not been that a bachelor uncle adopted him, he would have inherited no land of his own. As it was, he moved to Mikinoos to live with his uncle and met and loved my mother.

Mother was a beauty and might have married many a man, or so my grandmother liked to claim, though even I knew the truth from overhearing family quarrels. Everyone in Mikinoos believed both Mother and Grandmother to be witches, and witches do not make good wives, as the saying goes. No one supposed them to be very powerful witches, not the sort who could summon storms or shake the ground. Not the sort who could stand on the High Place like the wizards in stories. They were the kind of witches who were convenient to blame when the neighbor's milk soured or someone's crops went bad. Once upon a time such women would have been respected in our community, but under the present circumstances, with the Queen opposed to all religion and most Wisdom, witches were looked upon with suspicion. My Grandmother liked to act mysterious about the rumors and used to shake her head in warning whenever I asked questions about her magic powers. "Some things aren't for talking about," she said.

When my father and mother married, Fysyyn sold the boarding-house to the grain-master Kraf for a tidy parcel of gold, as she used to brag, smacking her paper-thin lips.

Mother and Fysyyn went to live on Kinth's farm after he and Mother reached the appropriate nuptial agreements. They settled on the northern form of marriage, under which Papa agreed to share his house with her, and to raise whatever children she bore under his roof, and each agreed to respect the other's right to occasional liaisons with others. Their eldest child would inherit the farm after both of them were dead, but Mother would hold title if she outlived Papa. This was considered a good bargain since Kinth was from a family who served in Lady Kiril Karsten's household before the Lady vanished, whereas Mother's family was not particularly distinguished except for a dubious claim of kinship with the Chieftainess of the Svyssn.

I spent an unremarkable babyhood in the usual gurgling manner. My mother was a long time recovering from my birth, and kept me beside her till she was able to get out of bed. Sometimes I dream I remember her from those earliest days, a tall pale woman with dark hair and large brown eyes, propped against fat feather pillows. A gentle person, not meant for the fate that fell to her. She held me carefully and sang in my ear. I remember her wonderful fine hair spilling free and wild over her shoulders, floating soft in the air. When I was older, at night after the supper dishes were cleaned and put away, she would sit by the fire spinning thread or doing some other hand work, listening with me to the stories Grandmother told.

It was from Grandmother I learned Grandfather Veneth had been renowned as a hunter and that her own father Aretaeo was more famous still, so famous it was dangerous to say his name out loud. She told me tales of Cunavastar and the YY-Sisters, the Forty Thousand and the Awakening, the Twelve who did not die, the Uncreated and the Long Wars, Arthen and the City in Arthen, the Wars of the Sorcerers, the Priests who made the song that offended God. She told me the history of Falamar Inuygen who made himself King, of the Lady of Curaeth, of the Prophet and his book of riddles, of Lord Mordwen of the Eye, the Drii People, and Pel Pelathayn. On a rare occasion she would tell one of the tales concerning the Red King, warning me never to mention the King's name aloud, not even to my father or mother. Long ago the King had ridden into Arthen, to wait for the Queen to tire and call him out of the Woodland to rule again. But now the Queen hated his memory to the point that it was treason to mention his name. "No more stories about Kirith Kirin," Grandmother would say when I pressed her for more. "The Queen has spies outside every farmer's house; she knows everything we say and think, and she hates nothing worse than his memory."

Mama for the most part let Grandmother have her way in picking stories to tell, though now and then, when I was listening to some gory account of a battle between Jurel Durassa and Falamar Inuygen, Mama would shiver and say, "Hush, you'll make him have bad dreams."

"This one?" Grandmother shook her head. "Not my Jessex. It would take more than a few stories to give this boy bad dreams."

"Then stop before you give them to me."

"I'm only telling the truth. In the old days a child was thought ignorant if he couldn't name the wizards from ten thousand years ago and count them off on his fingers. Nowadays we aren't even allowed say the King's name. Why do we live like frightened animals in these modern times?"

I always thought, mostly from his expression and his way of shaking his pipe, that Kinth agreed with Grandmother, and I know for a fact he hated Queen Athryn the same as everybody else. Kinth was a tall, broad-shouldered man with clear blue eyes and the same wide-boned face that marked his clan for miles about. He had a dark streak of temper, and when he was teaching me the outdoor work of the farm I was always wary of his broad flat hands. He could be patient to a point but after his patience was gone he punctuated his lessons with sharp pops across the back of the head, to jog the memory, he said. But he was a good father in the distant way of fathers.

If he had been left to tend his land and prosper I think Papa would have been a happy man and bothered nobody. We were better off than most, having a big house and rich fields, three barns, twenty head of cattle, four oxen, half a dozen horses, even a mill for a while till father sold it to avoid the taxes. Besides Grandmother's cottage, there was a house where Sim, the eldest son, lived with his wife Kare. Many folks were worse off, as Mama and Papa reminded us at supper. As it happened, however, we were not left to prosper in peace and neither was anybody else.

We north-men have a saying, still current, that trouble begins and ends in the south, and this is true whether we are ruled by Red King or Blue Queen. But in the days of my boyhood this was no longer simply tavern talk. Queen Athryn had ruled for a long time, and while I did not understand what was wrong with that, I knew that something was. There was a law governing the change from queen to king and back again, and she had broken it. As a ruler, her open avarice was a perpetual scandal. She had suspended the Yneset a generation ago and made laws and set taxes as she pleased, without consulting anybody. She had a tax collector for every village and district and a new table of taxes every year, to pay for her palaces in Ivyssa and on Kmur Island, to pay for her wardrobe, her court, to pay for her armies, her numerous forts and the continuous patrols around the border of Arthen. Yet, complain as they might, every farmer on the Fenax Plain paid his or her taxes promptly for fear the Queen would send her Wizard north to devastate our country. When he finished in Turis only the Verm could live there. Stories of the Verm were used to frighten children into obedience.

Taxes are bad enough. But a people will put up with a lot if they are left to live freely, to ride about their country as they wish and hunt wherever they choose. When the Queen banned all entry into Arthen, the north country came near rebellion. The Arthen forest is the heart of our memory and folks resented being kept out of it.

The year I began to tend flocks on my own, rumors of a new rebellion in the north were flying thick and fast. In the mountain city Cordyssa, an army of rebels was said to be in training, and the stories drew women and men hoping to join from across the Fenax Plain. My half-brother Jarred could talk of nothing but running away to Cordyssa.

In response to the rumors, Queen Athryn tripled her garrisons in Cordyssa and in the northern fortresses. In our part of the world, so close to Arthen, the Queen had dared build no forts, but since she could not leave us lightly watched she quartered troops in our houses during the months of unrest when her tax collectors were making their annual rounds.

I remember scarce detail about the ill-bred southern louts our family was lucky enough to obtain as its patriotic allotment; for me they were mere uncouth blurs beside an otherwise cozy fireplace. But my mother later told stories of how the southerners ate everything with sticks and knew only enough of Upcountry, our language, to get themselves well-fed. They lived in the barn with the pigs and cows. We were able to house them that way because we had money and could bribe the officers; poorer folks weren't so lucky and had to give up their beds.

That same year Grandmother Fysyyn took sick and died.

We had wonderful talks those last days before she fell into her final sleep. I don't know whether she was in much pain; Grandmother was not the kind to show much, and knew a medicine for everything. Dying loosened her tongue. She told me the story of the fall of the Jisraegen from beginning to end. What I learned from her served me well in later years. Not least was a cryptic statement I would not understand for a long time. She gripped my arm and told me she was not a real magician but her grandmother was, not Matvae, Kiniseth's wife, but the other one. She dare not say

her real grandmother's name. I sat with her day and night, listening
to her labored breath; in the end I stayed with her more even than
Mother did, though of course Mother had the farm to run. As
Grandmother's death drew near she dreamily talked about mundane matters, like my grandfather's habit of coughing in her ear in
bed and the best technique for working the milk out of a deer's tit.
Her death, when it finally came, was welcome relief; she was wracked
with a sharp cough and could find no relief for the stiffness in her
joints for weeks, fading into long periods of sleep, and one day
dying while she was sitting on the chamber pot. We dressed her
body in white cloth for the burning, as north-folk have always done;
white is the color of death, we think.

As I remember, the Blue Queen's soldiers came to Grandmother's
burning out of respect for her age, age being highly prized in the
south. By certain signs the soldiers let it be known we might conduct any ceremony we pleased and so we lit lamps on the night of
Fysyyn's burning, one at her head and one at her feet, a custom
thought necessary to help YY-Mother find Grandmother's soul. The
Blue Cloaks helped to tie together the pyre, and when we hoisted
Grandmother's thin body to the bed of sticks they sang the old song
with us: "Kimri," "Light in the Darkness," sung, as the saying goes,
when there is need for hope. This touched my mother and father
some, since the soldiers could have gotten into a lot of trouble for
singing that hymn. They could not sing it very well, of course, since
the southerners all have a tin ear for sound. They whispered words
of superstition in their own harsh language, standing reverently as
the flames fanned out over my Grandmother, Fysyyn daughter of
Donraele, child of Aretaeo.

When word got out that the Blue Cloaks had come to her fu-
neral and we were criticized, Mother simply said there was no help
for it. Neighbors will talk about the wind if they can't think of
anything else to talk about. My father muttered something under his
breath, his face darkening.

The farmers had been meeting secretly for some time by then,
according to stories I heard later. The meetings evolved innocently
in the course of hiding the priest who journeyed secretly from village to village to bless the recently dead, married and born. Priests
were executed if Queen Athryn caught them.

Our neighbor Commiseth was one of those who met to hide
the priest, and soldiers were quartered in his house, too. His contingent was not so well-behaved as the southerners who lived with

us, however, and he had four soldiers as his allotment, partly because he was too poor to bribe anybody. Worse, a young lieutenant numbered among the four, and he set himself up like a petty baron in Commiseth's household, ordering Commiseth about like a servant. One heard horrible stories about the treatment the family endured. Soon the lieutenant took a fancy to the eldest daughter Sergil. At first the certainty of displeasure of the parents was enough to deter him. But as the days passed, the lieutenant became convinced Sergil thought he was nice and set out to win her to his bed. When she protested he took her there anyway. The priest, who was hiding on Commiseth's farm at the time, tried to help the girl and was discovered.

When Commiseth learned what had happened he tried to kill the lieutenant as any decent fellow would have. Because of the presence of the priest, the lieutenant accused the family of treason and hanged Commiseth's sons in front of him, and raped his wife, and killed Commiseth.

The wife and remaining children were marched off to the south, along with the priest, where later the Queen's courts declared them traitors and had them sold into slavery. Sergil never finished the journey, dying on the march. I passed their house sometimes when I was grazing the flock in neighboring pastures. Vines overran the sod walls in a season, and every window lay open to wind and rain. Grass grew waist deep in the door-yard; the whole aspect was sad and broken, and we told tales that it was haunted.

The Queen prospered from the best year of tax collections in history. She commissioned Charnos shipwrights to build a royal yacht for sailing across the bay to Aerfax in the summer. After tax season the soldiers withdrew from the vicinity of Arthen, shutting themselves up in the forts. While we no longer had Blue Cloaks as guests in our houses, their presence was evident everywhere. Each day patrols swept across Athryn's girdle round the Forest, the patrols maintaining vigilance lest anyone enter Arthen against the Queen's wishes.

In spite of the turmoil in the world and Grandmother's death, in spite of tragedies among our neighbors, our life on Papa's farm proceeded in something like a familiar order. I grew into my work, from feeding chickens to hoeing weeds to forking hay. I learned to ride and track, with Sim to teach me, a more patient master than my father would have been. Even the presence of soldiers at our table had little effect on our secure family. Now and then, however, a shadow crossed my vision—the look on Mama's face at tax time,

the dread Papa evinced when blue-cloaked soldiers rode across our
farmland. Tales Grandmother told me ran through my head, cities
in the forest and a high white tower, shrines in ancient fields, tribes
of silent, invisible folk slipping beneath tree shadow. Even then,
from the earliest moments I can remember, my schooling led me to
consciousness of a world of many powers.

My mother herself gained a strength with the years, a keenness
of vision, along with the beauty that emerges beyond youth. She
paid no mind to the names people called her, laid no charms on
anybody, soured no milk nor ruined anyone's crops. Not even when
she had good reason. At times I could see her restless with some
thought she could not say. Once I saw her in her room holding a
box, but when I came in she put it away, and the look she gave me
reminded me of Grandmother telling the story of the Jisraegen
priests when they were making the song that frightened God.

I turned out to be a fair shepherd, better than my full-sister
Mikif who had the job till I showed a talent for it. The sheep would
come to me whether I called them or not, and the dogs knew what
I wanted them to do without my having to tell them. I never considered this a praiseworthy accomplishment since it came so easily,
but my father remarked on it more than once, and after my ninth
year the flock of some two dozen was entirely entrusted to me.

I wandered throughout the countryside, spending summer nights
away from home under the starry sky, learning to make my own
campfire and to hunt for small game. We would stay off grazing
for days, me and the sheep and the hound Axfel, a huge, hulking
ribcage of a dog, three years old when I was ten, with tongue enough
to trail the ground and a snout that would have done justice to a
wolf. We wandered in the farthest pastures of my father's farm and
beyond to the hillsides that approached Arthen herself. At night one
could count the watchfires along the girdle, the Blue Cloaks never
ceasing their vigilance. It was said that the soldiers hated duty on the
Arthen patrols worse than any other post in the Queen's service.
The Woodland swelled vast and dark beyond their puny fires, shadows of branches engulfing the world like a sea.

Once I asked my mother why the Queen found it necessary to
watch Arthen so closely, why didn't her army ever go inside it? She told
me the forest would guile them if they did, would lead them farther and
farther into its heart and they would never come out again; that the
forest called to them day and night, because Arthen was their home the
same as it was ours. Many of the Blue Cloaks were Jisraegen, too.

The Queen feared something beyond the border. But Mama refused to tell me what it was, and none of my brothers and sister had ever heard anything but stories.

By then I knew all the stories I would ever need to know, or so I thought. At night, gazing at the dark old forest, I counted the campfires and watched the tree-shadows, feeling as if I were waiting, though I had no idea what I was waiting for.

2

The trouble in the north grew worse with the years, and by the time I was fourteen I understood enough to worry. Taxes were higher than ever, and grumbling across the Fenax had become heated enough that the Queen enlarged the fortress garrisons again. She had not yet quartered more soldiers with us but rumors were she might do so before summer. The whole Fenax rode on an undercurrent of murmuring, rumors the Queen intended to bleed the country white from taxes one more year and then send Drudaen to rid her of this burdensome northern rule. Or, worse, rumors that she was saving all this gold to buy a Tervan stone so that Drudaen could build a High Place in the north. The taxes swelled again, when already an honest family could hardly feed itself from its own share of the harvest, let alone have anything for market.

My father and his friends had begun to meet again once the soldiers were out of our houses, to remember Commiseth to each other and to keep abreast of the news. At this time it became harder to keep the new priest in any safety where we lived, and many priests were caught by the Blue Cloaks and hanged from the walls of the forts. It was a shame, my mother said, to hear of good people hanged from Fort Cunavastar's walls, with birds feeding on their bodies. Even the meanest shrines, merely closed before, were destroyed during these years. No one understood why, at the time, and I can remember my parents discussing this new turn of events. Our temples were simple places where lamps were lit at night, when this was allowed. Many of these places were very ancient and their destruction caused much grief.

In Cordyssa, the major northern city, Her Majesty's tax on plain bread was twice the market price of wheat per stone, with the Queen being the largest vendor of wheat as well. That year there were over two hundred separate levies special to Cordyssa and her citizens, including a fixed tax on hand-mirrors, white hen's eggs, garden plots, excessive ownership of silverware and children's toys beyond a maximum number fixed by royal decree. A tax assessor could enter the house of any common citizen at will. This caused unrest enough, and incidents aplenty. But it was the wheat tax that broke the city's back. When people could barely afford to eat, they could no longer afford the luxury of fear.

Soon came the quiet news that another army was forming in Cordyssa, not like the early rumors told in taverns but a soft ripple spreading from farmers group to farmers group across the Fenax. The clans and the country posses shared their news. Papa attended the meetings of his own secret circle but refused to encourage any of his friends to head for Cordyssa. Jarred talked idly at supper of enlisting himself but my mother told him that would be utter foolishness, since any war or threat of war would bring Drudaen Keerfax to the north. After that the farmland we treasured would be barren desert from Arthen to the walls of the mountains. Help would come out of Arthen, if it came at all. The rest of the family listened to her speech in shock. Mother had never before mentioned Arthen in this manner. Jarred looked sheepish and never brought up the subject of heading to Cordyssa again.

It is odd, to one as young as I was then, to know that one's parents can be afraid. Grandmother Fysyyn's stories took on more weight with each passing day, and I began to understand that we had been in the midst of a kind of war all our lives. The Queen in Ivyssa was not satisfied with what she could take from us in taxes, in corn or in gold. If she could have taxed the blood in our veins or had payment in pounds of flesh, she would have done it. Why did she want so much?

I learned to be afraid myself. Sometimes, leading the flocks through the green hillsides, I felt the wide world hovering around me, ominous on every side. Sometimes I was afraid with a fear I didn't understand and would sing Kimri alone with my hound and my sheep, in sight of the shimmering sea of Arthen's blue-green leaves. I was fourteen that year, nearing manhood as we define it. I could hardly have guessed, when I was able to drink the watered wine of the fourteen-year-old at my naming supper, that this would be the last such celebration I would pass on Kinth's farm with my family.

While I was grazing the sheep in the hillsides later in the spring, a strange man mounted on a handsome horse rode into our farmyard, leading an even handsomer horse behind him, a black stallion with silver trappings, the horse of a lord or a rich merchant. The stranger said he was my mother's brother Sivisal, and at the sight of him my mother burst into tears.

The first I learned of this was when Jarred came running toward me across the outer meadow. I had not planned to return home for several days and was surprised to see him. When I spied him headed toward me across the swale I thought some trouble had come up at home, that soldiers had come to live at the house again, or worse, and Jarred's expression and haste only made me the more fearful. When he came near enough to make himself heard, he shouted, "Jessex, we're to gather up the flock and take it home, now. Our uncle Sivisal has come here and he's asking for you."

"Sivisal? Our uncle?"

"He came from Arthen. But he won't talk about it. He asks for you by name as if he knew you all your life."

"Does Mama know him? Is it really her brother?"

"Mama fell down in the milk when she saw him, and you should have heard her scream. Father came running in from the planting, he thought the Blue Cloaks had killed us all. Now they have Uncle Sivisal shut away in the house, in case any of the Queen's men happen to ride by. Uncle Sivisal isn't afraid though."

We gathered the flock for our return while he described the whole scene for me, from the beginning, our lost uncle riding into our farmyard with horses only noble folk could own, and with a rust-colored cloak streaming from his shoulders. We had all heard the story a thousand times, from Grandmother and from Mother, how he vanished while hunting in Arthen years ago.

The poor sheep rambled home confused with half a meal in their bellies. We hurried them relentlessly through the split-log gates into the pen, where their dried clover would not seem as rich to them as the sweet grass of the hillsides. Axfel, seven years old by now, but still fit and able, nipped at the heels of stragglers and lay down with his chin on his paws to keep watch on the farmyard.

In the stable Jarred showed me the fine horses Uncle Sivisal had brought. One of them was a well-built sorrel stallion, sturdy and of good stock, but the other beat him by a stade. He was a stallion taller than any horse I had ever seen. Even the horses of Papa's rich relatives could not compare with this one. His coat was glossy black and had a shine as if it were carefully brushed every hour, culminating in an extravagant black waterfall of mane. Silver trappings hung beside him in the stall, a shine like nothing I had ever seen. The horse

had been offered the freshest hay and sweetest grasses and deigned
to eat a mouthful now and then. He had fine eyes, a calm gray color
I had never seen before on a horse, and the shape of his head was
aristocratic, with delicate flaring nostrils and a sensitive, disdainful
mouth. My father knew good horses from growing up in Curaeth
and had begun to teach me points a horseman will note. This horse
was the finest in every way that I had ever seen.

"Don't stand there staring forever." Jarred pulled me along by
the sleeve. In the fading afternoon we walked through the yard to
the house. I don't remember feeling any particular fear. I asked
Jarred if our uncle looked like Grandmother Fysyyn. He said he
had not noticed.

Papa was in the house, and so was my oldest brother Sim, unusual since hours of daylight were left when good work could be
done in the fields. The stranger my uncle sat in Father's chair beside
the hearth, where a fire burned even in that season, his large frame
lounging quiet and easy. His brown hands cradled a mug of cool ale
from the cellar. Mother hovered over him as if he might dissolve.
She called me to her side and presented me. "This is Jessex, my
youngest child," she said, and he gave me a long inspection. He said
nothing. Something in his eyes gave me to know I need not hold
myself shy before him, quiet as children are taught to be when among
adults, and so I inspected him back with pretty much the same thor-
oughness. "This is your Uncle, Sivisal son of Veneth."

Sivisal was taller than Father and a little older, with a lean belly
and broad shoulders, powerful legs and arms like a soldier's. Something in his dress reminded me of soldiers as well. He wore a
brown leather tunic laced with bright beaded strings, and leggings
of tough leather, good for riding through brush country. A crossbow of polished wood propped against the stone hearth, decorated with metal inlay, some collected talismans dangling from the
stock; a sheath of arrows tipped with stiff feathers stood there, too.
Sivisal had a handsome, dark face with heavy brows and deep-set
eyes that seemed to take in everything at once. He looked so much
like my mother I would have taken them for twins; the only difference lay in the weathered skin of his face that contrasted with my
mother's smooth and prosperous complexion.

If he had asked for me by name when he rode in he showed no
sign of any particular interest in me now. He sat in that crowd of
strangers with complete ease and without any need to say much. I
decided he might be testing us and therefore refused to be curious

myself. Uncle Sivisal asked my father how often the patrols came by, and whether the watchfires along Arthen were visible from the farm at night. His accent was curious, as if Upcountry were not his common tongue. Later Papa told him some of the stories that had been current in our part of the country in recent times, the hanging of Commiseth and his family, the quartering of troops, the general poverty and stories of trouble in Cordyssa. Much of this Sivisal seemed already to know, except the story of the lieutenant and pretty Sergil. That made him angry, I think.

Sim and Jarred laid supper on the table, Mother hardly glancing in their direction. She said, "Sivisal, I can't believe it's really you. If only Mother were here, she would think you so handsome."

"I'm lucky to leave Arthen at all," he said quietly. "Except for the grain patrols, no one gets out."

Father smiled at Mother. "At least the old stories don't come from nothing. The Prince is still alive."

Uncle Sivisal studied his cup for a long time and his eyes filled with quiet pride. "Yes. He's still alive, and nothing Queen Athryn can do will touch him while we live to defend him."

Jarred and I looked at each other.

Uncle Sivisal gave me a long, cool inspection. "Do you know where I come from?" he asked.

"From Arthen," I said, my voice very small.

He nodded. "Did your brother tell you I asked for you by name?"

"Yes sir. Why?" Voice diminishing still, as the rest of my family fell silent.

"Never mind, for now. I've been sent to see if you can ride that horse I brought with me. When we've tested you on his back, I'll tell you more."

After that there was a lot of talk, little of which I understood. I was thinking about the horse with his fine gray eyes. Mother protested that I was only fourteen, and Father was saying I could sit a horse better than he could. Jarred predicted I would break my head and Mikif said she didn't think I'd be brave enough to get on this horse at all, but she would. I watched Uncle Sivisal and felt a vague stirring within me, as if I were understanding the purpose for which he had come. "Answer me, boy. I've been sent here to call you by name and to see whether you ride that horse I brought. Do you want to give it a try?"

"Yes," I said, very nearly breathless.

"All right," Uncle Sivisal said. "We'll test you now. No use delaying." Without a word he rose up from the chair.

I followed him into the farmyard and everyone else came out to watch. Uncle Sivisal ran lightly to the stable. In the doorway he placed a ring on his finger, drawn out of a pouch at his waist. He polished the stone against his tunic and went into the barn. Soon he emerged, leading the big black horse, bare-backed, Sivisal's ringed hand on the horse's silver-studded reins. My heart misgave me at the horse's size and I almost ran for Mama's skirts again, but I kept before me the image of the horse's calm, gray eyes. When Sivisal led the stallion close to me, I could see the horse watching, as if all this fuss amused him. The horse looked deeply into me. I knew he would bear me then and was not afraid. When Sivisal signaled me I lightly found his broad back and buried my hands in his mane, like the fine thread my mother spun, soft and richly twisted. The others watched as if I had become magical. I took the reins Uncle Sivisal offered me. My hands were trembling. The horse cantered around the yard and galloped to the kitchen creek. He was aware of me and everything in me. He tolerated me and kept me on his back for reasons known only to him. We headed a way toward the hills leading to the Woodland. Finally I walked him back to Sivisal, who bowed. "Well, Jessex, it seems you have known this horse before in some other life."

"What does it mean?" asked Mother.

Uncle Sivisal looked at the sky. "I shouldn't tell you here where any bird could hear us and go off wagging its tongue. But this is a son of the King Horse. As a common rule such a horse would not permit Jessex on his back."

Wind was blowing. We returned to the house, Mama calling me to her side and walking me to the kitchen with her full skirts sweeping round me. Lise and Vaguath finished laying the table and Mama kept me by her without saying anything. She was afraid, now that I had managed the horse. Sivisal came through the door, stooping, and took the seat of honor by the fire, Mama watching his every move. He replaced the ruby ring in a pouch of his cloak. We sat down to roast tree hen, corn, shallots, ham from last season cured in the smokehouse, fresh bread and beans, followed by infith fruit in sweet cream from Sim's dairy. My sisters watched Sivisal eat with a slight blush at his appetite; Mama's cooking roused enthusiasm in him and some of his reserve vanished. He almost seemed merry at supper and he made compliments to Mama that made her feel like a sister again, she said. Father told more stories of current happenings in Cordyssa and other northern villages, to which Sivisal listened avidly. At that time Lord Ren of Cordyssa had just returned from a long journey south during which he had conferred with Queen Athryn at court. Sivisal knew of the journey but did not know Lord Ren had returned. Their conversation continued well beyond the end of the meal. I had heard much of this news discussed at previous suppers and wanted impatiently to learn more about the black horse in the barn. But this topic was apparently forbidden for the moment.

When supper was done, Mother sent me to the hearth room where jaka was brewing. In our house, as in many of the houses in that part of the country, the fireplace was large, open on two sides, allowing a hearth room separate from the kitchen. Our hearth room was cozy and warm, being built of mortared stone with a high beamed roof and real glass windows. Father and Sivisal were already seated on stools talking while Mama poured jaka into mugs I held. "Athryn Ardfalla has doubled the corn levy in the past few years," Father was saying, "on top of the levy we pay on seed, livestock and buildings. Last year I built a lean-to for the potatoes back of the barn, and when the tax collector came through he added it to the lists at the same rate as a full shed even though it didn't have but a rain-wall and a roof. As if the Queen doesn't already have enough money. We can barely pay the taxes on what we've planted this year. Of course that will suit her just fine if we can't pay the tax; she'll send her magistrates to seize the farm."

"Are you really in danger of losing your land?" Sivisal asked. "I have back wages I could draw—"

Father waved his hand. "Sybil and I will manage. We plant no more than we need to pay the tax and feed the family. We get by."

"What use to try to make any money when the Queen will only take it?" Mother asked. "But thank you kindly for the offer."

"The Queen keeps her Wizard in very grand state, with armies of his own, I hear," Father said.

"She doesn't have much choice," said Sivisal. For a moment his face was full of trouble. He gauged his words carefully. "She has less power left to oppose him as the years go by and no power to match him. Neither do we."

"Are you treated well in the Woodland?" Mama asked. "How do you get food? There aren't any farms in Arthen."

"We bring in food from Drii and Cordyssa," Sivisal said.

"There's fighting?" Mama asked, with an eye for me.

Sivisal saw the glance and stood, taking me by the hand to a place beside him on the hearth. "Yes, there's fighting. The Blue Cloaks don't let us pass unhindered. The Queen would starve us if she thought she truly could. I've seen some fighting. All of us have. We fear we'll see more as times get worse."

"Did you come to turn my Jessex into a soldier, too?" Mama asked.

A hush fell over the room. Sivisal watched his sister calmly. "Would you refuse to let him come with me because of that?"

Father said nothing, studying his own knuckles. Mama said, "No. I wouldn't." But I had never seen such sadness on her face, and it made me wonder.

Father read the silence that followed as Uncle Sivisal's hesitation. "You can trust us, Sivisal. My wife and I have kept secrets before."

Sivisal waited until a new silence had fallen, as if gathering his words. While he watched the fire he played one hand idly through my hair. He studied my mother almost tenderly. "My lord keeps his shrine according to the old custom, and keeps a servant in the shrine to tend the lamps. A twentynight ago the present temple servant took sick with fever out of the blue sky, and she was dead inside of a day. That evening Lord Mordwen Illythin had a true dream. YY-Mother visited him as she has not visited him in many years, telling him to leave the shrine tent vacant and to send to Kinth's farm in Mikinoos country for the next servant to light the lamps. She named Jessex son of Kinth and Sybil as the boy, and gave the lineage of our family back to four generations. She told him other things as well, and one of them was the test with the horse. Next morning Lord Illythin told his dream to my lord. My lord knows me and my kin and summoned me, telling me I was to test my nephew Jessex with the son of the King Horse, and if Jessex could ride the horse, I was to bring him to serve the shrine of YY in Arthen."

I could tell by the way he was saying, "my lord," that he did not want to say the name. In the silence that followed I could have counted every crackle of the fire. I watched only my uncle, being afraid of every other face. After a while Father said, sadly, "Praise the Eye. We have nothing to offer Jessex here. You know all the land has to go to Sim." He looked at Mama.

Mama said, "I can't fight an oracle, can I?"

"No one will force you to give him up," Uncle Sivisal said.

Mama gave me a long, calm appraisal. "I'm only sad. I'd give up more than one son to the service of Kirith Kirin."

Father went pale and embraced her. "That isn't a good name to say out loud, even in the house."

"I guess she's entitled," Sivisal said, looking at me. "Well, Jessex, will you be ready to ride away with me in the morning?"

"So soon?" Mama asked.

"I can't stay out of Arthen long. There are too many patrols. And the shrine is dark in Arthen until Jessex comes."

Mama drew up tall, gesturing me close. For a long time she simply studied me with sorrowful eyes, lips moving on the words to some song I could not hear. Her cool hands brushed my face with patterned gestures, as if she were memorizing my features. "What do you think, little man? Do you want to live in the Woodland? Where you'll forget your mother altogether?"

"Oh no, I don't think I would forget you."

She looked at Father and Uncle Sivisal. "I've some things to teach him before he goes. Please excuse us both."

Sivisal and Father looked at her curiously. She gave them each a smile and we disappeared into her room straightaway, where she closed and locked the door.

As is the custom among Jisraegen of means, mother and father kept separate bedrooms linked by a single door. Mother's room smelled of the scented soap with which she washed her hair. We children were not allowed inside this room and even Father had to knock. I thought it splendid with its woven tapestry hanging at the head of the feather bed, its fine collection of lamps and glass vases, heirlooms of my mother's family. In the warm light of the globe lamp she embraced me, her expression growing grave and clouded. The smell of her hair was wonderful, like perfume, and her warmth overwhelmed me. "When I was waiting for you to be born I had a conviction you would cause me more sorrow than all the rest of my children combined. It will be true, you mark my words. I've known this was coming; I won't tell you how."

"What will I do in Arthen?"

"Serve in the shrine, light the lamps of worship, and sing the evening and morning songs. You'll work very hard. If you follow the path, you'll be a priest yourself one day."

"I don't think I'll like that. I want to be a soldier like Uncle Sivisal."

"Priests go to wars too. Don't you remember Grandmother's stories about Lord Illythin?"

"Does he have a horse of his own?"

She laughed at my silliness. "Lord Illythin has many estates and many horses, maybe more horses than you could ride in one life-time." She held me tight. "Will you be sad when you don't see me any more?"

"Yes ma'am, very sorry." At the thought, which was new, I became disturbed and thought I might cry. She kissed me and said, "Well you won't need to be sorry. I'll always be here in the same places you remember, and I'll clean the linen on the eighth day and make the cheese on the fourth. Wherever you are I will think of you and love you and feel proud that my Jessex is off in a secret place, doing a service to one on whom our hopes are resting."

I nodded very solemnly, and she adjusted my tunic to hang prop-erly. Then she gave me a gift. She unlocked the heavy oak chest in her room with a key from the ring on her waist, and drew out another wooden box from inside it, and opened it with another key, revealing another box, and this one I recognized, very small, wooden, with silver hinges, carved with strange writing; I had caught her holding it once and she had not liked it.

"I'm giving this to you now because there won't be time in the morning, I'll be busy with the breakfast when you're getting ready. This is a very special gift. It's dangerous even to open it and show it to you." She let me see the box, opening it part way. Inside was a necklace on a silver chain from which a small pendant hung. The pendant was curious, a bird impaled on a claw. A jewel in the center, glinting in the lamplight. I tried to touch the necklace but Mama said to leave it alone. The box was carved with runes inside the lid as well as out. Mama closed the lid after a few moments. She had a look on her face as though she were listening to some voice. "Take it out of the box as soon as you reach Arthen. Don't let anyone see it, ever. Your grandmother gave it to me and her father gave it to her. It belonged to a very wise woman who once served the Red King. Remember, show it to no one."

"But Mama, you should save this for one of the girls —"

"Your grandmother told me it was meant for you. She always knew." She looked at me tenderly, drew me close. "I don't know what it means and neither did she. But do exactly as I've told you, because she said it was important and would save your life, and I believe her."

She would not even let me look at it, but pressed it in my hand. "Keep it in the box until morning, where it will be hidden. But don't take the box with you into the forest. It can't return to Arthen. Take the necklace out of the box and throw the box away. Say nothing about this to anyone, not even Jarred or your uncle." She hurried me out of her room then. I found my bed and hid the box and the necklace under the mattress where Jarred would not roll over it in his sleep.

3

In the morning a storm blew over the whole world. Gloom of it seeped through the bit of window in our attic bedroom. As soon as my eyes opened I jumped from the covers and stood at the window, where the dark clouds were rolling across heaven.

Already I could hear voices in the kitchen, counterpoint to the wind that raced through the visible hills. In the dim yard stood saddled horses, reins trailing the dirt. A pack was tied to the back of the black horse I would be riding. The horse waited patiently, once turning his gray eyes toward the window from which I watched him.

"You'll be leaving pretty soon, I bet," Jarred said, coming up beside me at the window. "Do you think you can really ride that horse when he gets going?"

"Yes, I think so." I quietly dressed, sliding the small box into the sleeve-pocket of my coat. From outside came the sound of distant thunder.

"I hope I get a horse like that someday," said Jarred.

"I wish you were coming too."

"Not to live in Arthen, not for anybody's money."

"Is it a bad place?"

"There's every kind of goblin and monster in it from what I've heard. And probably witches and bloodsuckers on top of it."

"I think people make up those stories," I said, and Jarred laughed as we heard more thunder rolling over the hills, followed by Mama's voice calling us to breakfast.

The storm worried her more than Uncle Sivisal, who claimed the ride would be easier under the cover of rain. We ate our breakfast quickly. Papa mentioned waiting to see if the sky cleared, but Mama said harshly that the sky would not be clearing and we should get ourselves into the Woodland if we knew what was good for us. She said this in such a sharp tone no one dared to contradict her.

I could feel the necklace in its box, an awkward lump against my arm.

"You'll want to ride the straightest, shortest way," Mama said to Sivisal, "and make no attempt to hide. If you aren't in Arthen by nightfall God help you."

"My sister has more on her mind than she's saying," Sivisal said, and I could tell she was making him nervous.

"I often do," she answered. "Don't take me lightly Sivisal, I know what I'm talking about. Get into Arthen, quickly, storm or no storm."

Behind, framed in the barn door, my father was watching his wife, a touch of fear on his face, the first time I had ever seen any such emotion in him.

The time had come. Outside the cold rain began to fall and my family pressed round to say good-bye. Uncle Sivisal threw on his cloak and I slipped the hood of my boy's sleeved coat over my head. Father pressed a gold piece into my hand. Lise, Mikif and Vaguath started crying as we moved toward the horses. Jarred had tears in his eyes too, and we embraced a long time. Mother hugged me desperately, wanting to say something, I thought.

She found a reason to fuss with the collar of my undershirt, and whispered in my ear, "Never be sorry, Jessex, no matter what happens."

A rush of wind overtook us both. She helped me onto the stallion's bare back. I clutched the coat around me as the wind came down on us more and more. Uncle Sivisal looked at me with a calm smile. "All right Jessex, now we ride," he said, and, gesturing farewell to everyone in the yard, we left my home.

I never saw it again.

4

The storm that followed shook the countryside, dark clouds rolling and wind blowing trees nearly level with the ground, lightning flashing and thunder resounding, rain pouring from the clouds in such floods one wondered if the fields would wash away. Sivisal and I rode straight through the tumult toward the hills.

We rode through the east fields where the furrows of new-planted corn were battered to pieces by the rain and wind, along a creek that bordered our land and farther, past the hills where Jarred had found me herding sheep the day before. Soon we had left my father's farm behind and rode upland into forest, good for hunting according to Sim; Uncle Sivisal headed us there to avoid any stray Blue Cloaks who might be in the area. Under the trees we took our first rest.

The storm was awesome, clouds covering the Fenax as far as the eye could see. I remembered what my mother had said and touched the necklace-box once or twice. Uncle Sivisal looked at the sky, worried. "Weather like this isn't natural. An hour before dawn the sky was clear as clear can be."

"Mama said it would be a bad storm," I answered.

"Well, she was right. We had better take her advice and get to Arthen quick as we can. Is this the fastest way you know?"

"This is forest that belongs to the Queen. It isn't very thick. Beyond is the Girdle where the patrols ride."

"How far?"

"Minutes from here. But it's very wide."

"The patrols will be out today too, I'll bet gold on it. This storm stinks of magic. Come on, we're going to hurry. That horse of yours knows how to get where we're headed, if you can stay on his back."

"I can stay." I had to shout to make myself heard above the wind.

He pulled something from inside his cloak and slipped it on his finger. I recognized the ring that he had worn when he led the black horse from the barn. He leaned toward my horse and spoke words to him. The horse listened with a wholly serious air and when Uncle Sivisal released his bridle, he began to canter forward. I turned back to see if Sivisal was following. He was. So I asked, "What did you tell him?"

"To get you to Arthen no matter what. Stick fast to his back, little man. I believe we're in for a hard ride."

He spurred his own horse to a gallop and we headed west along the hills, not directly toward the Girdle despite the talk of urgency. I wondered why till I understood Sivisal didn't want to give the Blue Cloaks a good guess which farm or village we had come from. The black horse ran with long, powerful strides, hardly even blinking in the rain. My uncle's sorrel was no mean horse but was clearly no

match for this mount of mine; and that made Uncle Sivisal the more
nervous since I was the less-practiced horseman. The country was
rough and more than once I thought I had lost my seat. We covered
much ground in a short time but still Uncle Sivisal seemed reluctant
to turn south, where the Girdle lay, where the Blue Queen's patrols
would be riding their crisscross paths.

Finally we turned, passing a marker Uncle Sivisal read me, "You
who are subject to my law, know that this is my land and I dare
anyone to cross it, or to enter Arthen Forest, on pain of death." The
marker listed no author. There was no need.

At the edge of the forest we paused, hidden by scrub faris and
some vine with pale flowers; in the rain and wind one could hardly
get a good look at anything. The Girdle was a broad swath of land
cleared many years ago by armies of laborers. In the distance loomed
Arthen itself, dark and sedate like a mantle over the hills. The country between us and the Woodland was empty of Blue Cloaks. Uncle
Sivisal looked at me and said, "Ride as fast as you can."

From the moment we broke free onto the plain the storm redoubled round us, the wind so fierce it nearly took my breath, whipping through the horse's mane and swirling through Uncle Sivisal's
cloak. Lightning scored the earth from every direction as if it knew
where to seek us, and the thunder afterward would have sent many
a horse into terror. But these were steady animals. Sooner than I
would have thought possible we were deep into the grassland, despite the storm, and for a while it appeared that we would cross
without incident.

Blue Cloak patrols appeared suddenly from both directions and
the sky lightened as if to make us all the plainer. Then I knew my
mother had told the truth and this storm was more magic than not.
Uncle Sivisal glanced at me, grim. Over the wind and storm he said,
"They intend to catch us, Jessex. Stay close to me if you're able, but
if it comes to choosing, you have a horse they're not likely to match.
Get yourself into the Woodland where they won't follow you."

If we'd ridden fast before it was nothing compared to now.
My poor thin frame had never taken such a beating before, but I
relaxed into the grasp of the horse's rhythm and he carried me, I
was never afraid of falling. The black horse reached forward with
every nerve and muscle.

By my side my uncle urged his horse quietly, checking on both
sides of us to locate the patrols and finally slinging the bow into
position, an arrow slotted into it. He rode the horse as if he were

joined to it. With the two patrols closing at an angle I could not tell if we were ahead or behind and with the wind in our faces it was hard to see the edge of the Woodland. The storm increased again as if it had only let up long enough to give the Blue Cloaks a good look at us, and the feeling of malevolence grew. I felt a strange aching on my arm and heard laughter and thought I must be going mad, but Uncle Sivisal heard it too, I saw him glance at the sky from where the sound had come. A voice called out strange words. I felt a huge weight on my shoulders dragging me down and for the first time I thought I might truly fall.

I cannot tell you where my next thought came from or why it came. But I pictured the necklace as I had seen it the night before, the raven impaled on the claw. Mother had said to get rid of the box. I touched it through my rain-soaked sleeve. Gripping the reins one-handed, I slipped the box free of my sleeve and opened it. The necklace fell into my hand and I flung the box into the grass.

The laughter died away, and for a moment even the storm abated to the point that I could see trees ahead of me—tall, dark trunks and shaggy down-hanging limbs. Blue Cloaks were closing from our left; we had only escaped one patrol, it seemed; and my uncle wheeled his horse away from the patrol that was now closer to us. My horse made this maneuver more gracefully, for which I owed him thanks, or else he might have flung me onto the wet ground. The riders behind us were closing, though, and if they had a good bowman they might bring us down. But we were closer to the forest than they were and I thought we were free, when, out of nowhere, a white figure appeared, a mounted wraith whose shape was hard to see. The white blur moved at impossible speed and cold fear filled me. Uncle Sivisal saw it and paled.

I will never forget the calm of his eyes. He said a word I did not know and raised the ruby ring again. My horse answered, adding speed to speed. I and my horse left them all behind: my uncle, the Blue Cloaks, the running shadow and even the storm. Within moments we were crashing through underbrush, and soon cool trees closed round us.

The soldiers were still chasing my uncle, and I could see one of them had caught him in the arm with an arrow but the wound had not felled him. His sorrel ran for both their lives and knew it, but they were close to Arthen and had a chance if they could outrun the white shadow which had resolved itself to human shape, on horseback. When the white figure saw me safe inside the Woodland and my uncle closing onto safety, he or she stood up tall in the saddle and gestured, saying words that were hideous to the ear. An arm flashed from the pale cloak. Lightning crashed near my uncle and I thought the sorrel stumbled, but the brave horse recovered and kept running. The figure on horseback raised the arm for yet another try.

I gripped the necklace and sang Kimri. When the storm seemed to abate a little I touched the necklace more firmly, and sang Kimri in a loud voice, "We are in the darkness, give us a light. We who have hope have need, light in the darkness." The white figure diminished. The storm lessened; no bolt of lightning fell. My uncle entered Arthen with the arrow in his arm.

He joined me and we stopped to look back into the outer world where the Blue Cloaks and the white-cloaked figure were milling round on horseback. They could no longer see us. The wraith adjusted the white hood and I could see she was a woman then, red-haired, wearing a kind of silver headpiece.

Uncle Sivisal grinned and looked at me. "No questions yet. We don't want them to get a good look at you. Right now we have to get deeper in the Woodland where her birds can't track us."

"Just tell me one thing," I said, almost pleading. "This horse that saved my life, what's his name?"

He stroked the ring he had worn on his finger, and then put it away inside his cloak. "He is Prince Nixva out of Queen Mnemarra. He is a royal horse and will live forever. Pay your respects to him. His speed today saved us from disaster."

I stroked his mane and whispered my thanks in his ear. He heard me and I think he understood. But he, like my uncle, knew that now was not the time for thanks but for riding farther. He let me turn him toward the forest interior and Arthen embraced us at last.

CHAPTER TWO
ARTHEN

1

I performed my first soldier's task, helping Uncle Sivisal cut out the arrow in his shoulder and dressing the wound with a poultice of theunyn leaf. Theunyn aids healing but also drinks up poison on the barb. I knew the leaf but not the use; my uncle taught me. He kept a store of the herb in his saddle-pack. Directing me in the preparation of the poultice, he leaned white-faced against a tree root, the arrow causing him to flinch in pain each time he moved.

The cutting of the arrow out of his shoulder became an ordeal for us both. My uncle wore a quilted leather tunic in which the shaft had spent most of its force, but enough arrowhead had cut into the flesh that I had some nasty work. A few barbs had taken deep hold into the muscle. Uncle Sivisal had a sharp dagger and I used it to cut the shaft of the arrow, so I could open his tunic to get at the wound. Swallowing brandy as an anesthetic, he kept still while I worked the tunic free, then, with the bleeding wound exposed to air and dripping rain, I cut out the arrowhead. He hardly made a sound but his face remained as white as the witch's cloak. The most vicious barbs of the arrowhead remained clear of the tender shoulder; I avoided touching them at all. Using the knife as Uncle Sivisal directed, I lay the poultice onto the wound. Theunyn leaf has the property of easing the pain of such insults, at least to a degree. "That's my boy," Uncle Sivisal said, grinning palely, as blood sheeted down his shoulder. "Now pour brandy over it," he said, and handed me his flask. I did it and he made a face like his body was burning, but not a sound escaped him.

Afterward, he drank more brandy as I packed the gaping wound with clean, dry spider-web. I retrieved stuff for bandages from his saddle-pack and wrapped his shoulder tight. At first the blood quickly soaked into the wadding but after a few moments of quiet, the ground theunyn began to work and the blood flow eased. I secured the bandage. He drank more of the brandy and lay back on the ground with his eyes closed. He offered me a sip, saying I had earned it after my morning's work. I wanted to make him a decent bed but rain dripped all around us.

The storm continued fiercely, thunder crashing north of us over the plain. Uncle Sivisal looked miserable lying on the ground in his wet cloak and I asked whether he had a tent in his pack. The question roused him. He sat up, gauged the day and said, "No, give me a minute. The brandy has me a little dazed, that's all. We have some riding to do before we can camp tonight, wound or no wound. There are soldiers meeting us." He noted my wonder-struck expression and nodded. "Welcome to the Woodland."

"I like it so far."

"Well, I have certainly liked it better." He got to his feet slowly. He waved away my help, buckling on his sword and plucking off wet branches and leaves from his cloak. He moved gingerly, favoring the shoulder, but if he felt any pain he refused to show it.

When Uncle Sivisal whistled, his sorrel stallion came to him. Nixva went on watching me until I said his name, low. He approached me, nuzzling my hand. I mounted him with pride, my uncle watching. He said. "Don't get too attached to Prince Nixva. He belongs to your betters and you're not likely to ride him much in camp. You'll get something more like my Sythu to ride, if you get a horse at all."

Sythu shook his head at me as if to tell me he was plenty of horse, whatever I thought. Sivisal stroked the sorrel's thick mane. When he looked at me again I could not read his face. "Did you see the white-cloaked rider in the grassland?"

"Yes," I said, remembering her pale arms raised toward the dark clouds.

In rain-smudged light the gray of his beard became more evident. "What did you sing? 'Light in the Darkness?'"

"Yes. A little of it. Could you hear?"

"Yes," he gave me an odd look. "Did my mother teach it to you?"

I nodded, hoping he would tell me something but he mulled over what I had said and then declared we were ready to ride. A dozen questions died on my lips. I felt for the necklace to make sure it was still secure. Soon I must find a safer place to keep it.

We rode again, with nearly the same urgency as before. Every step jolted my uncle's shoulder; I could see him clenching his teeth. But the bandage remained dry and the poultice did its work, bleeding stanched. The keen forest air carried different smells, a pungency of cedar and perfumes of cilidur, vesnomen and elgerath. The last abounded in vines the size of houses or barns, spilling down from the trees in vast lattices. We took no time to study anything, Sivisal being in a rush and me dumbstruck. Everything was strange, green and beautiful, vaulted and awesome, and we rode forward through high leafy caverns whose size made our progress seem miniscule.

Wonder struck me when I saw my first duraelaryn, a high broad tree, the shade of which might have dwarfed Mykinoos. Duraelaryn grow only in Arthen Forest. We rode beneath their spreading branches for a long time, till we came to a grassy road marked with stone obelisks. We headed along the road toward the interior where the storm behind us hardly moved breezes. The horses frisked in the crisp air, the eerie forest light filtering down around us, almost hazy. Under the high canopy of the duraelaryn the forest floor is open except for grass and light brush, since little else can thrive in the shade. Here and there a long bright beam of sunlight slanted to the forest floor, illuminating shaggy falls of elgerath. It was the fourth sun, the amber light. Once we paused for rest beside a clear stream and I changed the dressing on Sivisal's shoulder, washing off the old poultice with brandy and crushing a new one from fresh leaves. The wound had puffed and swollen purple, but a clot had begun to form despite the jolting from the ride. I packed the wound tight again, poor Uncle Sivisal grimacing and biting his lips. I bound the bandage tight, as before. He thanked me for my trouble with a face the color of new milk.

The stream was remarkable, I had never tasted water so fresh. Sivisal explained with some pride that the water fell straight from the mountains round Drii. This amazed me, because I had some-times suspected Grandmother made up Drii. "Oh no," Sivisal said, "It's there. And the people who live there really do have silver skin."

I finished tending his shoulder and we mounted the horses again, riding through the long afternoon. The unfamiliar posture was making me sore but I tried to endure it since I had no choice. Near dusk we came to a place where this road merged with another. Above the trees, a large shadow loomed, split and became two shadows, two carven seated figures, a man and woman, grand in demeanor. These statues were ancient wardens of the road, one a male and one a female priest, my uncle said. We stopped at the base of these monuments to wait, letting the horses graze in the cleared ground at the base of the massive statues. We made a fire for ourselves and had

our supper as if we were expecting nobody, and I laid out my
uncle's bedroll, checked the dressing on his wound. I also fetched
more brandy from his pouch. He watched me do all this with a
kind of amusement.

I made his bed among menumen trees, their soft leaves hanging
white and silken round his dark hair and swarthy complexion.
Menumen is not a hardy type of tree and does not grow many
places outside of people's gardens. These were fine big ones that
had recently bloomed, white petals strewn along the ground. Uncle
Sivisal said he had not smelled that fragrance in years.

Evening chill set in and I wrapped myself in the plain blanket
Mother had given me. I sat near the horses at the edge of the grove
of trees. From that vantage I could see the priest statues and the
road running off in three directions. Last light was on us and we
waited to see what stars we would have. The red moon rose but the
white one did not. In the south this is called "blood-time," and
people are said to commit strange crimes during it. Grandmother
had explained to me we northerners are skeptical of this power of
the red moon. Though one never knows what the skies will bring,
as the saying goes.

Uncle Sivisal directed me to build a fire by the statue of the
woman, giving me ifnuelyn to kindle the wood. Ifnuelyn is a kind
of powder which kindles fire quickly following a slight spark. I
unwrapped the viis cloth that protected Uncle Sivisal's store of the
chemical, and soon enough had a good fire going. I sat watching the
flames contentedly as the sun descended into the trees and beyond.
We would have no lamp tonight, only the fire, but in the wild I
supposed a fire would serve.

A moment later, horses stepped through the underbrush from
every direction on both sides of the road. I stood, confused, my
back to the fire. Most of the riders halted, but two came toward
me without fear. One wore a leather jerkin and red cloak much like
the one Uncle Sivisal wore, but the other was more grandly dressed,
in a red cloak trimmed in black fur.

"You're the son of Kinth," the man said, speaking Upcountry
with elegance and a peculiar lilt. "Where is your kinsman?"

"Uncle Sivisal is lying under that tree. He was wounded this
morning."

"Wounded." The commander sat very still for a moment. He
rode to the pallet where Sivisal drowsed and called out in a tongue
I did not know. He dismounted and knelt to study my uncle. The

people he had called hurried to him quickly, among them a physic. I heard Sivisal speaking in that language, and I heard my name once or twice. But I stayed by the fire where the commander had found me.

Apparently it was better to await summons. A moment later the silver-eyed man sent everyone away but Sivisal and the physic and called for me, without any sign of impatience. I ran to the place where he stood over Sivisal. "There were two parties of Blue Cloaks," Sivisal was saying, in Upcountry now, his voice strained some since the physic was probing his wound to make certain I had picked out all the arrow's barbs. "The riders broke toward us as soon as we got onto the Girdle. They knew we were coming. The storm was blowing pretty good by then too, and I knew something was up. We slipped past one party but the other looked like it was going to catch us. I used the ring the Prince gave me and told Nixva to save the boy, but I was afraid it was no use by then, the White Cloak was coming fast."

"A White Cloak?" The commander leaned toward him, kneeling under the soft menumen leaves. "Did you recognize which one?"

Uncle Sivisal shook his head. "Once we were inside the woods she let down her hood and we saw her face, that was all."

I said, "She had red hair and a silver headpiece. Her skin was very fair, not like a woman who works in the fields."

The commander received this as bad news, turning away from Sivisal and me. He looked at me keenly. I could hardly read his expression for the fascination of watching his eyes. "Don't speak about this to anyone. Don't describe the white-cloaked woman again."

We affirmed that we would keep the story to ourselves.

To my uncle he said, "You've done good work, Sivisal, as I knew you would. Your nephew is safe."

"Yes sir," Sivisal said; and then they both switched to that more sibilant language that I did not know. From Sivisal's expression it seemed plain that the commander's earlier orders were being repeated. When they were done, the commander walked away from the menumen, gesturing for me to follow, and Uncle Sivisal indicated I should go with him.

We walked to the shrine in a circular garden between the statues. Everything was in perfect order, as if the grounds were carefully tended. The commander found a clear spring behind the shrine. The water running had smoothed the stone to the slickness of glass, and its gurgling over the pebbles made a pleasant song. The commander looked down into the water for a long time. He was a tall, fair-haired man with fine bones in his face, and long, tapered hands. His slender body gave the impression of strength. This man's skin and eyes were silver, like starlight, and his skin nearly glittered in light. I noticed this and the commander looked up again, smiled gently. "You've had a hard day's ride. Are you sorry you've come to the Woodland after so much trouble?"

"No. I like it here, I don't know why."

"Your first taste of soldiers' life hasn't discouraged you?"

"Blue Cloaks were quartered on my father's farm two seasons, nearly three. I know something about them."

"And the woman in the white cloak?"

I shivered. "I haven't seen anything like her before. But the village folk have always said my Grandmother and Mother both knew witchcraft."

"Did they?"

"Not enough to call down lightning," I said.

"Your father's name is Kinth?"

"Yes, sir."

"Your farm is near Mikinoos?"

"Yes, sir."

"I remember Mikinoos from old days," he said. "Once there was traffic between your village and my native city, Drii. Did you know I was Venladrii?"

I nodded. He bowed his head. "My name is Imral Ynuuvil and I'm King Evynar's son."

I was speechless then, and turned away in confusion. There were two shocks in what he told me. Uncle Sivisal had only just affirmed that there was really a city called Drii and here I was, meeting a man who claimed he was the son of the Drii King. More astonishing, however, was his name. Among us, the greatest honor conceivable is to be called by two names.

His laughter continued in a gentle vein. "Your uncle should have warned you."

"Jhinuuserret" is the old word for twice-named. Grandmother Fysyyn taught it to me. In our world, only a few are Jhinuuserret, and they are said to live forever unless misfortune comes to them. The second name comes as a gift from God.

The Prince dismissed me soon after. I kept watching him, realizing who he was. One of the Twelve Who Do Not Die, the inheritors. Later I saw him deliver a message in writing to one of the riders. She got a horse from the line and was gone in no time. What message she carried I could only guess.

2

When supper was ready we ate it seated around the campfire, good venison and warm bread, dried fruit, fresh cheese, wine to wash it down. Uncle Sivisal was propped close to the fire with me to serve him. His wound and the story of our glorious ride had made the rounds quickly, and he had to tell it again and again. At the conclusion of the last time he slapped my knee and said it was a long way to come for such a small package. Everyone got a good laugh at that.

There was a woman who had brought her guitar with her, and she sang with Prince Imral after a while, an old song from the mountains, with a sweet harmony. I couldn't understand the words but the singing was fine. Prince Imral had a good voice and the woman, Trysvyn, offered a clarity of tone and total ease in gliding from one note to the next. We Jisraegen believe that to hear music is to hear the mind of God, or as close as we can come when she is far away. No one spoke for as long as they chose to sing and afterward in the silence I found a place for my pallet near my uncle. It felt good to lie back and look at the stars with the echo of those songs running through me. After a day full of so much adventure I thought I would have trouble sleeping, but I was wrong.

In the morning we rolled our bedrolls and downed our jaka by first sun. We sang "Velunen," the Morning Song, before riding. I did what I could to help strike camp, packing Uncle Sivisal's belongings while he grumbled about his shoulder. I waited a long time before getting Nixva in case somebody had forgotten to tell me I wasn't supposed to ride him any more. When I slipped the saddlecloth over his back, the horse seemed content with the prospect and I asked no more questions. One of the soldiers checked my cinches, but I had saddled my father's horse a thousand times on the farm.

I was lost in memory of a dream from the night before, in which I had wandered in a beautiful city. I could remember the city keenly even in daylight, me walking in parti-colored clothes down a broad quay, a riverfront, colored stone underfoot, very beautiful. This was a festival-day in the city and music hung in the air, bangles and lyres and kata sticks, singing sweet and sour. Along the river

every house was open, many families sitting on their terraces in festival clothes, some waving to me and some simply nodding as I
passed. The city was bright and golden, smelling of horse leather
and rich spices, perfumes and scented oils. In the dream I had always known there was such a city. I woke with a longing to return,
wrapped in sadness.

The feeling did not diminish with fullness of morning. I rode
with Uncle Sivisal, watching Imral Ynuuvil at the head of the column on his silver mare. When Sivisal had nothing to say to me I
daydreamed about the city. We rode from morning to night. After
supper I spread my pallet and slept till daylight.

After supper the next evening, when once again I thought only
of finding a place for my pallet away from the campfire, the Prince
asked that I sing a song as part of the nightly gathering. He played a
white lyre and Trysvyn beat the kata sticks and they led me through
a ballad about the Lady of Curaeth, that time she rescued Pel Pelathayn
from the Svyssn far to the north. Though I did not know it, I had
chosen my subject well. Prince Imral sat back with that look of
impassivity the Venladrii adopt when they are happiest. Everyone
else liked the song, too.

As if cursed, I dreamed again that night, much the same as
before, myself in many colors, singing as I walked along the quay,
happy at a festival in a city I had never seen. The dream lasted longer
and I saw many docks, buildings, courtyards, boat-landings, parties
floating on the water. Some of these landmarks I recognized from
earlier versions of the dream. At last I reached what must have been
my destination all along, a courtyard in which sat a tall crystal fountain, water splashing in arcs, rainbow shards of sunlight shattered in
the fountain, throwing off a million fires. A huge crowd gathered
here to wait while oars pulled a red boat toward the landing. A
white figure stood in the prow of the boat, a handsome man.

This was early morning, long before dawn. When I woke from
the dream I wanted to walk but there were soldiers on watch and I
was afraid to move. I lay sleepless on my pallet and when someone
lit the breakfast fire I was awake.

3

We rode west for many days. I kept Uncle Sivisal company, and he
talked to me plainly about Arthen and Camp for the most part and

asked questions about my father's farm and about life around Mikinoos. The wound in his shoulder had stayed pretty sore, given our constant riding. Each night I made a new poultice as one of the soldiers had taught me, thuenyn mixed with leaf of asfer and kor, to ease the ache and promote healing. The wound stayed inflamed but got no worse.

No conversation provided comfort against the night, when I rolled out my bed and awaited the dream. Sleep came easily each time I lay down, when I had never been one to fall asleep easily. Without fail the dream returned, with the same freshness that had characterized its beginning. Sometimes I walked along the river quay and sometimes through other parts of the city, but ended up in the courtyard where the crystal fountain blazed, where sometimes the red boat pulled ashore and sometimes did not. Soon I had dreamt the place so often I could picture it during my waking hours in every detail.

Though I mentioned the dream to no one, it was obvious to Uncle Sivisal I had become distracted by something. He questioned me but I gave only a vague explanation, homesickness, the newness of life in the Woodland and the like. I was ashamed to admit to him that I was troubled by a simple dream. But when I began to hear the soldiers mutter about a city in Arthen, toward which we were riding, I began to pay more attention.

One of the soldiers spoke about the haunted city around the campfire one night, and I asked Uncle Sivisal what she meant.

"The western road leads to a deserted city," he said, his expression betraying unease. "We'll ride there but we won't go inside the walls. No one does."

"Is it really haunted? That's what the others were saying."

He shrugged. "Who knows? I never saw any ghosts there, but I never went inside the walls, either."

"Then why does everybody talk about it this way?"

He thought over his answer a bit and said, finally, "There must be some truth to the stories, I guess. The roads lead straight through the city but we always ride around it, outside. And it's a pretty big city and a pretty long way around, I can tell you that."

"Why is it deserted? Did the Queen make people move out?"

Uncle Sivisal laughed. "No, Jessex. Cunuduerum was deserted a long time ago, before Queen Athryn was alive. I don't know the story myself, but I think it had something to do with Falamar. You know him?"

"Grandmother told me some stories about him."

"He was the first king in Arthen," Uncle Sivisal said. "He killed the priests, and he was a pretty bad man."

"He was a Wizard," I said. "Grandma told me that."

"Yes," Uncle Sivisal said, and I could tell he was about to change the subject. "Anyway, that's enough about haunted cities. You can hardly hold your eyes open."

"Is there a river?" I asked.

"What?"

"Is there a river near the city?"

He gave me a curious look. "Yes," he said. "The city was built at the junction of two rivers. Why?"

"I just wondered," I asked, but he continued to study me. So I changed the subject myself, pointing across the clearing where Prince Imral approached with his lyre. "Look, he's going to sing."

That night the dream deserted me and I rested easily till first light.

The first sign of Cunuduerum one can see is the Tower that soars over the treetops, visible for a long way. We heard the soldiers point it out and Uncle Sivisal showed me where to find it, a slim pillar against the distant horizon, rising out of a sea of green. He grinned and said, "That's the Spike of the Nameless," and someone nearby made a sign to protect from the evil eye. Uncle Sivisal did the same and so did I. No one had to tell me what the Tower was for. Any child knows it is a place where Wizards work.

"Is anybody in it?" I asked. "Does the Queen's Wizard ever come there?"

Prince Imral, who overheard my question, said, "No, Jessex. No one has stood in Seumren Tower since Jurel threw down Falamar. A long time."

We camped near a wide dark river within sight of a stone bridge. Beyond the bridge stood the walls of the city.

I had never seen any structure as elaborate as the bridge, which crossed the river on carved stone pylons, arch after arch. The carvings struck me with their somber beauty, the faces of hunters, merchants, tradesmen, weavers, dancers at a festival, youths lovely and graceful. I did not recognize the animals. Uncle Sivisal explained to me that the creatures depicted no longer roamed Arthen, if they ever had; he was from a hunter's family like Sivisal's and would have known if they were around to be hunted nowadays.

We made camp in a grassy knoll near the bridge, since daylight would not last much longer; though I could tell most of the soldiers would have preferred to ride farther and camp elsewhere. The evening turned chilly and I fetched my coat from my saddle-pack, checking as usual to make sure the necklace was hidden in its lining. I helped Uncle Sivisal with his bandage. The wound had survived another day's riding and showed no sign of putrefying. I rolled out my bedroll beneath one of the infthil trees. As I lay on the pallet smelling the bright infthil blossoms a sickening feeling made me shudder, and I wondered if it was the smell of the flowers. Infthil bloom in the summer and bear fruit in early fall. These infthil were blooming far too early and yet were lush, as if the fruit were about to form.

Restless, I wandered by the dark, broad river, hearing soldiers return with a load of firewood. Along the river, a low stone wall peered out from overgrowth along the back, and the manmade structure drew me. The stone cooled my fingertips. The flowing of the river, hypnotic in the late afternoon light, led me effortlessly toward the bridge.

I had seen only Mikinoos village in my life, and had no reference for a structure so monumental. Men and women had carved these stones, had moved them into place to make a bridge. Across its back, wagons, carts, horses, human feet had moved, into the city which lay hidden beyond those walls.

In the distance, the Tower rose over the wall, dominating the whole city. The Spike of the Nameless, my uncle had called it. Prince Imral had called it by another name, Seumren. A High Place, where a real Wizard once worked.

From far away I heard Nixva calling me. By now I could recognize his voice. I laughed softly at the sound but when he called me again I felt colder and wrapped the coat close around me.

A feeling of placelessness overtook me and suddenly the sounds of our camp in the distance had no meaning. I walked farther along the road to the bridge. The momentum of motion was powerful. Suddenly the wandering became like my dream and aroused a longing to go on.

I mounted to the paved stones that led to the bridge. A cool breeze was blowing along the bridgeway from the city side. I stepped hesitantly onto the stones. I watched the river from arch to arch, thinking it odd to stand so high over the broad, dark water. At the end of the bridge a low arch beckoned me through the wall.

I crossed the bridge without considering what I was doing. To tell the truth, I thought I was dreaming. Within moments I stood at the entrance to the main gate that guarded the city side of the bridge. Once my eyes had adjusted to the twilit interior I glimpsed a portcullis suspended above my head, spikes of iron massive enough to crush people and horses. Along the walls were slits in the stone, maybe where more such gates waited, or maybe places for soldiers to stand with weapons. The wall was thick and I had a goodly walk in the dark. But soon I came to the end of the tunnel.

Beyond the wall, tall sheer buildings flanked the flagstone road on either side. I gaped at these immense structures as anyone in my place would have. I could see parapets at the tops of the buildings; and then, for a moment, I glimpsed a line of soldiers, nearly colorless in the daylight, glaring down with hollow eyes and black-rimmed mouths. When they vanished a chill passed through me.

By now I could not tell whether I was dreaming beneath the branches of the infthil, comfortable on my bedroll, or whether the dream had finally consumed me and I had found the city at last. I passed through the open bronze gates into the precinct beyond. One could see Cunuduerum spreading far off toward the horizon.

A feeling of overwhelming recognition engulfed me. Beyond the gate was a courtyard, beyond the courtyard a lane lined with mansions, and along one rank of these mansions ran the marble quay where I had wandered, following along a broad canal which led from the river toward Seumren Tower.

I wandered farther, passed mansion after mansion along the canal. At first I sensed only the absolute quiet of the place, its desertion. But everything was in perfect order, maintained as if the citizens were expected to return at any moment. Soon I began to imagine that figures moved in the distant houses. I heard voices as well, the murmur of a festival in the ghost city.

I did not think of my uncle or of anyone I knew. I was in the dream, I was walking down the quay. From the houses I passed I got some greeting; not the laughter and musical speech of my dream but silent, sullen stares. Once I passed a figure on the quay itself, gaunt and transparent so I could see through him to the dark canal. He gazed at me with malevolence and spoke a word that did not sound as if it came from any language I had ever heard. I was afraid of him so I passed him singing bits of melody from my dream. I continued singing as I walked. I had no conception of time and could only guess how long I had been gone. The sun sank low over the mansions along the canal.

I had headed, since the canal ran that way, toward the High Place. When I approached its shadow, long and cool, I also recognized the courtyard at its base.

The crystal fountain lay beyond broad archways which I recognized, with a start, from my dream. No water flowed in it now. The sun was nearly gone but still struck a little fire in what was left of the crystal. I passed through the archway in shadow and could dimly make out the courtyard beyond. It lay in ruins.

Only the boat landing, the termination point of the canal, stood as it had in my dream.

A wind came up, gentle and caressing. Maybe there was some breath of voice in it but if so, the voice was quiet. Here I stood in the courtyard I had dreamed about so many evenings. The sun would soon abandon me to darkness and more voices, I could feel them gathering around me. I felt curiously stirred and wandered toward the landing, where the boat would come. The end of the quay had been crushed, I could see stone fragments beneath the surface of the water. I stood close to the broken pavement in the slanting sun.

Each fragment of stone shimmered beneath the water, pale like spring flowers. I did not realize what I had been hoping for until I stood there. The boat could not come if there were no place for it to dock. The court of the fountain was silent but for voices no one wants to hear. These days only the dead gathered by the river, and no King ever arrives to ascend the steps to his grand city.

But I had not come here for any of that. I had come to Arthen to serve in a shrine. I kept hold of that thought. I was cold and wrapped my coat close against me. I turned and found where the sun was sinking.

As it vanished I sang "Kithilunen," the Evening Song, wishing for a lamp to hold in my hand. In the ghost city I could give full play to my voice and I let it soar. Who knows how long since "Kithilunen" had been heard in that ruined place? My voice floated in the air asking YY for warmth and comfort through the night, for safety in the knowledge of darkness, a prayer my Grandmother taught me, older than we are. A prayer that there should be one light in the sky, at least, each night. When the last note died I felt the peace that comes sometimes from singing and sometimes from worship. I took a deep breath and watched dark water. The impression of voices in my head increased.

I heard a real sound, a horse's hoof striking stone, and I turned.

A horseman appeared in the Courtyard, inside one of the arches, though not the one I had entered. The horse's coat blazed white in the twilight, like the horse of Death in the stories. The horseman carried no torch but I could see him clearly. I thought him another ghost in spite of the sound of the horse's hooves. When he rode closer I could see the elegant trappings of his saddle and gear. The man unclasped the russet cloak he wore, as if he found the court-yard warm. When he saw me he reined in the big horse and sat still. After a moment he called out words I failed to understand, his voice musical and deep. When I gave no answer, he rode across the bro-ken courtyard and dismounted.

There was fear on his face. He asked me something in that language I couldn't understand. His beauty astonished me and took me back to the dream, and when I recognized him I felt as if I couldn't get breath. He had not arrived by boat this time. Yet he must be a ghost, too. He appeared not much older than Sim but was stronger of body. He wore a light tunic and riding boots. He had a rich mouth, olive-colored lips perfectly shaped, flaring. His eyes were black as night, his skin tawny, between bronze and gold. He spoke to me intently in that ringing speech again, and I heard fear in his voice. I said, quickly, "I'm a farm boy from the north country. The only language I understand is the one I'm speaking."

His relief was obvious. In Upcountry he said, "You're not one of the ghosts?"

"No, sir. Are you?"

He laughed, a warm, lively sound. "No, I'm not a ghost either. So we're both all right that way."

His horse blew out breath impatiently. The man went on watching me, without hurry. "I heard you singing Kithilunen. You sing well. How do you know that song if you can't speak true Jisraegen?"

"My grandmother taught it to me. I know what most of the words mean."

"I heard you from very far away," he said. "I've waited for that song for a long time. Do you know where you are?"

I took a deep breath. "I'm in a courtyard where there was once a glass fountain. Over there is what's left. Did you know about the fountain?"

"Yes. You know, your disappearance caused quite a stir in your camp."

"Have you been there? Is my uncle angry?"

He laughed. "Yes, I've been to your camp. Your uncle is concerned, not angry. He had just noticed you were missing when I arrived and his friends were getting ready to search for you, even though they're afraid of this city. I offered to search for you myself." He stepped closer. I could not tell how old he was, any more. "How did you think you would find your way back so far at night?"

The thought had never occurred to me. I stared stupidly toward the river. "I would have walked along the canal the way I came."

When he stepped closer I felt a flood of the dream returning; at the same time he lifted my face to catch the moonlight, touching me easily; I hardly gave it note. "You're like a boy from ten thousand years ago. Arthen is the true home of your blood." He paused, a slight guardedness to his expression. "Do you know who I am?"

The question made my heart pound. Because I did know. "You're Kirith Kirin," I said.

He went on watching me without comment or sign of surprise. His horse called him and other horses approached, torchlight flickering on the arched entryways and then on the ruined flagstone of the courtyard. The black haired man stood there as if he heard nothing. A woman's voice rose clear and strong, a question.

"I'm on the quay," he answered, speaking Upcountry. "Where the boat landing used to be. If you look you can see me."

"Don't be clever, I don't have Venladrii silver in my eyes. Why are you speaking Upcountry?" She had switched to that language herself however. The woman rode her horse forward. "Some of Imral's men have joined us. They crossed the bridge anyway, the boy's uncle and some other folk. Have you found anything here? Do you think he could be the voice we heard?"

"Yes of course he could," Kirith Kirin said, and laughed. "He's right here in front of me, I found him exactly as I told you I would. Send Imral word the boy's all right, and tell his uncle too."

She rode her horse toward us impatiently, then thought better of it. "Well, are you planning to be down there for very long? No one wants to be here after dark."

"For heaven's sake Karsten, do as I've asked. I trust I won't keep you waiting beyond your patience."

She said, "At your service, oh prince," as she rode away, and he laughed again watching her. When he turned to me his voice was gentler. "Everything seems good tonight, even Karsten's sarcasm. We can't stay here long, you've caused a fuss. Will you ride with me on Keikindavii, Jessex?"

Maybe it was only that he said my name, that made me trust
him. Though, more likely, it was simply his charm, something that
everyone felt. We walked to his horse. Kirith Kirin saw that I was
shivering and wrapped his cloak around me. "How can you be
cold in Cunuduerum's perpetual summer?"

"It doesn't feel like summer to me," I said, and he watched me
carefully again and mounted Keikindavii, Nixva's father, who greeted
me grandly. Kirith Kirin drew me up behind him.

"Hold on to me. You'll soon be warm."

I hugged his waist. The warmth of his body was wonderful.
He paused a moment before he turned the horse to cross the courtyard. "I must have dreamed of seeing the city this way a thousand
times," he said, "and here it is at last." We rode to meet his soldiers
who awaited him with patient torches burning.

4

That ride through darkness was more dreamlike than the walk
through the city. His outriders led us quickly, with torches, across
the bridge to camp. The woman he had called Karsten rode close
to us. I watched her through the folds of the cloak, noting the
strength of her long brown legs, the power of her arms, the beauty
of her face framed in shining white hair. There were many riders
round her and behind her, and she shouted commands to them,
beautiful syllables like singing. In their company, my fear of the
dream vanished.

I could hear Prince Imral's voice along with my uncle's in the
crowd of riders but I could not see them. Keikindavii started neighing
long before we reached the clearing where long ago I had helped
make camp. The voice that greeted him was one I knew. Prince
Kirith felt me squirm against him and half turned. "Do you hear
Nixva? He knows his father is coming. He's wondering about you
too, if you can credit it."

I could, remembering Nixva's gray eyes from the morning we
rode into Arthen. I settled against Kirith Kirin again, brief last moments of warmth before we rode onto the lawn where the cookfire
was burning.

We dismounted by a smaller fire close to the river. Kirith Kirin
helped me down and kept me by him, not yet claiming his cloak.
When his riders assembled he had his Marshal of the Ordinary, a

woman named Gaelex, assign them to posts. He wanted a watch kept while we were near Cunuduerum, and sentries. He wanted his own tent pitched wherever Imral was. The soldiers were to be fed even if they had already eaten and anybody who wanted wine was to get it, to the last cup if necessary. He said this in a jovial way. He dismissed his retinue soon after, and turned to his friends. When I started to find Uncle Sivisal Kirith Kirin held me back and said, "Not yet. Wait."

I stood awkwardly, trying to hold up his cloak and look dignified. In the fire shadows I glimpsed Uncle Sivisal, walking toward the cookfire scowling at me. He bowed to Kirith Kirin, who greeted him by name. "We found your nephew," he said, "so wipe that look off your face."

Uncle Sivisal glanced at me, a warning and a question. "Sir, I'm sorry, I don't know what got into him—"

"He wanted to see the city," Kirith Kirin shrugged. "Who wouldn't, being so close?"

Said in this way, as if I were simply a curious tourist, the remark brought laughter. No one, it seemed, ever had such thought about this place. Lady Karsten added, "At least we know your nephew's no coward, Sivisal. We found him near the High Place. He was singing."

This time Sivisal gave me a look with some pride in it. "Well, he's a sturdy boy, sir. If we can get him back to camp without any more adventure, I expect he'll get by all right."

That was that, it seemed. Kirith Kirin's servant took his cloak. Uncle Sivisal led me back to our fire—with the new arrivals, there were three campfires now. He lectured me, but seemed pleased I had distinguished myself with an escapade. I would have gotten more scolding, I guess, except after a few minutes Kirith Kirin summoned him back for more talk.

When he turned, he wore a clearly worried expression, and my heart sank. I was in trouble after all, I guessed. We got our dinner-portion, nearly a feast compared with our traveling rations, and he led me away from the fire.

His face let me know this was more serious than my straying across the bridge. "Commander Imral sent Kirith Kirin a message the night we met him," Uncle Sivisal said. "It was about your family. Our family."

I became still, and a chill passed over me, like the touch of the ghost in the city. "Why?"

"He sent soldiers to guard your farm." Sivisal watched me somberly. "Soldiers who know their business and will be seen by nobody. Commander Imral asked him to do that."

This news threw me into some confusion. Sivisal allowed me to sip wine from his cup. "They're afraid the Queen's soldiers will make trouble for your family."

"But they didn't see us, they don't know who we are."

"The woman in the White Cloak knows how to find out," my uncle said.

"You mean you think she traced our path that same day—" My own words choked me.

"Don't worry. They'll be all right." But he hardly seemed convinced of that himself.

We ate our supper. He brought me a cup of watered wine when we returned to the fire. Some talk passed during dinner, about other things, Camp news, a fresh rumor from Cordyssa. I was picturing my mother, doing, as she had promised, the things she had always done.

After a while I asked, "When will the soldiers be there?"

"Soon," Uncle Sivisal said, but from his manner I wondered if soon would be soon enough.

After this, the pleasant fire and the sound of voices made me sad, and I asked Uncle Sivisal if I could walk by the river for a while. Mercifully he omitted any mention of my recent wandering, maybe because his spirits were low. He directed me to stay in sight of the campfire.

As my eyes adjusted to darkness, I could see the river and walked there. When a thought tried to come into my mind I shut it out. I watched the river and listened to the sounds of its passing. Close to its freshness I felt peace, even warmth after a while, more than the fire had been able to bring. I stayed till the white moon was high. Back at the fires, figures sat drinking wine, their voices reaching me without any distinctness of words. I crawled into my bed without returning to the fire. My mind was full and fought sleep for a long time. Finally Uncle Sivisal went to bed, nearby, and I took comfort in that. A few days ago he had been a stranger, but now he was my only kin in sight. I lay under the soft infthil leaves with fear in my mind, till sleep came. I had no dreams.

5

In the morning we sang Velunen and set out on the ride around the river city. Through the early hours we traveled in the shadow of the city walls, a vast circumference. Prince Kirith and his companions rode at the head of our company, the rest of us after. Toward midday we crossed over another stone bridge, this one less grand than the last, though it was also built when Falamar was King. Camp was particularly pleasant that night with the stone abutments of the bridge to reflect the fire and protect us from wind.

At sunset we sang Kithilunen. Kirith Kirin was there but simply watched and listened, saying nothing before and nothing after. A hunting party had gone out during the day and we ate well on what they had killed. That evening only one fire was laid, and Kirith Kirin sat among the rest of us. No one acted as if this were anything unusual. He was boisterous, telling many stories and leading some rounds of singing. It was obvious he was well-loved; in his presence even Sivisal became animated. Kirith Kirin made my uncle show him the arrow-wound and Sivisal did so proudly. The Prince complimented his bravery and remarked that the wound appeared to be healing well. I hoped he would say something to me also, but he did not. Through the evening I watched Kirith Kirin, wishing for some excuse to talk to him. Uncloaked children are expected to be quiet and bother nobody at such gatherings, and adults are expected to ignore them. Still, once or twice his gaze fell on me.

In the morning we formed for ride and crossed the bridge. The forest grew bright and open, the canopy lighter though the undergrowth was still sparse. I asked Uncle Sivisal about the change when we stopped to rest our horses. This part of Arthen was called "Tiisvarthyn" or "Goldenwood", and was a favored place for Camp in the early spring before the chill of winter has entirely passed. At that time of year goldenflower trees blossomed here, heavy with petals and scent, and in late spring the blossoms would shower down from the branches and cover the ground. These trees were still budding.

That evening we made camp for the last time in open forest. The white moon rose early and some stars were shining. We were close to a clear stream called Mithuun where I bathed while waiting for supper, amid clear light dying in the golden trees. I picked a spot far from the cookfire, being shy of my own nakedness, but

I lingered in the water once I was there. My mother had packed oil of elgerath for my journey; I used the last of it in the stream, the fresh smell lingering on my skin. The forest was hushed and still, full of early moonlight, the singing of wind in trees, shadows crossing and re-crossing. As I dressed in my clean tunic the new-ness of this world took me afresh, the strangeness of having bathed in a forest glade, of dressing by moonlight and listening to sounds from a camp full of strangers.

When I returned to camp the place was full of bright sound, the smell of supper and spilled wine filling the clearing where we had settled for the night. Again, no separate fire was laid for the Jhinuuserret but for a long time Kirith Kirin did not come to supper. Neither did Lady Karsten.

I got food for myself and found a seat in the shadows of the fire. Some of the soldiers had already drunk pretty deeply and in many directions one saw flushed faces reflecting firelight or heard voices tinged with the warm echo of good company and pleasant beverage. From beyond the blaze I could hear Trysvyn singing a song in High Speech. Though I couldn't understand the words I heard the sadness in it, both in Trysvyn's clear voice and in the song itself. I felt a sudden longing to know what she was singing. I heard the word Cunuduerum again and again.

Uncle Sivisal sat with me. We drank to each other's health and sat in the light with our cups balanced in our hands. We spoke pleasantly on many subjects, calm friendly conversation that made me feel less like a stranger to him. He told me then that my mother had taken him to visit the place where Grandmother Fysyyn's smoke went up while he was on the farm. It was hard for him to fathom that his mother was dead. His last memory of her was from many years before, when she was still fairly young. When he talked about her I could see the child saying good-bye to his mother before riding away to the wild forest. She had told him he was bound for a life that would change him from boy to man maybe more quickly than plains life would have, and that he was destined for long service to a great lord. He was the forerunner, the first of her blood to return to Arthen. He must be credit to her. I could hear her voice in the words as he said them.

I told him what there was to tell about her death. I guess it was clear she had meant a lot to me. We talked, also, about the soldiers Kirith Kirin had sent to keep watch on Kinth's farm. He gave me sober advice. "Don't think about it. There isn't anything you can do for them one way or another. If the Kyminax witch meant to find your farm she'll have done so. If she didn't have the time or the will, then nothing is wrong and nothing will happen."

"The Kyminax witch?"

"Julassa Kyminax," he whispered. "She's the strongest of the southern magicians, all except Drudaen himself. That's who was chasing us."

I had all but finished the wine by then. Uncle Sivisal studied me in silence, a more tender appraisal than usual. I poked my finger into the moist humus. We talked about Camp a while and I tried to pay attention. I asked about the soldier's training; many people on the ride had been at pains to tell me how strenuous a soldier's first years could be, though I figured they wanted to frighten me for their amusement, as people do. Uncle Sivisal's description was not much less grim, though he had faith from somewhere, he claimed, that I would do pretty well. He told me there were not often boys of my age in camp and to be careful, and when I thought he only meant I would have trouble making friends he did not press the point.

Sivisal left me to talk to another friend and I went off for a walk. Beyond the fire circle the forest was dark but full of sounds. When I couldn't see any trail ahead of me I gauged my best path by the sound of the creek flowing. By the time my eyes had adjusted to moonlight I had covered a nice piece of ground already and I kept walking till I found a clearing full of moonlight, bright as day.

Above, stars wheeled slowly in patterns partly broken long ago by YY-Mother or by chance. In Aeryn the stars change from night to night, never in a regular way, so we are taught early how to recognize the ones we know when they appear. I said the names of a few of the ones I could see tonight: Fisth, Yurvure, Aryaemen, circled by the Four Hundred Boys. These were companions from my days leading the sheep through the hills of the lower Fenax, Aryaemen in particular, called also the Traveler's Star, because she is most recognizable when she is there, surrounded by her veil, a dusty gold. We have a legend that when YY first grew angry with the world she broke the stars so that they no longer moved across the heavens in an orderly way, so that one night there is one white moon, and one night there is one red moon, and one night there are both, and we can tell they are the moons we are used to, but we can never count the days by their movements, as people once could, long ago.

In the same way, in daylight, we have counted four suns, four kinds of light that fall on us, and so we are the land of four suns and two moons, which is the oldest name for Aeryn that we know.

I heard footsteps on branches from the direction of Camp and turned, expecting someone had followed me. I could see well enough to distinguish a tall, hooded figure near the curve of the creek. The figure drew down his hood. Kirith Kirin approached me timidly, moonlight coloring his face, outlining his shoulders. I was too surprised to react, I stood there stupidly. He said, "I watched you sneaking away. You passed my tent."

"I got tired of the party. I never saw a tent."

"No. I didn't think you had." He walked quite close, pausing behind me. I counted his slow, calm breaths. "Stars," he said, in a voice tinged with reverence. "So many. One never sees them often enough."

"I was looking at them too. You can't see the night sky from many places inside the Woodland."

He chuckled. "Yes, I know. There are clearings like this one but one must know where to find them." He unclasped the cloak and let it fall to the ground, freeing his arms. He wore a light, spare garment beneath, cut like a tunic but draped more elaborately, fastened by jeweled pins at either shoulder and by a belt of silver loops at his waist. His arms and legs were bare. "Do you like the Woodland so far?"

"Maybe. I think so. If I had stayed on the farm I would only have had to worry about the sheep."

He pulled a twig from a neighboring stand of cilidur, the glossy leaves spiraling round the tough black stem; one by one he stripped each leaf from its place, calmly gathering the leaves in his palm. I thought he meant to save them, since cilidur leaves when dried make a fragrant tea, but when he had done stripping the branch he proceeded to tear each leaf to bits. The dense smell floated in the air round both of us. At last he said, "Your life will always be full of new worries here, Jessex. You'll never know the whole catalog. Even here alone with me you face danger of a kind, but of such a subtle kind you may not realize its presence."

He said this plainly, but there was something questioning in the directness of his gaze. I sat beside him on the fallen log, rearranging a fold of his cloak to make room. "The danger for me here would be that I might stay too long."

He let the bits of leaf flutter from his hands. The rich smell rose up in final fullness. "Yes," he said, with a heaviness in his manner that made me wonder if he wanted to be alone.

"Do you want me to leave?   I'll go away if you ask."

His answering smile was hard to read. "Perhaps you should."

He said nothing else. The peace of the night had passed beyond us both. I went back to the fire without a word, feeling only a little scalded, nothing more.

CHAPTER THREE
CAMP

1

We arrived at Camp the next day, in mid-afternoon.

For me to reconstruct my first impression of the place would be both foolish and fruitless, since I brought with me only my ignorance, colored with bits of information garnered from the soldiers during our journey. Our party reported to the quartermaster tent where all the soldiers except Uncle Sivisal were dismissed. I remained too, mounted. I did not make much of the delay, my curiosity being focused on the duties that awaited me in the lamp-shrine.

Soon Prince Imral signaled us to follow. Kirith Kirin was watching me solemnly, maybe to see my reaction to this unfamiliar city of tents. We rode toward high ground, a rise of land where the tents of the gentry had been pitched.

So subtle are the colors of a Jisraegen weave that one could hardly see the airy pavilions behind the concealment of leaf and branch. I studied them as I was able but we were riding pretty fast, down a trail marked with slender wooden obelisks, each bearing aloft the charred remains of a torch. The torches looked pathetic and listless in the light of day.

The path took a steep turn and we rode through forest, such a long time I thought we were heading for open woodland. But finally we reached a clearing where a many-chambered tent had been pitched among a grove of vuthloven trees, their gray trunks blending perfectly with the dreamy fabric of the tent. Two wide flaps were staked open, the inside of each blazoned with intertwined letters forming the name of YY-Mother, in the form of the eye-sign, she-who-sees-the-world. So this was the shrine tent.

The others dismounted and Uncle Sivisal signaled I should do the same. Since this was the end of my journey, he directed me to untie my bundle of belongings from Nixva's saddle. I followed through the broad flaps, gawking at the rich interior. The altar was fitted with brass lamps and adapted so that one could slide in an axle and bolt on wheels; otherwise no one would ever have moved it. Fine carpets were strewn underfoot, soft as a bed and far more fragrant than my straw mattress in the attic at home. On either side of the altar and by each side of the wide flaps, incense drifted upward from brass pots, pungent and sweet. I had never seen any god-place more elaborate than the wandering priest's shrine which could be carried in a bundle the size of a saddlebag. Here was a beauty that brought the mind to YY— rich colors and scents, the play of sunlight and branches overhead, the sighing of vuthloven leaves.

A shadow crossed the altar, tall and broad. The shadow crossed me too. A man stood before me in a drab cloak trimmed in many colors of thread, his hood thrown back over broad shoulders. He had close-cropped hair the color of polished steel, a fleshy nose hooked to one side, and ears with fleshy lobes. His face was handsome in an odd, craggy way. He stooped down to study me, hand pressing the small of his back. Beneath the cloak I could see he wore the full gown that is customary for priests. He had eyes clearer even than Kirith Kirin's, liquid, like clear water, with only the faintest hint of color. He touched my brow with his fingertips. "You're the boy from my dream," he said. "Your face is the same."

Kirith Kirin, who had kept apart while the old man inspected me, approached us. The Prince said, quietly, "There's been little doubt, Mordwen. He fulfilled every sign you sent."

The man before me—Mordwen Illythin, about whom I had heard many tall tales—tapped my head with his fingertips. "You're the son of Kinth, called Jessex? Child of Sybil, of Fysyyn, of Aretaeo?"

"That is my mother line, sir."

He asked me a question that I would long remember, because it seemed urgent to him and the urgency tinged his voice. "Who was the mother of Aretaeo?"

"Matvae," I said.

"You're certain."

"Yes, I learnt my ancestors ten generations back at my grandmother's knee."

"You come from an old-fashioned family, where tradition means something." When he said this his face became gentler. Uncle Sivisal beamed at this praise. Mordwen looked at Kirith Kirin. "Curious," he said. "All parts of my dream fit, except that."

Mordwen asked something in the other language, which I had come to understand was true Jisraegen.

"Never mind," Kirith Kirin shook his head but answered in Upcountry, "we have other proofs that we've brought the right boy, beyond those in your dream."

Mordwen raised both brows. "Oh really? This I need to hear."

He told the story of Julassa Kyminax while kneeling on those rich carpets. The story affected Mordwen but did not appear to surprise him. After consideration he said, "One cannot expect to keep many secrets from Drudaen. But I wonder how he knew to send Julassa to that particular patrol."

"So do we all," Kirith Kirin said.

He let the subject drop there. After a moment more he stood, turning away abruptly and pulling up his hood. "We've had a long ride, anyway," he said, "and I'm tired. The boy's in your charge, Mordwen. He's too young to live in the main camp; keep him here." Kirith Kirin turned to Uncle Sivisal for his assent, which my uncle freely gave. Kirith Kirin added, still in that tone as if I were not present, "The shrine is always guarded, the boy will be safe."

"I think that's best, sir," Uncle Sivisal said, glancing at me.

"Once upon a time it was the custom," Mordwen said.

"It's a custom again." The Prince glanced at me. "Serve well, Jessex."

He turned to go before I could answer. Uncle Sivisal knelt to kiss my brow. After a moment he said to Mordwen, "The boy knows Velunen and Kithilunen already, in true Jisraegen. My mother taught him."

"Well, that's a relief," Mordwen said, gruffly. "You never know what ignorance you'll run into these days."

He withdrew then, to let Uncle Sivisal say good-bye. Suddenly, I felt as if this really were good-bye and was afraid; little as I knew him, I knew no one else better, and he was my blood. "Well, Jessex," he said, "I have to go to my own tent now."

"Where is it?"

"Down in the main camp."

I took a deep breath. "They won't let me live with you?"

He shook his head. "It wouldn't be proper. Not for a boy of your age."

"My age?"

He smiled. "I told you, uncloaked boys never come here. But you'll be safe in the shrine. And I'll see you at supper."

2

With Uncle Sivisal gone, Mordwen Illythin closed the tent flaps, sig-naling me to help him. He led me through the other chambers of the tent: the workroom where the lamps, oil and incense are stored—the oil in sealed jars, the incense in cedar chests. Wood-smell mingled with the sweet odor of the incense sticks. He showed me where I would live, concealed behind another flap. Once I saw it, I felt better. It was not large by anyone's standards but mine, and I had never owned any space that belonged to me alone. I had a small frame cot, a wash-basin, a pitcher, a chest and a small table. I must have gazed at the objects with something like awe, for Mordwen said, "Don't just stand there as if you're completely daft. Go ahead and set down your things. You have a lot to learn by sunset."

I set my pack on the floor carefully, afraid of disturbing the neatly-made bed by laying my pack on the canvas-covered mattress. Mordwen returned to the lamp altar and I knew he expected me to follow him quickly. But I hovered in my small room for a moment, breathing the smell of the wood.

The lamp ritual is older than anybody remembers, going back at least as far as the days of the Forty Thousand, when written Jisraegen history commenced; and as ancient as the ritual are the three songs that have been handed down with it: Velunen, Kithilunen and Kimri. There are many stories about the ritual's origins, the most likely being that the ceremony is the result of some agree-ment between Cunavastar and the Three Sisters, who were the first to worship YY-Mother in Arthen, long before the Jisraegen people came to be.

The ritual is simple and easily performed. A person of the proper age, of either sex, assembles a lamp, sets it into the alcove of an altar and lights it at sunset. At sunrise the same person puts out the lamp, cleans it and places it in a wooden case. The lighting of lamps and the ceremonial singing honor the endless cycle of light leaving and returning, which is the essence of our worship. YY-Mother sends darkness and light, but she is removed from both. The person who served the shrine in this way was called a kyyvi and in older days would have then studied the reading and writing of High Jisraegen and would have learned the Calendar and the Days and thereafter might have served as a priest and a day-counter.

I would perform the lamp ritual morning and evening every day. No one should serve the shrine after attaining the nineteenth year, according to a custom as old as we are, though exceptions are made. But I might serve till then.

Mordwen patiently taught me the use of the lamps. I absorbed details about oil-chambers, wick-making, and the rate of burning for various oils. He showed me the roch stone that makes the fire, and the different wicks for the lamps, including the ones that would coil atop the oil and float and burn through the night. He showed me the altar and taught me the proper ceremony for refueling a lamp while it was burning, for replacing the wick without extinguishing the flame, and for reading the sunstone to determine the moment of sunset and sunrise. It was nearly time for the ceremony when he finished. But when I went through the various steps of the ceremony, Lord Illythin affirmed I had performed correctly.

I spent my last moments gazing into the round sunstone, called muuren in High Speech, which formed the crest of the godmask. The muuren is a clear stone the Tervan mine, at whose heart a point of fire will burn for as long as daylight lasts. When that point of fire disappears, the kyyvi must light the lamp. The seeing stones that are on the High Places are made of the same stone, purchased at great price.

When folks began to gather for the evening ceremony, I hid in my little room, dressing in a fresh white tunic with two blazons on its breast: the sign for YY and the sign for Kirith Kirin, both worked in crimson thread. Listening to the voices of those gathered, I studied the ka-lamp I had chosen to light, a spherical lamp of blown glass with the oil chamber in its lower half, the fire-colored liquid shimmering. Mordwen, who waited in the before-shrine where the broad tent-flaps had been tied open, fetched me when the proper moment arrived. I walked into the before-shrine, bearing the unlit lamp in my uplifted hands, watching both the lamp and the floor under my feet, treacherous with stacked carpets. I laid the lamp safely into its niche, fastening the lock-pin through the base, and, quietly turning my gaze first toward the muuren crystal and then toward the sun itself, began to sing the Evening Song.

In the ceremony, when one's mind is right, one is outside the body, almost as if the spirit expands or contracts with the light; and one never sees those gathered until this first turn toward the sun. One is free to watch those assembled for only the few moments in the song when one faces outward. In those moments I saw faces in the before-shrine and in the clearing beyond the tent, more people than I had ever seen in one place at one time, hundreds, it seemed. I never faltered in my singing but this image of faces struck me deeply, and when I turned toward the God Mask again I clung to the objects, the roch stone that lit the ifnuelyn-treated wood cupped in my palm. I dropped fire onto the wick just as the heart of fire died in the clear crystal muuren.

The lamp burned with a cool blue flame. The ka-lamp is noted for the purity of its light, which filled that translucent pavilion with a glow like the full white moon. It was as if a star had fallen into my hands. I finished Kithilunen cradling the lamp between my hands, my heart full of reverence, the sound of the song dissolving in the twilight. An echoing silence followed, and no one moved.

I felt a first clear moment of joy in being there, in having been called to this life. I kept my back to the many gathered eyes. Their thoughts, like mine, should be with YY. I closed my eyes and kept my brain as empty as possible. After a moment I felt a pressure on my shoulder. When I turned, Mordwen was watching me, smiling this time, though still with the trace of his previous scowl. "You're finished," he said. "Well done."

Only when I left the altar-dais did I see Kirith Kirin. He had placed himself close to the tent wall, behind many other faces I did not know, the rust-colored cloak wrapped round him as if this were winter. He vanished soon after.

But Karsten was still there, having changed her riding leathers for a softer robe of pale blue, the drapings low on her bosom, flesh splendid with health, her shapely arms adorned with three silver bracelets, simple bands inlaid with the jewels of her house. When she knelt to embrace me I smelled a fine scented oil along her soft neck and shoulders—flowers I remembered from the long ride, though I could not recognize them.

"You've done well, both during the ceremony and after." She had changed to Upcountry, she spoke it with no accent at all.

"There were a lot of people," I said.

She looked at me curiously. "Your father is of the Erejhor Clan? Is that right?"

"Yes ma'am. My grandfather is very rich, he used to work for the Lady of Curaeth."

She smiled. "You don't realize who I am, do you?"

Puzzled, cocking my head.

"I don't wear my house-signs most of the time. But I'm the Lady of Curaeth, I knew your grandfather, and your eldest uncle, though he was a babe when I came into Arthen." I bowed my head and said I was glad to meet her. She was amused but too polite to laugh. "I meant to speak to you before but my mind wanders these days. Too many distractions."

She was Kiril Karsten, the Lady of Curaeth. She was twice-named, too. Here were four of the Twelve.

Mordwen had knelt beside me. Apparently he liked Kiril Karsten since in her company he became good-humored. "You see how they're all staring. Tell me they don't know everything about this whole affair from beginning to end."

"They're curious. Since when did Kirith Kirin ever send to the Fenax for a kyyvi? The Nivri would expect the next kyyvi to come from one of their houses. I'd be curious too, I expect."

"They know every wretched detail," Mordwen said again, laughing gruffly.

"Don't listen to him, Jessex, he'll poison your mind." She laughed and rose to greet a jewel-bedecked dandy wearing another of the round skullcaps common to the southern folk; she greeted this gentleman warmly and politely, shifting out of Upcountry into another mode of speech, different than I had heard before, and Mordwen beckoned to me to escape with him, which I did.

Many of those who had come for the ritual were drifting away to find supper. My own belly was calling me to the same purpose. Mordwen stopped by the shrine to survey the chamber a final moment, his glittering eyes scanning the lamp-lit faces as if he could read each one.

3

I ate supper in the lower Camp, in one of the common tents, with my uncle. The tent was spacious, supported by delicate beams of fragrant wood from which hung ornate lamps made of metal strips and glass, called vuu-lamps, these being by all accounts the best light for early evening, burning with a warm glow that lights the flesh as if from within. Though in other parts of the tent were other lamps, I noticed, for those who preferred something different. The Jisraegen are connoisseurs of light, and there are dozens of varieties and families of lamps in use among us, and hundreds of variants, or probably thousands; the Jisraegen language contains over a hundred different words for light, as I would learn. That tent was large enough that two hundred people could eat inside it at once, seated on benches at long wooden tables whose surfaces were bleached from repeated scrubbings. We ate some kind of broiled meat and a gruel that would have thickened any man's middle, along with bread my mother would not have given to the crows. Uncle Sivisal, who had come to the shrine tent for lamp-lighting, watched me eat and encouraged what he termed my fortitude. "Not exactly what your mother used to make, I expect."

"Well I don't think I ever ate it before." I lifted the edge of the cutlet cautiously.

"The cooks haven't had much to work with lately. This part of Arthen isn't famous for game. Early in the year most everything tastes stringy to me, anyway; half-starved from winter."

"Then it isn't always this bad?"

Uncle Sivisal chuckled softly. "No. Let's hope there aren't any cooks listening."

As a matter of fact there were none, and we were speaking Upcountry anyway. We had chosen a table close the center of the tent, directly under a lamp where the shadow was richest, velvet-textured and tinged with violet. At first we were alone at the table and a long time passed when no one joined us. I satisfied my curiosity by studying the adjacent tables, which were nearly full: hefty women cramming bread into their mouths, burly men laughing; some slim, some fair; some tall, some short; some with clear, pretty voices; some with deep, throaty timbres; a few fat ones, a few thin ones; a few homely, a few nice, a few really passable, a few pleasing, a few striking, a few handsome, a few true beauties, along with every variation. Some with scars and some missing limbs. I tried not to stare at those. I had never seen so many people, even in Mikinoos when my father sold corn. About half women and half men.

I noticed one thing very plainly, sitting there with my fork in my mouth. As I was staring at them, they were staring at me. More than one of them. I should have expected this, but in front of that mass of strangers I was cowed and longed to have them look at someone else. Sivisal affected not to notice anything and went on chewing his supper, but his eyes twinkled as he watched me.

"Eat your gruel. You'd be amazed how good for you it is."

"It sticks my mouth together."

"Wash it down. That's the way. You can't let a glob of gruel beat you."

"Why doesn't anybody sit with us?" I asked at last, seeing that nearly every table in the tent was full except ours.

Sivisal chuckled and leaned forward. "Because they're afraid."

"Of what?"

"Of you. Because Lord Illythin's dream brought you here and Prince Kirith rode to meet you himself." Chuckling again. "They know who you are, make no mistake. You can't keep a secret in a camp like this. Too many Cordyssans; they can hear through stone walls."

Some silence followed and we settled down to finish our suppers, with the noise in the hall rising and falling like a tide. When we were done with supper we carried our plates to the appointed tables, where a fat old man with a hairy wart was standing by a vast cauldron full of boiling water. A couple of hags, his helpers, took our plates from us and dipped them into pails of soapy water, the old man barking at them to be quick about it, since the water wouldn't be boiling to midnight. We passed beyond their table and out of the tent by another flap.

The night was clear and fragrant, stars burning overhead in the gaps between tree branches. Uncle Sivisal obtained a torch from the tent-porter and led me along the overgrown path to the shrine. One could see the warm glow of the tent a long way off, a gauzy, milky light, clinging like film to the crown of the hill. At the perimeter of the clearing we parted, after he introduced me to the sentries, whom he knew. I entered the shrine alone.

I said good-night to YY-Mother and watched the sentries vanish into the darkness, the torchlight flickering beyond layers of flowered branches.

4

Lord Illythin woke me long before daybreak, calling my name from beyond the tent-flap. He set a traveling lantern beside my bed, light spilling over my sleep, rousing me insistently. He opened the chest and pulled out a fresh white tunic, gathering together the pitcher and basin along with a decanter of cleansing oil. When I sat up, rubbing my eyes, he said, "Out of bed, child. I need to show you some things before the morning ceremony. The day ritual is not as simple as the evening."

He handed me a long-sleeved coat of soft cloth, explaining to me in a mellow, morning-gentle voice that I must take a ritual bath each morning before putting out the lamp. I stood, put on the soft bath-coat and followed outside. Down a narrow path we descended, toward the sound of running water, and soon I saw a brook shrouded in vuthloven, blossoms floating on the surface.

Lord Illythin led me through the ritual. One stepped a certain number of steps into the water and washed one's body beginning with the head and ending with the feet, this while facing east, keeping strict silence and breathing a particular number of breaths. The patterned breathing and movement has the effect of easing one gently into wakefulness. At the end of the bath one steps from the water, drying the body beginning with the feet and ending with the head, using the bath-coat to drink the water from the skin. Finally one lifts the lantern and returns to the shrine. Once inside the tent, with the bath ceremony completed, one is permitted to speak.

Mordwen asked me if I had questions and I told him I thought I could remember the ceremony for the next day. He quizzed me to see if I was telling the truth and I gave him good answers. He warned me that there were other variations of the bath ceremony used when we were camping in places where running water was not convenient, and another ritual altogether to be used when we were in a palace like Inniscaudra. I would learn these in due time.

He taught me the correct knot to use when tying back the eastern tent-flap, through which daylight comes to light the sunstone. He told me the proper order for morning ceremony, including what time I should enter the shrine, where I should stand and when I should wet my fingers for snuffing out the lamp wick. By the time he finished explaining everything once, folks were gathering in the clearing outside.

We could both feel morning come. By instinct I knew it was the second sun, the pale light. Soon Mordwen nodded for me to begin. As I stepped toward the shrine, watching the blue-white flame burn in the ka-globe, I said a phrase Mordwen had taught me, lifted the lamp from its fastening, careful to carry it on a padding of cloth to protect my hands from the heat of the glass, and walked with it to the tent opening.

Light from the lamp spilled into the clearing beyond. Kiril Karsten was the first person I saw, but I recognized others too, faces but not names. Prince Imral and Kirith Kirin led a few people into the shrine when I went back inside, following Mordwen's signal.

At the appropriate moment of brightening, I wet my fingers with scented water and when the heart of the muuren clouded through with the first touch of true daylight, I snuffed out the ka-lamp. Amid the soft clink of lamp-shutters closing I sang Velunen.

For me the feeling of singing was like the night before, I let my voice hang on the breeze, watching the sun through the treetops, the muuren's misty heart, the trail of smoke rising from the lamp and vanishing. At the end of the song I carried the lamp behind the shrine and listened to the voices from beyond. I disassembled the lamp and cleaned it as one is supposed to do. Mordwen found me pouring the oil into a funnel that guaranteed every costly drop reached the safety of the jar. I wiped the lamp clean with wet cloths and dried it with dry ones, polishing the metal and breathing on the glass, finally packing the various parts away in the wooden chest. I locked the case-lock and fastened the key ring on my waist. Mordwen said nothing till I had put the case away and turned to him. "Well done," he said. "Now, put on leggings and your coat. The groom is bringing a horse. My householder is packing you some breakfast, too."

This was news to me, a horse.

We walked round to the clearing from the back of the tent, Mordwen wishing to avoid conversation with anyone remaining in the shrine, as he admitted. "I'm as nervous as a cat," he said, "when I thought I was long past superstitions."

"I'm very superstitious," I said. "What do you mean?"

He narrowed his eyes at me, as if he had caught me making fun of him, though I was completely serious. "The morning ride is for luck," he said, "and in the days of the Praeven, signs the kyyvaeyi brought home were read as augury, sometimes very accurately. We don't have the means for reading ride-signs these days, the lore books are locked away in Cunuduerum. So we won't know whether you're bringing us good luck or bad."

"What did the last kyyvi bring?" I asked.

"The last kyyvi did not do the morning ride," Mordwen said. "It's been a long time since Kirith Kirin required it."

We were near the clearing, where only a few folks were still milling about, suspended between Velunen and the journey toward breakfast. A murmur of astonishment went up ahead of us. I could see nothing but Mordwen's back and the headdress of a Cordyssan noblewoman, pearl studded roosts of hair. The headdress tilted precariously and vanished. The crowd parted. Mordwen, his expression gone suddenly sour, stepped to one side.

Kirith Kirin had taken Nixva from the groom and was walking toward me. Nixva tossed his black head, the fine velvet of his mouth quivering, as if to say we were headed for a fine life together, a fine ride, morning after morning. I gazed at them both in wonder, Prince and stallion, hearing nothing of the hubbub in the crowd.

I took the reins from his hand. He nodded, ever so slightly. Though he said nothing, the fact of the gift was plain and I could hear the reaction from those gathered.

Mordwen knelt next to me and whispered, "Now you get on the horse and ride east. Let Nixva have his head. Return at midheaven and look for me."

We contrived to seem as though Mordwen were helping me onto the horse as he whispered these instructions. Kirith Kirin stood close by. "Return with luck," Kirith Kirin said.

I nudged Nixva gently with my booted feet. The big horse tossed his head and cantered through the clearing, unmindful of those who drew aside out of his path, taking that deference as his due. I watched them in the clearing, Kirith Kirin and Mordwen, Karsten and Imral joining them in the pale light and watered shadow of new day.

5

I rode in open Woodland with golden light pouring down. The second sun has a clear, cool light that is said to be calming. It was beautiful, that morning.

Mist rolled between shaggy tree trunks and along huge falls of vine. Nixva pulsed, the beat of his stride pouring through me, waves of strength radiating from him along with unmistakable joy, and I believe he could have galloped forever, uncomplaining. I felt the same exhilaration, as if I too might live forever, as if the world might be endlessly new.

We rode through Goldenwood beneath trees that glowed like a roof of flame. We followed a path Nixva seemed to know, a lane where a horse could pass unhindered by underbrush. He stopped in a broad clearing through which a brook ran. I found myself a grassy seat by the water, unwrapping my bread and cheese, eating both hungrily while Nixva made a meal on clover. Light filled the sky, winds blowing monumental clouds across the blue expanse. Birds sang nonsense in the trees, bright noises, high trills and echoing arias. The wind blew across the treetops, sending flowing waves across the grass, tangling Nixva's heavy mane. From this scene, or some scene like it, I was to recognize a sign worth remembering for

Mordwen. The word for luck is suuren. It is also the word for a star that appears for the first time in the sky, one that we may never have seen before and will not name. I was looking for suuren to take back to camp.

I might have worried as long as I chose, sitting there beside the brook with my mouth full of cheese, but Nixva was watching me as if he knew what our business entailed and my idleness displeased him. I packed my food away, slipping it inside the leather pouch at my waist, and rinsed my hands in the brook. Returning to Nixva, I took his head in my hands, looking deep into his eyes. "My lord prince of horses," I said, "this is a fine morning for a ride, and no one could ask for a better horse, but I don't know what I'm looking for."

He answered with something like, *Get on my back and you may find out; you certainly won't find anything standing in the grass.*

I got on his back obediently, whether I heard his answer or made it up. He tossed his head and let it be known he would continue as the guide.

I had forgotten, in our more leisurely riding along the Arthen road, how fast Nixva could go when he wanted to, a black blur along the grass, as on the morning when we crossed the Queen's Girdle and entered the Woodland. I felt peculiarly attuned to him, the wave of his motion, the two of us riding the center of the wave where each stride of his galloping burst us through to the next moment. I felt present with him in that way. Even in the forest he could find a path safe for us both, since I made myself such an insignificant package against his back, the stirrups pulled up short and my weight supported just over the warm saddle by tensed legs. Riding above the saddle, resting on it for a moment, lifting myself again. We rode so far the countryside changed again. The trees were iron-colored, both bark and leaves. The grass took on a gray cast, and the wildflowers bloomed in shades of blue, silver and bronze. It was wonderful country, taking my breath away. Nixva tossed his head proudly, cantering beneath the trees, letting me get a good look at the abundant flower beds, offerings of star-shaped silver petals, delicate lattices of leaves, fine as moss. Nixva was vain as if he had invented the whole country himself.

The wonder of the place seized me completely and I lived in my eyes. Nixva cantered with a purposefulness that led me to believe we had not yet reached our destination, even amidst this vision of wonders. The forest became open and airy, trees competing less fiercely for the light, which fell in abundance. The sky was blue as if it were burning with the color, tumbles of clouds parading, helpless to resist the wind that impelled them, that tossed the trees, that swept the grass.

We came at last to a wide clearing, set with stones about the perimeter, with a rock shrine at the center. One could tell it was a shrine by the YYmoc carved on flat stone. The rock was craggy, moss-covered, with a smell of age. Beneath the altar, hidden at the back of a carved rock shelf, an old lamp sat, of a gray metal the Smiths make that refuses to rust. I had to get down on my knees to find it, but I thought it must be somewhere; what use is a shrine without a lamp? No oil, of course.

Looking at it, with Nixva behind me making complacent noises, preening himself between mouthfuls of grass, I said, "So this is suuren for today," running my hands along the rough stone.

Nixva stamped his approval. I walked round the shrine slowly, getting a good look at it, in case Mordwen Illythin should ask me a lot of questions. Surely this must be a famous place, a shrine in the middle of such an odd part of the Woodland. I replaced the lamp carefully and mounted Nixva, meaning to turn him toward camp.

But he stood curiously still. The wind died also, and every sound vanished. The day, the whole Woodland, drew in breath and paused.

Vaguely I heard music, clear singing. Then silence. Far off, at the edge of the clearing, three figures on horseback watched me, draped like ladies of a rich house, their horses stamping, tossing their manes. I saw them only a moment, then they were gone, much faster than they could have turned those immense horses, vanishing more completely than mere tree shadow and distance could account for. A breath of perfume reached me when the wind resumed. Birds began their singing again. Nixva snorted, tugging at the reins.

Three ladies in rich clothes, riding horses that were beautiful even when compared to my own horse, the son of Keikindavii. Arthen has the name of a place where magic can happen. I had a feeling I had seen my first piece of it.

6

I returned Nixva to the Prince's horsemaster, Thruil, who took him away to feed him oats and give him such other care as royal horses receive. Nixva suffered the groom's handling with the ease of any master to his servant, turning his head to me and blowing out his breath; *That wasn't such a bad ride*, he was saying, *and we'll do it again tomorrow*.

I hurried through the tent city to the Nivri precinct, remembering Mordwen's instructions on how to find his tent. He was waiting for me in the clearing beneath the banner that flew in front of his pavilion. "You returned at about the proper time. Was this your instinct or the horse's?"

"A little of both."

"Then you gave Nixva his head?"

"He seemed to require it."

This made Lord Illythin smile ever so slightly, and he walked into the sunlit woods, signaling me to follow. "You have respect for him, which is a good thing. If you didn't respect his wishes, you wouldn't sit on his back for very long." He paused in a patch of sunlight, its radiance illuminating his thick hair, his lined face, the dull-colored robe he wore.

After a moment's hesitation, I asked the question foremost in my mind at the time. "Is Nixva mine?"

Lord Mordwen looked down his long nose at me. "It would seem so."

"Why were people so angry?"

"Royal horses bear children only once in a lifetime. And Nixva is the youngest of the Keikin's offspring. The gift of a true-horse is a sign that a house is very powerful. Some of the Nivri had their eye on Nixva. They'll refuse to understand why Kirith Kirin gave this precious gift to a farm boy from the Fenax."

"Should I give him back?"

"Heavens no. You would mortally offend Kirith Kirin. Never mind what anyone thinks, the horse is his to give as he pleases. In many ways you're the wisest choice possible, since you offend all the Nivri and the Finru equally."

I remembered his own reaction from the morning, and worked up my nerve. "The gift didn't seem to please you so much earlier."

Mordwen eyed me thoughtfully. "I will have to remember you have a tendency to ask brazen questions. No, the news didn't please me at first. But his reasons were good ones. Now that I've watched you for a while, it seems to me you're the right master for Nixva."

"Why? I've done nothing but light the lamps."

He chuckled, scratching his hairy knuckles on the bark of a tree. "Never mind. We'll let you wonder what your virtues are in order not to limit their scope by praise. Suffice it to say I do not like children but I find you tolerable and am not in despair at the prospect of having you in the shrine. No more questions." He touched his finger against my lips; I had indeed been about to let fly with another one. "We are about to take you to your tutor. But first tell me what you saw on your ride."

"A shrine made of stone, one that looked as if it were carved a long time ago, sitting in the center of a field where the grass was gray and the trees all around were gray, a strange country."

"Describe the shrine."

This being the question I had anticipated, I took a deep breath and pictured the heap of stone in my mind. I told him about it, omitting nothing, going into much detail about the lamp, a simple cylinder of metal, much plainer than the lamps used for Kirith Kirin's altar. I described the countryside thereabouts in more detail too, in case the Seer should think that was important. After I had been talking a while, he said, "Good, good, that's enough. Do you want to know where you were?"

I had been just at the point of telling him about the image of the three ladies, but his grand manner halted me. "Where was I?"

"Hyvurgren Field. One of the oldest shrines, built by the Diamysaar, a holy place. That part of the Woodland is called 'Raelonyii' because the trees give off soft light whenever two white moons are in the sky." He said this in a dreamy voice, hardly aware that he was speaking to me. But his eyes narrowed slightly. "Hyvurgren is half a day's ride from here. It's only just past mid-morning now."

"We got there in no time," I said, "Nixva was fast."

"How can he have been that fast?" He made me describe the place again, which I did. This time, when I got to the part about seeing the image of the three women, I felt a sudden dread and fell silent. Mordwen, fretting about the distance to the shrine, ignored my disquiet. "That's Hyvurgren all right," he said, "there's no other place it could be."

He recorded my ride in the book he carried, writing in square, bold letters, "The kyyvi rode to Hyvurgren Field, one of the Naming Fields, in Raelonyii." I could not read the letters but he told me what they meant. He explained a Naming Field was a place where the Jhinuuserret received the name from God, the Umiism, as well the signs that accompany a true-naming. These fields are very holy places, five of them altogether, each with a shrine built by the YY-Sisters.

I remarked that I was surprised no one had stolen the lamp in all these years if the Sisters themselves made it; Mordwen only smiled. "I wouldn't doubt people have tried."

He led me back to his tent, the book under his arm and the words written in it, "The kyyvi rode suuren to Hyvurgren Field." I had intended to tell him about the women but had not done so. The omission seemed purposeful, and I said no more.

One chamber of his tent had been converted into a school-room. We went there without any further warning or delay, and I met my tutor, Kraele, a woman of Mordwen's household. Lessons in High Speech began immediately, without any prelude. Kraele told me the name for simple objects, and made me repeat them. She taught me a phrase I have always remembered, "Whatever sun the day brings, it's best not to quarrel with it." I went away from the lesson repeating the words.

It was good after so much newness to retreat to the shrine tent, to tend the altar again, to polish the deniire lamp, picturing the colored light flaming from its jeweled heart. The deniire is the most compact of the ritual lamps, being shaped like a pyramid with a jewel at its crown, a white, clear stone called "iire", the Eye of God. Mordwen had described the light it shed, a splendid, austere rainbow, colors shifting as the flame consumes the oil. This is a very expensive lamp to own, because of the iire.

As I worked I sang an old song Grandmother Fysyyn taught me, "If I sow beside all waters," peaceable words in the language of the farm country. I went on singing even when I heard voices in the outer shrine. I was not nervous, I felt no shrinking; rather, it was as with Nixva, the rhythm of the moment carried me. I sang softly in one language, picturing new words in another. As I carried the deniire lamp out from the workroom Mordwen nearly ran into me headlong. He took a good look at me and slowly smiled. Saying nothing, he walked ahead of me into the shrine room.

Many faces, as before. Some of them I recognized, but only one I looked for: Kirith Kirin, fresh from riding. But even he seemed quite far away. I was separate from them, I was, in my mind's eye, facing the shrine in the wide field in the country of iron trees, the place Mordwen Illythin had called Hyvurgren. I was carrying the deniire to its holy place, to the altar where YY-Mother watches, her single eye the gem that crowned the lamp. I was in the field and the three women were listening.

The last moment of light quavered, resonated, the vuthloven glowing. The muuren went dark. I touched the fire to the lamp and felt the colored light pour outward like a caress, bands of fire, silver, ice-blue. As I sang the Evening Song the light dressed me in richness, coloring the faces before me in the gauzes of sunset, blood-reds, fiery golds, royal blues and crimsons striving with one an-other. It took one's breath away. For this reason the deniire must be burned sparingly, Mordwen told me later; the lamp-lighting should not become a spectacle. But that moment was perfect, even Mordwen agreed, I could see it in his face. I finished Kithilunen and felt everyone's breath go out. I closed my eyes for joy, the rhythm of breathing engulfing me like a sea.

A moment later I was behind the shrine, leaning against the high bronze base, my mind a blank, too full from the day to care.

Footsteps approached and I drew myself erect, expecting Mordwen, maybe come to tell me something I had done wrong. I tried to pack away the exalted feeling, to clear my mind, to set my-self on a more businesslike, less rapturous base. But when I turned there was Kirith Kirin.

"You're a treasure," he said. "I've never heard better singing."

I said thank you, using the High Speech word. He raised a brow at that. "Well spoken. You've had your first lesson."

"Yes, all day, after the ride. My head is swimming in words. I wonder if I'll remember any of it tomorrow."

"Puzzle it out. It'll be good to hear you speak like a Jisraegen."

His stern tone made me feel like a child again, after the exhilara-tion of the first moment.

A shadow appeared beyond the shrine. Imral stepped into the narrow lane. "Mordwen thinks he should come behind, Kirith Kirin, for propriety's sake. Most of the lords are still waiting for you to come out."

Kirith Kirin never stirred. He smiled at me. "Tell Mordwen I'm on my way. Tell him to stay where he is."

Imral glanced at me, skeptically. For some reason the glance made me feel furtive, and I was troubled till Kirith Kirin said, "You'll have to get used to people watching, too, won't you? All kinds of people."

When I raised my eyes he was gone.

I went into my room and sat down on the cot. Mordwen found me sitting, staring, just that way.

CHAPTER FOUR
KYYVI

1

Prince Imral's naming feast took place that evening, far from the shrine tent within which I remained, with only the sentries for company. Yet, in the end, I joined the feast, though not as an invited guest. Late in the evening, without warning, Uncle Sivisal came to fetch me, accompanied by the Ordinary, Gaelex.

"The Prince has asked to see us," Uncle Sivisal said, and something in his face frightened me. "Do you have a coat? Get it."

I slipped the sleeved garment over my arms and we hurried along the path. Gaelex and my uncle preceded me without conversation, and I kept the proper silence of a child.

We were led to the Prince's pavilion from behind, to avoid disturbing the celebration, still in progress. At the rear entrance, Gaelex stood to the side and said to Uncle Sivisal, "Kirith Kirin is waiting." I followed Sivisal through the tent flap.

He was two chambers beyond, in a small room fitted for a council meeting, cushions strewn about the floor, low writing tables here and there, a clay lamp burning, dim light for late evening. He was dressed in a tunic of rich blue. His dark skin shone. At first he did not look at me. He said, "Thank you for coming, Sivisal," without moving, and Sivisal bowed his head. We three were alone in the chamber. A breeze stirred the tent walls, and Kirith Kirin's voice rose over me, deep and firm. "Sit by me here, Jessex. The scouts have returned from your home."

He indicated a place on the cushion close to him. I sat quietly, saying nothing. From his face I knew he had bad news. I was afraid to move or make a sound. I could feel the tension in his body next to me. I knew I had begun to cry, I could feel the liquid on my face. But I felt a distance in myself. He watched without knowing what to do. At last Uncle Sivisal sat next to me and embraced me, as Kirith Kirin muttered something in High Speech. Then, in Upcountry, "But you don't know what that means, do you?"

"No, Kirith Kirin." I watched him stupidly, without a thought in my head.

Trouble filled him, his face darkening as I watched. "Your farm is burned, Jessex. Your family is dead or vanished." He swallowed, watching me at first, then looking into the shadows of the chamber. "My scouts found some bodies. One girl was still alive in part of the barn that was left standing. She died before the village doctor could reach her. Her name was Mikif. She told my soldiers what she could remember."

The words echoed in my head. I wiped my eyes with my sleeve and got my breath. "The witch killed them?"

"The soldiers killed them. The witch looked on. Later she questioned your mother. The girl, Mikif, could not remember much after a point. But my soldiers said your mother was taken south."

He had said all he could say. For a moment I was too stunned to feel. I remembered the story of Commiseth and his daughter Sergil. My poor Mikif. I pictured her as I had heard Sergil described, her face broken, her back a mass of welts; I hardly knew I was still crying or that Uncle Sivisal was still near me. "Jessex," he was saying, "Jessex," he whispered it like a chant in my ear. I gave way entirely, leaning against him, hugging him fiercely. I quieted after a while. Uncle Sivisal asked, "Why would they take my sister?"

"I'm not sure," Kirith Kirin said. He clenched his jaw muscles, and his gaze hardened. "We'll know soon enough, though. Two of my picked guard are trailing the party south." He spoke to me now. "If anything can be done for your mother, it will be, Jessex. But it's likely she's being taken to Drudaen."

I closed my eyes. "What would he want with her?"

"I don't know. But he hasn't sent Julassa Kyminax so far for no reason."

"We only had a farm. My father paid his taxes, high as they were. Mother made good cheese. What does the Wizard want from us?"

He shook his head, and Sivisal bowed his. "There is you, Jessex. You were called to Arthen, to my service." Kirith Kirin went on soberly. "Julassa questioned your mother about magic. She suspected your mother of witchcraft."

He fell silent then. He was as puzzled as I was; and as afraid. After a time he said, in a voice full of feeling, "Will you forgive me for this, Jessex?"

"Forgive you, Kirith Kirin?"

"This happened because you were called here. Will you despise me because of that?"

I remembered the necklace spinning in the light of my mother's room. Her face, slightly troubled, as it passed from her hand to mine. I said, "God sent the dream to Mordwen. My mother wanted me to come where I was called."

After a while he prepared to return to the naming feast for Prince Imral. He had left his guests to give me this news himself. He went to the flap, saying to Sivisal, "The party from the farm is waiting to talk to you, if you want to question them. I've told them to answer your questions without concealing anything. You and the boy have the right to know as much as you wish."

"I'd like to talk to them now," Sivisal said.

He turned to the door and spoke to Gaelex again. The soldiers entered within moments.

2

Uncle Sivisal made them recount the whole story. When they seemed reluctant to describe any particular fact, he questioned them closely until he was certain they were sparing no detail.

Smoke was still rising from the ruined farmyard when the soldiers found the place. Our neighbors had not found the courage to visit; the Queen's troops had only been gone from the village a day. Kirith Kirin's people rode through the farmyard, finding the bodies of my father, Sim and Lise, cut apart by swords, partly eaten by carrion birds. Some of the soldiers built a pyre to burn the bodies while the others searched through the ruined farm buildings. They found Jarred, Histel and Vaguath hanged in the orchard, within sight of the house. Mikif had identified the bodies. Sim's wife and child were burned in their house; the soldiers found charred bones and naming necklaces, scant remains. Mikif was found in what sounded like the milking shed, though it was hard to tell. It took them a while to find her; she had heard them ride in but had been afraid the Blue Cloaks were returning; when she saw one of the soldiers in a red-trimmed cloak she called out for help. She was in a bad way when the soldiers found her; they sent a member of the party to Mikinoos to bring the physician, but Mikif did not last that long. The soldiers questioned her through her last moments. They said she seemed eager to talk.

She gave them the few details they knew about the raid. The Blue Cloaks appeared a few days after I left, at sunset, when Father had already come in from the fields and everyone was in the house. The Kyminax witch rode into the yard and called out my mother's name. Mother went outside, not knowing who the woman was. The soldiers had immediately tried to drag her off, and my father rushed at them, flanked by Histel, Lise and Sim; the soldiers cut them down where they stood.

Julassa questioned Mother for a long time. Mikif only heard a little of that; the Blue Cloaks had dragged Mikif into the barn by then. The witch asked again and again, where had my mother learned magic? Where was her youngest son? When Mother refused to answer either question, the witch ordered Jarred hanged, and then Histel and Vaguath after him, when Mother still refused to speak.

Mikif remembered nothing beyond that, and died soon after she finished telling what she knew. She spent her last moments describing the size of the Blue Cloak war party, their uniforms, their weapons, the few names she could remember. Twenty soldiers had ridden into the farmyard. None of them were from the regular northern detachments, as best Kirith Kirin's soldiers could tell. The Blue Cloaks had worn Drudaen's crest, the black raven against storm clouds. He had sent the raiders himself.

The Red Cloaks had ordered the dead burned and mounds raised over the places where their smoke went up. I need not picture carrion birds feasting. A hound had been found wandering about the farmyard, obviously a family pet. They had brought the beast to Arthen, to me.

"Where is he?" I asked, hoping against hope; there were several dogs on our farm. Gaelex answered, "I've asked for it to be brought here. Do you have more questions?"

"No, ma'am. Thank you. Thank you all."

I found myself singing Kimri under my breath, as I had on the morning when I rode into Arthen, when the witch all but had me in her grasp. Uncle Sivisal heard me, and came to sit with me again.

Gaelex returned to say the dog was too big to bring into the tent. A sudden gladness possessed me. "Axfel!"

In the yard I saw nothing at first, then the outlines of trees, then a huge blur leapt on me with its paws on my chest, and a wet tongue found my face. I embraced Axfel for all I was worth. In his damp, shaggy fur was the smell of my home; memory flooded me and I could not move. I was lost in the hills around our farm, Axfel dragging his tongue through the grass, Jarred running toward me with the news that a stranger in a red cloak had ridden into our farmyard…I finished my crying there, quietly, and nobody bothered me till I was done. I dried my eyes and sat still on the ground for a long time. At last I asked, "Will they let me keep Axfel at the shrine tent, Gaelex? Do you know?"

"I'm not sure. I don't know of a kyyvi who ever kept a dog before."

"Kirith Kirin has dogs."

"Most folks do," Gaelex admitted. She frowned. "But they don't live in the shrine tent. You can't let a monster like this anywhere near the lamps."

"He wouldn't have to come inside. He would live wherever I told him to live. Isn't that right, Axfel?"

The hound stared at Gaelex solemnly, and Gaelex contemplated him with equal fervor. She said, "I imagine you'll be able to keep the dog with you."

Axfel quietly sat with me, and we watched the moons over the trees. Distant voices threw their echoes over us but no one found us. I was picturing horses riding in darkness, twenty followed by two. I was picturing my mother on her horse, lips pursed with secrets, the witch's eyes on her. At fourteen I had no notion how I should feel. Now as I am writing, many years beyond fourteen, the image comes on me with fresh bitterness.

3

Later, in my cot, I dreamed I was lying in my father's barn. A fire was burning and I could hear screaming outside. Through the open barn door I saw my father sprawled in the dirt, arm crooked over his head at an impossible angle, a hint of red in his mouth, a red gash in his shirt. Soldiers were shouting in the yard and some of them called my name.

In the dream I had been lying in the same position for a long time and my legs were beginning to go to sleep. But I was afraid to move in case somebody should hear me. A lump in the pocket of my tunic was stabbing me in the breastbone. With the least motion possible I drew out the lump from my pocket, the necklace my mother had given me.

The raven flying downward onto the curved talon of some larger bird. Silver chain dangling over yellow hay. I clutched it in my fist as a shadow fell across the doorway, a cloaked figure, hood drawn forward so that no face could be seen. A voice issued from the cloak, and the voice could have been man or woman. "I will be in his mind," the voice said, "even if I never find him. I will be in his mind wherever he is. He will never be rid of the fear of me."

I woke at this point, huddled beneath the wool blanket with a cool breeze blowing through my window. My heart was racing from the dream, and in spite of myself I checked every corner of the room for the hooded figure, hearing the echo of the dream voice in my head. I did not have the nerve to investigate the shrine. After I had got my breath I retrieved the necklace from its hiding place, cutting open the seam of my mattress and drawing out the cloth pouch. I studied the locket in the moonlight. The silver gleamed in my palm.

This was why he had taken my mother. This necklace. In my mind I could see her hand touching the necklace in the rune-box. She had been afraid when she opened it. Maybe she had guessed what might come.

A jewel like that one would have been famous for leagues, would have made my mother a rich woman, as rich as my father's farm could ever make her, and yet I had never heard of it, not even from Fysyyn. But according to my mother, the necklace had belonged to Fysyyn once, and Fysyyn had given it to her.

Unnamable fear seized me. I heard the sentry walk by my window and nearly called out. But for what? What could I tell anyone, except that I had a bad dream, that I had seen my father lying in the dirt. *I will be in his mind wherever he is.*

I closed my around the necklace. No, I thought, you will not. You do not have power over me.

4

Kirith Kirin woke me the next morning, his face hovering over me in dim light. I thought it was another dream, but when I opened my eyes he drew back, as if he wanted to escape without being seen. I sat up and he smiled. "I didn't mean for you to wake up. I wanted to make sure you were resting."

"Is it close to dawn?"

"Yes. I couldn't sleep so I came to sit in the shrine."

A far away birdcall echoed in the night. I pulled the blanket around my shoulders and leaned against the fabric wall. "Mordwen will be here soon, Kirith Kirin. He told me last night he was coming early to make sure I woke up in time."

He glanced warily at the door and listened for several heartbeats. From outside one could hear only the breathing of the guard. Kirith Kirin said, "I shouldn't be here. Mordwen would skin me alive. I'll go soon."

But he was not in any hurry. With him so close I felt tension seize me again, unfamiliar tautness restricting my chest. He asked how I had slept and I told him about my dream, the dark hooded figure, my father's body lying in the dirt. The dream troubled him, and when I was finished telling it, he seemed more dispirited than before.

Whether he would have said anything more, I can't say.

Mordwen Illythin walked into the chamber, frowning so darkly I wanted to crawl under the bed. Kirith Kirin flushed. Mordwen faced him. The Seer was so angry he trembled. "Have you forgotten yourself completely?"

"I couldn't sleep and I came to the shrine to think. I looked in on Jessex to make sure he was sleeping. He woke up. You don't need to go on like this."

"What if someone were to find you here, or see you leaving? Have you no feeling for the boy?"

Kirith Kirin blushed and closed his mouth, thinking better of whatever he had been about to say. "Be careful." He sighed, heavily. He stood, turned toward the doorway, his face in shadow. "Good morning, Jessex."

"Good morning, Kirith Kirin." My throat taut and aching. He walked out the door without looking back. He spoke to the guard and walked away. Mordwen stood by the window till his footfalls died to silence.

He lifted the felva from its place inside the chest. He started to hand it to me and then hesitated, tucking the robe under his folded arms and sitting on the edge of the cot. "I ought not to help you break the rules for the ceremony, but since you've already spoken, and since you haven't yet touched the felva, I want to say this much to you. Kirith Kirin is very lonely, Jessex. In spite of his friends, in spite of Kiril Karsten and Imral Ynuuvil, in spite of me and Pelathayn. You seem to have touched him deeply. I believe that's a good thing. But you're still a boy under our laws."

"I woke up and he was here. I didn't do anything." A sudden ache of loneliness filled me.

He lay his hand on my brow. His touch was gentle. Words dissolved that he had planned to say. "You'll have to cut the bath short, it's close to sunrise. I won't go with you today. From now on this is your quiet time."

I slipped the felva across my shoulders, finding my boots in the dim light. The clearing was silent as I headed through the underbrush, following the path to the creek.

5

Days passed. The shock of bad news eased, though a dull ache remained. The curious came each morning to see the boy the Seer had summoned to Arthen: child of a local witch, descendant of stewards, standing in a place reserved for the daughters and sons of the gentry. I'm told my presence there caused unrest, but no one ever said so to my face.

The word for blood hatred is "duruth" in High Speech, and this is what I swore against the Kyminax witch and all those in her house. My lessons in High Speech progressed each day, the language coming to me like something I had known once but forgotten. I suppose that's only natural since Upcountry is a corruption of the Jisraegen original, but I was pleased to learn it effortlessly, to show Kraele I was no fool. She was a patient teacher, but always distant.

Soon enough my private sorrow gave way to other concerns. In the world beyond Arthen, events were coming to a head.

News from Cordyssa was worse than ever. Poor families from across the tax-impoverished Fenax were migrating to the city, living in the streets, begging for bread. Begging soon became rioting, as food grew scarce. The garrison of Queen's soldiers in Fort Bremn had tried to enforce the peace but ended up killing several of the migrants. To make matters worse, royal couriers and a fleet of Ivyssan accountants had arrived with new tax edicts and orders for a complete audit of city and citizens in the spring.

I know for a fact a messenger came to Arthen with a letter for Kirith Kirin from the City Nivra, Ren Vael. When the messenger arrived the Prince was on a hunting trip in the southern Woodland, Maugritaxa. The letter was urgent and the messenger rode on with an escort from camp.

Kirith Kirin had gone hunting the day after Mordwen found him with me in the shrine tent. Imral Ynuuvil accompanied him along with a party of favored gentry. Nothing was ever said to me about this trip, and I was too naive to suspect that it had anything to do with me.

I performed my duties in the shrine, worked at my lessons, trained with the youngest group of archers, beginning drill in the use of the crossbow. Each morning I rode suuren through the Woodland, returning to Mordwen to describe something for him, a forest glade, a scrap of cloud, a landmark, a beautiful tree. Sometimes he could add to what I saw, as he had when I found Hyvurgren Field. Other times he simply wrote what I told him, always staring at the words after he had written them. He was trying to make some pattern of them. The Praeven, the priests of Cunuduerum, had been able to find a rhythm in the suuren. But if there was a pattern, it escaped Mordwen.

Only one other time during this interim did I deceive him by omitting something unusual. One morning a few days after Kirith Kirin had left Camp, I let Nixva pick our path for us and he headed east toward the nearest arm of River where one of the old roads cut through the forest, easy to follow as if it had been freshly cleared. These roads have existed since early Jisraegen days, the encroachment of undergrowth being prevented by an old enchantment within the obelisks that will last as long as the stones do. The Praeven made the obelisks and over millennia gardened the Woodland to its present state, and in its design Arthen is still as they saw it, for that part of their work pleased YY-Mother. The fact that Nixva had brought us to the road led me to anticipate some worthwhile destination. Mordwen told me there were memorials and shrines hereabouts, some of them dating back to the millennia before the Jisraegen built cities or towns.

I found no shrine or temple but I did happen across an old stone well, and at the well a tall, broad-shouldered woman was turning the crank to draw up a bucket of water for her cart-horse, which stood lazily chewing grass in a patch of sunlight by the roadside. She called a greeting to me in Jisraegen, and I replied that I did not know the language very well yet, though I could wish her a good-day in it. This made her laugh. "Maybe you speak this language then," she said in Upcountry. "I think I hear the northern rhythm in your words. Are you a farm-boy, lost in the forest?"

She stood as tall as Imral, with an angular face distinguished by heavy, dark brows, a well-formed, strong nose and a full, feminine mouth. She looked as if she might be my mother's age, her black hair touched with gray, fine lines around her eyes. But her body was obviously vigorous and there was no heaviness in her movements as she cranked the water-filled bucket upward, hefting it over the low stone well and filling the rock trough. Her horse drank gratefully as the woman watched me. "Can't you speak?"

"Yes ma'am, I can. Excuse me, I was surprised. I didn't expect to meet anybody out here. Are you from Camp?"

She hung the bucket on the rope again. "No, I'm from much farther away than that. From far beyond the mountains."

"I never heard of anybody from that far away. Are you on your way to Camp?"

"Why should I be?"

"Because no one is supposed to live in Arthen unless Kirith Kirin allows it, and he only allows folks to live in Camp. That's what I thought."

She was picking a burr out of the mane of the cart horse, which lazily lashed its tail even though this was much too early in the year for flies. "Kirith Kirin would be glad to see me if he knew I were here, but he doesn't know, and he won't know, because you're not going to tell him."

Her tone of voice was the same my mother used when she meant to be obeyed. I was not offended, but watched her more carefully. "I'm supposed to tell Mordwen Illythin what I see when I ride in the morning."

"Not everything you see. Mordwen knows that."

"Do you know him too?"

"I know many of the people in your camp. I know Nixva. I know you too, Jessex son of Kinth." She said this while she was checking her horse's harness. "I know why you came to Woodland. I may even tell you someday."

"Tell me now."

"No." She climbed into the cart and lifted the reins. The horse stopped drinking as if she had commanded him without my hearing. "But I'll see you again." At last she smiled, quite coyly. "Unless you tell anybody you saw me. Then I won't. And you'll never know more than you do man."

I bit my lip. No, I would not beg her; in fact I would not make a sound. After a heartbeat I bowed my head, and she received the forced courtesy graciously. She turned her handsome face away, swatted the horse on the rump with the reins and the cart heaved down the path.

The thought of following her never occurred to me. I doubt Nixva would have allowed it. While the woman had been talking and watering her horse Nixva stood calmly, never impatient, never stamping his feet as he usually did when he wanted to be running. He listened to the woman's voice and watched her. The wonder was not simply that she had said his name; he had also recognized her.

I rode home with that to think about. As usual I left Nixva with the groom and hurried to Mordwen's tent where I found the Seer bent over the suuren book, studying the listings he had already entered, his brows furrowed together, a veritable ridge of hair. He gestured me to sit on a cushion without greeting me by as much as a word. He asked what I had seen. I told him about the road and the well. About the woman I said nothing. He entered the road by its proper name; I never paid the least attention to it and consequently cannot remember it now. He said, "This makes no sense to me. I don't remember a well. I almost wish we had not brought back the ride, it troubles me so much."

I asked him why but he would not tell me. Soon he sent me to Kraele for my lesson in High Speech.

6

One afternoon, when Mordwen Illythin had closed the suuren book, I asked him to tell me about his dream, the one that had brought me to Arthen.

We were seated on cushions under an awning in the clearing behind his tent. Dappled light crossed our faces. He heard my question and quietly turned to the householder, asking for tea. "Do you know anything about true-dreaming?"

"No. In the stories I've heard, you only get what happened afterward, when the dream came true."

"These days there are only a few true-dreamers left, as far as we know—one in Cordyssa, one in Drii, some old codgers in the mountains. No one in the south."

"Is a true-dreamer the same as a Seer?"

"Not precisely. A Seer is a harder thing to be. A true-dreamer dreams in sleep, when the mind is free to unlock itself, when the sleeper learns what has been in the hidden parts of his knowledge. A Seer can be overcome by the vision even while waking. This is the way it is with me. Or the way it was."

The householder returned with tea and sweetbreads. Mordwen sipped his tea in silence, holding the delicate cup carefully poised. "Your dream came to me in the shrine, in the afternoon. The kyyvi was sick with fever and the physicians were baffled; they had told me the girl was likely to die, but they didn't know exactly what she was dying of. I knelt to pray for her life but when I was on my knees, sight left me. In place of the altar I saw your farm, Jessex. I was hovering in the air above your house and a voice was telling me your name and your lineage, the fact that you would be kyyvi, the test by which you could be known, other signs. This was not the only dream I dreamed, either. Later I foresaw that you would meet Kirith Kirin in Cunuduerum. I told that part only to him."

He looked as if he had more to say, but suddenly became silent. He was watching me in a new way. "In my dream I was told this: 'Here is the youth who is awaited, who will return light to Imith Imril, who will sing by the water'. Imith Imril is the name for the Court of the Fountain in Cunuduerum, where you met Kirith Kirin. That's the place YY stood when she made Arthen and the first world. There you sang by the water."

Here is the youth who is awaited, who will return light to Imith Imril, who will sing by the water

He locked the suuren book into a casket—he had been holding it in his lap during this conversation, hands gripping it like an anchor. He gathered his cloak about him and stood. "You'll be late for your archery drill if you don't hurry. Theduril won't like that."

He bid me good-day and went inside his tent.

7

Kirith Kirin returned to Camp early one morning, riding into the clearing before the shrine tent just as celebrants were arriving for the morning ceremony. I was waiting for the muuren to change when I heard horses. I had no time to wonder at the sound, however, since the stone quickly clouded through, as it does when sunlight is gathering at the horizon, and I took my place before the altar, keeping my eyes on the ground lest I should lose my concentration. The mind must be in the proper place in order for the ceremony to please YY-Mother.

When I finished singing I carried the lamp to the rear chamber and disassembled it quickly, cleaning it with practiced movements.

When its components were locked safely inside the lamp box, I hurried through the before-shrine and clearing.

Nixva was awaiting me, Thruil standing beside him, stroking his velvet nose. Other horses were also waiting with him, the Keikin being one, ornate compared to his plainly attired son—Kirith Kirin had a jeweled bridle and a saddle trimmed with silver, while I rode with nothing but a blanket, a flat-style saddle and a leather bridle. Kirith Kirin was beside Thruil, and Imral was just behind him. Kirith Kirin watched me intently.

His return had caused a stir one could feel in the air like the charge that follows lightning. I could hear folks whispering about the Cordyssan messenger. But I paid little attention, taking the reins from Thruil, touching Nixva along his muzzle, mounting.

"Good morning Jessex. Have a peaceful ride."

Nixva wheeled and we rode away, like any other morning.

CHAPTER FIVE
ILLYN WATER

1

Clouds boiled and wind blasted onto the treetops, piercing my thin clothing with a cold like the dead of winter. Storms foretold themselves. Nixva ran as if a demon were chasing him beneath the darkening lower branches of trees. I huddled against his back, losing the first edge of joy and feeling a sharper companion take its place, a metallic taste of fear, a prickle along my scalp.

Spring storms are often violent in the north country, where high, sharp mountains surround the Fenax, where the cold wind can sweep down by accident or by design, boiling the warmer air to madness, wringing storm on storm out of the sky.

I saw lightning crashing on the horizon and heard the echo of thunder. Fine rain began to fall. I sealed the seams of my coat and fastened the throat clasp. I considered turning Nixva back to Camp since there was no ceremonially-prescribed time limit for the suuren ride. But I had seen no luck yet. Could I tell Mordwen I had become frightened by the fringes of a storm and forced Nixva back to Camp against his will?—obviously against his will, since he was galloping faster and faster toward the storm's full force.

I pressed my face into Nixva's damp mane and felt his powerful striding toward the center of the wind, a jarring through my whole frame, my flesh melding to the horse. We broke momentarily clear of the trees, riding through an open clearing, and suddenly I realized we were in Raelonyii again, the country of iron-colored trees. Nixva had brought us to the field where the stone shrine had stood unmolested since the days of Cunavastar. The rain splattered hard on my shoulders and lightning crashed from the sky. The wind was stronger than any I could remember, bearing down on me with a weight I could hardly withstand. Light flashed around me, and I remember Nixva rearing, and the wind dashing me from his back, and terror. I was falling, for a long time, it seemed.

Arms caught me at the last moment. I gazed up into a woman's face, round and ruddy, dark eyes and heavy lashes. She watched me impassively, as if I were a cat. I heard Nixva neighing joyously. My head struck something hard. Darkness engulfed me, the storm vanished, and I lay dreaming in a stranger's embrace.

2

In the haze that followed I was aware only of my breathing. The storm howled yet I was untouched by wind and rain, unable to move. Now and then I felt a vague touch along my skin, the brushing of a hand or a wind along my face. Once I heard voices, distant and detached. "How are we doing, sisters?" asked one voice.

"All right," said another. "Vissyn is steering pretty well for a change."

"I don't know what you're talking about," said a third voice, presumably Vissyn, a cheerful contralto with a feeling of depth. "I've never had a mishap at this altitude. It's only lower down I have trouble."

"I would hate to contradict you with facts," said the second voice, mellow and resonant.

"Pay attention to the child," snapped the first voice.

"He's quite all right," said the second, "I have him in a trance deep enough for a fourth-level novice."

"Oh do you," said the first. "Maybe you should take another look at your trance-work, sister."

"My heavens, he's hearing every word we say," said Vissyn.

"But that can't be," said the second voice, "I set the trance on him myself."

"I saw you," said Vissyn.

"You don't suppose he could have fought it off?"

"He is thought to be talented," said the first voice, and fingers brushed the lids of my eyes, and darkness returned.

Again, for an indeterminable time, I knew only darkness, quiet and a surrounding chill that made my bones ache. No more voices sounded in my ear, though now and then as I struggled within whatever bound me, I could feel the wisp of touch, catch a glimpse of a face, or—oddly—the jagged peak of a steel-colored mountain, crowned with shining snow. Fragments of the conversation I heard floated in and out of my consciousness. I understood I was moving. I understood there were three voices accompanying me, three women. I remembered my last moments of consciousness in Hyvurgren Field, where Nixva had reared up to avoid a flash of lightning.

Three women on horseback, richly dressed ...

One woman in a cart, stopping along the forest road to water her poor thin horse ...

I know why you have been brought to the Woodland

Again the brushing of fingers across my lids and unearthly singing, a soothing sound, words I could nearly understand like a pulse in my brain, lulling me into unconsciousness, into the place where no thought could find me.

So deeply was I entranced this time that I could not sense at what moment the traveling ceased. Time passed without my awareness of it. I thought vaguely of the lamps, dark in their cases, of the altar, of Kraele waiting with my lesson books and Theduril cursing me in front of the other archer-apprentices. Days and days might have passed since the flash of lightning in the holy field. When I swam upward into fuller awareness I knew I was stationary, I could feel a vast house over me and caverns beneath me, an awful cold penetrating my bones like stories of the cold at the roots of mountains. I felt as if I had become quite small. For a long time I tried to keep my mind blank, to keep awareness at arm's length, for fear I should feel the fingers on my eyelids yet again and be plunged downward into darkness for another interim. But more time passed and no touch came. Somnolence ebbed. I began to wonder where I was, to reason as to what had brought me here, to fear the future.

When I had lain still for what seemed endless days, with the cold enduring, numbing every part of me, my mind refusing sleep and clinging stubbornly to awareness, a voice from nowhere resounded in the darkness. While the voice lasted, I was pierced with the sweetest warmth. "Whose child is this, sleeping in the darkness?" someone asked.

Fear stole my voice for a moment, but at last I said, "The child you stole from Nixva's back, in the holy field in Arthen. Which one are you?"

"No child-stealer," the voice said—a feminine, deep, velvety voice, throbbing like a purring cat—"and what is Nixva's back to me?"

"You're the woman I met in Arthen," I said, "the hag who drove the cart with the skinny pony."

"Where is Arthen?"

I held firm to my resolve, and said, "You know well enough, since you have spied on me there and now have snatched me out of my rightful life."

"You're full of accusations. But you don't know what you're talking about."

The sound of my voice gave me confidence. "Yes I do. I saw you and your sisters my first morning as kyyvi, in Hyvurgren Field, and then I saw you on the road in Arthen, when you stopped to water your poor mistreated horse, and now you've stolen me away by magic, and I suppose you intend to sell me to Julassa Kyminax, or to Drudaen Keerfax himself. I know your voice. I've felt your hand on my brow. But I won't go to sleep again."

"Oh yes you will." I felt the touch along my lids, darkness closing in on me, though I fought it this time, knowing that it came on me by some power. I sang Kimri in my head. From above I sensed irritation and this time felt the touch a second and a third time before the darkness took me. I heard other voices speaking strange words though I could not distinguish them, and understood that she-who-spoke had not been alone, that her friends were with her.

I kept this thought with me when awareness flowed back more fully, and by then I had accustomed myself to the pattern of dark-ness-and-light, of sleep-and-then-awareness. I was not so much afraid. Again I was certain my body was not in motion, and in fact I was sure I was in the same place as before.

A different voice—the contralto, Vissyn—greeted me upon my return. "I certainly hope you're in a better temper today."

"I'm fine," I said. "Which one are you?"

Gentle laughter surrounded me, and the chill abated from my battered body for a while. "What do you mean, which one? I'm the same voice as before, there's only one of me."

"No, there are three of you," I said, "I saw you in Hyvurgren. You're different from the first voice. Your name is Vissyn, isn't it?"

She laughed again, but this time she didn't seem so sure of her-self. "I have no such name. In fact you have no business asking my name at all."

"Haven't I? When you snatched me off my horse's back and dragged me to YY-knows-where?"

"For your information I found you lying here in the snow. Did you know that's where you are, at the bottom of a snow drift? The snow is beautiful and white, and the sky is clear over your head, and wind is blowing across you, and your skin is quite blue. How did you get to the top of the mountain?"

"I'm not on any mountaintop," I said, "I'm in a room, and your sisters are with you in it and all of you are watching me. Why are you trying to trick me?"

"How do you know so much? You can't see, can you?"

"Not with my eyes," I said.

Again her laughter rang out, echo-less, as if we were under the broad sky; but still I was sure I was right. "What do you use to see then, if you don't use your eyes?"

"I don't care if you believe me or not. But I can see you. You have blonde hair. You are bending over me. Your eyes might be blue or green, and your lips are rather thin, and you use no paint on your face. You have your fingers just above my forehead waiting to send me back to sleep, but you hope you won't have to, because it hasn't been so easy keeping me asleep. Has it?"

"What do I care whether you sleep or not?" she asked.

"Your name is Vissyn," I said, ignoring the interruption, "and when I was brought here you were the one that carried the rest of us through the air. I heard the others making fun of you."

She said nothing else. After a moment I felt the touch again, the cool fingertips, but this time I was waiting. "I won't," I said, "you can't send me anywhere, because I won't go. My grandmother Fysyyn was a witch, and my mother was a witch, so powerful that Drudaen sent his servant Julassa to capture her, and I'm a witch too, ask the other trainees in Theduril's archery drill, they all say so; I stopped the lightning from falling on my uncle's horse. You won't send me anywhere." But already other fingertips were joining hers, already the warmth of her voice and presence were abating, and I felt sleep rise over me. "Why are you doing this? YY-Mother will punish you. I'm her servant, and she'll protect me sooner or later." Speech came more slowly. For a moment I thought I was gone, then I heard someone mumbling words, and caught at the sound like a handhold. "Even if you were Drudaen the Great I would not be afraid of you. I am the youth who is awaited, who has come to return light to Imith Imril, and I was found singing by the River as was foretold—"

The darkness evaporated entirely and the cold fled. For a moment I was free, and I saw the waking world, three women in rich black robes bending over me, jeweled rings on their fingers, an incredible radiance around them. They were startled when I sat up, throwing off the smooth cloth that had lain across my naked body, looking round at them all. Then the tallest of them, the broad-shouldered, dark-haired woman I had met on the road in Arthen, said a word I could not understand though I could hear it, and she lifted a white jewel aloft. She touched it to my brow quickly and the room vanished with a crackle like lightning. I was in darkness again, and alone, and sightless.

3

This time I was farther from my body than before, and the cold was absolute. I had a hard time breathing. While I had been unable to move for a long time, now I felt pain in my limbs like white fire burning. Fear did possess me then, and images formed in the void about me, horrible—my own body mangled, piles of lizards coiled round me, or Mikif with the soldiers on her, or the neighbor's daughter Sergil watching her father gasp, falling into the loop of rope, his neck cracking and his feet kicking, kicking, and becoming still. My mother, hands tied behind her, gagged and bruised from beatings, mounted onto a horse with the help of a Blue Cloak. When I fought away one image another took its place. Even now I don't like to remember everything I saw in that time.

Finally a vague figure formed in the shadows, the voice of my dream taking shape, the one who had warned me he would never leave my mind. He missed me in front of him at first, and I thought this odd, since my presumption had been that these images were always focused on me, that their purpose, the reason for their creation, was my torment. This one was searching. He was not hideous, either. He had a handsome face; not young and fresh like Kirith Kirin but smooth, white as porcelain, opaque, a beauty like stone. A small scar on his temple, throbbing. Words began to travel from him, and the sound was odd, threading out from his mouth like a tendril. I began to understand. His black eyes flicked from side to side. He was aware of me. He was searching for me.

Real fear grew in me, because I knew who he was.

Distance would mean nothing to him, he had vast power. Wherever I was, this was a place he knew about, and if he found me here, there was no protection for me, no Woodland around me to baffle him.

A measure of wakefulness returned. I fought to remember myself, my life that I was beginning to love, the light of the deniire lamp flowing in colors, the splendid bustle of Camp, the beauty of Arthen. Some of the cold left me and the white pain ebbed from my motionless limbs; but at the same time the mist-draped image became more distinct, and the voice clarified. "Jessex," he called, his voice tinkling like water over rocks, "son of Kinth, come to me, your strength become my strength, do not return to your body but join with mine…" His strong body became plain, became desirable; and I became lost in the motion of his lips forming the words, his restless gaze coming closer.

He was in front of me, he waited. He was lovely, yes, but not lovely in the way of the living, not like Kirith Kirin. He lifted his white hand toward me and would have touched me, would have laid his cool fingers on my brow, except that I was warned by what had happened before, I said, "No, whoever you are, you may not touch me here."

"But you are longing for me."

"No, I'm not. I forbid you."

His smiled never wavered. "You've been calling for me ever since you were taken from Arthen. I heard your voice. Tell me where you are and I'll come for you."

"I haven't called you."

"Tell me where you are and I'll come for you," he repeated, and his eyes were shining.

"I'm in the bottom of a snowdrift at the top of a mountain, the place where I want to be."

"You're being held against your will by skillful women," he said, "tell me where you are and I'll find you."

"I don't know you, why should I want your help?"

"You know me, you've always known me," his figure swelling in my sight, the cloud of him engulfing me, so that I foundered, the cold returning brutally, fiercer than before, a feeling of finality to it. "You'll enter me one day and never leave me, and your strength will be my strength, and we'll be more powerful than any, and all weather and winds and all forces of time and space will answer to us."

For a moment I was blank, and the sense of the brooding figure was overwhelming. But he was no more real than I was, here. Reality was far away for both of us: for me it was my body on a table in a wide, high chamber, beneath the scrutiny of three women. "I don't want you," I told him, "I don't need you, I despise you, you're my enemy, and my life will destroy your life. You're Drudaen the White-Handed, and you're very strong, but I'm not in your power and I never will be. If you could find my body you could kill me but I won't tell you where I am. I'm at the bottom of a snowdrift on the top of a high mountain and eagles are my friends. One day we will meet and I will see you dead. Till then don't trouble me."

It eased my fear to let my thoughts babble. I had no notion of any plan. But he was dismayed, I could feel it, and something born

into me understood this was my gain. The cloud that was his presence
was already re-gathering, however, and the cold held me more deeply
each moment. When his face began to form from the cloud my heart
sank. I could fight him while I was aware, but if sleep came over me
I had no idea what would happen. Tattered thoughts passed in and
out of my mind, phrases from Velunen, from Kimri. I closed my
eyes and felt the cold rise, the darkness increase. "Yes," he said, "that's
it, don't fight it any more, there's no need; so much cold and so much
pain, for nothing. When you could be so warm. When my voice
makes you warm even now. You are so far away from your body,
why go back? Why make such a long journey, when you can be
warm and happy here, with me. Since you won't tell me where you
are, sever the link yourself. One slender cord binds you to your body.
Unfasten it. Let your spirit be free to fly from this place with me.
Come with me southward. Let me take you to your mother—"

Her image was more concrete than his, and I saw her bruised
and battered as before, the rough-handed soldier dragging her onto
the impatient horse. Anger scorched me and he withdrew again;
and as he did another presence found us both, a pure light.

"Hail to you, Drudaen Keerfax, prince of fools," a voice said.

"I hear no one, I hear nothing," the cloud said.

"You hear me, you know me well enough." The other cloud
shimmered and took form. A beautiful woman stepped forward,
as if through a curtain of light, and I knew her to be the broad-
shouldered woman, the one who had sent me here, whom I had
thought to be my enemy. "The child is not for you. He is here
through my neglect and I claim him. You have no power over him
here, you can claim nothing."

"Jessex—"

She spoke aloud awful words and light crackled from her, show-
ers of particles of light, and a sound like music. "Listen Drudaen, I
have news. Yron is coming. You know that name, don't you? This
child is a sign. Save your strength while you can."

Anger swelled out from him and the cold became so sharp I
cried out. But he vanished and the woman returned to me. An
overwhelming gentleness engulfed me, and her voice hovered just
outside my ear. "Sleep a good sleep, a pure sleep this time, little
singer. We only meant to test you, not to kill you. When you wake
up you'll be in a good place."

Why did I believe her now? I let the warmth she radiated lull
me into rest, real rest, and knew nothing beyond that.

4

I awoke in my body, truly and at last, by the shores of a blue lake. Grass tickled the skin of my palms and a warm breeze blew over me. I was looking up into the branches of one of the great duraelaryn, and when I recognized the man-sized branches, the tiers of broad leaves rising toward the blue heavens, I sighed deeply. I had come home to Arthen.

From nearby I heard women's laughter and tried to sit up.

A shadow fell across my face. "Not yet," said a mellow voice, and a plump woman laid the back of her hand against my cheeks. "Be still, rest a while longer. You have a lot of strength to recover."

"Is he awake?" one of the women asked.

"Yes," said the gentle-faced woman, "finally. Bring him some tea, Vissyn. Bring one of the cakes too."

My head was clearing. Warmth had returned to my limbs. I recognized the woman bending over me as the second voice on my journey, one of the women I had glimpsed when I woke in the strange room. She was ruddy-faced, round, and ample, with the face of a grandmother. I started to tell her I knew her but her hand closed over my lips. She was smiling and I realized with a start she knew what I had been thinking. "Yes," she said, "that's who I am, but you don't need to say so. My name is Vella. My sisters are Commyna and Vissyn. Vissyn you know by name already, apparently."

The other women were joining us, their shadows passing over me. Vella lifted a cup to my lips. Someone slid a cushion under my head, and a moment later the broad-shouldered woman, the one who had rescued me, sat cross-legged at my feet, arranging her luxurious skirt in folds on the ground. Her black hair was piled on her head, fastened in place by pins adorned with small jewels. She wore a white blouse whose full arms billowed in the breezes. "Commyna," I said hoarsely, remembering her name.

She lifted her finger to her lips. Even now there was something forbidding about her, a sternness that endured despite her merry eyes and the smile that lit her face. "Welcome to Illyn Water, boy. For a while we were afraid you'd never get here."

"Don't be in such a hurry, Commyna," Vella said, breaking off the cake into my mouth. "He's still weak."

The flavor of the rich, sweet bread flooded me, tasting of honey and spices. I took a deep breath. "Where is Illyn Water?" I asked.

Commyna glanced at Vella in something like triumph. "This one's strong," she said. "Not too many questions boy, or Vella will make me go away. Illyn Water is our home when we're in Arthen. It's a hidden place, and few people have ever seen it."

I ate more of the cake and felt some strength return. "Where's Nixva?"

"Yonder," said Vissyn, the blond woman. "He's perfectly happy, grazing with our horses. Nixva is the son of an old friend."

"We were in a house," I said. "When I woke up. Where was it?"

They glanced at each other. Commyna sighed. "We hoped you would not remember that."

"You touched a jewel to my head."

She looked deeply into my eyes as her sisters murmured in that strange language.

"You frighten me," Commyna said. "Not many could retain what transpired in a sleep such as you were in. Yes, I touched a gem to your head. You had wakened when you were not supposed to waken, in our house far away in the mountains. We took you there for safety, to make sure you were the child we had been told to find and teach. As it was, our wish for safety nearly killed you. I can't explain all that happened to you now, there isn't time. But no mortal Jisraegen has ever seen the house you were in, and when you wakened there we had to return you to the trance quickly. The jewel I used sent you too far, and we were a long time finding you. Do you remember what happened?"

I nodded. She smiled grimly.

"How strange." Vella helped me to drink more tea. "I had looked forward to returning to Arthen for so long. Now I feel afraid."

"The bad time is beginning in earnest," Commyna said, "and we haven't helped matters much with our bungling."

"Who could have guessed a novice would escape from fourth level sleep?" Vissyn asked. "We could hardly have done more."

"We nearly killed the boy before we started," Commyna had not taken her eyes off me. "And we've alerted Drudaen to our presence besides. YY only knows what he suspects concerning the child."

"What are you starting?" I asked.

"Teaching you," Vissyn said, twirling a blade of grass against her lips.

"Teaching me what?"

"Magic," she said.

The breeze returned. I watched the duraelaryn again, leaves streaming like small sails. I looked at Commyna. "You said you knew why I had come to Arthen, before, when I met you on the road. Is this why I'm here? To be taught by you? To learn magic?"

She met my gaze calmly. "Yes." Her face grew stern without her moving a muscle. "We had not planned for you to know so much so soon. But so be it, we'll change our plans. You're here to be taught. What you'll learn is magic. A magician is coming, and you are to be his helper."

"Is the magician Yron? Is that his name?"

Vella and Vissyn drew in quick breaths, and Commyna turned from one to the other. "He heard me say the name on the fourth level. You see what I mean? He remembers even that." To me she said, "Yes, the magician's name is Yron. Never say that name away from Illyn. Never, ever tell anyone that you've been here or that you have seen us. Never say our names. If you break any of these rules or reveal anything that we teach you we we'll send you far into the mountains and you'll never see this country again."

"You're being very severe," Vella said.

"Hush Vella," Vissyn said. "You know we've had trouble in the past."

"Thank you sister." Commyna turned to me again. "Are the rules fixed clearly in your mind?"

"Yes ma'am."

Commyna turned to Vella. "Is he well enough to travel?"

Vella laid her hand along my brow, her warmth reminding me of the cold place. "Yes, for the moment. But when we return him to his own time the full sickness will hit him." To me, she said "You have been to the fourth level without training. We can't absorb the shock of it for you without dulling your senses to our teaching. You'll be very sick for a time."

Commyna nodded. Then she sat up straight, with a look of listening. After a moment she said, "Nixva will know when you're ready to return here, Jessex. In the meantime, rest well. You've been a long way, body and spirit."

"Finish this cake," Vella said quietly. "We can't keep you here much longer. Can you ride?"

I wasn't even certain I could stand. But I nodded anyway, and finished the cake as she had asked. Some sort of charm was in it; I felt much stronger when I had eaten the last crumbs. I sat up, and finally stood.

Nixva was beyond, in the center of a broad meadow where golden sunlight was falling. When he saw me he tossed his head in greeting, cantering toward me. Vissyn handed me his bridle and when he was near I slipped it over his head.

I mounted him, sitting as steadily as I could manage. I faced the three women, looking from one to the other. "Close up your coat," Vella said, "you'll be riding through a storm. When you get to Camp, when you are in the worst of the fever, tell them to give you unufru. A doctor would have it but won't necessarily think of it for an illness like yours. Remember, unufru. We'd give it to you here, but you have to drink it in real time."

The sky was perfectly clear overhead. But I remembered Vella's words, *When we return him to his own time* and understood. Commyna smiled, knowing my thought, and said, "Precisely. You'll be returned to the moment in which we first took you. For those you know in Camp, you will have been absent only a few hours. Your time here is a bubble that we make, away from all the rest. Remember, say nothing about us, and above all say nothing about what has happened. If you can't keep this secret your life is not worth a flake of gold."

"I can keep secrets." But my head was spinning and I knew I would be lucky to keep my seat, much less remember not to talk out of my head. Nixva was impatient to go, and let me know it. The women turned their backs, and I nudged Nixva with my heels. He took off galloping across the meadow, the sky darkening with every stride. I felt no change. But suddenly we were riding beneath trees, and rain was beating down on us, and lightning flashed.

Nixva reared as before, and came down gently to earth, and we were in Hyvurgren Field in a spring storm with the wind howling round us. I nearly lost my seat.

Whoever the women were, they had been right. The sickness hit me at once, and it was all I could do to cling to Nixva's back as he galloped. He must have understood that his rider was in a bad way. He covered the distance between the holy field and Camp as quickly as he could. But I felt like I was dying just the same. When I reached Mordwen's tent I tried to dismount but nearly fell, the groom Thruil catching me in his arms. Mordwen cried out in shock and, surprisingly, affection, and had me carried into his tent.

Thruil lay me in cushions and someone threw a heavy duvet over me. I lay watching them as if they were a thousand leagues away. I had a hard time realizing that this was, for them, the same morning I had ridden from the shrine, Kirith Kirin's greeting ringing in my ears.

CHAPTER SIX
WYYVISAR

1

Someone changed my wet clothes for dry ones. A householder brought hot soup and mild tea. The tastes reminded me I was supposed to ask for something at some point but I was sick and drowsy and could not remember what. The cold had returned, and I shivered no matter how many coverings they piled on me and despite the braziers they ringed round me. Mordwen sent for a doctor from main Camp and she came in a hurry. She performed many indignities on me that I tolerated only because I felt too awful to say anything. I was still trying to remember the name of the stuff Vella had told me to ask for when the doctor mixed a sleeping potion and poured the warm milky stuff down my throat.

The sleep that followed was peaceful and no dreams came to me, pleasant or unpleasant. I slept for a long time, and my body did heal some in that interval but the fever did not abate. When I finally woke it was night. My teeth were chattering with the cold but I felt hot to the touch and moist with sweat. My hair was damp. No lamps were burning, so I knew it was late. With shock I remembered Kithilunen and wondered who had lit the evening lamp, who had sung? and I felt ashamed, too, that I had failed to do these things myself in the shrine entrusted to me.

With shock, I saw Uncle Sivisal asleep on cushions near the bed that had been laid for me.

When I said his name he woke up at once. The change was visible on his face when he realized what had wakened him. "Jessex, praise the Eye, you're awake."

"The doctor gave me something to drink."

He lay his hand on my forehead. "Yes, I know. But that was days ago. You're still so hot."

His hand was cold to me. "I'm tired," I said.

"You should eat something." He stood, still groggy, and walked outside. Presently I heard a runner heading away toward Camp, and

Uncle Sivisal returned. Light was at his back, I could not see his face. "What happened?" he asked.

"I was in the storm and felt sickness come on me. I was riding in Raelonyii, near Hyvurgren Field. Lightning struck close to us and Nixva reared up, and afterward I felt dizzy and got sick."

"Did you eat anything, or drink creek water?"

"No, nothing." I stirred, still shivering, pulling furs and blankets around my neck. "I'm cold."

He knelt close to me, stroking my forehead. In a few moments I was asleep again.

When I woke Mordwen and Uncle Sivisal were sitting by the open tent flap, talking in hushed voices. With surprise I understood Kirith Kirin was there as well. I did not know if it was the same night or not, but night it clearly was, and again no lamps were burning. Finally I called them, my voice hoarse but loud enough to reach them.

Uncle Sivisal heard me and called someone outside to fetch the doctor. Kirith Kirin bounded across the dark tent to my cushions. "Are you awake again?"

"Yes, sir. How long have I been asleep?"

He started to answer, then shook his head. "A while."

Mordwen knelt so that I could see him, and smiled in a gentle way that let me know I was very sick indeed. "I'm thirsty," I said and he helped me swallow water. By the time I had drunk as much as he would allow, the doctor had come into the tent.

She knelt over me and touched my brow. "The fever's the same," she said presently. "Are you cold?"

"Yes."

"Do you think you could eat?"

I shook my head.

"Do you want to sleep again?"

"No," I said, but I could hardly hold my eyes open. The doctor was frowning, and a little nervous too. I felt sorry for her. *At the height of the fever...* I remembered the word I was supposed to remember, and I said, "I would like unufru tea."

"What did you say?" She bent closer.

"Unufru. For the fever."

"What is he saying?"

"Do you know what unufru is?" she asked, ignoring the Prince.

"Yes," I said, and I found, despite everything, that I did know. "A root. You grind it and dry it and make a tea from it."

"It helps some bowel conditions," the doctor said, "but never anything like a fever."

Mordwen studied me intently. "Do it."

Kirith Kirin watched me strangely too. "Witches give unufru to cure the victims of love charms. They go through a fever purge, and sleep for a long time. I've seen it done."

"How do you know about unufru?" the doctor asked me. "Do you have an alchemist for a relative?"

"My mother knew herbs," Uncle Sivisal said. "She taught him."

The doctor had to send to Camp for the root, and someone had to be wakened to make the tea, so I had some time to wait. Uncle Sivisal sat close by, talking to me quietly to keep me from falling asleep again. Kirith Kirin sat behind him.

"Who's been lighting the lamps?" I asked.

"Mordwen," the Prince answered. "Trysvyn sings the hymn. I like her voice but it's not like yours."

"Is someone feeding Axfel?"

"Yes," Uncle Sivisal answered. "He's a good dog. I have him at my tent right now. Do you want to see him?"

"Not in here. He might break something."

"Nixva's missing you too," Kirith Kirin said. "Thruil's been riding him some. Open your eyes, sleepy. Stay awake till your medicine gets here."

A sweat broke from me worse than ever, but at the same time I was so cold my teeth were chattering. The doctor returned only a moment later with a closed cup in her hand, and Sivisal made way for her. The unufru smelled like vanilla. I had no trouble drinking it.

When I finished it the doctor asked if I thought I could keep it down. I felt no sickness and told her so. Aside from the sensation of having something in my stomach I could feel no difference.

Kirith Kirin watched from behind the doctor. She tested my forehead presently and said, "The fever's still the same."

I stayed awake long enough to say hello to Kiril Karsten. She came to the tent fresh from sleep, wrapped in a brown robe lined with white viis-cloth. Watching her sit beside my uncle and Kirith Kirin, I could think of no lovelier sight, and I would have fought sleep longer if I could. But I felt like a white wasteland, blasted clean. I fell asleep with the image of the lake women floating before me and dreamed I was walking along the lakeshore, breezes blowing across the glassy surface. Commyna was speaking quietly in a language that seemed easy to learn, to remember, such beautiful

words, like silver flowing on my tongue. She was telling me what to
do to help my body. She was saying such simple things I was sure I
could learn.

2

While I slept the unufru root took hold and the fever broke. Even
this much was a long time coming. The untrained body does not
return easily from fourth-level sleep, as I was to learn when the
lake women began my training in earnest. When Commyna touched
the jewel to my forehead she had sent my spirit out of the body
into a realm that only a trained magician should enter, and I was
lost there till she found me. My body was not prepared for a
separation of this kind; the shock of my reentry was added to the
shock of my departure. Often in such cases the physical mind will
reject the new presence of the spirit and a fever will ensue like the
one that I had. It would have been easy for the lake women to
have prevented this fever by the arts they knew, but in so doing
they would have crippled a part of me I would need when my
training began. Without the proper remedy, the result of such an
illness is often deeply unpleasant, death or permanent insanity or
the loss of wits. The inflammation heals but what is left is different than what was there before.

These were facts I learned later at Illyn Water. At the time I only
knew I had never been sicker in my life.

My body healed through rest and good dreams and soon I was
able to keep down food and feel some warmth again. The mind
purges itself through sleep and the spirit knits itself to the flesh again.
I had slept through most of seven days. Most everyone had given
me up for dead by the end of that time, remembering what had
happened to the last kyyvi. I'm told the doctor believed I was a
hopeless case and by the time I called for unufru she had tried most
remedies that are commonly used to treat brain fevers. No wonder
she was so willing to try whatever I suggested. She had run out of
remedies by then and had begun to fear for her future.

The first morning I could stand, I took the ritual bath again,
and sang Velunen in the shrine. I had lain down so long I felt weak
standing, but it was good to move around, to breathe the last
moments of night air, to rub the soft felva on my skin, to feel
clean again. When I walked to the shrine I felt like myself, and

when the muuren changed I went to the altar. At the correct moment I snuffed out the lamp, and a beam of sunlight broke through the trees. I sang Velunen.

My voice was weak and hoarse, I thought. But I was happy, singing.

I resumed my duties in the shrine after that, though Mordwen would not allow me to move back into the tent yet. During the day I did a lot of lying around and studied High Speech with a vengeance, till in a short time I left off speaking Upcountry altogether. For practice Kraele read me books and asked questions to make sure I understood what she was reading. A lot of it was ancient history, stories of the Twelve Who Lived, the reign of Falamar; tales of Drii; though the Venladrii do not talk much about their history before crossing the mountains. Kraele read me one book on the origins of the southern peoples, the various races that settled along the shore of Aeryn at the end of the first age of the Jisraegen, after Falamar disbanded the Praeven and made himself King. The southerners were called "Anynae," which means nothing, really, "people of Anyn", which is the name of the southern bay, into which they sailed long ago from countries across the sea. They've taken our name for them and have forgotten their own. The Anynae built cities and carved farms out of the wilderness in the southern part of Aeryn, and for a time it seemed the Jisraegen would let them live in peace. But a Jisraegen war party was ambushed by the southerners through a misunderstanding or through design, and in the course of the skirmish that followed, Itheil Coorbahl, one of the Jhinuuserret, was killed. He was one of the Twelve Who Lived, and he became the first of the immortals to die.

One morning Kraele read me the words to one of the most famous songs from that age, "Falin Uthys," "Last Ride," which tells the story of Itheil Coorbahl's death and of all that befell the Jisraegen afterward. The lay begins in the days after Falamar was made strong in his magic by YY, when the Praeven sang the song that nearly brought about the end of the world. Word had come to the city that a new people had appeared on the southern coast, and some of the Jisraegen were curious and wanted to meet these strangers. A party of them headed south, lead by Itheil. But at the time neither people had learned how to communicate with the other, the Anynae thought the Jisraegen were attacking them and killed the whole party. It was the death of Itheil and these others that Falamar set out to avenge. Itheil had been

Falamar's lover off and on for many lifetimes, and Falamar mustered an army in Cunuduerum, asking for help from Jurel Durassa and the Jisraegen who lived in the mountains, in Montajhena, who had never been part of the unhappiness in Cunuduerum. Jurel refused to ally with Falamar against the southerners, and so Falamar made war on the Anyn people with his own army alone. What followed is most often known as the Age of Blasphemies. Falamar led the Woodsfolk to a bloody victory against the poorly armed people in the south, and he himself attacked them with all the power of his magic. Many of the Anyn escaped north to Vyddn, where Jurel protected them. The rest were left to fend for themselves. By the end of the war, the Anyn males and females of fighting age were mostly dead, the females slaughtered even though in those early days the women did not fight alongside the men. The rest were parceled out among the victors as slaves. The Arthen Nivri divided up the southern land, giving the bulk of it to Falamar. Falamar was named King of Arthen and Aeryn and returned to Cunuduerum with two titles, having merely styled himself King of Cunuduerum in the past.

His rule in both countries was generally unchallenged for generations, and he nearly conquered the Venladrii and the Svyssn, except that Jurel Durassa prevented him from bringing his armies north through the passes, and kept him out of the north. It was at this time that King Evynar swore loyalty to Jurel, and the Drii became vassals of a Jisraegen King.

Jurel Durassa was a wizard much stronger than Falamar at the time and remained firmly in power in Montajhena and in all of Aeryn north of Arthen. Falamar turned his armies on Jurel after years of enmity over the presence of free Anynae within Jurel's holdings. But Edenna Morthul opposed Falamar as well, from her seats of power in Inniscaudra and in Genfynnel. Falamar harassed them with armies whenever he could spare troops but otherwise was occupied with problems in Arthen. In time his own people grew tired of the yoke he laid on them, and some of them turned to Montajhena and the remaining Twelve for aid. Then Falamar built a Tower in Cunuduerum, a High Place from which he could see a long way over the trees, and in the Tower he made many magical devices and means to amplify his strength. He drew on the One whom we do not name, and he did magic from the Tower, using its power to hurl storm and suffering against Montajhena, and for the first time Jurel could not stop him.

Winter came in summer in those years and wolves and snow lions and many other creatures prowled in the forest around Montajhena, the city in the mountains. Hideous creatures roamed in the night, dead-walking drinkers of blood. At last Jurel Durassa built a tower of his own, of rough granite, bringing Orloc masons to work in the dead of winter storms, Jurel walking among them stoking the fires that kept them warm. Further, the Tervan gave him a large muuren, a priceless treasure, and he had it worked into a sphere, and then himself blessed it and carved the YYmoc onto its face, and by magic made it perfectly white and full of light, and embedded it in the top of his High Place, which he named Yrunvurst, "Hand of God." So Falamar invented the High Place but Jurel was first to focus the power of it through a muuren stone.

After that the battle went in Jurel's favor again, and for many years he held Falamar inside Arthen, and the land between Cunuduerum and Montajhena was scorched with magic. Falamar gathered an army from every part of the world, buying it with gold or compelling it by plain bullying. A long war was fought in the mountains and on the Kellyxan plain. At one point Jurel Durassa, having found a way to bind Seumren to his own Tower, making it useless to Falamar, sacked Cunuduerum, causing the river to flood the city afterward. But Falamar repopulated Cunuduerum and raised another army from Antelek and Karns to lay siege to Montajhena. His strength in magic had increased as he studied the books his father Cunavastar had left for him. He built the Tower Yruminast over Cunevadrim and, using it, was able to take control of Seumren again. He had grown as great as Jurel in power but could never control the magic of that level and when he fought with Jurel and broke Yrunvurst, Falamar died as well.

The lyrics for "Last Ride" encompass this whole cycle of legend, and a person who can hear it without emotion is without a heart. My grandmother had known snatches of these tales but not the whole cycle. I listened in awe, as if the words were burning out of my own bones.

With all this in my head I did not die of boredom, and soon my body healed to the point that I was becoming impatient to ride. I had been out of bed a week before I broached the subject with Mordwen, but he put me off. "When we're sure you've got your wind back, you can get on a horse again. You're still too skinny, boy."

We had become friends by then, a morsel at a time, and I ignored his gruffness. I believe he was lonely and glad of my company. At the time I only noticed that his age was bothering him some, I never wondered why. Though I knew he was Jhinuuserret and age should not have bothered him at all.

Some days passed. My uncle visited every day, though I was conscious of his discomfort in the tent. I ate, rested, walked about Camp, visiting Nixva, visiting Axfel once, outside Uncle Sivisal's tent while he was on patrol. Axfel was glad to see me, licking my hands till they were spotlessly clean, and I scratched his ears and the back part of his jaw the way I always did, the big beast closing his eyes and rumbling like a cat.

Nixva was glad to see me too. He gave me a good looking over, and as much as told me to be on the lookout for him. The message shocked me with its clarity, and a wave of excitement ran through me, remembering the lake women, the golden meadow, the promise of something extraordinary. Get ready, Nixva was saying, as if he knew.

One morning when I had sung Velunen and put away the lamp, I walked out the back of the tent and Nixva was there. He stepped toward me silently, with an eerie purposefulness to his expression, and I moved toward him entranced, leaping to his bare back, gripping his thick mane with my hands. Just as we were about to ride away I heard a voice calling me from the tent, and I turned to see Thruil, breathless, who said, "He got away from us. I thought he would come here."

"Yes. Tell Mordwen we're riding. I'll be back."

He watched me helplessly. I signaled Nixva to go before anyone else tried to stop us, and we cantered away down the road to Camp, soon departing from it for forest country.

Nixva was jubilant at the chance to gallop again, but he was not playful. He traveled at a steady pace in a purposeful way. The thought of where we were going made me catch my breath. Nixva splashed across a shallow creek and headed between two broad hills; I felt a change, a fluttering in my stomach, and there we were, riding across a bright meadow, the clean blue water of Lake Illyn before us, one lone duraelaryn rising like a tower. Horses were grazing under the lower branches, and a red cart sat in the high grass, tilted backward so its tongue jutted high into the air. The lake women were in the grass, Commyna working a large loom while Vissyn and Vella spun thread on wooden spinning wheels.

Vella saw me first and called out, "Well, here he is, just as you said."

"I'm never wrong," Vissyn declared, "maybe next time you'll believe me. Good morning Jessex. I told my sisters you would be here today but Vella was skeptical."

"She loves to predict the future," Vella said, "she's always bragging about it, but her record isn't always so good."

"You're looking thinner, boy," Commyna called as I dismounted, setting Nixva free to graze. "I suppose you were very sick."

"Yes, for a long time. But I got the doctor to give me the root you told me about, Miss Vella, and it broke the sickness."

"Unufru is very good for brain sicknesses caused by magic," Vella said. "Most doctors don't know how to diagnose magic diseases, however, so the poor root gets dreadfully neglected."

"Kirith Kirin says witches use it to cure to victims of love charms," I said.

Vissyn tossed her head somewhat contemptuously. "Unufru wouldn't cure a love charm I made, I can promise you that. What was Kirith Kirin doing talking about love charms with a boy of your age?"

"He was talking to the doctor."

"Well I'm glad to hear that. I hoped he hadn't lost all decency."

"Do you know him?"

Vissyn smiled warmly. "Yes. We all know Kirith Kirin."

"How?"

"Because he's who he is." Commyna said this without a trace of sternness. But steel crept into her voice. "However, you're not here to have your questions answered, you're here to learn. I will begin your lessons myself, today. Vissyn, please take over the weaving. Jessex and I are going for a long walk."

She had been working the loom deftly all this time, even during her lecture. The cloth she was weaving was more beautiful than anything I had ever seen, even the Jisraegen cloths, which are the finest in the world: Commyna's fabric was like a fire mixed in a rainbow, a live, shivering pool of colors, changing before one's eyes. I have never seen anything else like it before or since. She followed my eye and smiled proudly. "You like my handiwork? This is for the magician Yron. We're making a cloak like no other cloak in the world."

"It's beautiful. I'm sure he'll like it."

"He'd better." She set off walking and I followed her. We headed away from the red cart where the two women continued to concentrate on their work, singing under their breath. Commyna walked slowly but I still had a lot of work keeping up with her; she was a very large woman, with legs like tree limbs and shoulders that would have done a wrestler justice; but she was very beautiful at the same time, with a bold face, large hazel eyes and a full mouth. She had such subtlety of expression that she could put three feelings on her face at the same time without so much as moving a muscle. We had not gone far before she started talking, not at all impatiently, in a clear, deep voice, resonant and large even in the open woodland. "You are here to learn magic. That's putting it plainly. You're not here to admire the countryside or to chatter with my sisters the whole day long. What we have to teach is difficult, and you'll have to give the study your whole heart, or you'll never get anywhere.

"You have talent for what we'll be teaching you. We know this because of what happened in our house in the mountains, when we couldn't put you into a safe level of sleep that would bind you and later when you made a crude charm and broke out of fourth-level trance. You have the ability to become a respectable sorcerer if you want to do it. But if you don't want to do it—if you are lazy or disobedient or careless—it would be better for you by far to say so now, before you have gone deeply into our teachings, while you can still be released from our tutelage without any harm to you."

She sounded like Kraele warning she was going to work me day and night. But I understood Commyna was very serious, so I answered, "This isn't work that I'm choosing, ma'am, this is work I've been called to do. You won't find me lazy, or disobedient, or careless, or unwilling."

"How do you know you have been called?"

I could have told her about Mordwen's dream, or my mother, or Julassa Kyminax, but I suspected that she knew about these facts. So I answered, "I feel it."

She paused in the walk, taking my face in her hands and studying me without pretense. "A good, simple answer. I think I would believe you even if I didn't already have evidence you're right. Even though you're so young."

"I'll be fifteen soon. After Vithilonyi."

She touched my face with the tips of her fingers. "Oh, well, in that case," she said, and laughed softly. She became serious again. "I've never taught anyone before who had lived less than two lifetimes. This will be hard on you."

"Did you teach Kentha Nurysem?"

She became sad, and looked across the wide blue lake. "Yes. What do you know about her?"

"My grandmother told me stories about her. She's the sorceress who cast down Drudaen from the High Place."

"She was Kirith Kirin's last hope," Commyna said. "While she was with him in Arthen, he had some leverage, he could make himself heard in the south. But this was long ago, before we knew what Queen Athryn was capable of, before Drudaen had shown his true nature. In those days even Drudaen came sometimes to Arthen, and once when he did, he and Kentha fell in love. It's said that the love was genuine on both sides, and that Drudaen risked even loss of favor with Athryn to be with Kentha. Athryn was terribly jealous when she learned of the affair, and threatened to banish Drudaen from court and strip him of his estates. Most likely she wouldn't have been able to do either, but there would have been a terrible fight between them, a fight neither Athryn nor Drudaen could afford, since their weakness would have added to Kirith Kirin's strength. So Drudaen left Kentha. Meantime she turned up pregnant and had to leave the Woodland. No one knows how the child could have been conceived. It was thought to be nearly impossible for the Jhinuuserret to bear children. She murdered the child and wandered in the mountains for a long time. She is said to have taken lore books from Cunuduerum with her, and to have laid a trap for Drudaen using them, in Montajhena. She fought him and cast him down from his Tower there, and then he betrayed her, killing her by use of a love token she had given him when they were together in Arthen. By the end of their fight, both Yrunvurst and Goerast were wreckage and the city was in ruins. The fires burned for a year. Nobody has been able to live there since."

"My grandmother never told me all that," I said.

"Not many people know all the details. Kirith Kirin kept quiet about the reason for her exile, and the affair between Drudaen and Kentha had been conducted discreetly, if you can believe it. It is sometimes said that Kentha enjoyed the last scraps of humanity left in Drudaen, that he offered them to her. Maybe it was his bitterness at the end of their love that caused the change in him. He was not an evil man in those days. But he was not as powerful as now. Though Kentha cast him down, he benefited from the breaking of the tower and from her death, though he never ate her soul. He's still stronger now than he was when she was alive."

"So now Kirith Kirin doesn't have anyone to help him."

"Not until Yron comes."

"Who is Yron?"

Commyna studied the sky thoughtfully, and sighed. "I wish I knew," she said. "We've only been told that a magician will come to Arthen, that the first sign of his coming is the appearance of a Jisraegen boy summoned by oracle to serve in the shrine of Kirith Kirin. You. You're to be taught magic, to serve Yron when he comes. That's why you were called here and that's why we've returned. That's all we know."

"Does that mean Yron will come as soon as I'm ready?"

Commyna smiled. "Then nothing I've said has discouraged you?"

"Oh no. This is what I want to do."

She stood perfectly motionless a moment. Wind lifted her hair, and she listened to some note of music in it. She turned to me, saw me again. "Sit down on the grass. I'll begin your teaching now. We won't require words."

3

In Aeryn, in real time, an age of peace was ending. Across the Fenax, poor families were selling their land or waiting to lose it to the tax courts. Hungry refugees jammed the streets of Cordyssa, where merchants, reeling under summer levies, were hardly able to absorb so many country folk. Verm soldiers were drilling in south Turis. 'Round Cunevadrim a shadow was brooding. Even the best spies couldn't penetrate Vermland; the few who tried did not return.

Kirith Kirin was often away from Camp for days at a time, and there were many rumors about his activities. I learned to be skeptical about the gossip, as with, for instance, the rumor that Drudaen had been spotted in the streets of Cunuduerum. This threw me into a panic till Commyna assured me, "He would never be able to enter Arthen without our knowing it."

The Cordyssan Nivri were outraged that the authority of Ren Vael was being challenged by the Queen's military governor even in his hereditary terrain. He had ruled in the city for time out of mind. Members of his family in Camp demanded that Kirith Kirin send a party of soldiers to support and protect him but the Prince refused, saying the messenger from Lord Vael had specifically warned against such action. The Blue Queen was thought to be looking for any excuse to send an Army into the Fenax.

Only once did I speak to the Prince during that time, when the soldier Sildivaris returned from the south with word that my mother had been held in Ivyssa for a few days and then taken west to Cunevadrim. Cunevadrim is the seat of Falamar's house, Falamar being Drudaen's father, who is said to have taught him all his skill.

Duterian remained in the south, watching the Wizard as closely as he could, gauging the strength of the Verm army boiling across the Barrens. Sildivaris had seen the army too, and her description of it was frightening and vivid. The Verm had become beasts that walked like men and carried swords, and he had forged terrible weapons for them, of metals taxed from the Cordyssan mines. He held thousands of the Verm troops outright in his mind and drilled them day and night. This was told as common knowledge in the countryside, and even the Verm feared being chosen for this service. His right arm, Julassa Kyminax, was sometimes with him and some-times not, and he was rumored to have other apprentices besides, servants foul as demons, hardly people at all. The human troops could hardly bear to be in the company of some of these creatures, though so far there had been no mutiny.

Sildivaris was returning south by her own request. She was a striking, reed-slim woman with nondescript hair and features, eyes of a jewel-like intensity and a body that vibrated with strength. One could see she was a good soldier.

A time of disorder, heading into a time of chaos. I was split between my normal life in Camp and the intervals between when I was at Illyn Water, lost on the shore of the lake in the wakening of eerie knowledge.

Sometimes it was as if the normal life were swallowed up by those hours, as if Illyn were submerging the rest of my life into its tapestry, into the shimmering cloth the lake women were weaving. I performed the ritual bath and put out the lamp in the morning, I sang Velunen and rode away on Nixva to the shore of Illyn Water. Sometimes Axfel went with us. The sisters took a liking to him, making fun of his appearance in a good-natured way. He was free to roam about the lakeshore as he pleased, to follow scent-trails and hunt if he wanted to, or to swim in the water or sleep under the trees. His visits were easier than mine. I had to earn my keep.

The early lessons were the hardest. It would be hard to explain everything that transpired, but there were ordeals and ceremonies at the beginning of my study of magic, very hard ones, designed to strengthen the body and help it endure the shocks and changes that would come. I slept in caves and under trees. I hung by my hair from tangles of vine, and once I hung by my feet from the top of a duraelaryn for three whole days, while the ladies went on weaving, heaping wood on their campfire at night, singing strange songs in their hidden language.

Under such conditions I learned or else suffered the consequences of ignorance. When the women gave me a hint as to what to do I remembered it and thought about it; when one of them told me to repeat a Word and fix it in my mind, I did. When hanging by my hair I repeated a Word Commyna gave me, and the Word, for just a moment, made me buoyant in the air; when hanging by my feet I controlled my breathing and placed myself into a trance of the seventh level, as Vella taught me to do, and I moved my pain into a new place in my brain and hung there. I survived these trials and many more. Was it any wonder I was sometimes dazed and tired in Camp, that sometimes even the most catastrophic news struck me as so much wind? Mordwen fussed at my absent-mindedness, and worried when I had nothing to say in the evenings. He had no idea how full my mind was.

The world and all that is in it is music. In magic one learns to sing in harmony with that, and against harmony with it. In my early lessons I learned to meditate, completely oblivious to my surroundings, and in time to meditate in a smaller and smaller state, to focus my meditation on seeing a smaller and smaller space, on filling a tiny space with my whole self, in order to listen to the deepest part of the world. Each circle of concentration, when I reached it, would lead to a deeper, smaller place, from which I could hear, and reach, more.

So I sat on the shores of Lake Illyn in whatever physical state the women placed me, and I breathed till my mind was clear and I was completely inside it and growing smaller, a mantra to which I trained myself, the becoming of a voice that worked in that space as well as in the waking world. Listening and singing, breathing and listening, singing and breathing, hovering. Aware of the language that is spoken there, in the mind's mouth, in the place the mind makes.

At Illyn Water I began to grapple with that language, the one spoken in the meditation space, the movement across the inner tongue so strange, the logic so unlike ordinary logic. The spoken name of this language was Wyyvisar, a word that might be translated, "waves weaving." The women also called it Hidden Speech, because it is forbidden for anyone to teach it or to reveal it without the wish of YY-mother, and the magician who does so assures that each Word taught will be forgotten afterward by the teacher, and will never be recovered.

Magic is the act of making a harmony that alters the underlying music that is the basis for the world we know. A wave is set in motion and that wave brings a change forward from the past to the present. On the most basic level of magic, this act consists of naming an object with conviction. Vissyn taught me this, the purest level of magic, practiced by village witches and local seers. Touch a knot of wood on a tree and say a word to it. Come every day and touch this knot of wood, speaking to the tree and naming it, in the same way, with the same degree of concentration, from the same state of mind if possible. Picture the knot as smooth and round. Over time, if the will is powerful, the tree will know you. The forest will know you. The place will give you a power you could not get another way. The knot will grow smooth and round.

In such a way my grandmother had worked at her craft, never leaving enough evidence to get herself hanged, never operating openly. In such magic, however, the path is patience, the power of place, and careful choice of object. Power is derived from earth, from herb and root, from lore and knowledge of the land gained over time. The powerful magicians of this genre are the oldest ones; these are the true witches, bearers of unshakable knowledge. Even the powerful will not lightly face such a witch in his or her own terrain.

To enter a higher level of application, one must learn a language of command, or else invent one. This is the language of the small, to be spoken in the small space, in deep trance, in the place the mind makes for itself. That is as clear an explanation as I can offer without use of Words. There are few such languages to learn; Wyyvisar is one, and Ildaruen is another. The priests of Cunuduerum knew of a third and were destroyed because of what they made in it. Languages of command are hard to master, and teachers are scarce. I was the first student of Wyyvisar in generations, Commyna said. Kentha Nurysem had been the last. As for Ildaruen, no one taught it but Drudaen Keerfax, who had learned it from his father Falamar, who had learned it from his father Cunavastar, and pupils of Ildaruen were even forbidden to speak Words to each other. On pain of death.

An apprentice in kei-magic, Commyna told me, sits in the seventh circle of power. When I asked what a circle of power was, she told me it was simply a measure of skill, but of the deepest kind. A person progressed from one level to the next all at once, in a flash of insight or a moment of clarity, she said; the progress was never gradual. But I would not have to think about that for a while. In the seventh circle, when one is not practicing deep meditation, one is confined to simple constructions of magic like blessings or love charms or potions that heal wounds quickly. In many magics at this level actual objects are filled with a music that may give virtue or cause ill. The sound may or may not be one that the ear can hear. The sound may manifest itself as a scent. Many objects can be made to carry such music, even crude ones like stones or sticks or flowers. Even animals or people. I made many such charms, some under close supervision and some entirely on my own; I made love charms that could drive a rabbit mad, using only a simple sprig of cilidur and holding it to my lips and whispering to it. Other small animals suffered from my new knowledge as well, but only at Illyn Water, and none were harmed that I know.

I worked as hard as the women asked and did as I was told without thinking, even when what they wanted seemed hard or impossible. I learned to trust them. Maybe pupils had given the lake women trouble in the past. I was determined they would remember me as one who had given them no trouble at all.

Vithilonyi drew near, the Festival of Lights, a holiday in all Aeryn but celebrated with special reverence in the north. For a night every house across the Fenax would have a candle or a lamp burning in every window, tax or no, and every house in Cordyssa would be the same, alight with tongues of flame, each windowpane shimmering. This was a holiday at Illyn Water as well. Even the Anyn peoples celebrated it, nowadays, and it was close to my name-day.

In fact I was troubled about Vithilonyi for some days in advance, from the moment I learned that the holy day also marked our last day in this part of Arthen, for on the morning after Vithilonyi camp would be struck and moved to its summer home. How would I find Illyn Water from a place far away? I had heard we would be riding twenty days before we reached Suvrin Sirhe, the northeast part of Arthen, a valley nestled high in the foothills of the Pelponitur.

I was afraid to ask the lake women what to do for fear of what they might tell me. Suppose they said I would have to abandon camp altogether, living with them along the lake shore, wherever their house was hidden?

I finally did ask Vella, who was teaching me the hidden grammar and syntax of Wyyvisar beside the lakeshore, alternately whispering

into my ear while I murmured sounds, then ordering me into a
trance while she sang songs over me. When we were both tired she
made tea on an open lawn near Illyn, spreading out her shawl, which
grew to become a large wool blanket, big enough for both of us to
sit on. She had brought an oet, a transportable jaka pot fueled by
hot ifnuelyn wood, and she set it up on a flat stone, brewing a pungent, steaming tea. We had been in that part of her country for a
day; I had slept the night before on the open lawn, with only Words
to make warmth and comfort. I had eaten nothing but was taking
in sustenance from the air. A magician must be able to sleep in ice or
snow, if necessary, she said, and do without water or solid food for
a long time. She was making the magic that caused this, it being
beyond my skill at that level; my body must become accustomed to
many new pathways and intersections before I could do the work
myself, she explained.

She handed me a large cup of tea and a chunk of waycake.
Vella was a gentler teacher than Commyna, more given to praise and
kind words than to Commyna's doses of sarcasm and scorn. Though
in the end she was as harsh a mistress in what she asked for. When
we were done with the tea, I sat in fire and in boiling water for her
till end of day, as she showed me the pathway for carrying the heat
of both around my body, for refusing to interact with the fire and
the water, even for burning and healing again. All simple and easy
when she was the one doing the work, all I had to do was open my
mind and feel what was happening as fully as I could.

In the Illyn afternoon, when the western sky was salmon-col-
ored, strung with tatters of cloud, she talked at length about famous
magicians of the past, and about magic itself. Finally I got up the
nerve to mention to her that Camp was moving, and I didn't know
what to do about it.

"What do you mean, do about it?   What is there to do but
move?"

"But it will be hard for me to get here."

"Oh." A slow smile spread across her round features. "We'll
find you when we want you, Jessex. You don't have to worry
about that."

"But Camp is moving all the way to the eastern mountains."

Vella looked very prim and reassuring. "Illyn Water will be there
waiting for you. Stick close to Nixva and let him find his own way.
Trust that hideous dog of yours, too. He has a good nose, despite
its appearance."

I felt stupid when I realized what she was telling me. I should
have known better than to assume that Illyn Water was an actual
place in my world, that could be found by anyone as easily as Nixva
and I had found it.

The lake, the surrounding landscape, these were not illusions.
Vissyn had drilled me in the differences. Illyn Water was a real place,
always there, shifted slightly out of Arthen. A bubble they were
making, out of sight.

We returned to my lesson in Wyyvisar. At the end of it I was
aware of knowing no more than before, though Vella said I was
making good progress. She would be leaving me here overnight
again, now that the sun was going down. Tonight the weather would
be colder. Did I need her to teach me the Words again, or did I
remember them?

I remembered. She smiled with satisfaction and turned away,
leaving me cake and tea and a packet of cheese wrapped in cool
green leaves. By the time her figure vanished round the broad bend
of the shore, the sun was in the last splendor of its setting and
evening was closing round the world. I sang Kithilunen quietly. I
had no lamp so I lit a small fire instead, using the local tinder for fuel,
and as my spark I employed the Word I had known for many days,
spoken at the tips of my fingers, springing from there to the wood
and burning.

I was far away from the world, from any world of my memory.
I sat by the glowing fire in the twilight, the lake sparkling before me,
shimmering surface reflecting the emerging stars. The wind smelled
of forest and decaying leaf, of flowers heaving out scent, of the
season warming, seeds awakening. I thought of Camp and of my
friends there. I thought of Kirith Kirin and sang Kimri, picturing his
face. When I thought of him I felt a sense of foreboding. I carried
the thought with me when I walked that night, brooding beneath the
stars, mysterious Words whirling in my head. I was hardly conscious
of my youth any more, I had become an old man through love of
magic, this new work I was learning, this fire that sprang from the
air when I moved a Word in the space I could make in my mind. I
was fourteen, lying down with my love in the grass, saying the Word
that would bring warmth to the air around me even while I slept,
the Word that would comfort my body while it lay on the cold hard
ground. Sleep came easily. I dreamed of riding with Kirith Kirin
across an endless plain.

4

On the morning of Vithilonyi, in honor of the day, the kyyvi does not extinguish the lamp with the coming of sunrise, but lights two more, carries them one in each hand before the altar, and places them on stone pedestals. I managed this pretty easily and sang Velunen. Sun rose in perfect waves of color like a fire burning beyond the trees. I walked to the portal of the tent, watching Nixva stamping in the yard. A large crowd had come to the ceremony that morning; custom is to sing Kimri on festival morning, and most folks had come for that. I took up the first words of the song.

Of the festival mornings I've known in my life, that one is among the most enduringly beautiful. I sang "Light in the Darkness" for the birds in the trees, for the warm spring air, for the feeling that a change was coming, that light would be needed.

Holiness arose in the clearing at that moment, a fullness like the throbbing in the air at the end of music. We love music because it is the echo of God's mind, we say, and we mean it reminds us that she is still there, somewhere, though silent. Everyone took up the song. I ran to Nixva and lead him past the fringes of the crowd. We rode away to the sound of singing.

Nixva carried me to the lake by a different route each day. That morning we rode through familiar country, the land of iron-hued trees, of grass like spun silver and flowers like bright jewels, Raelonyi, and my heart leapt. I said the name aloud and Nixva tossed his head, galloping between the dark tree trunks, pounding the earth with his sharp hooves. He ran like something full of fire. We passed around Hyvurgren Field, entering from the east.

Horses grazed round the shrine. Three figures were kneeling by the altar, singing in Wyyvisar, a hymn that raised the hair on the back of my neck. I knew the Words. They sang of renewing the Woodland once again, of the progression of seasons, of scales of time weaving in and out of scales of space, phrases I could understand but not connect in any way. I rode quietly toward them, listening to their sad, somber song. When they stopped singing, a good while after I arrived, they turned to me as if they had known all along I was in the field with them.

"Thank you for listening so patiently," Commyna said. "We chose the Hyvurgren Shrine for our ceremony this year, since it is close to your Camp, Jessex."

"Do you do this every year?"

"Yes, every year on Vithilonyi. It's necessary to us, to return here, though only a few people know it." She smiled at me in the gentlest way. "All the creatures who were born in Arthen must return now and then, or they die."

"Sister," Vella called quietly, "please rejoin us. It's time to continue."

"Should we add Jessex to our circle?"

"Do you think that's wise, Commyna?   He won't know what we're doing."

"All the better," Commyna answered. "He will feel something from it. Yes, I think it's a good idea. Take my hand, Jessex."

Vissyn broke in very quietly. "There is a spy watching us, sisters."

"A spy? In the forest?" Commyna looked all around.

"Yes. A most cunning man, known to us all."

"Oh, him," Commyna said. "I might have known."

"He's suspicious of the boy," Vella said.

"It won't really do any harm to let him watch, will it?" Vissyn asked, with a sly look at the others.

"I don't see what it could hurt," Vella said, after a moment's thought.

"It will serve him right, since he is so impertinent as to sneak up on us while we are minding our own business. Taking advantage of knowledge he gained unfairly." Commyna faced the shrine with a guileless look that was cat-like, nevertheless, in its promise of mischief. She took my hand again, and Vissyn took the other. We stood in a ring in front of the stone altar, where in a metal lamp a fire was flickering. A throb of power ran through my hand, a pure tangible strength, a vibration that rose over all of us, and Vissyn whispered, "You add to us nicely, son of Kinth. You have good strings."

Vella told her to hush, and awareness of time left me, completely, as it had not since the day of the storm when the lake women first took me from Nixva's back. A pure music came from among our joined hands along with singing like a cold wind. But I was not afraid; I was a part of the force that was singing, and the song carried me with it.

The song made me think of many things, above all of the women themselves. When they sang they gave out a feeling of strength and light that filled my vision. They said they had performed a ceremony in Arthen each year, but for how long? When they sang they felt as old as the earth underfoot, and the song was renewing everything, the forest, mountains, rivers, oceans, the worlds, the changeable stars, the emptiness of heaven. Their song called for a light like no other light, they called for the Hand to light the Lamp-that-lights-the-Lamps, a line of another old hymn, and when the light came to my inner eyes I lost sight of the world for a long time.

The singing ended but I was sustained by brightness, seeing only the sere white light, a small sun landed in my brain. The lake women led me to my horse by their voices, and I knew this was another of their tests, but I was blissful and laughed, finding Nixva by the sound of his breathing, which I knew like my own. I mounted him and got my balance, the light making me laugh, obscuring everything. Next thing I remember we were at Illyn Water, drinking tea and smelling the breezes. I saw only the light for a long time, but I could hear them clearly, and described for them how I had felt during the song, and what I was seeing now. We spoke in Wyyvisar, the Words moving from one mind into another, as formal as spoken language and as audible if one had the ear. I was beginning to understand better and better.

I must learn to see past the light but retain it, Vella said. I could do this only by Words. Since a song had brought the light, most likely a song would be needed for vision to exceed the light. Patiently she helped me to understand how such a song would be made, what Words would be used, and what form, what melody, what level of application, what object. I must breathe deeply, sit quietly, make an image in my mind and sing.

I listened to her attentively, feeling sudden joy. What she described seemed plain and easy. I knew this was another test, but this time I was not concerned, this time I relaxed as each of the women had taught me to do, centered my breathing and cleared my mind. The song came to me, waiting for me already. The sound made sense, it was a harmony I sang softly, into the emptiness of the small place. Wind blew against my real face. I had learned to be in both spaces at the same time. Now I must deal with the light. I was glad while it shone in my eyes, but I was just as glad when it became a mist, when the mist cleared. The lake women were seated in a circle watching me. They were smiling with quiet pride.

"Congratulations, Jessex," Commyna said. "Happy Vithilonyi."

"Happy Vithilonyi, ma'am. What are you congratulating me for?"

"You've just made your first song," Vissyn said. "You've moved Power."

"I can't believe it," Vella said, sitting up straight, gazing big-eyed at the rest of us. "You've been with us such a short time."

"Be quiet, sister," Commyna ordered sharply. "He's really very slow, I think he could learn Wyyvisar much faster." She paused, her eyes twinkling. "However, you should be pleased with yourself. The moving of Power in Words marks your transition from seventh level apprentice to sixth level adept. You are no longer quite a beginner. A fine gift on festival day."

I sat up a bit straighter. It surprised me that the news should mean so much. No one said anything, but I felt some pride coming from the women too, and finally Vella said, "Well, like it or not, Commyna, he does pretty good for a mortal boy."

"He would have to. He has a short life. The lessons only get harder from here." Commyna's expression was typically dry. "However, in honor of festival day, and of your passage to the sixth level, you will get the day off, Jessex."

"Camp is moving tomorrow," I said.

"Never mind that," she answered. "We'll find a time and come for you. You will be living on Nixva for the next few weeks anyway. Don't fret, you'll get your time at Illyn."

Again I was surprised at how much this news relieved me. This was plain to read on my face, and Vissyn said, laughing, "I believe he's enjoying himself, anyway."

"I am," I said. "I've never had so much fun doing anything."

"It's good that you like your work," Commyna said in a serene voice.

This was the end of my instruction for the day. I asked Commyna what suuren I should report to Mordwen for this ride, since the invention of the suuren-object had become part of our daily routine. Ordinarily she did not take much time to choose the object I was to report but today my question made her thoughtful. After consideration she said, "We have a problem today, Jessex. This morning you were seen joining us in Hyvurgren Field by someone from Camp."

I remembered the discussion about the spy in the forest, just before we began singing at the shrine. "I don't know who could have followed me," I said. "Nixva is a fast horse."

"The visitor may not have been following you, necessarily," Vissyn said. "There are a few folks who know we come to Arthen for this particular holiday."

"Who was in the forest this morning? You know, don't you."

Vissyn smiled. "Yes. We know."

My heart sank; I didn't know why. "It was Kirith Kirin, wasn't it?"

Commyna answered, "Yes. Because it was him, we didn't interfere to hide you."

I gazed at the lake beyond them, confused. "If he asks me
questions, how will I answer? You've told me to say nothing about
magic away from the lake."

"Nor has the rule changed," Commyna said. "Don't worry so
much. Kirith Kirin knows more about us than I can explain to you
in one morning. He won't expect you to tell him anything. If he
asks you a question, answer him yes or no. If he asks you more than
you think you should tell, refuse to answer. He won't press you. It's
very simple."

This was delivered in nearly the same voice she would have
used to scold me. I said I would do as I was told. She explained
further, in a gentler tone, "He may be disturbed by what he knows.
If he should seek counsel from one of his friends, if he should tell
them something about what he's seen, you must acknowledge nothing. If he's disturbed and seems angry, you must not worry, the
anger will pass."

I felt a sudden sense of dread. She would hardly warn me
unless it were likely. "Why would he be angry?"

She watched me for a long time. After a moment she said, "It
can't be easy, knowing so little of your own fate, when other folks
know so much. I'm sorry, Jessex. I can't answer your question.
Kirith Kirin has had hopes for you that may be changed, or may
seem to be changed, by the fact that you are our pupil. Just remember what I've told you. If it seems Kirith Kirin is cold to you, or
angry, don't let it trouble you. The anger is his own and will have
nothing to do with you. The feeling will pass from him in time."

5

Vithilonyi is a drinking man's holiday. When I got back to camp, the
party had already started. I went down to main camp to find Uncle
Sivisal, and he greeted me at his tent with a glass of Klyr wine. We
went walking through the Camp drinking and saying hello to people.
It surprised me how many folks I knew—apprentices from archery
drill, cooks from the common tent, members of the doctor's staff,
servants of the Nivri and Finru, the Nivri and Finru themselves; all
of whom greeted us graciously. A spirit of the holiday returned to
me for a few moments while we traveled through that noisy crowd.

The wine settled my nerves, Uncle Sivisal had hardly watered it, and in the crowd I felt smaller, less significant, more hidden.

Far ahead, I saw Kirith Kirin approaching, Imral with him. As if he could feel my eyes on him, Kirith Kirin looked across the crowd to me.

A whiteness closed over his face. He had never shown me such a cold expression. He looked away. But the two were still approaching us, and soon they were close enough for voices to carry. Imral asked me cordially if I had a pleasant ride that morning. I said yes, my heart pounding. Imral greeted my uncle, who answered in a formal way. Through all this, Kirith Kirin remained silent.

He was struggling. Whatever sign he was reading in what he seen at Hyvurgren Field had misled him; he could not look me in the eye. Dread filled me and I wanted to run away. Uncle Sivisal had his hand on my shoulder. I swallowed wine and breathed deeply. Mordwen Illythin found us and instructed me to come with him for the suuren book; the holiday could not interfere with this task.

Before we opened the book, Mordwen shared a cup of wine with me in his tent. I could hardly speak, feeling dull and empty inside. He asked me to tell him what suuren I had seen that morning, and I did. A white dove flying across a small pond. He wrote it carefully. I was feeling worse and worse. I asked if he would mind excusing me, I wanted to find Axfel and give him a run in the woods.

I ran home to the shrine tent, ignoring Axfel, disdaining the shrine in favor of flinging myself face-down onto the cot.

I lay shivering for a long time. Once I got up long enough to tie the flap to my room closed. After that I did not move, lying without thought for hours, breathing as the lake women had taught me. The shivering stopped and a species of relaxation came to me. Afternoon drew on into evening. Sounds of celebration penetrated from the Camp occasionally, and once I heard someone's voice calling for me in the outer shrine. I lay still and quiet, pretending sleep, and the bearer of the voice went away.

I did actually sleep for a while. When I woke the taste of wine was stale in my mouth and Mordwen Illythin was bending over me, saying, "It's nearly time for Kithilunen, you must wake up."

I sat up, rubbing my eyes. For a moment I could not remember what day it was or how I had gotten into bed. The sound of laughter and music penetrated from outside and I realized the festival was still going on.

In the lamp room I washed my face in the water basin and went through the necessary preparations for the lighting of lamps for festival night. We would have all nine lamps burning, three of each kind, inside and outside the shrine. Mordwen helped me, running through the steps for the festival ceremony at the same time. I worked efficiently, letting nothing enter my thoughts but what was needed for the work at hand. Peace came to me as I worked.

We were filling the last lamp when the sound of singing filled the air.

On Vithilonyi, it is customary to carry torches to the shrine, lighting the torches in daylight and burning them long into evening. At home, when we went to Mikinoos for the Festival there, we each had our own torch to carry. At the shrine that night more lanterns and torches burned than I had ever seen before, in the clearing and in the forest beyond, hundreds of them, flickering light on every side. A feeling of magic possessed me as I set out the lamps and awaited the dimming of the stone. The six I lit when the sun went down joined the three lamps that had burned through the whole day. Standing beside the last lamp, gazing out into the clearing where so many faces were watching reverently, I sang the Evening Song and "Light in the Darkness." I sang for Commyna, letting my voice rise to fullness, hoping the sound would reach her. It did not seem safe to sing for anyone else just then.

Kirith Kirin was there. He stood close to the altar, and I passed him each time I brought out a lamp. Even his posture was cold.

When the song was done I hurried behind the altar, pulling on my coat and slipping out the back of the tent quickly, before anyone could find me. I waited near the brook where I bathed each morning, Axfel beside me kissing my fingers with his cold muzzle. I heard a fair voice call my name once, but I refused to answer. I stood quietly beside the creek till I was certain I heard no other sounds from the tent above. Axfel walked me back up the path.

Gaelex was waiting for me. While I was untying the flap she slipped out from the shadow that had concealed her, saying nothing, watching my hands on the leather thong. "Hello, Gaelex."

Her smile was slightly ironic. "Where have you been?"

"By the creek. Watching the darkness."

"On festival day? You should be with people."

"I was happy without them," I said.

"You're expected at Kirith Kirin's feast table. We were afraid no one had told you. I've brought you a fresh tunic—"

"I like the one I'm wearing. Why do I have to go to a feast?"
"It's festival day," she said. "You're kyyvi in Kirith Kirin's shrine."
"I'm not hungry."

Her face hardened some. "Put on the tunic and come with me,
Jessex."

This was a command and I obeyed. I found the tunic on my
bed, blue velvet, decorated with a line of gold embroidery around
the collar, a pattern of circled chain links, with a sleeved coat that
matched it, the most beautiful garment I had ever seen. "What
you're wearing is not rich enough for the Vithilonyi feast," Gaelex
said, from outside.

When I was dressed she walked me to Camp, where everyone
in the world had put on festival colors. The big eating tables had
been set up under a broad tent made of colored streamers draped
over tree branches. Kirith Kirin's engineers had built a stone hearth
inside the tent and a big fire roared there, warming pots of spiced
wines and other drinks. The center tables were bowed down with
food and cooks were wandering from table to table, flushed from
their efforts, admiring their handiwork for a last moment.

I ended up in a seat between the southern Countess Duvettre
and Lady Brun, also one of the Anynae, with Lady Karsten a few
seats down on the table's opposite side. Uncle Sivisal even had a seat
at the Prince's table, since he was my kinsman; he was near red-
haired Pel Pelathayn, both of them red-faced from wine.

When I turned, Kirith Kirin was watching me from his seat at
the far end of the table. I met his eyes, and again the whiteness
washed over him. He nodded coldly and returned to his conversation with Lord Cothryn beside him, the kinsman of Ren Vael who
lived in Camp.

I actually enjoyed the feast because of Lady Brun's company,
and also the Countess's, though to a lesser degree. Neither of them
condescended to me or treated me like a child; the rules of adulthood can be relaxed when an adult deigns to do so. It is always odd
to speak to southerners because one must pitch the voice to what
they can hear, so that one can always tell that there are Anynae in a
crowd by the sound of the speech. Brun and Duvettre were ladies
of Finru Houses who spoke the lower modes of Jisraegen fairly
well, and they were obviously curious about me, having heard the
requisite rumors, including the now-famous story of my not-quite-
normal illness and the manner by which it had been cured. Lady
Brun knew a lot about witches and magic. She was a quiet woman

with a long nose and thin lips, an air of reserve, even of shyness. She talked about local witches in the south country and told tales of their efforts to survive under Drudaen's rule. She made life in the south sound very bleak.

Householders moved quietly around us pouring wine and setting down plates of food. Musicians had set up in front of the hearth and were playing their instruments, the lyre and guitar blending, the various percussion instruments beginning to compel rhythm. Many traditional songs were sung, among them a portion of "Last Days," the melody being even more beautiful than I had imagined. The singer was a Venladrii whom I did not know. Trysvyn was with the musicians also, but she was not singing yet.

Jugglers performed, and later a troupe of tumblers did some routines, standing on each others' shoulders and the like. All these folks were professional entertainers, one could see their polish, though I wondered how they got into Arthen. After we had eaten there was wrestling as well, some professionals as well as some people from Camp. We drank after-dinner brandy and wandered around under the colorful pavilion while the householders cleared away the tables.

The party was merry and showed every sign of lasting long into the night, in spite of the work there would be tomorrow when we were to strike camp. I found Gaelex talking to Lady Karsten and asked leave to return to the shrine tent. She said I could go.

"I'll walk with you," Karsten said.

I was surprised by the offer. But she turned to look at Kirith Kirin, who was nearby and I did, too, and found him watching me. Cold and hard. Karsten touched my shoulder to turn me away.

We walked along the familiar paths. We each had a torch. The fire registered on many levels of my awareness; fire is a good conductor of power, and for that reason many witches never do more than fire-magic. But I had to keep that part of myself locked away, in this world, for now. I breathed the pungent smoke.

Axfel met us on the way to the shrine, shoving his wet nose into my hands. Karsten knelt to scratch his shaggy head. He readily accepted her attentions. When the big hound had received enough petting he led us to the shrine clearing, full of light, the lamps burning from the nine points of the altar. The varicolored light flowed from the shining viis cloth, shifting everything from dream-tone to dream-tone.

"This is a peaceful place," she said, sighing.

"Come away from the lamp-stand, Axfel," I called.

She watched me for a long time. There was some look in her eyes I had never seen before, and I wondered if he had said something to her. Finally I moved away from her, saying good-night, departing into the tent. Axfel stayed beside her, thumping the ground with his tail.

I did not wonder, though I should have, what she saw in me to draw her affection to the surface. It seemed natural to me at the time. But I was not remembering how old she was, how long she had lived. It was a remarkable gift she was giving, to pay any attention at all.

I felt very heavy and sad inside the shrine. Sounds from Camp drifted through the clearing, mostly music and laughter. No one came to pray while I was at the altar, sitting quietly in the slanted lamplight. I was trying to recall the look of that overwhelming light I had seen at Illyn Water, radiant whiteness filling my eyes and my mind, eliminating every thought, every pain.

The recollection returned to me enough that I could rest. I lay in my cot feeling the renewal of the world in me, the rhythm of change that is like the rhythm of breathing, endless, sometimes catching one unawares. I slept well. No dreams. Rivers of hidden Words flowed through me, the murmuring of magic in my rest.

6

In the morning when ceremony was over, the whole army of Woodsfolk set about striking Camp for the move to Suvrin Sirhe.

I had expected noise and confusion and certainly got the first in good measure; Camp folks tended to sing or swear or both when doing this heavy, tedious work. But there was no confusion. The process of striking Camp proceeded in an orderly way, from my own packing away of the shrine implements, under Mordwen's direction, to the massive tearing down of the cook tents, the common tent, and the merchant's pavilions. Gaelex and her marshals were everywhere.

Mordwen instructed me patiently the way to pack the shrine, and together we capped the oil urns with hot wax and laid them in beds of straw inside crates. The Jisraegen, having been a nomadic people through much of our history, have long incorporated portability into the design of most objects. Every piece of furniture broke down into small, flat components, except the wooden chest in which my tunics (including the two fine ones I had been given) would travel to our new campsite. By midmorning the fragile parts of the shrine had been disassembled and packed into velvet-lined boxes, and the tent itself, now empty, was shimmering and collapsing as householders released the supporting ropes and braces.

I had kept out my traveling pack, filling a water flask at the creek. I got a ration of food as well; Mordwen warned me sometimes Kirith Kirin rode ahead of the main column and might ask that I travel with his party. This surprised me, given his coldness toward me, but I risked no questions.

When the viis cloth was folded and slipped into its waterproof leather cover, we followed the cart carrying the whole load into Camp. We stopped by the cook line to get the bread and cheese they were handing out for lunch. Even as we arrived the cooks were packing the last of the provisions onto wide-wheeled carts. Within a few moments we were ready to ride.

We followed a set path, Lady Karsten leading the column, Kirith Kirin out of sight. Prince Imral was with the Lady, and I spied Pelathayn soon after I saw them. Pelathayn was riding with the pike cavalry, his red hair and beard bristling in the morning light.

Thruil saw us coming and fetched Nixva and Mordwen's horse, Kyvixa, Nixva's full sister.

Mounted on the coal black horse, I felt my first real peace of the day, the vibration of Nixva's familiar strength. Commyna had said to trust him, that he would find a way to bring me to Illyn Water, and the promise of reaching the lake shore was sweet to me that morning. Mordwen and I took our place in the column, near the shrine wagon. Again I wondered where Kirith Kirin had gone. But soon anticipation of the coming journey swept even that thought from my mind. We who were mounted rode forward, on signal given by Gaelex at Lady Karsten's command. In a short time shimmering leaves obscured the hillside and valley where we had camped, and I was launched forward into yet another new country.

7

The lake women kept to their word. Early in the afternoon, when the mounted column was climbing a rise of land ahead of the cart train, I rounded a curve in the road and Nixva plunged into a dark grove of shrubbery and saplings. I felt a dizzy queasiness inside me, and when I looked up from Nixva's mane the lake shimmered blue in the distance. I said a Word to ease my passage now that it was safe to do so, and took that first curious relieved breath out of real time.

Vissyn had ridden from the duraelaryn to greet me, I could see her coming from a long way off. She was dressed in simple clothes, brown linens and light-woven wool, a filmy rose-colored scarf in her hair, the color of the sky at sunset. She greeted me with a broad smile and said, "Well, we got you here as we promised."

"It was a pretty piece of work," I said. "Lucky you have Nixva on your side."

"Luck has nothing to do with it," she said, leaning over to scratch Nixva's nose. "Horses have fates too. You are his." She looked up at me, changing her tone. "Was your festival-day pleasant?"

I had some work to do, hiding my confusion from her skillful eyes, but I managed to say, "Oh yes, very nice," in an even tone, with some hope she would not detect the lie.

We never talked much about Camp and she didn't pursue the subject that day. We exchanged more courtesies as we rode along the lake shore to the duraelaryn where the cart, horses and loom stood in the golden grass. Vella was working the loom today, singing into the thread and watching the fabric with all her attention, the new cloth shimmering with every imaginable color. Commyna, pedaling the spinning wheel and pulling thread, greeted us with a curt nod when we dismounted close-by.

Commyna noticed the unaccustomed saddle and pack on Nixva and stated that we must have gotten Camp moved without much trouble. "Not that I'm surprised. From what I hear, Kirith Kirin didn't even stay to the end."

"No. He left before the column. I don't know who went with him."

"No one went with him," Vella said from the loom. "Except the Keikin. You can never get any information from that horse, either; I'd as soon ask questions of a boulder on a mountainside."

"Was he angry with you?" Commyna asked.

"He wouldn't talk to me at all."

"This is what I was told," Commyna said, though she did not say by whom; nodding vigorously. "Very surprising."

By now I knew better than to expose myself by asking questions. The lake women gave information when it pleased them, and not before; they were generous to a fault with rebukes, however.

Vissyn settled down to work at the second wheel, and none of them spoke for a long time. They appeared to be staring at the ground, but I had learned enough to know that they were doing magic, something they called "in-singing," belonging to a higher level of application than I had yet attained. Vella, from the loom, said, "The boy means more to him than I would have guessed."

Vissyn, pedaling the wheel, sang a few notes of music. "He has cared for you, Jessex. Perhaps more than he should. But now he knows you are our pupil."

"Why does that makes so much difference?"

"It's a dreadful calamity, to love a magician."

"Be careful, sister," Vella warned, running her hand through the lovely fabric she was weaving.

"I know what I'm doing."

"I hope you do," Vella said evenly. "There's nothing to be gained from saying too much." She went back to her weaving.

"Don't dwell on this too much, child," Commyna said, her fingers moving briskly to tie off her thread. "He'll make his peace with you in time." She was tidying up her work area as if she meant to leave it for a while, and I guessed from her preparations she would be my teacher for today.

When she beckoned me to follow her I did. Vella and Vissyn said pleasant good-byes to us, the sort that would serve as well if I did not come back for an hour or a year.

To tell the truth, it would have been hard to say which was closer. I had thought my training stringent before. Now I began to understand just what the women meant when they talked about hard work.

Sixth-level applications are different from seventh-level training, more difficult than the simple progression from the lower to the higher circle would imply. Many a respectable wizard never works out of the sixth level and much powerful magic can be done using the applications of this circle. My training began with fire.

Commyna took me to a stone circle and sat me down. She turned away and spoke a Word, and before I knew it flame was rising all around me.

I had learned to remove my body from harm in such a circumstance already, and did so quickly, suffering no more than a few singed hairs. I sat in the fire, tasting the feelings of it as I pleased. Commyna, from a place beyond the flames, watched me with keen interest.

"Do you hear it?" she asked.

"I hear the wind rushing through it," I said.

"There's another sound, in harmony with the wind. That part is the fire. The fire is all music, all plucked strings. So are you. You'll have to learn to hear it."

She tested me with fire in other ways. I walked over coals and even lay down on them, as I had already learned to do. She had to help with the new pathways for the fire, leading it through and around me, but when she did I could hold my place. Without ever questioning her I understood she was making sure I knew what I was doing, before we progressed to other phases of fire-work.

Fire can be used to move power, to amplify Words, and when used for that purpose is referred to as a device. Moreover, the fire is a source of strength as well, due to the state of the burning matter, which makes a more violent music than a breath of wind. Other devices are more efficient as amplifiers or points of focus, like precious metals, gems, stones, and runes, but they are much harder to tap as sources of strength. They are made of music as well, but a harder sound to hear.

I spent much time meditating, either near or inside fires; and this last practice, while it may sound arcane (considering that some nations are said to burn their witches, according to the Anynae, who come from elsewhere), is one of the most basic magic arts, since sitting inside fire offers a quantum of protection from other magical attacks. (The saying in Aeryn is, if you can burn the witch, you never had much to worry about in the first place.)

Fire-magic was one of Commyna's specialties and she taught me every use you can imagine, from dreaming in fires to bringing fire out of rocks, out of the ground, out of air, out of water. Before she was done I could call up fire from rain-soaked ground and make it swell high as a house; I could make smoke billow out in a cloud or make no smoke appear at all. Fire is a sound, and once I learned to hear it I could make it as well. I could dance-for-seeing around a fire, finding images in the flames. This seemed the most wonderful use of magic I had yet learned, once I learned to govern the direction of my far-seeing, once I could focus on an object and see it minutely.

This was only the beginning, and my heart could feel it.

I became infatuated with this new work I was learning, as any young person is apt to do. I became lost in the complex executions, the harsh physical disciplines, the inner listening and the stream of music that I found, that flows through every thing that is around us;

and when I was not actually present at Illyn Water in those days, I was there on some level, meditating or singing under my breath, running through the steps of some spin-dance in my mind. In fact it is harder for me to distinguish between days for this period than any other, and it would be impossible to tell all that I learned unless I were to stop this story and write another text. The ride with Camp to Suvrin Sirhe was long and tedious; my concentration was saved for the periods when I was with the lake women and I was dull company the rest of the time. I became used to the ordeal of being plucked out of real time and thrust back into it, taking up the moment of my return just as if there had been no interval at the lake, no long, nameless, divisionless time along the blue shore where I was learning such unimaginable arts. I encouraged few distractions on the ride and consequently received few in return. Kirith Kirin did not return to the column even after we were days out of the old campsite, and finally Lady Karsten, Lord Pelathayn and Prince Imral rode in search of him—as much out of boredom as concern, I thought. Gaelex had charge of the whole subsequent journey of the column and cart-train and thus had plenty to keep her busy. Mordwen was worn out by riding, which he did not like to do any more, since he claimed his bones had aged. He went to bed at sundown and slept till time for Velunen.

I was young and adaptable. My new life, though unusual, was not without its ordinary moments, and after a few days the routine became comfortably familiar. I awoke, sang Velunen, ate a fast breakfast, saddled Nixva and joined the column. During the ride that followed I was patiently alert for the moment when I would be summoned out of real time to the world of Lake Illyn. I might be at the lake for any amount of time. But I knew that in the waking world not a heartbeat would pass, that I would return there to take up my life without break or gap.

Some people would have thought this madness, I guess, and a philosopher might have argued that I never actually received any instruction, I simply dreamed the lake and the women. I might have harbored this same suspicion if my mind had not relaxed into, and grown to love, the work I was learning.

I think my progress at the sixth level surprised the lake women some, though they never praised me. My study of Wyyvisar was progressing, and Vella had started teaching me to write Words as well, this being a whole discipline unto itself, with a thousand rules to remember. You can imagine the difficulty of the notion of writing a language that is not even truly spoken. The writing can be runes, though the runes are pictures and carry no power in and of themselves. Most often what is called writing involves something else, like the blessing of a ring to make a man able to speak to a horse. That is written Wyyvisar, and I had to learn it. As if this weren't enough, each of the women told me stories, till I had learned a good sketch of the history of magic, from the deriving of Wyyvisar by YY-Mother to the making of Ildaruen by her Opposite, from the battles between the Evaenym and the Mountain Witches to the fall of Kentha Nurysem, the sorceress who loved Drudaen Keerfax and bore his child.

I would ride from these lessons to the cart-train and the soldier column winding its way along the forest road, to Mordwen who often as not would drill me in High Speech grammar or writing or Jisraegen history along the way. On some of those nights none of the moons rose, and we sat by watchfires and sang songs by starlight, sometimes sharing brandy, sometimes listening to stories.

Often I was so full I would lie in bed unable to sleep, thoughts chasing each other head to tail, and when sleep did come I dreamed of my work all night, lighting lamps and watching fires, sleeping in a damp cave or meditating while holding a smooth stone in my palms.

Once I dreamed of Kirith Kirin. In the dream I was riding with the column as usual and felt, while no one else was in sight, the familiar lurch of departure, the summons of the lake women, only when I drew breath again I was not at Illyn Water, I was facing Kirith Kirin. That dream image of the Prince was as vivid as if he had been facing me in real time. He was wearing buckskins, the creamy brown leather setting off his bronze skin. He was watching me as if he were very angry. I said, "Don't you think I can feel a difference?" and the dream dissolved.

We heard nothing from him for many days, however. Other news reached us, about bread riots in Cordyssa following the commencement of the new wheat tariffs, and the refortification of Ithlumen, the fortress guarding the approach to Cordyssa and the mines. Rumors were raising the walls by as much as forty feet, and estimates of the thickness of the stone were staggering. Some said Drudaen was finally ready to build a shenesoeniis there, a magician's tower to secure his control over the north.

Meanwhile Athryn Ardfalla and her Court were moving from Ivyssa to the palace Dernhang on the island of Kmur, where she often spent the summer. She would celebrate, in only a few days, the three hundred twenty-third year of her reign.

CHAPTER SEVEN
AEDIAMYSAAR

1

I turned fifteen on the ride to Suvrin Sirhe, late in the month of Khan. Uncle Sivisal remembered, and got permission from Gaelex to ride with me that morning. He had bought the fifteenth bead for my naming-necklace from one of the merchants who traveled with the Camp, and he presented it to me with an awkward smile. I was surprised and touched; I had been planning to buy the stone myself, once I got someone to tell me how to get my money from the paymaster. (There was a small pay allowance for the kyyvi, same as the rest of the army.) I thanked Uncle Sivisal and we had a good time talking.

Mordwen was riding close by, and when my uncle returned to his place in the column, the Seer wished me a happy naming-day. I showed him my stone, and that told him I was fifteen now, a year from adulthood, if he had not known it already.

Later in the day a messenger reached us from Kirith Kirin. I saw the letter, since it was addressed to Mordwen Illythin and he was beside me. The Prince was in a country called Ym and he wanted Mordwen to ride to meet him at place called Aediamysaar. This means Mount Diamysaar; the Diamysaar were the first of created women. Diamysaar means "Sister to the Eye," and the Eye is another name for YY, for Mother-God.

My name was written at the bottom of the message in the midst of some other words I could not read. Mordwen saw me studying it. "Well, how much of it can you make out?"

"He wants you to meet him at Aediamysaar. Where is that?"

"Near where we're going. It's a very ancient place, a huge earthwork with a circle of stones at the top. The Diamysaar built it at the beginning of their war with Cunavastar. I think you'll like it."

"Am I going, too?"

"Couldn't you read that? Yes, I'm to bring you with me." He was intrigued and curious. He headed back along the column to find Gaelex, while I sat still. Why did Kirith Kirin send for me? Could it mean he wasn't angry any more?

Gaelex had provisions and a light tent issued us and we left the
main column as soon as these were ready. Ym country was a full
day's ride east of the road, Mordwen said.

Despite his complaining, Mordwen could ride as well as anyone, and our horses, being children of Keikindavii, could have galloped the whole day and night straight through if we had asked for
that. We were content to ride till sundown. I pitched the tent following some instruction from Mordwen. Mordwen built the fire,
painstakingly; I knew a harmony to make the wood burn, it would
have been so easy to intone it in that place of my mind. He touched
the roch to the ifnuelyn and the fire mounted upward, throwing
sparks and blue streaks of smoke toward the upper branches.

Only then did it occur to me, there by the fire, that the lake
women had not summoned me the whole day. This was the first
time I had missed my lesson at Illyn Water since the women first
took me as a pupil.

I found Nixva tethered to a faris sapling, and stroked his long
face, his velvet muzzle. I had brushed him and thrown a blanket
over him. He was peaceful and without any sign of trouble, and I
reflected that getting to Illyn had never really been my job but was
his. Mordwen and I ate dried meat and drank cumbre, a good meal
if somewhat unvaried. He had brought a skin of wine too, and
drank deeply. I slept peacefully the whole night, spring breezes blowing softly against my face.

In the morning I woke before dawn, rising in time to sing
Velunen, facing east, as new sunlight colored the sky, the first sun, a
clear white light. Mordwen had brought an oet so we had hot jaka.
We had a fair breakfast, way-bread and salted meat.

In daylight one could tell we were in different country. Where
along the road from Golden Wood I had seen every sort of tree,
here one saw only faris, cedar, hemlock and fir. We had ascended
into the foothills of the mountains and rode uphill. Soon, from the
crest of each hill I could see Mount Diamysaar in the distance, a
huge slab of rock on which trees had stubbornly grown and down
whose jagged sides clear water streamed. I could see the stones at
the summit, huge flat things, set out in rings.

Mordwen told me something about the place, which was built
by the Diamysaar during their war with Cunavastar, who had built
an earlier stone circle within his fortress Cunevadrim. He used the
circle as a device to focus his magic; to fight him, the Diamysaar
caused a mountain to rise up in the middle of Arthen, and they built

their own stone circle at its top. In the war that followed much of Arthen was destroyed—the forest, in those days, ran south to the present Cuthunre valley, and north to Thynilex and Svyssnam. Cunavastar brought Ildaruen magic into the world, the language of undoing and unmaking, and his success hinted at the existence of another power beyond the YY; but in the end the Diamysaar bound him and imprisoned him far beneath the mountains.

One could see that the solitary mountain, rising so starkly above the hills, was no ordinary work of geology; the land thereabouts showed the signs of old, localized upheaval. Trees along one flank, torn up by the roots when the ground broke open, had petrified in the streams of water, lying in broken pieces in the shadow of the mountain.

Aediamysaar rose too steeply for horses to climb. We tethered Nixva and Kyvixa with the horses of those who had arrived ahead of us. I recognized the Keikin and other of his offspring. My heart beat more strongly when I realized who would be at the summit.

Mordwen warned me the path was steep. I followed through a grove of twisted scrub-faris and a vine bare of leaves. The path had a winter aspect even on that warm morning, and I found myself wishing for a coat. We climbed in silence.

I had wondered vaguely how the Prince would behave when we reached the top. I adopted an attitude Commyna would have approved, of respectful wariness. As we neared the end of the climb, with the wind screeching breakneck through the thin, twisted trees, I told myself over and over again, enjoy the scenery, you may get nothing but that.

It would have been sufficient, I think. I had never seen anything like the view going up. We spiraled higher over the undulating rhythm of green and golden treetops, finally climbing so high one could see the eastern mountains. On a clear day one can see the walls of Drii from Mount Diamysaar. If I had been on horseback I would have fallen off at the sight.

The top of the mountain was a broad table of flat stone. A flight of curved steps led up the sheer rock face on either side of this plateau—that is to say, from either the eastern or the western approaches, for one can reach the summit by either of two paths. On the rock table stood stone slabs set upright, some capped with capstones, forming a broad outer circle and a smaller, less defined, inner circle. One could see this much from a distance. One could also see cloaked figures standing in the circles. Karsten came toward us. Wind blew through her hair.

When I started to speak she shook her head, placing her finger against her lips. She took my hand and we walked toward the standing stones.

A sound like music came from inside, the echoes of voices, but I knew this was nothing my ears were hearing. For a moment I felt what panic would be like. But my body remembered what the lake women had taught me to do, and I breathed as if I were a bird slowly beating its wings. I savored each moment. We reached the shadows of the stones, ascending a shallow flight of steps, passing through the rock pylons.

Beyond, past the second ring of stones, I could see the dull gray of the circular pavement. The light struck it oddly, not as if it were stone but as if it were the surface of a lake. A figure stood at the center of the pavement, a man, and I knew him long before I could distinguish any feature of his face.

I had not seen him in days. Now, I knew the difference his presence made. I felt resonant with him, and expectant, and so full of feeling I was almost sad. The well of feelings was in fact so strong that I forgot my training, and as I neared him the voices returned, dizzying; songs of warning, in Words I knew.

The songs were very powerful, and when I understood that their purpose was to warn me not to tamper with the magic here, I stopped in my tracks. The lake women had never told me what to do in a case like this, but had taught me something about entering magic circles and magician's chambers; one does neither lightly. Here was a device for moving power built in the age of Cunavastar, and I was being led blithely onto the stone circle as if this were someone's tent.

Karsten turned and frowned at me. When I still refused to move she bent and whispered, "Come along Jessex. Kirith Kirin is waiting for you."

"I don't want to go inside."

She touched my forehead sadly. "You don't have any choice."

Mordwen paled, gazing into the stones. "Why is Kirith Kirin doing this?"

Karsten spoke, without meeting anyone's eyes. "What do you think? There aren't so many uses for this place that we know."

Mordwen studied the motionless figure at the center of the shining pavement, the Seer looking as if he wanted to speak to the Prince, but deciding the effort would be futile, these changes plainly visible on his features. He knelt and spoke to me with tenderness that touched me. "You're only being asked to walk across the granite circle. Once you've reached the place where Kirith Kirin is standing the test will be over."

"Test?" Anger flooded me suddenly. "Why am I being tested this time?"

He started to speak but Karsten cut him off. "You're not to tell him anything, Mordwen. Kirith Kirin's orders."

"Naturally," Mordwen said.

"That's enough talking." To me she said, "Walk through these pylons and across the granite, Jessex. Say nothing, whatever happens."

I waited a moment for my head to clear. The talking had distracted me, and with the lapse of concentration came a resurgence of voices, a dizzying power:

Traveler go no farther
this is no place for a visit
You who are lost in Words
Enter with care and due precaution

I could hear other phrases that cannot be translated, specific warnings about specific penalties to be imposed on the pretender to power.

I could feel the barrier erected against the entry of one like me, and on my lips was the phrase to disarm the incantation, a request for entry and a pledge to do no harm to the holy place. But I could not say it without disobeying the injunctions of the women at Lake Illyn, I must never say Wyyvisar away from them, and on my obedience to this rule hinged the remainder of my training. I ascended the stone steps with my lips clamped shut, my mind under strict harness, every breath a concentrated effort.

Beyond the first rank of pylons I could feel the change. The voices of warning changed to voices of menace, and since I spoke neither to challenge nor to placate the magic of the place, and yet was an initiate of the Circles, I had no defense. The possibility that I would be foolish enough to come to such a place as this had never occurred to the lake women. I reached the inner ring of pylons without suffering more than generalized dizziness, pausing before setting out across the polished circle. I suppose I must have looked tired. Kirith Kirin, awaiting me in the center of the circle, looked at me oddly, as if puzzled this was taking so long. Though to tell the truth I never studied his expression. Watching him would have made me angry again, and I had no time to spare for that.

When I stepped onto the pavement, a new singing began, and the wind increased.

The Prince was looking down at the pavement expectantly, but there was no change in the polished surface.

The singing rose in power, but he was deaf to that. I bit my lips together, feeling a tearing pain like when I was in the dark place in the mountains. I kept walking grimly forward, feeling the wind blow harder, but in my mind was another vision, myself as a tiny image walking horizontally across the gray stone disk, bare to every power, my thoughts plain and undefended. I could feel awarenesses, Commyna and Vissyn momentarily, and another power to the south, the same image I had met in the fourth level trance. My enemy.

I must have stood still sometime during this moment of confusion. I became conscious again when Kirith Kirin called me from the place where he was still standing.

Laughter filled my inner hearing, and a long phrase in a language I had never heard. A power was reaching for me, knowing where I was. I stepped across the black granite ring to the place where Kirith Kirin stood.

"I'm sorry," he said, embracing me, "I've wronged you. There was no change in the stones."

His touch was cold to me. I pulled away from him. "In a moment I won't be able to see you or hear you. If you don't take me away from this place I'll be killed."

He frowned at me, and started to speak again. But the voice from the south was already engulfing me, and my undefended spirit was weakening. "I don't know why you brought me here," I said, "but while I'm here I'm in danger."

"From what?" he asked, and then I couldn't see him any more. I was aware of my body falling. I was no longer quite inside it, heeding the call of the singer.

I could feel his arms when he lifted me from the stone. I could feel hands on my face as well, but I believe those were magical touches; Vella was singing in my ear. Wind blew on my face. I awoke in the grass, with Mordwen bending over me. "Thank the YY, there you are."

Wind lashed the trees behind his head, and clouds were gathering over the mountain. The wind was warm, out of season. The storm that was coming already had a fierce feeling; soon forks of lightning were lashing down like snake's tongues from the sky. I sat up, watching the whole landscape, the violent clash of grays and greens. Karsten and Imral were watching too.

Kirith Kirin was behind me. I could feel his presence.

"Lie quiet for a moment," Mordwen said, but I shook my head. I stood, letting the wind whip my face. Away from the stones I had less awareness of what striving was producing this storm, but the sickness filled me.

"We need to get away from here," I said.

"We'll leave as soon as the storm breaks." Kirith Kirin spoke from behind me. "We can take shelter under the pylons."

I shook my head and said emphatically, "The storm won't break as long as we're near the holy place. We can't take shelter here."

"Jessex, the road down would be murder in a storm."

I watched him calmly, feeling a power in me I had never felt before. "Yes, Kirith Kirin, I know, and I also know why it was made that way. You don't know what you've done in bringing me here."

This touched his pride, and I could see his anger plainly. But he swallowed it back. "I had good reasons for what I did. The stones didn't change. My mind is more at rest about you, or at least it was. Where did you learn so much about this place?"

"I don't know anything."

He would have answered but his voice drowned in a gust of wind, followed by the first sheets of rain. He looked round at the sky.

The storm was awesome, crashing over the forest with thunder and lightning, wind hurtling across the treetops, breaking with force against the side of Mount Diamysaar. Unconsciously we drew closer together as the rain intensified. The force of the storm sobered the Prince. Imral and Karsten also drew close. "This is uncanny," Imral said. "There's magic in this." He studied me with suspicion, rain running down his face. "But the stones didn't change, there were no runes."

Karsten looked from one to the other, and said in a flat, even voice, "You both saw what happened when he reached the inner circle. If he says we need to get away from here, I'm inclined to believe him. It was his crossing the stone circle that triggered the storm."

"That's an interesting theory anyway," Imral said, and went on to say more that the wind drowned out.

I turned away, shivering in my tunic. I was too close, my head was aching. Someone was calling me. I turned, blindly, to find them all watching me. My anger boiled at the sight of their stupid faces; "I can't stay here," I shouted, "I told you that. You had no reason to bring me here if you trusted me. If you have any sense you'll trust me now and get down to your horses at once."

Even then they merely stood there, four of the blessed of the world, dumfounded in the rain. Something changed in me, seeing them like that. I turned and ran down the path, pressing my hands to my ears as if that could help.

The rocks were slippery, and I was already dizzy from staying too long on the summit. The rain increased, sometimes beating down so furiously I could not see two feet in front of me on the path. The wind was like a prey-bird trying to claw me from the rocks. I clung to the tenacious shrubs, when there were any to be had; otherwise I hugged the side of the mountain or got down on my knees and crawled.

The storm continued, furious, a battering like nothing I'd seen since the morning I left my father's farm. I found Nixva with his family, other daughters and sons of Keikindavii. Taking his bridle in hand, I told him we had to get to Illyn Water, and I mounted. I waited on his back for a moment, watching the path, empty still. Since I could do nothing else, I prayed for their safety.

My own required that I get away from this place as soon as possible. Nudging Nixva with my heels, I headed him for the forest.

We rode for some time through the resounding storm, and I began to wonder if we would find Illyn that day. Rain beat down in a thousand rhythms, leaf to leaf, drops and streams, an endless pulse receding in every direction. The sound was soothing. My heartbeat steadied and my head cleared as we drew away from Aediamysaar.

We were heading east, toward low hills. The storm had followed us. Overhead trees lashed wildly, branches tangling and splitting. Nixva was surefooted as any horse could be, and cut through the rain and wind effortlessly. I lay my head in his mane for a moment, feeling safe and warm against him.

When I sat up again we were at Illyn Water, where the storm was also blowing. Commyna met me, she on horseback, cloaked in a flowing gown, eyeing the heavens like a field marshal. "Thank the Eye," she said, "I was worried sick. Tell me what happened."

I told her, quickly. She let me finish and reflected a moment. "That agrees with what we saw."

"You know what happened?"

"Yes. The Sister Mountain is one of the places we monitor."

"Why did Kirith Kirin take me there?" I asked.

"To test you. To see if you were a sorcerer. When an adept crosses the inner stone ring, bright runes appear in the pavement. In most cases." She was smiling as if she had been very clever.

I looked at the ground, suddenly bereft. "Why would it matter so much?"

"Haven't you guessed? He thinks you practice magic in Camp. He thinks you've enchanted him. He thinks that's why he's fond of you."

For a moment even the storm made no difference, I heard nothing. I felt nothing. Finally I said, "And I can't tell him any different without telling him about you."

"Certainly you can," Commyna said, with lightning illuminating her features. "By the way you behave." Seeing me still confused, she said more plainly, "Don't judge him, or anyone else. You don't know everything. You care for him, that's plain. Let that be enough for the moment."

The storm grew fierce. I asked, finally, "Why didn't the stones change on the mountain? Why didn't the runes appear?"

Commyna smiled. "My sisters and I prevented it. But that was also what awakened the power of the place, and what drew the attention of the Wizard."

I framed one more question in my mind, though by now I knew the answer. I asked, as we were heading through the gray rain for the lakeshore, "What power could you have over the stones on Sister Mountain?"

"Can't you guess?" Commyna asked in return. "We made the mountain and put them on it."

2

Following my time at the Lake I was returned to a region near the Prince and the other Jhinuuserret, a few hours ride back of them on another of the cleared roads. Vissyn brought me to the place, actually riding along the road for a while, to make sure I had my bearings. This time I was not returned to the same moment that I had left, but emerged into temporal Arthen on the following morning, when the skies over Ym were country-clear and blue.

Vissyn parted from me in the shadow of a sheer hill with a rocky slope, around the base of which ran the road I would follow. At the top of the hill stood a low ruin, stone walls distinguishable as fortifications as well as the time-wrecked base of a tower. I asked what the place had been and Vissyn answered, "This was one of the fortresses guarding the approach to Montajhena during the war between the Evaenym and Falamar. At the height of the war Montajhena commanded all the country from this hillside to the south Kellyxa."

"Did it have a name?"

Vissyn smiled. "Everything Jisraegen has a name. But I can't read the name of this place from the stones." She turned her horse to go. "Follow the road from here," she said. "Kirith Kirin is ahead of you, you might catch him by nightfall, or at least by morning. He and his friends think you're lost in the wilderness."

"I'll tell them I found the road and followed it thinking they might have done the same."

She agreed this would be a good story. Bowing her head, she signaled her horse and vanished.

I leaned forward and stroked the firm muscles of Nixva's neck. He turned to eye me sidewise, making it plain he was ready to go. I said to him, "Teach me to be calm like you are."

He shook his head, the black mane shimmering. He seemed ready to laugh out loud. Sighing, I nudged him with my heels and he gladly galloped forward.

The day passed in a kind of silence that had become rare for me. I spent the time in solitude, not a soul in sight, only Nixva and me under fair skies. I had some food in my saddlebag and stopped to eat it in a dense part of the forest where faris and oak were mixed, both nearly submerged under heavy nets of dark elgerath, the wildly colored varieties that grow in higher altitudes, blues like bolts of lightning, reds like rubies and oranges like fire. My thighs ached from riding. I ate strips of dried venison and drank cumbre from my flask while Nixva ate grass and sweet leaves. Though the glade was beautiful we did not linger.

In the afternoon Nixva stretched his legs and maintained an awesome pace, eating up the road with his strides, but still we had not caught the others by sunset when we stopped. I found a rock promontory and sang the Evening Song. I had no muuren stone with me, and so had to guess the proper moment. I lit a torch the hard way, with ifnuelyn and tinder, and we rode beneath the light of that and the two moons.

More hours passed, and still we found no camp, no horsemen, nothing but dark road and whispering trees. Finally we stopped for the night. I gathered a pile of wood and built a fire, meaning it to frighten away prowlers. My store of food was low but I had enough to settle the grumbling in my belly. I spread my blanket on the lush, springy grass and with the fire to lull me I soon slept.

Twice I woke and built up the fire. Nixva murmured to me each time, telling me we were safe.

In the morning I had no jaka and no bath either. I changed tunics anyway and began my ride quickly, singing Velunen from Nixva's back. Once again the lake women never summoned me to Illyn. By midheaven I had not caught Kirith Kirin either, and was beginning to wonder if he had abandoned the road for another path.

But in afternoon I found a camp by the roadside, near one of the obelisk markers. Mordwen was fanning a small flower of flame while Imral Ynuuvil set up a viis-tent beside one that was already staked in place. It was a marvel to watch him perform the task, neat-handedly, no wasted motion. No one else was in sight.

I dismounted some distance from the fledgling fire and walked with Nixva's reins in hand. Mordwen saw me coming and straightened, soundless, electrified. When he found his voice he said, "Look who's here, Imral."

The Drii Prince turned. His pale eyes gave me a slight shock. He patiently finished tying the stake he was presently working on. Touching the unicorn necklace at his throat, he said, "Jessex. It's good to see you. We were worried."

"I've been trying to find you since yesterday," I said, swallowing. "I got lost in the forest around Aediamysaar. I'd almost given up."

"You frightened us half to death," Mordwen said, "running away like that. You could have wandered around Ym for months before we found you."

Imral's tone was matter-of-fact, "We spent hours searching for you before we realized there was too much country to cover. Kirith Kirin was very concerned."

"I'm sorry. I tried to tell you. I couldn't stay there."

Imral considered this. Then he said, with evident feeling, "Why don't we leave it alone? What happened on Aediamysaar is something I'd like to forget."

That closed the talk, and I was left to settle into camp. I unsaddled Nixva, leaving him to tell his kinfolk about where we had been while I made myself a pallet against a tall boulder, in a bed of abundant grass.

The fire was crackling steadily by the time the hunters returned with their trophy, two lorus-hares shot through the skull. I was beyond the boulder out of sight, singing Kithilunen quietly, a whisper not even my shadow could have heard. Kirith Kirin asked if Imral would skin the hares and Imral answered that he thought I could probably do it as well as he could, and called me.

I ran up shyly. Kirith Kirin stood there dumfounded. I watched him. I could see he was confused. "I'm glad you found us."

"It was luck. I found the road and followed it."

He said nothing else. It was clear he was not entirely comfortable with my presence and so, stung, I withdrew to my work, borrowing Mordwen's good Cordyssan hunting knife for the skinning. Karsten knelt to help me, saying nothing.

The hares were warm, their rich blood staining my hands. I felt vaguely sorry as I gutted them and cut them to pieces, scraping their hides free of vestiges of fat, detaching the limbs, the tender breastmeat, spearing the stuff on sturdy branches and hanging it over the fire to cook. When I needed instruction Karsten patiently told me what to do. Mordwen stirred wild onions and mushrooms in a pot, and tea was brewing as well, the various smells hovering over us. Evening had quickly blossomed into night, starless and moonless, it appeared, as some nights are, though we dread them.

When a feeling of quiet had descended, with Kirith Kirin and Imral Ynuuvil sipping wine out of sight, Karsten said to me in a low voice, "Don't mind him so much. What happened on the mountaintop rattled him."

"Did you know why he was bringing me there?"

After a moment's consideration she nodded. "We've used Aediamysaar for that same purpose before, and as far as I know others have used the stone circles as a test for sorcery for ages. If a person is wearing so much as a charmed rune-necklace the stone-writing will appear, I've never seen it fail."

"Would it be possible for anyone but the Diamysaar to tamper with the mountain? To keep the stones from lighting?"

She weighed her answer carefully. "I've known my share of wizards, and none of them ever attempted to stand on Aediamysaar. Not even Jurel Durassa. Falamar was afraid to go near the place because of his kinship to Cunavastar. Drudaen has apparently inherited his father's fear, and has always avoided Ym country."

This made me thoughtful for many reasons. I could feel Karsten watching me but was too preoccupied to say anything. She eyed me with sudden suspicion. "Are you saying the runes should have become visible?"

I gave no answer. But now that the thought had occurred to her it would not be denied. "He thinks you've bewitched him, doesn't he? That's why he's done all this. That's why he brought you to the mountain."

I sat unmoving, staring into my curved fingers, the laced shadows. "I don't think he meant you any harm, Jessex. But if you had ever seen the havoc a magician can wreak among humans, you'd understand why we fear them."

We had done as much as we could about supper. Karsten said she was going to find a friend with a skin of wine, and she would provide for me when she did. She kissed my brow, almost shyly. I began to wonder if I myself understood all that I had told her by my silence.

I sat watching the roasting game, knees tucked under my chin, the warmth of night wind on my face. Under my breath I was singing, "Muraelonyi" mixed with a country dance song I had known since I was a boy. Thoughts came and went without pattern. I could have sat there till the stars came back and felt as happy.

We ate supper together. I had never felt so relaxed with the twice-named, free to be quiet in their presence, free of the worry that polite conversation might lapse too long. We sat listening to the songs of night birds and insects, the whispering wind in the trees. After a while even Kirith Kirin was at ease. Wine passed round, no one caring how much I drank. When Karsten murmured once about my age Mordwen reminded her my naming-day had just passed, the forty-third day of Khan. Being fifteen, I was now responsible for monitoring my own drink, as practice for my coming adulthood.

Kirith Kirin started to tell a story about Kentha Nurysem, who had often spent mid-winter near Sister Mountain. From the way he talked about the famous sorceress, I could see that she was on his mind for some reason, that this was not the first time her name had come up.

"I know about her," I said. "She was Drudaen's lover, and she broke Goerast under him."

Prince Imral said, "That's how she's remembered anyway. The years before that are mostly forgotten now."

"She was a very sad woman at the end of her life, Jessex." Kirith Kirin spoke to me directly for the first time. Even then he could not look me in the eye for long. "She had lost everything."

His voice was full of feeling, sadness blossomed in his face; I could see he was telling more than the facts of her story. "We knew her, we were her friends. Our lives depended on her, too. Without a magician, one cannot oppose Drudaen." He swallowed, shaking his head. "But her fate was like the fate of most sorcerers. Magic consumed her, and humans shunned her, out of fear. In the end she had nothing to do even with us, her friends, and shut herself up in Ellebren Tower. I believe she'd never have been seduced by Drudaen if she had not become so distant from the rest of us."

"Those who schooled her would have more to say about it," Karsten said softly.

"What do you mean?"

"Nothing." She refilled her wine glass. "Only that we don't know the whole story of what happened to Kentha. No one does, except the Diamysaar who taught her."

A tingle ran down my spine. I asked another question that was on my mind. "Who is Yron? Have you heard of anyone by that name?"

I thought I was prepared for any reaction. But Imral spat his wine onto my hand, and asked, "What name did you say?"

"Yron." The name means, "God's claw."

They looked at each other. I wiped my hand on the hem of my tunic. Finally Imral said, "That name is known to few people. You're looking at the majority of them."

"But you've heard it."

"Yes." He watched me patiently for a moment, as if he expected me to go on—the others were watching me the same way. Finally he asked, "What do you know?"

"That the name is mentioned in a prophecy."

"Who told you that?" Kirith Kirin asked softly, watching the fire.

"A woman I met in Arthen, by a well."

"You never told me about meeting anyone," Mordwen said.

"She was just an old woman," I said. "Driving a cart. I thought she was a merchant or a merchant's wife. But she knew about me, and about the oracle. She told me I was a sign Yron was coming. But she wouldn't tell me very much about him."

"Have you ever seen her again?" Imral asked.

"Not the cart-woman," I said, and that was the truth. "Do you know who Yron is?"

Mordwen turned to Kirith Kirin, who had drawn back from the fire. The Prince nodded.

Mordwen sighed. "We were told about the coming of the magician Yron by Kentha herself, as she was leaving Arthen the last time. There are some hints about it in Curaeth, too, but all very cryptic. Kentha had seen very clearly what was coming. She said he would cross the mountains on the air at the beginning of a hard winter, bearing Drudaen in another form. She said she built Ellebren Tower for him. She said a number of other things that we could never puzzle out. No one has ever explained how bringing us Drudaen in another form is supposed to help us. The name Yron has come up in two of my own true-dreams, but only vaguely."

"Is that everything?" I asked when he stopped.

"That's the essence of what we know."

I took a deep breath. "Do these prophecies have anything to do with me?"

Everyone looked at the figure withdrawn into shadow. I watched the ground, awaiting judgment.

Mordwen said, "I don't think this is a good idea."

"Tell him," Kirith Kirin said.

Mordwen turned to me, scowling as he used to when I first knew him. But his voice was gentle, despite his expression. "I never wanted you to know this, or I would have told it to you myself. Kentha told us the first sign we would have that Yron was close would be the finding of a boy in Imith Imril singing by the river in the abandoned city. This same boy is said to be a servant of two masters." Here he swallowed. "The same image occurred in my true-dream. I saw a boy singing by Imith Imril. I saw you, in fact. And then Kirith Kirin found you, in my dream, as he did in real life."

Again Mordwen turned to Kirith Kirin's shadow. Again we waited by the fire. At last the deep voice spoke. "That's enough."

Kirith Kirin stood , and I had a feeling he was watching each one of us, though one could see nothing of his face. He walked away. So all of us, each with more questions than answers, said our good-nights.

3

Sleep never found me beside that boulder; I twisted in my bedroll till my inner clock told me dawn was close, and then I found the creek Karsten had described to me and in morning mist took my bath, counting breaths and washing each limb in the manner proper to the

ritual. I had lacked the leisure for this ceremonial many days during
the course of the ride from Golden Wood, and I felt very peaceful
that morning performing my proper duties, breathing, breathing, while
dawn birds chorused in eerie voices. I had no clean tunic to put on,
nor any felva to dry myself with, so I beat my dirty tunic on a rock to
shake out the dust, while the crisp morning air dried me.

I reached our campsite in time to sing Velunen, not loudly, but not
softly either. Before, no one had stirred. When I was done with the
song, Karsten was watching me from a place beside the fire, stirring
the smoldering ashes. Her hair had the wild, tangled look of sleep,
and she hardly seemed awake enough to be aware of me—curious, I
thought, when in Camp she would have been awake a good while by
now. But when I returned to the fire, she said, "It was good to hear
you. This time, I guess, we'll all be riding suuren with you."

"That's true. I wonder what we'll see."

She sent me to fetch water for the jaka pot. I hurried to the
creek as Mordwen was emerging from his tent, wearing the loose
sleeveless shift in which he slept, his pale, freckled arms flashing
upward, skin and muscle shimmering. His arms were not old or
frail, though the hair that matted his skin was peppered gray.

Through our makeshift breakfast—strips of cold roast hare and
dry bread from last night's supper—the echo of the peaceful morning
remained with me, along with memory of the conversation the night
before. Kirith Kirin said very little when he returned from the creek,
taking his mug of jaka and climbing to the top of the boulder to
drink it. He and Imral spent a few moments talking about our day's
ride, and I gathered we would be meeting the rest of the Woodsfolk
at the campsite in Suvrin country by nightfall. Karsten packed away
the few cooking utensils we had used, spreading earth over the glowing coals of the fire. I chewed the dry meat and drank my jaka, trying
to look inconspicuous, until Mordwen called me to help him tie up
the tent. I had never done this before, and he instructed me patiently,
till finally the task absorbed my whole attention.

We headed southeast, still following the road. By midmorning
we were nearing mountain country, the first peaks appearing on the
horizon, jagged white crowns, bluish slopes, fairy-tale sweeps of
sheer rock that were almost toy-like. At least I thought so until we
stopped on the summit of a local hill and took a good look at them.
I realized then that we were still a long way off from even the
closest of the peaks, and still we could see them clearly, etched against
the gray-blue sky, lost in the undersides of clouds.

I had lived close to these mountains all my life and yet had never seen them before; the sight, the whole breathtaking landscape, flooded me with a nameless joy, like when I was a little boy and came upon some wonder while wandering in the woods around the farm. Hearing a description of mountain country is not the same thing as seeing it for oneself. I had never dreamed the land could rise so high, could mount such a challenge to the sky. One could feel the new raw edge to the wind, sweeping down from the snowy peaks.

Karsten noted my awe and said, matter-of-factly, "But Jessex, these are little mountains. You should see the Barrier Range, beyond Montajhena. Compared to that, these are only foothills."

"They look tall enough to me. Has anyone ever climbed them?"

"Certainly. That's the way to Drii."

I swallowed. She laughed, and pointed north to a cleft between two peaks. "That's the mouth of Svorthis, the pass to Drii. There's another pass from Drii south to Montajhena, called Cundruen. I've made the trip myself. It's hard, but it can be done."

"Is that the only way to get to Drii?"

"No, you can go south, round the mountains. It's a much easier trip, I'll grant you. But sometimes there's no tonic for the heart like a ride through icy country. Don't you think you'd like to make a mountain journey someday?"

"Maybe I will." I watched the distant snowcaps and shivered. "But no time soon, I hope."

We had left the road to climb to the hilltop, Kirith Kirin wanting to get a first look at the peaks himself. He and Imral had ridden down the ridge toward a thicket of faris and hemlock; they signaled us to follow and we returned to the road.

The Keikin set a pace only a royal horse could have kept up, and by afternoon we had ridden through leagues of countryside of indescribable richness, dense tapestries of vine, flower, branch and leaf, different from the lighter, golden country we had left. This forest had an older, darker aspect, brought about by the density of undergrowth and the difference in tree-types. The duraelaryn do not grow in mountain shadow. We had ascended to a higher elevation than the Golden Wood, and the delicate, flowering trees that had thrived in that well-watered, benevolent climate could not have survived this altitude. The trees that dominated this landscape were shaggier, evergreen: faris, pine, fir, duris, cedar and hemlock for the most part. Wildflowers found shelter and sustenance in every conceivable spot, climbing out from beneath fallen tree trunks, splitting the seemingly impermeable surface of a boulder, carpeting a hillside. Streams flowed among the hills in abundance, carving through the soil to reveal the rock beneath, water beading over dark granite, spray washing smooth across terraced shale. Occasionally I longed for the leisure to stop and admire some beauty particularly, but after a while the speed of our passage was part of the wonder, and every new beauty added to the composite image of reckless wilderness.

We reached the new campsite near nightfall, in a valley between three broad hills, sheltered by one of them from the winds that swept down the mountains. A storm was blowing when we met Gaelex, and she hurriedly reported to Kirith Kirin on matters that needed attention. Camp was mostly set and the cook tents were in enough order that Thuerthin was promising a meal for the evening. The Jhinuuserret tents were settled and the Nivri pavilions were being staked. The shrine tent was being oriented, the shrine itself awaiting Mordwen's presence before unpacking was begun.

But news had reached the column as it wound its way through the eastern forest, first from Cordyssa and then from Pel Pelathayn's party, which had ridden south to review the border encampments in Maugritaxa and lower Illaeryn. From Cordyssa came news of bread riots in the city streets. From southern Arthen came reports that Drudaen and his army were marching east across the Cuthunre Valley and central Kellyxa, a host some six thousand strong, including heavy infantry from Vermland.

We heard this much at once since Kirith Kirin summoned the messengers before we had even dismounted. We'd ridden straight through central Camp to the Nivri precinct—as I was to learn, the royal Camp was always laid out in the same pattern, as heedless of the geography as possible. Gaelex told us the news, adding that the spy Duterian was awaiting Kirith Kirin in the glade where householders were pitching the Prince's tent and that a delegation of Cordyssans wished to meet the Prince in Suvrin country, and awaited permission to enter Arthen at River Gate.

Mordwen and I went to oversee the shrine-mounting while the rest followed Kirith Kirin to hear the news.

We worked quickly even in the gathering darkness. A dozen torches burned in the clearing, blue-green flames and clear white light or orange-red tongues licking upward, coloring the flesh warmly. The soldiers were tired, some of them sweating, rivers of dirt washing down broad shoulders, scarred arms, collecting in exposed, ludicrous bellybuttons, between firm breasts, in hairy armpits. Voices mingled with laughter, wisecracks, snatches of song, brief moments of flirtation.

When the tent was in place I brought in the lamps and tool-cases, helping a woman I did not know roll in the jars of oil. I set everything to rights in the workroom and unpacked my own belongings. Soon the tent took on the familiar orderly look I remembered, and I got a start the first time I walked through the back flap, when instead of golden vuthloven I entered a thicket of hemlock and cedar, lower branches festooned with false grape vine in full leaf and flower. I heard the stream that ran behind a nearby fall of elgerath and felt the peacefulness that comes with return to order. I was home again, though home itself was in a different place.

I lit a reyn lamp to watch the shrine through the night, not performing any ceremony since sunset was long past, simply bracketing the lamp and kneeling for a moment in the ghostly light. Before we headed to the common tent for supper, I stole a private moment to place the raven necklace in its proper hiding camouflage, stopped up inside one of the lids to the oil-jars behind a seal of wax. The lustrous chain fell into my hand, the polished gem gleaming in raven's eye. For the first time I connected the image, the talon impaling the raven, with the name Yron. Claw of God. Holding it made my cold hand colder.

As I finished placing the clay seal, Mordwen called. I thought he was ready to head for supper but when I found him, at the edge of the clearing pulling his hood around his face, he told me I would have to get supper on my own since he had just been summoned to Kirith Kirin's tent for council. "Apparently things have heated up in Cordyssa by several notches since we broke Camp in Tiisvarthen. The spies aren't giving us very encouraging news either; Drudaen is marching east with an army but no one knows where or why."

"Ask if the spies have any news about my mother," I said, adding "Please," when I wondered if Mordwen found my asking him to be presumptuous. He said he would, after a moments' reflection, and a torchbearer led him off.

Finding the common tent on my own turned out to be no small task in the dark. This being our first day in the new campsite, the firepots had not yet been set out along the paths, and by the time I had found my coat—worn to ward off the night chill of this new altitude—no torchbearers or torches remained to light my way to the main camp. I found a yard lantern in the shrine-tent workroom, oiled it and lit it, polishing the flue and the mirrored reflectors with the sleeve of my coat. With this lantern as my guide, I sauntered, whistling, through the thickets of fresh-smelling cedar and across the beds of wildflowers shining like stars in the lamplight.

In the common tent one could feel the general weariness, the sense of relief that the journey was over and the day's work done. Theduril found me in the cook line to tell me archery drill would begin the next afternoon when my compatriots and I would meet with other trainees to lay out the exercise fields. With some surprise I noted I was actually looking forward to the resumption of drill, and I asked Theduril when I could start working with the longbow as well as the crossbow. Fifteen was old enough, wasn't it? He squeezed my arm muscle and said most archers started earlier than I had. I was left to wonder what that meant as he sauntered away.

I waited for the sullen-faced cook to ladle gray gruel and beans onto my wooden plate, and found myself an empty space at a table. The beans weren't nearly as bad as they looked, and the gruel was edible and quieted the belly. I chewed cornbread and felt content, listening to the hubbub of voices, watching the familiar faces under the swinging lamps, bright early-evening light. I lingered, letting the sounds, the smells, the pulse of that life soak me through, returning my own gladness to the general air as if the feeling could surround me like a visible aura.

For once I did not feel conspicuous, nor did I hear my name mentioned by anyone as I passed. When I was done with the meal, the cook-tent orderly took my scraped dishes with a gap-toothed smile and said good evening, gesturing with a misshapen hand. I procured my usual pail of dinner scraps for Axfel and fetched him from the dog-handler. The big hound was glad to see me, nearly knocking me over in the process of the greeting. We returned to the shrine tent swinging my lantern, this time not whistling but singing, Corduban and the Ninety-Nine Wineskins. I made sure the shrine was in order, checking the oil in the reyn lamp and polishing one of the fixtures that had got smudged during the alignment. I fed Axfel, scratching his bony head and sat with him while he ate.

When one lives in a place as public as a shrine, one gives up on any such illusion as privacy. I had gotten used to the sound of footsteps in the clearing, the hush of voices, maybe singing softly or chanting, gazing at the lamp-flame or praying in the side-rooms. Soldiers are a mystical, superstitious lot. That night the shrine heard more whispered words than usual, and counted more knees on its plush rugs; I thought it notable but not astonishing, and kept to myself in the back.

The thought that any of the visitors would come looking for me never crossed my mind, and I was surprised to hear footsteps rounding the side of the tent, leather soles brushing dry faris needles, a subtle walk. I pulled Axfel's big head close to my ribs and watched the flickering torch advance, light illuminating the silvered hand, the ground beneath the booted feet, a unicorn on a chain. Imral Ynuuvil found a bracket for his torch, an iron stake driven neatly into the ground at the customary distance from the back tent flap. He sat next to Axfel and scratched between his ears. "It's peaceful here," he said. "You can hear the brook so clearly. I'm glad that hasn't changed."

"Does Kirith Kirin camp in this valley every year?"

"No, not every year. That would be tedious. But we've been here before. Have you ever been this close to mountains?"

"No. We never traveled much at home. My grandmother told me about giants that live in the mountains, and dragons, and other monsters."

"Giants lived in the peaks once," Imral said, "but the Jisraegen drove them away after many wars. There are dragons in other places but there have never been any in Aeryn or Arthen that I know about. As for monsters, there are so many kinds it's hard to say where they stop or start. I've seen what I would call monsters in the mountains, but they aren't as frightening as you might think."

"The Orloc live in the mountains, don't they?"

"Yes, off in that direction. Beyond Drii in the Barrier Mountains." He turned to me with warmth. "You may have guessed I didn't just happen to come here tonight, Jessex."

"I thought not."

"We'll be leaving again in the morning. Kirith Kirin wanted to speak to you himself but he couldn't leave the gathering at his tent."

"You're leaving? Why?"

He lifted a fallen branch from the ground, breaking the needles to pieces between his fingers. "To meet the Cordyssans. Kirith Kirin doesn't want them in Camp when he hears their news. It appears there's a lot of trouble in the north."

"I heard there were riots because the price of the bread was too high."

"That's part of it. The real news is actually worse. One of the tax collectors was killed by a mob. The city is under martial law, and the garrison commander is attempting to rule the city himself without consulting Ren Vael. We're afraid the whole place is going to revolt. Who knows? By now it may have happened already."

"Why do the Cordyssans want to meet with Kirith Kirin?"

"For his advice."

"Wouldn't the Queen be angry if she knew they were asking him for advice?"

"Oh yes, very angry. But they're willing to risk it." He had demolished the dead faris branch. "Things are very bad, Jessex. Say nothing of what I've told you. But I'm afraid the city is risking war with the Queen. It's no wonder they're consulting Kirith Kirin." He studied me for a moment. "I didn't come here to tell you any of this, though there's no reason you shouldn't know. I came to tell you that Duterian brought some news of your mother."

"I hoped so," I said, "but I was afraid to ask you."

"She's been returned to Ivyssa and taken to Kmur, where the Queen is in residence." He hesitated before continuing. "Apparently your mother is ill. We don't know why she's being moved now."

My heart sank. "Do you know what's wrong?"

"Duterian said she traveled in the company of doctors and a guard. He wasn't able to find a way to question the doctors but he managed a look at the guard's orders—he's a very clever man, Duterian—and learned from those where she was headed."

I slumped against Axfel, feeling the thudding of his heart against my collarbone, picturing my mother traveling under armed guard, my poor mother flying from one part of the country to the other, she who had thought it a grand journey to ride on my father's cart to Dagorfast for seed. "She's still a prisoner," I said dumbly.

"Yes," he said. "It's probably a good thing for your mother to be out of Cunevadrim. The climate is much healthier in Kmur."

I hesitated a long time, a hard thought forming in my mind. I tried to tell whether Imral was lying or not by studying him, but he seemed the same as ever. Finally I asked, "Is my mother dead, Imral?"

"No. Duterian saw her alive. She was sick, but not dying."

"You're telling me the truth?"

"Believe me, if she were dead and I knew it, I'd tell you. A friend wouldn't hide something like that."

He was trying to tell me something besides the news. I looked at him eye to eye and felt a flood of warmth for him. I reached round Axfel to embrace him. He laughed, asking, "What's all this about?"

I thought momentarily about all the things it was about and my throat filled so full of words it ached too much to speak. I shook my head, and finally said, "Nothing, Imral Ynuuvil. Mostly my mother and Kirith Kirin."

He said nothing to that. Presently he stirred. "I can't stay. We're riding within the hour. I'll tell Kirith Kirin you took the news as well as usual."

"Tell him I wish him a good journey." I felt a vague ache at the thought that he was leaving. "But the news won't be good, will it? I mean from Cordyssa."

"No," he said, "it won't."

CHAPTER EIGHT
SUVRIN SIRHE

1

I returned to Lake Illyn that first morning in Shadow Country while Kirith Kirin and the Jhinuuserret were hurrying away to meet the Cordyssans. Commyna met Nixva and me as we were rounding the lake's eastern shore. I was full of news and breathless, blurting out everything I had heard in Camp while she listened patiently. When I had finished, she said simply, "Now that you've told me what I already know, put those matters out of your mind. It's just as well Kirith Kirin has left camp. Your training here will claim all your attention. To those in real time you'll seem distracted, at the very least, for some weeks to come."

"You mean I won't want any company?"

She shook her head. "No. I mean that from now on, time when you're not here will pass like a dream. This state of mind is necessary."

She did not lead me to the broadloom where Vella was taking her turn weaving the magical fabric. Instead she sat with me beneath the spreading branches of a live oak and we talked. By now I was fairly proficient in Wyyvisar, and much of our conversation was conducted in that language, which is nearly impossible to render into normal speech. But essentially what she told me was as follows.

I would be learning new disciplines, mainly regarding the mastery of the body. We began with a type of meditation that would teach me control of my thinking, both in my consciousness and in the parts of my mind of which I was not normally aware. Without this control I could advance no farther in the circles of power and would be useless to Yron when he came.

My success in this part of the lake women's instruction would determine whether or not I would be allowed to proceed, Commyna told me; and not merely because such mastery of thought is necessary to magic. Without such control one is not worthy to do magic at all, one cannot be trusted to move power except in the most elementary way.

I have since heard from travelers that in the larger worlds, beyond Aeryn, what is called magic is nine parts illusion, and indeed in
many places the idea of sorcery is held in contempt, relegated to the
world of children's stories, superstition and trickery. In Aeryn and
Arthen this is not the case, since magicians have been powerful in
our country since YY made the world:

> *In the beginning the YY made darkness*
> *YY made light*
> *and in the place between light and darkness*
> *a world took form while YY sang*
> *a beautiful forest, and YY made three women to dwell in it*
> *sisters, for she was lonely*
> *YY made song and taught them*
> *singing*
> *in Words that called storm and shook the ground*

The hymn from which this passage is drawn is called "Luthmar"
and contains the story of the first days of Arthen. It was not written
by the YY-Sisters nor did Cunavastar set it down; no one really
knows the author or authors, but the early Jisraegen recorded the
legend when the High Speech alphabet was invented, in the years of
the Forty Thousand. In the old days every child was taught
"Luthmar." The "Words" that are referred to are probably Wyyvisar,
which was derived from Words used by YY in the making of Aeryn,
the first world, and the model for all the rest.

You will not find this part of the legend written down anywhere else, since it is my own speculation. At the time of my teaching at Illyn Water I had never heard or read Luthmar; the saga had
long since fallen into obscurity. Only the Sisters and those to whom
they have revealed it know the truth concerning the making of
Wyyvisar. Wyyvisar has ever since been the province of these Sisters,
and hardly anyone who has learned it was not taught by them.

But as I have said before, Wyyvisar is not the only language in
which magic can be performed. Cunavastar, who was not allowed
to share in the secret of Hidden Speech, derived a magical language
of his own.

Of the making of Cunavastar there are no legends, and his birth
is remembered only as the first coming of opposition into Arthen.
In the poem he is called the Son of Yruminax, the Other Power.
References in other songs echo this saying, and he is called, among

other things, "Prince of Blasphemies," "Nemesis," "Emptiness-Who-Walks," "Cunctator," "Lord of Nothing," "Vortice." But of Yruminax his father we do not speak, nor have we retained any legends about him. Common folks are afraid even to say his name and refer to him as the Nameless, the One-Who-Is-Not. There is only one other reference to Yruminax in "Luthmar":

He was the husband of YY
An empty face in the bright sky
a prince of air
whose true name is the unknown, whose face is emptiness
whose life is hidden and unspeakable
One day YY will consume him
fire eating air
He is the father of evil and weaklings are his food

So ancient are the oldest texts of "Luthmar" that we do not know whether the reference to "father of evil" is also a reference to Cunavastar; portions of the text here are missing and no complete version of "Luthmar" survives.

The Cunavastar of legend began his life with good acts, whatever the truth of his birth. It was he who invented the worship of YY. He built the Elder Shrines. Anger overcame him when the Diamysaar refused to teach him Wyyvisar. He comprehended much of their thought without any teaching, and finally began the long process of deriving Ildaruen, the Language of Other Power, which will be used to dismantle all the worlds that exist when the time comes. He taught the process of deriving Words to his son, Falamar, who later shared the secret with the Jisraegen priests, and came to regret it.

Ildaruen is a powerful tongue, with the advantage that one may teach it. Those who make magic in Ildaruen outnumber those who make magic in Wyyvisar for that reason.

The Sisters and I did not discuss what I had learned about them on Mount Diamysaar, except once when I tried to ask a question about it and Commyna cut me off—mildly, without her usual sarcasm—by saying, "Don't worry about who we are, Jessex. Concentrate on the teaching and everything else will follow."

Indeed, the knowledge that these three gargantuan women were, or might be, the Diamysaar came too late to strike any permanent awe in me. They remained plainspoken and simple, easy in manner,

as if I were their mutual child. When I was with them, whatever the
circumstance (and these were often eerie), I never feared them.

Commyna was right about the effect of the new disciplines I
began to study. I learned that the mind has deep rivers of memory
and sensation whose existence one never suspects. I learned that every
moment of my life was stored in memory in perfect detail, that each
memory could be recalled in its entirety, as if the past day itself were
being recreated. This was not always pleasant; who would choose to
relive the whole of his or her past without the ability to change it,
witnessing anew its blemishes and scars? Who can look at the faces of
the dead as if they were still living and not feel pain? I was young, but
even in my brief life there were things I preferred to forget.

I had no way of knowing how long these meditations lasted.
For the most part, in such circumstances, time has no meaning, since
the trained mind can alter time's density, making a moment seem like
a day, a week, a month. Compared to my hours at the Lake, the
intervals when I returned to Camp were shadowy and brief, and I
walked the torch-lit paths to and from the common tent with the
silence of a ghost. My mind was on my teaching, insofar as it was
safe for me to think of this teaching away from Illyn Water.

In this way a long time passed, and I became a master of many
strange arts. I could speed my heartbeat or slow it, I could control
the circulation of blood through my various limbs, I could scan my
memory for a particular moment, I could (if I wished) monitor the
digestion of my food, the formation of urine or waste. These are
functions that the mind does control, whether we are aware of this
control or not. By the time the lake women were ready for me to
proceed to other studies, I knew myself maybe more thoroughly
than I wanted to. Often I found myself dazed by the ceaselessness
of these processes, as if my body were a continual jangle.

Vella understood my uneasiness in this regard, and once, near
Illyn's nightfall, while we were drinking the fragrant tea she had
brewed, she said to me, "One of the arts you will need to learn soon
is the art of forgetting."

"Pardon me, ma'am? I don't understand."

She broke apart one of the sweet white cakes that constituted
the mainstay of my diet while I was at the lake. "Now that you
know so much about how the mind works, you'll need to forget it
until you need the knowledge. The hidden parts of your mind can
go on causing your heart to beat and regulating your breathing without any help from you."

"I do get dizzy from watching it all sometimes."

She taught me this lesson herself, and showed me the usefulness of some things I had already learned, including ways to prevent or cure sickness in myself—including the correct method for preventing the fever that had nearly killed me following my first visit to Illyn. Vissyn taught me different arts and sometimes took me riding as relief from the stillness of my other lessons. She could ride in shadow, hidden from mortal sight, and she could multiply a horse's speed by her craft, something I would learn, she said. When I asked her, innocently, what circle of power she was in, she simply smiled and refused to answer. I had a feeling most of the tricks she showed me were not things I could learn from the sixth level, and I was right. But in her company I saw Cunuduerum again, and we rode to Nevyssan's Point, the northernmost part of Arthen. Once we rode to the outskirts of Drii, a fair city of three concentric walls high in the mountains, and I watched the Venladrii moving along the cobbled streets, wearing their cloaks of green or silver cloth, speaking in their apocopated language, word flowing into word almost indistinguishably. This was the only time we strayed from Arthen, and Vissyn was careful to keep us hidden.

Once she took me to see Inniscaudra, the Winter House. We did not ride into the vast stone citadel but stopped at the crest of one of the neighboring hills. The House rises from the summit of a crested hill named Vath Invaths, where scented elgerath hangs from tree to tree in sweeping festoons, and in the season when I first saw the place, the vine blooms in explosions of rich color: crimson, azure, saffron and rich violet. Atop all this sits the Winter House, white walls shining, tall turrets reaching higher than the surrounding hillsides and over everything soaring the High Place, Ellebren Tower. The House is broad, its many wings spread across the hilltop, its outermost walls obscuring the lower floors from sight. The deepest parts of Inniscaudra reached to the heart of the earth below, Vissyn told me, and when I asked her what was in those parts, she tossed her golden hair and with glittering eyes described the treasure rooms, the armories, the barracks where an army of many thousands might sleep indoors. This was the House that No Man Built, and in the turreted rooms and all along the grounds had wakened the Forty Thousand long ago, on the first morning of our kind. I had never seen anything bigger than the market-house in Mikinoos or the mill on East River; the sight of this grand sprawling palace took my breath away.

"Have you ever been to the High Place?" I asked.

"No," Vissyn said, "That wouldn't be a good thing for me to do."

"Why not?"

"I'm not a power of this world," she said. Her expression had suddenly become very serious. "I was once, but not any longer. For me to stand there would be blasphemous, and I would become like Drudaen Keerfax."

"But you don't use Ildaruen when you make magic, how could you be evil like him?"

"Don't misunderstand, Jessex. Neither Wyyvisar nor Ildaruen is good or evil, any more than light or dark is good or evil. There have been good magicians who use Words of either tongue. What has happened to Drudaen is a sickness that comes to the ones who live so long."

I studied the Tower again, slender and shining, its highest summit crowned with silver, tatters of cloud floating past. Even then I wondered if I would ever stand there. After a moment I asked, "Is Yron a power of this world? Can he stand on the High Place?"

When I watched her for her answer, for the first time I saw doubt in her. She said, after consideration, "We assume so. Otherwise why would he come?"

Why indeed? Shaken by her apparent uncertainty, I asked no more questions that day.

For the most part Vissyn took me on these rides for relief from the rigors of training; the arts in which she was most knowledgeable were related to riding, travel, survival in harsh environments, and transformations, all of which were too advanced for an apprentice of the sixth level. I envied the ease with which she concealed the mechanics of these applications: I never once heard the whispered, telltale Word in my mind, never saw the relevant gesture with which she moved power.

When the Sisters deemed me sufficiently skillful in the control of my own thought, my training turned to other directions.

To reach the fifth circle from the sixth, one must master the deep magics—the dual trance, insinging, power-singing and patterned movements, including movements into spin. My teachings in these arts began without fanfare.

In the deep magics one learns to use the control of the mind one gained in earlier training—to see with the mind alone, to transfer thought, to release memory and, finally, to free portions of the spirit from the body for travel or work on other levels. One can also think of this as compaction, as moving the awareness into a smaller space, in order to draw more energy from it; though in fact what we are speaking of is a smaller duration of time, since awareness exists in time alone. This duality of expansion out of the body and compaction within the body is the crucial difference between applications of the fifth level and those of the lower circles. A magician who can encompass this duality, who can leverage the spirit free of the flesh, can work magic from both levels at the same time—or from three or sometimes four levels—and thus will always have the advantage over the magician who can work only from the body, in the visible world.

The beginning of these arts is the same as the beginning of nearly every part of magic: control of breathing, relaxation and the cleansing of the mind.

I spent uncountable hours gazing into the glowing heart of fire, emptying my mind of thought and letting it remain empty, relaxing control of muscles one by one, while Commyna or Vella monitored my progress, making certain that I did not lose my grip on the involuntary organs. Apprentices who attempt to enter a deep trance-state without supervision have been found dead of the attempt rather often, their hearts stopped cold, their spirits unable to reenter lifeless flesh. I had no desire to take such risks, and the Sisters found me to be cheerfully obedient and very attentive to instruction.

Trance-state is not hard to master. Seeing with the mind is more difficult, and the twin art of compression of the awareness and working out of the body is harder still. I quickly learned to enter trance-state, at first using fire as an aid to concentration, later using small gems for the same purpose, and finally learning to go into trance with no aid at all. At the end of one of these training sessions, I returned to consciousness to find Commyna watching me with a baleful expression, holding in her fingertips the gem I had used as an aid. I asked what was wrong, and she answered with another question. Lifting the gem slightly—a small red stone, set in gold and dangling from a delicate chain—she asked, "What does this remind you of?"

I studied the gem again, and the chain. The stone was pretty, striking fire from sunlight, and the chain seemed well made. "It doesn't remind me of anything," but as soon as the words left my mouth the image of another necklace came to me, the one I kept hidden. That stone was the same color as this one, and the chain was the same weight.

Commyna watched me with keen eyes, noting every flicker of feeling that touched my features. "Tell me what you just remembered."

I felt helpless; hearing again my mother's voice, *Let no one see it, ever,* as she handed the locket to me. "It's like something my mother wore once. That's all."

She eyed me suspiciously, and finally said, "Are you sure there's nothing you're not telling me?"

"Yes, I'm sure."

She let the subject drop, but she was clearly dissatisfied with my answer. I hid my relief by returning to meditation, and after a moment of hesitation Commyna began to give me the usual round of instructions and tutorial abuse in Wyyvisar. She was harsher than was warranted by my efforts, I thought, and I wondered if I were really the simpleton she seemed that day to think me, or if she were disturbed by whatever intuition had prompted her to question me about the pendant.

In the press of events that followed, the incident was forgotten.

One afternoon at Illyn, in the midst of another exercise in the cleansing of the mind, while I was in sixth level trance an image of my mother unfurled.

I was not expecting it and had not been warned that any vision might come to me, nor was I, to my knowledge, using a different application in maintaining the trance. I had managed to enter the deep state without the aid of any jewel this time, but I had even managed that trick before. My mind was clear. I ceased chanting in Wyyvisar and was gradually slowing my breathing, carefully, still feeling the slight pressure of Vella's fingertips on my wrist pulse. The image came to me clearly, my mother on horseback in country I had never seen before, colorful fields, golden, violet and bright green, circular houses with red roofs. My mother wore garments of gray and a drab cloak of the same color, a hood drawn over her head. The horse she rode was a well-fed roan mare wearing a criss-crossed bridle of a type I had never seen. My mother held the reins in her hands though her wrists were chained together with links of bronze. Riders flanked her on either side.

I saw this as if I were hovering above the riders, a party of a dozen altogether; yet, when I wished, I could see her face as clearly as if we were facing each other across the dinner table. She was sick and weak. She had no notion I was anywhere near her, and I could feel fear radiating from her, along with deep anger. In her eyes was a wildness that had never belonged to the mother I remembered.

Since I was in trance-state I simply catalogued these different elements of the vision; one does not bring feelings into the trance. I watched the party of riders for some time. Something warned me not to question what I was seeing but simply to catalog as many elements as I could. The riders were wearing white cloaks. The figure at the head of the party, also wearing white, was a woman, and I gradually realized I had seen her before as well, raising her arm to call down lightning the morning I entered Arthen with Uncle Sivisal. She was a milk-skinned beauty in this light, arms covered with jeweled bracelets, green eyes flashing, white tunic clinging to her spare figure. She was not aware of me, though I could feel her power. Strange words formed in my hearing. Before the vision faded I saw, in the distance before them, a gray-walled fortress on a hillside, a red-domed tower rising beyond the turreted walls.

When the vision was gone, awareness of my breathing returned to me, and after that came pressure, more and more insistent, Vella's fingertip on my wrist, and her voice calling "Jessex! Jessex!" along with the Wyyvisar command that brings an end to trance.

She was leaning forward, gripping both my wrists in her hands, calling the Words urgently over and over. When I opened my eyes she said, "Praise YY," touching my forehead with the back of her hand. "You were too deep," she said, when I gave her the sign that means one is oneself enough for conversation. "Your breathing slowed to nothing and your heartbeat was gone."

"I saw my mother, riding with a party of white-cloaked riders."

When she understood what I had said she became utterly silent. For all I know she may have been reading my mind. "You're telling the truth."

I told her everything I had seen, every detail. She listened without responding. When I was done, she said, "I'd better tell this to my sisters."

"Have I done something wrong?"

She stood, gracefully for such an ample woman. She carefully brushed grass from her skirt. "No." But she would say nothing else till she had brought me to Commyna and Vissyn, who were under the duraelaryn in the meadow, Vissyn working the broadloom and Commyna spinning thread. Both watched us approach with some surprise; my lesson had just begun and here we were returning. Commyna watched calmly as Vella built up the fire, sending me to the lake to fill the teapot. I could hear them talking as I returned.

Commyna blandly directed me to tell her what had happened, and she and Vissyn listened, broadloom and spinning wheel falling silent. I had learned to give a plain narrative and did, ending with the red-domed fortress. A moment's silence ensued.

Vissyn broke it. "Well, that's something, isn't it?"

Commyna watched me sharply. "You've had no reports from the Prince's spies that warned you about any of this?"

"The last report I had was before Kirith Kirin left Camp. Soldiers took my mother to the Queen's palace on Kmur. They told me she was sick but no one knew what was wrong with her."

Vella spoke in a hush. "Commyna, I think you should tell him everything."

"So do I." Vissyn stepped away from the loom.

Commyna watched me. Finally she said, "I plan to. Sit down, Jessex. Sit down all of you. Pass me a cup of tea."

Vella poured the tea and handed it to her. Finally Commyna said, "There's no question but that you've seen a true thing. This morning my sisters and I noted in our own far-seeing that Julassa Kyminax was riding north in the Kellyxa in the same country you've described. The red-domed fortress is Pemuntnir, where the Osirii and the Osar fork. Those are the rivers that wash through Ivyssa on their way to sea. We didn't know who the woman was; her identity was hidden from us, and we couldn't have learned it without challenging Julassa directly."

Kellyxa is the southern plain. If she was riding north—

"Julassa is going to meet Drudaen," I said.

Commyna nodded. Vella laid her hand in my hair.

I remembered the woman I had seen, the gaunt-faced stranger with the wild eyes, my mother, and my eyes filled. For a while no one spoke. I let the tears fall without any thought of shame, wiping my face on my sleeves. "Is there nothing I can do?"

"No," Commyna said. "Nothing would suit Drudaen better than for you to try."

Vissyn knelt in front of me and lifted my face. "I'm very sorry, Jessex."

"So am I." Sudden weariness in Commyna's face. "It can't be a good sign that Drudaen has sent for her. But Jessex—" She took a studied sip of tea, and then looked at me. "The wonder is that you've seen it. Do you understand? We've taught you nothing of this technique, and yet your mind has found it. The vision came to you."

"But I couldn't control it, I didn't know where I was—"
She shook her head. "No one could, without a device. You had no jewel, no godstone. You were in sixth-level trance. I myself could do no better from that level."

Vissyn spoke gently. "Not only that. Julassa Kyminax suspected nothing the whole while, but you saw through the protective magic that disguised your mother. This shows a rare talent. Seeing with the mind is not like seeing with the eyes, Jessex. Your mother's face would have been obscured from those far more practiced in magic. We ourselves saw nothing through the veil, and could only have gotten through it by using a higher level application. Julassa would have been aware of that."

Vella stroked my hair. "In other words, we're proud of you."

The words gave me a warm feeling. The lake women had never praised me before, and to tell the truth I had begun to wonder if I were impossibly dull-headed. Commyna did not let me linger long in the courts of self-satisfaction, either. She turned over the spinning to Vella and led me to the center of the golden meadow, to see if I could repeat the meditation.

I did so, with no prompting. The trance came quickly, and I was able to see without a device. Clearing my mind was not as easy as it might have been, with so much anticipation to get rid of. But at last I was in the proper state, my breathing slowing, and an image forming, a clearing lit with morning light, silvered trees bending in the breeze, Kirith Kirin standing perfectly motionless over a runnel of water. He wore no tunic, only buckskin leggings, his torso bare, colored like the bronze chains that had wrapped my mother's wrists. He bent with a silver basin and filled it with water. A voice called out from the undergrowth behind him, and he turned. His face struck me full on.

I have said that one carries no feelings into trance, and this is true. But the part of me that was in this vision felt a ghost of emptiness and longing, wonder at his beauty, till a figure crossed the clearing heading toward him and the vision faded.

When I returned to Commyna and the meadow, the transition being much smoother this time, I told her what I had seen. She asked if I had been thinking of the Prince prior to the trance, or if I had willed myself to see him in any other way, and I answered that I hadn't been conscious of doing so. Though he was never far from my mind. I said this simply and plainly. Commyna had no comment, though she paused on the remark.

She had no means of affirming the truth of this vision, she said, but she had monitored my mental state and it appeared that I was using the proper far-seeing technique. She started to say something else but thought better of it. "I have part of my answer," was all she said. Patiently, she commenced my official instruction in trance-sight.

At the end of the session I was tired, ready for rest. Illyn's nightfall was approaching, and I would not return to real time for a while. We headed to the lakeside, where Vella and Vissyn were building a fire. I would not sleep there but would use another technique the women had taught me for doing without. They would feed me and after tea and conversation my training would continue.

But before we reached the shore, I said to Commyna, "I have one question I didn't ask before. About my mother."

Her face filled with sympathy, though sternness overlaid it. "All right. If I can answer it."

"Why would Drudaen summon her? Why does he keep her alive?"

"He'll use her to torment you." She had no expression on her face. "It would be better for your mother to be dead."

Abruptly she turned away, heading for the brightening fire. I stood in the meadow for a while.

2

The Queen's Second Army, under command of Drudaen Keerfax, marched across the southern plain, pausing at Pemuntnir to meet another army, the Fifth, on its way from New Ivyssa to Genfynnel, the northernmost of southern cities, ten days march from the border of Arthen. I learned about this body of soldiers at Illyn Water, during deep trance while Vissyn was teaching me to guide my disembodied awareness. Drudaen had six thousand soldiers with him. The Fifth Army, four thousand strong, was under command of General Nemort of the House of Tours, formerly the Military Governor of Novris. He was leading an army in our direction.

I had heard no rumor in Camp of Nemort's march. When I asked Vissyn if Kirith Kirin knew about the army headed north, she answered that he most likely did not, since spies bearing the news had not yet reached Arthen. The Sisters could only guess at the purpose of sending so large a force, but it seemed likely General

Nemort was to reinforce the garrison in Cordyssa, perhaps to become Military Governor. "Drudaen will be giving Nemort his final
briefing," Vissyn told me. "One wonders who decided to assign
Nemort to this, Drudaen or Athryn Ardfalla. Drudaen isn't fond
of Nemort, from what I've heard. And Nemort is known for his
mistrust of magicians."

Later we were bathing in the clear water following a long session of meditation, during which Vissyn had guided my internal
vision to scan the place we guessed Drudaen would visit with his
troops. We hovered over Montajhena and I examined the ruined
city as summer was taking hold of its battered stone remains, from
the Court of the Twelve to the old palace, Turmengaz, and the fire-
scarred foundations that flank it. I saw the blackened stump that
was Yrunvurst and the charred wreckage of Goerast, the two High
Places of the city. One saw patches of green grass, beds of flowers
on velvet-lush leaves, multicolored tufts of lichen, winter birds searching the earth for stray seeds, scattered remnants of food among
tumbled marble columns, broken bits of statuary, shards of stained
glass, a fanfare of gold leaf smudged with soot and sand. One
could feel the far off echo of power, the faintest smell of sulfur, the
sweet taste of air where lightning has struck.

Soon it became apparent we had guessed right. Drudaen and
his thousands set out northeast from Fort Pemuntnir, headed for
Vyddn and the ruins of Montajhena.

Ostensibly his reason would have been to station troops at the
south of Cundruen, the mountain pass that leads from Montajhena to
Drii. But he had never before come within a day's ride of the ghost
city since Kentha died in it, so this march was significant, evidence his
fear of the ruins had lessened or his need had increased. The Sisters
were not sure why. For the first years after the fall of the two towers
in Montajhena—Yrunvurst was rebuilt after Jurel died there, and then
destroyed again—travelers avoided the place altogether since it was
feared to be cursed. Nowadays some hardy caravans did pass the city
ruins and undertake the crossing of Cundruen to Drii, and this was
thought to be proof that any general curse had subsided. Though
Drudaen feared something Kentha had left behind for him in the
wreckage, it was said, a gift he had given her.

I listened to this history patiently, since questions rarely did me any
good. Most of the time the lake women told me exactly what they
wanted me to know and not a word more, lest I become glutted with
information, they claimed. True, I had plenty to think about.

One day, I was in sixth level trance, guided by Commyna, who was choosing to work without words as she often did. I felt myself become aware of a new sensation, her hands articulating hidden instructions into my wrists, the trance deepening, attaining a level unfamiliar to me, and finally, with a sense of buoyancy, I rose up in the air and looked down at myself.

Commyna spoke to me in Wyyvisar, without physical voice. Suddenly it seemed to me that I was not floating outside myself but that I had gone very deep inside my brain instead, and had become small.

She was teaching me the duality meditation that allows the spirit to separate from the body and to travel. The Wyyvisar phrase for this practice translates as "casting inward and outward with the spirit", though in the translation the idea becomes flat and the words contain no sense of the process of accomplishing these two separate things, let alone doing them as one. The idea in Wyyvisar is like a bright light. The Wyyvisar concept of spirit includes in it our concepts of consciousness, sightedness, will, and motion in time. The spirit extends itself in two directions, one to the created space in the mind that becomes the speaking place for Wyyvisar, which is in fact the place where the magician's strength begins; the second, to outside the body, to a place that can be either above, to the side, or out of sight of, the physical body. In the meditation one can emphasize one extreme over the other, one can shift from outside the body to deep inside the small place, but both meditations are done at the same time. The spirit may only move outside if it has first moved inside, as if the magician's sight is leveraged outside the body by the movement within, the two existing in balance.

The world of within I had seen before, but from a higher level of magic, when the Sisters took me to the house in the mountains. I had felt my spirit disembodied in this way, and I was able to remember how one moved in this space (by wanting to move), how one saw (by clearing away thoughts), what one heard (phrases of music, chords, sometimes singing). Commyna had a presence adjacent to me, and she asked if I wanted her to take a form, if that would help to orient me. I answered no, I thought I was all right.

This is a mind-space, she reminded me, and I heard her as clearly as if she had spoken. *Remember that this is how your mind perceives the magic that you do, what you see here, but this itself is not real. This is your perception. By remembering that, you can learn to divide the awareness further still, by changing the mind-space.*

Then, as if there were no contradiction at all, she went on. *What you do in the mind-space is real. The mind-space is as valid as any other. When you speak Words there, the world beyond will change but the mind-space will not. The mind-space will always be the space where all things already exist as you wish. When you speak Words there, you will speak to the eleven directions of the world.*

When we spoke in Jisraegen, she called that space the "kei." It was a word from old stories for when a magician was in the clouds on the High Place. Grandmother Fysyyn taught it to me.

Commyna left me to make what sense I could of the contradiction and her riddles. My lesson began again.

She taught me simple things: how to make a thing appear in the mind-space by picturing it, how to give an object the illusion of substance, how to make it move. An edge to her instruction, a trace of strain. Near the end of this session she paused. "I'm going away for a moment. Don't be alarmed."

Her presence vanished. The nebulous light dimmed. In the silence, I could see various shadows on their way to becoming shapes. I hung unmoving in something like misty air, waiting for Commyna, without whom I could not return to my body.

Music clarified, and suddenly a landscape formed. A thing like a gem spinning and unfolding on its facets blossoming a figure who emerged in the eerie light, a woman with dark, thick hair framing her face, tumbling down her back. She was wearing a cloak of fire, holding something in her hand that glittered. She walked toward me smiling softly. She was like my mother in the face. She lifted her hand and I glimpsed a jewel in it. Her smile became wistful, and I saw anger in her eyes. She hung the jewel around my neck. She seemed about to speak, but then Commyna returned and the image dissolved.

We returned to our respective bodies, the process being simpler than getting out in the first place. Commyna waited till I had restored my breathing. "You did well, very well. I'll tell you more about that later. But there was a power near us. Did you sense it?"

I said yes and described what I had seen.

She asked for details about the woman's appearance. I told what I remembered, but the image had been indistinct, or seemed so now. The figure had worn no jewelry, had borne no characteristic blemishes that I could see. Commyna asked that I visualize the woman as specifically as I could. I did as she asked. Her cool fingertips brushed my brow. After a moment she thanked me. "I can't tell you everything this means." She was agitated. "But here is one more piece of news, if you can think about your training again for a moment." She touched me tenderly for the first time. "You know you have traveled out of the body? You know that's what today's lesson was about?"

"I think I could do it again."

"I believe you could, too." This was unlike Commyna, I thought. Her face was less stern than a moment ago, almost more tender than I had ever seen it, except when she was weaving in the meadow. "It is impossible to do the dual meditation or to displace any portion of the spirit out of the body from sixth level sleep. Today I led you to a fifth level trance. This is the test of passage from sixth level to fifth, Jessex. Now you are a true adept."

3

One's power increases not arithmetically but exponentially from one level to the next. From fifth level, as a novice, I could call wind out of the mountains as long as I was pretty near them, and I could make clouds darken, and bring storm. I could see under every leaf for miles when I was meditating, so that I knew where local deer drank water, where eagles nested in the high peaks, where to find a salt lick or a hillside covered with mountain cilidur. I could call Nixva without spoken word. I could make charms and potions that healed wounds quickly, or inflamed sudden lust, or love, or other feelings, or I could cause fainting, nausea, or illness.

I practiced these arts on small animals and other subjects. I had never been cruel before, had never willingly caused any creature pain, but now, to a degree, this was my study. In magic the doing of virtue or evil can turn on the inflection of a Word. The lake women were unstinting in my education. I learned both paths.

Vella said to me one day, almost conspiratorially, "Once we might not have taught you the arts of unmaking, though we've always known them well. One expects a good pupil to understand that where there's the One there's the Other. There is darkness and there is light. But we left many to discover the negative magics on their own, without discipline or perspective. We won't make the same mistake with you."

Looking back on that time, I find it hard to estimate how many real days or months passed while I lingered at Illyn Water, lulled by the singing of the Diamysaar. Certain uses they make of time make the notion of objective time irrelevant. Magic was the seeing and bending of the waves that make events. Magic was seeing time from the outside, singing a harmony in the present that will bring a change forward from the past.

When I was at Camp I was like a shadow walking in sunlight. The Twice-Named were far away through late spring, and since I made no new friends during that time I had no one to talk to except Axfel. He and I walked through the moonlight, my fingers scratching his burr-tangled head, his tongue hanging just above the ground. This was my silence, the peace that I could have, since Axfel expected nothing except me.

I was not the same boy who had entered Arthen so long ago, or even the fifteen-year-old child who had walked blithely up Sister Mountain. In Suvrin Sirhe I became apart from other folks, full of secrets. My mind was fevered, flooded with Words I could not forget and dared not say. It is dangerous even to think a phrase in Wyyvisar outside of the kei, for the construction of the thought itself is power. When one is guarding one's mind as closely as I was—since the lake women continued to warn me never to use Words away from Illyn—it is difficult to make friends. Particularly when one lives among folk who already suspect one of dabbling in magic. I was called witch boy more insistently than ever, never to my face but pretty freely behind my back. Uncle Sivisal was the one who told me about the gossips. Not everyone knew we were kinsfolk, and he sometimes heard tales he'd be better off without. He said, as before, the best thing was to get used to the talk but never to allow anyone to call me a name to my face. But the resurgence of the nickname, when my friends were few and far between, made me doubly careful. During the afternoon and evening I hardly spoke to anyone, except during the ritual or in the common tent. Gaelex thought I was sick and had a camp doctor examine me. The doctor reported that, in fact, I was very healthy.

I never lost touch with the rumors that reached Camp by messenger or by merchant, but I also got news from the lake, and my only care with what I heard was that in Camp I should not appear to know more than anyone else. I heard of Nemort marching long before outriders swept through Camp searching for Kirith Kirin. The news of further rioting in Cordyssa reached me long before it reached Gaelex. I was the first in Camp to know of the hanging of the tax collectors.

The story of those times is famous now, and the events of those days have been handed down to history as the beginning of the long war that followed. The Cordyssans had come to Arthen to warn Kirith Kirin that conflict could no longer be prevented, that Cordyssa must rebel or face financial ruin at the hands of the tax collectors, that the numbers of the poor had swelled on the city rolls, farmers who could no longer afford to work their farms flooding the city from every corner.

The Nivri and Jhinuuserret were days reaching any agreement as to what to do. Their meeting took place in an encampment at a place called Nevyssan's Point, the northernmost finger of Woodland, because Kirith Kirin could not leave Arthen, and consequently this meeting has become known as the Council at Nevyssan.

It is remembered Kirith Kirin won all hearts at this council. He had been long forgotten by the powers of the north, he who waited patiently in Arthen, obedient to the Law of Changes. When the City Nivri complained that the Blue Queen's rule was burdensome, he laughed at them, he who had fought for every meal these generations, he who was prisoner in Arthen, he who should have been King a century ago. "You know her now, do you?" he told the first to complain to him. "Well, she's the same as she's been for years."

It is said he dominated this meeting by cunning, realizing he alone had sufficient personal force to carry off seizure of the gold and arms from the Thynilex mines and Smithies, as well as incite rebellion in the capital of the Queen's northern government. Many stories are told of his political finesse, charming this House or that. Few remember the truth, that Kirith Kirin advised against rebellion, despite his bitterness toward Athryn and Drudaen. War with the Queen would bring down a swifter ruin than any tax. He wrote that in the letter that summoned them to Nevyssan. It was the Cordyssans who would not listen to reason.

Even Ren Vael joined those pressing Kirith Kirin to lead a revolt. It was he who finally convinced Kirith Kirin no other choice remained. If the Nivri houses did not lead the movement to throw out the Queen, they would be forced to watch the mob do it with any leaders to be found. Cordyssa was stuffed with farmers who could no longer make a living from the land and poor folk who could no longer afford to pay the tax on bread. Kirith Kirin agreed to the rebellion, all right, but only when it was plain he had no choice.

What he predicted at Nevyssan has been remembered, mostly correctly, the years since. "Don't dream that this conflict will stop at the gates of Cordyssa. If we lift our hand against Queen Athryn in the city, she'll bring us a fight that will cover Aeryn in blood. We won't be freeing one city if we take up arms against her. There'll be no end to the war once it's begun, until Athryn's throne is fallen or we're all dead on the pyre, smoke in the wind. The Wizard will come north and all will be ruin." The words did no good. The decision was to make war, and at last Kirith Kirin, out of weariness, agreed.

Neither he nor any of the others returned to Camp following this gathering. Instead, the Nivri and the Jhinuuserret were dispatched to perform various tasks. Pel Pelathayn and Kiril Karsten formed parties to inspect the perimeter guard, the permanent encampments of soldiers who kept watch on entrances into Arthen. Kirith Kirin rode east to country near Drii to confer with King Evynar. Mordwen Illythin rode south to Maugritaxa where he took charge of intelligence gathering, while Ren Vael and his entourage returned to Cordyssa.

Not long afterward, Prince Imral followed Ren to the city with battalions of the Woodland army.

Uncle Sivisal was one of the soldiers picked for that journey and so was his companion Rel. When the orders for the soldiers to march reached Camp, I said good-bye to the two of them, wondering what they were being sent to do. At the time, we weren't even certain they were headed for Cordyssa. We only knew the north was in uproar. Hardly a day passed without fresh rumors about violence in Cordyssa.

This was in summer. Riots continued through the season and the military ruler found it impossible to keep the peace. Word had come that General Nemort would be marching within the year at the head of an army to reinforce the city garrison in Fort Bremn. But Kirith Kirin's soldiers had reached the city ahead of the news. Soon after, Imral's troops stormed the fortress during a series of food riots in the outer city.

The riots had been prompted by yet another increase in the price of grain. The city garrison in Bremn, weakened by losses incurred in attempting to keep order during summer tax collection, was caught by surprise, with half the Blue Cloaks in the streets trying to control a mob in the market. The soldiers trapped in Bremn offered resistance but were slaughtered. Imral and the Woodland Guard were said to have fought savagely, with Ren Vael and the Cordyssans at their side.

Word of the massacre soon spread. The mobs and Cordyssan soldiers finished off the Blue Cloaks in the streets. No one from the garrison survived to carry the word that the fortress had fallen. The mob hanged the tax collectors from the walls of the city. Flesh-eating birds killed those who did not die immediately.

When news of the Cordyssan revolt finally reached Camp, some weeks after I learned of the event at the lake shore, one would have thought the encircling mountains had tumbled into the sea. Nearly every soldier had relatives or friends in Cordyssa, or else had visited the place once, so every tent housed an expert in Cordyssan politics and civic character.

From this initial victory there was no turning back. Imral marched quickly to attack Fort Ithlumen, on the road south of Cordyssa, before word of the massacre could reach the garrison there. The northern army gained entry into Ithlumen by the following ruse. Imral Ynuuvil composed a message to Ithlumen's commander, giving it to the Bremn garrison's military scribe for copying, the scribe's life having been spared for this purpose. Imral himself signed the document, imitating the handwriting of the former military governor's second-in-command, the governor having perished in the fray; and the letter was sealed with the dead commander's ring. The letter was dispatched by a Blue-Cloaked messenger and a portion of the army followed, cloaked in the garrison's own blue weave. The rest of Imral's army marched behind this force.

The forged letter detailed the latest riots in the city and the loss of Fort Bremn, differing from the actual course of recent events only by claiming that a certain number of Bremn's soldiers had escaped and were presently marching toward Ithlumen in advance of rebel forces.

The fortress commander saw soldiers in blood-stained blue cloaks as the survivors of the garrison that had secured Cordyssa for Queen Athryn, and the force following as their pursuit. The fact that the fortress commander recognized few faces did not surprise her in the time that was left her to register surprise. Fearing the rebels who were said to be chasing the remains of the garrison, she ordered the gates opened.

Inside, the Cordyssans threw aside their Blue Cloaks and slaughtered the soldiers in the gatehouse, reinforcements already in sight. The fortress was thrown open and the soldiers taken unawares, many having no way of recognizing friend from enemy. The southerners perished to the last soldier. With control of Fort Ithlumen, Imral

Ynuuvil won control of the whole Thynilex territory, including the mines and armories.

At the same point King Evynar, following the advice of Kirith Kirin, dispatched soldiers to besiege Brisnumen, the fortress that guards the road from Cordyssa to Drii. Imral sent an army under command of Ren Vael to besiege Fort Cunavastar, near Lake Rys. This fortress secured the approach to Svyssnan and Listrenen.

Imral and those with him marched south from their victory at Ithlumen, scouring the road between Cordyssa headed toward the last of the fortresses, Gnemorra, which sat at the north end of Angoroe. Soon he reached Gnemorra and placed the fortifications under siege.

With a larger body of soldiers Imral might have broken the garrison's back at once. But one body of the Woodland Guard was marching north to reinforce the Cordyssans at Fort Cunavastar, where it appeared the Blue Cloaks were ready to surrender. Another force was marching to catch the Fort Bresnomen garrison, which had fled westward under cover of night, before it reached Fort Gnemorra.

Kirith Kirin, at the time, was in Maugritaxa, keeping an eye on Nemort and the Fifth Army in Genfynnel. He was also trying to learn the whereabouts of Drudaen, who was variously rumored to have turned back to Turis, to have encamped on the east shore of Lake Dyvys or to have occupied Kursk, the city that lies at the joining of the Deluna and the Rovis. Some of the Anynae had rioted there, which made sense, since if the Queen was squeezing the north for silver, she was squeezing the south as hard. Gaelex sent a messenger to the Prince, informing him that she was assigning a thousand soldiers out of main Camp to the pursuit of the Brisnomen garrison, and that she was leading the troops herself till Kiril Karsten could be summoned to take command. It was vital to catch the Brisnomen soldiers to prevent them from reinforcing Fort Gnemorra.

The dispatch of this many troops left Camp mostly barren. I had come to a lull in my training, a point where the lake women rested me from the strain of being so often out of real time. My lessons at Illyn were easy and brief. The women were preoccupied with the completion of the cloak they had been weaving, the magical fabric on which they had labored since I first came to the shore. The loom no longer appeared in the golden grass. A huge worktable replaced it, ludicrously large in comparison to the small wagon that had, presumably, carted the table to the meadow. On it was heaped the unending, shimmering cloud of cloth the Diamysaar had woven, a heap glittering like a starlit night, predominantly violet-blue-black in color, though occasionally swimming with other hues, plumage like rare birds, hearts of fire, fields of flowers. I gazed into the fabric with the same fascination with which one stares at burning fires, at waterfalls and vast abysses. Faced with an excess of beauty the mind can often only drink.

When I asked what the cloth was, I was told it was to make a cloak in which the magician Yron would work magic. Beyond that it was none of my business, and they were very busy getting it started, since once Yron arrived the cloak would be urgently needed.

I had the feeling he was near, and they were busy preparing. In fact, several mornings running the women dismissed me with barely a lesson, and I noted from strains in their conversations that the Sisters were disagreeing about something and didn't want me to know about the argument.

As a consequence I had some free time, and since I was resolved not to spend my small leisure in worrying about whatever secret they were keeping, I went abroad aggressively, seeking out such company as I knew from the few hundred folks left in Camp.

In the month of Ruus, high summer, General Nemort and his army departed from Genfynnel. I learned of this march in the company of the lake women. As for Drudaen, his presence remained clear to the Sisters and me. He was still in Vyddn, the province round Montajhena. One saw him from fifth level as a black cloud descending, the land beneath him gone dark, runneled with blood, the cloud itself brooding and boiling, its power turned upon itself. Had he been aware of what was happening in the Fenax, he would have been more active, it was thought, but one could not be sure. He should have been able to see the armies marching, if he wished. Nor could one but guess what he was doing, encamped in the countryside near the city he had dreaded for so long.

News reached Camp that Karsten had joined Gaelex and the thousand soldiers and was subsequently successful in turning the Brisnumen garrison northward from its march toward Gnemorra. Both armies were heading into the Anrex Valley, with Venladrii soldiers also in pursuit. But this news was old to me as well. At the time Camp learned the news, the Battle of Anrex was already being fought. Karsten ambushed the Queen's garrison at a bridge on the Mymitur River, at the east end of the valley, two detachments of cavalry sweeping down from the hillsides after archers had softened the Blue Cloak advance from cover of the trees. The Venladrii squadrons arrived to find the Brisnumen garrison in full retreat, and the Blue Cloaks were cut to pieces between the Venladrii and the Woodsfolk. A handful of southerners survived to be marched to Drii as prisoners of war.

The remaining northern army divided into two forces, one headed to Fort Cunavastar to aid the Cordyssans with the siege. The second army was hurrying south to join Imral Ynuuvil whose army was encamped at the north end of Angoroe, awaiting General Nemort.

Shortly after, Cunavastar surrendered, its half-starved garrison taken without bloodshed, marched off to Cordyssa as prisoners. This left only Gnemorra of the Queen's northern forts; but that garrison would never surrender knowing Nemort was on his way.

Nemort himself crossed north Turis, anticipating no more than a leisurely march toward Cordyssa while the Fenax weather was not so forbidding.

I had heard the Sisters speak of these matters so often it was hard to remember what I was supposed to know, and I found myself continually biting my tongue—particularly at supper one night, when Fethyar the assistant groom (who was in charge of the horses left in Camp while Thruil rode with Lady Karsten) declared that he had heard from a good source in the merchant sector that the Brisnumen garrison had escaped Karsten and was within four days march of Fort Gnemorra. The rumor was false, but I was forced to listen to him while he passed on his incorrect information to a dozen unsuspecting souls. With the rest I feigned horror at the appropriate places, and hoped Karsten could catch the Blue Cloaks in time.

By now we were entering late summer, with autumn and last harvest coming fast. A few days before the end of Ruus, those of us who remained in Suvrin Sirhe received orders from Kirith Kirin to strike Camp and march with all speed to Nevyssan's Point.

4

The order for the move was brought to us by the Nivra Vaeyr of Cordyssa, who was accompanied by Inryval son of Thorassa, one of Gaelex's aides familiar with the routine of striking and moving the tent city and wagonloads of equipment. Vaeyr was, as I had learned, one of the Nivri with a reputation for practicality and

efficient administration, and no one questioned his competency or
that of Inryval; still, this second move did not proceed as smoothly
as the first.

I supervised the dismantling of the shrine and the taking down
of the tent following sunrise on the day we were to march. Two
householders gave me some help, but as to how to do it I was left to
my own memory. No disaster overtook the cumbersome shrine,
nor did lightning strike anyone involved in the task, so I guess we did
all right and YY-Mother was not offended.

When the shrine was packed, I pitched in wherever I was needed,
once I made sure my own possessions (including the necklace in the
leather pouch and the Book of Suuren, which had been in my care
since Mordwen left Camp) were safe and secure. Axfel I turned
over to the dog master, who packed him in a traveling wagon. One
does not like to watch one's dog enter imprisonment, but we would
be many days marching, and the hound was not yet sufficiently accustomed to Woodland life to be content following the column. If
Axfel strayed into Arthen and were lost, my last link with my family
would have vanished. I wanted nothing less, these days when my
fear for my mother's well-being grew and grew.

The lake women were cryptic when they learned of Kirith Kirin's
orders. But when I told the Sisters Camp was leaving shadow country (knowing, as I did, that they were aware of the orders to march
before I had been), they behaved curiously. Commyna, Vella and
Vissyn watched each other with expressions that could only be described as mischievous, and Commyna said, "I can just imagine two
hundred tents in the middle of a cliff in Nevyssan. Charming place
for a camp."

"Don't make fun," Vissyn said. "Jessex will have a wonderful
time in the gorges and ravines."

"Well, at least he's come to his senses," Vella said, and I knew,
without asking, she wasn't referring to me.

I was not with them long that day. They were working with the
glimmering fabric draped over their knees, their preoccupation obvious. I performed a cyclical of meditation and trance exercises,
said a routine good-bye.

We left Suvrin Sirhe in the month of Ranthos, the fourth day.
Summer was fleeing while we marched from the shadow of the
eastern mountains. It felt like no summer I had ever known.

CHAPTER NINE
NEVYSSAN'S POINT

1

Nevyssan lies beyond the Arth Hills, twenty days march from Suvrin Sirhe, in northernmost Arthen. Nevyssan is hill country, an ancient habitat of shadowed firs and aged cedars, the only part of the old north forest to survive. That whole part of the world is different from other places, as if the blast of a God still hangs in the air. A hundred volumes could not hold all the stories that are told about the Arth Hills, where the Sisters were born beneath the Eldest Tree. Nowadays one cannot get to that tree, or anywhere near it. One cannot reach the interior of Arth Hill country on horseback, nor can one cut a path through the brambles, the foxvine, the elgerath tangling and choking on itself. Even the Jisraegen at the height of their woodcraft never traveled in those hills, and whatever creatures live in Arth have no need of intercourse with other peoples.

The lake women never took me there, though to do so would have been within their power, nor did they tell me any stories about the place, nor answer my questions. When the march took us close to the hill-shadows, I asked Vella what was there. She gave me a bland look, answering with uncharacteristic firmness. "What I know about the Arth Hills comes from long before any time you need to know about, young fellow. No one will tell you anything about Arth, so keep your questions to yourself."

The column reached the edge of the hills on the twelfth day of marching. By then I felt as if I had been riding toward Nevyssan for a century at least.

Time at Illyn intensified again. The long days of autumn passed, the briefest of pauses, the soldier column marching through bronzed leaves, autumn flowers and heavy fruits. Moments away from training were like rest between long breaths.

I was left to surmise I was making progress from cryptic references in the lake women's conversations, from which I gathered that some difficulty in hiding us lately came from me. Exactly what I was doing that made the veil such a drain on the Sisters' concentration I did not know and could not learn. They were not displeased with my skill as far as I could tell, though any word of praise that I had hoped for died in the air.

There is no need to linger over the events of those days, either at Illyn Water or on the march to Nevyssan. I was becoming accustomed to the bizarre routine of entering and leaving real time; it no longer troubled me that between singing Velunen in the morning and Vithilunen in the evening, an interval might pass that seemed months long in my mind. None of what I did at Illyn bore much resemblance to anything I had ever seen or done in the world beyond. I was young and, lately, had gotten used to changes.

When we reached Nevyssan, guides joined the column to lead us along the trail to Kirith Kirin's encampment, five days march to Nevyssan's Point, a hilltop with a commanding view of the surrounding Fenax. These guides were not people I knew, but they did bring some news even I hadn't heard. We were heading for Kirith Kirin's camp, all right, but he was absent at the moment and Mordwen Illythin was in command. Kirith Kirin rode with patrols along the Angoroe border, marking the northward progress of General Nemort.

One of the guides had a message for me from Mordwen. He wanted me to ride with the bearer of the message in advance of the main column to Nevyssan's Point. Sealed with his ring. The Nivra Vaeyr sent for me and told me to pack.

The summons from Mordwen flooded me with relief and the prospect of seeing him made me so happy I could hardly contain myself. I had been alone a long time and thought of him as company. That he had sent for me almost made up for the news Kirith Kirin was somewhere else.

I rode away following Velunen, accompanied by the messenger, Cuthru son of None, who had been lent Mordwen's horse Prince Naufax for the occasion, along with a ring to tame him, to keep pace with Nixva. I was acquainted with Prince Naufax from other rides and scratched the blue-black stallion's silken nose by way of greeting. Cuthru was a taciturn man, a descendant of Cordyssans who had migrated to the south generations back, his mother having inherited land from a childless uncle in Amre. A "son of None" is a boy whose father will not acknowledge parentage; a daughter would be called his "false child." Northerners are not well-liked in the south, any more than southerners are liked here in our country. The bloods have never blended, even in the present day.

He told me a little about life in the south as we rode the marked trail toward the encampment. Not that he was talkative by any standard. He made jaka briskly and whittled with his wrist knife and thumb blade, weapons some soldiers prefer to the ordinary hand-held dagger. He wore southern clothing for all his Jisraegen airs: a sleeved shirt, leather leggings and soft doeskin boots. I liked him but was shy to talk to him, and gave up. I had a troubling sense of being too thoroughly seen by him. He had piercing eyes; one could imagine him an eagle, scrying prey miles off.

We rode through the darkening Woodland through hills and valleys, following a cleared trail that led miraculously through swaths of vine, waterfalls of tangled branches, shadowed hillsides covered with white moonflower that thrives in the rarer light. Our second night on such a hillside, the white moon did rise though the red one did not, and the flowers really did glow, an eerie light flowing like a mist, throwing ghostly shadow against the roots and lower trunks of the twisted trees that towered out of the rock. The landscape struck me with such an aching force I wondered how I would sleep. I walked around our campsite once the moon rose, heeding Cuthru's warning to be careful of badgers and wildcats that were known to prowl the hill country, and above all not to step on one of the moonflowers, since that could be bad luck in another way. I told him I would be careful. I felt as if I were in fairyland, walking from dark tree trunk to fall of vine, stepping between the full, glowing blossoms of the broad moon-flowers, the petals shaped like the ends of torches, delicately veined, limpid. The petals were warm, one did not have to touch them to feel it, and the flower shivered as if to the beat of a gentle pulse. I was careful not to disturb a single blossom.

Sleep came easily in spite of the flowers and the vibrant light. Just after dawn, when the flowers ceased glowing, we rode again, and by midmorning we reached the encampment, atop a tall hill at the northernmost place in Nevyssan, called Nevyssan's Point.

The encampment was nestled in a small cul-de-sac formed by rock, down which washed a narrow, shallow brook. Tents had been pitched in the available clearing, standard issue, nothing as fancy as what we were used to in Camp. When we rode into the clearing, where a cook fire was burning, Thruil emerged from one of the tents, saw us and hurried forward. Without awaiting any greeting he called out, "Mordwen's been expecting you all morning, Jessex. He's in that tent yonder, the one with the banner over it. He may have folks with him but go in anyway to let him know you're here."

I hesitated only long enough to thank Cuthru for the company. He acknowledged with a curt nod and helped Thruil with the horses. I hurried through the crowded tents and trees, toward higher ground where stood the brown tent with the crimson banner hanging in the breezeless morning.

Mordwen's voice sounded among others. A guard was posted by the tent flaps, armed to the teeth. She announced me to someone inside and I entered, stepping past two clerks who were copying out letters and Gaelex who was composing another. Mordwen was seated on cushions in the tent's center, wearing a dagger and wrist-knife with the blade sheath in place. He had war bracelets on his upper arms, glittering birds of prey inlaid in white enamel on the beaten gold. He had a look of deep concentration on his face. He was listening to the officer in front of him, the Nivra Cothryn of Cordyssa.

Mordwen was looking more vigorous than I had seen him, holding his shoulders higher, occasionally touching the hilt of his dagger as if to reassure himself that it was still safe in its scabbard. I watched him for a while, caught his eye and nodded, and went away.

He did the Prince's business all afternoon, while I wandered in and out of Camp. I went for a ride on Nixva and had a pleasant run. Since we were close to the border of Arthen we rode to the Woods End, beyond which lies the open plain.

The Girdle was bare and empty, windswept, grass darkening in waves. With the Queen's forts conquered or besieged, no patrols rode in this part of the world. Peaceful not to have to worry about Blue Cloak patrols. There was something uncanny in looking at that open landscape through which one could move without restriction. Here was Arthen and there was the plain. No soldiers on horseback stood between the two.

Cothryn and a few gentry were in Camp that evening, as well as enough soldiers to suit Mordwen's rank, about two hundred folks; every tent pulled its own kitchen duty, sometimes sharing a cookfire with a neighbor. At night the lights from the fires lit the hillside, smoke drifting to the stars, and one could hear music from every side, lyre, guitar and kata sticks. After dinner I sat outside till the officers finished their discussions with Mordwen regarding the layout for main Camp, which would arrive in the next day or so. The sound of voices blended with the music and wind in the upper branches. Because we were on a hillside one could see the sky. Duraelaryn do not grow close to the border of Arthen, nor do they care much for rough country like

Nevyssan. I watched the stars shining, naming the ones I knew, remembering nights when I was shepherding the flock through the meadows close to the Queen's land.

When the officers were gone I found Mordwen sharing a polite glass of wine with Cothryn. The Nivra was in a courteous mood, and while I was present he followed the convention of not referring to me or speaking to me directly, until he was ready to leave, but I was conscious that he watched me. He asked if I would sing the morning song and I answered that I probably would, though there was no lamp and the cookfire would have been lit long before dawn. He expressed what he called a sincere desire to hear Velunen as he was used to hearing it since I became kyyvi. Mordwen overheard this remark and raised an eyebrow.

When he had gone, Mordwen stood in the tent opening, watching him walk away. I thought Mordwen wanted to say something. He stood thinking for a while and then asked if I had brought the suuren book.

Once he had inspected my entries and found them to be satisfactory in neatness and form, he read them with absorption. Presently he said, "I see no more of a pattern than when I was keeping the record." In answer to the question he could already hear coming out of my mouth, he went on, "It's nothing you've done. Maybe it's a lost art."

"Lost?"

"What we know about suuren-keeping comes from books written by the Cunuduerum priests. Not many of their writings have survived outside the city, and one does not venture to visit the libraries. Falamar broke the ranks of the Praeven but he never fathomed the magic they used to hide their secret places. Drudaen could never break those magics, either, when he was still able to enter Arthen. Some of the books that do exist mention a few of the suuren patterns that were used by the priests to foretell the future. But they were able to see a pattern where I see nothing at all." He closed the book and gave it back to me. "Go on recording the entries yourself, as you've been doing."

"Yes sir. Were all the priests magicians?"

"What priests?"

"The ones who lived in Cunuduerum. Did they all know magic?"

"What a strange question. They were magicians of a sort, primarily masters of lore. They were not originally Word-masters as were Falamar or Lord Durassa; at least at first. But they developed

a language that gave them strength when they used it together, and
they made magic that way. They used the kyyvi and the suuren to
derive the true-names of all the trees in Arthen, and the names of all
places they could reach, and all things they could think of, and used
those names and words they derived in other ways to make a new
kind of chant. They were Jisraegen after all and had an ear for
magic. Do you know anything about Words of Power?"

The hair on the back of my neck prickled. "A little."

"Words of Power are magic words, and only magicians like
Drudaen know how to use them. When the Praeven learned to
make magic, the balance of the world was disturbed, and they did
not seem to know what they had done. They made a song that is
said to have terrified YY-Mother, because if she had let it end it
would have brought about the Great Breaking then and there. So
she gave Falamar a new strength and allowed him to end the song
and to destroy the Praeven, and after that he ruled Cunuduerum and
Arthen himself.

"Books containing the language they made were hidden in the
Library the Praeven closed when they vanished. I imagine there are
folks who would like to find the books but no one has."

I had more questions but Mordwen was clearly tired and would
want to sleep soon. So I asked him about Kirith Kirin, since that
was the other subject on my mind.

At first I thought he had not heard me. He wandered from the
coal brazier where a teapot hung to a wooden writing table holding
an ornate metal lockbox. Mordwen opened the lock and drew out
a cut sheet of parchment.

Kirith Kirin had no scribe with him on his present journey, and
the letter Mordwen handed me was written in the Prince's hand. I
held the letter stupidly, as if I didn't know what to do with it.
Mordwen took the suuren book to study on a cushion beside one
of the lamp-stands.

The letter was dated the first day of Ikos, not long ago. At the
time Kirith Kirin was in a place called Avyllaeron, a hilltop in west
Arthen where Falamar once hoped to build a fortress. The name of
the place was written beneath the date. "Mordwen," the letter began, "I'm writing in some haste and urgency. The sealed packet
contains letters of cachet and authority for your use in my absence.
I'll be back in Nevyssan as soon as I can verify the whereabouts of
Nemort. Meantime do what you can to settle Cordyssa and above
all keep the Nivri and Finru from quarreling with each other.

"This business has me worried sick. I should have been harder at the Nevyssan council. A war now is a chancy thing; and we're already in over our heads. Athryn won't stand for losing the whole north. We're doing well enough against the garrisons but her patrols will be getting word to Nemort now that we've broken their backs, and he'll be sending the news to Ivyssa. Even if we manage to beat him, soon one of the magicians will come. Where will our defense be then?

"I didn't mean to brood over this so much. I suppose I'm lonely, if you can credit that. I don't have enough friends to have you scattered to the nine winds. I look forward to a cup of wine and a warm fire when I get back. Camp should beat me there. Give my greetings to the son of Kinth when he arrives."

The last words filled me with momentary warmth, till I read the letter through again and felt the weight of his sadness. Mordwen was watching my face. "Why are you showing this to me?"

In the dim lamplight Mordwen seemed younger, and far more confused. "I wanted you to read his greeting for yourself."

"Why is he so sad?"

"He's set something in motion that won't stop before a lot of blood is shed, and he wouldn't be Kirith Kirin if he didn't feel the weight of that."

"But he has no choice."

Mordwen had wandered to the tent opening. "No. That was what Ren Vael told us. The mobs would have stormed Bremn themselves sooner or later, and there would have been a lot of killing, and a lot of reprisal. One hates to think of the whole city population sold into slavery but such things have happened lately, in Turis, for example. Kirith Kirin had no choice all right, unless he could watch Cordyssans be slaughtered without feeling it."

"But that doesn't make things any easier. Is that what you mean?"

Nodding, stroking the embroidery on his sleeve. "This is a war we've fought to prevent for many years, even though every sign told us it was coming sooner or later."

"Is Kirith Kirin afraid he can't beat General Nemort?"

"We can handle Nemort. We can pen him up in Gnemorra anyway. But after that, once word reaches Athryn and she summons the Wizard, what will happen then?"

I began to understand. What if Drudaen marched north to rescue Nemort? The General might not like wizards but he would accept help from any place he could get it if he were besieged. "But don't the Cordyssans understand that?"

"Yes. But it doesn't make any difference. Even fear will only push people so far. The Fenax has had enough. Cordyssa has had more than enough. People are starving, are losing land their families have held for ages. Kirith Kirin has had enough too, I think, though he dreads the price we'll have to pay."

"Has he left Arthen?"

Mordwen looked shocked. "Of course not. He can't leave. Kirith Kirin hasn't yet broken any of the Law of Changes, and as long as he doesn't, we've still got hope. Pelathayn and Imral have led the troops outside in Angoroe, and Karsten won the victory at Anrex. The Jhinuuserret are under no one's injunction to remain in Arthen. The Law of Changes says nothing about how to behave if it ever becomes necessary to overthrow the King or Queen."

The next thing I heard was the singing of crickets in the autumn evening, still warm like summer. I walked to Mordwen's side, watching the cook fire outside our tent, the flickering torches, hearing the murmuring of the guards who were kneeling by the fire. Gaelex and two others. Gaelex was on her way to her own tent, and called a greeting to Mordwen.

Presently he offered me a final goblet of wine. When he said good night I spread my own pallet on the layers of carpet in the tent, trimmed down the lamp, and slept. I could hear Mordwen breathing in the next chamber, a comforting sound. I rested much easier than I had in days.

2

I sang the morning song while jaka was brewing over the cook fire, and rode suuren in the surrounding hills while the rest of camp was rousing itself to another day. Following instruction, I returned to the hills and copied an entry for the day into the suuren book. Again no summons came to Illyn Water.

Because I could write some I was employed as a scribe, and because I could be trusted Mordwen used me to copy confidential letters or writs of order he was reluctant to give to the other clerks. My day passed with this fresh discipline to occupy me, copying letters to various noblemen in Cordyssa and on the Fenax estates to call up soldiers, letters to magistrates in Cordyssa setting prices on various market items. With practice my writing improved. I copied each letter neatly, and in fact was faster than the other scribes from so much rune-writing at Illyn.

Cothryn was in the tent most of the day, since he was kin to Ren Vael and could help with management of the city. I was working close to Mordwen most of the day and Cothryn always managed to hover near. I could not name the change in his manner toward me and was uneasy, thinking myself vain and giddy. He was paying attention to me, though, and after a while I could not deny it.

Outriders from main Camp reached us at dawn the next day, and the column itself arrived about midmorning. Gaelex had been up half the night getting ready, and with the help of Inryval and Vaeyr she soon managed to make some order of the site.

That was my favorite of all the places we ever set our tents, because the Woodland grew so wild there, the earth pitching and rolling from sheer hill to deep ravine. Small, tenacious trees throve in Nevyssan, and elgerath abounded, spilling down whole hillsides. Perfume from lavender blossoms floated on every breeze. The stewards pitched tents as best they could, using any near-level spot. The merchants who sold at the camp market had only a good-size clearing and did a lot of grumbling but made the best of things. As for the shrine tent, the shrine sat at an angle and had to be jacked up on wooden supports. Gaelex said nothing better could be had under the circumstances.

Axfel arrived in Camp sick with some kind of fever. If I was fifteen Axfel was rising eight, and the fact of his age was not lost on me. A big dog like him does not live much longer than eight or nine years. I always kept a close eye on him and was careful to give him the proper remedy whenever he got sick—there are herbs for the healing of animals just as there are for people, and some are the same for both. Axfel had come down with a surprisingly human-sounding cough. Following lamp-lighting I nursed him most of the night, making him a bed behind the shrine-tent, building a small fire to keep him warm, wrapping him in wool blankets that had been packed in a chest since spring. We were in high country, where the summer nights can be chilly. The dog was better by evening the next day, eating a meat gruel made from supper scraps I gathered in the common tent. Because of my nursing duties I was sleepy during Vithilunen, however, and was distracted afterward when Cothryn spoke to me. "Is the Prince's leftenant working you too hard, young Jessex? I ought to speak to her about that."

"No, sir, my dog is sick and I was up all night tending him. I've had no rest to speak of today, either."

He was smiling in a way that I did not find altogether attractive. "Even when you're tired you're still very beautiful."

Not really believing I had heard his actual words, I turned and walked away. I went behind the shrine to clean the lamps. Cothryn had been one of only a few celebrants at ceremony and remained after the rest were headed toward the lower camp. I had to dawdle in the workroom, finding chores to attend to, before I could be sure he had gone.

I continued my duties as scribe in Mordwen's work tent, and more often than not Cothryn was there. With the coming of the shrine to Camp I saw him at morning and evening ceremonies as well, and in that context he was more boorish. Following lamp-lighting he spoke to me publicly in spite of the fact that I was in sleeves. He complimented my singing. He complimented my looks in subtle ways. Though these attentions were troublesome, I only became alarmed when his first gift arrived.

A servant wearing the gems of his house brought me a worked wooden chest bearing a jeweled dagger resting on a bolt of cloak fabric, under cover of a polite note informing me of my loveliness and charm. I was taken aback by the richness of the gifts and the forwardness of the note. Here was writing in his own hand, and signed "Cothryn son of Duris." Here were luxuries, preening them-selves over their costliness.

I knew what offering the gift implied, having heard my share of barracks talk even in my state of relative isolation. When an older man or woman wants to take a young lover, courtship begins with a gift. But this custom is for men and women who are old enough to wear cloaks. I sent the gifts back by the householder who brought them to me, being certain it would please nobody to see me courted by this man.

Next day a servant returned with another pair of gifts, a porcelain jar of perfumed oil and another bolt of fine cloth. The note was polite and even more presumptuous. He took my first refusal, he said, as a sign of my enduring virtue, proof that my beauty was not wasted on a soul of chattel. I thought this "soul of chattel" to be a particularly vile phrase, and so I kept the note this time, though I sent the gifts back.

At Velunen he was waiting near the shrine and would have spoken to me but I hurried to mount Nixva. He stood in the clearing watching me ride away. Some other soldiers who had come to ceremony took note of this.

Following Vithilunen he lingered in the clearing again, and that time I was starving and could not think of enough tasks to outlast him. When I headed for lower camp he followed me, speaking charmingly of the weather and other trivialities. He had heard rumors about Nemort's march and related them to me; his news at least three weeks old, though I could not tell him so. A time of silence, after which Cothryn wondered aloud, in well-modulated tones, why I had returned his gifts when they might have pleased me had I only kept them.

I answered that I had not yet reached my cloaking-day and that I would dishonor my uncle if I began accepting gifts before I was of age. He answered (he actually said it) that my beauty was beyond my years and that convention was not for me, or something on that level. Luckily we reached the eating tent soon and I, seeing Mordwen, excused myself from Cothryn at once.

A Nivra who is taken with a common boy doesn't often have the best intentions. I was astonished he would speak to me in public after I twice refused his gifts. When Mordwen asked me what Cothryn wanted I answered vaguely and turned him to another subject, asking about a letter I had been copying.

That evening, in my room behind the shrine, no gift awaited me. I relaxed.

My vacation from his passion was brief. A few days later another gift arrived, this one placed in my room when I was not there to refuse it. The accompanying note again flattered me and begged my company. I had only to wear the embroidered sash and silver bracelet and he would fathom my wishes, he would have me brought secretly to his tent.

This was odious enough. But he had drenched the letter in scent, false sweetnesses like rotted elgerath blossoms. I had just come back from Illyn Water where fresh flowers were in bloom.

It was obvious he meant to persist. For a day or so, between other tasks, I wondered what to do, and considered asking the lake women for their advice. Finally I rejected that as silly. Even Words of Power would have been of no use to me unless I wanted to make something dreadful happen to him. I would be breaking my promise if I did that.

Worse than the gifts was his sending someone into my room to leave them. The next day a note arrived in the same manner. He was encouraged that I had not returned his gifts outright. (Was I supposed to carry them back to his tent myself?) Perhaps he had reason for hope?

I closed my mouth on my anger and recorded suuren in the suuren book, reporting afterward to Mordwen's work tent.

Cothryn was there. I would not meet his eye, though I lingered to make sure he saw I wore neither sash nor bracelet. I set about my duties and felt better, performing the now-familiar copying, the charge of business in the air, the hushed voices, the careful dusting, drying, and proofreading of letters cachet, writs notable and seals delivered.

Cothryn came to the shrine tent for Evening Song, and when I lit the lamp he moved nearly beside me. I fled at the earliest moment, out the back tent flap and into the forest. Mordwen found me shaking in the trees. I had been afraid Cothryn would send his householder to my room while I was there, or worse, come himself. Mordwen asked me what was wrong. I swallowed my pride, showed him the gifts and let him read the note.

Mordwen's voice grew crisp. "He's sent you gifts before?"

"Yes. Twice. I refused them both times."

"He had these things placed in your room?"

"Yes. He knew I'd send them back if I were there. He sent them during the morning ride when I was away."

We had returned to his tent, awaiting supper. He paced back and forth in the clearing, more agitated than I had yet seen him. Finally he said, "I ought to send for him and deal with him myself. Never mind your age, you're also kyyvi in Kirith Kirin's shrine. I suppose he didn't think of that. Well, Kirith Kirin will be here any day. Let's see how he likes this news."

"Kirith Kirin will be here?"

He raised a shaggy eyebrow. "Yes he will. No one else knows. Say nothing."

"Do you have to tell him about Cothryn?"

Mordwen's eyes actually gleamed. "Of course I have to. He'd be furious if I tried to keep such a thing from him."

When I told about Cothryn's attentions to Commyna, her reaction was briefer and even more to the point. "Do not let that man speak to you again, in the shrine or anywhere else. Gross creature. Cordyssans are prone to that sort of tawdriness."

But when I returned to my tent another gift awaited me, with a note of the usual sort. "At last you are tempted and keep my small tributes. Maybe these additional treasures will convince you of my devotion."

The bundle contained silver earrings and a jeweled buckle, costly and well-made. I wrapped the jewelry carefully in the viis cloth and sat trembling. If I could have flayed him and rolled him in salt his suffering would not have satisfied me.

Naturally he was in the work tent again that afternoon, and naturally he reappeared at evening ceremony. I dreaded going to the shrine tent, since I figured he would approach me directly again. As it turned out, however, he never got the chance. When the sun vanished and I lit the lamp, Kirith Kirin came riding up the hillside.

3

I sang the evening song as best I could, though as soon as the soldiers realized the Prince was in the clearing they began to shout. Kirith Kirin simply sat there. When the cheering died down he raised a silver-braceleted arm toward the evening stars. "It's good to see you all here in one place again. This Camp is home, I'm glad to be in it. Prince Imral and I have come to see Mordwen and some of the officers; I won't be staying long. While I'm here, continue in your usual routine, but at the same time prepare yourselves. General Nemort and an army of four thousand have entered Angoroe at the southern end. Within a few days we'll be preparing to face them."

He spoke with a calm that lent his words force. He looked at everyone for a moment. "Jessex, lead us in singing Kimri."

I fixed on red Aryaemen flaming in the black sky, a familiar star that appeared as if in omen. I lifted my voice into the night and voices joined me singing, including Kirith Kirin. I could not help but watch him after a while, relief at his presence, a heavy hand lifting from my heart. On the last bars of the song he dismounted and embraced Mordwen Illythin, as did Imral. I went behind the shrine, finding my coat and pulling it over my bare arms. I watched Kirith Kirin standing calm at the center of every gaze.

Almost every gaze, that is.

Soon after my retreat Cothryn sidled near me. At the same moment Imral broke away from the crowd around Kirith Kirin to greet me. Cothryn, naturally, paid his respects to the Drii Prince, so cordial in manner it was impossible to be offended. He asked after Imral's journey and Imral gave him some bland pleasantry. I was at the point of taking my leave when Cothryn said, blithely, "You must tell me the secret of making friends with our kyyvi, Imral Ynuuvil. Our Jessex is not friendly to me as he is to you."

Prince Imral laughed mildly, taken aback. "You must simply become more interesting, Cothryn. Perhaps you can learn how." Imral steered me away, saying quietly, "What a vulgar man."

I bit my tongue. The moment passed and Imral merely thought it curious. But the incident had not been lost on Mordwen. He called me to his side and asked me what Cothryn had said. He conferred momentarily with Imral and sent both of us to supper while he went to Kirith Kirin alone. Imral said nothing to me directly but his manner had become very grave, he took pains to speak to me kindly. I felt as if I had suddenly come up lame. He ordered me a glass of Drii brandy, the nose so strong I was uncertain whether to sip it. A steward brought supper but no sooner served it than a messenger arrived with a note for Imral and one for me. Mine sealed with the red seal I had seen before, the paper fine and smooth. "Come to my tent at once," the note said. "Imral Ynuuvil will accompany you. Bring with you any gifts given you by Cothryn son of Duris."

When I folded the note, Imral was calling for his cloak and my coat. I took a whole swallow of brandy in spite of the vein of fire in my throat. Imral watched me but said nothing.

We fetched the parcels from the shrine tent and descended to the glen where Kirith Kirin had set his field tent. We passed the outermost watch-fire and I could hardly draw a calm breath.

In the tent sat Mordwen Illythin wrapped in a violet cloak. Kirith Kirin was pacing back and forth, too angry to sit, bracelets flashing. When Imral and I entered, both Mordwen and Kirith Kirin nodded greeting, Mordwen frowning at me slightly as a kind of warning. I stood respectfully beside the lit brazier while Imral took a seat. Kirith Kirin asked me crisply to tell him what had happened between Cothryn and me. As I spoke he watched the fire in the brazier. I told him everything about the gifts. Once he interrupted to ask, sharply, "Why didn't you send back the sash and the bracelet?"

"What was I supposed to do, sir, take them to his tent myself?" My heart pounding. "He had the gifts sent to my room when I was riding. I couldn't refuse them when I wasn't there."

Apparently this fact had not penetrated. His voice gentled. Lifting the earrings to the light. "He sent you these today? In the same way, leaving them in your room?"

"Yes."

He watched me for a long time. There was something of his former tenderness in his gaze, it took me back to the quay in the

River City, and I felt like a lonely child being welcomed home. "It isn't fit I should say what I think of this, nor do I wish you to hear our discussion. But Cothryn won't bother you any more, I promise you."

He let me stay long enough to drink the cup of politeness, though the time passed mostly in silence. Anger had etched onto his face. When the wine was finished, a guard walked me to the shrine tent, and the tent was placed under guard as it had been before our numbers got stretched thin.

I fed Axfel and ran with him on the moonlit slopes, my legs feeling tireless and strong from the uncountable hours I had spent riding Nixva or dancing along the Illyn shore. Later I cleaned the lamps, oiling the wooden cases, refilling the oil flagons from jars that I had buried in the rocks for safety. Feeling uneasy.

In the morning I sang Velunen and put away the lamp, leaving immediately on the morning ride. Both Kirith Kirin and Cothryn were among the celebrants in the clearing that morning, the former looking grim, the latter unsuspecting, still trying to catch my eye when I sang.

I spent the morning as had become customary for me, riding on Nixva to the shore of the azure lake, meditating in fifth level trance to understand the intricacies of a step in pattern-dancing. That day, for the first time since we moved camp from shadow country, the lake women retained me for a considerable period out of real time, and I traveled with Commyna to the High Place over Cunuduerum.

While I had done detailed work in the basic principles of Tower magic, I had never been inside a High Place and had not actually expected to visit one. The lake women were wary of the Towers and had told me so many times. One does not climb to the High Place unless one is prepared to fight.

We traveled to Seumren in the manner of the lake women, crossing space by a magic of which I would learn nothing from them. We did not ascend the Tower Stair to the summit since that would have awakened the Tower; we emerged from Commyna's mist into the pirunaen, the magician's work room.

Commyna had chosen Seumren rather than the High Place over Inniscaudra because of the dense magics that veil the River City; our presence in Inniscaudra would have been more difficult to hide. The work room was a sparsely furnished affair. A huge worktable and lines of chests and cabinets. The center of the room clear, though in other Towers that space would have been occupied by the silver-worked frame for the firepot and the underpinnings of the Eyestone.

Once Commyna had shown me what there was to see of the room-under, we climbed the narrow stair to the top. Seumren is the eldest of High Places and there has never been an Eyestone on the summit. The ruling magic of Seumren comes from inlaid runes like those in the circles on Sister Mountain, the device Falamar was copying. Jurel Durassa was the first pirunuu to imbed a stone in a Tower.

The summit of Seumren was a hundred staves across, paved with smooth stone on which runes were inscribed in silver. So long as we trod on the marble strip around the stair mouth, we would not activate the magic in the runes. On other shenesoeniisae, a stone colonnade bordered the circular summit, and some towers, like Ellebren, were three-horned, but Seumren was open, flat and wide. The tower soared over the city, whose buildings spread out like stone miniatures along the mist-shrouded riverbank. "I feel at peace here. I want to dance on the runes."

Commyna laughed. "Well, don't do that this trip. In fact, you should think twice before wakening the elder devices like Seumren or Aediamysaar. Their powers are not to be entirely understood from the levels to which you can attain. This was part of what defeated Falamar: He built Seumren to mimic what we had made at Aediamysaar, but in the end he could not master our runes. The YYstones are much more suited to the powers of this world."

"Then you could stand as mistress of this place?"

"Possibly. But in doing so I'd call down endless curses on myself. The shenesoeniis of this world is forbidden me, if I want to remain a power in the One rather than the Other."

"Why? You were born in Arthen."

Commyna shook her head. "I don't think I could tell you all the story. Every creature made by YY has made a terrible mistake at some time or other. Mine was as bad as any, and my sisters were caught up in it. Because of it, my sisters and I are forbidden to influence events in this world, on this side of the Barrier Mountains. The world we live in is beyond them."

"In Saenal? That's the name for the whole world, Mordwen says."

"Only in one direction. You'll find in time that there are eleven directions, including tomorrow. In another direction, along another path, lies my world. You'll see it some day, a very long time from now."

She seemed troubled, and I wondered what she was not saying. "You're not telling me everything that's on your mind, are you?"

Commyna wandered down the marble strip to the end of the stair mouth. "Nemort will arrive at the north end of Angoroe in a few days. He's marching in battle order, having been alerted to the possibility of ambush by the patrols Kirith Kirin drove south.

"Whatever keeps Drudaen at Montajhena is still holding him there. But if Kirith Kirin's soldiers defeat Nemort, as I believe they will, Drudaen will send someone to help him, to hold Gnemorra and drive our soldiers back into Arthen. He'll send Julassa Kyminax, I believe. When that time comes—"

Her voice drifted to silence. I said, finally, "There won't be much warning, will there?"

Commyna shook her head. "Hardly any. And worse, these present soldiers have not faced magic. Only the Jhinuuserret have ever fought against one skilled in our arts."

"Can't we do anything?"

"We can wait for Yron."

"Do you have any sign he's close?"

Commyna lifted her face to the wind pouring over the tower. "I wish I knew. We're finishing the cloak we made for him. We're hoping."

When the lesson was over we returned to Illyn Water, and I meditated at fifth level for some time before returning to Camp. Vella and Vissyn were sitting beneath the duraelaryn, stitching Yron's cloak while clouds blew over Illyn, a storm of no one's creation. The lake women watched the clouds mildly, wind lifting strands of their hair. Vissyn asked me what I thought of Seumren and I said I had found the shenesoeniis to be wonderfully exhilarating, the air tasted sharp and fresh, I wanted to go onto the stones and would have except Commyna said no. The rapture of my description must have taken the women aback. "He isn't exaggerating," Commyna said. "I watched him. I believe he could do well even on such a place."

"You didn't find Seumren to be oppressive?" Vella asked.

I shook my head, and Commyna agreed, "We were guarded from most of that, sister. Cunuduerum had no hold on us, and no eye living or dead knew of our journey."

"Did you take him to the Library?"

"He'll have to find that place on his own."

"What library?" I asked.

She signaled she would answer no further questions and I fetched a pot of water to make tea. We performed that ritual and I returned to Nevyssan.

My conversation with Commyna had disturbed me, and I forgot Cothryn until I reached Camp. When I walked Nixva to the horse line, soldiers throughout Camp were replacing bits of armor, mending saddlebags, replacing leather laces, sharpening blades, tipping arrows in preparation for fighting. I hurried to the scribe tent where Mordwen, Imral, and Kirith Kirin sat surrounded by secretaries, officers, and gentry. The Venladrii Prince, who nodded to me when no one else was paying attention, noted my entrance. Because of all the bodies and the burning of several braziers, the tent was warm. From outside I could hear the howling of winds and the ominous rumbling of northern thunder. A storm was blowing over Nevyssan same as Illyn, and the day darkened.

Mordwen gave me a letter to copy from Kirith Kirin to Ren Vael, who was in Cordyssa preparing to lead more troops to the siege of Gnemorra. In the letter Kirith Kirin was urging him to send officers into east Fenax to recruit from the farms and villages. Mordwen signaled me to copy the letter discreetly, and I carried my writing board to a corner and trimmed myself a lamp-wick. When I was walking across the tent with the lamp, threading my way between by-now familiar bodies, it occurred to me I had not seen Cothryn, and Kirith Kirin looked up momentarily from a discussion of the terrain around the north end of Angoroe. In the clean light falling through the transparent viis, his face seemed softer and clearer.

I copied out the letter and returned it to Mordwen, who gave me more work of like nature, a budget for the movement of Cordyssan squadrons from the city to Angoroe, an authorization for a payment of gold from the Prince to the city's general treasury, and a plan for a contingent march that would lead the army down the extreme western edge of the Fenax, guarding that route to Cordyssa should Nemort slip past our army and the Venladrii.

I stayed at this work longer than I meant to, missing my archery drill and only remembering the evening ceremony in time to splash water on my face. The crowd for lamp-lighting swelled with Kirith Kirin in Camp. I sang the Evening Song while the lamp flickered on the altar. Cothryn son of Duris came nowhere near the shrine that evening.

Mordwen was absent from his tent when I went there, and I wondered if he were with the Prince. I found supper at the cook tent, keeping company with one of the other clerks, a pleasant girl just past her cloaking with whom I had struck up something of a friendship. She was full of gossip, as was nearly everyone those days, and she was careful to share the latest she had heard, something she learned when she stopped by the command tent to retrieve her money purse. A party was leaving Camp that evening, ordered away suddenly, led by Cothryn. Kirith Kirin had sent him to south Arthen to join one of the border patrols. It was unheard of to send such a high-ranking person to duty of that sort; already rumors were circulating as to the reason. She asked if I had heard anything and I said no.

The anger I had harbored vanished. My supper companion continued with her speculation at some length. It was she who told me Cothryn had come to Arthen in disgrace, having been sent away from Cordyssa following a scandal involving a merchant's son. I felt better after hearing that; though I had no idea if the story were true. I finished my supper quickly.

At the shrine a torchbearer awaited me to take me to Kirith Kirin's tent. We hurried through moon-dappled shadows along the rocky path, the night full of music, birds calling, somber breezes in autumn leaves. The torchbearer relinquished me to Imral Ynuuvil, who asked after my health. I was at the point of asking him what was going on when he touched a slender finger to his lips.

Inside the tent Mordwen awaited us both, and before I could greet him he embraced me. He had a fine tunic in his hand, crimson worked with silver, trimmed with stones called pearls that are said to come from the sea. Their luster caught my eye and I reached to touch one of them, having never seen anything like them before. Mordwen laughed. "The boy does have a feeling for finery, doesn't he?"

Imral said, "I find that to be an encouraging sign since we are taking so much trouble over him."

"Trouble? Have I done something wrong?"

"What makes you think that?" Imral asked.

"I heard gossip in Camp." I decided it was best to get right to the heart of my fear. "Cothryn has been sent away. Is it my fault?"

Mordwen snorted his disgust, and Imral knelt so that I was looking down into his face. His expression was tender. "Cothryn got what he deserved, Jessex. I'm sorry you had to hear the news from strangers, and Kirith Kirin will be sorry too. But don't think anyone can bear you a grudge, unless Cothryn is a fool and chooses to. You did nothing wrong."

"In fact you behaved like any decent boy should have."
Mordwen lay a familiar hand on my shoulders. "Though decent
behavior is rare enough in this degenerate age."

Kirith Kirin called from the inner chamber and Imral turned,
smiling. "I'll let him know you're here. Give him the tunic, Mordwen,
he should be better dressed."

I slipped my plain white tunic over my head, standing briefly
bare but for my linen drawers and leggings while Mordwen fumbled
with the clasp of the other garment. When I had smoothed the
short skirt and settled the brocade neatly on my shoulders, Mordwen
gave me a final inspection, and we went inside.

Kirith Kirin said hello and led me to a cushion by a wooden
table on which was set a flagon of wine and cups. Mordwen and
Imral sat with us, as if I were some favored relation, and I was full
of their affection again, lit like a lamp. I had not known how lonely
I had been.

The Prince asked after my lessons and listened to me read from
"Luthmar," praising my accent and diction. He asked about archery
as well, and how I liked riding Nixva, and Mordwen praised my
work in the clerk's tent, maybe more abundantly than was required.
But it made me happy to hear the pride in the Seer's voice, to feel
Imral's friendship, the Prince's spirit open to mine. It pleased him to
have me there, and for the first time he made no shift to hide it.

Finally, when we had drunk the cup of friendship and were
proceeding to the cup of mirth, Kirith Kirin glanced at me, and I
would almost have sworn he was nervous. "Jessex," he began, "before you hear it from others—"

"He's already heard," Imral said quietly. "Apparently Cothryn
could not keep quiet."

Kirith Kirin looked at me somewhat dumbstruck. "I'm sorry. I
wanted to give you the news myself." He shook his head, plainly
disturbed. "No matter. It was gossip that got us into this mess to
begin with, why should I think that tongue-wagging would have
stopped in the meantime?" He looked at me and smiled. "At any
rate, Cothryn won't trouble you any more."

A householder poured wine. Kirith Kirin leaned back into the
shadow of the lamp. He watched me without word or change of
expression. Imral sipped wine from his cup and Mordwen ran
fingers through his own shaggy hair. I settled back against my cushion. Finally I said, "Forgive me if this question is impertinent, but I
think I ought to know. What's changed since you summoned me to

the test on Sister Mountain?"

He looked at me again, seeming very young. "I haven't changed my mind." He touched my hand shyly. "You are a mystery to me. Whether you're witch, or angel, or farm boy, I don't know. But I know I've missed you these past months. There's no reason to say more than that, except that you can't know what it means to one whose life is as long as mine, to feel with heart, to miss anyone. I won't forget it again."

4

Within a few days Nemort neared the mouth of Angoroe, and Kirith Kirin prepared to leave camp with many soldiers, riding west along the rough trail out of Nevyssan.

I was with him most evenings, though never alone. Mordwen was a more circumspect guardian than ever and I was rarely out of his sight when I was in Camp, unless I was preparing for the lamp ritual or sleeping. When Kirith Kirin needed a letter copied or notes taken at a private meeting I was the one summoned, and it pleased me to be taken for granted, to be asked in an easy tone to fetch him a pen for signing a letter, or for a cup of water or tea, or to bring something from his tent that he had forgotten.

The seriousness with which he worked infected everyone around him, and the reality of the coming war sobered me. When one is drilling with sword, pike, and bow, the whole of warfare seems a game; one does not think much of the sword truly piercing the soldier's side, the complexities of making certain that there are sufficient arrows for the archers, the need for tents to house the wounded. Yet we were heading for days when soldiers—living women and men—would die, suffer pain, receive wounds that would cripple them for life. The soldiers moved toward this conflict joyously, with no thought for the danger or the suffering, because that is the nature of a war in the beginning. A blindness comes. The worry was left to Kirith Kirin, to Karsten, to Imral, Mordwen, and others who had seen such times before.

One night I wakened to hear noises in the outer shrine and rose to find Imral Ynuuvil at the lamp, making a strange sound that I realized was sobs, trying to stifle the sound with his sash. For a moment I was torn, not knowing whether to go to him or return to bed, pretending I had heard nothing. In the end that seemed the coward's path, and we were friends, after a fashion. I knelt at his side and lay my hand in his fine hair.

He was glad of the company. He said nothing, but made no attempt to hide his tears or his sadness. "I've dreamed of men and women dying, and blood spilled, and sicknesses loosed on the world by magic. I dreamed Karsten was killed on the field, and Mordwen taken, and you were in my dream too, son of Kinth, imprisoned in a dark room."

"Do you think it was a true dream?"

He shook his head. "No. This was only what comes of too much work, too much thinking about misery. And I miss Karsten, and am afraid for her. The Jhinuuserret can die in battle same as other mortals. Our lives are prolonged but not protected."

"Do you think the battle will be—do you think many people will be killed?"

He gave me a long, sobering look—his own despair was in it, and he hid nothing. "This is only the first battle. And yes, I think a lot of people will die before the world is a happy place again."

A vision of my neighbor's farm passed through my head, a ruin consumed by weeds. I tried to imagine it when the soldiers were killing the family, hanging Commiseth and raping Sergil. I pictured my own farm, my father bleeding on the ground, my sisters screaming, my mother forlorn and battered, clinging to the back of some stranger's horse. Imral noted my expression and asked me what I was thinking, so I told him.

"I forget sometimes that the war has already started for some."

"Do the Venladrii have wars of their own, or do they only fight in other people's?"

I had thought this was a simple question, but suddenly his eyes were full of pain. I thought he was angry with me, and so I apologized. "No, Jessex, I'm not angry. The Venladrii fight wars of their own. For many thousands of years we did not, but that was long before we crossed the mountains into your land. We thought we were a peace-loving people where we came from. But we brought a terrible war to a place that had never known war before, and we've mourned it ever since." He took a long, deep breath. "My mother died then. A long time ago."

His voice trailed off. But I was very curious, having heard few stories of the time before the Venladrii crossed the mountains. He sent me to bed. Before we parted I said, "I'll pray for peace to come to you, Prince Imral."

"Pray for peace to find us all," he answered, "especially Kirith Kirin, who'll soon begin to blame himself for every death, for every wound he sees."

"YY won't let his heart be so hard."

"If I know him, he'll shut out YY before he'll give up his grief." He turned as if to go, and then added, not as an afterthought but weighing each word. "You've been a good friend to me tonight, Jessex. I won't forget it."

Before I could think of any answer he was gone. I returned to bed, where sleep was a long time coming.

5

On the following morning Kirith Kirin and his soldiers headed westward to battle. This time Mordwen was with them.

When I think of all that followed from that first morning's march, it seems the enormity of the occasion escaped us. The morning was overcast, clouds laden with rain, the first hint of chill. We sang "Light in the Darkness," and with no fanfare the column of soldiers marched away, the supply wagons following behind.

Despite my talk with Imral I could not help but be cheered by the martial spectacle, the brave and beautiful soldiers marching gallantly, broad-shouldered women binding up their hair, swords slung at their sides; slim-hipped men with their many blades polished to perfection, colorful feathers in pomaded hair, polished bows slung over embroidered tunics. They marched off singing and vanished into the trees.

The whole world knows what happened when Nemort marched his four thousand troops out of Angoroe beyond the last embracing arm of Arthen Forest. Lady Karsten led mounted archers and cavalry down on him from a hillside while Pel Pelathayn blocked his escape, leading infantry to drive him back against the cavalry. Half the Blue Cloaks died before Nemort led two well-formed, disciplined detachments down a rocky stream and overland to Fort Gnemorra ahead of our army, which pursued the southerners to the walls of the fortress. Nemort had to fight his way through Cordyssans already encamped there in order to enter the fort at all. Had Kirith Kirin but a thousand more soldiers, or else had he been able to leave Arthen to join the battle himself, Nemort would never have reached Gnemorra, or so I have always heard.

I was not part of this conflict in any way, nor did I see it. We who were left behind in Nevyssan waited for news, which was slow in coming. The battle was joined on the third day following Kirith Kirin's march and ended five days later when Nemort and his thousand-odd survivors beat through the Cordyssans to reach the safety of the fort.

The first post-riders returned to Nevyssan a day later, bringing the tale of the battle, the whole camp gathering round a bonfire to hear the words of the messengers. The officer bore a letter to Camp from Kirith Kirin, and he read it to us. One could hear the Prince's voice behind the words. "Today we have won control of the north from Arthen to the country of the Smiths, until more troops come from Ivyssa or the Queen sends other aid. We are celebrating in westernmost Arthen as you must in Nevyssan. YY keep us safe in the time that is coming."

This was a cold note for a victory day. But the message was understood. As one of the clerks told me, later when the Camp Steward was passing 'round ale and wine, "Drink now while you can, forget your cloaking day. The next army to come north won't be so easy to beat."

"But we'll have some time to train the Cordyssans, won't we?"

The clerk smiled, fingering the hem of his own cloak of adulthood. "Nemort came without one of Drudaen's witches. The next general may not be so particular."

A shock spread through me slowly. Because as he spoke, I realized that such a one might already be on the way.

Next morning at Illyn Water I learned Julassa Kyminax was riding north on wind and storm.

Commyna gave me the news, standing by the lakeshore, autumn breezes lifting her hair. Though at Illyn I could see for myself. Our lessons these days were brief, my meditations long in their wake; but today no meditation would be possible, she said, for the curled spaces were disturbed by the magic Julassa was making, and by the powerful vigilance Drudaen kept. I must be more careful than ever to conceal myself.

I felt my stomach tighten. "What will happen? Do you know?"

"There's likely to be slaughter." She spoke coldly, without feeling, as she was apt to do when she was most disturbed.

"Where's Yron?"

"If I knew how to call him I would."

"Then we have to fight her from here."

She turned on me, speaking sharply. "Don't tempt me to do what would be my ruin, boy. Yes, we could, and we could break her like a strumpet. But I've told you what the consequences would be. I won't tell you again. If Yron doesn't come, there'll be no help."

We returned to the great-leafed tree where Vella and Vissyn were busily shaping the cloth into a long, full cloak. The fabric swam with color and hints of images, constellations, cold blue fires, the faces of strange people. I asked, "When does Julassa reach the fortress?"

"Sometime today, we think," Vella answered, sparing Commyna, who scowled and set about the business of making tea. "She's not riding as fast as she might. I suppose she's conserving her strength. There's no hurry from her point of view."

"No, I guess there isn't," I said. "There's no one to fight her."

"One wishes Kentha were still alive." Vella's voice was oddly high-pitched. "Or that Kirith Kirin had the ruby ring Drudaen gave her."

"Never mind dreaming, sister," Commyna said in her severest tone.

When I had drunk the tea I took leave of them, Vissyn walking me to the spot of shade where Nixva grazed. She said nothing, except that I must try not to dwell on what I knew and must certainly keep the news to myself, hard as that would be. "Pray for the soldiers. Pray for Kirith Kirin."

"It will be hard simply to pray when I see Julassa in my mind, riding northward to begin her work."

Vissyn took my face in her hands. "I have no answer for that. Many of your friends will die by her hand, I think, and I'm afraid for Kirith Kirin. If he loses heart—"

We embraced, and I leapt onto Nixva's back. "I'll pray." I kept a careful balance of expression. "I'll pray for guidance."

Bending to kiss her brow, I turned Nixva and we rode away.

CHAPTER TEN
FORT GNEMORRA

1

Once Nixva had carried me safely beyond Illyn's border, we consulted with one another.

The morning was bright and clear, not a cloud in the sky, perfect azure. The air was tinged with a slight chill. We had emerged from the wards 'round Illyn onto a sheer hillside east of Camp in a grove of linvern where sunlight fell as if through lace onto Nixva's mane. From the height rolled the hillsides and deep vales in which we had set Camp; beyond, swimming in haze and gold, the fertile land of West Fenax.

I could not feel the Kyminax sorceress any longer, though when I was in Illyn's domain I had eyes that could reach her wherever she might be. On Illyn's shore I had felt her like weight on my mind, but now I was deaf to her singing, blind to her riding.

She would reach Gnemorra today, perhaps soon. So far she had not stirred weather to her call, traveling like a low shadow. Maybe she had set wards so she would know if her riding were being spied on, or maybe she feared no opposition, maybe her singing was as clear as the wind in the leaves above my head. I could not tell. My eyes, my ears, my learned-power was at Illyn. Or rather, was locked within me by a vow. Within the space the mind makes, the kei.

When Julassa reached the fortress, many hundreds would die and our soldiers would be driven from the field.

I breathed deeply, holding my face against Nixva's neck. "What do you say, friend? Do we go home and pray?"

He tossed his head impatiently. I ran my fingers through his mane. "I can pray here. But what good is praying going to do? I can only tell YY what she knows already. There's no help unless Yron comes. But what if Yron doesn't come?"

Nixva pranced from side to side, neighing sharply. I laughed, feeling my stomach lurch at the same time. "I am a power of this world," I whispered. "Forgive me, Sisters. But how can I obey you when all I can see from obedience is ruin? Forgive me, YY-Mother, if you think what I'm doing is wrong. If Yron won't come, I'll go myself."

I mounted the black horse and turned him toward the Fenax. Swallowing, I began the controlled breathing and insinging that released into my mind the kei of Wyyvisar, Words of Power, the use of which I had always denied myself outside the province of Illyn Water. It was easy, and I was there.

2

I rode through valley and over hill swiftly, skirting Camp to the north by a wide margin. Nixva galloped joyously, riding the wave of my silent singing, aware that we were not headed home to the familiar horse-line, snorting his impatience to run even faster.

Once we reached the hinterland of Arthen he headed due west along Wood's End. Since Arthen was a veil Julassa could not penetrate, I figured to keep hidden that way till I had got my bearings and knew where to find her.

I cleared my mind of every thought, as I had been taught to do, and listened for the sound of distant singing.

Soon I found her. She was riding partly hidden, servants in her company under partial wards, closer than I had guessed from what the lake women had told me, moving partly with aid of the ithikan, a chant that increases motion. She was confident of her strength to bring servants with her, riding at speed in her train; the effort would weaken her in ways I might exploit. Many thoughts could be discerned even from that distance, particularly her baleful hatred of the countryside and her sense of foreboding that came from the nearness of Arthen.

Her servants were not men. I could get no sense of what creatures they were but I guessed them to be Verm.

My heart sank at the realization of her preparedness for what was to come. She had been laying the foundations of power in herself for more years than I could number. I was a babe compared to that.

Grimly I turned to my own preparations. I prayed, YY grant me guidance and teach me to sing.

Soon Nixva and I could no longer remain under the protective cover of Arthen, and from there we would ride in danger unless I could hide us. This I had been preparing for, and from the moment we trod the Fenax the rhythm of my song was subtle, masked to seem like wind or running water, so that even the Sisters would have trouble finding me. To hide me from Julassa, who anticipated no enemy, I deemed this sufficient.

I no more knew the road to Gnemorra than I knew the way back to my father's farm without a guide, but I did not need to know it. I was behind Julassa, whose presence was already moving steadily northward, and I had only to follow her. Her speed was great but mine was greater, I saw to that. I could make the ithikan, too. Hugging Nixva, my body under various controls, I hovered in the dual trance, my spirit flung out above my body so that I had long vision, like that of a bird flying high above; my spirit in the small space inside the body, singing. I traveled like a shadow. Twice I flashed through farmyards unseen, leaving no more trace than strong wind leaves, bending the wheat to the ground and howling on. Nixva galloped savagely, mane whipping like black fire, fearless of the magic that immersed him.

We were long past noon by now. Time moved too quickly for me, who had much to prepare.

Ahead of us, in my elongated vision, the sky was changing before my eyes.

One who has not seen power move can hardly imagine the sight, the sudden boiling of clouds out of nothing, the spreading of a shadow over the land sudden as the sweeping of a hand across the sun. Julassa Kyminax increased her song suddenly, her power swelled, engulfed earth and sky, so that in the space of moments darkness spread from horizon to horizon. She was drinking the light into herself, for strength.

Her shadow fell as far north as Umilaven and as far south as Nevyssan and the Prince's encampment. Kirith Kirin, emerging from his field tent to receive messengers, saw the shadow and knew his enemy had come.

I hid from this, letting shadow mingle with my own singing, though this was taxing. I had thus less space in the kei for my other preparations. Meanwhile she was beginning to lay out her own applications, staking claim over a good deal of ground and beginning a song to move power at a deep level. She was still unaware of me; what she was preparing was for our army.

She used words I did not know, and I assumed this was the Ildaruen in which Drudaen instructed those who served or followed him. But the lake women had taught me other means of surmising thought, and I read her pattern from a distance, and understood at once that I should challenge it.

She was summoning a storm, gathering rain and lightning in the clouds and calling a bitter wind from the mountains.

For a moment I hesitated, even after I knew what I had to do.

After the first Word there would be no turning back. She would know me then, and she would not relent until she brought me down.

But by now our speed had swept us onto the stretch of plain before Fort Gnemorra, and I saw the hastily-lit watchfires of those who waited there, feeling the fear that had overtaken them with the coming of the witch's shadow. These were my friends. They could smell their death.

She sang out for fire and light, and a broad, blood-red illumination surrounded her, lighting her hellish ride across the plain.

With a jolt I realized I was so close to her I could see her with the eyes of my body. She had been careless, and she did not yet know it. She had let me come too close.

I rose up straight on Nixva's back and called out in Words for light and fire of my own, and my Words were true. The thrill of it ran through me, that this was the world beyond Illyn and I was in it with my whole self, including the magic I knew, and I exulted as confusion flooded my adversary. She heard the voice of an enemy where she had thought to find none. Moreover, she heard Wyyvisar, and she knew herself opposed. She was dismayed in spite of herself.

While her thought faltered I bore down on her, both in speed and in power, so that Nixva swept across the plain at the same time I sang out against her storm and reached forward to hold the heart of her horses. The horses cried out at my deep touch, and Julassa failed to counter me in time to save them all. One of the horses died and his rider was thrown headlong. Julassa gathered her wits about her well enough to mount a defense that prevented me from coming so close again, but she was shaken.

Nixva swept by the dead horse and the stunned rider, some creature like nothing I had never seen before, bigger than any man or woman, rising from a tumble that would have killed most mortals. I felt a fetidness from him and called out savage Words that sent pain through all his limbs and bound him, casting him to the ground, helpless. His cries were real. The sorceress had left him unprotected.

She struck next, working from the fifth level and within her body, hurling power back toward me and forward toward the army surrounding Genfynnel. This was a mistake, for her thrust toward me was absorbed in my defenses while her assault on the soldiers was insufficient for the distance. But she was still closer to them than I, and I feared when she was close enough to use killing phrases, many would die. I increased my efforts to reach her, forgetting, for the moment, any thought of attack.

Nixva responded as he always did, and our speed was as great as any we had ever achieved under the watchful eyes of our tutors. Julassa did not turn in her saddle but I could feel her awareness, and I drew close enough I could make out her hand clutching the white hood to her flame-colored hair.

One could hear the soldiers shouting terror beneath the walls. Not one man flinched, not one woman stepped aside, when the witch finally reached the line of drawn swords and bows. The shrieking of her voice was terrible, as was the carnage she wreaked. I reached forward to challenge her and her body stiffened in the saddle.

I was no longer aware of thought or of the words that were pouring out of me, a sound of eerie singing from my living voice, the unearthly echo of Words in the kei space. I was bent on the witch whose every move I must understand, whose every thought I must anticipate. She kept to her horse with difficulty. I took the chance, and dismounted from Nixva.

From the ground, without the need to spare much thought for balance or for Nixva's safety, I could focus more attention on my work. We were surrounded by onlookers, which I did not like, but I could not let my attention waver for a moment to warn them away. I need not have worried. In the moments that followed, fear cleared us a broad circle.

I began setting wards about her, and naming Bans to bind her. Twice she broke my song contemptuously, but not with enough authority to free herself from my binding. The third time she fought furiously, but in the end I would have had her, except she did the movement into spin and hurled herself some distance away, her horse trembling with the effort. A wave of heat and light like fire swept over me, and soldiers drew back, at the moment that her second Verm companion, whom she had left to defend himself, dismounted among the foot soldiers. Other, dimly-heard sounds penetrated my consciousness, and I vaguely realized the soldiers from inside the fort were attacking as well, the sky raining down arrows and stones from catapults.

Had I ever seen a battlefield before, that moment might not have rattled me as it did, but that brief confusion nearly cost me the fight I was waging, and my life in the bargain. My thought wavered from Julassa and she redoubled her attack, so that I felt her touch in my body and could hear the incantations she was intoning as she set up her wards around me.

She was nearly cackling, and both relief and greed radiated from her when she thought she had me beaten. She meant to drink my life as she had drunk the lives of many local powers who had opposed her over the generations she had lived. But I had not risked the Sisters' anger to get beaten like some minor dabbler, some parlor-magician. I broke down her wards one by one.

She reached for gems to amplify her singing, and for a time I felt myself sorely pressed again. She was able to break the storm over us, and it was a powerful storm, but her control of its elements was not as close as she wished, and I was able to direct its main fury away from the plain on which the army was fighting. She ensnared soldiers who strayed too close to her and killed them, and for a while this fed her power, until someone grew wise enough to order the soldiers to stand away. I felt this happen and was relieved.

She settled down to a long fight. I could read the thought when it occurred to her, that what she could not defeat quickly she could wear down by turns. Force gathered in her, and she began her extended attack.

Time has an indescribable role in such a contest. She tested me on every level, probing each of my defenses while she launched attacks whose countermeasures cost me strength. Had there been any chink in my armor she would have found it, but there was none. I was in the dual state and far above us both, the present moment stretched as long as practical, and I understood that she had not begun this meditation and that she could never beat me from within the body. The realization came to me at the same moment that it came to her, at the end of a long sequence of application-and-countermeasure in which she tried a few tricks so simple I broke them with scorn. She must have heard the harmony of the dual state, which is unmistakable. She had begun her own fifth-level defenses late, and I could read her thought. She launched a fifth level attack so skillful it left me dizzy, but I was proof against it. Hardest to fight were those incantations she broadcast through hand-held gems, but in those moments I found a strange ally in the gems themselves, especially from my eye in the air. The Sisters had told me I had a gift for gem-magic, scarce praise, and on that battlefield before Gnemorra, when the witch employed these jewels as devices, I felt the power she was moving and understood it.

My hesitance to launch any assault on her she read as weakness, even when my defenses were deft. She set wards around me again but I broke them down—this time, noting her stance, her look of confidence, I was careful to break them with apparent difficulty, one by one, and to seem to struggle as I did so. She noted this. Soon after she set out on a dance of encirclement.

During this dance, wards of confinement are fixed into place one at a time by a movement of the physical body so they can no longer be broken easily. If she completed the round I would no longer have freedom to move beyond the ward circle, and from there it would simply be a matter of time before she ate my soul. If I fled from the field, as I could, to save myself, she would go on with her slaughter of Kirith Kirin's army. But to stop her from setting the wards I would have to break her in the midst of her dance. She was doing me some honor at least. The encirclement dance is one of the high magics and, since earliest times, magicians have used it to test one another.

She moved quickly and surely in the dance, into and out of spin, light and fire flashing round her, the storm raging overhead and wind howling across the plain. I watched her figure calmly, her smooth limbs and sinuous arms, bracelets shivering up and down, gems flashing. Her voice was eerie, echoing in me, and beyond it, behind it, the shadow of another voice with whom she was communicating.

I knew who this would be.

I sang against that distant song most powerfully, my voice in the air and in the plane of the fifth circle where I knew to find him; I sang *Yron has come, oh you lord of shadow*, and I could feel his distant confusion. Uncertain who or what I might be, he hesitated. When the link between those two was weakened I could feel the jolt in Julassa Kyminax, the faltering of dance and thought. Moving quickly toward her, I broke the ward she had been setting and drove her back with fire and other applications. But the wards she had already set remained fixed and she took refuge behind them.

She was holding gems in her hands.

She tossed them in her loose fingers, looking above at the sky as if listening.

Now, in trance and out of my body, I expanded time and moved to the gems. A way to do so became clear to me, to move directly through a space I had never seen and to move in the kei, nowhere else, which is not motion at all, but which makes the world, as Commyna said. Ignoring her wards, I sang to her gems in a way I had never tried before, behind the Ildaruen that filled the stone, not even contesting its presence, simply refilling the gems with Wyyvisar and reaching from them to Julassa.

The effect was immediate. My head was full of her words, and I was engulfing the whole current of her thought and song, directing and molding, setting down my hand into her mind. She felt my presence and tumbled to the ground in her confusion. I felt surprised at her fear, and realized I felt no pity for her. I had thought it would be so much harder. She fought me but it was for nothing; heat and cold blasted me, and she sang death to me from three levels at once, but I had her gems, and she had nothing of mine. The memory of my father flooded me, and my sisters and brothers dead on our farm, and my mother imprisoned.

I set my wards round her all at once and their power filled the gems. She struggled to break the circle but could not, and I fixed it in place and she was mine. I imposed no Bans. There could be no question of mercy. She could not live to return to her master. Before I killed her I let her know who I was, the son of the farmer she had slaughtered. She was dismayed and angered and fought me off for a time, but I was still in her gems even from that distance; she could not win. I said a magic of unmaking and fire poured from her, the ground trembled beneath her death spasm, splitting the walls of Gnemorra so that Lady Karsten and her soldiers could pour through the breech. Julassa's cries could be heard to the end of Aeryn, by those who had ears to hear. I ate her life and strength as was my right. No part of her was left to be reborn, in Zaeyn, beyond the Gates of the Dead. Her defeat was no secret from anybody. That day Drudaen knew he was opposed in the north, by a power he had not reckoned on.

When the fight was done I stood forlorn on the plain beneath the storm that would go on raging, the darkness that would slowly dissipate. From the fortress resounded the cries of soldiers dying. Red Cloaks poured through the gap in the wall.

On the plain round about lay the bodies of those who had already fallen, and I wandered there briefly, dazed, hearing the groans of those to whom the sword had not been quite kind enough. Some few of them I sang into sleep or numbness, till I realized in a daze that I hadn't strength to comfort them all. My heart flooded with misery. I had killed my enemy but I had also broken a vow to the Sisters of the YY. Victory had an uncertain taste. I summoned Nixva as we had been taught at Illyn Water, and he came to me out of the smoke and blackness, rain sheeting down across his glossy coat. I mounted into the saddle and we returned to Arthen, following the way we came.

CHAPTER ELEVEN
JIIVIISN FIELD

1

By the time I reached Camp darkness had long since descended, and I found the shrine tent empty, Axfel asleep at the rear flap, whimpering in a dream. I said his name and he sprang on me, licking my face, yelping his delight.

I hurried indoors to the work chamber, where I set about putting to rights my neglect of Evening Ceremony. I lit the kaa lamp in the shrine and sang the Evening Song quietly. When the lamp was lit and placed in its appropriate niche, the night did not seem so strange.

Visitors came almost immediately, no one I knew well, though the Camp Steward, who was part of Gaelex's staff, asked me politely where I had been. He had been worried when I failed to return from the suuren ride, and when the witch shadow came no one had been able to search. Seizing on that, I claimed to have been lost in the hill country when the shadow fell. The steward said he had never seen anything like it. He hadn't been able to see a foot in front of his own face until someone got the torches burning.

He accompanied me to high camp where the cook fire was still burning. Those of us who were left in Camp, mostly trainees and reserves, huddled in clots round the burning logs, the night echoing with quiet voices, women and men talking furtively, gazing north. "Still no lights," a blonde woman told a redhead, both of them wearing the archer's green tunic blazoned with the crimson insignia of Kirith Kirin. "I guess it's over."

"Is that good or bad?" the redhead asked.

The blonde paused to swill down ale and wipe her mouth. "I don't see how it could be good. That was witch-shadow, everyone says so, and the witch was one of the southerners, you can bet on that. Maybe Drudaen Keerfax himself."

The redhead stared at the fire with a sad face. "Do you think they're all dead?"

"Either dead or hightailing it back to the forest. He can't get in here, you know. I heard it from Lady Karsten herself. Lord Keerfax nor none of his followers can come inside Old Arthen. The trees bedevil him or some such."

"If he's got us trapped in here he'll figure out a way."

"Don't you bet on it."

"Sure he will," the redhead insisted. "If that's him and the war's over except for us, he'll find a way."

"Short war," the blonde said ironically.

"We never even made it out of training," the redhead lamented. "Anyway, I thought Lord Keerfax was busy in the south."

"When half the country revolts who do you think Queen Athryn is going to send to put down the revolt? We already beat General Nemort."

They went on with their quiet conversation, but I stopped listening, finding a solitary spot near a twisted oak where I could watch the fire but not be watched myself. What the redhead had said puzzled me, too. Drudaen had not come himself. Was his present work in the south so vital to him that he could not leave it, even when the Queen's northern rule was at stake?

Would he come here now?

I felt no sign of his imminence nor could I discern any movement of his southern presence. However, I knew such superficial signals could be misleading and so meditated on the fifth level, though my sight seemed richer in some way. I had a look around. The planes were full of turbulence, the death of Julassa Kyminax still registering on those unseen levels, the balance of power having shifted. Drudaen's shape was in flux, restlessly searching for some sign of me. Apparently he could not discern much beneath the remnants of witch shadow, however, and even less in Arthen.

I passed the night in the clearing, stirring when time came for the ritual bath and the extinguishing of the lamp.

By morning the shadow had vanished from the sky but the storm covered most of the forest and southern plain. Rain fell in sheets and lightning flashed, beginning as I mounted onto Nixva's back to ride suuren, gathering in force as I neared Illyn.

When we reached the lake shore, I felt heavy dread. The lake women were waiting under the duraelaryn, neither cutting cloth nor embroidering the magical fabric. They were watching me from the lawn near the shore, their horses behind them, jeweled bridles trailing in the golden grass.

Gone was the simple clothing they had always worn. That morning each was dressed grandly in a gown of shimmering color, trimmed with precious stones and embroidered with costly threads, and each was cloaked in a supple, light cloak like the one they had been weaving for Yron. They wore the same three-cornered hats I remembered from the morning I first glimpsed them in Hyvurgren Field. They were lovely, monumental images: Vissyn blond and shining, her face young and full of beauty, Vella ample, florid of face and thick of body; and Commyna, dark and tall, face all angles and planes. She greeted me with stern words. "Ride no farther. Do you come as friend or enemy?"

I reined Nixva in, dismounting. From their impassive faces I read nothing. "I come as a friend. How can you ask?"

"Do you have something to tell us?" Vella asked, her musical voice become stern.

I took a deep breath. My heart sank. "Yes, ma'am. But I see you already know."

"Tell us anyway," Commyna said.

"I've broken my oath to you. I've used magic."

I thought this would be enough, but Vissyn asked, calmly, "Where did you do this?"

"One day's ride from here, as horses travel. On the plain before Fort Gnemorra. I fought with Julassa Kyminax, the Witch of Karns."

Commyna's voice cut me like steel. "In doing this, did you dream you could deceive us?"

"No, ma'am."

"What was your intent in breaking your oath?"

My mind was too heavy to make excuses; I wished they would mete out punishment and have done with it, since punishment was clearly coming. But they waited for my answer. "I saw no other choice."

"Please explain further," Commyna said.

I continued wearily. "I think you know my reasons. Yron has not come, nor is there any sign of him. I am the only power of this world that I know who is willing to fight Drudaen."

"Are you willing?"

"Yes. I think I've shown that."

Commyna nodded, turning away from me. Almost as an afterthought, Vella—eyeing her elder sister—asked, "What was the result of your work yesterday? Did you win your fight?"

"Yes, ma'am."

"The Karns Witch has returned south?"

Could she not know? It was impossible to guess from her expression. I answered, "No, Lady Vella, she'll never return south again."

"So you killed her."

I nodded, feeling only sorrow when I had expected triumph. "I had no other choice."

"Since then, what have you done? Did you sleep last night?"

"No. I maintained vigilance from the fifth level."

"Why?"

Now I knew she was forcing answers for reasons of her own. "I had to know if Drudaen would ride north once he knew she was dead."

"If he were to ride north, would you face him?"

After a moment's thought I nodded. I could not find words. Vella asked, "Aren't you afraid of him?"

"Yes. But what choice do I have?"

Vissyn said, ironically, "We've told you before, a magician is coming."

"But where is he? Kirith Kirin needs him now."

Silence fell. I stood in the field with Nixva's reins trailing in my hand. The lake women were motionless, but for the wind that played their skirts along the grass.

Commyna turned to me again, walking toward me a few steps, her shadow looming long. "Your reasons may have some bearing on your punishment."

"Yes ma'am." Till that moment I had tried to act the part of an adult, but at the sight of her stern face childish grief welled up. "I know I did wrong, Commyna. But I would probably do the same thing again. Kirith Kirin had a great need. I answered it, and that seems a good thing to me. I don't mean to sound defiant, I'm only telling you the truth."

"The truth is what we want." For a moment I thought she had softened. She glanced toward her sisters, though, and said to me, "You may leave now. Your training is ended. Say farewell to Illyn Water, Jessex."

I knew this was just, but it seemed hard. Knowing her will could not be swayed I said nothing, and presently she continued. "Return to your Camp. Kirith Kirin is riding to meet you, along with others you know. Tell him and the twice-named that we'll meet them and you in Jiiviisn Field tomorrow at noon. Be prepared to depart Arthen with us then, Jessex."

"Where will you take me?"

She frowned very deeply. "I've said all I'll say. Bring the Jhinuuserret to Jiiviisn Field and you'll learn the answer. They know the place, it has a long history."

The Sisters stood as before, waiting. I mounted Nixva and rode off the way I had come.

By the edge of the meadow Nixva stopped of his own accord, as if he knew this would be the last time he saw this place.

In the clear light of day on the shore of Illyn Water it was hard to remember any shadow, or any battle on the plain, or indeed even to remember the scene that had just taken place. At Illyn no shadow of unmaking has ever fallen, and nothing but peace is welcome there, until the universe is broken. The clear lake sparkled, the sun shown, the leaves breathed music. The lake women, moving slowly, gracefully, spread out the magic cloth by the far shore, beginning the ritual of preparing tea, Vella filling the porcelain oet with water.

Before this sight made me feel young and fresh, destined for adventures. That last morning, when the faultless sky poured its benevolence down, I was a boy no longer.

2

Over Nevyssan light rain was falling and heavy clouds rode a steady wind toward the sea. We headed home without any hurry even in the rain and chill, Nixva not as frisky as usual when we were returning from the lake, and my spirit full of trouble.

In Camp I found no sign of Kirith Kirin nor was there any word he was riding here. But if the lake women said a thing was true, it was. In the glade of trees behind the shrine I held Axfel's bony head in my lap and pieced together the sequence. Gnemorra had fallen in the night. The twice-named had ridden south immediately to take the news to Kirith Kirin. Royal horses could make the ride in a short time. If the news reached Kirith Kirin a few hours after, which was possible, he would have left at once. Headed for Nevyssan with all due speed.

He was coming for me. There could be no doubt of that.

When I closed my eyes I could feel his distant presence, could feel the scar on the land where the Witch of Karns had died, could feel the vigilance of Drudaen in the south.

I lingered, watching branches crisscrossing overhead, hearing cries of the royal falcons from the Birdmaster's tent, the distant murmur of human voices. After a while I took Axfel's face in my hands and asked him, "Will you come with me to the mountains? Do you think you could learn to live there?"

The dog's eyes were bright and eager, ample tongue draped out one side of his mouth, his big frame burning. I felt comfort from him, as if he knew I was sad. He would follow me anywhere I asked even if the journey killed him. But I would spare him that, I would leave him for Uncle Sivisal.

I hurried to the shrine tent, gathering my belongings on the narrow cot, my tunics, knife, arrows, and quill laid out on the piece of buckskin that would serve as my traveling roll. Last of all I retrieved the necklace from its hiding place in the lid of the oil jar, hiding it in my sash.

How odd that so few minutes should be consumed in the packing away of my present life. I had only to tie up the buckskin and I was ready to go. Putting this out of my mind, I walked to the clerks tent to see if there were work to do, to keep me busy till Kirith Kirin and the others arrived.

3

He reached camp after the Evening Ceremony, bringing with him Imral, Mordwen, Karsten and Pelathayn, with the news that the Witch of Karns had fallen and Fort Gnemorra was taken, along with the garrison and Nemort. The news spread like wildfire through the tent city and into the merchants quarter, along with speculation as to why all the twice-named had returned and why they had come without other escort. A messenger from Kirith Kirin found me in the shrine tent. He bowed his head, which no one had ever done before in seeking me out. "Pardon me, son of Kinth, but Kirith Kirin asks that you come to his tent."

I laid down the polishing cloth and settled the reyn lamp back into its case. The lamps were clean. I asked, "Do you have a torch? May I follow you?"

The messenger led me. I could have found the path to the tent myself, but it was pleasant to have company.

That Kirith Kirin was in Camp I had known without being told, and that he would send for me quickly I had guessed. Outside his tent I neatened my hair and closed my eyes. It seemed a good moment to pray, though I asked for nothing except general benevolence. What fate I had was out of my hands.

The messenger presented me and I entered. They were all there, seated on cushions in the tent's outer chamber. They watched as if I were a stranger.

Kirith Kirin signaled the messenger to leave. Footsteps faded outside, while the Jhinuuserret looked at each other. At last I said, "Gnemorra has fallen and Julassa Kyminax is dead. Please speak to me. I'm frightened, too." Karsten made a sound like a cat mother calling her young, leaping from her cushion to gather me close. I hugged her body tight, glad of her warmth, glad of her voice in my ear. She wore a bandage on one hand. "Then I wasn't wrong. It was you."

The others were watching, and I gave the answer to them all. "Yes, it was me. Yes, Kirith Kirin, it was me."

He was watching me as if his heart were breaking. He could not speak, but gestured for me to come close, and when I did he embraced me almost as wildly as Karsten. When he could speak again he lifted his glass, as did the others. "You've finally come, after all this waiting." His eyes were blurred with tears, and his voice full of pent-up joy, so much one thought he would burst from the release. "The Witch has come to the Wood."

"Hail," murmured Imral, and Mordwen said, "Hail, Thanaarc." Pelathayn and Karsten tilted glasses toward me.

"What is Thanaarc?" I asked.

"A title in my Court," Kirith Kirin said. "Last held by Kentha Nurysem. It means 'Witch of the Wood'."

"We have been waiting for you," Imral said calmly. "Only Kirith Kirin suspected you were already here."

They thought I was speechless with joy or some other such foolishness. I said, "I broke a promise when I faced Julassa yesterday. I'm to be sent away."

"What?" Kirith Kirin asked. "Who told you that?"

"The lake women," I answered. "At Illyn Water."

"Illyn!" Karsten paled at the name, leaning close to Imral, who put his arm around her.

"Broke an oath?" Mordwen said. "You? To whom?"

"To the Diamysaar. I've traveled to Illyn shore to learn from them nearly every day since I first came to the Woodland." I was staring into my cup, avoiding eyes. "I was to serve the magician Yron when he comes to Arthen, the lake women were teaching me. I'd sworn to them I wouldn't use what they taught me out of their presence, but yesterday when they told me Julassa Kyminax was riding I couldn't bear the thought of what would follow. So I disobeyed them."

"The Diamysaar." Mordwen was completely dumfounded.

"Of course. Who else could teach the magic?" Turning to Kirith Kirin. "You knew about this, didn't you?"

"By accident," Kirith Kirin said. "Or else by their contrivance. I saw Jessex with them on Vithilonyi."

"In Hyvurgren Field," Imral said, his expression sobering. "I should have guessed. That was why you summoned the boy to Sister Mountain."

"But I don't understand," Karsten said, "Jessex failed that test."

"Because the Sisters interceded," I answered. "The stone circle is their device. They spoke to the stones and the stones did not change when I crossed the circle."

"Tell me about this oath again," Kirith Kirin said, and I did. Finishing with the exact words as I remembered them. "I was told to meet them in Jiiviisn Field. I was told to bring all the Jhinuuserret with me. The Sisters will meet us at noon to take me away."

No one said a word. They looked at each other in awe and fear.

"You're sure that's what they said?" Kirith Kirin asked.

"Yes. Commyna made her instructions very plain."

"Commyna," Imral said, looking suddenly very far away. "I haven't heard that name in a long time. Can you name the other Sisters, Jessex?"

"Vella and Vissyn."

"If any more proof were needed, there you have it," Karsten said.

When I looked puzzled, Kirith Kirin explained to me quietly, "The names of the Diamysaar are known only to us. Only the Sisters bestow the Second Name. Only those who know the names of the Sisters have received the name from God." He and Karsten were watching each other.

In the wake of so much information, only Pelathayn maintained a practical frame of mind. "Jiiviisn is a half-days ride from the border of Nevyssan," he said, "even on royal horses. We had better get to sleep if we're to meet them on time."

"Yes," Kirith Kirin whispered. "We'll have some preparations to make here if we're to ride out tomorrow."

He sounded so completely bewildered. But he finished the business at hand patiently, sending for a clerk to take down letters, assigning the arrangements for our trip to Karsten, directing Pelathayn to pick the fastest road to Jiiviisn. Once during these dispositions I started to rise and leave him to his work, but he turned to me quickly, laying hold of my arm and saying softly, "Please stay." So I sat down again.

He went on with his business, dictating orders to go out tomorrow by courier to the patrols along Arthen's southern border, sending other orders to Ren Vael who was in charge of the soldiers arranged along Angoroe, and still others to Lady Unril, who had been left with command of the Gnemorra garrison. I lay quietly sharing his cushion, glad to be so close.

The letters were signed and sealed, Imral checking that the clerk had written correctly, the packets assigned to riders who could be trusted. Imral sent the clerk away, and finally only he and Karsten remained, Mordwen having long since returned to his own tent, Pelathayn gone to the tent of his current mistress. Imral ordered brandy brought in and dimmed the lamps till shadows fell softly and outlines blurred. He poured the glimmering liquid into glasses. "Good Drii brandy from my own stock. You'll never have better."

Karsten raised her glass. "I drink to the Witch of the Wood."

Imral raised his glass as well. "Whatever tomorrow brings, you're Thanaarc tonight."

Kirith Kirin solemnly touched his glass to mine. When he had sipped, he said, "We would have asked for none better."

"Nor could we have had a better, from what I saw at Gnemorra," Karsten said.

"Were you close by?"

Her laugh was deep and vibrant. "Imral and I were there together, you nearly trampled us when you followed the witch into the encampment. Not that I'm complaining."

Even Kirith Kirin found her irony funny. "Karsten isn't one to look a gift magician in the mouth."

"Neither am I," Imral said, "especially not then."

"Were you surprised to beat her?" Kirith Kirin asked.

I met his eyes for an instant and could not watch him any longer. "I don't know if I was. I don't really know what I felt. If I had known—"

"Go on," he said softly.

I looked at him. "I knew I was breaking my oath when I rode out of Arthen. But I didn't know then how it would feel for the Sisters to send me away."

"Would you do it again?" Imral asked.

I studied the pool of amber in my hand. "Yes. I told them so." I looked him in the eye. "I knew the oath was an oath, Prince Imral, I knew I would be punished. But I saw no other choice. You're my friends. You're more than my friends. I couldn't leave you to face Julassa Kyminax with no one to help you."

The Venladrii looked as though this answer amused him, a smile of whimsy on his face. "That's from Kentha's prophecy," he said. "In the last hour, with the witch riding, when it is the Sisters' word against the choice."

"I remember," Karsten said, "word for word."

"I have what she said by heart, too," Imral said, sadly. "I've thought about it often enough. Looking for some sign of your coming, Jessex—your true coming, I mean, your riding across the plain on wind and storm, as she told us. I always wondered why Kentha mentioned the Sisters or spoke of this as a choice. 'Against the advice of every mouth.' Now I know."

"You'd never know I'd be here such a short time."

Kirith Kirin set down his glass, nearly spilling what was left in it. "Don't give up yet. Maybe they have something else in mind." He was quiet, he said nothing else, so I had no idea what he meant. He buried his head against me as Axfel did when he wanted me to know he loved me. I cradled him like that until the worst of the moment passed.

When I looked up again, Karsten was in the doorway, Imral helping fasten the cloak across her shoulders. She signaled me to be silent, and Imral looked away. They were both leaving, having dimmed the lamps further. Outside, Imral gave the bodyguard orders not to allow anyone to disturb Kirith Kirin, not even the householders.

I looked down at the Prince in wonder. He was still lost in his own sadness, not yet realizing the gift his friends had given us. I bent to kiss his brow and he sighed, pulling me close with the arm that encircled me.

4

I woke up before dawn. We had lain all night on the cushions, one of Kirith Kirin's cloaks spread over us both. At first I didn't know where I was until I felt the weight of his arm across me. His warm breath collected at the base of my neck.

In sleep, his face was childlike, the lips full to flowering, the heavy lashes curved outward extravagantly, the brow smooth. Before I rose from our warm nest I kissed him on the lips. He stirred but did not emerge from sleep. I moved carefully from under his arm and the cloak, my hands on his smooth strong flesh, the hairs of his arm like fine black silk.

It was a wonder to have lain so close to him, to have touched him. I kissed him again before I left, lightly, the merest brush of lips on his black hair. Creeping out of the dark tent, I passed the guard and the sentries who saw me and waved me on. In main Camp the first cook-fires were burning. I hurried to the shrine tent where the kaa was throwing light against the scrub pine and twisted faris. Despite the day that was coming, I was happy.

5

We set out for Jiiviisn Field as soon as Morning Ceremony was over. Riding hard over the rough trails out of Nevyssan, we reached the north road before the sun was clear of the horizon.

Jiiviisn, like Hyvurgren where I first saw the Diamysaar, is one of the Elder Fields, a place where a shrine has been maintained since the first days. This was, as I gathered from snatches of conversation on the ride, one of the few places where the Sisters were ever seen. It was in Jiiviisn Field that the Nivra Kiril of Curaeth became Kiril Karsten, when the Sisters brought her the name from God. She told me this when we stopped to rest our horses, her eyes clouded with the memory. "I never dreamed I would dread a meeting with them."

"I'd as soon not see them at all in these circumstances." Mordwen was watching me. "For the life of me I don't see what else you could have done."

I was silent. We were ready to ride again. The morning passed gloomily, and we reached the field when the sun was high. One cannot say enough about the beauty of the country thereabouts, the wild green rolling hills, the shaggy duraelaryn lifting massive canopies to the clouds, the drifts of poppies and visnomen, murve and infith, tangled vines and waving grasses. I thought I was immune to landscapes at the time, but that ride through hill, vale, and field took my heart.

The field itself was roughly circular, laid out like Hyvurgren but far different in character. Jiiviisn in autumn is a fairyland of color, leaves painted in bronzes, browns, golds, sunburst yellows and blood reds, late-blooming flowers carpeting the field on which trees and undergrowth do not encroach, an azure-colored spring flowing through its center, passing beneath the shrine made of rough hewn stone that dominates the place. The shrine is flanked by bridges broad enough for horses and wagons to pass across, remnant of days when the Elder Shrines were meeting places for the early Jisraegen, who held marriage feasts in them, or burned their dead, or celebrated Vithilonyi.

We waited for the Sisters near the shrine. Kirith Kirin stood close to me. Sometimes he closed his eyes as if he were praying. He did not seem sad so much as agitated, and I wondered whether it mattered to him, really, that I was leaving.

Music from the forest. "They're nearby. Do you hear?"

The Diamysaar rode out of the trees, singing, their voices clearer than any bird's, and in spite of everything I was proud these high creatures had ever troubled with me. Commyna led the procession, black horse carrying her grandly, her hair crowned with gems, her wrists and fingers adorned with gold and silver, the skirts of her violet gown sweeping the grass. A slender silver sword was buckled round her waist. I had never seen her armed before, and never had reason to suspect she needed be. Vissyn and Vella followed slightly behind, Vissyn wearing brown buckskins, a close-fitting tunic and trousers, while Vella wore a full, high-waisted gown of gray, many strands of pearls weighted on her bosom. They rode like queens. Vissyn was leading a fourth horse, roan colored, already saddled and bridled, a bundle wrapped in black cloth tied to its back.

This horse was for me, I thought. It had not occurred to me I would be parted from Nixva.

The Sisters saw us on the bridge but did not hurry. They stopped their horses in the grass and dismounted without haste. Vella, who was wearing a sunhat, had a little trouble keeping it on her head but she soon set it right, also calming the wind that had disturbed it. She took the lead in approaching us, Vissyn pausing to untie the bundle from the fourth horse.

When the Sisters were near, the twice-named knelt, bowing their heads. Seeing this, I knelt also, and bowed my head as they did.

"Get up, get up," Vella called. "Jessex, why are you kneeling, when you never did before?"

"A little courtesy is charming," Vissyn said. "Kirith Kirin! How good to see you."

"I ought to be glad to see you too," Kirith Kirin answered, eyeing her with his jaw clenched. "But I don't like your errand today."

"We're sorry for that," Vella said, turning to help Commyna with her cloak. "But the boy took his lot in his own hands, we didn't choose for him."

"We do what we do," Commyna said, eyeing me suspiciously. "What, has the child been complaining to you? Didn't he tell you what he did?"

"I told them I broke my oath to you," I said.

Vissyn spied my pack on Nixva's back. "I see you've brought your belongings. There was no reason to. You may leave the bundle where it is."

"Come, son of Kinth," Commyna called.

She had tethered the riderless horse to the shrine and was ascending stone steps to the top. She waited for me to join her, and when I was at her side she lay her hand on my shoulder. Turning to those below, watching from the windswept field, she unsheathed the slender sword she wore. "Kneel here, Jessex."

She had not even given me time to say good bye.

A mad thought possessed me, to say Words and escape, for it was clear now what would happen. But she was Commyna, Sister to YY, and I had always obeyed her. Slowly I knelt and bent my head. I saw the shadow of the sword as she raised it.

Wind stirred over Jiiviisn. I heard commotion on the ground. "Prepare to be reborn," she said, "as some humans are."

The sword fell. If it touched me at all, I never felt it.

Vella lifted the bound parcel to Commyna. "Blessed be YY-who-watches."

"Blessed be," Commyna said. "Stand, Yron."

When I did not stir she took my arm and lifted me. She was smiling, her face bright. She turned to those below. Kirith Kirin was watching in rapture. "So Kentha's words are fulfilled, the stories have an ending and a beginning. The Witch has come to the Wood as she foretold. The mortal has died in order that a life in magic shall come to him. He is to be called Yron, by those who know him, and YY will judge him as his last judge."

I was too stunned for thinking, I could only stare at them dumfounded. I felt as if I really had stepped out of the grave. Kirith Kirin's voice was full of warmth. "So you see, you're not leaving us, Yron. Not for a long, long time."

I couldn't find any words. Commyna embraced me, laughing at my confusion. Vella said, "No, he isn't going anywhere. He has a lot of work to do. So do you all. Now you have the help YY can give you. A fourth level adept that we trained ourselves. See you take care of him. It's a certainty that since God sent him, he'll be needed."

Commyna knelt to me, saying more softly, "You're much too quiet, boy. What happened to that tireless tongue of yours?"

"I'm surprised, Commyna. This isn't what I expected. Can't they call me Jessex any more?"

She laughed heartily. "You don't understand, do you? Well you will, in time. And your friends can call you Jessex, if they wish; only those here will know your true name."

"She called me a fourth level adept," I said.

"So you are. Your combat with Julassa Kyminax was the test. The gemwork you performed was from the fourth circle, and Julassa was undefended there. She hadn't the skill to counter you. You saw through to the fourth plane in the fight, and you filled it and that's how you won."

"I wondered. It didn't feel like anything I had ever done before."

She gave me a serious look. "I've never praised you Jessex, but now I'm not your teacher any more. You have a skill that is beyond rare. Kentha was with us many years before she absorbed as much. But against Drudaen you'll need more than talent. He's a fourth level power too, and he has lifetimes of cunning you don't have. Don't fight him at Cunevadrim; that's his stronghold and the stronghold of his family, a place where no one goes as a willing guest. Don't think you've learned everything, or even a tenth part of everything. Magic is always unfolding. At the fourth level the adept can no longer be trained but must make a path. You have the cloak we made, which has in it all we know. There are lore books at Inniscaudra and others in Cunuduerum. Find them and study them. You'll need magic to find them and magic to use them, for Inniscaudra we Sisters built, though we're forbidden to go there, and Cunuduerum is a place of many enchantments dating from the time of the Praeven. But you'll need all the knowledge you can gather in days to come."

A wind was beginning to blow, and from below Vissyn called, "I believe it will be time to go shortly, Commyna."

"Yes, I think you're right," she answered. "Give me another moment." She turned to me again, as Vissyn and Vella returned to their earnest discussion with the others. "The traveling we need to do can only be managed at certain times. I need to hurry to tell you the rest. The cloak we made is yours. Wear it even though you haven't reached your day of adulthood; you'll need it. You never were a child while we knew you, anyway. The cloak should serve you well, especially outside Arthen where you don't have the virtue of the Elder Shrines and Elder Trees to protect you. Remember that not everything has yet been revealed. There is another thing I want to tell you, though you won't understand why." Here she flushed slightly, embracing me with unaccustomed tenderness. "Long ago we Sisters were exiled from Arthen, though we love it dearly. The wrong done was mine. The lore is known to the twice-named and some others. Learn it. You'll understand after a while." She released me and we watched each other.

I said, "I'll never forget you. I hope I live to see you again."

She gave me the wry look with which I had grown familiar. "Maybe you will."

She set the cloak parcel in my arms. We descended from the shrine and she greeted the others while I said good-bye to Vella and Vissyn. Vella touched the top of my head, her hand weighed down with rings. "Commyna has been whispering in your ear a good while. I hope she remembered everything she was supposed to tell you."

"She told me a lot. If I can make sense of it all."

"We'll miss you, boy. You be as careful as you can."

Vissyn leaned against me, thumping my back with her fist. "You won't be able to be very careful, if I know you. We will miss you, Jessex. But it was high time we were rid of you. I don't know how much longer we could've gone on pretending we were training you to be the magician's apprentice."

The wind grew stronger, clouds darkening. Vissyn said to Commyna, "We should go now, Sister. We've many places to visit before we leave Aeryn."

Commyna nodded. "What do you say, Imral Ynuuvil, do you think we should tell your father first?"

The Venladrii colored with pleasure. "He would be honored to receive you."

"I think that's a lovely idea," Vella said, mounting her horse. "I haven't seen Drii in just thousands of years."

"Good bye," Vissyn called, and Commyna and Vella echoed the words. Wind was blowing furiously and the sun had nearly vanished. The Sisters drew their cloaks around them and rode silently toward Wood's End, till a shadow engulfed them and we could see nothing else.

When they were gone I turned to Kirith Kirin, who stood some distance away and yet still watched me. I thought, I don't know what it will be like to be free.

No one spoke. The wind lifted my coat, sang in the treetops, swept the grass. I could feel a presence, the shadow of a hand in the southern sky. In the south clouds were darkening.

"A storm is coming," I said to the others, "sent from the south. If you'll permit me, we'll ride back to Nevyssan by a way I know that will enable us to beat the bad weather."

"I have a feeling I'm going to like this," Pelathayn said, grinning. "You know Kirith Kirin, this may be just the thing."

"Like in the old days," Mordwen said, and Kiril Karsten winked at me.

Kirith Kirin beckoned, and I ran to him gladly. He took the bundle from me, tying it to Nixva himself. Our ride home was on a howling wind, riding in the ithikan unseen by any eye. We were in Camp before the first drop of rain fell on us, after moving at impossible speed. I had never felt so alive. This was the beginning of my true art.

CHAPTER TWELVE
THANAARC

1

The storm was violent, lasting through the night and into the next day. Its main fury broke to the south, but enough strength remained to give Nevyssan and thereabouts a thorough drenching. The crash of lightning kept the horses skittish and made deadman's watch a misery for the sentries.

I was awake through it, having forsaken the comfort of my cot for a night's wandering through Camp and the surrounding hills. I had preparations to make, and the hours till morning were short.

A storm that is the product of magic is not like other storms; it follows the same laws but its engine is independent of natural circumstance. There is a difference the trained ear can hear. I built a fire and filled my mind with the burning. The wind mounted in fury, bending the faris and stripping oak leaves from their branches, lashing the earth with rain. The drops stung my face as I sat before my fire, murmuring and gazing into the flames that continued to burn by virtue of my protection.

I could hear the Wizard singing, his Words rumbling in my bones, his anger evident. The image of the storm changed from fireworks to darkness, and I could feel his power reaching out, full of malice. Once, for a moment, I sensed another presence near him, someone I knew, alone, frightened, full of pain.

I meditated at the fourth level and felt him like scorching heat. This plane had been his playground for too long, he had needed no defenses here since Kentha died, and I could see him plainly. He was vast in the south like a dark shadow, tall, with eyes like wheels of fire, his face handsome and terrible, his mouth cruel, these features shimmering beyond the veils of his power. Words were pouring out from him, a sound like the baying of many wolves and the rending of flesh. Someone was crying in pain, someone I knew, and I understood that he had vented his anger on his prisoner.

So, without preparation, I began my own torrent of anger and song, my image rising up on fourth circle like a piercing light. From this distance, with no High Place on which to stand, I could do him

no real harm. But my singing sent a jolt through him, coming as it
did from the level on which he had moved unopposed till that
moment. I could feel his anger and astonishment before he diverted
wind and rain, raising veils so I could no longer read his features
plainly. Soon he was a cloud in the south, same as his presence on
fifth level, his purpose hidden from me. Try as I might I could not
pierce his veil.

I contented myself with other practices, building my own defenses, augmenting them with the magic inherent in Arthen, a long
and devious application that had the effect of amplifying my voice
and movement through the Woodland, so that no matter where I
was, I would seem to be in all places at the same time. This was
slow work, but when I stopped, near daybreak, I had lain the foundations of a matrix that would alert me to any change in Drudaen
even if I were not kei. I could have done much more if I had the
Sisters' trick of looping a string of time out of the present moment,
but this was an application of higher circles, and Drudaen could not
manage it either. I could slow time for myself, though, and I did.

Emerging from the long night's meditation, I could feel Drudaen
in the south like a brooding cloud, and the storm he maintained was
rumbling in my ears. I withdrew my protection from the fire and
watched the rain fall hissing onto glowing embers. Such was the
rain's force that an instant later the fire vanished. Drawing my sleeved
coat closer, I hurried back to the shrine tent to prepare for Morning
Ceremony.

2

I found guards posted at the shrine, one of whom halted me when
I tried to walk through the clearing. The soldier recognized me and
drew back in surprise. "You're the son of Kinth, the kyyvi. I thought
you were in the tent."

"That's where I'm going."

She looked extremely uncomfortable. "I have orders to let no
one pass. But I don't think the Prince meant me to keep you out."

I laughed softly, at her innocence in thinking she could. "There'll
be no Morning Ceremony if you do. May I?"

After a moment's consideration she stepped aside to let me
pass, giving out the birdlike call that let the other sentries know I
was coming.

I checked the lamp wick out of habit, though it had only a short while left to burn. Axfel was sleeping in the shadow beside the bronze altar, and since the rain was still falling I didn't have the heart to disturb him. I had caught him using this refuge before; YY-Mother never seemed to mind. I paused to scratch his fur where it tufted between the ears, murmuring his name.

Someone was in my room. The sound of breathing. At the flap opening I paused, watching Kirith Kirin, his large frame dwarfing the cot, hair tangled about his head, tunic twisted half off his shoulders. I could see him clearly, and his innocence, his look of utter rest, closed round my heart like a hand. I sat beside him on the tent floor. At first I was afraid to touch him and tried to convince myself it would be impolite to waken him. But I could feel dawn coming in my bones. I traced a curl on his forehead, saying his name.

He opened his eyes at once, seeing me and fighting his way upward from sleep. I gathered my bath coat and oil while he watched, blinking. "Where have you been?"

"Working nearby."

"Don't you need to sleep?"

"Not always. What are you doing here?"

"I wanted to look in on you. Tired as I was, I couldn't rest. When I saw you weren't here I decided to wait."

"It's close to dawn," I knelt to get a clean tunic from the chest, "I don't have much time."

"It's still raining outside?"

"Oh yes. We'll have rain through most of the day I expect. Our friend to the south is not happy."

He sat up on the cot, running a hand through his hair. "This will be your last morning as kyyvi," he announced while I was folding the felva. "Savor it, if you've enjoyed your time here."

This news stopped me cold, and I sat back on my heels, looking round the tent. "I suppose I should have thought of it."

"A magician can't serve in the shrine. We'll select a new temple servant today. As for you, you'll have duties of your own, my dear."

"This will take some getting used to."

He stood close to me as he adjusted his tunic, watching me with affection and amusement. "Yes, it will indeed."

"How soon will the news go out?" I asked.

"Today." He was smiling with mischief, though I thought nothing of it at the time. "This is part of the custom. You're in my court, now." He was studying my face, seeing more in it than I wished. "You're afraid."

"Yes, I think I am. I'm more afraid of the Nivri and the Finru than I am of Drudaen."

"You've charmed half of them already. You don't need to worry."

He sent me off to the ritual bath with those words in my ears. The last instruction was that I should not ride suuren this morning, but wait behind the shrine for his instructions. If he thought the moment right, he would speak to those who assembled for Morning Ceremony. I was running behind, of course, having lingered too long to talk to him, and so I didn't wonder enough about what he had in mind. One can't think of what is to come and do justice to the bath ritual. I finished and returned to the tent as folks were gathering, with barely enough time to spread the lamp-cloth in the workroom.

That morning's was a good crowd, with many of the Nivri and Finru houses in attendance, and soldiers from the barracks tents and merchants who had been hardy enough to follow us to Nevyssan. But Velunen sometimes draws a good crowd anyway; what made that morning notable was the intensity with which they watched me, as if I had suddenly grown horns on my head. Only when the sun struck fire in the muuren stone and I extinguished the lamp did I understand.

Word of Gnemorrra had reached Camp, even though the sentry with whom I had spoken was ignorant of it. They were no longer watching the son of Kinth, a farm boy dragged into Arthen at the behest of an oracular dream. They were watching the Witch of the Wood who had killed the Witch of Karns.

I sang Velunen with that thought in mind, holding my head high, making certain I showed no fear. I believe I sang well, though I'd rather have given the song itself more attention since that was my last morning to sing it for the shrine. I lifted the warm lamp from its cradle and carried it to the workroom without a backward glance.

I could hear the hubbub in the before-shrine even from there, the word "Gnemorra" from every side, along with "pirunuu," "Karns," and "Kyminax." Accompanied by waves of anxiety.

Humans fear magicians. The lake women had warned me in more ways than one; and anyway it's to be expected. My task was to claim my place among these people. As I was thinking this, fingering the tasseled edge of the lamp-cloth, silence fell in the tent.

I straightened, feeling the rush of anticipation, understanding that into this pool of quiet would drop Kirith Kirin's voice. Wiping my hands clean of lamp oil, I hurried to the tent opening, paused there, and saw his shadow falling against the sheer hanging behind the altar. The mouth of the shrine tent had been opened wide, so that those who were in the clearing could see; the chamber flooded with rose wash from the east, the sun rising beyond violently colored clouds. One could hear the rain beating down on the leaves and in the clearing, so quiet were those assembled once it was clear Kirith Kirin would speak.

"People of Aeryn and soldiers of the Woodland Guard, I ask that you listen a while." His voice had a way of filling any space, and cut through the rain as if it were not there. Not a soul stirred. "As many of you have learned, Fort Gnemorra has fallen to us, General Nemort is our prisoner, and Julassa Kyminax has perished. These urgent events were the reason for my return to Camp. Other events have prevented my addressing you directly until now. You will soon learn of all these things.

"Those among you who are knowledgeable about the history and traditions of our country understand that we are at the beginning of a long conflict that has been prophesied for many years. Certain signs, known to the Evaenym and others, have been awaited as proof that the years are fulfilled and the time of disorder is on us. One of these signs was the coming of a wizard to Arthen, whose form would not be that of other wizards. As those of you who have heard the story of the battle for Gnemorra will understand, the magician has come, and indeed is the same the son of Kinth who has walked among us for many months."

The effect of this was electrifying: one could hear the collective intake of breath. I hurried quickly to my room, found the bundle in which the Diamysaar Cloak was still tied, quickly cutting the knots with my knife.

The cloak fell out like shimmering starlight, a cool silkiness to my hands, shot through with color like bolts of lightning, smelling of the wind over Illyn and the fragrant tea brewed of sweet lake water. The scent hit me, rich and sudden, and stung my eyes since suddenly the lake seemed so far away, and I figured I would never go back. But another breath and that was gone. I shook out the cloak's fullness, found the clasp.

Kirith Kirin called me by name, his voice booming.

I could feel the movement of power all around, a presence like nothing I had ever felt at Illyn Water nor on any of the lower circles of magic. The Prince of Aeryn is a magic thing in and of himself, and I could feel the protection of YY that guarded him now that I was able to use my full senses in the real world. I fastened the Diamysaar Cloak over my shoulders, noting, when I did, a slip of paper that fell onto the floor. I picked it up, not pausing to read it. The cloak hung round me like the singing of many voices. Wearing it, I felt the shadow of Commyna falling on me from behind. I could hear her voice plainly, saying, "Stand up straight boy, and look lively. Did we teach you all this time to have you shame us before the simpletons of Aeryn?" I stood up straight. With that voice in my ear I returned to the shrine.

The gentry and soldiers had drawn back from the altar, and at the sight of the Sister-Cloak they gasped. I gave them something to talk about myself. I kindled a light from the cloak, colors that shot out like fire, as well as a wind that swept down cold and white from the highest clouds. At Kirith Kirin's feet I knelt.

He said, in the same deep-timbered tones, "Before all gathered here and all the worlds beyond I do affirm by my life and honor as Kirith Kirin, Prince of Aeryn and Lord in Arthen, that you have been rightly and truly taught, you who were once known as the son of Kinth, who will be called hereafter Lord Thanaarc of Arthen, Ruler of Lands and Peoples that will be named hereafter, Defender of the Law of Changes, Keeper of the Keys to Ellebren Tower over Inniscaudra."

He had warned me of none of this, nor had anyone else. The words rushed over me like thunder, as if his voice and a hundred other voices were uttering the words. I felt the weight settle over me. I heard the echo of far-off singing. Kirith Kirin drew me to my feet.

He sang a song I had never heard before, strange archaic forms of words, verses of great beauty powered by the strength of his voice, a part of Kimri not sung for ages, maybe. Heads were bowing throughout the clearing, and I bowed mine too.

Here in darkness
help is come
marked by the Eye in Heaven
light is breaking
in a time of war

shadow from horizon to horizon
bringing night
here in the darkness
help is come
light is breaking
in a time of war

When he was done, it was as if a light faded, and those who were in the shrine caught their breath. Kirith Kirin spoke again, more quietly. "Return to your stations, begin to disassemble Camp as you will be asked to do. By morning we'll march out of this country, and by nightfall you'll know where you're going. Tell what you've heard to others. Tell them this is only the beginning of news."

Signaling to the rest of us to follow, he strode through the crowd. I hesitated only until Kiril Karsten took me by the elbow. Outside the detachment of bodyguards met us, and we hurried from the shrine to Kirith Kirin's tent. I still clutched the note that had fallen from the cloak when I put it on. On the fine-grained paper were written characters for my eyes alone. "The name for the Cloak is Fimbrel," the note said. "When you wear it we are near you."

I folded the paper, swallowed it and dispersed the writing into myself. Drawing the fabric close round me, I felt the rain beat down. The voice in the south had not relented. Full morning broke grayly over Arthen.

3

As we hurried through the storm, not toward Kirith Kirin's tent but in a less familiar direction, through the confusion of Camp being struck, wagons loaded, miserable wretches scurrying about in the rain, I wondered why such urgency when no destination had been announced. Where our destination might be I could not guess, but it was plain from all these preparations Kirith Kirin had not been alone in his sleeplessness.

Breakfast had been ordered for us in Prince Imral's tent, and a guard was posted on the grounds in the interest of privacy. The chief clerk from the clerk's tent was awaiting Kirith Kirin with packets of letters and other items of business. Kirith Kirin glanced at the letters, selecting only two documents for unsealing. When he had done this he nodded leave to the chief clerk, who bowed and exited.

Karsten passed round jaka cups, and I sipped the aromatic brew, steam to caress my face. I found a space beside Pelathayn, who had finished a first cake and was reaching for a second. The hunter was more thoughtful than usual, and when he noted me watching, he said, "Now and then it's good to be reminded YY is still in the world."

"What do you mean?"

"This morning. What Kirith Kirin said in the shrine. Have you ever heard the King use his voice before?"

He had called Kirith Kirin the king, so naturally. "No, not like that."

"Well, let it be a lesson to you." Kirith Kirin dropped the letters on the cushion beside me, seating himself on it a moment later. "There's more than one kind of magic in the world."

"Did anyone bother to warn you this was going to happen, Jessex, or were these louts as ill-bred as usual?" Karsten took her place beside Mordwen and Imral, who were reading letters Kirith Kirin had opened.

"Kirith Kirin told me the news would go out today."

"Imral and I decided the announcement couldn't wait. We were awake half the night thinking it through." Kirith Kirin looked at me. "That's what I came to the shrine tent to tell you, but you weren't there."

"I was walking in the hills," I explained to the others.

"Making mischief, no doubt." Mordwen had wet his mustache with jaka and dried it on a napkin. "Do we have you to thank for this storm?"

"No. This comes from Drudaen."

A shadow passed into the chamber. Imral asked, in a somber tone, "Then he's on his way?"

"No. He hasn't moved. I've set my guard so I'll know when he does, unless he takes a lot of trouble to hide from me. Even then there would be some change I should detect."

But the shadow remained. Quiet settled over them. After a moment, Kirith Kirin said, as if repeating a phrase required by ceremony, "We are met in the name of YY, in council." He turned to me.

The others in the room answered, "In the name of YY, so be it."

Kirith Kirin said, "Welcome, Jessex. You're part of us and part of our councils. God is good." His glance took in every face in the room. "Well, friends. We've won a battle. We've broken a fortress and taken a General prisoner. We've gained a sorcerer and a new ally. At the moment we are in control of Aeryn from Arthen north to the mountains, provided we can bring the gentry in line. Our luck has turned, a little."

"About time too," Mordwen said, reaching for the last of the cakes.

"You've said we're to move." Pelathayn was rearranging himself more comfortably on his cushions. "Do you know where you want to take us?"

"Yes," said Kirith Kirin. "To Inniscaudra."

Only Imral was not surprised. Mordwen looked as if the gates of Hero's Home were opening in front of him. "Praise the Eye, I thought I'd never see the place again."

"Your sarcasm is well taken," Kirith Kirin said dryly. "I don't mind going to Inniscaudra now that there's a reason."

"Apparently I missed a lot last night, foolish me for sleeping," Karsten said. "Why Inniscaudra?"

Kirith Kirin lifted his fingers one by one. "Inniscaudra has gold, arms and space to train an army. She's three day's march from the narrowest part of Angoroe. There are chambers for proper council and halls for audience."

"Audience?" Pelathayn's bushy brows rose toward his scarred forehead.

"I can't settle the north country from a tent in Nevyssan."

"So you'll be King."

He paused a long moment. "No. I'll be Regent. At Inniscaudra we'll convene a Council of Nivri and Finru, as soon as it can be arranged and before winter sets in. By winter I want this to be an accomplished fact. By the time the Queen marches north with Drudaen, I want the whole Fenax at my back."

"But what if she marches before winter?" Mordwen asked, and Karsten started to second the question, but then looked at me.

"I understand," she said.

"She won't march because she can't," Kirith Kirin said. "We have our magician now. She can't rely on a quick victory, and she won't risk an army in the northern winter. She herself may not know this yet. But Drudaen doesn't have the field to himself any more, and he knows." His eyes were glittering as if with inward fire. "We have a breathing space, all unlooked for."

"There is, of course, the possibility that Drudaen will ride north alone," Imral said. "We shouldn't ignore that."

I stroked the rich drapings of the cloak. At Imral's words the shadow had returned, and with it silence. So for the sake of my friends I found my voice. "I don't think he'll come, not openly."

"Give reasons," Kirith Kirin said.

"He's engaged in a long work in the north Kellyxa, near the ruins of Montajhena. At Illyn we were keeping him under close watch. We couldn't learn his purpose, but his strength is divided between that place and his stronghold at Cunevadrim. Strong as he is, he won't divide his strength further by facing me in the Fenax, not when he has no reason for hurry and so many reasons to stay in the south."

"Why do you say he has no reason?" Imral asked.

In imitation of Kirith Kirin I lifted my hand, enumerating reasons on my fingertips. "His pride in his power is not shaken. He can beat me as easily in the spring as now, to his way of thinking. If he waits, there's the chance that I'll do something foolhardy, like ride south to face him in his stronghold. He holds my mother captive; he'll use her to entice me. He knows there's no High Place north of Arthen, nor is there time to build one, so I can't prepare the plains against his coming. He knows I'm young, whereas he has skills in magic gained through many battles and many lifetimes. In short, while I may have beaten Julassa Kyminax, she was the servant and he is the master. The Wizard will bide his time and move when he's ready."

"Queen Athryn can hardly spare him from the southern provinces at the moment," Karsten said. "From what we hear there's unrest everywhere, and the news of our revolt will raise hopes in many places."

"Suddenly my name is remembered as far south as Novris," Kirith Kirin said, with obvious irony. He shivered as if at a sudden chill, though I felt none. "I see nothing good ahead for those places. The Queen will be afraid, having already lost so much, that she'll lose more." He turned to me, pain on his face. "She'll need Drudaen more than ever."

"Or she'll have the chance to see it's time to be rid of him once and for all," Mordwen said. "You should consider that. She may be afraid of him herself, by now. He may be ready to move against her, too."

"You make it sound as if this whole rebellion has been part of his plan," I said, and, hearing my own words, fell silent.

The others were watching me. A feeling of oppression had come on me with the new thought. As if his laughter mixed in the rain. "You're beginning to understand," Kirith Kirin said. "Drudaen has become corrupt beyond even his father, and he has patience, and cunning, and time. Mordwen has a point, Athryn may be afraid of him herself, but I don't think she's finished with him. She's broken the Law that held the world together, she'd have no refuge anywhere without her crown. So she'll turn to Drudaen to preserve her kingdom, for a while longer, anyway." He took a deep breath. "The northern rebellion answered Drudaen's need. I think we all knew that, but couldn't stop it. If the rebellion hadn't come, he would have found some other way. Up until now, he could be like a spider, he could afford to wait. But now there's Jessex, and everything has changed."

4

For a time, though discussion continued, I was oblivious to words. Maybe I had never seen our predicament so clearly. Against such power, such cunning and patience, I felt small and insignificant. A boy, foolishly setting himself up against the present enemy. "Beyond even his father," Kirith Kirin had said.

It's not much in some cases for a son to surpass his father. But when the father was Falamar Inuygen, who brought war and ruin to the Evaenym and ended an age of peace, then the son who exceeds him is a force indeed. This was he whose voice I heard in wind and rain. This was he who would haunt me, waking and sleeping. Suddenly a magic cloak did not seem so rich a gift and all my training seemed paltry. How could I dream of taking the field against a wizard whose father was one of the first to waken long ago in the morning of humankind?

From this bleakness of spirit I was wakened by a simple question. Karsten asked me if I could do anything to stop the rain.

"Stop it?"

"Yes. We'll have a long march from here to Inniscaudra through the mud if this keeps up."

"It'll be worse for the soldiers marching from Cordyssa," Imral said. "Does the storm reach that far?"

I listened, as if the answer were in the rain itself. "It reaches that far and farther. Drudaen means for the storm to last a long time, I think. Nor is it all he has in mind, unless I miss my guess."

"We're close to harvest season," Mordwen noted.

"There are other things he can do, too, without facing me directly." I touched the cloak, the fabric trembling as if the threads coursed with life. Swallowing my doubts, I went on. "I can hinder him easily enough, but I can't stop him from here. But I could do a lot to change that from the High Place at Inniscaudra."

"How quickly could you lead riders there?" Imral asked me.

"How many riders?"

Imral looked a question to Kirith Kirin. "A dozen?"

"No more than that."

"If we left at sunrise we'd reach the house by nightfall."

Pelathayn whistled. "Kentha herself never offered better. Is this a trick you can teach?"

Everyone laughed. Kirith Kirin asked, "Mordwen, can you settle a new kyyvi into the shrine before then?"

Mordwen looked at him in surprise. "I have a Venladrii girl in mind already."

Kirith Kirin turned to the others. "Karsten, you and I'll spend our afternoon sending out orders to the armies to meet us at Inniscaudra. Pelathayn, you'll arrange provisions for our ride and choose lords to ride with us. Get some of the Finru or they'll sulk till spring. Let me know your choices before you give out any word. Imral, you and I should write a letter to your father, telling him everything that's happened. Jessex, do whatever you can to break the spell of bad weather."

This much in a clipped voice. To all, more mildly, "Remember, we're moving in haste but with care. We'll meet again in my tent tonight." He paused, letting a smile light his face. "Aside from word of our destination, what we have said here is for our ears only. You know this, but I warn you anyway."

5

Mordwen was in the shrine tent overseeing the dismantling of the altar, at the same time teaching the lamp ritual to a young Venladrii girl whose face was familiar. The clearing was full of folk, porters and stewards busy assembling the wooden crates into which the shrine fittings would be packed. When I hurried into the clearing, my thin coat half-drenched by rain, my hair plastered to my skull, some of the stewards drew back. My status had changed; their fear was palpable. I took deep breaths.

Mordwen appeared. "Jessex," he called, "Can you show these stout fellows where you buried the lamp oil? I haven't had time to take them there myself."

I led the soldiers round to the glen where I had buried the precious stuff, then returned to Mordwen at the altar with the new kyyvi. He was demonstrating the best method for settling the ritual lamps neatly into the niche. The girl was slim and lovely, her face oval-shaped, lips full and dark. She had a high, broad forehead that overshadowed her eyes and gave her a serious look. Her hair had more brown than silver in it, tumbling thin and shining along her neck. She was not like any other Venladrii I had ever seen. When she spoke one could hear the sibilance of her voice, converting plain words to music. She spoke True Jisraegen with a slight accent, as if she were slanting the vowels. I studied her briefly, though at a moment when Mordwen could not pause to introduce me to her.

I went into my room, where nothing had been disturbed. Atop the open chest lay the bundle I had packed when I expected to be exiled from Arthen.

The leather pouch containing the necklace was in the bundle. Breathless, I retrieved it from its wrapping of linen drawers and sat on the edge of the cot, fumbling with the leather thongs. I don't know what brought the necklace to my mind at that moment, but I held it in my palm. Brushing it with my fingertips, I studied the runes scored in the back of the silver setting.

When I touched the gem I felt only a strange murmuring from within, a far away echo of song, faint and weak.

Hearing footsteps, I quickly replaced the medallion in the pouch, concealing it in my sash, murmuring a Word that would make it very hard for anyone to find. Mordwen came to the door. "She's a fair child, isn't she? I have her chanting the words to Kithilunen. She already knows Velunen by heart. I thought you would be packing."

"I don't have time now. I have work I need to do."

He told me the stewards would attend to it, not to concern myself. Stepping forward, he asked leave to touch the Fimbrel Cloak, and I said he could. He lifted the glimmering cloth with a sharp intake of breath as if it were cold as ice, and the folds about his hand glowed softly. "Oh, I hear singing." He smiled a rapturous, almost pained smile, letting the fabric slip through his fingers. "Do you hear singing when you wear it?"

"Sometimes. And other things. While the Sisters wove it, they were always singing." Pulling it over my shoulders, I went with

Mordwen to the tent-flap, listening to the Venladrii girl's clear piping
voice. "What's her name?" I asked.

"Amri. Sharp little thing, but she doesn't say much. I guess that's
good. One wants a kyyvi to be able to hold her counsel."

I said farewell to him and hurried into the morning where rain
still fell. Axfel was waiting for me, having taken shelter under the
awning. He leapt to his feet, his whole body shaking with delight,
and I let him run with me. We did not return to Camp but headed
south where the hills were higher, running at first at ordinary speed
and then more lightly and swiftly, both of us, the cloak streaming
behind me like jewels aflame.

As we ran I began my insinging and was in trance before we
reached the hillside. On the summit of a high hill I climbed one of
the tall oaks whose upper branches were broad and sturdy. Sitting
where my view of the southern horizon was unobstructed, I deepened the trance.

The cloak shimmered and grew full, enfolding the oak with
radiance.

Speaking a Word from the dual trance, I made a fire in the air,
shaping it like a wheel and setting it to spinning, singing to the flame.
I was aware of the tree, the rain, the wind that swayed my high seat,
the smell of freshness in the air, the shifting needs of my body,
balancing and rebalancing. The rain was cold, the storm bore down
with fury, clouds oppressing the tree tops, coloring the light, suffus-
ing but not overcoming the landscape. But this was Arthen, we
were spared much, as I could now see. Far away the storm was of
such fury it shredded the land and the rain lashed earth into rivers,
raised creeks above their beds.

The power that raised the storm was hidden from me, though
I could feel its movement. Other powers of his or of his servants
were at play, but these were localized; he was not yet reaching his
arm northward with any more than ill intent. I tried for a long time
to deepen beyond these veils of his, but I did not care to match him
openly before I could stand on a High Place.

He was searching for me everywhere, but I was hidden within
Arthen. He found nothing to satisfy him. I kept vigilance over him
quietly, and then wove songs that would aid me on the coming ride.

The light deepened and darkened with afternoon. When I had
done what I could I grasped the wheel of fire and bid it vanish, and
descended from the oak summit. Axfel had waited for me all this
time at the base of the tree, sheltered under a rock, happy to see me

as always. I wrapped the cloak round myself and bent to face him, the rain streaming over my face and down my nose. "What do you think of your master now? Maybe he'll be of some account in the world, you think?"

The question had never occurred to him, clearly. I leapt to my feet and we ran for home the way we had come, more fleet than any leaping deer.

Despite the rain I bathed in the hidden pool, saying good-bye to the ritual; though to tell the truth even now I follow that pattern of movements faithfully, only not so early. My bath done, I drew on the bath-coat and returned to the shrine, some time remaining before the Evening Song. My room had been cleared of my few belongings. Mordwen, who was still with Amri in the workroom, told me my personal effects had been taken to his tent. He was distracted, being in the midst of demonstrating the proper order for assembling the reyn, so I did not linger. The girl Amri looked very attentive but a bit overawed. I doubt she ever had much conversation with a Jhinuuserret before.

Near sunset, when folks gathered, Amri brought out the lamp.

A hush fell, and people watched for my reaction. I was calm as she was. A shadow fell across me, as Kirith Kirin stepped into place.

Silence followed, while Amri watched the muuren for the signal to light the lamp.

If she was frightened, the fear did not affect her timing; I could not have begun the ceremony any closer to the proper moment myself. The fire at the muuren-heart died and the lamp flamed into light. Across the clearing torches were lit as soon as the lamp could be seen burning steadily—the Jisraegen long ago perfected the art of making torches that can defy rain, burning brightly even in storm and wind. A heartbeat followed while the Venladrii child gathered her breath.

She sang Kithilunen in a voice the clarity of which might have given a nightingale reason for envy. I marveled that such a big sound could come from one so slight and small, her singing like a bright cloud, filling the clearing to the tops of the trees. The soldiers and officers were marveling. When the song was over one was left longing for more. Amri, flushed with her effort, withdrew from the altar as she had been instructed to do, taking her place beside the shrine. She was close to me, and eyed me curiously, her long, dark face seeming incongruously old for such a small, light body. I winked at her, and she hid a small smile by bowing her head.

6

The storm had grown stronger, and from the south an ill wind was blowing. Rain fell in ragged sheets, making the treetops tremble and sag, running in rivulets down the hillside, pooling in rocks and tree roots. In the south the master of the storm was moving a storm over the Woodland and beyond. His voice hung like a cloud.

To what end was he singing? I needed to find a hilltop and make a fire circle. So I sent for Nixva to be saddled and we went out to find a place.

Nixva grumbled about the rain, mane wet with glittering drops. I explained as best I could but warned him this was the lot of magician's horses, and that he must take the bad with the good. He tossed his head as if to say he thought me somewhat arrogant, since he had been a royal horse all his life while I had only lately come to grandeur. I conceded the point but mounted to his back nevertheless, saying Words that lent us both night-vision and him fleetness beyond even his father's.

I also kept him dry, much to his pleasure. While I knew the land somewhat, he knew it better, and when I asked him to find me the tallest hilltop he could think of, he did. He took me to the very edge of the Arth Hills, a longer ride than I had in mind, but in that country stands a tall rock called Vulnur, where in ancient days criminals were executed by leading them to the pinnacle and flinging them off. Like the rest of Arth country, Vulnur has the reputation of a haunted place.

I tethered Nixva at the base of the rock beneath the shelter of an overhanging stone. A sheer, narrow stair led round and up the pinnacle, and the falling rain had made the steps slippery and treacherous. But my art was proof against that hindrance, and I ran lightly up the steps as if they were dry as burned bone.

The white moon was rising far in the east, hanging below the ceiling of cloud and coloring the rolling treetops with silver. Once from a similar place, Lady Vella had told me the roof of the forest put her in mind of the sea, rolling blue and green, and I wondered that night if this were so, if I would agree when my journeys carried me as far as that.

Squatting down on the crest of Vulnur, gathering such thin starlight as I could find filtering through cloud, I plaited what is called the Starlight Ring, and let it grow, and as it grew I wrapped the cloak

Fimbrel about me, the voices within it swelling, the cloak overhanging the tall rock like the shadow of drooping wings, filling the air and night.

I caused the Starlight Ring to flicker and burn, first as the ghost of fire and then as fire, burning air to feed its substance, a wind coursing up the sides of the rock chimney. The flame danced blue, green, orange, gold, blood red, licking upward higher as I sang Words to strengthen it. Within the Circle of Fire I placed my awareness out of body, wrapped and shrouded, and I chanted within the Fire and Darkness, letting my thought go up toward heaven, encircling darkness and enfolding fire. That time I focused all my thought on the outer eye, though all the while in the kei space my voice was making Words.

I could hear my enemy plainly, his voice insistent like a current of wind, prodding the storm gently, invoking with gentleness, patient like the good shepherd who does not wish to agitate the flock. The singing rang coldly, the voice had an edge, yet these things were subdued, and I understood Drudaen had tamed his anger, marshaled his wits, and was working his magic with craft and policy.

He had a purpose beyond the storm-sending, but I could not discern it. When I turned southward, there was only the gulf of blackness in which he had submerged. He was moving power, more than before, and a part of his mind was turned from his former purposes to a new work. I watched for a long time. The whole while he looked through me, nor could he find me even after I bent his storm a little, even when he knew I was moving. He could not pierce the veil over Arthen, and since he knew he could not, he wasted no strength on the effort.

For an instant his arrogance filled me with anger, and I longed to assail him directly, to set my thought against his and build devices on Vulnur that might break his storm, send it flying back to mock him. But this was my pride thinking and not my prudence. I had power but he had more. He had devices of many years making and I had none. Subtle and small as seemed the song within the rain clouds, were I to show my hand against it, Arthen could not hide me. This was cat-and-mouse he was playing, but I would not be a mouse.

Since I could not fathom his new strategy, then, I worked quietly against the old, and from the fire circle I plaited other fires, Wheel and Diamond, Rune and Curved Swan, speaking softly over them and sending them high, small devices that would float far overland, drawing wind upward with them, tearing the clouds that hung heavy over the northern fields. I sent nothing toward my enemy nor did I make any song whose sound would carry to him. What of my magic he could discern would seem but small and pitiable. Some of his anger would diminish into contempt. What did it prove that I had beaten Julassa Kyminax? She had never caused him to quail. She was a useful servant but she was not the only servant he had.

I plaited my runes and fire-shapes, and finally stood, stretching my arms upward, letting the cloak billow out and out, till the shadow laid the fire circle low. The wind dispersed in tatters and Vulnur sighed with rain. Whether I had done any good time would tell. I listened a last moment to that other singing, the magic he was making whose purpose I could not discern. Troubled, I descended the curved stairs, returning to Nixva who had awaited me patiently beneath the canopy of stone.

He greeted me with characteristic affection, resting his muzzle in the nape of my neck. I stood close to him, gathering strength before beginning the ride home through the storm, glad of his warm breath, of his comforting bulk. He invited me to his back with a toss of the head, being impatient to return to his place on the horselines. I obeyed and we began our quick ride beneath the trees.

But when we passed the jagged rocks at the base of Vulnur, I saw a strange sight. Over the rocks lay a soft blue glow, and within the faint light were many figures moving: translucent, fragile eidolons with voices like the faint cries of birds. These were, I guessed, the unrestful dead ones thrown from the height, maybe wakened by my magic-making or maybe following their usual routine, dancing and wailing on the foot-stones as they had done through the long ages since they died. We watched, Nixva and I, the horse inherently fearless and me guarded by my power. They took no note of our presence, which was a relief, since ghosts can be troublesome. I would have stayed longer to watch if I had not become aware of the lateness of the hour. Speaking quietly to Nixva, I turned his head and we made the journey to the Nevyssan hills, where watchfires burned like flowers on the dark hillside.

7

In Camp I found commotion. Soldiers stirred among tents and wagons, polishing armor or weapons, packing or simply talking. Some who saw me bowed respectfully but withdrew from my path nevertheless.

At Mordwen's tent I received a summons to see Kirith Kirin. A full contingent of guard was posted there, with orders to let me pass. I gave Nixva to one of the soldiers to return to the lines, warning the woman that the stallion was hungry, wet, and apt to be feisty.

Within the tent, light from many lamps flickered through fabric walls. Kirith Kirin and Lady Karsten sat on embroidered cushions illuminated by the warmly colored lights of mid-evening. Tea brewed, smelling of fragrant arrowflower, and on a low table rested a wrought silver tray of cakes. Imral Ynuuvil was reading a scroll, making notes in the margin with a bone-handled pen.

"I'm starved," I said, reaching for a cup and drawing tea from the heated oet. The others laughed, and Karsten said, "Well, pull off your cloak and eat a waycake. It was a dreadful night to go riding, don't you think?"

"Yes. It's raining all the way from here to the sea." The taste of the cake was fresh and sweet. Many rich smells drifted in the air: Karsten's perfumed oil, the Prince's smell of cedar, Imral's ink and paper. "My lord Keerfax is busy, but I can't tell what he's doing. I've done what I can about the storm. We'll see what effect it has."

After my entry I listened to their talk a while, brooding on details and other news Kirith Kirin had learned from his scouts in Maugritaxa. Silver wolves and white wolves from the deep mountains had been seen in Pelponitur above Suvrin Sirhe, and also along Angoroe, raiding the hill-farms and howling through the night. From Drii had come word that Orloc shadows were stirring in Cundruen, wary of Drudaen's presence south of the mountains. This was good news only to a degree. The Orloc could be expected to defend Cundruen against him, since they have been enemies with the House of Cunavastar since ancient times. But, as Kirith Kirin warned, one can never look to the Orloc for help.

Near the midnight sounding of the guard, Inryval the Marshal came to report Camp ready for departure. The officers had sent the soldiers to bed. The poor fellow was caked in mud, so tired he could hardly prop himself up on his marshal's staff. When he vanished, Imral said, "Sleep would be good for all of us, I think. We have a long day coming. I haven't ridden in a wizard's train in many a year."

Kirith Kirin beckoned me to sit by him, and so I moved, judging that the audience and its attendant feeling of busy-ness were ended. "Will you sleep tonight? Or do you intend to sit by some watch-fire on a hilltop?"

"It would be good to sleep. I believe I could."

"Mordwen's gone home ahead of you." Imral meant me, but he was watching Kirith Kirin. "Mordwen is one for a good night's sleep before a ride."

"So Mordwen has made room for Jessex?" Kirith Kirin asked. The room went quiet. Imral and Karsten were eyeing each other warily. "I was hoping no one had thought to arrange anything." His eyes seemed very hollow. In the silence one could hear only the rain, whispering and calling from every leaf.

When Imral answered, he was cautious. "Prince Kirith, you can't banish Cothryn for sending gifts to the boy and then turn around and do worse yourself. Jessex is six months from naming—"

"Yes, I know." Kirith Kirin sighed.

I rose from my cushion in confusion. Holding my tongue, I said good-night to Kirith Kirin and Imral both, feeling sudden anger. "I'll say good-night as well, Kirith Kirin," Karsten said, rising, gathering her cloak around her shoulders. "Jessex, I'll walk you to Mordwen's tent. I have lamp-bearers with me, you won't have to go in the dark."

Imral Ynuuvil said good night without looking up, having resumed work on his parchment. Kirith Kirin said good-night and reached for the glass decanter beside him. I paused in the doorway, wishing he would call me back.

We went out into the darkness. In the rain there was not much need for talk. The storm had increased, wind pressing us from behind.

In my tent chamber I did a short meditation visualizing the watchfires, the lights in the darkness, helping them to burn strong. The storm resounded, and beyond it, the insistent murmur of voices in the south, the calls of strange birds, the sense of turmoil and veiled movement. To the north the storm was increasing, spreading toward the mountains.

I would have felt better if we were riding already. But since we weren't, I would sleep.

But first I made a journey. Slipping on the Cloak, I spoke to it in a soothing voice, till the colors blended and flowed out like shadow, engulfing me and the room. I rode on mist out of the tent chamber, bypassing the doorway and the guard, hurrying through the forest unseen, moving between raindrop and wind. The soldiers on the nightwatch did not see me, the Prince's sentries were deceived by me, his own bodyguard was oblivious to me. In the chamber where Kirith Kirin lay, I stepped out of shadow, let the cloak become cloth.

I only wanted to see him, to stand motionless over him, a moment before I slept. He lay quietly breathing, his arm looped over the coverlet, his face overlaid with care even while resting, as if tonight his dreams were full of toil. I watched, and set the mist about me again, and bent to kiss his mouth. He stirred, but I was gone before he awoke, if he ever did.

CHAPTER THIRTEEN
INNISCAUDRA

1

In the morning we set out for Inniscaudra.

We rode, as Imral had put it, on the witch's wind. One needs a good touch with gems to do the ithikan well, but even the Sisters, who had praised me hardly at all, had occasionally remarked that I had a talent for gems and gem-magic, and in particular for this application.

The mist was heavy on the hilltops and a thin drizzle of rain still fell, somber birdcalls resounding from the interior forest. We mounted, a company of twelve, Kirith Kirin first and the rest afterward—me last, because I had to touch the ithikan gems to each of the horses. The royal horses were not troubled by the cool diamonds, nor by my singing, but the mortal horses had no memory of a magician's touch, and so were skittish. The Finra Brun's mare, a lovely palomino with golden eyes, tossed her fine head when I approached her, dancing away from my hand. But I called the horse by a name in Wyyvisar, and she heard me and stood still while I rested the jewel on the bone between her eyes. Brun was watching me with deep suspicion, and I was struck as always by the length of her chin, which was really extraordinary, forming almost a point. "I always thought you were a solemn boy. Now at least one knows what was on your mind."

At that moment I could not speak, and backed away from her with a bow. To my delight, she returned the bow with an amused smile.

Many folks could tell you the names of the gentry who rode in that morning's company. The poet who wrote "Kirithmar" takes that ride as her beginning point, the perfect moment between the victories at Anrex and Gnemorra and the long war that followed. The morning was pervaded with a sense of force gathering with us as we moved. Kirith Kirin rode, and Imral Ynuuvil, Kiril Karsten, Mordwen Illythin, Pel Pelathayn, Brun of the Finru House Tulun, Vaeyr of the Nivri House Diliar, Unril of the Nivri House Chalan, Kaleric of the Nivri House Yenmar, Idhril of the House InCossons,

which is neither Finru nor Nivri, and Duvettre of the Finru House
Shanz. I rode at the head of the party bearing the gems. Nixva
galloped on the witch's wind as if he were black flame. I could
hardly believe the feeling of rapture.

We saw many wonders that day, but the appearance of the landscape was shifted slightly by the magic, so that all of it seemed sur-
real, even to me. The road to Illaeryn runs south along a gap between the Arth Hills and Nevyssan, the only passable part of that
country. To the north runs Charnos Ridge, sheer and dark like a low
range of mountains. We could have cut the ride even shorter had
we headed straight across the ridge, but that is hard country for
horses. With fewer riders I might have tried it. But neither mortal
horse nor mortal rider was accustomed to riding in ithikan. The
Jhinuuserret suffered the disorientation and blistering speed without
much comment, but some of the others required help.

We rested once in the morning, in a dark ravine where the road
runs beneath the flanks of old Shag Arth, the westernmost of the
Arth Hills and one of the grandest. Autumn svelyra were in bloom as
were groves of moonflowers waist high, running far up the hillside,
along with a dozen other flowers I had never seen before, and ferns,
greenberry bushes, shag oaks, vines like falls of emerald water. Under
the swelling clouds the sides of the ravine rose over us like shadowy
wings, leaf giving way to naked rock on the upper reaches of Charnos.
The rain had broken for the moment, cool wind blowing from the
west where the mountains hover. We noted this only when we stopped,
since while we were riding the rain did not reach us. Lady Brun remarked, "The Camp folk will be glad to see this," and everyone
laughed. I pricked up my ears, however, and did some listening.

The menace of the southern power seemed less. But this was
not the result of any effort of mine.

We were close to Illaeryn, the High Forest, where the land rose
sharply toward the mountains, a wild country of immense pines
with haggard, twisted branches; of hemlock and junwort, faristae
and cedar. Botanists say there are more families of trees and undergrowth, flowers and vines and other growing beings in Illaeryn than
anywhere else in the world we know. In summer the smell of perfume and ripening fruit is staggering on the lower slopes, while upland the noonday is cool and brisk.

Illaeryn is a corruption of an older name, YY-Laeren, "God
Walks", which has been the name for this land since before the
building of Cunuduerum. In "Luthmar," the poet speaks of YY

descending from the mountains into Illaeryn after she made Arthen. She walked the length and breadth of the region for a day. According to the poet, she liked everything about Illaeryn except that it lacked a good high hill, and so she struck up Vath Invaths, the hill on which Inniscaudra stands, along with her sister hills, Immorthraegul and Kellesar. She made the foundations of the Winter House, delving the deepest parts before inviting her Sisters into the Woodland to see the work she had begun. The Praeven in old times went on pilgrimages here, to find her footprints.

Kirith Kirin was happy on the ride. The night's rest had done him good. While he had not been conscious of my late visit, he had ridden close all morning. Calm, lost in meditation of his own, hardly aware of the ride, one thought. When we rested he stood apart, staring into the stream that tumbled down from Charnosdilimur. Karsten offered him cumbre and he accepted it. She left him to his peace and he remained beside the flowing water for a while, scanning the clouds beyond the tangled treetops and jagged horizon. When he returned, he gave Karsten the signal to mount, and as the riders were returning to their horses, he sought me out. "We're close to a place where we must stop again—close by your way of traveling, I mean. Karmunir Gate. We can't pass through it until I speak to the stones."

"What kind of stones should I look for?"

"You'll know them when you see them," he answered, mounting the Keikin.

I swung myself atop Nixva and leaned forward, speaking softly into his ear. Holding the jewels to my lips and breathing warm breath over them, I reorganized ithikan and we rode through the clouded forest along the western road.

Beyond Shag Arth, the road sweeps upward with Charnos Ridge and the forest grows dense and dark, impassable beyond the road because of the undergrowth and rocky terrain. We swept along this high road like winter air, a line of horsemen riding at high speed in a country where even common horsemen had been a rarity for generations. One could sense the awakening in the land, as if the trees themselves were aware of the coming of a long-awaited day.

Karmunir Gate stands at the crest of the road where the western land flattens in a high plateau while Charnosdilimur mounts skyward to a crest of sheer gray rock. Trees grow right up to the road in that country, forbidding forest even in daylight, leaving no hope of passage except along the road. The gate flanks either side, two tall, carven women of stone keeping vigilance beneath the curve of a high rock arch. The women were seated on simple, high-backed thrones. At first I did not recognize the pair, being caught up more in their artistry, the cunning carving and gleaming blue stone. But on the backs of the thrones were written Words in Hidden Writing, "These are the seats of Vaela and Vaeissyn until the Breaking of the Worlds." Vaela and Vaeissyn are alternate and more ancient spellings of Vella and Vissyn.

The mortal lords immediately dismounted, gazing raptly at the two monuments. Unril called to Vaeyr to follow her to the base of one of the stones, but Vaeyr, who was an older man, vigorously built and still accounted a powerful soldier, shook his head. "We should stay well clear of these fierce stone women until Prince Kirith Kirin gives us leave to approach them. At least this is what I guess if any of my father's stories were true."

"Your father's stories were true," Kirith Kirin said. "No one should approach the stones."

As far as the eye could see, there was no gate. Beneath the arch and between the vigilance of the statues was only air and some hanging vine that had crept beneath the arch along one side. But the eye cannot see everything, as the Sisters say. Beneath the arch much power lay dormant, like that at Sister Mountain in the circle of stones. From a distance it was hard to tell the nature of the magic that protected the gate, but magic was here.

Kirith Kirin had drawn his cloak round him and walked slowly to the arch, pausing at the base of each statue. Lord Vaeyr whispered proudly, "My grandfather was with Kirith Kirin when the Prince spoke to the stones to close Illaeryn. Now I'm here to see the High Country open again. I never thought I'd be alive to see the coming of days like these."

"Who are the women in the statues?" asked Countess Duvettre.

"The Nameless Sisters, perhaps. Though there are said to be three of them, and here we find only two."

I started to tell them who the women were myself, but Pelathayn caught my eye and I understood to keep my mouth shut. Kirith Kirin was returning from the arch. He gave word to Karsten to order the ride recommenced, and she did so. I mustered ithikan and we passed into Illaeryn.

Later, when we had covered a good deal of road, we stopped at a creek and ate a light, quick meal of bread, cheese and creek water. The water was cool. Every wind had a bite of upland. I found Pelathayn standing alone and took the opportunity to thank him in sparse words for his warning at the Gate. He acknowledged it curtly and I asked, in a low voice, "Why are there only two statues?" "The third lady is forbidden this land." He was picking bits of leaf out of his beard. "The reason is told in a very old story that few folks know. Someday in better circumstances I'll tell it to you."

By midafternoon we could see the dark mass of three hills rising farther west, at their crown a glittering pile of stone.

I had seen Inniscaudra before, in Vissyn's company, but we had traveled there in the Sister's sudden fashion, nothing like this sweeping ride across gently swelling green countryside, trees rising slender and fair. Mist dusted the bright colors with gray, subduing the red linvern leaves, the golden infith, the duraelaryn whose leaves blanch white when they die, floating to the ground like immense moths.

From the eastern road one can see only the narrow flank of the House, the mass of the two towers, Domren and Ellebren, standing so close they seemed fused. The High Place was very high indeed, seen from afar, its summit crowned with horns of silver. Domren, the Tower of Guard, rose but to Ellebren's knee though it was much more massive, shining like a sunstruck cloud while Ellebren was gray like rain. Closer and closer we rode as the sun descended, shadows lengthening behind us. The hills surrounded us soon thereafter and one saw the House only in glimpses.

From the south one can see the full breadth of the citadel, from the Deep Gate to the summit of the High Place, tower on tower rising as if out of earth's heart. The road descended through Durassa's Park, a garden-like valley through which the road traces its path before beginning the winding ascent around Lake Thyathe and Vath Invaths. We rode beneath the shadow of the hill with the sun sinking beyond the mountains that filled the new horizon. The summit of Ellebren was lost in clouds.

Day was darkening as the storm clouds renewed themselves. My hearing detected more, however. I felt eyes in the clouds, a circling vigilance, as if the road were watched. I felt the southerner brooding and stretching his thought toward me.

Alarmed slightly, I urged Nixva for more speed, touching the gem and singing intently, employing the cloak so that we rode hidden. We passed south of Vath Invaths, the riders exclaiming as the house unfurled itself like a marble banner, while I strained to detect whatever presences were watching us from above.

The veil over Arthen could not prevent a bird from seeing riders
on the road, and if the bird flew under the will of Drudaen Keerfax,
he would have news of our passage more quickly than I wished. We
were riding beneath my own veil, however, no more visible than the
blowing of air through the long grass. I could feel no sign that Keerfax
was aware of me or of our passage, though I was certain he had kept
watch on Inniscaudra all the years it had been closed. As we neared
the vast house my apprehension increased.

We circled west and north and east again, beginning at last to
mount the slope of Vath Invaths. We passed beneath Aegul Wall, a
stade of towers and sheer smooth walls guarding the eastern approach to the hill. The road rose steeply but also broadened, and
the horses made swift progress. We swept beneath the shadow of
the Haldobran Cleft, the Deep Gate gleaming from shadow. The
power of the House was slumbering, but I could feel it.

Kirith Kirin rode stride for stride beside me, eyes on the road or
on the summit, his body lit from within as if power were kindling in
him. He breathed the Illaeryn evening with keen delight, sitting straight
as a scepter on the King Horse. He signaled to me to slow the ride
and I did so, laying hands on the gem.

"Have you ever seen its like?" he asked.

"No, sir. A thousand giants couldn't break down those walls."

He smiled. "Maybe a thousand tried, those first days when even
the rocks were young. These walls will stand until the last moments,
it's said." He paused, gazing upward. "I want a little time. I want
the House to get used to us."

The slower pace did us good, I think. The others took deep
breaths, as if wakening from sleep. Sounds of nightfall closed round
us: calls of birds, wood crickets, the baying of hounds or wolves.
When night was full, we lit torches at the base of the Tower of
Guard. I could have made a better light by my art, but this would
have been like a beacon to whatever eyes were watching the Vath
Road. The veil I was maintaining over our passage was beginning to
tax me after the day's long work. The torch flames flickered, throwing faint light onto the foundations of walls and towers. We passed
the bulk of Domren, our horses climbing the road that runs beneath
the Aegul Wall toward Krafulgur Gate.

At Krafulgur the road passes between two immense horned towers
whose sides rise smooth as polished glass from the rock of the hill.
Krafulgur is no Gate at all to the eye, it appears to be a huge open
arch spanned by a stone bridge. A portcullis that can be lowered is

cunningly hidden within the stone. We rode beneath the towers, whose upper reaches were deeper shadows in the darkness. The horses' hooves echoed beneath the broad arch. The road swung south in an ascending curve, and we climbed to the Syystren Gate. This was the end of the journey. We stood holding our horses' reins in the unbridled night, wind stabbing through our cloaks, an occasional raindrop on the cheek, a moment of moonlight awash in monkish cloud. Kirith Kirin was standing at the center of the cobbled road, turning a circle of dark metal over and over in his hand. He simply walked to the gate. Imral lit his path with a torch.

The Venladrii Prince halted below the outer pillars, and the flame of his torch sent shadows dancing against the walls, giving light for Kirith Kirin. The Prince strode to the side of the huge gate, and soon a blue light glowed. He spoke words I could not hear, and I knew by instinct I could not have heard them by my art, either. He was moving power himself.

He set the metal circle into the center of the light, which suddenly brightened.

As if the blood of a dead man became warm and began to flow sweetly in his veins, the power of the house began to move. Wind rushed up Vath Invaths from every slope, and above Inniscaudra the clouds were torn and the stars shone down on us, as if the night had never known storm or rain. From within the gate an age-old breeze stirred, sighed outwardly and kissed our faces. The outer gate split down the center and swung open. From within light was shining. On the high walls and in the towers of guard, one by one, watchfires began to burn.

The magic that preserves and guards the house becomes immanent when the Keeper of the Keys returns to the Citadel, but no one had bothered to warn me. All of Inniscaudra is built of magic of one kind or another. I stood there with the tatters of my spell of hiddenness fluttering around me. If there were indeed any watchers in the clouds, they had gathered the news for which they had been sent. The eye in the south would know we had entered the House of Winter.

At that moment, however, I hardly thought of Drudaen or spies or even of the others who were with me. I was struck dumb at the House, at the awesome energy I could feel moving within it. Eyes closed, listening to the singing that ran through the stones, a field of force in which the House was suspended. I could have stood there listening till all the moons rose together. We entered Inniscaudra with our heads craned this way and that. By the time the gates closed behind us, the Winter House was festooned with roch fire on every wall and parapet, and we who entered the Eldest House were singing from "Kimri," "I am lighting the lamp that lights the lamps."

2

The priests of Cunuduerum believed Inniscaudra to be the center of all worlds, and the House has many names in Jisraegen legend: House of Mur, Elder House, House that No Man Built, YYmoc, Mansion of Winter, Velyii, Mansion of the Fathers and Mothers, Sister-House, Edennavadrim and many more. Every Aeryaen people has stories of the House from as far back as their memories reach, including the Svyssn who call it the House of Light, and the Smiths in the Valley of Ice who remember the building of Inniscaudra, in which they participated. Even the Orloc helped to build the Deeps of the house and have songs concerning Inniscaudra, though few humans have ever heard them and returned to tell tales.

Long before there was a Queen or King there was a Keeper of the Keys. Nowadays under the Law, the Successor in Arthen held the Keys to Inniscaudra; a treasure greater, in its way, than any to be had outside the Woodland, now that Montajhena was no more than a ruin in the mountains.

Beyond the Syystren Gate was a wide moat and stone bridge, and beyond the bridge the wide lawn before the Halobar, the Hall of Many Partings, which was the entrance to the House. We crossed the bridge leading our horses behind us. A few of the others stopped to light torches, the flames reflected on the still water. On the bridge the support pillars were carved to resemble bearded men and women with long braids, all with their eyes closed, and in the mouth of each venerable sir or madam a fire flickered, sending out wavering light. Moonlight poured down from a tear in the clouds and the lawn was flooded with silver. The entry road, a mixture of stone, coral and pink sea shell, wound beneath silver menumen with silken leaves fluttering and dense green hedges neatly trimmed as if gardeners had manicured them yesterday. Lady Karsten murmured a song I had never heard, something about the House of Many Names, as we approached the glimmering entry court.

When I had ridden here before, even from a distance I had been awed by the mass of the place. Riding toward the Hall beneath the sky torn with storm, I was struck with wonder at the intricacy, the delicate stonework, the soaring towers, the window glass of jewel-rich colors, and the outer walls of the towers and fortifications shining smooth as glass, dark as blood.

No enemy has marched on Inniscaudra since Cunavastar made war on the YY-Sisters and laid waste to the northern portions of Illaeryn. No enemy will march on her again until the breaking of the age and no enemy will ever take her until the breaking of worlds, whenever that may be. I had a sense of walking on a height even from within the walls, the wind from the western mountains blowing the roch-fires, light and shadow dancing across the encrusted road. We halted beneath the broad stair leading to the Halobar Doors. Kirith Kirin had climbed to the seventh step. "Let your horses wander on the lawn," he said quietly, "we won't attempt to open the stables or any of the lower holds tonight. You'll find the mortal horses are wonderfully invigorated by a day's grazing on this grass."

He led the King Horse onto the lawn. The others followed. Everyone walked as if in a dream, turning this way and that, from the shining face of Halobar to the terraces that lead to the Under House, sweeping falls of stairs set with statues of grave-faced people of all the races we know. We turned from marvel to marvel.

The horses on the lawn called each other with eerie voices. Kirith Kirin spoke again. "For those who have not been here before, we're at the Western Doors, and this is Halobar, the Hall of Many Partings. Beyond Halobar is Thenduril, the Woodland Hall, and beyond that is the Tower of YY. You've heard of these places before, in the stories your fathers and mothers told you. We won't enter the house from this direction tonight. One should first see those sights by morning, in sunlight, and from the looks of things we may have clear weather tomorrow." Here he smiled at the stars overhead. "For tonight, we'll find places for ourselves in the Under House, along one of those terraces beneath Thenduril. Follow me and I'll show you."

Everyone shouldered as much baggage as she or he could carry and we followed Kirith Kirin along a bright path down a broad, coral-colored stair. We passed silent as shadows, cloaks sweeping the stone, torches flickering. From the walls, mute carvings watched us, reliefs depicting scenes out of history, some familiar but many not. I saw King Falamar entering the River City, the First Breaking of Yrunvurst, the slaughter of the Anynae, along with other sad moments from those times. Figures of slender beauty, strong-boned Jisraegen faces, mournful eyes.

The Under House descended beneath the north wall in a series of gardens and terraces that led eventually to a stairway at the foot of the wall and the towers. A wind swept up the stairway and I heard the whisper of a voice in it, a cold sound that made me shiver. We had paused on one of the terraces and I was leaning over the carved stone balustrade, the wind in my hair.

When I heard the sound again it filled me with dread. I gazed down at the far blue glow of the glimmering road. The wind blew from there and struck me with a peculiar tingling.

Someone was talking near me but I was listening to another voice. Pelathayn was in front of me saying something about a place to sleep.

"I won't be sleeping here."

The red-haired soldier blinked at me, and then began to grin. "Then you're going up to the top tonight?"

"To the top?"

He pointed.

High above, near an oval of stars, one could see the High Place, lit like the specter of a lamp, culmination of a slender tower whose sides were darker than night when the Tower was at rest. The stones drink light that would otherwise be reflected. Ellebren had been storing light for a long time. The voice I heard flowed from there. The wind blew down from the height.

"Fireworks," Pelathayn said. "I haven't seen a magician on a shenesoeniis for a long time."

"I need to get there rather quickly."

He understood me. I could not exactly go to Kirith Kirin and announce this in front of the others. We were standing on a terrace outside the gate to the courtyard where they were. Pelathayn walked to tell Kirith Kirin. He did this without drawing attention to himself, standing to the side till Kirith Kirin noticed. The two must have exchanged some sign but I could not see it. Imral was watching also and, as if on cue, stepped forward as if to help Kirith Kirin with the ring of keys he was holding. Kirith Kirin laughed at himself and called to Pelathayn to look how Imral had to help him with the keys, it had been so long since he had to bother with locks at all. "We've lived in the open forest for a long time, haven't we?" he asked, and everyone laughed, and he clapped Pelathayn on the shoulder. Pelathayn leaned into Kirith Kirin's ear.

It was neatly done. Kirith Kirin glanced at me across the terrace. I smiled and drew up my hood.

Imral opened the gate and everyone entered the wide inner court, where roch-lamps were burning. Kirith Kirin drew away from the others, gesturing me to proceed ahead of him.

I hurried down the narrow stair beyond the garden that surrounded the inner gate. On a stone bench beneath the carved head of some unheard-of beast, I waited.

Though I listened, he was behind me before I ever saw him, and his appearance out of shadow startled me some. No one was with him. He laughed. "Yes, I can fool even you sometimes, little magician. Do you need a guide?"

"I need to get into the Tower."

"So soon?"

I lowered my voice. "He has spies in the air, Kirith Kirin, and he knows we're in the House. I feel a change in his thinking."

Kirith Kirin looked at the burning firepots, the torches, the myriad lights that were swelling round us. "I hadn't thought of that, but I should have. One can't keep one's entry into Inniscaudra secret, the whole countryside wakens."

He pulled up the hood of his cloak and we hurried across terraces and gardens toward the stairway where the light was pulsing.

We moved forward at a near run, moving along the Falkri Stair. Kirith Kirin told me the name, and pointed out other places. The wind was pouring along the road, cold like the heart of winter. We rounded the corner of Thenduril, heading down the series of stairs and terraces running along both sides of the road from Under House to Tower March. Falkri descends as the High Wall rises, swinging south toward Aegul and Krafulgur, whose closed gates shimmered in the light from the roch fires on the battlements. High above, one could see the Authra shining like light in an outstretched claw, and beyond it the Falkri road rising toward Thrath. The wind was howling and the stars had vanished. From the south I could feel the palpable motion of power, and Kirith Kirin seemed aware of it as well. As we ran he glanced at the clouds, at the far-off light of the High Place lost in gray.

The shining road wound below Evaedren and passed the Lower Bridges before rising again behind the Thrath Wall. Beyond the last of the bridges one who had eyes could read the first of the Awaiting Runes, the magic-writing in the rock that was the beginning guidepost. I murmured the Hidden Word when we passed it, and soon found others. High above, the White Gate was shining, its liquid light filling that whole part of the house.

As we entered further into the Tower Precinct, past the Ward-Runes and the Words-vigilant, the power of the place was no longer hidden. The air was full of voices now, audible to Kirith Kirin as well as to me. The song was an old one, of a voice and character I could only partially appreciate. Kirith Kirin was listening to it with a stricken look. "Do you know who that is? It's Kentha. I've never heard it here before. These rocks remember her. One can hear Edenna Morthul also. Edenna built the lower tower. Kentha raised it higher and placed the stone on the shenesoeniis." He looked confused. "Something's different here."

We had come to the Estobren Arches, stone devices intricately carved, where we paused. I said the words of formula that were written on the stones, and answered the ritual chain with chain-phrases. When I did so, the arch-wards permitted me to pass, and a change registered itself through the whole Tower height.

The base of Ellebren was very broad, for all the Tower's slender appearance from a distance, and its sheer sides rose smooth as glass out of the dark granite spur. Around the base was a narrow walk where firepots were set. These were not burning, being under the control of a different magic than that which governed the rest of Inniscaudra, but now that I had passed the Arches they were under my Word, and when I called for fire, roch-light sprang from them and from the large bronze pots that flanked the White Gate. Kirith Kirin, still holding my arm loosely, signed for me to wait.

He proceeded to the nearest of the Arches. I did not see what he did or where he reached, but for a moment light shone in the portal, and when Kirith Kirin returned, in his hand was a silver ring of keys.

He gave them to me with the rain beginning to fall on the Shining Road. "These are the Keys to Ellebren Tower. Before you they have been held by Edenna Morthul, the Lady of Orelioth, and by Kentha Nurysem." Rain was falling more steadily now. Kirith Kirin gazed upward into the murk. "The storm's returning."

"He's putting out a good deal of strength in the south, he has been for most of the day. I don't know what he's doing but I'm worried."

Kirith Kirin turned suddenly, gazing far southward, where one could see only darkness. "I wish I had long sight. Come and tell me

as soon as you know anything." He wrapped the cloak close around
him. He was watching me sternly. "Come and find me in any case.
I won't be able to sleep."

I slid the key ring into the pocket of my cloak and stepped close
to him. Taking his hand, I laid my lips against it, and he sighed and
embraced me. We stood there with the strange singing from Ellebren
filling our heads, the light from the White Gate illuminating the steady
fall of rain. We said nothing. Finally he pulled the hood closer
round his head. Rain drove against the stones of Falkrigul and the
face of Ellebren. I thanked him and walked the last ascent of road
to the Thrath Gate, shining in the deepening blackness.

3

Thrath Gate is smooth as eggshell, cool to the touch, lit perpetually
with sourceless radiance. To open the Gate the celebrant must first
call runes out of the stone and find the lock that is hidden. Since the
Lake Women had known I would stand on the High Places one day,
they had taught me the opening rituals for all of them. Standing
before the shining muuren-surfaced doors, I called wind to swell
beneath the Cloak till it covered the rock bay where the massive gate
was set, throwing darkness over that part of the House. Laying my
hands close to the Gate without actually touching it, I sang quietly
and felt the immediate change within the Gate and the Tower, a note
of welcome in the music, as if my coming were expected. The
White Gate shimmered and changed. Runes appeared where none
had been readable before, and beneath the words was carved flow-
ingly in High Jisraegen the following inscription:

*Here is the Gate of Ellebren on High, the Shenesoeniis begun by Edenna
Morthul and completed by Kentha Nurysem when Kirith Kirin was Keeper of
the Keys for the Thirty-Third Term. One shall stand here till the Breaking of
Worlds. The Eye of Heaven watch over the High Place, She Who is Near.*

The lock was hidden within the Eye in the Circle, a picto-
graph used to represent YY-Watchful, the Eternal Awareness. I
slid the key-shaft into the barrel, whispering Wyyvisar runes carven
above the Eye, feeling the key grow warm. The Gate brightened
till the light was more than I could bear, though the Cloak contained it. One gathers the light for the power that can be had. The
Gate shimmered and opened, a seam appearing where none had
been before, the white stone opening outward in halves to form a

narrow corridor. Within, torches sprang into flame, casting light
onto white pillars and a false fountain of glittering crystal.

I walked inside, the Cloak sweeping round me, striking sparks
from the rock. Within the Tower was silence, the echo of wind
along the Winding Stair. The chamber where I stood was lit by the
eerie white-burning torches and by veins of muuren in the domed
ceiling. The crystal fountain glimmered at moments but was dark
the rest. At the base of the fountain were carved figures of birds
flying over mountain peaks, Wyyvisar runes etched in silver. One of
the panels read, "Wizard, you are standing in the Chamber of White
Crystal at the Foot of the Winding Stair at the Base Rock Thrath
beneath Ellebren on High, and you cannot pass beyond this Point
unless you claim the High Place." Other runes were carved on chalcedony panels set in the walls of the round chamber. I moved
slowly from panel to panel and around the fountain, studying each
carefully, listening to the wind. What had seemed cacophony clarified to a choir of subtle voices, a shimmering of power and of
magical devices. To sort it all out would take time, but my instincts
told me I had none. I surveyed the stone panels quickly, remembering what had been taught me of Towers at Illyn Water, and then,
taking the Cloak in my hands, I began the Song of Entry.

This song can be heard with the ear, at least in part. The sound
filled the chamber, lighting the runes. Two doors appeared, open
arches, where I had seen only stone wall before. A gust of wind
blew from one, where the base of the Winding Stair had been concealed. From the other arch came a scent of flower incense and
something else, more pungent, from beneath.

Beyond that open portal was darkness. Here was the kirilidur,
an open central shaft leading all the way to the summit of the Tower.
On the cylindrical face of the inner wall were carved crossing spirals
of runes, inlaid with Tervan silver and patterns of gems. The kirilidur
is the chief device in magic of the fourth level, the invention of
Edenna Morthul, and in order to ascend the Tower one must first
take possession of the inner spirals of runes. One does this by
reading them into memory through the intervening stone, all the
threads at the same time. When one has accomplished this from the
bottom of the Tower to the top, the patterns of gems become
active as well, and the whole Tower and all its complex stored phrases
of magic are active. One must then complete the circle dance to
take possession of the Eyestone on the High Place, and then one is
master of the Tower and all its devices.

One begins to read the runes at the portal leading to the Winding Stair.

I breathed deeply, standing beneath the stone lintel carved with the likeness of a winged serpent swallowing its own tail. One may read the Hidden Runes by whatever method one wishes, at any speed one wishes, using any device one may have within one's possession.

From one of the brackets beside the portal I freed a torch, which was burning with roch-light and to which I spoke Hidden Words, naming the fire and gazing into its heart. From the sixth level I used the flame as a scrying-fire, and also used it as a focus for my meditation, so that when I reached for gems in one of the pockets of the Cloak, I was able to clear their former enchantments quickly and use them as seeing-stones. I entered the dual state, reading the runes out of the body, climbing the stairs within it, and reading each word of each thread into myself, into the space that does not forget. The Tower was wakening, slumbering voices rising out of the stones. I began the climb with the flame-colored glow of the crystal fountain at my back, my awareness divided between the narrow stair, the torch, the gems and rune-silver interlacings of the kirilidur shaft. I streamed the musical Words into myself, flowing upward along the Winding Stair like smoke, intoning the names of the runes like running water, each thread harmonizing with the others, as if there were a choir of voices. The sum of these runes taken together is called the Ruling Song, and the Ruling Song of Ellebren is fair and lovely in the kei space of the mind. The stairway grew broad and bright, studded with high-peaked, narrow windows through which misty rain drifted on the wind.

As I was reading the long Wyyvisar lines, I passed over other spiraling threads of runes I could not read, and they made me curious, but I had no time to stop and think.

Soon I was near the top, and a sweet, clear singing filled the Tower. Once again I felt distinctly as if the place were extending a welcome. I thought I heard my name echoing far below, not Jessex but what Commyna had called my true name, Yron.

On its last circuits of the Tower, the Stairway narrows once again, leaving barely room for two people to climb abreast. Here the slit-windows were cut close together, and rain spattered on the wide stone sill, droplets hanging in light and air. I slowed and paused, my eye and awareness still in my devices. I chanted the last measures of the Ruling Song, feeling the High Chambers and the pirunaen opening beyond the last flights of the Stairs.

The High Chambers of Ellebren are breathtaking in beauty, built by Kentha Nurysem at the height of her power and employing the resources of the Inniscaudra treasuries and the talents of the best Tervan and Anyn artisans of the day. Wondrous to see the rooms first in starlight and storm, rain sheeting through the high windows, miiren-light glimmering, the chambers themselves full of muted gem-light, clear pools of silver on the floor, curtains of woven moon-light and tapestries whose colors glowed like stars, heaven. Even in my haste I marveled.

The final chamber was the pirunaen, the work room, ceiling vaulted, support columns running in concentric circles throughout the broad space, a sweeping curved stairway rising from the stone floor to the open summit of the Tower. Rain and wind howled down the stairs. I paused at the foot. Above I could see rolling dark clouds.

One's awareness at such a time cannot be described in ordinary terms. Part of me read the runes along the rim of the firepot, in the center of the room under the Eyestone, the lower part of the muuren sphere resting in its silver frame, and beyond the complex mecha-nism for raising or lowering the stone. I studied the drawing tables, the rune books and stencils, chests in which gems were stored, shelves and rolls of parchment, perfectly preserved, ready for use. Part of me listened to the harsh voice that swelled in the clouds, to the cries of wheeling birds and the shrieking of wind at the opening that led to the summit. I moved on many levels. I remember fear, and deep calm beneath the fear, and my own even, rhythmic breathing, the Cloak spread about me like a constellation. Amid all this, when my foot first touched the lower step to begin the climb into the open air, I was aware that the world into which I was ascending was not the safe world of a boy under the protection of the women of Illyn. My enemy had eyes in the sky. He had known the Tower was awakening from the moment I passed the entry arches, and he would know the moment I stepped onto the rain-swept pavement. I would be naked as a child before him, my thought plain to read, my en-chantments laid bare. Until I wakened the Eyestone I would have no defense against him, because I could do no magic here myself until I controlled the stone, while he would have the Tower to use to focus his thought on me.

I climbed toward the fresh rain and wind. Light flickered on the High Place. Above, clouds rolled and massed, lashing rain in increasing density as if the hand that guided the storm were deter-mined to dash out the watchfires and torches burning far below.

A squadron of infantry could have drilled on the summit with plenty of room to spare. From the stairs to the Eyestone glimmering beneath sheets of rain was a long way. The light within the Stone was no longer steady, but flickered like a lamp wick in its last moments, by which I knew Drudaen was in the stone. He could use it to a degree because he controlled all the other Towers. He had been in the stone for a long time, to that extent.

I smoothed the Fimbrel Cloak in my hands, remembering. The torch would be no good to me any longer and so I extinguished it, laying the smoking brand on the step where the rain kissed it cool. The white stone shimmered on the High Place, shadows swimming beneath its milky surface.

When I called to the Stone in Hidden Words, my enemy heard me, too. "Rock of Ellebren," I called, "I have come to take you. I am Yron who climbed your Winding Stair and gave your Song to you."

The light increased. A new kind of darkness descended, a blast of ice engulfed me. My body, from which I had distanced myself, grew numb and heavy. I could feel the Wizard's hand on my heart, his far-off strength increasing. I was dismayed and sank to the steps, fighting to breathe. My heart labored. The song had momentarily left my mind, and I felt myself, for an instant, perfectly within the Wizard's power, while he laughed and stretched out his hand.

A dull pain filled my chest and I could no longer see.

But with fear came clarity.

Until I was the master of the High Place I could not hope to defend myself against him.

Unclasping my Cloak, I held it aloft like a banner and let the wind fill it, the fabric unfurling. Lightning shot through the threads, crackling and spitting, and veins of fire pulsed in the air around it, growing, arcing to the Horns. The hand on my heart closed tighter, pain, and I sank completely to the stairway. But the cloak still hung in the wind, weightless, throwing off light and shadow, filling more of the High Place each second, till it covered the Rock and the altars around it.

My enemy was dismayed, thinking I had defied his magic. He kept his hand in me, but the moment of hesitation was enough to give me room to work.

I set foot on the Rune Pavement, saying, "I have climbed the Winding Stair and said the Words of your Ruling Song. Protect me from my enemy and I will dance your dance for you."

In the stormy darkness, the flickering of the Eyestone lessened, and the light increased. Above, as if in anger, the ripping wind renewed itself, and rain fell in torrents.

I clasped the Cloak and moved slowly forward, my strength returning, the weight of the hand lifting from my heart and my breath coming more easily. Drudaen's laughter died away, though I could sense him, waiting.

With each step toward the Rock, I diminished his command of the Height; my control over the Tower increased.

One masters the shenesoeniis from the fourth circle of power. Taking a deep breath, I knelt before the Stone, letting the Fimbrel-Cloak fall across the smooth white surface. I had never seen an Eyestone before and studied this one, a sphere of purified muuren suspended in the pavement, supported from beneath by the metal framework I had seen in the Work Room, here encircled with a band of runes and another of Hidden Words that said, "Man, when you come here do not be deceived; Woman, you stand before Ellesotur, whose power is derived from deep places, whose crown is in the clouds; one who fails the Dance will be utterly cast down and lost to all the Circles and to the Wise."

To be cast down is to die, consumed either by the shenesoeniis itself or by the power of one's enemy. Such a one cannot pass through Tornimul, cannot be reborn in Hero's Home. With this in mind, I began the Long Dance of Encirclement.

In the dance the celebrant follows the Rune Path that spirals from the Stone to the perimeter of the Tower. This was a pattern-dance into spin, like many I had practiced at Illyn, but with the added difficulty that the celebrant does not know what movements are required until she or he begins to trace the Path. One is being tested to make certain that one without skill does not become attuned to the shenesoeniis; one is also aligning the Eyestone and other tower-devices to oneself. Once begun, the dance cannot be ended prematurely except by dying in the middle of it.

I stood above the glowing stone, letting the name "Ellesotur" roll on my tongue. I said the Words that are used to open the spiral. Gathering the cloak in my fists, I regulated my breathing into the dual meditation and sent my consciousness far from the world of the High Place and the Wizard's storm. Turning from the Stone that blazed like the sun, I saw the Rune Path lit before me, containing its beginning in its end. My body was no longer my body. If there was any rain falling, I did not feel it. I trod the Path that only I have trod;

though I did not know this at the time. When it was finished, I looked beyond the edge of the Tower into the gulf that lies beyond Ellebren in that sphere. The power of the shenesoeniis awakened and was mine.

4

At once and for many hours my awareness went out from the Tower, through a false dawn into a wakeless day. I could see a long way. I could feel the movements of my companions in Inniscaudra far beneath me, wakening other, older powers within the sprawling stone mansion. In Arthen I could feel the movements of the living, the scouts of Drii afield in the east, the murmuring of trees in elder groves, the lapping of River as it swelled beyond its banks in the driving rain. In the south, in Vyddn country, the encampment of Drudaen and his armies was visible as a whirlpool of shimmering stuff, the center of a summoning of immense power, and all his southern strongholds were like torches burning. He was aware of me and of what I had accomplished. This was a day that had been foretold in the writings he had read of the Prophet Curaeth, and among other meanings it had, it meant his days of waiting were ended. His power need no longer be quiescent.

He stretched out his hand, and even though he was without High Place on which to stand, such was his strength that a shadow of his making fell across the southern land from Amre to Westernmost Karns, north to Genfynnel, boiling over Arthen and reaching in tendrils across the Fenax. The darkness fell as far east as Drii, Pelponitur and the Orloc mountains. Beneath the boiling clouds, forks of lightning fell in waves.

From this distance I could not fight him, not when he had prepared for this moment so long. But I could not sit still, either. I had taken the Tower, I wore the Cloak. To answer Drudaen, to counter his strength, there was only me. For now and for the years to come.

So I did answer him, simply, without artifice. I stood near Ellesotur and sang, a simple song, but one that reached clear south to where he stood in his pavilion raising his gloved hand with the rings that ruled all his Towers on them. I sang, "I am Yron who killed Julassa, whose coming has been foretold; this is Arthen, and no shadow will fall here. Let the Wizard come who can cast me down while I am Yron and this is Arthen, while I am standing in my Tower Ellebren and am Yron Named of She-Who-Names. Let the Wizard come."

This was my declaration and I sang it. I had not planned the words but they were present, deeply felt, and the Tower was moving in me as if we were one thing, the runes of the kirilidur mine to use, any part of that magic mine, I could feel it through me like a liquid fire. When I was done with the song the whole landscape of storm and darkness shuddered. The light of Ellesotur flared out like a new star, the silver miiren horns bursting into lances of colored fire. Deep within the Tower awoke its hidden devices. My song was heard in Ivyssa beneath Karomast, in the Genfynnel market beneath Laeredon, on the heights of Cunevadrim, echoing on the slopes of Aerfax. Drudaen heard me in his pavilion. Presently, because he could not cast me down and would lose much by opposing me at such a distance, he withdrew his hand from the north. Much suffering was spared that land. But over the south his shadow remained.

CHAPTER FOURTEEN
KEHAN KEHAN

1

That night the light of the Tower was seen as far south as Genfynnel and as far north as Cordyssa, where the townfolk thought the eerie glow heralded the end of the world. King Evynar Ydhiil in Drii saw the light from the rain-drenched terrace adjoining his bedchamber as he was retiring for the evening; he rose from his couch, pulled on a robe and watched all night, as Imral told me. Unlike the Cordyssans, King Evynar had seen light like that before and knew what it was. He saw the shadow also, advancing first and then retreating. He was not surprised, having taken warning from the visit of the Sisters. What he did not know for certain he could guess.

When morning came, overcast with purple haze and tenebrous drizzle, he could see that the shadow had been contained and even pushed back by the light over Inniscaudra. He could also see, eastward over Cundruen, another place where the shadow could not hold, where another light shone upward into the darkness. He did not need to guess where this light came from. Eastward, at the end of Cundruen, lay Montajhena.

What power stirred in those ruins he did not know. But he guessed Kirith Kirin would need to be told of this as soon as possible. Kirith Kirin's messengers had not yet reached him with news of the opening of Inniscaudra, but Evynar needed no telling after he saw the Ellebren lights. He sent fleet-footed scouts westward along the Arthen roads to Illaeryn, carrying word of his own support and news of the ghost-light in Montajhena. He summoned his ministers to war council, for he feared the shadow would not remain quiet for long.

2

Lord Ren Vael was waked by the shouts of his own householders when the strange light on the southern horizon began to burn like a fallen sun. He had barely pulled on his robe and stepped into his fore-chamber before he heard the first echoed cries from the city's lower quarters.

He saw the light from the roof-walk of his house and knew what it was. Having heard tales of the final battle before Gnemorra—he had been with squadrons securing the Anrex Valley—he was not surprised. Shadow rose up and storms swept across the Fenax out of nowhere, and Ren Vael understood. A chill made him shiver. He folded his robe over his head to keep off the rain. He was a balding man with a sad face and that night he did not so much look like one of the long-lived. Calling in his steward, he summoned the city gentry and burghers and they kept vigil with one another through the long night. At morning, when it became clear that the light in Ellebren had prevailed against the shadow, Ren Vael and his companions set about convincing the rest of Cordyssa the end of time had not yet come. This story is included in a letter Lord Vael wrote to his lover at the time, whom he had sent to one of his estates for protection during the unrest in Cordyssa.

3

Gaelex, on the march toward Illaeryn, saw the Tower radiance as a blue corona beyond Shag Arth, beneath which the soldiers marching from Nevyssan were encamped. The light was bright enough she could review her map by it, pacing back and forth in her tent, rubbing the bump in her hooked nose. I heard this story from her later, when we were riding south; I added the part about her nose, but she was always doing it. She sent word to the sentries to keep a sharp eye but not to worry about the light. The heavens opened up and the rain fell in torrents, swelling the streams that poured down Shag Arth. Gaelex had the trumpeter sound quarters and gave orders for camp to be moved to higher ground.

The sun rose in the morning but its watery light fell through haze. The soldiers struck camp having slept little more than half the night. As the march was beginning Gaelex got word that Amri, the Venladrii girl, the new kyyvi, had wandered off during the rain and spent the night among moonflower. The child was feverish, talking in her sleep. Gaelex gave the order for the march to begin and rode back along the column till she found the physician's wagon in which the child was riding. The whole violet day the soldiers marched through dregs of storm and tatters of shadow, Amri feverish, talking to herself, Gaelex riding beside her. They encamped that night at Karmunir Gate, the light of Ellesotur silhouetting the somber stone guardians of the High Country.

4

Sivisal lay folded in sleep in Fort Gnemorra's barracks when the sentries first sounded quarters. He hurriedly drew on tunic and light armor, moving instinctively in the darkness. Outside soldiers were forming up in ranks, everyone gazing at the southern sky.

At first Sivisal thought it was a storm, but he had never seen its like either for lightning or lack of thunder. Cartwheels of radiance danced and glittered, first white as stars and then ruby red, emerald green, turquoise, golden, burning like fire; yet not a sound could be heard. Then, beyond the light, as if a gulf were opening, the stars began to go away.

The stars of our sky are changeable but they do not vanish. He felt cold in his stomach and numb all over, and a picture flashed in his mind, the shadow surrounding him as darkening mist and dissolving him as if he were starlight. Grown soldiers were calling out in fear, nobles and commoners, women and men, and Sivisal could hear the horses crying on the line.

A voice called out from the darkness, harsh and deep. "Curse you all for fools," the voice said, "don't you know what that light is? Did your mothers and fathers never tell you stories? That isn't an enemy, that's a friend. That's your nephew, Sivisal. That's the weyr light from the Tower over YYmoc, and it means the Witch Boy who killed the Karns has taken his place against the other one."

The words sent a shiver over Sivisal, and he turned to see Cuthru son of None gazing at him in amusement from across a watch fire.

He wrote me this in a letter. Not long afterward his detachment of cavalry, commanded by Theduril son of Vinisoth, was ordered back to Arthen. But Sivisal knew of no such orders that night, and wrote me by the first fractured daylight, recalling how he had carried me into Arthen from his sister's farmhouse; and now I was walking in the clouds.

5

Queen Athryn Ardfalla saw no light but heard my voice issuing from
Karomast; all Ivyssa heard that sound, when I said I would defend
Arthen against him. She saw the shadow also. I have read a letter
she wrote to her companion, Sylvis Mnemorel, Lady of Durme
and Amre: "I've heard the new one speak and now Drudaen is
answering. Even as I sit here the blackness has swept across Anyn
and Kmur. I can't see the stars. You'll be wondering, in Novris,
whether I've at last lost my mind entirely, to allow such a blast across
my own country. You will have seen the Diamysaar, as I did. The
day has come at last. I can feel the cold in the pit of my belly. Now
I have to live with what I've done. Don't come to Ivyssa for a
while, my dearest. I'll be returning to Kmur in the morning, if there
is a morning. We're not very much loved here."

6

Kirith Kirin studied the lights over Ellebren from his own apartments in Evaedren, the Tower of the Twelve. He and the other
twice-named crept there after the mortal lords fell asleep, dead-tired
after the long day's ride. Riding in ithikan is a drain on anyone's
strength; the mortals slept through all that followed, deep into the
hollow morning.

The twice-named watched from a balcony as the windows of
Ellebren ignited one by one, the burning of roch fire spiraling toward the silver-crowned summit. Kirith Kirin was too impatient to
sit and paced the corridors, finally taking his leave of the rest, despite
their protests. He found his way down Falkrigul to the Estobren
Arches, where he sat down to wait. I found him sleeping on the dry
stone hours later when I descended.

I was glittering from my walk on the High Place, charged with
vision and smelling of strong storm winds. I knelt by him, wrapped
my hand round his shoulder, touched his face with my fingertips.
When he was awake and knew it was me, he sat up slowly, rubbing
his eyes like a child.

The storm was breaking up, white light beyond rolling dun-
colored clouds. While rain could not reach us, a light rain peppered
the rest of the world, sheeting round the arches in a curtain, the last
collapse of the storm's heart. We watched the rain fall and the

clouds roll. This was late afternoon, the finish of an ashen day in the fringe of shadow.

My mind was in many places: on the Height, in the Eyestone, within the Tower and the House, in the air over Arthen and watching the darkening south. But one has a lot of mind one does not use. It was easy to be mostly there, with Kirith Kirin, gently pleased by his warmth. Finally he said, "So, do you think we've started something?"

"Oh yes. We're all going to have a pretty bad time of it, I expect."

He laughed softly. "Yes, I know. Why does that strike me as funny at this particular moment?"

"You like storms."

He sighed, a deep sound like the release of a weight. "At least it's started, there's no more waiting. At least we're here. For once without any prying eyes."

"In this particular spot," I said, listening to the Arches, "no prying eyes will ever see you and me if that will make you happy, Kirith Kirin."

"It makes me happy now."

The clouds broke up, a cold, dry wind sweeping down from the mountains to force the shadow south, lifting the amber clouds in tatters as the rain thinned. By sundown the clear sky shone through. The sunset was colored in violent reds and burning golds. We sat into the deep twilight, the shadows of watchfires flickering across our faces. I lay down with him as I had done in his tent the night I thought I was leaving Arthen forever. The warmth of his body was sweet. We held each other quietly in the wind. On high, the summit of Ellebren shimmered like a ghost hand in the clouds.

7

I must have fallen asleep for a while. When I woke he was watching me, stones framing his face. When he saw I was awake he laughed softly. "This is my court magician, this sleepy child."

I yawned. I had not known I was so tired, though it had been almost two days since I slept. Nestling close to him, I listened not only to his strong heartbeat but also to the wind on the High Place, the smell of shadow keen in my nostrils. Kirith Kirin let me lie against him. He asked, "What are you thinking?"

"I'm listening."

"What happened on the High Place?   Drudaen was aware of you?"

"Yes. Very much."

"We saw the stars going out," Kirith Kirin said. "We saw the shadow come up and retreat."

"The Tower's a strong place to stand. He chose not to fight."

He watched tonight's stars beyond the tatters of cloud. "In the Book of Curaeth the prophet says, 'A night will come when a hand will be extended and withdrawn, when a shadow will fall on Laeredon but not on Immorthraegul. One standing in a strong place will have a voice for many. But still the shadow will fall on Laeredon.' I've read the book so often I have most of it by heart. Tonight the shadow is on Laeredon and all lands south."

He wrapped his cloak around my back till I was buried inside against him. Beneath the thin riding tunic I could feel his breath coming faster. His heart was pounding. He said, "We should go back soon and find the others, they'll want news. But I don't want to go anywhere. Do you have a magic for that?"

"I can make the moment linger for myself. Only the Sisters can bend time for others."

"I've known wizards enough to understand that for myself. But still one wishes."

Stretching his strong arms along the smooth stone, he let somberness cover him like a cloak. My hand rested on the sheet of tensed muscle at his midsection, quivering with blood and breath, the leather belt warm as his skin. I leaned over him and felt as if I were staring into a seething cauldron, fires licking the rim of his face. Breathless, I kissed the maelstrom. His mouth was tender and trembled. "I can make the evening live in memory," I said. "I can do that without any magic. The shadow may have fallen but it doesn't cover everything, Kirith Kirin. Tonight it won't cover you."

From a place deep within, next to the bone, some long-held tension released. The return of his spirit into his whole flesh was palpable to my hands. He watched me instead of the sky. "Imral won't like that, will he?"

My jaw set. "I'm your Thanaarc, and the cloak I'm wearing now has no sleeves. I've walked on Ellebren where few others have ever walked. Nobody can tell me where to sleep any more."

"Not even me?"

"Except you," I said, tracing the line of his jaw.

The question surprised me. "No, I suppose he doesn't."

"Of course he doesn't. He believes himself to be the best of men, to be exactly what the times require. All his friends tell him so. The people in his coterie let hardly a day go by without reassuring him that he is the great statesman of his time, that no man so gifted has been born among us in a thousand generations, that by rights he should be the ruler of Aeryn rather than Athryn Ardfalla or Kirith Kirin."

"Can such people really exist?"

She blinked at me, as if she could not believe my stupidity. Her voice was more charitable than her expression. "One forgets how young you are. Yes, Jessex—may I call you Jessex?—yes, there are indeed such men. I know, I've seen it, in my house, in the houses of my friends." She watched the fire a moment. She looked up at the sky. "Now the deed is done and the shadow lord will have his way. Athryn Ardfalla has brought about her own ruin."

"She's still Queen."

"A Queen doesn't let a thing like shadow happen to her people. Do you have any conception, any idea, what shadow is like?"

I looked at the glimmering light on the summit of Ellebren. "Yes, I think so."

She had followed my gaze. Her expression sobered. "From above, it's not the same as beneath. No, you'll never quite understand that fear, I expect."

"What fear?"

"You're a magician. You can never know what it is to fear one like you. You can never know what it is to be helpless."

Her face had washed clear of color. Fire danced in her eyes. She was remembering something, a vivid memory.

I had been like a boy with her through our talk. But the sight of this pain that filled her made me remember what else I was. I said a Word, softly, and took her hand in mine. One does not do this lightly with a well-born lady. She was startled and nearly pulled the hand away. But it was just plain skin and bone, toughened by hours on the rein, by practice with the sword, and it wanted warmth and comfort then. "Maybe you've had reason to be afraid of Lord Keerfax. I think you have. But you'll never have any reason to be afraid of me."

The hand relaxed. Tension fled from her face. The woman shone through, awkward, never beautiful, proud, strong, gentle. "Your heart would need much twisting before I'd fear it, I think." She gazed at the sleeping Kirith Kirin, curls tangled in my sash, with clear fondness. "One can see why he cares for you."

"You have one thing wrong, though." He gazed thoughtfully upward at the Tower summit. His fingers moved on my shoulder. "No one has ever stood on Ellebren. Kentha only completed the Tower, no one ever used it. The Sisters didn't tell you that?"

"The Sisters claimed they didn't know much about Tower magic."

He laughed, raucously. "The Sisters know whatever they want to know. They chose not to tell you maybe. They are crafty."

I watched him with what felt like a stupid look on a my face. "No one? No one at all?"

He shook his head. Some sadness returned to his face, though no distance intervened between us. "Kentha was able to use the lower rooms for the casting of the Eyestone lattice and other purposes when they were complete, but by the time she placed the Eyestone on the Height her time had already passed, as she said. She was pregnant with the child and returned the Tower keys to me after she and the Tervan specialists raised the stone." He paused, still touching my shoulder. "That was the day she told me she had prepared the place, and one would come to stand in it. She meant you."

He named the various parts of the Tower with ease. I remarked on it and asked if he had ever been taken inside. His face became firm, almost imperceptibly shifting to sternness. "Ellebren is within my realm, in my house. I have been as high as the Room-Under-Tower. There is no part of Inniscaudra where I can't go."

"Yes, my lord," I said, and the sternness dissolved. He did not object to the 'my lord' in this case. That made me smile.

"It's a lot of stairs to climb, you understand. I don't use it as a picnic spot." He glanced at me from the corner of his eye but did not allow even the glimmer of a smile.

We returned down Falkrigul afterward. The whole walk I was listening to the Height, shifting more of myself into kei. In some manner Kirith Kirin understood this and asked, "Do you hear anything? Is Drudaen changing?"

"Shadow's stable and growing, that's the main difference. He'll be stronger. I'm afraid of what's happening beneath."

"He'll be making fear," Kirith Kirin said. "He eats it like food."

"How could Queen Athryn let this happen?"

Mist droplets had settled like a jeweled veil over his black curls. "I don't know. It may be that she has no choice."

We passed beneath the bulk of Evaedren, its marble face shuddering with the shadows of watchfires on the high wall. The wind moaned, both here and where it was shredding clouds. He sighed and pulled me against him. In every move, sadness and happiness were mixed but not blended. One could read moments of both on his face, one could feel each coursing through his body. His mind was in the clouds, too, hovering over the south. "I know from reports what Drudaen did in Turis when he put the shadow there, when he rode through the country on storms and fires. I've never seen it for myself. Now, the whole south…"

A fire was burning on the terraces below Thenduril. Shadow figures moved on the perimeter of the blaze. The Finra Brun and the Nivra Kaleric stood with wine cups held loosely. Hearing our footsteps, they turned. Brun called, "Good evening, gentlemen," in her throaty voice, and Kaleric bowed politely to Kirith Kirin.

The moment they recognized me was easy to guess: they each turned from me to the Tower where many-colored light was glimmering. Kirith Kirin saw this moment too. Laughing heartily, he said, "You'll just have to get used to this, Brun. We have one among us who can be many places at the same time."

Kaleric, a young lord with fine, strawberry-blonde hair and features that indicated he might have Venladrii blood as well as the basic plainsman stock, gave me a skeptical look, nostrils flared slightly. He asked, "What news is there from Ellebren?"

He said the name with considerable ease. I was surprised at this. Kirith Kirin gave me leave to speak by a short, royal, nod of the head.

I said, "A darkness has fallen over the south that won't be lifted by sunrise. Lord Keerfax tried to send shadow northward as well, but we got here in time and the Tower has stopped him."

"Shadow in the south." Brun's eyes were like glass, unseeing. "Over Cuthunre too?"

"Yes, my lady. Over the whole land from Bruinysk to the sea."

"You'll fight it?"

"As best I can." I swallowed. "But he holds all the southern High Places. I won't be able to do much good."

"Shadow," she said. "Eye in Heaven, what has the Queen done?"

Kaleric, whose family lands were in the Lower Fenax, watched her with vague sympathy. "What is shadow?" he asked.

Kirith Kirin answered before I could. "Day won't come beneath shadow, except a kind of watered light. Crops don't grow. The wind fouls. Animals and people die after a while, or change."

Kaleric paled. "What do you mean, change?"

"You've heard of the Verm? Before shadow came there were no Verm."

Silence fell. Kirith Kirin asked where were the others a⟨nd⟩ told him; Vaeyr and Idhril were napping indoors. Unril and D⟨…⟩ were with the twice-named, touring the Lower House. Im⟨…⟩ led the horses to Erennor Vale to graze.

Kirith Kirin brought bread and cheese from his saddl⟨e⟩ stowed there from the night before. That and the wine mad⟨e as⟩ good a supper as I was likely to get. Kirith Kirin kept me near⟨,⟩ said little, watching the fire as if he were reading signs of the fut⟨ure⟩ in it. Soon he had fallen asleep with his head in my lap. Kaleric we⟨nt⟩ off walking by himself; one could hear his boots scuffing marble ⟨in⟩ the distance. Brun sat near us, comfortable in the silence. I foun⟨d⟩ her hawkish countenance pleasant in the firelight, bright fierce eyes shifting restlessly, brocaded cap snug on her close-cropped hair. The Anynae are never without their caps, even indoors, unless they are going to bed. I might have resented her nearness if her spirit had not burned so clear, if her sorrow had not been so apparent.

A few questions passed between us and soon she was talking about her home in the south. She spoke Jisraegen very well, for a southerner, and I was careful to pitch my voice in the lower modes. She had left her husband, who still lived on the country estate in north Cuthunre; she doubted anyone was using the house in Teliar these days. That house had been her pride, a legacy of her mother's family, designed by Ithambotl and built of the fine Briidoc marble that nobody can get any more. The house was centuries old, situated in a large garden on a hilltop. From it one could see the mountain spur on which sits Cunevadrim; one could see the descent of the Osar through verdant green, checkered fields. When Brun spoke of her house, stolen from her by royal decree when she fled north with Theduril, one could see how much she had loved her life in that strange country. She even spoke fondly of her husband once or twice, his habit of wearing his boots to bed, his love for his favorite horse. "We will see him soon I think," Brun said, with a wry look. "My lord Chorval is one of Drudaen's staunchest supporters. He can afford to be now that he has control of all my property."

"It's hard for me to realize there are people who serve and honor Drudaen."

Brun laughed, deep and hearty. "There are folks who would swear they love him, who write songs in praise of his virtue. There are folks who do just that. Do you think he believes himself to be a bad man?"

Kaleric returned to the fire and our quiet conversation ended. Kaleric was also disturbed by my news. He eyed Kirith Kirin warily as if making certain the Prince slept, and asked questions I didn't really understand at first. This shadow I had talked about, was it really everywhere? Over the whole south? Drudaen really made it, himself? Tomorrow the sky would be dark same as today, this wasn't passing weather?

I explained what I could about it, patiently. Yes, shadow was real. Yes, it reached as far as I could see from Ellebren, which was a long way. Yes, Drudaen made it. The sky would be dark tomorrow and the day after and the day after, until Drudaen lifted his hand.

"But what about the crops?" Kaleric asked. "They won't grow without sunlight."

"No," I said, "they won't."

"Then he's a fool," Kaleric said. "What will people eat if the crops don't grow?"

"They won't eat," Brun said. "Many of them will die."

Kaleric looked at her sharply. He had to remember to speak so she could hear. "How do you know?"

She smiled. "We southerners have felt shadow before. Not like you northerners who had the legend of Arthen to keep the sorcerer at a distance."

"But nobody would knowingly cause so much destruction—"

Brun's laugh in this case was not gentle, it was full of scorn. "You come from a family that should have taught you better, Kaleric. Have you never heard of the wars between Falamar and the Twelve? Have you never heard of the Hills of Slaughter? Have you never seen Turis? The Verm were humans only a century ago, just like you and me. Turis was green and her bounty put the Fenax to shame. But not a stick of wheat has grown there these four generations. Shadow did that."

"You never saw anything like this for yourself, I warrant," Kaleric said, his voice full of anger.

"No. But my grandmother did. Other folks remember it too. If you call their stories lies you might as well forget the rest of history, too; all we have is stories like those. My grandmother watched shadow smother Arroth and barely escaped with her life. First he destroyed the shrines and then he brought shadow. Few folks who lived in Turis were as lucky as my grandmother, who got out."

Their voices had risen and wakened Kirith Kirin. I could feel the return of tension in the sinews of his neck, the quickening of pulse. He sat up slowly. "What's all the quarreling about?" he asked.

"Nivra Kaleric doubts there is any shadow, since he can't climb to the top of the Tower and see it for himself." Brun's tone was haughty, her accent impeccable, and Kaleric flushed with embarrassment.

"I only said I doubted it could reach as far as the boy claims," Kaleric said.

"The boy claims nothing." Kirith Kirin's eyes narrowed. "The boy has seen. If it were not for him you wouldn't have to doubt the power of your enemy; the shadow would be hanging over your head."

"How can anyone, even a wizard, have such power? To blot out the sun over a whole countryside—"

The Prince sat up. "How? If I knew that I would be a wizard myself."

"It isn't such a great trick." I tried to sound matter-of-fact. "He's simply drinking the light into himself, and darkening the air, and in the process gathering energy. It's not that he means to do it, but it's a consequence of what he is; when he makes magic, he makes shadow. The scale on which he is doing it is another thing, but you have to remember Drudaen is master of all the High Places in the south. And now he has to defend all of that from me."

Brun nodded sagely as if she understood the principles involved and could do the trick herself. Kaleric looked at me as if I had begun speaking Upcountry. "You mean you could do it yourself?"

"Certainly. I won't. But I could. Turning back shadow is a much harder trick, because you have to beat Drudaen to do it. Fortunately I wasn't forced to do that; I simply let it be known I was on the High Place and that I was prepared to fight."

Kaleric had strayed beyond the boundaries of his knowledge and, seeing Kirith Kirin looking stern, began an apology. Kirith Kirin waved the words to silence. "Never mind, forget all that. You'll soon know more than you ever wanted to know about what Drudaen is capable of."

At that, Brun tactfully suggested to Kaleric that he accompany her on a walk down Falkri to the Under Gate—a place I had evidently passed but not noted—to see what had become of the rest of our party. Kaleric assented to this and bid both me and Kirith Kirin a polite farewell. One saw his breeding in the grace with which he let the awkward moments pass. Brun leaned down to me as she was about to depart. "Thank you, my little magician. Our talk was some comfort to me. I hope we get to be better friends in the coming days."

Kaleric lit a torch in the pit-fire and the two of them departed. Kirith Kirin drew me close and said, "Brun likes you, does she?"

"She's very sad. She's afraid for her home. She told me a lot about it."

"Which home? The house in Ivyssa?"

"No, Teliar. Did I say that right?"

He repeated the city-name and I heard the difference. "The house in Ivyssa is grander. The Teliar house is older and finer, though, and Ithambotl built it. She needn't worry, though."

"Why not?"

"Her husband will see to it the houses are kept up. Shadow won't fall too heavily on anything belonging to Chorval."

I would have asked who Chorval was but we were interrupted by the return of Imral from pasturing the horses. He called out a greeting in the Venladrii tongue and Kirith Kirin answered so quickly both voices rang together on the stones of the courtyard. Imral ran up to the fire looking more animated than I had ever seen him, saying in High Speech, "You should have come with me Kirith Kirin, the meadow is even more beautiful than I remembered. The moonflowers were opening when I left; I could hardly tear myself away."

"Moonflowers! There's hardly enough light for that."

"There's more than you think. Our Jessex seems to be winning the local battle."

I was nearly buried in the Sister-cloak; I suppose he thought me a pile of fabric till I stirred. "At least someone appreciates me."

"Jessex! Good lord, I thought you were Brun fallen asleep by the fire."

"There are worse people to be mistaken for."

"So, what happened on the height?"

Imral sat by Kirith Kirin and poured himself wine from the skin. The question sent me above, to the wind on the flagstone and the crying of voices from far away. Kirith Kirin answered for me. "Drudaen has declared himself openly, or at least that's how it looks. Jessex turned back shadow from the north but not from the south."

Silence fell. The exuberance drained from Imral's face. "Do we know what's happening under it?"

"I'm listening, trying to learn," I said. "But he's been preparing for this a long time, ever since he got hints from the Sisters that he might be opposed. It will take me some time to see through his veils."

Imral looked upward at the light from the Tower. It colored
his face silver-white. "When I was in Erennor I saw the light on the
summit and thought you were still there."

"I am still there," I said, and Kirith Kirin laughed.

They asked more questions and I told the story of my hours on
the High Place. Their understanding of magic, of my work, was
more complete than I would ever have guessed. Kirith Kirin asked
me what I meant when I remarked that Drudaen knew he might be
opposed and I told the story of the day in Hyvurgren Field when
the Sisters caught me up in the storm and took me to their house in
the encircling mountains. We had not had much time for tale-telling
and talking was a relief. For so long I had locked up these secrets in
my head.

The evening grew long and still the touring party did not return. I lay by the fire listening to the night. On the High Place
birds were crying, shadows of wings wheeling. Kirith Kirin's hand
cupped my brow, fingers drifting in my hair. Again I was in both
places, glad of the hand and listening upward to the echoing cries,
knowing the birds were friends of my enemy. Murmuring Words,
I searched for the shadowed wings. Even with my eyes closed I
could detect the change of light above, and laughed. Imral and
Kirith Kirin had been talking; they paused and Kirith Kirin asked,
"What's so funny, boy?"

"We're being watched. He's sent spies over Ellebren."

"Spies?"

"Birds. I can't tell what kind."

His fingers moved in my hair. "Do you need to go up there again?"

"No."

"I thought he couldn't see over Arthen," Imral said. "That's
what the lore would have one believe."

"The veil doesn't extend over Ellebren. It can't. But mine
does now."

My song was rising from Ellesotur. The light wheeled and
danced. The birds' eyes dimmed and their cries changed, became
audible shrieks. No harm came to them but without vision they
could not guide their flight. Wind carried them far away from the
Tower before I let them go.

My song continued till my veil extended over Ellebren, the
House, all the land surrounding the three hills, Lake Thyathe. Kirith
Kirin's hand continued to rest on my forehead. Imral was singing
softly under his breath. Drowsiness was sweeping through the

parts of me that were not concerned with vigilance over the Tower. This was also a new sensation. Heedless of voices, wanting only the hand.

8

I dreamed I was walking on air while Commyna held my hand and sang a song. She was trying to teach me how to pull down the stars from the sky but for some reason I could not get the trick, the stars kept dripping through my fingers, and each time I looked up, the stars had changed. Kirith Kirin was there wearing full battle gear, breastplate and greaves, leather war-thongs in his hair. He understood everything Commyna was saying in spite of the fact that she was speaking in Wyyvisar, and when he stretched up his hand planets descended into his fingers and fell glittering like a crown around his head.

When I woke he was lifting me from the flagstones, the embers of fire reflected from the kirin-ring on his hand, and Imral was saying, "I wish you would think better of this."

"The boy belongs with me," Kirith Kirin said, but there was no conviction in his voice.

"No one is arguing about that," Imral answered. "But for you to be seen taking him to your bed now, without any ceremony—"

"I think this is a bunch of rot," said another voice, Karsten's.

I felt the warmth of Kirith Kirin's nearness, touching the curve of his chest with my fingertips. He had lifted me easily as if my weight were nothing. I felt the same magnetism between us as when we had lain beneath the portal-arches at the base of Ellebren and remembered what I had told him. "What kind of ceremony do you want, Imral?"

"I thought you were asleep," Kirith Kirin murmured.

He set me on my feet. The cloak had fallen off my shoulder, as had my tunic; the night air was cool on my bare flesh. We were alone by the fire, the four of us. "Where's Mordwen?" I asked.

"Gone to bed," Karsten said, patting down a stray lock of my hair. "Along with the others. We're well into third watch, you've been asleep a while."

"Not long enough," Imral said, giving me a rueful smile. "I didn't mean for you to hear this debate of ours."

"Why not? I'm its subject."

"Yes. But it isn't proper for a boy of your age to hear such a matter discussed openly."

"He's right," Kirith Kirin said. "We'll let it go for now."

The look of bitter darkness returned to his face. It was plain he would let Imral have his way for propriety's sake, and that Imral would allow this to happen as well even though he didn't look much happier about it than Kirith Kirin. Yet while I was asleep Kirith Kirin had been prepared to carry me away without asking. "We won't let it go. We'll finish it now once and for all. What sort of ceremony do you require, Imral? Karsten?"

"You're too young for any such thing," Imral said. "You're a boy not yet old enough to be out of sleeves."

I pulled the Fimbrel Cloak onto my shoulder and smiled. "The man who can put me in sleeves again doesn't live, sir."

"He has a point there," Karsten said, stifling a laugh.

Imral looked extremely uncomfortable. He appealed to Kirith Kirin as if for mercy. "I'm only trying to prevent more loose talk. I know how you feel about the boy."

"I don't," I said.

"What?" Kirith Kirin spun me around. "What do you mean?"

"I know you were prepared to carry me off when I was sleeping but you don't seem so eager now that I'm awake. I've had lots of hints but they don't seem like so much right at the moment." I turned to Imral and Karsten. "As for the two of you, you didn't mind leaving me with Kirith Kirin the night before we rode to Jiiviisn Field."

Karsten merely smiled. Imral said, "But we thought you were leaving forever—"

"Honor is honor," I said. "It makes no such exceptions. And gossip is gossip. Kirith Kirin's bodyguards certainly saw me leaving the tent that morning. As far as that goes, no one will see me leaving Kirith Kirin's bed tomorrow morning if I don't choose to be seen. Now, what ceremony do you require to make this an honorable union?"

I asked this of no one in particular. The three of them looked at each other. Kirith Kirin said, "You're not old enough for the gifting, as Imral has said."

"Why not?"

"Your birthday is not until spring."

"I have had my birthday," I said, "three days ago in Jiiviisn Field. The son of Kinth will be sixteen in spring but I am Yron, and Yron is already a man."

"The gentry won't see it that way," Imral said.

Karsten spoke vehemently. "They won't like Kirith Kirin sleeping with his magician with or without benefit of ceremony, and we all know that!" She cocked an eyebrow, watching me. "If he's old enough to stand on Ellebren where no one living or dead has ever stood, then he's old enough to be called a man and not a boy. The Diamysaar said as much."

The three of them looked at each other, and something passed between them that I failed to understand.

Imral said, mildly, "There is that."

I turned to Kirith Kirin and took his hand. "The Sisters said you were afraid I'd ensorcelled you, that it was the reason you tested me on Sister Mountain. Are you still afraid?"

He shook his head. Words came softly. "No."

Karsten said, "Then let Imral and me be witness to your pledge, my dears."

Kirith Kirin trembled. Finally he managed words. "Imral? What do you say? If this doesn't suit you I can't go ahead with it—"

Imral drew in audible breath. His eyes were moist, glittering. "We'll have to do the ceremony again, properly, or else people will truly never forgive us. Mordwen especially."

I had been holding my breath without realizing it. I embraced Imral and kissed his cheek. The Venladrii Prince was trembling, too. "Thank you."

"It would help if the Sisters had not taught you so young. We'd all know better how to treat you."

"These are degenerate times," I said, trying to sound like Mordwen.

We built the fire up to a pleasant roar again and exchanged gifts—most such oaths are taken in firelight even when the gifting takes place during the day. Kirith Kirin gave me a silver bracelet engraved with runes sacred to his house, Imhonyy. I could think of nothing to give him that had not first come from him until I remembered the necklace hidden in the cloak. While the locket was to be kept secret I could see no harm in giving him the chain, and so, in shadow, I pulled the leather pouch from its hiding place.

The red stone in the bird's eye glimmered in my hand. The pendant felt oddly heavy, and for some reason put me in mind of the High Place where the same soft radiance pulsed like liquid starlight. But the others were waiting, I had no time. I returned the pendant to its hiding place and found my place by the fire.

The oath one takes is simple. "I will live in you as you will live in me. I give you my promise with this gift. May the gift last as long as the promise." The words are deceptive for all that. To break this oath is a dishonor from which no one can recover.

Kirith Kirin said the words and placed the bracelet around my wrist. I said the words and gave my gift. The silver chain was long enough that it did not bind him. He touched it and embraced me. He wondered where I had gotten it but hesitated to ask; Karsten was passing round cups of wine for the pledge-mark. We touched cups and drank in silence. The thing was done.

No one said anything. I touched the bracelet, glad of its simplicity. I would wear it forever. Kirith Kirin was touching the silver chain at his neck. "This is true-silver, where did you come by anything so fine? Did you and Karsten have this planned?"

"I had nothing to do with it." Karsten examined the silver chain too, idly curious. But her eyes narrowed. "These are house runes. Bend down, Kirith Kirin, I can't read them."

I studied them at the same time. She was right, there they were. I had spent much time studying the locket to the exclusion of the chain; my heart was in my throat. This one secret I had kept even from the Sisters; I supposed I was keeping faith with my mother's last request.

"What does it say?" I asked.

Karsten turned to me, gazing at me skeptically. "You don't know? These are signs of the House of Turisaeviisn. This belonged to Kentha."

Imral bent to study them as well and confirmed what Karsten claimed. Kirith Kirin touched the runes and watched me. "Where did you get this?"

"From my mother. She gave it to me the night I left home."

Imral frowned. "Where did your mother get it, do you know?"

"From my grandmother Fysyyn."

He laughed that melodic laugh of his. "This grandmother of yours has always been a mystery to me. Where did she come by a necklace from one of the Jhinuuserret?"

I had no answer. Kirith Kirin, watching me intently, read more in my expression than I meant anyone to see. He took my face in his warm hands. "There's more, isn't there? Don't be afraid, tell me. We're joined to one another now, we can't have secrets."

I brought the leather pouch to the fireside. As if the night had suddenly turned cold, I shivered visibly. Karsten noticed the change. "Good lord, Jessex, what's wrong?"

"I swore to my mother I'd never show this to anyone." Opening the pouch, I let the locket fall onto Kirith Kirin's palm. "When she gave it to me she was very afraid, the night before I left the farm. The next morning she made me and Uncle Sivisal leave as soon as the sun was up, and she told us to get to Arthen as fast as we could if we valued our lives. She never said so, but she was thinking about the necklace. She knew something terrible was going to happen. I think this is the cause."

Kirith Kirin's face drained of color. His grip tightened on my shoulder and he pulled me so close to him I could hardly breathe. Imral noted the change and asked, alarmed, "What's wrong?"

Kirith Kirin shook his head and passed the locket to Imral. He and Karsten studied it by firelight. They sat back, stunned.

"This is the Bane," Karsten said. "Mother of heaven, Jessex—"

Imral turned the necklace in the light. The radiant stone caught points of fire in its facets. "I saw it when she made it, here. Kentha said it would return to us. So did the Diamysaar. Had you shown the necklace to them, Jessex?"

I shook my head emphatically. "No, never. I've kept my word to my mother just as I said I would. But one time Commyna saw it in my thoughts, though she never pressed me."

Kirith Kirin touched his lips to my forehead. "You haven't broken faith with your mother."

"No, indeed you haven't," Imral said firmly. "I doubt she knew what it meant to send this stone back into Arthen. I wonder if you know yourself."

"I know what the Bane is," I said. "Drudaen Keerfax gave it to Kentha when they were lovers—"

I stopped short, watching Kirith Kirin. He nodded. "Yes, I know what you're thinking. In the same ceremony that you and I just went through. She gave him a similar gift and he later used it to kill her after he had broken faith with her. Do you know the rest of the story?"

"She had born him a child in the Woodland. She killed the child and buried the gem in its grave—"

Kirith Kirin noted every change on my face. Imral said, "This answers many questions."

"You mean you think she never buried the gem."

"Or the child." Imral turned to Karsten. "You were right all along."

"He means I never believed Kentha would kill her baby," Karsten said. "Not when she went through fire and ice to have it in the first place."

I was washed white and numb. Imral handed me the locket and I studied the light within the gem, the strange writing inscribed on the back of the setting. "If she didn't bury the child, what did she do with it?"

"With him," Karsten said. "His name was Aretaeo, I think. Don't you understand? In Mordwen's true dream, the one that brought you here, your lineage on your mother's side is given, but not in the usual way: child of Sybil daughter of Fysyyn, Fysyyn child of Aretaeo. Aretaeo false child of Matvae."

"False child" is the phrase we use when the different-gendered parent does not acknowledge the child. So that a son would be referred to as the false child of his father's wife when the real mother would not or could not acknowledge parentage. A thrill ran down my spine. I spoke so quietly I could hardly hear my own voice. "Grandmother knew this. When she was in her last sickness she told me her father's mother was a witch. Not Matvae but the real one, she said. She wouldn't tell me what she meant. I guess my mother knew, too."

Imral studied the stars for a time. "I suppose it would be unmerciful to waken Mordwen and Pelathayn even for news like this."

"The secret's kept these generations, it can keep a few more hours," Kirith Kirin said. He studied my face a long time, and I studied his for any sign of change.

We sat quietly for some time listening to the fire. The necklace took heat from my palm and burned. It was hard to realize what I held, what it meant. This was the gem that Drudaen feared, the legend of which had kept him out of Montajhena since the breaking of the Towers. This was the reason he had killed my family—his own kin, as it turned out. When two lovers change gifts in this way, they make a vow that will never change. The gift is the sign of that. When one of them is a magician, to give a stone as that gift is to give a part of oneself, and such a thing in magic can always be used. There's no defense against an object that carries such a vow. But even with my magic senses freed, I felt no stirring within the stone, no sign of whatever force it contained that could be used to harm Drudaen. In setting the stone into the metal, Kentha had bound the stone's connection to Drudaen in some way. I studied it again, particularly the runes on the back. "What is this writing? Do you know?"

Kirith Kirin took the locket and fingered the engraving. "These are priest-runes from Cunuduerum. Kentha was learned in their language."

I touched the gem again, breathed on it and listened. Not even a murmur of song emerged from its heart. "The writing disguises whatever power is in the gem. I don't know what use it will be to me." Kirith Kirin took the necklace and tied it in the leather pouch again. "Don't worry about that now. Time will show you what to do." Silence as we watched the fire, the shimmer of heat over the roch-stones. Small sentences were traded. Kirith Kirin promised me a tour of Inniscaudra in the morning. Imral noted that the Army should arrive in Illaeryn soon; I told him the soldiers were at the edge of Illaeryn already and ought to reach the Three Hills by day after tomorrow. From the High Place I heard nothing of note. I let my thought linger there, drinking comfort, till Kirith Kirin stood and pulled me up by the hand. "We're going to bed," he said, and we did.

9

I brought my pack with me and followed Kirith Kirin into one of the rooms that opened onto the terrace. We were only a few hours from dawn. In the room, Kirith Kirin lit a tube-shaped lamp of a type I did not know, that cast off bright light better suited to early evening. Kirith Kirin dimmed it and the rooms took on a more pleasant aspect. The room was large and sparely furnished. Carved and painted screens hid a wash basin in the corner. Someone had already drawn a pitcher of water.

We were alone together by our own efforts for the first time with the freedom to do as we chose. There were no more barriers between us except those within us: my ignorance and fear and his reluctance to frighten me, his reticence to touch what had not been touched before. When we had slept together in his tent the night before the ride to Jiiviisn Field, we had simply held each other and in fact had not even undressed. Tonight we had sworn to live within each other and we would do more. I stood over the water basin with water running out of the pitcher and let the rhythm of my breathing restore the calm that each moment threatened to dissolve in me.

I was a boy again, a plain ignorant child. Nothing I had learned at Illyn Water prepared me for being naked with a man. What little I had picked up in Camp through overhearing barracks talk had only added to my confusion. I found myself wishing for Uncle Sivisal, who was family and who could have explained some of this to me.

Kirith Kirin took off his cloak and laid it on a table beside one of the folding screens. He pulled off his boots and I felt an unknown tide of heat rising in me at the thought that he would go on taking off his clothes. At that moment he did not, however. He returned to the basin wearing the tunic and leggings. His arms, corded with muscle, reached to lift the cloak from me. "Can one simply treat this like an ordinary cloak or does it need to be hung up?" he asked.

"It doesn't matter," I whispered and tried to take it from him. He shook his head, smiling, and laid the cloak atop his own. The fabric, quiescent, merely glimmered.

I knelt to unlace the thongs of my leather boots, feeling my heart begin to pound. Kirith Kirin was unrolling a bedroll on the bare bed. When I laid down the boots he watched me and smiled. His breathing had become more audible and I thought I could see the heart beating beneath the tunic. We watched each other. He reached for me, unclasping my tunic at the shoulders.

I had never felt so naked, my nerves on fire. His hands played at the edges of my linen drawers. He ran his fingertips down my bare torso and I gasped. I touched his face. He watched me, still playing his hands along my body.

His beauty caught me in a fever, and in a rush of blood my thought dissolved, my heartbeat increased, my hands reached for the pins that held his own tunic in place. He had to help me with the unfamiliar fastenings. When the fabric fell away from him all my nerves began to sing.

I had known he was strong and beautiful but this reality was beyond anything I had imagined. In the pale light his body was like moonlight made into perfect flesh. The strong neck descended to broad, round shoulders and a deep chest. Where my nipples were pink and soft his were dark and flat. My nipples made points only when he touched them; his were already pointed and firm. Silken hair dotted the cleft of his chest and the ridge of his abdomen, descending into the loose drawers. I touched him artlessly without thinking he would feel for me as I felt for him; I was beyond planning. But when I brushed my hands along his bare flesh he caught his breath and closed his eyes, and when I continued to touch him he pulled me close.

We bathed one another standing at the basin. The linen drawers tangled around our ankles. I was familiar with my own erection but the certainty of his was awesome. Our bodies entwined with water

streaming down us and we dried each other using the tunics we had
shed. We walked arm in arm to the bed, a bigger bed platform
than any I had ever seen, with our sleeping rolls on top of it, and in
it we lay with one another, moving with a rhythm that rose up in me,
I know, though I had no idea as to its origin, it came from so deep.
For what teaching was needed words were irrelevant. I was awash
in a world of sensation strange and wonderful as anything I had
ever learned at Illyn Water. I made love to Kirith Kirin with my
mouth and hands and with all my heart.

I will have offended some by saying so much. While the Jisraegen
are not prudish, Kirith Kirin was and is a legend among us. One
does not lightly undress him. But that night in the strange bed in
Inniscaudra's lower reaches, the legend was naked for good. The
dark prince and the lighthearted youth were the same. When we
were done, lying tangled in newness with the first hints of dawn in
the air, I leaned up and looked at the man, the strength and beauty,
the soft lips whose tension I had kissed away. Kirith Kirin lay with
his arm loosely around me. His eyes were full of peace. I had used
no magic art but magic had occurred between us anyway. We had
said nothing to each other during this whole time but now I said, "I
love you with my whole life. I always will."

"Me too, for you," he said, and pulled me against him.

I thought I was too happy to sleep. But his comfortable strong
body drew me down into rest as easily as it had drawn me upward
into pleasure. I fell asleep with his breath warm along my neck and
the sound of the wind on the High Place echoing in my ears.

10

In the morning we went over all my lessons from the night before
to make sure I had them by heart. Afterward we lay abed for a long
time, later than I had ever slept in my life. No one disturbed us.

One does not crow about one's good fortune if one wants to
keep it; so the proverb goes. When I leaned above Kirith Kirin in
that ample bed with the makeshift bed-clothing tumbled over his
arms and thighs, I knew I was watching my life. Love of him
burned like an ache and a spacious loneliness.

Seeing this morning sadness in my face, he drew me closer. His
skin was smooth as viis. A strong heart sent its pounding into my ears.
"I'm afraid to move," he said. "I'm afraid all this will dissolve."

"Me too. But it won't, will it? We're pledged now, no one can change that, can they?"

"No one. Not Queen, not Lord, not YY-in-Heaven."

I put my finger on his lips. "Don't blaspheme."

His laughter shook me. "Not blasphemy. A great dare. It was her promise that brought you here. You're mine now until I leave this world or until it breaks into pieces. I will hold my Lady Mother to that."

His eyes were closed. The corners of the lids were wet. I touched the trembling lashes and brushed my mouth on his. "Then I'll hold you both to it. Now, if I'm any judge the sun is shockingly high in heaven and we had both better get up from this bed before Imral scolds us for scandalizing the lords on our first morning."

"Imral has had enough of scolding us, I think."

"I hope so," I said.

"You don't bear him any grudge, do you?"

"No. He was right. But I was tired of waiting."

Kirith Kirin bounded out of bed. He crossed the sunlit room naked and dazzling. When I got back my breath I followed.

We dressed one another. Kirith Kirin turned his nose up at my plain tunic and swore he would see me better dressed in days to come. "You're in my court after all, you might as well look like a courtier."

"People will think I'm putting on airs."

"People will think you're putting on airs no matter what you do. But people with discernment will know you're dressing to suit your rank. No argument. Good clothes are just the beginning."

"Oh?"

"Certainly. You must have lands, houses, jewels, silver, cattle, horses, soldiers, householders." He walked up and down the room declaiming with a boot in his hand. "And titles of course, you'll need a list of titles as long as your arm. You're nobody without a lot of hereditary thises and thats to string out after your name."

"This will naturally endear me to the other nobles no end."

"Naturally. The more rich noble folk there are the better everybody likes it." He had amused himself so thoroughly he sat laughing on the bed. I knelt to help him with the boot as an excuse to be near him, lacing leather thongs up his shapely calf. He ran fingers through my hair. "You know I'm not joking entirely, don't you?"

"Yes. I'm not joking either. There's no need for you to go out of your way to offend people on my behalf."

"No one will be offended. I'll be doing a lot of reordering. Karsten must get her estates back, and Pelathayn, and Mordwen. Athryn has confiscated land from all the minor houses and most of the great ones. I can't do anything about the southern lands but the northern ones I can."

"Even so, you shouldn't give me gifts I don't need."

"Not gifts. You have claim to most of Kentha's lands by birthright."

"Sivisal has the same claims. Give the stuff to him."

He stood, lifting me with him. He looked me in the eye, his expression both amused and stern. "You've said that sort of thing too many times to make me comfortable. You're Thanaarc; Sivisal isn't. I'll see that he's provided for but you are my main concern. I know you mean to be modest but it won't help. You're not a farm boy now. You're my sworn companion. I would have had to do most of this even before we knew about the necklace. Now that we know about your lineage the job is both easier and harder. You are a descendant of two great houses, your kin include Cunavastar, Falamar, Edenna Morthul, Kentha, even Commyna herself—"

"Commyna!"

"She never told you that tale? Few folks know it. Falamar Inuygen was her son. Cunavastar was the father." He smiled. "You've inherited the family looks, I think."

I had thought the revelations of the night before would put an end to surprises. Now this. I sat on the bed and blinked.

"Come on," he said, "it isn't so bad having famous relatives."

"No," I answered, "but it looks like mine tend to hang around longer than most."

"Long lives run in the family." Kirith Kirin picked me up as if I weighed nothing and held me over his head. "I for one am glad of that."

From happiness we emerged into sallow daylight over an empty terrace. Chill wind swept down from the mountains. The sky was so pale it was almost white. Kirith Kirin walked ahead of me to the fire pit where an oet awaited us full of jaka; he passed beyond it and walked in a circle round the fire. "I don't like the way that sky looks."

"Neither do I." I poured jaka for us. He took the cup without a word. I sat with the heavy mug in my hands, watching curls of steam; I turned my eye inward and used the jaka as a fixing-point. Chanting softly, I relaxed into the dual state.

I saw two things. At the center of a body of water, vaster than many Lake Illyns, an island rose as sheer as a High Place. On the rock-island sat a fair palace of dark stone. The surrounding land lay shrouded in darkness but the palace was bright. Within the palace, seated in an open window, an old woman sat with her hands folded in her lap. Three blue gems rested in the folds of her skirt. The gems glowed with weak light and the hands that occasionally stroked them were gnarled with age. The woman moved with difficulty and had a look of indescribable pain on her face. She was polishing the gems when the pain in her hands permitted the work. Through the window were ships approaching, flying blue banners.

That vision faded and another took its place. At the spur of dark mountains a Tower rose above a fortress of Tervan-worked stone. The brightness of the tower was not comforting but forbidding, pale as death and white like a field of ice. Within were rooms whose contents I could not see except one small chamber at its middle height. On a flat stone table draped with cloth lay my mother's corpse. I watched her with the dispassion one feels when one is kei; knowing she was my mother I still felt no grief. I could not tell if she were truly dead or if she were simply imprisoned within some enchantment the nature of which I could not discern. The vision was fleeting. Shadow fell again, and I returned to the terrace where the cup of jaka was still sending up its trails of steam.

Kirith Kirin knelt beside me, hand on my shoulder. No more than a moment had passed. He knew what I had been doing and simply waited for me to understand. It was a wonder to me; I had never expected tolerance from him after the storm on Sister Mountain. I told him what I had seen. He was thoughtful and sat back on his heels, sipping jaka.

"Was the first woman Queen Athryn?"

He nodded. "In the palace Dernhang on Kmur Island. Shadow would not trouble her while she has the gems with her. You say they were dim?"

"Yes. Like candles when they're dying. What are they?"

He lay his hand in my hair. When he looked at me he tried to push the worry aside. "A secret known only to a few. Protection for us, from magicians." He touched my hair tenderly to show he meant no malice. "The gems are called Karnost, and they're the source of law. YY gave them to us both, Athryn and me, when she set down the cycle that the Queen would rule Aeryn, then the King would rule after. We take the gems to Aerfax when the time comes for the

Succession, since they're tied to the Rock. But part of their strength depends on returning to Arthen, like nearly everything that comes from here. Like you and me."

I asked what he meant but he shook his head. "Not today. You've had enough strangeness. Today I want you to be as happy as you can be."

"But I never understood the Jhinuuserret could age. Athryn is old."

"We age for a time," he said. "Then we come to Arthen, to this house, to be made young again. Then a time comes, as for Mordwen, when YY no longer allows the life to be extended."

"Mordwen will die?"

"He'll cross the gates. When he's ready."

We were quiet again for a while. I thought of my mother lying on the cold stone. "The Tower was Yruminast," I said.

His face grew somber and he drew me against him. "Drudaen is apparently holding your mother there."

"Is she dead, do you think?" My voice trembled in spite of my attempts at self control.

"Jessex," he began, and stopped. I could feel the blood pounding in his veins. He drew a long, heavy breath. "If she isn't dead, by now it would be better if she were. I'm sorry. I wish I could tell you some easy lie but you wouldn't believe it and I don't want lies between us. Your mother hasn't your training. Without it her time with Drudaen has been torment. Be glad she's sleeping, if she is."

I heard Commyna's voice from long ago, *It would be better if she were dead.* The pain I had been unable to feel in kei flooded me. I couldn't remember when I had last cried for my mother and my family. Maybe I had been afraid. This time Kirith Kirin was there and I felt safe to let myself go. He set aside the jaka I had not drunk and rocked me in the breeze.

Later we talked quietly. He questioned me about other parts of the vision. His astuteness made it plain he understood my work on the High Place, and when I remarked on that he simply said, "I'm trained to be King over magicians as well as other folks." We finished the jaka and I wondered aloud, idly, where the others had gone. He smiled, lifting a note he'd found beneath the oet. "Imral says they've ridden to Immorthraegul to see the shrine. They're leaving us alone for the day." He was beaming and flushed. "So I can show you the House myself, without any distractions. Do you have to go up to the High Place?"

I shook my head. "No."

"You'll know if that changes?"

"Yes."

He let himself smile, as if he could only now believe nothing would come between us and these hours of privacy. What kind of life did he have that a day's quiet could seem like such bounty? Watching his face full of boyish happiness, I understood how scantly I knew him. I took his face in my hands. "Let's get away from here before they change their minds and come back."

He looked surprised as if he had thought me too shy to touch him on my own. So I kissed him, laying my hands along the smooth, full curve between his shoulders and neck. He sighed and took my hands in his. "When I met you by the river I knew you were for me. I knew you were too young but I thought I could wait patiently, I thought it would be enough to have you near, to look at you and know you had been sent for me. I cared for you even though you were mortal, which is hard for us. Now I wonder how I ever lived."

I looked into his eyes. "When you saw me with the Sisters and became so cold, I thought I would die of sadness."

"I was afraid. I thought you or they had worked an enchantment on me. To make me care for you."

"Commyna told me that was how you felt."

It pleased him that I had talked to Commyna about him. "She thought I was foolish I guess."

"No. The Sisters love you very much, Kirith Kirin. Commyna said it was not for me to judge you, that I should simply go on caring for you and show you that I would never attempt to—to get you to care for me that way."

"Commyna was right. When the news from Cordyssa called me away from Camp, I learned I wasn't as cold to you as I thought. And when I found out Cothryn sent you gifts—" His face flushed dark with blood. "I wanted to call him out or whip him bloody. One can't do that, of course, not to a person over whom one has power. I had to settle for banishing him to Maugritaxa, though Imral even tried to talk me out of that."

This raised a question I needed to ask, after the discussion of the night before. "Does Imral wish you'd have nothing to do with me?"

"Lord no! Imral cares for you very much; we all do. He's been trying to protect us both."

"Are people really likely to make so much fuss?"

"You'll see. It won't be pleasant. There are some folks, particularly southerners, who don't think men should lie down with men, or women with women. But we're not going to think about any of that right now. I'm going to show you Inniscaudra." A new thought brought a look of surprise to his face. "I can't remember the last time I was alone with anyone here. In fact I can't remember the last time anyone was alone in YYmoc."

"YYmoc?"

"An old name for the house. It means 'YY-written-in-stone.' The Evaenym believed YY-Mother wrote the whole history of created places, all that was or is to be, in the foundations of Inniscaudra."

By the end of the day I could believe it. Ancient the Jisraegen may be; the halls of Inniscaudra, built to no human scale, make the Forty Thousand Mothers and Fathers seem young.

We began in the Hall of Many Partings, which is also called the Hall of the Eldest, Jiivarduril, and the Hall of Last Days, Talhoneshduril. YY-Mother built this hall with help from the craftsmen from Smith country where the Tervan dwell in their city-in-the-mountain, Jhunombrae. The Tervan are not one of the created peoples but are much older, akin to the Orloc and the Untherverthen, having been born out of the roots of the Encircling Mountains when the living world was made. At the end of the war between YY and the Other, the Tervan came south from the mountains, leaving their city Jhunombrae empty for many ages, to live in Illaeryn and help heal the hurts of Arthen. They built the oldest parts of the House of Winter as a gift for YY. The high walls of Halobar Hall are built of many colors of stone. Immense tapestries hang between the tall, narrow windows. The hall was cold that morning; I wrapped myself in the Cloak and wished for a fire in the huge fireplaces that flanked the throne-dais and broke the long walls. These were so large that a company of soldiers could have stood inside each one. The mantles were decorated with stone carvings depicting the Tervan, Orloc, Untherverthen and Giants who were the Woodland's first inhabitants. The stone was smooth and cool to the touch.

One could not see out the windows; the sills were far above any human head. "Look how dirty," Kirith Kirin said, scanning the impossible height of one of them. "We'll be forty days and forty nights cleaning this place." But he looked happy.

The throne dais was enormous; in ceremony one could get most of the Nivri arranged on it alongside the throne itself, which was of oak and cedar, inlaid with gold and silver, globes of muuren on each arm. Set into the floor at the base of each side of the throne was a huge firepot, with curved flues hanging overhead to catch the smoke, a marvel of engineering. Since Halobar is not a hall of formal audience, the throne is on a low dais and has no canopy. When we were standing on the dais, Kirith Kirin grinned at me and had a seat. He sighed with satisfaction and set his hands on the arms, surveying the whole sweep of the huge, soaring chamber. "I love this room. Don't you?"

I gaped at everything, wonder-struck at the beauty of the woodcarving, the stone heads of the Orloc kings and Tervan Empresses, the fall of golden light across the brilliant-colored tapestries. Kirith Kirin understood my awe and let me look to my heart's content.

What struck one about the room was its earthiness, its literal quality: handcarvings more primitive than the work of modern artisans, tapestries woven in a long ago age, before we had advanced in weaving. When Grandmother Fysyyn told me stories about Inniscaudra I imagined a glittering fairyland festooned with gems and gleaming with gold leaf. Halobar was wooden and warm, almost simple, but grand in scale and proportion. One could smell the age. The Mother of Worlds who had once walked in this room was not a remote goddess, distant from men: she was a crone, a wise woman, a brewer of herb teas and an artisan in thread and stone. Through me surged an ache for the long ago that I had never known. It was as if I had remembered this room in my bones, as if I could see her walking in it.

With this feeling like a cloud around me, I followed Kirith Kirin into the Woodland Hall, Thenduril, expecting more wonders. The room so vast that a dozen of the squadron-sized fireplaces lined each of the long walls. But the chamber was empty and bare of ornament but for the throne dais where the Red Throne and the Blue Throne sat, each covered with gossamer cloth.

"There are no tapestries," I said. "And no carvings or glasswork."

"I had them removed a long time ago. We don't use this hall any more."

"Why not?"

He was silent, remembering. His face impassive. "The last time I held audience in this hall, I learned Athryn planned to keep me shut up in Arthen forever. Drudaen had convinced her he could keep her young outside Arthen, but that hasn't turned out to be the case for either one of them. That was when her sickness began. I thought she was sending a messenger to summon me south to make me King again. It was time. But the messenger she sent was Drudaen and the message he brought was that I would never be needed in Ivyssa. Now or in the future. So I exiled them both from Arthen and shut up this room and had all the pretty things taken out of it. We don't even open Thenduril for feasts these days. I have vowed I won't hold audience here again till the Summons comes." He drew a long breath, looking around the airy room. "Nor will I, even if there's no Summons for a thousand thousand years."

He headed out of the vast chamber and I followed, sorry for his hurt and anger. He meant to leave Thenduril directly, then changed his mind. "You must see this," he said.

We stopped in front of two enormous doors, large enough that a whole tree could have walked through without stooping. The doors were of polished duraelaryn, each planed and carved from the heart of a single bole. Except for golden nails and some pretty carved leaf-borders, they were unadorned. No scene of history was depicted on them. High above, the name of YY was carved into the lintel, along with the eye-sign.

"These are the doors that lead to the Tower of YY and to the Deeps of Inniscaudra," Kirith Kirin said. "They've been closed since YY brought up the Karnost Gems and gave the Law of Changes to the Jisraegen, after Falamar and Jurel were killed." He reached to the smooth, polished wood on which no mote of dust had settled. "When these doors open again, the present age will be swept away. I believe so, anyway. No one's tour of the House is complete without a moment here."

11

To describe all that he showed me in the course of that day would require another volume of equal length to the one you presently hold. I, who now know Inniscaudra better even than he, have never felt such magic within its walls. Never again has there passed a day when two walked there alone. To have Kirith Kirin himself show me the house where he first awoke to life—this was a gift for which I will thank the Mother through all my days, now that he is with me no more.

We ended the day as we began, in bed in the Under House, practicing those arts which he taught me and of which he seemed the perfect master. You may think it shameful that a boy uncloaked should revel in his debauchery but I make no apology to anyone. When I was called to Arthen to serve him I did not know what my fate would be, but even if I had known, I would have embraced it. When I met him in the Fountain Court in the ghost city, I knew him out of my whole being. If I had understood how to give myself to him at fourteen, I would have. If I could find him now, aged and changed, I would give myself again. Maybe one day, in my last hours, when the World-Breaking is begun, he'll find a way to cross the mountains again.

That day, in the quiet of the dusty room in the Under House, his arm across my chest, he said, "Now I can live. Whatever comes."

I kissed the tough skin of his palm in answer.

A wind blew through the room. To say something like that is to bargain with God, it is said.

To silence him, since I could feel his sorrow mounting, I spread Fimbrel over us both; the shimmering song surrounded us, and we lay in peace. What he heard from that fabric woven of the Sisters' love, I would not presume to say. As for me, there were within its folds many voices, some from the High Place, some from Illyn, some from other reaches. To those I added his voice, his sweetness, so that the Cloak would always carry this moment, the sum of this day.

Till sunset we lay in peace, when the return of our friends roused us. He lay his finger on my lips and smiled into my face, listening to their noise. "All ages of peace come to an end," he said, sighing, "even this one."

"We should join them, I guess."

The stillness within his face was like a light. "Unless you've learned to bend time for me."

I sighed and sat up in the bed. We found our clothes again, from the heap in which they had fallen, and dressed. At the moment before we returned to the terrace, to the sunset over Inniscaudra, he held me close, my hands on his chest. Nothing else made sound, only two hearts beating. Maybe this is the music from which the universe was born, throbbing through it still.

12

When we emerged into the air of sunset, I felt a little quaver of fear, not knowing what the others might make of the change between Kirith Kirin and me. We walked side by side to the place where Vaeyr stoked the fire, Pelathayn beside him skinning a shell-hen to roast for our supper. Grinning at us, Pelathayn said, "Well, Kirith Kirin, I know you don't like me cooking on the fine stones hereabouts, but if you want to eat I guess you'll give me leave."

"I give you leave," Kirith Kirin said, with a deep note of peace in his voice.

Vaeyr bowed his head. "We'll give you both your pledge-meal, in that case."

"And be honored to share it," added Lady Brun, smiling at me with warmth.

Mordwen kissed my brow with a tenderness that said everything. To Kirith Kirin he said, "You chose the right thing."

"I know, I feel it." Studying the fire-circle and the terrace, he asked, "Where are Karsten and Imral?"

"Returning the horses to the lawn," Mordwen answered. "Looking very much like the two of you look, I guess. Karsten has been dancing all day, she's so happy to be in the High Country again." He paused, his shaggy face full of emotion. "I feel it myself."

"Everyone does, I expect," Kirith Kirin said.

From the fire, Pelathayn started to sing a hunting song, his big voice booming against the stones; Kaleric and Vaeyr took it up with him, and Lady Unril joined the chorus too. Brun stepped toward Kirith Kirin and me with wine cups in hand. "This is a better gift than my singing would be, to one of you," she said, as we took the cups. "Blessings of the day be on you both."

Kirith Kirin, touched, bowed his head to her. "Your kindness will be remembered."

"We're all in magic today," she answered, without the least affectation. "All this will be remembered, I think." To me, with a twinkle in her eye, "I should have stayed up later, I guess. To witness this event."

Mordwen, deep-voiced, echoed, "Indeed. Sometimes it doesn't pay to want rest."

"You'll both be with us when we take the pledge again," Kirith Kirin said.

Brun acknowledged this, pleased. Mordwen would have expected as much; she felt the honor of it, coming from him. After, a look in her face made me sad. She and Mordwen led us nearer the fire, where we were pledged with full cups. Duvettre led another song, this one meant for the occasion, celebrating newly-pledged and gifted companions. For a southerner she had a fair range. Imral and Karsten arrived in time to gain cups and help the song.

Whether the happiness and congratulations were genuine on the part of all was hard to say. Kaleric had his suspicions, I think; his could be a voice that might claim I gained the Prince's bed through sorcery. Vaeyr struck me with his stolidity and grasp of custom and I respected his opinion more than the others. Unril I knew nothing about, and Duvettre was the sort to blow her thoughts this way and that, according to her audience. Whether they knew or guessed my age hardly seemed relevant. I wore the Cloak, and it had no sleeves. I wore the bracelet of the House of Imhonyy. No one could change that.

While the hen cooked, Vaeyr made other treats for us. Our provisions included more variety than I had guessed, and he had brought enough herbs and gathered roots and other stuff to concoct a green stew and porridge. This took time and we passed the moments with drinking and singing.

Beyond this peace, overhead, the Tower throbbed and cast off its weyr-glow, the silver horns flashing. That was our lamp tonight, I thought.

At sunset we sang Kithilunen, silent in the moment, with the sound of the fire and the wind as accompaniment. From high above came other light, the glow from the High Shrine of Inniscaudra, which Kirith Kirin had pointed out when he led me to the Tower. YY-Mother moved amidst us, a palpable presence we could feel. At the end of the song, Kaleric said, "Maybe I'm learning our history now, Brun, by living it. I felt the Mother then." We all agreed with him that she had come. Even the Anynae felt it.

So we ate our pledge-supper in the open air of the empty House, and later Imral brought out a treasure he had found in his own wanderings, a Venladrii guitar. In the darkening of night, under the shifting light of my design, we sang songs and drank wine. Unril gave us a piece of "Luthmar" in her clear mezzo; Vaeyr offered some of "Last Ride;" Imral Ynuuvil sang a Drii song older than the mountain crossing; Karsten and Mordwen sang from another traditional song, a story of two lovers in Old Arthen, sweet and sad.

Last of all, Brun joined Karsten to sing one of the holy songs that had fallen out of use, "Kehan Kehan," which means, "Dead of Winter." I had never heard the song before, nor had I heard Brun's rich alto blended with the soaring soprano of Karsten. She kept the song in the lower modes of our music, for Brun's sake; the Anynae cannot sing or even hear the higher measures. The harmony seemed richer than could be possible from two voices only, and I wondered then, as I would again, whether Karsten knew magic herself. This thought was fleeting, however, and soon was overwhelmed by the tender beauty of the melody.

In older days, according to those who remember, we better understood the proper place of death in life. Maybe that was the reason "Kehan Kehan" was no longer sung very often. But Karsten was not among those who had forgotten, and Brun's life had taught her the place of loss. The song tells the story of a time when a shadow falls over the world, the beauty of the death of seasons, the decay of flowers, the final dying of the Mother herself, the light that will withdraw from all places and times. The words are so much a part of our thought and of the depth of High Speech itself that they cannot be adequately rendered into another tongue. "Kehan Kehan" speaks of the end of time as if it is only a moment away; the song almost rejoices in the notion. I, having recently gained so much, did not want to think of loss; but the song stirred me deeply. Maybe some of that came from the knowledge of shadow. Or maybe it was the vision of my mother, motionless on the white bier in Cunevadrim's Tower.

When the song ended I turned to Kirith Kirin, in whose side I was sheltered; his face was stained with tears. The music faded in the air. Idhril, after the moment of respectful silence which is one's gift to singers, said, "That was a sad choice, my Lady Karsten, for a night when we should be happy for the gifting-couple." One could see the disturbance on her face.

Kirith Kirin answered, "No, it was a good thing, Idhril. It's too long since we've heard 'Kehan.'"

Brun said, "I wasn't born to YY-worship, but I have learned, over the years, that her beauty is in all things. Even in what is taken. My father taught me that song."

"Your father was a brave man," Imral said. "He paid a high price."

Later I would learn that story, from Kirith Kirin. Brun's father died in Arroth, at the hand of the Wizard. He was one of the last of the Finru to oppose Drudaen; his death was a horrible affair, to make a point, and at the end of it Drudaen ate the man's soul and denied him his crossing into Zaeyn. It is a death so total it is hard to contemplate.

Above us, wheeling and spinning, the lights of Ellebren shadowed and danced against the night sky, and beyond the tower, the stars of tonight, different than the night before.

No one took up the guitar after that last song. We sat before the fire till it burned low. Soon folks began to drift to bed.

Tomorrow the army would come, and other armies were marching here, too. As if we knew this, as if we knew there would be no other night like this for us, we two left the fire hand in hand. In answer to some need of his, I took him to the one place in Inniscaudra where he had never been. Together, as lovers, we entered Ellebren and in my company he rose up the kirilidur, as close to flying as a person can come. One rises by reading all the runes one has stored in the kei. We mounted to the Height, where the stars shone clear as his spirit. Holding hands across the Eyestone, I showed him his Kingdom, all of it that I could reach, from sea to shadow to mountain. No one else had ever given him that. While we were there, I protected him from all malevolence, as he had once protected me. Drudaen, far in the south, saw Kirith Kirin's presence on the High Place and quailed. Nothing I had done so far troubled the Wizard more.

He showed me something I had not seen before, without a word. Beneath shadow, points of light where shrines had stood, throughout the south, and I understood what Kirith Kirin had known all along, that the Queen had not dismantled the shrines by accident but because that was what Drudaen required her to do.

We never spoke of that journey, then or later. We descended from the High Place and found our bed. Even a twice-named Prince needs strength to stand on the shenesoeniis; Kirith Kirin never returned to the summit with me again. But I gave him that gift that night, and later I gave him others. It was as if we both knew. That was the only day of perfect peace we had, as lovers together, for many years.

CHAPTER FIFTEEN
SHENESOENIIS

1

Next morning, we heard the sounds of the Army marching through Durassa's Park.

We climbed to the battlements of the high walls to watch their approach, a sight to remember, the column stretching for two stades or more, crimson cloaks, bright-armored horsemen, banners unfurled and horns washing the air. All morning, in perfect order, the column crossed the Park, rounding the shore of Lake Thyathe and beginning the ascent of the hill. The spectacle filled us with pride. Kirith Kirin, beside me, said, "I wondered if even I would live long enough to see this sight again."

He would present himself from Krafulgur Gate where the soldiers could see him as they neared the top. I helped him bathe and dress, with Imral waiting in the outer room.

When time came for him to stand on Krafulgur's summit, I made myself scarce. The soldiers should see him and his commanders; his magician should be elsewhere. I ascended Ellebren and went to the high chambers beneath the pirunaen; from those airy windows I watched the red ribbon of the army wind round and round the hill, mounting the harsh flank, toward their Prince in his perch on impregnable Krafulgur. The army let out a cheer that reached past me to the clouds, and if I had my way, Drudaen himself would have heard it. Though in fact the Army moved under my veil, which by now had become entrenched in the skies over the Three Hills. The procession continued, the column moving through Krafulgur and beneath the High Walls to Haldobran Gate.

I ascended to the Room-Under-Tower and then to the summit itself, and while the Army entered the Gate into Inniscaudra, I wandered bare-armed on the polished pavement of the High Place, but I could see whatever happened below, in as close detail as I wished. The face of Kirith Kirin and my friends, standing on the steps of Halobar Hall while the Army formed up on the lawn. The look of calm on their faces. Even the mortals.

There were some four thousand with Gaelex, the same troops who had guarded Kirith Kirin while he waited, all these years; the same troops who had won him control of the north, who had fought Nemort, who had faced the Witch of Karns. Now they stood with their prince in a storied place, and their coming here was hard won. A moment of perfect fullness transpired, a solemn silence as the soldiers formed, rank on rank, with the Marshal of the Ordinary, Gaelex, at their head.

Kirith Kirin addressed them when they were assembled; his words are recorded elsewhere, in "Kirithmar" and other places. I will not repeat them here since I did not hear him. I am told he spoke of the bravery of his soldiers, of the valor of those who won Anrex, Cordyssa, Ithlumen and Gnemorra. I am told he praised his generals and officers by name. I am told he mentioned me among those; and I guess no one who was there when Julassa Kyminax howled onto the battlefield would have disputed my place on the list. While he was speaking, I listened to the wind and walked along the aerie edge of the shenesoeniis. Birdcalls filled the sky, and the music of wind whipped the treetops in waves, like Vella said the sea would look.

But one thing I did to add splendor to the moment below, before I moved to Ellesotur to complete other tasks. Out from the Tower Horns I caused to form three eidolons of the banner of his house, Imhonyy, the Unicorn with the Ruby Eye. Slowly and like smoke the phantom banners unfurled, while the silence of the Army told me he was still speaking. When their cheer told me his words were at an end, I let the ghost-images become visible to other eyes than mine. I hear they covered half the sky.

I sat down to my work, to the Eyestone and my vigilance. Clearing my mind, breathing, I moved through the circles into fourth-level trance.

2

At once, within shadow, I detected turbulence and change. The Wizard's shape remained in Vyddn country, but I noted two differences. Power moved north of him in Montajhena; not a living presence but a feeling like ash or slag that pervaded the planes. Even though we had surveyed that country from Illyn Water, we had never detected movement there before. At first I was afraid the presence was the Wizard himself, that he had managed to move without my knowing it; but careful scrutiny convinced me otherwise. The disturbance in the ruined city came from the bases of the broken towers, with the major disturbance coming from the ruin of Yrunvurst, glimmering like the ghost of a beacon in my sight.

Furthermore, over the ruined city, shadow was torn and weak. Something in Montajhena diluted him. Had I known it, Venladrii messengers moved toward Inniscaudra to give us this very news.

But more momentous was a change I noted farther south, at Aerfax, from the Tower of the Change. From there, a light like a star burned across shadow. A sound of insinging could be heard, and the voice was not Drudaen. Queen Athryn was singing from the Rock of Change on the summit of Senecaur.

Neither the song nor the words were clear to me. But I thought I could guess their purpose, and felt a thrill along the spine.

My excitement made me careless, and Drudaen knew me to be on the Height. His brooding presence shifted and reached toward me. Maybe he still held me in such contempt he thought he might contest with me from that distance. A moment of chill swept me, as his hand closed onto my unattended body; but his touch was weak, his power stretched, and he could bring only paltry strength to bear. I wanted to sing my defiance to him but, as I opened my mouth and reached out my hand, I thought better of it. Let him think me too foolish and small to spy this gesture of his. I defended my body from him in more subtle ways and let the moment pass.

What part he played in the change of Aerfax I could only guess. But again I heard the song from that Tower, flowing like moonlight across the tops of clouds, a pure sound, seeming far too young for the old woman of my visions. This was news that could not wait; yet I must not hurry too much even so. Patiently I scanned Arthen for other signs, other movements; it was then I noted the coming of messengers from Drii. This was all. I returned to my body out of trance. Only a short time had passed, in real terms.

I took a deep breath and stepped beyond the colonnade, to the place where one of the silver horns rises from the side of the summit. The parade ground before Halobar was emptying, the army marching along Falkrigul toward the armories and barracks. Now was the time to find Kirith Kirin and tell him the world had changed yet again.

3

Since it was not my wish to be seen leaving or entering Ellebren, I moved on mist that kept me hidden, one of the virtues of the Cloak and my art. At the time I knew no other way to accomplish my purpose, though there were many; and I knew only the one path from Thrath Gate to the place where I would find Kirith Kirin. Along the Falkri Stair I moved, along the column of soldiers marching goggle-eyed through the House. No one saw me; and I was spared their fear.

Overhead, the magical banners of the unicorn house had begun to dissolve into air.

Nearer the courtyard, where Kirith Kirin stood among his officers and the twice-named, I allowed the mist to dissolve and stepped behind a column-base. To approach him at such a time was against my instincts, so I waited, quieting the Cloak to drab. Karsten saw me, caught my eye.

Within moments she detached herself from the body of those attending Kirith Kirin; discretion itself as she led me to an alcove. "The banners were a glorious touch," she said. "You couldn't have timed it better." But in her eyes there was a question.

"Thank you my lady, but I would have waited for the praise. I have news for Kirith Kirin and I think he'll want it now."

"What is it?"

I shook my head. "I don't dare say."

She gave me a look that warned me I had better be serious. "You're sure?"

"There's a change he must know about."

Nodding, she make a quick survey of the courtyard. "Go back to your room in the Under House, I'll bring him as soon as I can."

She returned to his orbit and I moved behind the column once again, assembling mist and gliding hidden into the apartment. There I removed the Cloak and tried to compose myself, sitting for a moment on the tousled bed in which we had lain, all innocence, a few hours before.

He sent Imral to find me and bring me to another place. Imral asked no questions but beckoned, noting my serious face. Without asking, I enshrouded him in the Cloak and we moved, both of us, in that cloud. By signs he gave me directions and we entered near Halobar, up a broad stair and through a series of doorways. A smell of must and disuse surrounded us. Through a pier of columns one could see the Great Hall below.

In a room full of books Kirith Kirin awaited me, and his friends were with him. When the mist released us he searched my face anxiously. "What news was so urgent?"

"I hear the voice of Queen Athryn from Aerfax Tower. She's singing a song I don't know." Giving him a cautious look, I added, "When this began I don't know either, but it's new since last night." That last he hardly heard. He blanched and turned to the others. They understood the sign, as he did, and I guessed from their stricken faces I was right. For a moment Kirith Kirin did not know where he was or who was with him. He studied a gem on his hand, closed his eyes and touched it. A look of listening came to him, and many thoughts passed over his features. He murmured words, and everyone bowed their heads; after a moment so did I.

"Eye in Heaven," he said, still touching the gem on his finger, "she's so weak I couldn't feel the change in the stone."

"The song's weak too," I said, "or I'd have heard it before I climbed to the shenesoeniis."

He nodded. No one spoke; and I could see them waiting for him. He said, "You were right to find me. This changes everything."

He sat. For a moment vague shadow flickered over his features. He saw me and looked into my face. Beckoning me to his side, he turned to his friends and studied them.

No chair was close enough; I sat at his knees. He rested his hand in my hair. If this was not seemly, I hardly cared. Finally he said, "So she's sending me a Summons to come south and take my crown." His laughter, bitter, washed quietly over all of us. "She wants to make me King of Shadow-land."

"You yourself said this might happen," Imral said. "What better strategy now than to draw you out of your place of strength?"

Kirith Kirin kept touching his finger to the stone. Despair washed over him. "How weak and small she is." Turning to me, his eyes flooded with tears. "You shouldn't have had to bring me the news. When the Queen stands in Aerfax Tower and sets the Change in motion, her voice should reach me on its own."

"Maybe there's some disturbance through shadow," Karsten offered.

He shook his head emphatically. "No. I wish that were true. But this is Athryn herself, this is what she's come to." Grief took his voice for a moment. "No shadow could have stopped her voice before. No shadow ever did." Turning to me again, he said, "She's my sister. Did you know that?"

I nodded, I had heard it said by someone. His voice, when he spoke, was quieter. "So. This is sooner than we thought, but no real surprise."

Mordwen spoke in his firm voice, looking at me gently. "The difference is Jessex. That's why she calls you so quickly."

With an edge of anger Kirith Kirin said, "You can't blame him for this—"

I saw Mordwen's thought at once, however. "He wants me out of Ellebren."

"Of course," Imral said, as Mordwen nodded.

This sobered Kirith Kirin, being new. He gazed at me with eyes more like those I remembered from the morning. "He wants to deal with you on the ground and out of Arthen. He knows I have to bring you with me." He took a deep, ragged breath. "He knows I can't refuse the Summons either."

A long silence grew. His fingers traced a curl idly, the touch sweet to me, troubled as I was. From above the strange song had strengthened some, and Kirith Kirin seemed to know the difference as well. "Now she's beginning to find her voice."

"I wonder what messenger she'll choose to send," Pelathayn said.

"It hardly matters," Kirith Kirin said. "The Summons is the Summons. If we were ready, we could ride south tomorrow."

With a glimmer of idea, Imral said, "Maybe that's what we should do."

"Tomorrow?" Pelathayn asked, nearly sputtering.

"Speed is everything now," Imral said, quietly, his thought settling in. Kirith Kirin had begun to listen. "If we can move quickly we may have the advantage."

"With the force we have here?" Pelathayn asked. "Tomorrow!"

"Hush," Karsten said, and one understood from the sharpness of her gaze why she had command over Imral and Pelathayn both, where the army was concerned. "Name the advantages, Imral. I follow you partly."

"So do I," Kirith Kirin said, but he was looking at me.

Imral moved along the windows as he spoke. "We've surprised our enemy. The defeat of Nemort was unlooked for. The death of Julassa was unthinkable. Now we've occupied Inniscaudra and we have a magician on the Ellebren Height. None of this was expected. Drudaen has thrown shadow, but I'll wager you Drii silver he did it before he was ready. Jessex, help me. Am I right or wrong?"

A thrill ran through me, that he spoke to me as an equal. "You're right, I think. There are signs."

"Name them," Kirith Kirin said.

"One I saw today. Shadow is thin over Montajhena, and there's light he can't alter or take into himself."

"Yrunvurst," Mordwen whispered.

"Yes," I said. "From the base of the broken towers, but particularly from that one. His shadow can't engulf it. And it seems clear from other signs, from the little we've contested with each other so far, that he wasn't ready for so much at once. He's stretched."

"So if we move now, or at least as quickly as we can, we may gain some advantage," Imral said.

"While he's encamped in Vyddn," Kirith Kirin murmured, "before he can send an army north."

Karsten said, "I like the plan. Can we do it?"

"My father can have troops in Maugritaxa in ten days. So can we, if we push. The Cordyssans and the new troops will be slower but that can't be helped."

"They won't do us any good without training," Karsten said. "Better to leave them and take what we have."

"We would be no more than ten thousand," Kirith Kirin said, "against twice the number Drudaen can put into the field."

"Only if we give him time to assemble a whole force," Imral said. "His armies are split now."

Karsten and Pelathayn nodded at this logic. But it was left to Pelathayn to state the obvious. Looking at me, he said, "Ten thousand or forty thousand, what difference does that make? The armies won't fight the battle that matters."

They had been skirting this topic. The thought brought gloom to Kirith Kirin. He asked me, nearly a whisper, "So, little magician. What do you say about that?"

I said Words into the kei and let time play itself out. I saw myself at Illyn Water, that last morning, and Vella's voice returned, so clear it hung in the air, *Aren't you afraid of him?* And my answer, *Yes. But what choice do I have?* What choice indeed, when from the High Place I could hear, even now, the murmuring of his voice? I could see what had to be done, as if it were a page I was reading. I returned to the room in the Winter House, to the moment of my friends; and he knew where I had gone.

"I can't wait ten days. I'll need to ride south sooner than that.

I'll have to take Laeredon Tower from him. And you can't leave
here till I do."

The others were stunned and rendered silent. Kirith Kirin leaned
over me as if I were a child. "No," he said, "not so soon."

"Yes, Kirith Kirin." It became my decision with those words.
"If he senses we're marching from Inniscaudra he'll leave Vyddn
country himself and take the Tower against me. I can't face him
from the ground. If I can break his hold on Laeredon, I can hold
that whole country against him, and I'll have two Towers then. He'll
have to go south himself to find a place to stand against me, and his
army will be split."

The logic of it struck them dumb, as it had me when the thought
finally formed. Kirith Kirin sagged against his seat. "Can you do
it?" Imral asked.

"I don't know. But I can try." I was suddenly full of dread. "I
know one thing. If I don't break him there, you can't come south.
There'll be no more hope."

Kirith Kirin knew this already. He sat motionless. Karsten
reached for his hand. Mordwén said, at last, "The Summons is
the Summons and the Law is the Law. We'll have to ride south
regardless."

I looked him in the eye and spoke from the center of my being.
"No, Mordwen. Better to ride straight to Tornimul. Kirith Kirin is
the Law now. And if I can't make a way south for us, then he must
stay here, where the Wizard can't reach him. This is the will of the
Mother, and you know I'm right. Without Kirith Kirin we're lost."

Their silence told me I was speaking the truth. After a long
time, Kirith Kirin asked, "When?"

"Now." Into his eyes. "When I have Laeredon you'll see the
signs. Promise me you won't come out of Arthen otherwise."
He looked away from me so I took his face between my hands.
"Promise me."

After a while he nodded. A breath like a wind passed through
all of us.

When I stood, it was the beginning of a journey. They knew it,
each of them, and said good-bye. Kirith Kirin held me so close I
thought he would break my ribs. I touched the chain around his
neck and murmured Words. I kissed him good-bye in front of his
friends, and left him blank and speechless in the chair. I left Halobar
on the same mist that brought me there. They don't call it the Hall
of Many Partings for nothing, I guess.

4

I enfolded myself in the Fimbrel Cloak, flowed through the House unseen and entered Ellebren, where this time I rose on the runes through the kirilidur straight to the pirunaen. I called the names of the runes as I rose, and they burned from their stone setting. Whirling and rising, I wrote the strange words into my memory. I looked for the other threads as well, the runes that I could not read. The writing of the Praeven, the thought came easily. Like the writing on the locket.

Reaching into Ellebren's depths, to the place where Edenna Morthul laid the first stones within Thrath Rock, I called *Hear me, I am the one who climbed your summit; release your deepest secrets to me for I must take a journey; I have no time for riddles or devices; whatever is hidden must be opened; I am he who sang in Imith Imril when no one had sung there since Falamar died; I am Yron who crossed the mountains; I am riding and my need is great; if there is a spirit left here who can answer such a summons, help me now; release your secrets, Ellebren, and come to me when I call from far away.*

While I moved through the pirunaen like smoke, I continued this undertone of song. When I first opened Ellebren I felt the Tower receive me as if it had been waiting all this time. In my mind, too, were Kirith Kirin's words when he told me that no one had ever walked on the Ellebren Height before me. *That was the day she told me she had prepared the place, and one would come to stand in it.* She was Kentha, who completed the building of Ellebren after Edenna Morthul abandoned it. She was my great-great-grandmother.

On impulse, in the midst of my preparations, I lifted the Bane Necklace from its hidden place within the Cloak. Holding it aloft, I let my thought go into it and heard, as if sighing coursed through the whole Tower, a release of wind. Along with the echo of Kentha in the stones, a trace of her resonance that would last as long as the Tower. I could feel the Praeven runes in the kirilidur, throbbing. "When I'm riding, remember me."

I gathered gems from their caskets, rings and brooches that could be fixed to my clothing; these I could prepare along the ride. For the Bane Necklace itself I selected a new chain, from a casket marked with Edenna's rune-sign; the thought seemed important, to place the necklace fashioned by Kentha on the chain forged by Edenna. They had built the Tower.

When I placed the Necklace around my neck, peaceful voices
soothed me. I added a white-stoned earring from the casket as well,
speaking a Word to fit the ensorcelled metal to my ear. The Bane
Gem weighed on my breast, heavy and dense.

At once the Room-Under-Tower seemed less a stranger to me.

I found a casket where dried cakes lay in heavy enchantment; I
filled a pack with these, lining it with soft viis from nearby. In another casket, marked with the signs of Kentha's House, I found a
dagger, simple and silver, set with a single ruby gem in the hilt, the
Eye of God. Its belt was of wrought silver and I fastened it round
my waist. When I touched it I knew Kentha had put it here for me.
It had waited all this time. A gift.

Other secrets, other gifts, on every side, if I ever returned.
Ellebren opened itself to me in a flood of radiance. I could see the
Library in its hidden vault, other chambers of special use, other
treasures that might, someday, serve me well. The joy of it swept
me round the room dancing, as if my grandmother had suddenly
returned to sing me one of her favorite songs.

In fact it was my great-great-grandmother, I think.

But one treasure drew me at that moment. I felt the harmony of
the object, a kind of calling, and opened a casket, rooted through it to
find a carved stone box. Inside, a ring with a white stone that Edenna
had fashioned, and I read the rune for Laeredon on the ring. She had
made a ring to rule Laeredon Tower from a distance. Common
enough to do so. Kentha might have done the same for Inniscaudra,
though I'd found nothing here. Drudaen would have altered Laeredon
to make it useful to him, but the ring would still prove helpful.

Last of all, I walked the Height for a moment, gem-bedecked
and glittering, speaking softly to the veil over Inniscaudra, to the Horns
and their vaults of light, rounding the colonnade with the Cloak flowing like smoke behind me, and finally kneeling at the Eyestone. I
made no magic there but set a gem on each of the altars, a way to
make him feel me present on the Tower. I prayed my trick to work.

My last moment before descending, I remembered sitting here
with Kirith Kirin, only a night ago. Already nearly lost in the flood
of events, a moment of that peace returned to me. That was my
gift to this place, I thought. I brought him here. The stones will
remember me for that.

So I went down to the pirunaen and on a breeze, floated down
the kirilidur to the base of Ellebren. The voices of strange and
wonderful women hung in the air around me.

5

When I emerged from the Tower, Imral Ynuuvil stepped from the shadow of the Arches and beckoned me. "I'll lead you to Nixva," he said, and again I enfolded him in my Cloak and we traveled hidden from eyes. This journey carried me to parts of the House that only the twice-named know; they have their own ways of moving in concealment within Inniscaudra. After a time we had no further need for my arts to mask our movement. We descended through hidden corridors and stairs to a gate in the rocks below Krafulgur, where Karsten awaited us with the horse.

Nixva greeted me with haughty impatience. Karsten embraced me and Imral spoke quickly. "We've packed cumbre and a little of my brandy in your saddlebags. Nixva himself would stand for no more than that, so we guessed it was all we should do."

"I have whatever else I could think to bring," I said. Hesitating then, I asked, "How is he?"

Karsten answered, "Not well. He doesn't know we're here; we didn't dare tell him, otherwise he'd have come himself."

Imral asked, "When will you get there, do you think?"

"Two days, maybe more. You'll see signs of our journey at Ellebren."

"Fireworks," he whispered, smiling. He kissed my brow, as did Karsten.

I made Karsten swear to get Axfel as soon as the baggage wagons were unloaded and find a home for him here. Sorry I could not say good-bye myself, but she said she would. As my last gesture I gave into Imral's keeping the Keys to Ellebren Tower. "You know what these are?" I asked, pressing the silver ring into his hand. "I can't have them on me if I fall."

"I'll give them to Kirith Kirin," he said.

I shook my head. "Keep them till you see me again. If you give them back to him, he might think I've despaired." After a moment I added, "They're mine to leave in this fashion if I choose. If I fail to take Laeredon, give them to him then."

A moment, I lingered. Nothing was left to say, except one thing; and I had to have heart for that. I mounted to Nixva's back, feeling the trembling of his impatience. "I'll see you in Genfynnel." Making mist and veil as they opened the gate, I started on my way.

6

Since I made that journey I've seen maps and know what route we took; at the time I had only Nixva to trust. I told him where we must go, and that we must travel hidden within the Woodland until the last possible moment; he snorted and answered that his part was easy, but could I carry off mine? He had no wish, he said, to return riderless into Arthen.

The horse headed through the Woodland following the roads south and I began to build the ithikan that would lend him the speed he needed. This was delicate business to do, since everything depended on my remaining hidden from Drudaen's vigilance, but at the same time I had to make sure Nixva was safe at the highest speed we could reach. Vyddn is a long way from Genfynnel, the city over which Laeredon Tower broods. If I could reach the edge of Arthen without the Wizard's guessing my purpose, I could beat him to the Tower.

Nixva understood what had to be done and gave his spirit to the task. Soon we traveled in one low wave along the Woodland roads. The joy of speed consumed him, but our passing hardly stirred the leaves on the trees.

I began my own preparations. I avoided trance and moved no further into the circles than sixth level, since Drudaen might have detected that even beneath Arthen's canopy. The gems I'd left on Ellebren would give the glimmering of my presence, for a while. I worked from another state, a kind of mid-mind in which I could thread song and thought but not yet move Power; in its way, this consciousness was akin to the means by which I had hidden my training at Illyn Water. No magician ever learned that art as well as I did; no one else ever had to.

Gathering all my knowledge of the Towers and their making, learnt at Commyna's knee, I threaded thought on thought. Drudaen held all the southern High Places in one fashion or another, but his hold was not the same on each. Some Towers he had built himself and some his father Falamar had built, and over the Towers of their making Drudaen exercised unshakable authority. In these High Places, the ruling runes in the kirilidur were of Ildaruen, about which I knew nothing. But Edenna Morthul built Laeredon during the Long War with Falamar, and the runes in that place were Wyyvisar when the Tower was made. Furthermore, Edenna was the wizard who first invented the rune-threads, and the Laeredon kirilidur was the finest example of what the rune-threads could do until Ellebren was built.

Kentha held Laeredon after Lady Morthul crossed through the Gates, and its Keys are said to have vanished with her when she died. Drudaen took the High Place for his own use after that. Because he had no keys, he broke down the gates, then had them remade. One could be certain he had altered the Tower to his own use in the years since. But he had never taken the time to bring the Tower down or raise a High Place of his own, as he had done in Ivyssa and earlier in Montajhena. He had simply faced the kirilidur with an Ildaruen veneer. The Sisters guessed this was because he lacked the strength to undo Edenna's work.

We flashed through the middle Woodland, Nixva a rush of black fire over the bridges crossing River. Leaning into his mane, I whispered my love to him and he answered me with more speed. Nearer came shadow with each step. The passing of time became meaningless, and I floated in images that were pieces of my thought: the presence of Ellebren behind me, the light over Montajhena, the heaviness of the Wizard on the Vyddn Plain. He stood in no High Place and could reach none unless he beat me to Laeredon. His purpose in Vyddn must be vital or he would not have lingered. His contempt for me and pride in his own strength must also be great, or else he would not have remained on the ground when I opened Ellebren against him. Now I had no sense of any change in him at all, and if he was striving with anything, it was with some ghost in Montajhena, as far as I could tell.

We rode all day and through the night. Near dawn we crossed River again, and the light wood of Maugritaxa surrounded us. Soon Nixva left the road for a path, since the place he wanted, where the Woodland reached down closest to Genfynnel, was tangled and wild and had no proper road. We slowed the ithikan some, in the undergrowth, though we still made good speed.

By then day had broken. By then, also, Drudaen's first folly was closing its hand around him, because when we entered Maugritaxa we were already far closer to his Tower than he was.

When Woodland's End loomed before us I sang Kimri under my breath, the part where YY answers,

I am lighting the lamp that lights the lamps
I am behind that light

On the last line we burst free of Arthen and were revealed to him. I entered fourth-level trance and began to sing.

7

Genfynnel lies south of Arthen, several days march, at the place where Isar and Osar diverge. Before the closing of Arthen it had the bulk of the River trade, but that business passed to Bruinysk in days after the Ban, since all northern caravans passed through Angoroe. Genfynnel is ancient, having been a Jisraegen settlement since the days of the Forty Thousand. I could feel its presence within shadow once I left the cover of the Woodland, and when I entered trance I could see it as well, with far-flung sight.

I could see the Wizard too, since in his carelessness he had left himself naked beneath shadow, thinking me far away. For a time his whole thought was known to me, and the poison of it filled me. He hung over the land like ice, a cold and brittle spirit, the beautiful shell of his face and body remaining from his youth but filled with the dread of years and the lives he ate to preserve his own. Like all who come from Arthen, he needed to return to the Woodland for wholeness. His exile had turned to torment. He was in Vyddn to listen for the echo of Jurel and his father in Montajhena. This I saw in those first instants, and the truth of that moment was to guide me through all that followed.

We moved forward like a fire rushing across the grassland, beneath the broiling of shadow, and our freshness came from the trees of Arthen, from the stones of Inniscaudra, from the Eliebren Height. He could feel these forces around Nixva and me, and he longed for them himself. That was his first thought, even before he guessed my purpose, understood his own nakedness, and cloaked himself in protection. In letting me see so much, he made a mistake for which I could make him pay. If I lived.

A moment later, when he began to move himself and I could feel the size of him, I felt my first wash of fear.

I hid the feeling and set part of myself to watch him while other parts busied with other tasks. Even from Vyddn he could use Laeredon against me, and he did so at once. But when he did, I could hear the sound he made on the kei planes, the thread of song by which he controlled Laeredon, and I isolated it from all else that I could hear. I reached forward too, and began my deep-singing.

Touching gems within the cloak, I rose up on Nixva's back and gathered what sunlight I could find that trickled through the stuff overhead; I plaited Fire and Light and let the rings drift upward, I plaited Daylight Rune, Curved Swan, filling them with my fourth-circle voice, and the passage of these devices gashed shadow where they touched it. Blue sky opened overhead, and true sunlight reached me. The oppression and cold lessened, though these were only feelings of the body and could not be allowed to enter my thinking. The world of YY, above the clouds, caressed me and Nixva as we hurtled forward.

Then the hand of Laeredon closed around me and all was darkness.

I could not find his thought or hear his Words, nothing except the sound of his calling to Laeredon, so subtle was that first assault. Nixva cried in terror and might have stumbled except I soothed him. My breath became labored and my body's pangs began to draw me back inside it, out of the kei-space, my eye no longer within and without; stones weighed on my limbs and my thought became confused. I had not understood, till I was out of Arthen, how much it had protected me, but now I did. But that thought brought another, a memory, Commyna's voice in Jiiviisn Field. *The Cloak will serve you well, especially outside Arthen.*

Gathering the folds around me, I raised the hood over my head and draped Nixva with it as well; we would ride by my eyes for a while, and I told him so. His panic eased and so did mine. The singing of Illyn surround us. Whatever he had sung from Laeredon could not touch me within the Cloak. Presently, when I restored my consciousness to kei, I launched myself anew on all levels.

I sang to the distant Tower, against the current of the Wizard's voice which even then I could not hear, except the one sound I had kept in the kei space, his song to the Tower. I called to the stones using a far song, which was the same as Drudaen was doing; I could feel the change in the presence of Laeredon in the fourth circle, as the Wyyvisar runes of the kirilidur stirred. It had been a long time since anyone had called that magic out of the Tower. The Sisters had been right. He had never been able to remove the Wyyvisar, or had feared Edenna Morthul too much to try.

But his own power still moved in his rune-threads, and his Words were still hidden from me, except his calling-song to the Tower. Again came the crashing assault, as if he meant to smite me flat from the air, and without the sound of his Words I had no notion of what kind of attack he employed. The Cloak shielded me and I kept my seat on Nixva; but Drudaen's strength seemed incomprehensible, to find me and reach into me so deeply. His hand on my heart, a tearing in my gut, sensations like fire and freezing cold. From all sides I could feel the kindling of him on the land, in every High Place south of Arthen, and overhead shadow began to close the tear I had made.

In the kei space, in the small space, I pictured Ellebren, at the same time that my long vision focused on what I could discern of Laeredon.

For a moment I was walking on Ellebren Height again, the wind in my hair...

At once I felt the uprising of light from that High Place, and I found a resonance that let me throw off his touch, steer my thought toward Laeredon again. This light was not simply in my mind or on the planes; the brightness swelled at my back over all the landscape, and shadow dissolved not only near me but beyond. A road to Genfynnel opened, sunlight fell on those lands, and a rush of light poured down, warm and golden.

I took heart and sang, threw off light and fire; with the hands of my body maneuvering gems, I pushed shadow farther and reached forward again toward Laeredon, focusing every thought on the Tower, on singing the ruling runes of the Tower awake. I spared not one moment or bit of consciousness on attacking Drudaen himself, as he had attacked me. It was the Tower I wanted, only that, and I raced toward it at a speed which soon led me round farm and forest to the place where two broad rivers rushed together.

Now I could see Genfynnel as if I were high above it, a black-walled, fair-built city of many dwellings; over it rumbling the Height of Laeredon, fire flashing from her crown. The fireworks had frightened the people living there and evacuation was already underway. People were pouring out of the southern walls onto the plains; some were spilling over the bridges as well, heading into the countryside, most with nothing but the clothes on their backs.

The High Place flashed and Drudaen struck at me again, finding me easily. Still I could not hear his Words or guess his strategy, and the hurts he caused me drained me of strength. I lost hold of Ellebren, could no longer see the High Place within the kei. He brushed the heart of my body again; quickly I returned there and fought him off, a victory for him, since from the body I could not see so far or so well. So now I was out of the dual state, and the

Laeredon High Place flashed again and I felt pain and cold clutch me. He had reached Deep Magics now, and meant to kill me on Nixva's back. The Cloak helped some but I was not yet well accustomed to its uses and without the hearing of his Words could not defend myself. The Tower struck again, flashes of pain like lightning through my body; my heart thudding to a stop, then starting again at my command; my breath came short and I clutched the place where my heart was laboring, his hand striving to reach it, to pluck me out of my flesh into his maw. He came close, and Nixva cried out in terror, feeling my distress; *do not leave me*, the horse said, and I could feel the love of the animal pour through me.

I clutched the Bane Necklace in my palm and suddenly I could hear the Wizard's hidden voice.

A river of Words surrounded me, and I saw that he was traveling himself now, had encircled me with wards and had begun to say Bans to stop my journey before I ever reached the Tower. I kept my hand on the Bane and cleared my head. Now I knew where he was singing and could fight him, and broke his wards in the direction of Laeredon. Nixva streamed toward the city surefooted in the ithikan and I restored my breathing, calmed my heart and kept my hand on the Necklace.

Entering the dual state, this time I pictured only Laeredon, seeing it from above as if I were flying high above myself, and seeing it also in the kei space, in the small; *What you do in the mind space is real,* Commyna had said. *The mind space is as valid as any other.* So I pictured the Tower encircled by a sphere of dissonance that would interfere with Drudaen's calling-song. I began that work, and left it in the kei, returning to other parts of my awareness. I had stretched out the moment and moved almost at leisure. His circle of wards crumbled. His hold on Laeredon wavered and he knew what I was doing; this was what the attacking magician always attempted to do, there was no guesswork in it. But I had Edenna's ring and sent my song through that, and sent that wave of stuff through the kei space, too, and the sphere I was building around Laeredon in that place grew more solid. Ellebren on the horizon swelled and pulsed; shadow ran from my approach, and as I crossed the Bridges leading to the city gates, the summit of Laeredon felt the kiss of sunlight.

I sent out a shrieking that caused those on the bridge to huddle against either side of the span. Verm soldiers had closed the city gates but I broke them down with Words till they were smoldering ash and sections of the walls thereabouts fell smoking into Osar.

Nixva rushed through the gap like a dark wind and any Verm who pursued us fell in agony as I passed. I had reached the city ahead of Drudaen, though by how much I did not know and could spare no energy to learn.

The Laeredon shenesoeniis rises over Telkyii Tars, a palace Edenna Morthul built here before the war with Falamar. The place has a graceful, country-house look, hardly martial, and its walls, to one who has seen Inniscaudra, seem low and puny. The Verm held that gate as well, and I will admit it was harder to break down; but Nixva did not have to slow his progress to wait for me to do my part. We rode over ruined stone and heaped Verm and soon we had traced a path to the base of the high, pale Tower that was the sole object of my journey.

From Nixva's back I set up wards of my own, and any Verm who crossed them perished, though I did not eat their souls. Proximity to the High Place was its own punishment; here it was as if I stood near to Drudaen, and the force staggered me. For a while I could not spare strength to dismount from Nixva, so hard did I struggle to follow Drudaen's singing and to defend my wards. But while I held the Bane I could hear him, and while the Cloak enfolded me I could hear other voices too: Vella, telling me how to keep the channels of the body open; Vissyn, telling me that any door with a lock can be opened without a key; Commyna, warning me that the surest way to offend a Tower is to ignore the Runes that lead to the Gate. These were lessons I had learned at Illyn Water that returned to me now like a breath of breeze over the lake itself. My body obeyed me and dismounted from Nixva's back.

The horse quieted, tossing his head. *Come back soon*, he told me, and I said I would. In momentary clarity I surveyed the approach to the Tower Gate. One reaches the base rock of Laeredon by a causeway across a chasm, the causeway guarded by high horns of bronze, gleaming bright and inlaid with runes I could not read. I guessed these writings to be Ildaruen and this portal to be new, and therefore looked elsewhere. In Lady Morthul's day the celebrant reached the Tower using different runes.

Beginning the song of entry, the same with which I commenced the opening of Ellebren, I called to the older Runes of Place to light themselves; *One of Power is here*, I sang, *and my Words are your Words.*

At that moment, when I was most vulnerable, listening for the answer from the Tower, Drudaen struck deep into my body again, using not only the Laeredon Height but all the southern High Places blended in song, mixed with malice and cold. I sank to my knees under the impact, but I could not stop what I had begun. In the kei I sang the sphere around Laeredon, using Edenna's white-stoned ring; his control of the Tower wavered as the sphere grew solid in the small space. While I was occupied this way he closed his hand on my heart and stopped it again, and read my thought almost entirely; I could feel him, but not stop him. I held my Ward Circle intact from him and I kept my body alive; I focused on the kei space until his control of Laeredon was weak, his calling-song all but shattered. That was the only defense I could offer.

The moment stretched, the attack continued. Agony coursed through me, pain of cold and fire, the jangling of the nerves, as if my body were exploding from within, one part tearing away from another. But my lungs pumped air and my attack continued as I sang to the Tower in Wyyvisar. The old stones heard my voice and finally knew me to be their ally. The pain continued, the coursing of his hand through my body, seeking the tiiryander; but this was a necessary part of the battle; if I could not live through it I was not the pupil who once hung by the hair three days over fire to please Commyna. I made my eyes see past their torment to read the runes along the causeway; I answered the chain with a chain. The ground and Tower rumbled as older magic asserted itself over the new. I reached for a gem with an arm that would barely obey me. Lifting the gem, I amplified my Words through it and focused on the runes which now appeared at the base of Laeredon, forming the frame of a gateway. These were runes I could read.

His hand tightened on my heart and it ceased its beating. No matter. I sang the runes and was lifted to my feet. A flash of fire poured up from the pavement and the bronze horns burst from their roots. For a moment he was shaken but his hand closed round my heart again as I stepped forward over fire. The whole song of the place joined me. Through the death of my body I walked across the causeway to the Gate of Laeredon, and with my voice through the gem I said, "I am here. Yron is here. I am he who stands even now on Ellebren High Place, I am the friend of your Maker. Let me in, for I have come to take you back."

The runes became clear and I said their names. The place awakened in the old way and wrapped me round with some of its strength. The hand of Drudaen fell away from me and I drew breath. I stirred my heart from deep trance and numbed the hurts and pains of my body. Behind me, anxious, Nixva chortled.

Above, along the sides of Laeredon, runes were glowing like fire.

"Open," I said, "I have no Key. Your key died in fire, and this Gate is not your Gate. Open yourself."

I lifted my hand and called out light from the white-stoned ring, and the Tower knew it and shuddered visibly. "See," I said, moving my voice through the stone, letting Lady Morthul's own voice be heard as well, "See, I have your ruling ring. I am the one who stands in Ellebren-on-High, I am the Witch of Arthen, as your Maker was. Open. I have no Key to give you, but I can bring your old magic back to you."

The ground trembled. The ring grew bright. In the kei space I pictured the Tower encased in a perfect sphere of light that drank all else. The Tower shuddered, the whole height of it. The Wizard knew, at the same moment as I did, that I would open it or bring it down. His dismay crossed all the planes, and for the first time since we began our contest, he began to doubt himself.

Fire and lightning poured down from clear skies all around, striking the Tower Height at first, and then coursing along the sides. Eerie smokes and colors whirled around me. I calmed Nixva and kept my body motionless before the portal. A stream of fire poured down onto the portal runes, and lightning ringed them, and, groaning, the stone gate cracked, heated to hot red slag and poured down the chasm. When the Gate gave way, the shuddering ground shook the causeway and split the walls of Telkyii Tars. But I held the Tower intact in my mind, and so it remained in the visible world.

Calling Nixva to me, I walked into Laeredon, singing as I went. Drinking the heat of the rock into the Cloak, cooling the gate.

Now I had to ascend the Long Stair.

When I entered the base vault, the domed ceiling glowed with inlaid silverwork. On the ceiling I read, "Celebrant, you are on the Base Rock of Laeredon Tower, raised up from the Depths of YY-Mur by Edenna Morthul when she was tired of war. We are in the heart of darkness. If you walk here, know my spirit and sing the song I love."

Whatever Ildaruen overlay this was invisible to me; but even so I must not leave runes here to welcome their Master when he came riding. So I spoke to the Wyyvisar and gave back the Words Lady Morthul had written. Something of her sorrow remained there, the dread of bloodshed. The feeling stirred me so that I felt physical tears.

I sang her song for her, not the Ruling Song of the Tower, but the song she loved. "Heart of darkness" is another translation for "kehan kehan." Reaching back to that night by firelight which now seemed centuries behind me, I sang what I remembered, *The coming of winter is in deepest darkness, but there is no night so deep I cannot find you. Light is coming, but even light can hide you.* I sang for her, simply, and the room quieted to my voice. Then I said, "Lady Maker, burn away the mark of the Wizard." Calling out Words, my voice filled the room, and the Tower again shuddered. Light flooded the domed chamber. For a moment, within that radiance, I saw the outlines of Ildaruen Words, blues and violets dissolving.

The Tower welcomed me and threw open its portals. The kirilidur was revealed, and so was the Long Stair.

Hurrying across the causeway, I brought Nixva inside the Tower Base, leaving him waycake from the saddlebags to eat. He wished me luck. I began the ascent.

I read the runes of the kirilidur through the intervening stones. What made the task hard this time, as I mounted, was the voice of my enemy from the High Place, and my dismay at the fact that the sky outside had begun to darken. Shadow moved through the windows of the Tower as I climbed. Blue sky washed brown and then dun-colored, light thinned and birds ceased their singing. His voice grew strong. His riding brought him near the City.

I put this thought away and mounted, stair on stair, singing without sight, returning the Wyyvisar to its rightful state within the kirilidur. Had Drudaen stood in his body on the High Place, I would have had to struggle with him for each step; had he known the ways the Sisters travel, he would simply have crossed space to stand there; but he was fourth circle, as I was, and he must cross the same ground I had crossed. While I sang the Ruling Song and mounted the Stair he drew closer, shadow thickening till there was no light except that of the torches I lit in the Long Stairway. Higher I climbed, breathing and singing, sinking deeper into trance and moving faster. Wrapped in the Cloak, with its murmuring to soothe me, I activated the kirilidur so that the Wyyvisar rune-lines fought with the Ildaruen overlay. As I reached the pirunaen, the stone veneer of the kirilidur crumbled and broke away, revealing the older runes beneath. From the deep shaft came the echo of rock crashing and falling. I could not pause to complete this work, however. Now I had to climb to the High Place and break him in the Eyestone, or all that I had done would count for nothing when he arrived.

The Room-Under-Tower had filled with smoke, wind whirling
up from the kirilidur, weyr light pulsing on every side. I glided
across the pavement and circled the room in each direction, singing.
The Eyestone was in place in the metal lattice. I could try to use the
machinery to take it out of the socket, but that would be dangerous,
too; the machinery is used to lower the stone periodically, so that it
may be turned and polished with oil. Within the Room and throughout the Tower I could hear the dissonance of the Wyyvisar interfer-
ing with the Ildaruen which Drudaen moved through. If anything
would bring the Tower to ruin under me, this would. To die in the
collapse of Laeredon would be the same as dying at Drudaen's
hand. As he closed in on the city, this dissonance would worsen. If
I meant to take the High Place, I had to do it now.

Finding the stair, I stretched time and gathered myself into readiness. Moving in and out of my body, entering the dual trance again,
I climbed. I stood on the lip of the stair, looking out across the
High Place; at the same time, rising into shadow, I searched for my
enemy and found him.

He had ridden faster than me, and already neared the Bridges
which led across Isar, entering the city from the east. Furthermore,
he had thrown off dismay and the urgency of the struggle had
drawn him out in all his strength. Even in his furious riding he saw
me on the High Place, and when I heard his voice, he spoke to me in
words I could hear and understand.

"Boy," he said, "you have come as far as you can come. Know
me now."

He set his hand inside me again, and the agony of his touch
ripped me so that I sagged onto his rune pavement. I fell on my
arm and it twisted backward with a wrench of pain. He bound me
there with Words like fire and ice along my skin. Lightning crashed
into me from every side, and the focus of the Eyestone moved
against me. His hatred filled me and I lay numb and motionless
while he poured his Power through me, clawing at the tiiryander, the
place where my spirit was tied to my body.

I watched from high above myself, pitying the agony of my
flesh. But I refused to waver. Hard as it was, heavy as my hand had
grown, I called upon my pitiful body to move, to use the arm left
me, to wrap the Bane Necklace in my palm. Below, through the city,
his white horse thundered in the cobbled streets, and everyone he
passed, friend or foe, swooned and died and he ate them and grew
stronger. My hand slowly neared the necklace while roch fire rose

up round my body and shadow thickened in my nostrils. He had my corpse in his thought and bent his strength to wreck it, but my hand moved a centimeasure at a time and finally, painfully, wrapped the Bane within flesh already cooling into death.

I could feel the bite of the runes against my palm.

The part of my mind that had been meditating on them all this time became clear to me. I remembered Kirith Kirin's words. *By the time she placed the Eyestone her time had already passed, as she said. She was pregnant with the child...* If she was pregnant with my great-grandfather, then she had already made the Necklace too. No doubt she fashioned it in the Work Room at Ellebren. Nowhere else could she have hidden the work from Drudaen.

Kentha made the locket to rule the Tower.

Even more important, she had the hidden lines of these same runes in Ellebren, the Words of the Praeven, to keep the link strong; I could hear the runes now, in the part of myself that remained at Ellebren.

Piercing agony filled me suddenly, as Drudaen found the tiiryander and closed his hand there like a talon.

With ebbing strength I sang to those rune threads that I did not know, and the Necklace burned my palm. I could feel the burning as far away as my spirit soared. The Wizard had reached the Base Rock beneath Laeredon and swooped down from his mount with the thunder of song, able now, he believed, to crush me with the strength of the Eyestone since my body had fallen onto his runes. But now I let him hear my voice, for the first time. "Here I am, Great-Great-Grandfather," I said, "flesh of your flesh and blood of your blood. Feel this."

I struck him with Words refracted through the Bane Gem, and the feeling of his pain was sweet. He had reached the causeway leading to Laeredon but staggered. His hand loosened within my body and my spirit-link strengthened. I moved power through the Gem again and his cry reached me all the way at the summit. The touch of the Bane Gem he recognized from the first moment, and his fear was palpable. "Oh yes," I said, "I have it. You feel it."

The Gem was strong but much of its use was hidden from me; it could not lead me to the place where his spirit tied itself to his body, and so I could not kill him, though I tried. For a moment my hand was on his heart. I stopped it beating as he had stopped mine; he could feel my touch, and while I was inside him he could feel the Gem. His terror swelled, and I helped it to seize him. Since I could not kill him, I needed to make him wary enough that he would give up any notion of breaking the Tower beneath me. I spoke through the Gem again and then, stronger, made my body stand. He could not pin me to the runes and protect himself at the same time. I was able to move my arms and legs again. I could see the High Place with the eyes of my body. The Eyestone shimmered and swirled, and while he was weak I reached into it. "I will give you your dance," I said, "as the Lady designed it, and you will belong to me."

So I moved. From the first step, pain shot through me, and with pain came the certainty that I had thrown the dice, that now I would win or lose. Even without opposition, there are only two ways to end the Dance of Encirclement on a High Place: one finishes the Dance or one dies. I bent my whole thought to that, keeping the Necklace where I could find it. On this razor's edge my spirit spun, in parallel with my nearly broken body below, tracing its steps on the Rune Path that Drudaen had concealed beneath his own.

I fell out of time. We struggled through the day as I completed the Long Dance. He was at the Gate but could not come in unless he meant to try to take the Tower again, and that would likely bring it down and kill us both. Holding the image of him at the gate in the kei space, I felt moments of his confusion. But I had other business. Blind, deaf, I returned to that place again where the Wizard had first found me, when the Sisters lost my spirit in the mountains. He was there too. We were clouds orbiting each other, and lightning poured from him to me. Coldness crept through me and I knew myself to be close to him, closer than I had ever dreamed of being. I could smell his breath. He laid his hands along my body. Confusion overcame me and I could no longer be certain I was dancing; I was lost in the fourth circle, and the terror of that nearly swept me into him forever. I could feel the dimming of light in Ellebren, the collapse of my presence there. I could feel the sighing of the Sisters along Illyn Water, their sadness when they heard the news that I had failed. I could feel the darkness enter Kirith Kirin finally: him on the battlements of the high walls watching the Tower-light dim and fade. His beauty turned to stone before my eyes. Despair would have taken me along with him, except that I could still feel his bracelet on my wrist, the burning Necklace in my palm, and I could still feel my heart beating. Somewhere, I told myself, I am alive and I am dancing, and I have the Bane Gem and Ellebren is mine, and if he wants to keep Laeredon he had better come and take it, or else I will kill him now where he stands, because this High Place belongs to me.

All worlds collapsed into one. I was in my body and the dance had carried me to the Horns of Laeredon. I hung in perfect balance over the edge of the summit, and my hand, stretched out, held the locket cupped. My other arm, broken by that first fall, hung useless at my side.

Dawn was breaking over the eastern hills. A day and night had passed as we fought. Below, watching me with physical sight, Lord Drudaen Keerfax.

He wore rich white garments, leggings and a cloak trimmed with glittering gems. His face, lifted toward me, had beauty beyond any earthly look of man. I could see why Kentha had loved him. Even from that distance I could see he would like to smite me too, that way, if he could, since all his other weapons had proven useless on this day. He opened his mouth to speak but without a sound I choked him silent with the strength of Laeredon, which was now mine, and he staggered. The glimmer of beauty fled him and some thing grim replaced it. With the arm left me, I held the Bane Necklace for him to see, dangling from the silver chain. "Here it is," I said. "Come and get it."

"Not today," he was getting his breath. "Some other time."

"We'll see when that day comes, if it ever does. Remember that I have it."

"Using it's the trick," he countered. "You'd have killed me already if you knew how. But you don't." To show his force, he struck at me again with all the vast strength left him, all the southern Heights, all the lives he had eaten, all the Words he knew. All the years he had lived. I staggered then, and nearly tumbled from the edge of the Tower I had won.

Contemptuous, he turned his back and found his horse again. The Necklace went cold in my hand; I could not longer muster the strength to reach through it. "Keep the Tower while you can," he said. "I'll get it back, after I'm done with you."

He would have ridden away then, and won a sort of victory, except I remembered myself, who I was and who had taught me. Crying out my last shreds of strength, I struck him once, twice, again and again, not through the Necklace but with the whole breadth of Laeredon. I saw him fall from his mount and stagger and still I struck him, and because I could not kill him outright I was free to cause him torment like no one had shown him in whole lifetimes. He felt every scrap of pain a body can feel while I raged. When I was done, he was limp as a rag on the ground, hardly better than I.

I said to him, "You're right old man, I can't kill you yet. But you'll feel worse than that from me before I finish. You're not alone in your power any more. Now get out of my sight before I kill your horse and make you crawl to Cunevadrim."

Whether I could have made good on this last threat or not I don't know. He struggled onto the horse's back and hid himself from all eyes other than mine. I watched him depart the city, howling in his fury. He attempted some very foul enchantments to make the city desolate but I countered him, and so he passed out the gates. He declined to return to Vyddn country from which he had come, but instead turned his riding southwest, the road to Cunevadrim.

I crawled to the stone and kissed it, favoring my arm. Huddled against it, I felt myself near loss of consciousness. But while I still had awareness, I broke shadow again, over Genfynnel and points north. I called below to Nixva to let him know his master lived. I sang to Ellebren and lit that summit with rainbows and wheels of fire. At Inniscaudra they would know I had won my fight. Laeredon answered to me. The Wizard had fled south. We would live to fight another day.

CHAPTER SIXTEEN
LAEREDON

1

Soft warm rain woke me, sweeping across the High Place.

Midmorning over Genfynnel brought clouds full of moisture from the sunlit east. The warmth surprised me. I had never been so far south this time of year and had no notion the breezes could be so balmy with winter closing in.

My sense of time returned to the normal flow. Drudaen had fled the Tower scant hours before. My body, full of hurts, objected when I stood, but there were things I had to do. He would be riding to Cunevadrim and when he reached his home Tower I could expect further opposition. In the hours intervening I needed to heal my own hurts as much as I was able.

I limped to the stairs leading to the pirunaen, which had cleared of smoke. Wind had swept the worktables clean of anything moveable, but the casks and workboxes had weathered the assault. At the edge of the open shaft, over which the firepot sits on its metal spider web, I listened. Murmuring and singing, the Wyyvisar reawakened. But I thought it unwise to try a descent that way till I had cleansed the place of the Wizard's changes. I headed into the High Chambers and whirled down the stairs.

Pain shook me, but I had long ago learned what to do with that when it became troublesome. As I descended I sounded the Tower, found it solid and whole. Now that it was mine I could begin to admire the handiwork that had made it, the care of its building. I had the sense that the stones themselves welcomed me, being glad to serve the Other no longer. Everywhere I found signs of the crumbling of his Ildaruen shell and the reassertion of the older magic beneath.

In the base room Nixva greeted me with unusual affection. We ate cake from the saddlebags, my first food since leaving Arthen, and we drank cumbre together. I had some of Imral's brandy as well. I led across the causeway to a grassy lawn.

We were safe enough. A pile of dead Verm marked the boundaries of my ward barrier, which still held. Beyond the Verm, a few faces moved. Here were some people come to steal gold from the dead creatures and to wander in the Palace where common folk rarely come. I stumbled toward one of them and called a Word to let my wards down. A boy approached, younger than me. He thought me lost, I guess. In my bedraggled tunic, with the Cloak all drab and dull, I hardly looked like the magician who had wrenched the Tower free of Drudaen's hold. The child gaped at me curiously. "Boy, if you can find a doctor who'll come here I'll give you a hill of gold."

He gaped at me like I had gone lunatic. I flung an amethyst at him, though, and he knew it was worth something. Taking a fresh look at me, he hurried off.

The food and drink restored me some. Most of my hurts would heal themselves, more quickly as I regained strength; but I wanted help to set my arm. It dangled useless at my side, shooting pain like fire into the place where I was putting pain just then. I waited at the causeway to the Tower while Nixva grazed and kept his eye on me. The balmy rain had passed and sunshine stirred the city to new motion. Signs of my passage and that of Drudaen were easy to find. The walls lay crumbled for a hundred cubits and the gates sent up trails of smoke. The front of the Palace portico had cracked, and some of the halls were smoldering even after the light rain. The street was lined with the dead and their pickpockets. It pained me to see the damage I had helped to do to such an ancient place. But I walked to the walls anyway, and those who were roaming thereabouts paid no notice. Except for my broken arm I looked like the rest, scavengers in a nearly-empty city. From the acropolis on which Telkyii Tars stood, I could see the nearest streets, the edge of a distant market. Once I saw a company of blue-clad soldiers moving; another time a train of wagons rattled beneath the road, carrying someone's possessions out of the city.

I could see, also, the gap in the city walls where the western gate had stood, until the Verm closed it against me.

The force of magic can stun even the maker of it. Incomprehensible to me, that so much destruction had visited this place so quickly. A city emptied of women and men, walls torn to shreds, an ancient house cracked, and carrion crawling over the dead. From Words I had said. The Verm love their lives too. I had killed today.

The soldier will tell you no battle is without blood, the magician will tell you no different. The boy would have told you, that day, he had never killed before, except the Witch who murdered his family, and he scarcely knew what to make of it. Here I stood, looking for someone to help me set my broken arm, and around me spread the city on which I had feasted in my rage.

Is it any wonder people fear us? I remembered Pelathayn's words in the council room at Inniscaudra, *Ten thousand or forty thousand, what does it matter?* No army of the world would ride here without my leave.

Yet I was a boy who once herded sheep on the Fenax hills, who had spilt his milk in his lap and gotten spankings for chasing the geese. My sister once gave me a licking for breaking her best arrows. My mother frightened me with stories of boogar bears in the night.

When the bedraggled boy found me I was teary, kneeling in the grass near the rent wall. He had brought a doctor all right, and she hurried behind him with her bag. She guessed I was crying from the pain but I tried to tell her I could hardly feel any of that. The pain I felt came from deeper, and I did not try to explain it.

She led me to the portico and the urchin followed, waiting for the hill of gold. The doctor told me her name, Evlaen daughter of Mrothe. I told her mine. She touched gentle fingers to the flesh where the break made itself evident. "It's broken," I said stupidly.

"I see." She gave me a sidewise look. "What happened?"

"I don't know. I was up there." I pointed to the Tower and she looked twice in that direction.

"Up where?" she asked.

I pointed again, this time making the gesture unmistakable. She faced the High Place and then faced me.

Evlaen, skeptical, asked, "How did you get up there?"

"I broke down the gate and went up. Lord Keerfax broke my arm while we were fighting."

She stopped dead in her work and looked to the boy, whose eyes had got wide. The boy said, in a small voice, "He did come out of the bottom. I saw him."

She turned to me again, bit her lip and looked around for something to make a splint. "Just set it. I can do the splint."

She refused to believe me, however, and found straight sticks. The setting took less time than I would have imagined. I was quiet through it all, and I think it was this that convinced her I might not be lying. Afterward, I handed the boy two rubies. "That will buy your gold for you. Put them away and run along."

He was a child who knew the value of a stone. He slid the rubies into his pocket and I asked his name. Simishal, he said. He had no parents. I said I would remember him and he ran off. The doctor, watching this, stepped away from me and cast her eyes downward. "Who are you?" she asked. By now she had seen the jeweled brooches stuck to my tunic and the Necklace on the true silver chain.

"I told you that. I wasn't lying. Don't run away from me." I was afraid if she did, I might start crying again. But she could not help herself, she was retreating. "I haven't paid you yet." But she started to shake her head. She backed away, keeping her eyes to the ground, and a fist of ache clutched my throat. I turned and ran myself, across the causeway into the base of Laeredon, where I hurled myself against Nixva and buried my face in his mane. He must have wondered what all the fuss was about.

Evlaen watched as I disappeared into the Wizard's Tower. I doubt she had ever been so close to it in her life. At least she knew I was telling the truth. I never saw the daughter of Mrothe again.

2

I ate more of the cake in the saddlebag, drank more cumbre and climbed to the High Place. Through the long afternoon and night I waited on the summit of Laeredon, my eye on the south road where Drudaen was traveling. By then I had rested and gained strength enough to enter trance, and from all the circles I could reach I watched and listened.

Soon I began to move power through the shenesoeniis, throwing a veil over the city and environs. The unfurling of the veil was quiet work, and I proceeded into afternoon and night with its making. By evening Drudaen had reached his stronghold in the southern mountains and his presence changed beneath shadow. He had climbed to his own High Place.

When I touched the Bane Necklace, I could hear neither singing nor voice. Maybe he walked his own Height with the same quiet as me, that evening. He must have felt the disturbance of me on all the planes, the newness of my voice broadcast from Laeredon. The fact that the Bane Gem had returned to haunt him must have disturbed him. If he had been me, his every thought would have been bent on scrying its use and learning its secret in order to finish him off. Maybe I would have been wiser if I had taken this course. But my thought that night was in other places. My veil deepened through the long hours.

The link to Ellebren was my concern, and as the veil took hold over Genfynnel and its environs, I reached out to that Tower again. My hand moved over the stone, as magicians say, and I made sure, as hours drew me toward morning, that my hold over Ellebren remained firm and strong. For a long time my eye hovered over both Towers, a hard feat that taxed my knowledge of fourth level vocabulary.

I made no attempt to see into Inniscaudra itself, or to find Kirith Kirin there. He would know, by my light on the High Place, that I was alive. To search him out would have disturbed the bond I felt with him. I can't explain this; it isn't forbidden. But that night, when I had at last tasted the full measure of what I had become, I had no wish to use these arts to find him and spy on him.

In fact, he came to me in his own way. Maybe he sensed my sadness, or maybe he was lonely. He appeared at Thrath Gate where my eye would find him. Anyone there would have drawn my atten tion, and he must have known that. He stood in front of the gate and breathed.

Some of the coldness left my heart. The sight of him healed places inside me where Drudaen had moved his hand. He studied the lights on the High Place, and their quiescence made him easy. I gave no sign I saw him, there was no need. He said nothing, sang nothing, merely watched. When he turned, someone joined him beyond the Arches. I made no attempt to see who was with him or to watch him as he departed. He would come to me in his body. It was enough for me to know that.

At dawn, when first light stirred in the heart of the muuren Eyestone, I sang Velunen. For this moment I had prepared in hidden ways, being wary. As day broke across the High Place, I reached into the Tower and sang in Words. In answer, the Tower burned like a second sun in the arm of two rivers, a light pierced the morning brighter than dawn, and a song went up into the clouds, heard on every level of magic known to me. Heard somewhat by human ears as well. Whether the voice was mine or Edenna's hardly concerned me, and I have heard both claims made. Velunen rang out over the ranges of the north Kellyxa, echoing west into Trenelarth and north into Vyddn. The light of Laeredon pierced the sky and could be seen as far as Drii. I tore away shadow in all those places and true morning fell for the first time in days. Over the land, one by one, I set my wards and spoke my Bans.

Those who had fled Genfynnel saw the light, wherever they had landed in the countryside. I spoke to them when Velunen died away, and my words were meant for others as well. "I am he who stands on Laeredon High Place," I said, and this time it was my voice, booming across the hills, "I have come to prepare the city for the March of the Successor out of Arthen. I have driven out the Master of Shadow and he will not return unless he can cast me down. You Verm and you soldiers of the Queen who served Drudaen Keerfax, get to shadow as fast as you can. At midmorning today I will ride out of Laeredon Tower and if I find you, you will regret it. You who fled your homes yesterday may return under my protection at noon, when I have cleansed the city of these people. Shadow won't fall over Genfynnel while I'm here. Return to your lives and prepare for the coming of Kirith Kirin, who will be your King."

3

At midmorning I kept my word, feeling safe to be away from the Tower. I rode as myself, in full awareness and not in trance, which would have dulled my feelings. This hindered me some, since I preferred to leave some part of me in the Tower to maintain watch on Cunevadrim; but I had already seen enough of what heedless magic can do.

I found the streets mostly empty, signs of departure where troops had been. Only a few of those who saw me understood I was the voice from the Tower, even though I changed my tunic for a clean one and lent fullness to the Cloak to make it seem more grand. I could have done more, and you will read tales that I coursed through Genfynnel on trails of fire with stars shooting from my fingertips.

The Verm had left wounded in barracks near the western gatehouse. I rode among them and they knew me immediately. The change of fear is pitiful even in Verm, and some were badly injured. Maybe I had caused these wounds when I broke the walls. I dismounted and spoke to their officers to calm them. Verm nurses had stayed behind to tend the wounded, the nurses risking death with the troops when I found them. But I let them live, and told them I would guarantee their safety. Their language was the same as ours, only hard to understand when they spoke it.

I found Blue Cloaks willing to surrender and city militia wondering what they might do to help, so I let the first group surrender to the second. At first the militia hesitated to believe I was the one to whom they must listen; but when I darkened the veil over Laeredon, they understood.

I insisted the Queen's soldiers give up their arms in the courtyard at Telkyii Tars. All morning the pile grew and the surrendering soldiers marched off in custody of the militia, while I scoured the streets on Nixva's back. Soon it became clear I needed someone to take charge of the city; the numbers of troops in custody swelled quickly, since most of the Queen's soldiers chose to surrender rather than face shadow. There had been a governor of Genfynnel appointed by the Queen, but she fled and never returned. Finally a militia captain brought a Finra who could take authority according to the city charter. We were in front of the High Place when the man was brought to me. I chose that place so he would not doubt me when he saw I was a boy. I told him what I wanted, which was really very simple. I wanted the Queen's soldiers held until Kirith Kirin arrived, when he could decide what to do with them. I wanted the wounded Verm protected until they were well enough to return to their own country. I wanted order restored to the city without delay, which meant looting and scavenging must stop. I wanted the dead burnt, Verm and other. I wanted hay for my horse. Last, I wanted workmen to open Telkyii Tars and make whatever repairs were necessary, to make it fit to receive Kirith Kirin. If these things were done, I would return to the Tower and leave them in peace.

The Finra agreed that these were reasonable stipulations and asked if I would guarantee the safety of those returning to the city. I said I would. I could see his discomfort when he was asking me for this protection so I shook the Tower a little to make him feel better about it. His followers drew back but he held his ground like a brave man. He asked if shadow would return and I told him no, it would not, as long I held Laeredon. He asked where the Keerfax had gone and I told him the Wizard had withdrawn to his house in Antelek and I was watching him. When he asked no more questions, I turned Nixva and we rode across the causeway into Laeredon. By then the Lord believed me. He carried out my wishes and I remained in the High Place as I had promised. By afternoon, the roads were swollen with people returning to their houses in Genfynnel.

I had no plan for settling Genfynnel in this or any manner when I rode out of the Tower that morning. My intention was to rid the city of people who might oppose our army when it marched from Arthen. But in the course of my riding I saw it was important to restore order in the City itself, for the sake of those who lived here. This was in my power to do, so I did.

In Laeredon, I lingered with Nixva till the oats and hay were brought. I made safe passage for the carters and they came into the Tower itself. They would tell that story for the rest of their lives. When they had unloaded and the empty wagon cleared the causeway, I set wards again and rose through the kirilidur to the High Place. My work was mostly done, and I sat down to wait.

CHAPTER SEVENTEEN
TELKYII TARS

1

Two armies marched through Arthen in the ensuing days, and another force moved down the narrow mountain pass that leads from Drii to Vyddn.

A force of mounted soldiers moved ahead of the rest, pressing toward Maugritaxa with speed. Among these riders was Kirith Kirin.

The dispositions of Drii troops into the Cundruen Pass made me think. So did the behavior of the Prince's own army, which split into two forces at the fork of roads in the central part of Arthen. One part of the army moved down the southern roads toward Maugritaxa. The other continued southeast toward the shores of Lake Dyvys.

The main Venladrii force split at the fork of Svorthis and Cundruen as well, with apparently similar goals.

The target of the east-marching forces could only be the Queen's army encamped on the Vyddn Plain, abandoned there by Drudaen when he rode to fight me at Laeredon. The south-marching forces were meant to garrison Genfynnel and hold the city for Kirith Kirin.

This much I could surmise. But as for Kirith Kirin's own plans, I could only guess.

By now, the advance party of mounted soldiers had moved well ahead of the infantry and neared the southern edge of Maugritaxa. Soon they would emerge into the north Kellyxa.

Descending from the shenesoeniis, I rode Nixva to the place where workmen busied themselves with repairs to Telkyii Tars. The workmen, seeing me, dropped their tools in fear but I assured them I meant them no harm. Cloakless, I sat astride Nixva in my boy's tunic, wearing the Bane. I asked the foreman of the work party to ask the new Lord of Genfynnel to come to me.

When the Finra came, I received him near Laeredon Gate. Out of courtesy I dismounted from Nixva when he approached; he was my elder after all. He approached without fear. He wore an elegantly embroidered cap and fine trousers under a jacket with sleeves. The Anyn wear sleeves even after reaching adulthood, a practical

custom in winter. I remembered his name, Zaevyeth son of Motaxin
of the Finru House of Kruenen. After greetings, I told him Kirith
Kirin was approaching north Kellyxa above the Rivers and that armies
were marching on Genfynnel to occupy the city. This was news he
needed since he must make his own dispositions for their provision-
ing, and he thanked me for the information. I made a request as
well. I needed a falcon of strong wing to serve me. The bird
would be returned in good health.

Zaevyeth sent me a falcon from his own aerie, a fine bird
whose name was Rik. I gloved my arm and carried her with me
to the Height.

Words tamed Rik to fly as I wished, and I tested this by
setting the proud creature to circle the Tower while I wrote out
my message to Kirith Kirin. The bird obeyed my charms and
returned when I had written down my question. My note said
this: "I see those marching east and those marching south and
cannot guess which place is your destination, nor do I know what
is your need. I can ride to you when you're nearer the city, if you
mean to come this way. If this is your wish, throw the gem
enclosed into your campfire when you're ready for me to ride. I
will see the sign and come. All this land is under my veil. The
Queen's army is still in Vyddn. Our enemy has withdrawn to
Antelek and sits under shadow. I can leave Laeredon and hold it
as long as I'm prudent. Yours."

Blessing the gem to which I had referred, I tied it inside the
parchment and secured the whole to Rik's leg by light cord and
binding Words. The falcon suffered this touch and burden without
complaint, as if she knew my need. I told her what I meant to do,
that I must supplement her eye with my own for a time, and she
agreed to the necessity. Speaking Words to wrap her in my enchantment, I flung her toward the sky.

This is simple magic requiring only a small part of the thought,
so long as I did not essay to see through her eyes or to control her
will. She flew north toward Arthen to find the riders, and the wind
carried her at great speed.

Afterward, I reached east into the deep mountains and began to
prepare for storm, snow, and wind. These I could bring down
onto the Vyddn Plain at will.

The veil could not hide this last movement from Drudaen, and
beneath shadow his presence changed. But I got no sense of what
he proposed to do.

By nightfall, seven days after I took Laeredon, mounted soldiers emerged from Arthen and camped. Those who needed a change of horse got one at the Maugritaxa outposts; royal horses had endurance but the mortal horses had been pressed to the limits of their strength. Rik had another half-day's flight before she reached their camp, and I checked her progress now and then. She killed, ate, flew on. Kirith Kirin's horsemen broke their camp before dawn, rode south, and camped again after nightfall. He was pressing them toward Genfynnel. That night my falcon found him, circled the camp and cried down to their hearing.

I was in her eye through all that followed, though I was careful not to take control of her mind, since that would have killed her. Traveling at such speed, Kirith Kirin would have left his own Birdmaster behind, and I could not let some foolish archer take aim at Rik, and so needed to see what she saw. The strange behavior of the bird was soon noted; she flew in lower circles and indeed, one numskull did lift his bow. As quickly it was snatched from him by a hand I knew, Karsten, who was first to sense that the falcon flew under my watchfulness. She called for her hunting glove and someone brought it to her. Kirith Kirin found her when the falcon settled peacefully onto her arm, eating tidbits from her hand. He untied the parchment and cord himself. The red gem fell into his hand.

He opened the note and I could see his face change. At this point I left Rik to their care and withdrew. To see through the eyes of a living creature is hard magic. As the Sisters teach, all living beings are the same size, the size of the eye of God. I could not waste strength when so much work awaited me on Laeredon. But I replayed the image of Kirith Kirin again and again in my mind.

Two days passed. Rik returned on the second and I had her taken to her master by a servant. I continued my work in the Tower and on the High Place, preparing applications and devices needed when we continued south from Genfynnel. The winds in the eastern mountains gathered. The armies of Drii and Inniscaudra neared Lake Dyvys and the southern end of Cundruen.

The mounted party came half the distance to Genfynnel before Kirith Kirin threw my gem into the fire and called me.

I heard the call near sunrise and my heart lifted. Nevertheless I prevented myself from rushing out of Laeredon like a foolish puppy. I prepared the Tower for my absence, setting a ring of kirin-stones around the Ruling Rock and descending through the kirilidur, kindling watch runes and other devices, keying them to my voice and to

the ring I wore. Since there was no Gate to shut, I set other gems
into the portal, these armed with Wards and Bans of the killing kind.
I closed the causeway to passage of any but the Wise and set more
Wards in the Tower courtyard, these to warn off stragglers. Sum-
moning the Finra Zaevyeth again, I asked that he set militia near
Laeredon, to prevent the foolish from wandering close to the place.
I would be absent from the city for a day. I was pleased when news
of my riding troubled him, and added, to reassure him, "Don't fret.
I won't go so far that I can't beat the Keerfax back here. Your city
is still under my protection."

He was relieved to hear this, and set the guard as I had requested.
Near midmorning, I rode out on Nixva's back. We cantered through
the city streets. Those who saw us coming fell back into their houses,
all but a few who bowed their heads and wished me blessings for
lifting shadow. I had expected the fear but not the kindness. My heart
felt fuller when Nixva carried me across the Osar bridges.

Kindling the ithikan around the horse and me, moving beneath
my own veil, I stretched myself outward and upward, entering the
dual trance again, so that as I rode, my eye hovered over Laeredon.
Now that I had spent more time at fourth level, this was easy. Nixva,
with my aid, carried us at enough speed to meet the mounted party
near nightfall.

2

He knew me by the shadow of my speed across the plain and rode
out to meet me himself. From Nixva's back I saw the mounted
party halt and the Keikin surge free of the rest. Relaxing the ithikan,
I slowed us to something less than a blur. I met him as the boy I
wished to be, riding the horse he had given me.

We dismounted and he pulled me close, murmuring words in
my ear. His heart beat like mine. "Here you are."

"I thought you'd never call me."

Holding me at arm's length, he stroked my hair. "We thought
we'd get close to the city, since there's time. No need to take you too
far from the High Place when you worked so hard to win it."

By now he had felt the splint on my arm beneath the Cloak and
his brow furrowed. "Broken?"

"Yes. During the fight. It's nearly healed now. Bone takes
some time."

A shadow crossed his face and he pulled me close again. He searched my eyes and I could not hide that the fight had changed me. But while he kissed me it was as if there had never been any coldness in my body. I laughed quietly, feeling like a boy again. He asked, "What?"

"Nothing. I've missed you, that's all."

We set out walking toward the war party, making camp. The royal horses followed behind, reins trailing the grass of the plain. West of us a farmhouse could be seen, anxious figures standing in the yard. "Poor folks, they'll be wondering what we want on their land. I'll send someone to talk to them."

"Who's with you?"

"Everyone. The twice-named, I mean. Except I left Mordwen Illythin in charge of Inniscaudra and of the Fenax. He didn't like it but he had to see the wisdom of it in the end. He's too old for this, he's in his last life. He's taking care of Axfel for you, he said to tell you so. Idhril has the Genfynnel garrison. Unril has the army marching east. We'll join them as soon as we've had our council here."

So I had been right. He'd meant to ride to Genfynnel and then to join the army again. "As far as I can tell the Queen's army hasn't moved."

"Save all that," he said. "We'll have time to talk. Right now, all I want to do is feel you breathing under my arm."

Near the encampment, other figures hurried toward us. Karsten hurled herself around me and Imral gave me that quiet look of pleasure which I had learned to read as his approval. "Here you are," Karsten said, noting my arm, "but what's this?"

"My first wound, and it's a pretty nice one too."

She looked into me same as Kirith Kirin had. Something in her searching brought out more of the hurt. We passed sentries already posted and Imral led us to the fire he had laid. Pelathayn roamed the other campfires but soon joined us. Kirith Kirin dispatched Gaelex to the farm nearby to ask permission to camp in the broad meadow and to use the creek water. She took two soldiers with her and was gone. Around us tents were going up. The curious were watching our circle. I saw Brun and raised my hand to her. She bowed her head courteously and then touched a finger to her lips.

Imral brought me brandy from his own stock and I thanked him. They drank with me, all of them, and we sat in the grass in the open air.

A change within the Veil warned me that Drudaen, from his southern Tower, sought after my whereabouts; he knew me to be out of the Tower. Reaching into kei, I made a change in Laeredon to show him I still held the place; he would know the change but still would not know my whereabouts. Nor would he see this camp if I could help it. The veil held. This work carried me away from my friends and they waited and watched. Again I was surprised at how much they understood. "He knows I'm on the ground again. I warned him off."

"He's in Cunevadrim?" Kirith Kirin touched my cup to remind me to drink, and handed me waycake.

"Yes. He's been on the High Place worrying over his loss, I guess. And building defenses he never had to build before."

Karsten laughed. "Not a happy wizard." With an expectant look, as the rest settled near us in the grass, the fire licking upward, she said, "Well. Tell us the tale."

Taking a deep breath, I told what had happened. They listened as if wrapped in enchantment and I was proud of what I'd done for the first time. I finished with, "So then I broke shadow as far as I could reach and claimed my ground."

"How far?" Kirith Kirin asked.

"East to the mountains but not as far south. He still holds the rest of the Towers there."

"A victory even so," Imral said.

"Maybe not so much. I took a place from him that he never built. He'll be sorry he never pulled Laeredon down and built a Tower of his own, which I couldn't have taken. But he's sure he'll get it back, he told me so."

Kirith Kirin kissed my brow and told me, "Don't diminish what you've accomplished. You've made a way south."

The thought seemed new to me then, though the fight for Laeredon was days old. I had taken a High Place from the Wizard himself. A story had been made that women and men would tell for a long time. I mulled this. Lifting my cup, I said a silent prayer to YY-Watchful.

Talk moved to other subjects. We had come together for council and, when Gaelex returned and got us food, we settled over the fire and the meal. Kirith Kirin told me some of what had happened since I left them. When it was clear I had won my fight, they made strategy, and the result was different from the early plans, as I had seen. Kirith Kirin meant to deal with the Queen's army in Vyddn before coming to Genfynnel. This had caused some argument, since it would be unprecedented for the Successor to move out of Arthen in that fashion, making war on the army of the Crown. But these were hard times, and no one saw the wisdom of our soldiers marching south with an enemy already at their backs. King Evynar and the Venladrii would follow Kirith Kirin's lead, and so plans were made to divide the Armies, one part moving to reinforce my presence in Genfynnel and the other part marching in a two-pronged attack on the Queen's forces in Vyddn.

Karsten questioned me when this much had been told. "Have you seen any movement among the Vyddn troops since Drudaen abandoned them?"

"No. He rode away from them suddenly, as soon as I rode out of Arthen, and I don't know what contact he's had with them since. He won't know what troops are moving in Arthen, but I expect he'll know about the soldiers moving through the mountains. My veil doesn't reach as far as that, but his eye does."

"The Venladrii know how to move hidden," Imral said. "But if you saw them, I guess he did too."

"Why would he leave an army there if he knows we're marching on it?" Pelathayn asked, and then answered himself. "To slow us down." Nodding his head.

"Troops mean nothing to him now," Karsten said. "He has more Verm, when he needs them. But with Jessex in the field, he needs time. Will he be able to reach across you to help his folk in Vyddn?"

I shook my head. "I've been preparing for that, since I saw the split in the armies. That's part of why I rode out here to meet you. I can help you from Laeredon, but I didn't want to move my hand there without leave."

Silence fell for a time. Imral passed more brandy round, and we drank as sunset approached, shadows lengthening. Gaelex returned with a gift of fresh cheese from the farm and with news of the farm-folk's joy that it was Kirith Kirin who camped on their ground. She reported this herself. "They heard a voice out of the clouds to tell them you were riding, sir." Crafty woman, she managed a glance at me sidewise. "They claim the whole countryside will rise up to follow you if that's what you need."

I told that part of the story too, and finished with the settling of the city under authority of Zaevyeth. Kirith Kirin listened carefully to these details and questioned me as to my dispositions. The choice

of the Finra pleased him; "That's an Anyn house," he said. "Those
people will know this isn't another Jisraegen war against them. You
did a good thing there, though I daresay you didn't realize it."

"I got the first eligible person I could find who hadn't fled the
place. I'd no idea what else to do."

"So we'll find no opposition in the City," Karsten said.

"None. Most of the Queen's soldiers surrendered when I made
it clear their only other choice was to head for shadow. The Verm
left long ago, except for the wounded."

Karsten gave Kirith Kirin a sharp look. "So they gave up rather
than return to her service. I smell a new strategy coming. Maybe we
don't need to fight the Vyddn folk, maybe we can offer them terms."

"I'd thought of that," he agreed, and Imral was nodding too.
"This is a good piece of news, Jessex. We wondered how much
support Drudaen had among the Queen's soldiers, after shadow.
Now we know."

"The Vyddn army has had a few days of sunlight to think about
what's coming," Imral said, mildly. "That may soften them. That
and the fact that their wizard has abandoned them in the field."

These thoughts lifted their spirits, and so we broke council for a
time. The moment of sunset neared and Amri, traveling with this
party, stood some distance away with the muuren in her hand. We
approached her and listened to the Evening Song. The girl's voice
astonished me, her silver eyes and dark skin glowing in the twilight.
The Venladrii have the same vocal range as we do. I stood close to
Kirith Kirin, a place no one begrudged me. When the song was
done, we wandered into the meadow, the whole party of us. The
kindling of Kirith Kirin's spirit was plain. Here he walked, free of
Arthen. A journey had begun which might lead him to his Crown.

The farmfolk had come out for the song too, and when it was
done, one of them got Gaelex to approach us again. The Marshall
strode to us with a wicked gleam in her eye and, head bowed, refusing
to look the Prince in the eye, said, "The farmer and her husband beg
leave to give their bed to you Kirith Kirin. She says she can't rest in it
herself when the Prince Kirith sleeps on the ground. It would do her
honor, by her own words, and she'll have a story to tell her grandchil-
dren when you're King." Here was the part that made Gaelex merry.
"I told him that if you accepted the offer, there might be two."

He allowed himself to raise a brow at her but no more than
that. He looked at me. "Well. A bed would be nice, wouldn't it?"

"Yes, it would," I said, my face heating.

No one laughed. Kirith Kirin directed her to accept the generous offer and to post a guard there. "Warn them we'll be a while at our talk here."

"They'll be moving into the barn for the night, I think." Withdrawing in her formal way, she set about making these things happen.

Returning to the fire, the others spoke more on the subject of armies and strategy. Karsten and Kirith Kirin told me what help they might need if there were fighting in Vyddn. We agreed on signs to tell me which of the strategies to follow, and I gave them kirinstones to use to send me signals. This took more time than the summary of it, and we went late to bed in the farmhouse.

Before we went there, Kirith Kirin took me walking under moonlight in the meadow, away from the encampment. Some distance from the farmhouse stood a duris-nut orchard and we wandered in that, along the stream that traced its path through the place. Silence helped to drive away the thoughts of the council. He slipped his arm around my waist and I did the same for his, liking the taut muscles of his side, the movement as we walked. "I remember that hand," he said, sighing. "I just wish you had two."

"I do, but one's not fixed yet."

Some heaviness had settled on him, and I waited for him to bring it out. We stepped under low branches, by the flow of water over rounded rock. Tonight we had the red moon, after an absence of many days, and after some time staring at the red reflection in the water, he said, "The night you fought him, I watched. One time, near morning, Ellebren went dark and I thought you were dead."

I remembered my vision, the lovely face turned to stone. I pulled him close, holding him as hard as I could with the one arm I had. "I didn't die. Here I am."

"You came close. You won't say it, but I can tell. I don't know what I would have done."

"You would have gone on being Prince."

"Forever with a taste of ash in my mouth. And no hope."

Clumsily, with the splinted arm, I touched his face. "If I lost you I would feel the same. But I haven't lost you. Here you are. Let this other feeling go."

He sighed, but the heaviness would not lift. There was something he had not said. I kissed his mouth, the tenderness opening to me. After that I knew where his fear came from, not from reading his mind as magicians can, but from the feeling between us, so new and open. He felt the difference in me. Finally he said it. "He hurt you deeply, I can feel the change. When you left me you were a boy, whole. Now there are wounds in you. I can feel them, little as you make of it."

"It was a hard fight. But I had to win."

"I don't know if I can do this. Her gifts can be so cruel. Here you are, and I love you with all my heart. But I have no choice but send you to fight the one enemy against whom I have no other weapon."

"I think it was her wisdom made her shape the gift this way. Not cruelty."

He shook his head, speechless. The hurt ran deeper in him than I guessed. I remembered the moment when lights of Ellebren died. He spoke haltingly. "I've known the great magicians, Jessex. I've seen what magic does. That was part of my fear and anger, when I saw you that morning with the Sisters." He searched my face, as if he had lost me. "I don't want this life for you. But the choice isn't mine. And it's too late to take my love back—"

"Please don't even say that."

He drew me close, lay his cheek against my neck. It is something when an immortal is tender. I let him stand against me, holding his weight against my slighter frame. "When I was on Laeredon, near the end of the fight, for a while I thought I was lost and my death had come. But I saw your face. You were on the walls at Inniscaudra and you were watching the Tower lights. When they went dark you turned to stone. The terror of that went through me. Maybe without the thought of you I would have died there, who knows? But when I thought of you I remembered I was alive, I remembered I had a heart, and I finished the battle and won."

"That was the moment. I was there."

"You see? Maybe YY sent me as she did because only a boy who loved you could fight your enemy well enough." Trying to smile, I said, "Anyway, I was never a very good archer. I'd probably have gotten killed the first time I took to the field, and then where would we have been?"

He made a sign against the bad luck of chance words, and kissed my brow. "I guess you'd have had to fight one way or the other, same as we all do."

"I don't mind what YY made me into. It's not so bad, as long as there's someone who won't run when he sees me." I told him then about the doctor in Genfynnel, and the feeling afterwards, when I saw the dead.

"Some of the change I feel in you comes from that. Better to feel the weight of what you've done than to brag about your killings. We're what we are, I guess." He sighed. "Some lovers can at least swear to love each other beyond the grave. We can't even do that, can we?"

He meant that magicians do not always die with their souls intact. "Listen," I said, "I promise you this. If he ever comes so close that I think my soul is in danger, I'll cut the cord myself, race him to Tornimul and love you forever from beyond the Gates. All right?"

He laughed at my grim scenario. But it did ease him, to think that such an escape might be possible. Kentha had managed it, after all. It is a terrible thing to dream that one you love can die forever, without any hope of birth in the land beyond. "All right. As long as you meet me there when I cross the mountains. Don't go running off with the first hero who turns your head."

This was nearly as much as we could do for each other, with words. The moon drew behind clouds and wind blew. Of one mind, we headed to the farm house with its circle of sentries awaiting his approach. "There's one thing I want to know," I said, "it's been on my mind to ask you. When you found me in Imith Imril, did you already know I would be there?"

"Yes," he said, laughing, and we walked side by side across the red-washed meadow.

3

The bed had seen a lot of use. A good goose-down mattress, and as a bonus one could hear the geese out the window. Kirith Kirin could barely stand in the room, the ceiling was so low. We undressed by a single lamp and lay down in the clean linen, smelling the pig sty and the chicken roost through the torn grease-paper. He made a joke about it and we lay together talking for a while, touching shyly. The room made him curious about my farm and my family and I told him some about it. "When all this is over," he said, "we'll go there. I want to see the place. If you can stand the sight."

"It would be good, I think."

We made love in the feather mattress with Kirith Kirin's feet sticking off. He had some trouble working round my arm and I felt the comic touches as keenly as the touches of pleasure; we were laughing through to the end. His body reached through me and while we were moving together, with his presence inside me and mine in him, I pictured his touch as cleansing me of all the places Drudaen had reached, when my body lay undefended. The healing went on and on. At the end I told him so, and he said he thought the boy was back. He could feel the difference himself. This was when his heaviness finally lifted.

Neither of us really slept. Our hours together being short, we talked into morning. We had never talked as much before and repeated all kinds of nonsense to one another, the things companions like to say. None of it bears repeating though every word is etched in my memory.

Sometimes, with the part of me that was kei, I stopped to listen to the sounds of the other planes. The certainty that my enemy was gathering force beneath shadow returned. I tried to hide this listening from Kirith Kirin but he knew too much, and finally asked, "What do you hear?"

"There's a change in his presence. I don't know what."

"Don't you?" He sat up in bed and pulled me against him. "Don't you think he can guess where you are and why you're here?"

I hadn't thought of that. Kirith Kirin went on. "He's preparing something to drive you back into Laeredon." The wisdom of this surprised me and it showed in my face. He laughed, touching my nose with his fingertip. "I told you, I've known the great magicians. I know how he thinks. He's afraid I'll take you with me into Vyddn. Mark my words."

Too soon his prophecy came true. A sudden light filled the narrow window of the chamber, and on all the planes Drudaen set out a huge cry, raising his Tower against mine and beginning the song that sends the circular storm. I had the Necklace near me and could hear his voice. The assault shook all my Wards and I shivered in the cramped bedroom, Kirith Kirin curled around me. Sadness filled him. "I was right." Sliding out of bed, he handed me my drawers. "It's nearly morning anyway."

I made him look me in the eye, standing naked against him, I kissed him brazenly, like a strumpet. His body responded and we clung to each other. "This time we know we'll see each other again. As long as you don't get yourself hurt in Vyddn."

That made him laugh. "I'm too tough and old for that."

We dressed, and he sent for someone to have Nixva saddled. All the sentries were watching the weyr-light on the horizon, a funnel of fire pouring upward. As I fastened the Cloak, I spoke Words of my own, reaching out to Laeredon for an answer to my enemy. The Tower responded and the soldiers, nearby, looked back at me. Murmuring prayers, they drew back, lest some stray lightning bolt should fall on them, I guess. Kirith Kirin stood his ground until Nixva came cantering, all saddled and ready, impatient to be off. I gave them all a show as I was leaving, kindling the Cloak till it threw off light as bright as the Towers. "I'll see you in Genfynnel," I said, and he took my hand a moment. "Mind you get there soon."

"Very soon," he said, meeting my eye.

I rode off in a storm of light. As I departed, I saw Imral and Pelathayn running to him across the field; I waved and headed toward my work, as soon they would head toward theirs.

4

We rode at higher speed on the return journey, and I spent the time deep-singing and setting into motion defenses I had already prepared during my days alone on the High Place. This time, heading to Laeredon, I had a sense of joy and fullness.

That the Wizard stood on his High Place and fought me Tower to Tower was proof of respect. Now I did not have to wonder whether he had laid some trick for me; his hand was revealed. I was determined, on that ride, to make it backfire against him if I could. He meant to pin me in my High Place. That was all well and good from his perspective. But I meant to do the same to him.

Sunrise broke over east Kellyxa with the two Towers still belching light. The early striving went to him almost by definition, since he stood in his body on Yruminast while I held Laeredon by voice and thought. His shadow broke over my Wards and from the western mountains came wind and gathering clouds. But I noticed, in my fourth-level seeing, a curious fact. While Laeredon and her power withstood little of his early assault, Ellebren held her countryside entire and his hand never troubled her. This difference could not be credited to the virtue of Arthen, since his troubling weather broke over Arthen easily in her southern reaches.

But I had heard enough through the locket by now to know it was the lines of Praeven runes that made the difference. Though I knew nothing of them, the locket made that irrelevant; the Praeven Words harmonized with the Wyyvisar and Ellebren reached him with a two-voiced magic against which he knew no defense.

So, while I employed the strength of Laeredon to hold my Wards and to repel shadow to some extent, I sent the main part of my thought back to Ellebren. I called to Ellebren to move against him, to unsettle his power in the mountains and to counter his stormbringing. The whole Tower answered, Wyyvisar and Praeven magic blended.

He knew the Laeredon High Place but had never set foot in Ellebren. No one knew Ellebren except her builders, and they never wakened her power to use. Only I had done that. The Praeven magic had a feeling like nothing else. Its presence in Ellebren troubled him deeply. While I stood on Laeredon in my body, I had not noticed this. But riding toward Genfynnel I saw the distinction.

I sang to Ellebren to move against his storm and suddenly his thought was not so clear. Answering my calling-song, Ellebren's deep places reached toward Cunevadrim and I could feel his palpable confusion, a wavering of his thought. He recovered quickly; his skill and power allowed him to do so. But the wavering recurred when I reached to him from Ellebren again, while my hand from Laeredon hardly touched him.

As I rode, the Bane Necklace dangled from my neck, its strange runes beating against my chest.

We reached Genfynnel soon. Even in the urgency of the moment, we merely cantered through the city streets at sunrise as the merchants were setting up in the market. Near the Tower base, beyond my Wards, I found a delegation from the City Lord awaiting me, wishing news about this present battle. Would the Keerfax return? I told them no. The City remained under my protection. But when I climbed to the High Place they would see signs of conflict.

They bustled away. Through the kirilidur I ascended. I climbed to the shenesoeniis and walked under the clouds.

My vision sharpened through the seeing-stone. The movement of Words beneath me in Laeredon matched itself to the movement of Words within the engine of distant Ellebren. I had learned to use the Bane Necklace well enough by now that I no longer needed to grasp it, and I heard his voice calling storm. Now he contested my hand in the east as well, confusing my own winds.

I entered fourth-level sleep with my body beside the Eyestone, my awareness grown very small in the place where Words are spoken. Seeing a long way, I understood his strength. Light cascaded on all the planes from the White Tower in which he stood, and his song moved in waves like a rainbow. There was nothing repulsive in his voice or in the Words. The sound of Ildaruen was not so strange to my ears this time and I had less difficulty concentrating. The vastness of him at that moment defied belief, his hand moving from four shenesoeniisae, his voice making shadow over half of Aeryn, his wards stretching out through valley and forest, storm kindling at his behest in the west and east at once, and his whole thought bending toward Laeredon. He meant to shrink me down to size and pin me here by throwing all of Yruminast against me. For a moment, on fourth-level, I could feel and see the motion of all this. His magic filled the terrain I had come to know. The sight pleased me no end. He was moving his hand in all places doing all things, making shadow over the southern countryside and stirring storm on both sides of the mountains. Now he was pushing my wards and setting himself against the Tower in which I stood. I had only to defeat him in one place and his pride would suffer.

Drawing the Cloak around me I began the pattern of breathing in my body that would deepen the dual trance. Quietly reasserting myself from Laeredon into the east, moving under veil, I divided my eye onto Ellebren and Laeredon at the same time. I divided my song with an equal mind; I had never done this before but saw it as if it were a new move in a dance. I sang from both places in different ways and brought the weight of Ellebren onto him. As I did, linking the runes of the Necklace to the runes of the distant Tower, I began to understand.

Kentha made Ellebren and made the Necklace too, and in so doing fashioned the perfect weapon against Drudaen, tying the Tower through the Praeven Runes to the gem he had given her, which was all his weakness handed to her in love. The power of Ellebren worked against him out of proportion to my skill because Drudaen could not defend himself entirely from the gem, and the magic in two languages perplexed him as well. The Diamysaar had not known this to teach, no one had, till someone climbed to Ellebren and used the High Place.

I sang against his shadow using Ellebren's whole strength, and even in daylight I could see the bright answering fire over the horizon. My object was not to push shadow farther back but to strike at its heart, at Yruminast-over-Cunevadrim where the Wizard stood. I opposed him in no other way, bringing all my thought from Ellebren against his High Place. Even on fourth level I could feel the shuddering of many curves.

Over Cunevadrim I tore open shadow and ruptured his veil to see him clearly. It was as if I reached toward him with a single fierce light and burnt him. A shuddering went through all of shadow and his song faltered. I could see the bulk of his thought before he closed the tear I had made.

This was the thought I read: he meant to ride south as soon as he could, and his intention remained to bring the White Tower to bear on me in such ways that he could use from afar to keep me penned in Laeredon. He meant to prevent me riding after him and opposing him on the ground. Fear of the Gem and Ellebren loomed big in his mind. He wished to undertake a work in the south that he thought might bring me down. That thought he held protected even with the veil torn, and I could not discern what he intended to do.

Before he closed the veil I could feel his surprise and then his chill, when he understood the blow had come from Ellebren. He would wonder if I had returned there. So I lifted my song over Laeredon and reached to the eastern mountains, conjuring storm to send over the army he had abandoned on the Vyddn Plain.

To his eye, I stood in both places at once. I could feel his confusion even beneath his defenses. I struck from Ellebren again but this time he was better prepared; I broke shadow but his veil held. We continued in this way, through a long day and into another. He stayed on the High Place as I did.

This was later called the War of Lights, named by those people who suffered the effects and made stories and songs about it. I kept fair skies in the part of the world where Kirith Kirin traveled, but the Wizard's storms tore across Arthen, Genfynnel and the Fenax, while mine raged over Vyddn and Antelek. For ten days I stood on the Tower without a moment's rest, till I was thin and worn as old bone. But for that ten days he stood with me, not daring to ride south as he wished, and we took the measure of each other. Because I did not lose, I won.

My wards bent but held. By concentrating my strength, I could thwart any part of his magic-making I chose; and so I chose my victories carefully. I broke shadow over Arroth, Turis and Antelek, the countries in which it had held longest. I broke shadow, for a time, over Ivyssa as well, to make a point. The people there would know the Wizard to be opposed, and it is remembered that they took heart at the sight of the sky. Because of the distance I could only hold back shadow for a time; but the story spread. I hurled storm with good effect and did so where I chose. The key to this was simple. I never opposed him in all ways and I never lifted my hand against him directly except from Ellebren. I never fought where I could not beat him.

I beat him with strategy, not strength. But strategy counts. This I learned walking on Laeredon and Ellebren at the same time.

The Genfynnel garrison came marching from Arthen during all of this. Lady Idhril led the soldiers, mostly infantry and a few mounted folk, across the storm-swept country into a terrain that burned night and day, three kaleidoscopes of whirling fire. I noted their progress and protected their passage, though I could not protect them from his weather entirely. The garrison crossed the bridges and came through Osar Gate at night, under threat of lightning in pouring rain, with the Tower lights casting eerie color onto the walls and buildings, the countryside and the surfaces of the rivers. Lady Idhril moved the soldiers first into Telkyii Tars and from that acropolis she dispatched patrols throughout the city, manning the walls. She spoke to Zaevyeth, met with the militia commanders, sent messengers to Laeredon to await my descent, making each move crisply.

When I descended I smelled of lightning and my hair nearly stood on end. I greeted her with appropriate courtesy and we stepped aside from her retinue. "I bring Kirith Kirin's blessings," she said. Idhril was tall, with hair the color of fire, and her arms were thick with muscle; she had the broad, pallid face of uplands people, the Svyssn, not of the finer boned, darker Jisraegen. "He sent me messengers from Lake Dyvys." She offered me folded parchment, sealed with the Prince's ring. Addressed in his own hand, not written by one of the clerks. I slid the letter into my Cloak.

Indicating the High Place, she said, "We've been watching the show all the way from Arthen. The southern light, is that Cunevadrim?"

"Yes, ma'am. I expect it will go on for a while. I can't do much more than I've done to protect the city from weather, any more than I could protect you, so you might warn folks about that."

"I've opened Telkyii Tars. I have a room ready for you, whenever you can sleep."

I took the moment to nibble cake and drink cumbre. We talked a while. I asked about the march, especially leaving Arthen. She had not walked out of tree-shadow in a long time, she said. She asked about the early battle for Laeredon and I told her some of the details, and then the aftermath, the work I had done to restore order in Genfynnel. She asked me a few questions about that—Kirith

Kirin briefed her in letters so there was not much she didn't know. I asked about the Verm. They were still in the city.

When in my body and away from the High Place, I lost track of the Wizard. I could hear his voice and it seemed to me he still stood where I had left him. But when I returned to the summit again, I knew he had gone.

He had taken his opportunity to ride away; I was sure of it. I searched for him in various ways. I failed to detect any change beneath his Veil that would indicate his whereabouts, except that the Verm under his eye were marching as well, west beyond the Narvos Ridge.

Soon, however, when Drudaen sang ithikan to increase his speed, I knew he was on horseback.

He rode in a fury. He had much strength left to him, as far as I could gauge. I called up what I had to spare to force him back, but his own Tower, answering to his Words, rendered me ineffective. He had chosen his moment carefully. I slowed his riding some but could not stop it.

At the same time, in the north, Kirith Kirin dropped a gem into fire that gave me the signal I awaited. So I turned my attention there.

My enemy rode south, as had been his wish. I lost sight of him in the Hills of Slaughter.

5

The Drii force reached southern Cundruen near Montajhena as Kirith Kirin marched north from Lake Dyvys, moving quickly up the Pajmar into Vyddn. When all was in place, on signal, I focused Laeredon Tower on breaking shadow as far south of Vyddn as my hand could reach. In place of shadow I left storm cloud of my own, the type armies hate, with torrents of rain and teeth of lightning or cyclone. This cut off any real hope of retreat.

I maintained this tense posture through the long wait that followed. Stretched, with Drudaen's Tower still singing at my back, I brought my will to bear from Vyddn through Trenelarth and Rars, even reaching into north Onge. This wait encompassed two days or more. The Prince meant to let the Queen's soldiers get a good look at his forces before he sent his terms to them. These hours of readiness would save lives, he thought.

At last he signaled me a battle would begin, and a small battle was indeed fought. Some Verm put up good resistance but the Queen's soldiers quickly sued for terms. The Verm retreated toward Cundruen, preferring that to my storm, and the Venladrii caught them there. They fought again, and the Verm died or were captured; none surrendered. The Queen's soldiers laid down their arms with few casualties. Kirith Kirin spent a day processing the prisoners, getting wagons for their abandoned arms, ordering the march back to Genfynnel and greeting King Evynar, who had led the Venladrii through Cundruen. They were aware of the need for speed, though they did not know Drudaen had gone south already. Within a day, the armies marched for Genfynnel with their prisoners, five thousand of the Queen's soldiers. I hear they were a jolly lot, congratulating themselves on being marched to a comfortable confinement in Genfynnel. Before they surrendered, Kirith Kirin had let them know shadow was broken there.

6

I had stood on the High Place nearly fifteen days. On the last, I watched Kirith Kirin's southward march, aching in every bone. Scanning the clouds a final time, hearing voices on the planes, nothing new. Drudaen moved beneath a veil and avoided the High Places. I could not find him.

The return to my body was hard; I found my flesh in fever from having endured fourth-level trance so long. I drank clear water from the cistern in one of the chambers and sipped cumbre to prepare my stomach for solid food again. Strange to see through the eyes again, to feel air on the skin, to gather sensation through the nose and fingertips. To hear so little, and such small sounds. I felt the heat of the fever and prepared unufru tea, finding the root stored in the Work Room. I drank the tea and descended.

Nixva had been moved to stable with the other horses, now that there were soldiers to guard him. I found the Base Vault empty, full of singing. Briefly listening to the changes of voice within the kirilidur, I touched the silver runes in the rock, the signature of Edenna Morthul.

I would not have wanted Kirith Kirin to see me that day, so removed from the world to which I was returning. I stepped across the causeway under clearing skies, clouds scattering north. This was late in the month of Ymut, near winter. Even in Genfynnel one began to feel the chill. The cloak swirled around me, casting off light. I tamed it some on the way to Telkyii Tars.

Knowing nothing about the place, I wandered. Idhril had left a servant to watch for me, a shy man who begged my pardon and led me to an apartment, Kirith Kirin's own rooms, in fact. I thanked my guide and sent him to Idhril with a note telling her Kirith Kirin was marching to the city and describing some of the battle.

Then I read his letter to me.

"I am taking this chance to send my love by letter, since Idhril will see you long before I do. We've watched the fireworks with concern. The troops think it's a fine show but I've seen these fights before. Troublesome that it's continued so many days. You'll come down from the High Place looking nearly transparent and you won't know where you are. Well, if I were there I would find a way to remind you. Greetings from your friends. I've told Idhril to take care of you and put you in my rooms. Be safe and wait for me."

The letter made him real. I felt better. Nearly transparent became flushed with color. The world enfolded me.

I slept in a high-ceilinged, stuccoed chamber flooded with light. I slept two whole days, woke, ate real food, and slept again. Idhril kept me company for a while that day, and later sent a doctor. I drank unufru again. The tea broke the worst of the sickness and I mended with rest and food. My arm had long since healed of its bone break and I had removed the splint during the time I spent on Laeredon. With sleep I began to feel more myself.

7

Even during sleep, part of me kept watch on the Tower. I dreamed of walking on the High Place, lightning flashing from my fingertips, as I rode across the world on a carpet of storm. I dreamed of Drudaen beneath shadow. I dreamed of Kirith Kirin.

Meanwhile, Idhril sent Kirith Kirin dispatches by post-riders and I included my own news in those. I wrote a letter to him when I finally got out of bed, and she sent that along.

The armies moved faster than I would have imagined, forced-marching down the Pajmar, taking the river road. We had news every day. Within five days after I descended from Laeredon, his outriders reached us with a packet of letters and news that he would cross the Isar bridges next day.

The letters contained orders for preparations for our southern march, which would take place within a few days of the consolidation of the armies in Genfynnel. Idhril set to work and people were coming and going from Telkyii Tars all day. A householder brought a note for me like the one before, but short. "We did good work in Vyddn. I will see you in a day. Yours."

For his march into the city I withdrew to the Tower. The Nivri and Finru houses claimed the best seats for his arrival, atop the northeast walls where the flatland stretched out for miles. One could see a broad vista of the country through which Isar flows. The view from the Tower was better, of course. I made no trance that day, wishing to see only with the eyes of my body. I sat near the Tower Horns and saw his shadow on the horizon, the host of soldiers spread out across the plain.

Trumpets sounded when the sentries saw him, and from across the fields his trumpeters answered, deep, booming sounds like the crying of giants. Thirteen thousand soldiers marched across the plain, five thousand as prisoners and the rest as friends. I had never seen so many people moving as one body before, though I am told by the knowledgeable that our armies are actually quite small. Crimson banners waved and bodies of cavalry flashed in advance of the foot soldiers. The trumpets blared again and again, outriders crossed the bridges and the host of Kirith Kirin crossed Isar, the Prince riding at the head of the column.

The whole army would not fit inside Genfynnel so he made his main encampment on the ground between the city and the river, leaving sentries on the bridges. Some of the host rode inside the walls, and the City Lord and Lady Idhril walked their horses forward to meet them. All the folk left in Genfynnel filled the streets between the East Gate and Telkyii Tars. There were more of them than I expected and they made a big noise to welcome him. Autumn flowers were strewn in his path and parents lifted babies for him to kiss. Everyone who could reach him touched his cloak or brushed the Keikin's mane. The royal pair, master and horse, pranced toward his palace, unoccupied these long years (Queen Athryn lately had not liked to ride so far north). The city, full of his legend for weeks, faced the fact of him.

Kirith Kirin made magic of his own, in his own way. He rode straight-backed and strong, without hurry, patiently letting everyone see him and seeming, himself, to see everyone. Today one hears stories of sick children he healed with a touch, blind men and women struck by his light and able to see again, the sorts of things invented by cheap romancers in the wake of history. But I was there, I saw the ride, even if I declined to share it directly. He rode with royal grace through the crowd and led his soldiers into Telkyii Tars.

Changes in the Tower light let him know he was welcomed from that place as well. He already knew as much. He dismounted in front of the cracked facade of the house, now repaired. Lords joined him and he entered the place. The troops, under the watchful gaze of Gaelex, took their positions on the walls and in the barracks of the citadel.

This was as much as I watched. He would send for me when he was ready for me to descend. Better, for the moment, I should sit where I was, under the open sky, with the knowledge that Kirith Kirin had come to Genfynnel safe and sound. The first leg of our journey was over.

CHAPTER EIGHTEEN
CHAENHALII

1

In the peaceful night, under a clear, cold sky, in a city restive with its occupying army, I sat on the summit of Laeredon holding the heavy locket in my hand, warming the gem, listening. From the streets below rose the light of bonfires, the sound of laughter, a night of good weather, soldiers bringing gold into the city, along with it a reason to drink, to forget. Fires burned in the countryside on both sides of the river as far as I could see, and I could imagine, watching them flicker under the stars, that the stars themselves were distant fires. I savored the thought because in the presence of such huge distances I felt small, like the locket in my palm, the dark gem catching starlight as I turned it over and over. Comforting and compact, this weight, the rasp of raised letters along my fingertips. The idea of vastness lent the feeling that I remained a finite object, after hours when I had spread my spirit over wind and cloud.

Kirith Kirin came for me late in the night when his business was finally done, and when I knew him to be waiting I descended. He stood where the gate had fallen, some of the broken stones as tall as he. Hood drawn over his head, a drab cloak, his bodyguard waiting at a distance. He had come alone, without our friends, I was glad of that. He stepped toward me and drew down the hood, his eyes glittering; we stood there watching each other. "I thought it was time you came down."

"Hello. I've been waiting for you all day."

He smiled. Exhaustion had drained the color from his face. He signaled the guard and I fell in step beside him. We entered Telkyii Tars by a side gate, through a series of walled gardens. Guards were posted along the paths and inside the apartment. Gaelex waited inside and bowed her head to Kirith Kirin. "The sentries are in place on the inner and outer walls, Kirith Kirin, and the house is secure. I've taken charge of the keys from Lady Idhril's steward."

He acknowledged without answering, standing in the high-ceilinged room beside the chair where I had read his letter. Gaelex glanced at me and I nodded, very small. She withdrew with her soldiers.

When the door closed, I was alone with him, in a room where a warm fire was burning. I led him to the fire and he stood there looking at his hands, dazed. I took his face in my hands, kissed his mouth. We sat on cushions with the fire burning, I drew his head down to my lap, and he sighed. The weight of him, the texture of his hair, provided the same comfort as the locket before, to anchor me in my body. His face offered a different kind of gravity, always pulling me toward it. We sat in quiet with the crackling of the fire, with no need but to be there. We did speak after a while, almost in whispers, knowing so many folk stood guard around us, beyond every wall on every side. He laced his fingers through mine and turned to face me, his back to the fire. He lay a hand along my neck, fingertips on the throat. "Have you eaten? Are you hungry?"

I shivered, pulled him close. "I'm cold."

He obligingly surrounded me, chuckling. "I like it when you're cold."

The closeness and heat of him made me understand how lonely I had been, and I said, "I missed you." I said this quite simply, meaning no harm, but his response was to look at me dumbstruck, his eyes suddenly full, and then to hold me tight against him as though I were trying to escape. A sorrow poured out of him like wind. "Please," into his ear, "I only meant I love you. That's all."

"I know." He calmed, lay on the cushions again, and I listened to his breathing, his heartbeat. The fullness of feeling between us struck me like a sorrow too, that when I was with him I should feel such a sweetness, in a world in which I could hardly ever be with him. "I'm so very tired," he said, "I don't rest without you," as though we had lain together for years. He needed sleep, more than he needed conversation with me. I drew him from the fireplace to the bed and tended him like the best of servants, taking off his boots, his leggings, his tunic, his ring of keys, the jeweled knife he carried, laying them all neatly on a ridiculously large chair near the fireplace arch. He watched, amused. We slipped into the warm covers on the downy mattress, and he sighed as I dimmed the lamp, easing against him. "I wanted to come for you earlier," he said, "but the talking went on and on."

"I spent a quiet night myself." I could hear the question this raised in him and spared his having to ask. To tell the truth, I was relieved to find him curious. "Drudaen rode south days ago, before you signaled me from Vyddn. I don't know what he's doing or where he is."

"There are only so many places he could have gone," he murmured, his eyes already closing.

"He's not in any of the Towers." But I was already too late. Kirith Kirin sighed, curled around me, and fell fast asleep in hardly the time it took me to finish the sentence.

I had less need for sleep myself. What I needed was to have him there, to be a solid creature beside him, to feel the warmth spreading between us, to feel and smell his breath. What I needed was the slight moistness of his skin where it touched mine. Though after a while I did close my eyes, for the luxury of it.

When he woke me, early, the dawn soft on his face, I was startled I had slept so deeply, without dreaming. Sitting up, I did a check of the High Place and touched the locket. He laughed at me as he pulled me into the covers again. "Sleepyhead. I've been awake for hours."

"You haven't even been asleep for hours," I answered.

He chuckled, stretching his arms. He stripped back the covers then, checked my arm to see that the bone had healed, as it had. "It looks fine. I was worried sick, you know. I still am."

"Kirith Kirin —"

He set a finger on my lip. "Don't waste your breath. I'll worry as long as you're you and I'm me." After a while, looking down the length of the room, "At least my feet don't hang off the bed, here."

The memory of the farmhouse made me laugh. "I do miss the smell of the pigsty."

"I gave our hosts there enough gold for a new bed." He stroked the nape of my neck, drew me down along him. "I expect they kept the gold and the bed, though. It will be a nine-days wonder in the countryside, mark my word. The bed where I slept with my wizard."

So close now, all I could see was his face. "I'm glad you're here."

He simply looked at me. "Do you really think you need to say it?"

"I want to say it." I leaned over him, the locket resting on his chest. He slipped it over my head and lay it on the nightstand, easy as that, the enchanted gem on which all our futures might rest, and I never said a word. He felt no coldness in me that morning, though he tested every part.

2

I walked into the sitting parlor to find Imral Ynuuvil waiting there, winter light from the window on his silver skin. I had wrapped myself in Fimbrel, white and soft, to look at the day out the window. Fimbrel whispered music, an echo of the Sisters, as I moved to Imral, who embraced me loosely but most seriously. He handed me a cup from the oet. "I'm glad to find you here."

"We have a roof over our heads, here, at least."

One must learn to sense the pleasure of a Venladrii, one will never be told of it. Beyond the window catofars were calling, the winter song we call it, because in early winter the catofars pass from the mountains to the warm southern coast, singing the whole way. They rested this morning in the oaks in the park beyond, cleaning their wing feathers, flashes of black and green.

"Kirith Kirin is awake? Did he tell you he's invited guests this morning?" He hesitated an instant, with a trace of discomfort.

When I turned, the white cloak whispered like the birds outside. He touched the fabric, closed his eyes, listened. "What guests?" I asked.

He stepped to the window himself, looking for someone, then turning to me sidewise, a sign he was uncertain. "My father has asked to meet you."

"Not for the simple pleasure of making my acquaintance, I take it."

Perhaps his father could also smile without moving a single muscle of his face. "No."

Movement in the other room, Kirith Kirin stirring. He emerged from the bedroom toweling his face, nodding to Imral, asking, "Where's Evynar?"

"Coming."

I poured jaka for him, gave him the cup, sat down as one of the bodyguard escorted the Drii king into the room, no ceremony at all. Kirith Kirin took my hand. I stood when Evynar Ydhiil approached, and I bowed in politeness. Tall, pale, with eyes like white stars, he took my breath. An elegant figure, broad-shouldered but trim, his face clear and smooth, his hair the color of ice, he showed his age only in his gravity of bearing. He was dressed in a jacket trimmed with small white pearls, wearing gold and silver rings and bracelets, earrings and an earcup, so that he glittered when he moved. On him this finery sat like simple, homespun stuff, but I had never seen even

Kirith Kirin dressed with so much gold, so many gems, and this before breakfast. "Sit down, boy, sit down," he said, and eased himself into a chair with no formality at all.

"You slept?" Kirith Kirin asked.

"Not enough." He looked around the room. Imral had knelt in front of the fireplace to stir the embers. When Evynar's gaze rested on his son, something softened in his face. "Imral and I are sharing rooms opening onto the goldfish park. Did he tell you?"

Kirith Kirin laughed. "I know you don't like Telkyii Tars very much, Evynar. But we're only here for a day or two."

"But I love goldfish, I always have. Especially in the winter when they're all asleep at the bottom of the pond."

"The rooms are fine, Kirith Kirin." Imral turned back to us. "My father is very comfortable. Aren't you, Father?"

He chuckled but never answered. He looked at me, studied me for a long time. Kirith Kirin introduced us, and I bowed my head again, not knowing what else to do. He continued to watch me in silence. "They told me you were a boy but I didn't believe it could really be true."

"It's not exactly my choice to be so young," I answered.

"But you know your art well, I'm told."

"I've had good teachers."

A moment later he asked for jaka and, since Imral was busy with the fire, I poured it myself from the oet. He accepted the cup with something like a smile. I guessed the first part of the inspection had begun, and, to tell the truth, I felt rather gentle about it. Why would he not be skeptical of me? How many Venladrii had marched out of Arthen to help us? How many lives had he risked, on me?

In response to their questions, I told them all that had happened since we met in Maugritaxa, that I had held Drudaen pinned on Yruminast for many days, but that he escaped me when I came down from the Tower. He had vanished beneath his own veil. Since then I had glimpsed his presence in Ivyssa. Where he had gone from there I could only guess. I had some other news, too, including the notable lack of response to our march from any of the queen's strongholds.

I watched Evynar closely as I briefed them, and he studied me with interest as keen as mine in him. He saw me clearly. When I was done, he bowed his head. "Thank you, young man. You explain what you've seen very well. But explain another thing for me. Why was Drudaen camped in Vyddn for so long?" The

question surprised me some, and I must have showed this, because
Evynar went on. "It became his folly to sit there, but he did it
anyway. In Drii we watched him, and wondered what he could be
seeking that was so precious. Because even to us it was clear he
should move back to his strongholds when you first took your
place on Ellebren."

"The Sisters said it was because of this." I held up the locket,
passed it to them. "He thought the Bane Gem was in the ruins
where Kentha fell. Or at least he thought so until I showed him
where it really was."

"What do you think?"

"I can't see why he would believe Kentha died with the gem on
her. She would have used it against him, that's how he would see it.
So I wonder if there's something else."

Evynar held the Bane locket, studying the stone's careful faceting.
"A kirin," he said. "Tervan work, I'd guess. The Sisters could not
read the writing?"

"I never showed them the locket. I didn't know what it was in
those days." I leaned forward to take the necklace from him. "But
Kirith Kirin told me what these letters are."

"The language is called the Malei," Kirith Kirin said. "The alphabet
is called akana. Edenna Morthul gets the credit for inspiring the priests
to work on it. In the earliest age, the Cunuduerum monks studied a way
to make a magic language of their own, and Edenna helped them."

"Why?" I asked.

"You should know the answer to that. Ildaruen can be taught.
The Nameless Tongue can't, or so I'm told."

"That's right." I was surprised again to hear the words from his
mouth so plainly.

"The Praeven were giving Edenna what she needed, a way to
make magic that she could teach. When Falamar saw the threat this
could bring, he made up the story about the song that frightened
YY and put the monks to death. But all their lore books were
closed up inside their libraries. You won't find this history to be
written down but we know it to be true."

"The Sisters believed Kentha had found access to the Praeven
books and that she was studying them," I said.

"She was," Kirith Kirin answered. "She had learned how to
travel to the ghost city, she told us that. Her child was born there, I
believe. And Edenna Morthul taught her the way to enter the libraries, which even Falamar could never do."

"So Keerfax wants to learn akana himself?" Evynar asked. "That's why he virtually besieged a ruined city for half a year? Has he figured all this out?"

I answered, simply. "Kentha built the Malei language into Ellebren Tower, to be controlled through the locket she made. He would have to know the Malei himself to defend against it."

Kirith Kirin shook his head. "Maybe that's part of it. But what he really needs is simply a way into Arthen." He crossed to he window, flocks of catofars framing his head. "He's always had that weakness. We all do, we who live a long time. Unless we return to Arthen we die like all the rest. He thought he had found a way around that for a while but he was wrong, apparently, or Athryn wouldn't be sending for me to be King. If he's looking for anything, it's for a way home. Something to circumvent the magic that keeps him out."

3

This interview ended and I left them in the room with a good fire going, to have whatever further discussion they might require. I would learn later that it is customary for the magician to withdraw, but I had no interest in staying for more talk, since Kirith Kirin would tell me whatever I needed to know. I climbed to the top of Laeredon and stood in the high wind.

A wave of cold air swept down from the Fenax, not a wind of my devising but a true blast of winter, the kind of wind we call an "early blade" in Upcountry, a corruption of High Speech, some say, but with thirty nine words for cold and forty for snow. A harsh winter would soon grip all the lands north, the season that comes down like a claw; my name Yron is another way of saying Winter.

South of us, shadow drank the cold wind, pulsing and shuddering, a living veil. He had made it, he had thrown it across the land, and because his nature had cast it out of him, it was part of him, drawing strength that he could use. But while it was sustaining him he could never shed it, and the weight of it fell on him, too, partly sustaining and partly devouring. The portion of him that remained a living creature responded to shadow as a living creature would, and it taxed him, even though it was his.

Entering trance, tuning my body to the stone, I began my work. I needed spare no effort for concealment or defense, since he had

left his shenesoeniis for the safety of travel where I could not find
him. True enough, I had no way to find him in the lands that were
under his control. But I could make him regret the place he had left.
I sang intricately and deeply without fear of interruption, because I
had a High Place on which to stand, and I stretched out the brooding treble of my song toward his stronghold Cunevadrim, empty
of him. Tearing shadow there, I bared the song of the place, tested
its defenses, and began a long, slow insinging, an encirclement from
afar, reaching from Ellebren with one hand and from Laeredon
with another.

In my body of bone I held the necklace in my hand, stone over
stone, and through this lens I traveled. Over the fortress of pale
rock, over the mansion of towers fashioned by Cunavastar so long
ago that to think of it is unimaginable, over this space I hovered as
though I were brooding in a cloud. On that plane from which I was
spinning out my thought I knew this was my place, too, that I had a
claim on it, through him, and I gathered that within my thought as
well and went on singing, the lowest, sweetest thread of music, sending
the Words out far, the land and all its people under my eye. With
such clarity I saw his home, his absence. One can hardly bring such
memories out of trance, but I can remember the jagged towers, the
high walls, the sheer, winding road.

Also, the rough edges of the silver locket on the skin of my
palm. Here was a thing that had been made for me, by someone a
long time ago. By someone as old as the trees. And me as green as
a leaf in spring to hold it, to lift it to the clouds, to pray to the all-
watching and all-encompassing that I might fathom something of
what it meant.

For a moment, inside all that, spinning in that current of forces,
I was only a boy, remembering my bed with Jarred, my dog, my
father's farm, my easy life. I was only a boy and the thing in my
hand was only a piece of metal, something I could sell for gold,
something I hardly understood at all.

But I had as much time as I wanted and no opponent who
cared to show himself, so what did it matter to me how long I sat
there with those thoughts in my head, those feelings, the numbing
sense of it, that I was no longer what I had been, that all my early life
was receding faster than the days could explain? A thing blossoming
in me, a nameless creature. One who could reach into the stones of
Cunevadrim, among the oldest of places, who could find the foundation of Yruminast and slowly, slowly, unbind the rock from itself,

only the tiniest of tears in the fabric, the smallest song rending the smallest space, but it would be enough, and no one to stop me, no one to turn my thought aside to anything else.

When I sang through the locket, through the gem, I reached nothing, but when I sang through the runes I could feel the change, because when I did it was as though I stood in my body on Ellebren, as though I were divided between the two towers as before, and since this was not a magic I had ever learned I could only guess it was a gift from the lady who had made the necklace and linked it so completely to the tower over the forest far away. Once I understood that, I found my strength.

In the real world, throughout the intervening countryside, but particularly in Antelek itself, winds gathered as Drudaen's shadow was replaced by the beginning shreds of storm. Colliding masses of air roiled overhead. Cuthunre farmers took shelter, suspecting only that a winter storm was coming, the first of the season. The Verm, being more accustomed to the changeable skies of magic, took note that the skies had darkened with unnatural speed, particularly near Cunevadrim; they battened their houses in the hills around the great fortress and studied, as they and their ancestors had done for generations, the lights over Yruminast Tower, pale glimmerings against the dark rock of Durudronaen.

I could feel him now, though I could not find him, for I had been at this singing for hours and had penetrated deeply into the foundation of that Tower of his. I had begun to trouble his hold on the place, the link that bound this Tower to all the rest, the engine for making shadow over all this land. He could hardly have failed to feel it. If he had scorned me to my face when we met, he now understood the depth of my training and skill. Yruminast shuddered beneath my touch.

The telling of this takes moments. The doing required many hours even to get as far as this, so that by sunset I had merely gotten the project underway. But I thought I had troubled my enemy sufficiently, with no sign yet of any opposition from him. I descended briefly from the Tower while remaining in full kei on the ground. I walked within my body but I was also in the sky above, a dizzying proposition. I moved hidden through Telkyii Tars and into the rooms I shared with Kirith Kirin. The apartments were empty but a householder awaited me there. She hurried away to bring news of my descent to Kirith Kirin, as she had been instructed to do.

I waited at the fireside in the room used as his study. I savored the strangeness of the moment. Against my inner lids moved the tumult of cloud, edges of storm slashing eastward over all the land I held in phyethir. Within the kei space moved the syllables of song, the deep-singing which, amplified through the two towers, resounded southward over the heartland of my enemy.

Kirith Kirin found me near the stone mantle. "You've been up there all day." He squeezed my arms in his hands as if wringing the cold out of me. "What are you doing?"

"Trying to find him. And other things."

He studied my face earnestly, and I could see the edges of his fear. "You're cold. Are you done for the night?"

"No, I have to go back up. Soon."

"How long?"

"All night, I expect. I'm in no danger. But I'm at him for something that will cost him, and I can't let up."

The Prince won out over the lover and he nodded with that crisp, sharp look in his eyes. "All right. But I won't go to bed again till you do."

"Kirith Kirin, don't be ridiculous—"

He drew his back up straight and stared me down. "I'll thank you to remember who you're talking to. I know a thing or two about going without sleep. When you come down from there, you send for me. All right?"

"Yes, Kirith Kirin."

"Tell me what you're doing. Up there."

"I'm trying to shake him loose from Yruminast. He has to show himself or lose the Tower."

Smiling. He knew exactly what I meant. Curious that this should relieve me of worry, in some way. "Which do you prefer?" he asked.

"That he lose the Tower. We'll have a safer march south, if he does." Feeling the vague stirring of apprehension, the wash of cloud and wind from the High Place nearly overwhelming the senses of my body.

"You're hardly even here."

"I'm here." I kissed him softly, clouds wheeling around us, birdcalls in our ears. He laughed, sharing all this sensation with me.

I left soon after, as dinner was being laid, his friends to join him and to work through the night if necessary, ironing out the details of our southern march. I returned to the Tower and rose through the rune hollow into the pirunaen beneath the night sky.

Clarity. My song had thickened across the landscape and the brewing of storm shook his veil as far as Ivyssa and lands further east. His southern Towers were hard pressed to maintain that fabric. The darkening over Cunevadrim surpassed that of shadow, and soon the collision of air masses, some hot and some cold, produced a vast engine of air and rain and lightning, but most of all, wind, rushing in gusts over the lower hills and crags, ripping trees to shreds, making stone walls sway.

All through the next day Drudaen disdained to defend his High Place; all day he continued to sap its main strength into his southern matrix. Finally late in the night he yielded and the Tower broke off from the remainder of his Towers, falling out of the loop of shadow. Yruminast, freed of its burden, asserted itself anew.

This move was what I had expected, though I had hoped the gesture would reveal his location. But nevertheless it was what I had sought. I continued to bring my whole thought to bear against Yruminast, my song swelling deep within the stones, in spite of the Tower's renewed resistance. *Stone break away from stone, stone eat stone, stone burn stone break. Stone break away from stone, stone eat stone, stone burn stone break. Stone to fire stone to smoke stone to sky.*

When the time came, the storm raging at the peak of its fury, from my two Towers I sent this song flowing, but so focused, in such a small place in the deep rock, to tear it completely, as I pictured it, the tiniest of tears but completely, and for a moment I saw into a new space and wondered what it was, and I made a movement there, and I felt the rock shudder, all in a moment, and the whole summit shook. Fire flashed upward from the base rock and poured from the eyestone. On the southwest horizon swelled a dome of radiance, lighting the countryside like day. The fireworks were plainly visible beyond the wall of storms, and even in Genfynnel in the middle of the night people rushed to the walls, under storm clouds that were beginning to dump their load of rain across the city. I continued my calm singing through all this; I kept my eye over Yruminast; my song in the stones did its deep work and the force that I released cracked the Tower foundations.

At the last moment, before Yruminast could be wholly broken, deeper magics were brought into play to bind the stones against me. This required no intervention on the part of Drudaen, being a function of the Tower's Tervan construction. Our two songs struggled, my magic of unbinding against the ruling magic of the Tower stones; and that struggle I did not win. But the shaking of combat damaged the Tower badly, and my song remained malignant within the Tower. Yruminast would be of no more use to him until he returned to it himself in his body, to cleanse it of the magic I had set into its rocks and walls, and to heal the foundation rock if he could.

He had kept the secret of his whereabouts, but at a high cost. With the power of Yruminast eliminated, I broke shadow as far south as Vulnusmurgul and set my hand over all of the Barrens and the cities of the Verm.

Near dawn the horizon went mad with color, storm clouds breaking apart in iridescent rags and the last forks of lightning slashing across the landscape. The Genfynnel walls were crowded with citizens who had watched the light show through the long night. What would have happened, I wondered, if all this celestial commotion had heralded the return of Drudaen to suzerainty over them? If he had come riding like white shadow across the countryside, what would these people have done?

Dawn uncoiled golden over a land in the clear aftermath of storm. The countryside of Antelek lay in shreds. Verm wandered, homeless and dazed, some wounded, under shadowless sky. They gathered their dead out of the wrecks of their homes and burned them, same as anyone would have done. I saw none of this, having descended from the Tower. But I have heard the tales all my life since. The magic that won me freedom from fear of Yruminast and which secured our southern march cost many Verm their lives. My storms damaged winter crops and broke buildings along a wide swath of terrain. In those places I am remembered as a marauder and killer.

Least damaged of all these places was Cunevadrim itself, the unshakable fortress on its awesome rock. I had fractured the Tower but not broken it, and the citadel beneath remained nearly unaffected. Drudaen had his stronghold still; to use it, he had only to return there.

I cannot tell you if I knew then, emerging from trance on that High Place, that I was once again a killer. But I remember the heaviness that settled on me when I emerged from Laeredon into a shower of rain. Moving hidden, I listened to the sentries chattering in small sentences about the lights in the sky, *that was some storm, right? Haven't seen anything like that before. Not in my lifetime.* No, I thought, I dare say you have not. You'll be lucky if you never live to see it again.

4

Kirith Kirin had replaced the sentries Idhril posted with his own picked guard, and one of Gaelex's lieutenants met me with an escort as soon as I appeared. They were decked out in rain gear, good solid weaves that shed water, and funny brimmed hats that kept their heads dry; we walked across the courtyards through the side route, passing through the gardens where all those goldfish were asleep in the bottom of the cold pools of water, as I imagined. Remembering Evynar from that morning two days ago, the rings on his fingers, the touch of the dandy in the way he carried himself.

That morning Kirith Kirin was alone, however, taking his morning bread, fresh from an oven now that we were in a city, in a well-staffed house, good fresh jaka from the Svyssn uplands, a sheaf of documents, billets, letters sealed and unsealed. He had been warned I was coming, though I had no idea how he could get news so quickly. Setting the papers aside, he dismissed my escort and pulled me near, unfastening the Fimbrel Cloak. We stood close together in the quiet hiss of the fire, nothing to say, till I sighed, and he asked, "Are you ready to sleep for a while?"

I slipped Fimbrel off my shoulders and stroked it with my hand till the fabric settled to a density something like good wool. The color never would be still, quite, a shimmering of deep purples, chocolate browns and ebony blacks. "I did what I wanted to do," I said. "The Tower over Cunevadrim will be no good to him till he goes there to repair it. I couldn't bring it down but I came close. So I think I can sleep for a while."

"No sign of the Keerfax?"

"None. He chose to remain hidden and let me do as I pleased in his homeland. I don't think he anticipated what I was able to accomplish, but even when Yruminast fell out of his link to the other towers, he kept hidden."

"He's ridden to Aerfax, I'd bet my good boots on that. He's gone directly there for fear we would cut him off."

"I expect you're right," I said. "It would be the place to defend. For all he knows we were planning to make a dash for Aerfax ourselves."

"That wouldn't have been a bad plan."

"Too late now."

"We'd have decided against it, anyway. The prudent course is the one we're following, to secure the country at our backs and push south in stages."

I patted him on the arm and yawned. "Better to have him there and know where he is."

"Athryn will have moved to Aerfax herself, by now," he said. "The court moves there for the ceremonies around the Succession."

"They can keep each other company, how pleasant."

"I doubt she cares much for his company any more." He bussed me on the forehead and sent me off to bed.

A householder came to help me turn back the covers and take off my clothes, matters I'd always been able to handle by myself before. I sent him away, since he was frightened to begin with. I asked him to fetch a pitcher of water and he brought it back, and I drank nearly all of it and asked him to fill it again.

I could sleep easily for the first time in weeks, knowing my enemy had ridden far away. Later I would have to face him where he was, but not tonight. This soft down mattress, this warm comforter, this comfortable room with the householder pulling closed the curtains, I could lie here all day and rest.

Hours later I woke from a dream about my mother to hear a lot of commotion in the outer apartment. In the dream my mother had been standing on a road in a barren country, and I had the feeling the ocean was near; she simply stood there and beckoned me, calling me to her, dressed in a simple shift gathered at the waist, her hair clean and soft, her face easy, not a trace of suffering or pain. Never a sound or a movement beyond the gesture of welcoming, of beckoning, and when I tried to see the road behind her I could not.

But suddenly awake in the light with the dry taste of sleep in my mouth and the voices outside, Kirith Kirin and some other people, midafternoon light from the window. Enough sleep, I thought, and stood at the washbasin, bathing quickly, trying to make out what was going on in the other room, using only mortal means of eavesdropping. That was fair enough, I thought. But when I went to the door the room was full of soldiers in the blue blazon of Athryn, along with some of our folk. One of them was speaking earnestly to Kirith Kirin, thanking him for his mercy. Kirith Kirin made some kind of answer and the interview was over, the Blue Cloaks filed out of the chamber. This was all I saw of Nemort of Novris, who had been our prisoner since Fort Gnemorra fell, asking Kirith Kirin to allow the Queen's troops to march with him, a changing of loyalties that remains a tale to this day. Nemort had already secured the agreement of all the soldiers we had taken captive, and he could deliver the body of five thousand to us intact, at once, to help us on our way. Kirith Kirin accepted the offer, and, indeed, I was told then and believe now, he had made Nemort's captivity easy and mixed him with the other prisoners hoping to engender such a change of heart. Nemort had never been a supporter of Drudaen and now found a reason for showing his feelings openly. The Queen had sent for the Successor herself. Therefore it was the duty of the Blue Army to help him reach Aerfax, or at least this is what Nemort opined, under the Law.

I was glad enough to have missed the dull part, to have come into the room in time to find Kirith Kirin flushed with the news. He told me what had happened. We were alone for a moment, then Imral and Karsten came back, and after a moment Evynar Ydhiil as well. I asked him if he thought Nemort could be trusted, and he answered yes with no hesitation. "He has nothing to gain by supporting Drudaen. I expect the other southern commanders feel the same way."

It was only when the others returned, in the confused conversation that followed, everyone excited, that I understood the urgency of this event. We were to leave on the march south next morning.

"Your Verm are coming too," Kirith Kirin said. "The ones you spared. They asked to join the rest of the Queen's army rather than return to Arroth. I said yes."

"The Verm?"

"Can you believe it?"

"No, I can't. How will people react?"

He laughed, and everyone else laughed with him. "They'll be astonished. So will Drudaen."

The Verm preferred to march with us than to return to their own country. Many people would be interested in that fact. But the news that we would depart so soon meant I had much to do, and so I said my partings and put on Fimbrel, vanishing before Kirith Kirin could send somebody to fetch guards to escort me. I preferred to travel more quietly, and hurried to Laeredon to prepare the Tower for my departure.

5

So next morning at dawn we began the An Chaenhalii, the Long
March to the Sea, the story of which has been chronicled by many
people, poet and fool alike. There have been some good accounts
and some bad ones, and the one you will get from me is likely to
disagree with the good and the bad on some particulars. So be it.

I packed my own baggage, including devices from Laeredon
and those I had with me still from Ellebren. Since Laeredon Gate
had been destroyed, I ordered masons to wall up the portal with
successive layers of rock and brick and stone. We accomplished this
purpose in good time, and I stayed to lay enchantments in the vicinity, warning off those who might attempt to tamper with the place
in my absence.

I met Kirith Kirin in our apartment, the last of our belongings
headed for the baggage train. Even the short time we had spent
here left me with sad feelings, and I closed off thoughts of what
was to come. We stood together watching the catofars in the garden, all soon to fly farther south, as we were to do.

"Ready?" he asked.

"Yes.

He looked around the chambers a last time. In his eyes glimmered the reflection of my own feeling, that we departed Telkyii
Tars and all places like it, maybe for a long time. "On the road
again. Let's go."

So, joining our party in the courtyard of the house, we mounted
horses and rode out of Genfynnel. I would never see that city again.

CHAPTER NINETEEN
NARVOSDILIMUR

1

We headed south along three different paths. One army, under the command of Kiril Karsten, moved along the eastern plain, securing the main road to Arsk and establishing a garrison to protect our flank from Fort Pemuntnir. Along with this force went General Nemort, who would be able to treat with the Queen's troops in eastern Aeryn and perhaps enlist more aid for us, should it be needed. The second army, under command of Evynar Ydhiil, was to move along the Osar southward, securing Teliar and Ravenford and preventing any sorties from Narvosdilimur and the Hills of Slaughter. A third party, made up of picked guard, Kirith Kirin, Imral and some of the Nivri, very small and fleet, would ride west of the Osar and west of Narvos, under my protection, to see what we could of the enemy's movements in Turis and Karns.

But that first day, while the armies were still relatively close, all the command staff rode with Kirith Kirin, and we had one more evening's council by the banks of the Osar. Amri was with our party and sang the Evening Song by Kirith Kirin's watch-fire, and we sat down in the open air, the Jhinuuserret, the Nivri and some of the Finru Houses, Nemort included since he was Finru by birth. It was at this session that Kirith Kirin's strategy, and thus our hope, became plain, and we understood what we were about and took heart.

Athryn is on our side now, he said. Maybe he knew this through Nemort, I thought. Drudaen has become too greedy, and now she must turn to us for help. So the question becomes, can we fight our way to Aerfax? Because when we get there, we have won.

He went on: We know he is there, or will be by the time we arrive. We know he will use the High Place to try to keep us from reaching Aerfax at all. But when we reach the gates of Aerfax, when I am there, Queen Athryn will take Senecaur away from him, because the Change will have begun, and when the Succession has passed and I am King, I won't give up Senecaur to anyone but Jessex.

Can we trust Athryn? Yes, we can. Because she has no choice, now. Drudaen's magic has begun to fail her and she's aging, and she has to return to Arthen or she'll die.

So again he asked us, can we fight our way to the gates of Aerfax? Can we fight our way down the coast of Karns and along the murderous narrow of Kleeiom, the hair's-width of road along the spur of the mountain? Can we fight our way that far? Because, if we can do it, we can win.

The words took my breath away, and maybe had the same effect on everyone. I studied Nemort, a pudgy, balding man with a sharp look to his eyes, and read only admiration for what Kirith Kirin was saying. I read more deeply into that face and saw he was telling the truth, that his change of heart was real. This was more than I should have done without anyone's leave but I was not going to allow Karsten to march south with him unless I was sure he could be trusted. So I kept my eye on him that night, and read his reactions, touched the edges of his thought, enough to know he was telling the truth, he preferred the Succession take place as it was supposed to, now that the Queen had relinquished her crown.

The talking continued, the fires burned, the sentries circled us. "We can fight that far," said King Evynar, "if that's what we have to do. We can fight as well as any of our enemies, including the Verm, as long we can match Drudaen." Evynar was watching me as he spoke, and only continued after a languid pause. "I think we have a chance to do that. Drudaen didn't flee south for his health. And now that he has, our wizard has made him pay."

I imagine this was a bit of theatre the two had worked out between them; they went on to relate together the news that I had crippled Yruminast, that neither of the armies faced shadow for a long way south. Few folk had heard this news yet. People were looking at me and I felt conspicuous; though I understood the need for the officers and the gentry to see me, to understand that I was real. I understood the need for them to inflate what I had done, a bit.

The news had people buzzing and they were heartened, as anyone could see. So we took our partings on that note and went off to our tents and sleeping rolls. I moved hidden to the tent I was sharing with Kirith Kirin and waited there, dozing, till he joined me. We slept in the open country wrapped round each other, prince and magician, embraced by two armies, charging toward an enemy we hoped we could defeat.

In the morning we woke to news that Amri was feverish. Kirith Kirin had planned to leave her in Telkyii Tars to ride back to Inniscaudra with the first party headed that way. She had become dreamy since her walk in the moonflower and that morning when we found her trying to assemble a lamp she was clammy, her eyes glazed, and she looked at Kirith Kirin and said, "I saw you in a boat. You were sailing across gray water." She turned to me and said, "You were asleep in a room. I could hear the ocean outside. The dream went on and on." She was out of breath, saying only this much. Shivering. Kirith Kirin had Gaelex find a doctor for her, and led the girl away.

We had no morning ceremony. Karsten said, "I suspected Amri had the dreaming eye." But no one else spoke about it.

Our party split in three and we rode along our separate paths, to meet again at Charnos before crossing Ajnur Gap into Karns. The armies would be united again for the march down the coast of Karns and along Kleeiom. As was customary, however, the magician would ride separate from the rest of the troops, to draw any magical attacks away from them. We had taken this notion one daring step farther. Kirith Kirin would lead a party of picked soldiers that included me, and we would take a route that would lead us east of Narvosdilimur and the Hills of Slaughter. Drudaen's Verm armies followed the same route south. I was to interfere with their travels.

I said good-bye to Karsten before she headed to command her thousands. So peculiar had our time together been that it already seemed to me we were like old friends, and so it was hard to part. She was wary of the danger in Kirith Kirin's strategy, fearing the Verm would box us in, but I reassured her it would cost them dearly even to try. She remained concerned, and I understood that the worry was for me, because I was young, a boy, but was riding in the war party of a prince.

"Be careful of yourself," she said.

I promised I would try. "I'll see you in Charnos. After Fort Pemuntnir has surrendered, and you have more soldiers riding with you than you know what to do with."

"We can hope for a miracle like that, anyway."

Time to go. Her entourage rushed her to her horse. Pelathayn was riding with her, his red head high above the heads of the rest. Around us the commotion of many other partings, Kirith Kirin three-deep in Nivri, with Imral beside him and King Evynar similarly surrounded. A fresh, cold day, but warmer than usual for that time of year. Not a cloud in the sky.

2

Our party rode due east from Genfynnel, heading toward Teliar. We were some one hundred picked guard, about half mounted archers and half mounted swordsmen, led by Kirith Kirin. Imral accompanied us. We made good progress on the first day, traveling at mortal speed, it being beyond my power, or anyone's, to enfold so many people in ithikan.

We would need concealment on our ride, especially after we crossed the Narvos Ridge. To provide that kind of protection is a matter of less effort than making ithikan, but even this much magic can make a mortal horse, or a mortal, a bit unsettled. While we were still traveling across the Kellyxa, we moved mostly out in the open, under the sky, but when Kirith Kirin signaled, I passed a veil over us, and then lifted it, to drill the soldiers in what it was like to travel hidden, and to accustom the horses to it. The day passed in that way, and I rode mostly within my body, only occasionally entering the dual meditation that sent my awareness high into the air. Still, I was kei and distant from the others.

At times I moved outside of time, onto the fourth circle of my awareness, from which I could feel his presence without the need to see him. Even there he was hiding, and yet the undertone of him, the under-note to his singing, throbbed and subsided, rose and died again. I took a long, deep look at the world, moving on that circle without opposition, and on all the others, too. Near me was my tower, Laeredon, and farther west was Yruminast, broken and cold until her master should return to heal her hurts. To the north was Ellebren, a wheel of stars changing to a wheel of fire; and more, as I remained, as I drew out the moment, lingered in it. To the east, the towers Goerast and Yrunvurst, wrecked these hundred years, a long time in my reckoning but not such a long time in the world, hardly a moment. After an interval I found the two towers in Ivyssa, Thoem still active and Karomast stripped clean of its ruling Wyyvisar and not much use to anybody, except that the Eyestone was somewhat in use; and last of all, Senecaur, rising out of the sea at the end of our journey.

Scouts had found us a campsite on a forested rise of land not far from the Teliar road, good high ground, and as we settled there I hid us from sight above or below. Drudaen could have found us if he searched from a High Place, but he was on the ground, as I was. With the evening cold we had hardly enough wood to warm ourselves, but this was something else I could remedy, not by conjuring wood but by extending what we had, Words to make the burning take a long time. The camp was laid with precision and a meal prepared out of stores we added to the fruits of a hunting party that had separated from the main body of riders in the afternoon. I wondered, noting the orderly unfolding of it all, what lay ahead of us, whether we would always manage so well.

We had a field tent now, small and cramped, about enough room for Kirith Kirin's armor, Fimbrel, and our boots. The first night we lay together like that, I hardly slept, feeling him against me, lost in sleep, glad of the safety we had, being together. It was a wholly human feeling and it warmed me through, in spite of the work I was doing, in spite of my need to remain aware of whatever was around us, seen and unseen.

Many days like this came and went and we traveled across the Kellyxa Plain toward Teliar without incident, under clear skies, with the days growing colder and shorter, a murderous time of year for a march. But if we were successful and Kirith Kirin became King, we could take our time in Aerfax and ride north again in spring. If we were not, winter would hardly matter any more.

We rode near Teliar and there I had a piece of work to do, for this city had been garrisoned by the Verm and was being defended by them as we approached, along with a sixth-level novice of Ildaruen, whose voice was weak but who nevertheless recognized me when our party came riding along the road; our party took a southern turn to avoid the city, but I rode to the gates and sat there for a while. Teliar was built by the Anynae. The walls had a rounded, wholesome look, and the gate towers swelled in the middle. The Verm had begun to ride out the gate when they saw me but I sent a wave of pure terror through them and they stopped. The one who was singing in Ildaruen, who was trying to trouble me with sixth-circle magic, was nowhere in sight, but I waited till he came, wearing a pale robe and carrying a staff, a device to hold his gems that he had worked so carefully. He walked toward me making that noise, and when he was close I spoke a Word and broke his staff, and Fimbrel spread around me drinking light. The Verm drew back inside the gate, and I sat there, my own song flowing out, deeply, and the acolyte fell to the ground. He lay there unable to see or hear, and I wiped his mind clean and stripped the memory out of him, which seemed more merciful than to kill him. I began to ride along the city wall near the bridges, lightning in the air, the song gathering a storm. People panicked inside the walls, spilling over, some of them falling into the river, scurrying out of it wet into the countryside. But I only meant to bring down the walls, and not even that entirely, but to make big holes in them, so King Evynar's army following us would have an easy time taking the city. Mortal walls are easy, since the stones are not magically bound, like the stones of a wizard's tower, or like something the Tervan built. I made the resonance needed to break down Teliar's walls, and I rode away from the city with smoke and dust rising up from the gaps I had made.

I had to ride a long way before I found our camp that night, and was met by one of the Finru lords serving as sentry, who took Nixva to the horse line and gave me a look of such open-faced respect, that I felt it all the way to Kirith Kirin's campfire. Only later did it occur to me that I had handed off the horse to a high-born Finra as if he were my servant, or, even more accurately, because at that moment he was serving me.

My actions at the walls of Teliar had aroused some interest in the south, I could tell, and once I learned Kirith Kirin was still meeting with his officers and advisors, I went into deep trance to take a look. Shadow had changed, had grown taut with a new tension, perhaps because Drudaen was seeking to learn more of my whereabouts, having already discerned the magic I had done earlier in breaking Teliar's walls. Before, the substance of shadow had shown itself as a softness, a rolling membrane over the landscape. Now he was drawing on his strength, which charged the shadow and gave it a different appearance. I stayed there until I had listened for the towers, all of them, until I could sense the note of music that was Senecaur far to the south; I listened in that direction most carefully.

We had news from scouts to the west, who had been posted some days ahead of us to cross Narvosdilimur. Verm supply trains were moving constantly southward, and an army of Verm was massing in Arroth, according to the reports, given by my old friend Trysvyn, one of the scouts. I had hardly seen her since we moved camp to Nevyssan, and now she had proven herself an expert intelligence gatherer, and my state had changed as well. She felt awkward until I spoke to her, wishing this were an ordinary ride and that we could stand around the fire and sing tonight. She grinned, and I saw she had broken a tooth somewhere, and she had a wound on her cheek, what had been a nasty gash, but healing these two months. She had been part of the army that marched to Cordyssa with Imral

Ynuuvil, and afterward had force-marched south to Inniscaudra and then through Arthen with Kirith Kirin.

In the morning she rode with her companion to bring what she had learned to King Evynar, along with the news that I had breached the walls of Teliar for him. Our party mounted and continued west, and the land rose sharply as we began to climb Narvos Ridge.

The ascent is not steep in the region of Teliar at the north, but the horses labored on the constant incline and we stopped to rest them frequently. A cold, clear wind was blowing from the Black Spur. We were close to Cunevadrim, and I was tempted, at moments, to ride there in my body, to see the place with my physical eyes; I had traveled to the place with Vissyn during my training, but to see in that fashion does not yield clear memories. I wanted to see that pile of rock, the house built by my ancestor Cunavastar. But that would have to wait for another day.

Kirith Kirin rode at the head of the party, picking the trail with Imral. When we reached the crest of the ridge, he signaled me to ride near him, and we looked over the valley beyond, wide and brown, the dry landscape of north Karns, home-place of Julassa, whom I had killed. "Not exactly a rich country," Kirith Kirin said. "There are some beautiful marshes further south, where the land gets wetter, and toward the mountains are the moors south of Cunevadrim. Nothing as far as the eye can see but wind and heath."

"Do people live here?" I asked, surprised at the look of desolation, and for a moment I must have seemed completely a child again.

"Yes, for as long as I can remember," he answered. "People find a way to live anywhere and everywhere, I think."

Behind us, Gaelex had begun to order our camp for the night, and I dismounted from Nixva's back, slipping my palm along his muzzle. I slipped the bridle off his head and by the time I got that far someone was running up to take it out of my hand, to lead Nixva and the King Horse away to a place where they could find some grass for themselves.

We walked a distance down the ridge, in the shade of scrubby, twisted trees with leaves glossy and evergreen, and I felt the discomfort of riding in a country where one does not know the names of things, the names of places. Anyone will understand such a feeling, I guess, but for a Jisraegen it is distinctly uncomfortable; we are drunk with names, some people say. Kirith Kirin had no reason to draw me away from the others except that he wanted to, and that was fine with me. It surprised me that the others left us alone, though it may easily have been that Kirith Kirin signaled for privacy.

We stood in the shadow of a tall rock with some heather and broom-grass growing out of it; visible as far as one could see were the scrubby trees and rocks along the height of Narvos Ridge. "You own land out there, you know," he said, after a while, idly, gesturing to that brown expanse beneath us.

"Do I?"

"Kentha's holdings. They'll be restored to you and your family."

To me and Uncle Sivisal, he meant, since only we were left. I had not seen my uncle since he was sent with the soldiers to garrison Fort Gnemorra, not since I had become Thanaarc. The memory of him made me think of home, of my mother, wherever she might be.

"Maybe Uncle Sivisal will have some use for land. I doubt I will."

He smiled. He started to say something, stopped himself. Finally he said, "Maybe you'll find some use for it yourself, by then."

We stood together in the wind. For the moment I ignored my magical senses, being close to him like that, a moment stolen. He was enough. Later it occurred to me that he had been talking about the future, a sign he felt some hope. But that was after we had returned to the camp, eaten our waycake and dried meat.

Our party was low on supplies, except for waycake, and Gaelex sent out a small party of scavengers and another of hunters; they would meet us south along the ridge, where we intended to ride most of that day. We were moving too fast for supplies to follow us from Evynar's army, which was near Teliar by now.

The next day we moved at a more leisurely pace, south down the ridge along an old road marked with Jisraegen road-stones. The road, Imral told me, runs along the ridge, then down into the Cuthunre Valley, joining a conventional road there. It seemed odd to me that the Jisraegen would go to the effort of building a stone-marked road here, till I remembered that this was the country were Falamar's lover was killed, and that a war had been fought here. The stones had kept the road mostly clear of new growth and would do so for as long as they stood, same as the stones that mark the roads in Arthen. Something comforting about the sensation of the quiet, old magic in the carvings.

While we were on the road it was a simple matter to hide us, using the road-stones and their magic to mask our presence; this left me with more energy for the other work I needed to do, searching out the movements of Verm troops to the east. So that day I rode in trance, out of the body, though I doubt anyone but the Jhinuuserret noticed the difference. From my fourth level presence I scanned the visible world, focusing myself through the gems in my possession and through Fimbrel, though quietly. At once a part of the landscape came into focus, then more.

Across north Karns were moving trains of wagons, huge many-wheeled things, dragged by enormous trains of oxen, accompanied by Verm soldiers on foot and horseback, and all moving in the same direction, toward the south, where our armies were headed. North as far as I could see the wagons were moving, and to the south, when I looked there, I guessed an army must be waiting already.

I had my instructions and followed them. We were here to confuse the movements of these same soldiers, to create confusion in this country. Kirith Kirin had given me license to do this much, but wished me to stop short of killing, if I could. We had seen that the Verm could be turned from Drudaen. So as we were riding, even as early as the first moment I understood the Verm were moving, I began my work.

As slowly as I had assembled the long-seeing trance, I extended my reach farther, into the deep mountains to trouble the winds, beginning the gathering of a storm there, moving quietly through that long day, alive on the four circles, while in my body I was riding Nixva in a party of soldiers through high country. One can make a small storm quickly but a big one takes time, takes a skill in gathering light, trapping heat, causing air to rise and mix, a feat I had learned so many ways I could picture it in my sleep, a feat I could perform at a long distance, even in a place I could see only with my mind's eye. The slow engine of my nascent storm grew and I drew it down out of the mountains, clouds thick with moisture from the southern ocean, chilled by the arctic airs from the mountains and from the north, a long interface of energies that I had built, an almost perfect creation, fueling itself on natural and unnatural energies. A snow storm blew down, and yet it was dark as if the heaviest thunderdome were passing overhead, a vast thing, sung out of the ground, forked with lightning even as snow was falling, a breath of warm hot wind mixed with cold winds that cut like knives, a mist over everything and a lace of air. Hours and hours I spent at this, awake through the night with Fimbrel wrapped around me, sitting at a fire at the outermost edge of our camp, despite the fact that I made Kirith Kirin anxious in one way and the rest of the war party anxious in another.

When the storm commenced, the one long wagon train shuddered and the Verm soldiers wondered what was happening. At first they struggled to keep moving but soon the storm fell fully on them and they scurried to dig themselves into some kind of shelter, even unloading and overturning the wagons in some places. They were destined to suffer for as long as I wished, since I could draw power down from the two towers that answered to me as long as I liked while Drudaen refused to contest my work.

Even though I had sent the main force of the storm to the north of us, across all of Antelek and Karns, snow and wind passed over the skies where we were, and our party stayed battened in good Jisraegen tents through the whirlwinds and crashes of lightning that passed overhead that second day. We were in no danger as long as I remained in kei and held the storm in my hand, but that took all my concentration, and we could not travel in such weather without my aid. As for the Verm, their wagons were wrecked and their supplies scattered over the road or swallowed in the snows. Cold wind followed the storm, as cold as that country had seen in many years; not so much for a northerner like me, but to the Verm it was fearsome.

After a while the storm went along without me, counted as a blizzard as far east as Teliar, where Evynar's army took shelter. Evynar had anticipated its coming to the day. Long life will give you an instinct for things.

I eased out of deep trance to find Kirith Kirin waiting near where I was sitting encased in the fire's protection, while he had only his cloak against the weather. This was near evening the second day. When I was in my body again he knew, and came close and helped me stand. I took off some of my rings and pocketed them. The fire had died to ordinary size, and unless I gave it protection it would soon vanish in the cold snow that was falling. "Ready to stop for a while?"

"Yes." Leaning on him, feeling the real weight, the real texture of him. Taking a long breath of clean, cold air.

"We pitched tents. You gave me enough warning for that. Did you know you did? Do you know what your body does when you're out of it?"

"Not always. I could remember it in a certain way, if I needed to."

He laughed. Took my head in his hand. So deceptive, the clean, young feeling of him. "I've always wondered what that kind of magic would be like."

We were trudging through snow that reached to mid-boot, deeper in places, toward the Jisraegen camp, nearly invisible in the snow. The sentries met us, shadows suddenly appearing. Our tent was heaped with snow all around, and inside a brazier was burning, the tiny space snug and warm. Around us a cluster of little warm spaces, not a single big fire, nothing wasteful. We ate waycake and some cheese Kirith Kirin got from somebody. A strong cheese, too; afterward his mouth tasted of it for a while.

3

We rested the horses another day, the snow melting so they could graze on the grass. Kirith Kirin sent riders to find Karsten and the eastern army, to report on what we had seen and what had happened. I have seen that letter, which reads in part, "We are perched in snow like we used to be in Cundruen crossing north to Drii, or like used to fall in the high streets of Montajhena. The Verm haven't seen a snow like this in a hundred years. We'll make good time along Itheil's road." This was the name of the road we were on, made by Itheil Coorbahl, lover of Falamar.

Next morning, with the wind still scouring the high plain between the Narvos Hills and the Barrier Mountains, we broke camp, making a cookfire and drinking morning jaka with the sun rising and someone singing Velunen. In the night we had talked, Imral, Kirith Kirin and I, and Kirith Kirin told me what to do next. So the riding party mounted horses and headed south along Itheil's road, and I descended the hills to ride on Nixva through the snowy country where the Verm lay scattered in the aftermath of the storm. That day I made more havoc, but still stopped short of killing Verm. I maddened the horses they were riding and the oxen pulling their wagons, sweeping along all the countryside I could reach, and when I was done most of the horses had bolted toward whatever direction seemed nearest home, and most of the oxen were fighting one another, snorting and stamping, or else rolling on their backs in the snow and gazing vacantly at the sky. Many of the animals died, I am sorry to say, but I did what was necessary.

I rode as far north as needed to sweep that whole country with magic. By then I was no longer troubling to hide myself on any of the circles, and my song filled those places, noise and commotion. He would have seen what I was doing. But he let me wreck his

northern army of Verm without lifting his hand to defend them,
and when I finally rode south again, after a whole day and night of
travel, I was all that was moving on that landscape.

This was orchestrated by Kirith Kirin, who had used magic to
make policy before. Some of the Verm who joined Evynar's
army rode into the north Karns country with a written message
from Kirith Kirin, that the Verm troops need only return to their
homes to have their lives spared. "I have sent my wizard to ride
along your lines," he wrote, "and he has driven away all your beasts.
Next time he rides, any of you who are not heading north will die.
Those of you who return to your homes, you will earn mercy
when I am King."

He had already said those words to me, and there would come
the day when I killed because he told me to. But that was not the
day, because the Verm took his warning seriously and withdrew
from north Karns.

I had a good look at them as they were trudging home in the
snow, bony, massive creatures, skin the color of ash, the men so
like the women it was hard to tell them apart. They made no
distinction among the sexes, any more than the Jisraegen did, in
dress or weaponry. They were Jisraegen, after all; were what we
become under shadow; this was what happened to the people in
Turis when Drudaen brought shadow there, after Kentha defeated him, after he killed her in such a faithless way. The Verm
are larger than us, deep folds over the eyes, large pupils, amber
irises, or sometimes irises the color of white ice or red blood,
sometimes black so that the eye seems one enormous pupil; the
changes in the eyes fascinated me as I studied them. They live
short lives, no more than fifty of our years, and I have heard
physicians say this is because they are so large the organs of the
body cannot support the bulk of it. So they are stronger than we
but prone to sickness and with joints easily dislocated and bones
broken, because they are larger than they were designed to be. I
could not tell all that by looking at them, of course, and am
mixing in much that I learned later. But as I watched them marching northward, making the prudent choice to go home, tugging
at their hair-braids under their helmets, or picking at their noses
or sneaking a drink of wine, they became less frightening to me.
A people like any other. Unfortunate enough to be ruled by
Drudaen, and shaped by him, since it was his shadow that had
caused their forebears to change.

In camp at last, after two days riding, Nixva let me know he was glad the travel was over for at least a night; I stood with him till Duvettre came for him, to have him brushed and dried and kept warm with the rest of the horses. Kirith Kirin had told her to expect me at about this hour, and in fact he was showing such a knack for predicting my arrival that I wondered if he had some way of following my movements. There is a magic in Aeryn that belongs to the King and the Queen, that comes from YY herself. But I could feel not a trace of it at all.

I found him waiting in an open glade where a fire was burning.

I told him all I had done and seen and he took it in without surprise. I asked him why he was taking such pains to be merciful to the Verm, and he answered, "They're Jisraegen, too. Whatever shadow may have made of the Verm, they're still a part of us. I told them so in Genfynnel, after you gave them permission to stay in the city till they were ready to travel."

"It would be nice to reason with all the Verm like this."

"The ones who're ensorcelled in Drudaen's service won't be persuaded," he said, and looked me in the eye. "You'll have to deal with those, or the soldiers will."

A breath of sharpness in the wind that followed. "I'll do it. Whatever has to be done."

4

When we reached the Hills of Slaughter, riders from Arsk found us camped on the Osar on the Kellyxa side. They were bringing word from Karsten that her army had control of Arsk and had accepted the surrender of Fort Pemuntnir and all the eastern garrisons from Kursk to Novris. I presume we had crossed to the Kellyxa side of the river for that reason, because Kirith Kirin had known the riders were on the way, or should be, provided all had gone well.

We had left the protection of the Jisraegen road and I had to spend more energy and time on watching the sky. I had displayed my whereabouts to Drudaen openly when I was making the storm but now that I was traveling with Kirith Kirin I preferred we should be hidden, and this required some effort. But for the most part, for the few days that followed, I remained quiescent and rode with the others, with Kirith Kirin, in the body, feeling every ache and grind of the ride.

The letter from Karsten read as follows; it lies among the papers I have kept from that time, in my library: "We have come as far as Arsk and the trip has been all we hoped. Nemort is helpful, courteous, and very cunning when it comes to dealing with Athryn's troops. The commander of Fort Pemuntnir met us when Arsk opened the gates for us; she had ridden all day and all night to reach the city in time, and after an hour of talk she was ready to commit her troops to us. She'd already heard from the Queen, she said, and had orders to cooperate with Kirith Kirin in every possible way. So now we know you're right, my dear, and Athryn is on our side. You can imagine the taste that leaves in my mouth, but if we all get through this, I'll have a long time to think about forgiving her. I've sent out riders to all the eastern garrisons, and in effect I've taken command of the armies in the Kellyxa. We'll have another three thousand blue troops when we reach Charnos, and good garrisons to hold the roads all the way back to Genfynnel if we need to retreat.

"The people here are already telling stories about your witch. His name is said to be Thron and he's also called the Thief of Karns, because he killed the Witch of Karns. I thought Jessex would like to know he's getting some attention. People say Drudaen is afraid of him because he comes from the mountains and the Prophet told stories about him; even here they call Curaeth Curaesyn the Prophet, and there are some temples where he's studied, according to Nemort. The Anynae are a mystical lot. I can never get used to these round houses, but on the whole the people are pleasant and glad to have us with them. Drudaen is feared by everybody, and shadow is remembered as a deeply uncomfortable state."

There are some logistical paragraphs that I have omitted, but even when she is writing about the merest trifle, her wry voice sounds through. I read the letter for the first time standing by the fire in our camp, the dark Osar flowing past. Kirith Kirin stood near me, close enough to give shelter from the wind coming down the flanks of Narvosdilimur. "I like Thief of Karns," I said. "It has a good feeling."

"Then you'll have it as a title, along with the land, which you won when you killed her. I hope you won't require me to put her family to death."

"Heavens, no. Could I?"

"Under some of the oldest laws, you could. But I probably wouldn't do it." He was chuckling, but Gaelex came up with some other matter from the pouch Karsten had sent, and we were distracted.

I copied out a letter for him, the night nearly balmy, the quiet stars gleaming, a moonless night, which is rare. We have watched the stars, the moons, for many ages, and no one has ever seen a pattern to when the stars are there and when they are not, though Luthmar speaks of this in the passage that says at the end of the first war YY removed our land, Aeryn, from reach of starlight. I was thinking about that, looking up at the stars, at Aryaemen, which we recognize by the color and by its halo, called Ajhyaenus, the Four Hundred Boys. I was wondering whether a moon would rise. He asked me what I was thinking when Gaelex had packed away the writing board, and I told him.

He looked up himself. He was seeing something I was not, and I understood, as I had at times, that he saw more deeply into the nature of the world than I. "We aren't like other places. We're hidden from all the rest. Though I was told, a long time ago, that after I go through the Gates to Zaeyn, we'll no longer be hidden. Maybe you'll still be alive."

He was teasing me, fair enough. I said, "By then, I'll be long gone from the world and you'll have someone else to say that to."

A flicker of something, of puzzlement. A moment of anger. He made the sign against the evil eye and whispered a word for luck over his shoulder. "Don't ever say that again," his tone changed, and I knew he meant it. "You'll understand better after a while."

I hadn't made him angry lately and wasn't used to the feeling; neither was he, so we worked to get over it. I remember it as the last moment on that march when we had the luxury for such a trifle.

5

We slept by the riverbank two days and then, the next day, barges appeared upriver, approached us, and I guessed riding on one of them was Evynar Ydhiil from the fact that neither Kirith Kirin nor Imral betrayed the least surprise at their appearance. Evynar had commandeered barges to bring the whole army easily and peacefully down river, escorted by mounted parties on the two shores. This had been part of the plan from the start, one of the chief reasons for taking Teliar, where a lot of barge traffic docks.

We chose to ride along the shore rather than get on one of the barges; I wanted to stay on Nixva's back, and I don't think Kirith Kirin had much stomach for a boat ride either. We accompanied the barges through the Hills of Slaughter, around the edge of the sacred precinct, into which no Jisraegen has walked since Falamar laid down the stones. This was country sacred to YY, who is said to have loved Falamar greatly, who mourned his fall, which began here.

A change in the pulse of Fimbrel when I was riding along the shore, careful never to stray even a step inside the boundary markers. The voices that were woven through the fabric grew stronger, the cloak shimmered with a light like one of the shrine lamps, and because this happened of its own accord I made no move to change it. The cloak was woven of Wyyvisar, and as the language changed near the Slaughter Hills, as the tone of the song within the fabric shifted from one voice to another, I understood the work of it better than before, a thing of language like a standing tower, a wrap of words, all of Wyyvisar spun into it, as those same runes are spiraled on the inside of the kirilidur all the way from the base to the High Place. Each thread of the Cloak's weave was a chain of Words; I had been at Illyn Water to hear the song that made the threads. We were near a place precious to YY, a ground she had marked with her step within memory, and the Cloak, which was all woven of Words, in changing revealed more of its nature.

We were headed toward the Ajnur Gap, where Osar crosses a narrow, flat plain beneath the Slaughter Hills, before spreading out across the delta that has become the city of Charnos. It was in this place, where our armies were to converge, that we expected to meet resistance from the Verm, and this was the case when at the edge of the sacred precinct the barges landed and our troops marched off.

We came ashore at Twar Ford, a small village still in the highlands where the barges dock before returning the long way upriver to Teliar. Below Twar Ford, the land drops and the Osar runs too fast, over rocks, for barges to pass. Freight is hauled by cart or wagon from Twar to the city, and when we came ashore the village was buzzing, because, we were told, a battalion of Verm were marching toward Charnos to hold it against our arrival. They were arriving too late for that, of course. But when we got the word that Verm were marching so close, Kirith Kirin nodded to me, and he and Imral and I broke away from the main army, which was disembarking from the barges and thus vulnerable.

We rode toward the main road and along it, and I put rings on my fingers and formed ithikan wind to carry us, these horses all accustomed to the shift out of the normal world. The three of us headed toward the Verm, and I made certain we were invisible to their eyes, hurtling along the road and down the long descent. We rode across the Osar bridge and saw the Verm soldiers. When I counted their white banners, saw the size of the Verm, and the number of their horses, I understood that the moment had come, and so we pulled up short of the road, still hidden under the shadow of the trees. I sent myself to the Verm as an eidolon on a mist, my eye within it, so that I was watching them as though I were the ghost, seeing the impossible shoulders, the thrusting bone of the elbow, the gray skin and shining eyes. The Verm soldiers riding at the head of the column saw me at the end of the bridge, and word went backwards along their ranks. I said, a voice out of the ghost image, "Turn and go back the way you came if you want to live. Kirith Kirin has already landed at Twar Ford and you are not permitted to pass beyond me here."

They were confused, the ones at the head of the column, but their ranks parted and a human officer approached, saw me, wheels of light spinning around my head, and hung back. He wore the jewels of a Nivri house, I could not recognize them, but he spoke to the Verm, and when they pressed forward I spoke the first Words of Soul Eater, Soul Devourer. One can see it in the eyes first, that the Words have begun to work, that the legs are full of lead, followed by sharp pains, laces of death that race through the tissue, death rising out of the ground, followed by Soul Devourer, which cannot be reversed when it is begun, and so these first ones died. The Nivra saw them go down. I spoke again. "Go back beyond the bridge, you'll have safe passage on the other side of Osar. Kirith Kirin comes to claim the city and he will soon cross the river too, and when he does, I will sing you all to sleep if I have too, you'll hear my song as the last sound of your lives, all of you including the Nivra, so tell your siblings as many as are in the Ajnur Gap. Kirith Kirin says go home to your houses in Antelek, to your farms in Briidoc. Go home and he will not remember that you marched against him when he was going to Aerfax to become King."

The words would trouble the Jisraegen in them, and the deaths of the score or so at the head of the bridge convinced the Nivra I meant business. I moved the image toward them, swelled a mist around it, and they fell back from the bridge, the Nivra giving the order to retreat. I could feel, through Fimbrel, that Drudaen was aware of this moment, that I had revealed myself; but he was loathe to let me know where he was, even yet, because of some thought he was hiding from me, some place in his thinking that he was protecting. The Verm fell back from that spinning, shining creature that was me, a moment that I saw from the eye of the ghost and from my body's eye, under the trees not far from the bridge, watching with Kirith Kirin and Imral Ynuuvil.

We waited at the spot and Evynar led the army, by now formed up in good order, with archers in the trees and on the road, the infantry protected, coming up as if they expected a fight, bows strung and pikes lowered. A group of infantry took the head of the bridge and detachments of mounted archers and swordsmen flanked them. We made camp on the flat ground where the Osar, having descended from the hills, slows to a gentler pace again. Our campfires were visible in Charnos, as we meant them to be. Kirith Kirin had come south.

CHAPTER TWENTY
CHARNOS

1

The sight of the city in the distance entranced me, white walls rising over the mouth of the Osar where the plain was still dry, Chunombrae rising from the rock at the center, framed against the Bay of Anyn beyond, shining blue. Charnos is the city most of the Anynae will point to as their heartland, built on the place at which, as they tell the story, their boats first came ashore in the long ago. Jisraegen live mixed with the Anynae here, but the flavor of the city remains Anyn, no matter that a Jisraegen-style house with corners and angles appears here and there.

A delegation from the present Mayor of Charnos, Aniwetok, daughter of somebody, came to meet us the first morning after we encamped at the bridge. There is a ceremony which the Mayor of Charnos undertakes at the time of the Succession, since the Successor always passes through Charnos on the way to Aerfax. Mayor Aniwetok invited us in words that Kirith Kirin had heard many times before, I suppose, when he rode south to Senecaur. "The King is welcome to his city Charnos, and the Mayor and all the boats will meet him at the gate."

Kirith Kirin sent word he would come straight to the gate, and as soon as the delegation had ridden away we broke camp and formed up for the march across the bridge and down the paved road that runs along Osar to the walls of Charnos. Another bridge crosses Osar there, and a huge gate rises over the bridge to engulf it, on either side the immense walls of the city sunk deep in the earth, water rising along the edge where the wetlands begin, a natural moat. These walls are a wonder and are prophesied to stand as long as the walls of Inniscaudra, since the Tervan built them out of pity for the Anynae after so many were slaughtered in Falamar's war. Walls like these, of joined stoned quarried from the deep gorges of Jhunombrae, could never be taken by any army, could never be broken by any magic, and the Tervan had intended the gift of them to make a place where the Anynae could always defend themselves. The stones were worked with images of the Anynae, their arrival in boats, the building of the walls and Chunombrae, the digging of the canals, the slaughter when Falamar brought the Jisraegen army down from the north. The walls and the reliefs on them run for stades in either direction, circling the city and stretching far out into the bay, enclosing a protected harbor with huge sea gates that can be closed when the need arises.

Ajnur Gap is narrowest where the main gate stands, and our foot soldiers made the march in a day, stopping for the night at the walls. We camped on the dry ground near where the Tervan causeway raises the road above the wetlands. Boats were gathering on the other side of the walls, we could hear them calling one another.

At dawn, when we were ready to enter, boats large and small lined the waterways, the winding river and the irregular canals, as far as the eye could see toward the center of the city. Kirith Kirin rode at the head of his Nivri and Finru escort beneath the maw of the gate. I stayed on the other side of Osar until the whole army had crossed the bridge, the thousands who had come south with Evynar, including the Verm party, whose presence was noted with much consternation by the burghers and citizens. My attention was elsewhere, to the south, where Drudaen's army had camped.

When Kirith Kirin was settled, in the house named Chunombrae, after the Tervan city, he sent Imral and a party of riders across the bridge to find me, and I rode into the city behind the last of our infantry. When we were inside, at the request of Kirith Kirin and for the first time in the memory of anyone living, the Tervan gate was closed across the causeway, and our army manned the gatehouses. With her sea gates open, Charnos could exist as an island indefinitely. The silver portcullis slid downward and the walls of hardened glass slid inward, a cunning arrangement said to be like the one at Krafulgur, which will be closed in the battle that precedes the Breaking of Worlds, according to Curaeth. We marched along the causeway escorted by the remaining boats, stragglers, some with oars, some with sails that seemed able to catch the least breath of wind. Anynae were good sailors before they came to Aeryn, as they will tell you, but they are all the better now for good Jisraegen cloth to make their sails. As they will admit as well. The road led to the old city, to the high mount topped by a mansion in the northern style behind a wall that would have done justice to minor city. The Tervan built this house as well.

The house rose out of what would have seemed a ridge of land if such a thing were possible on a river delta; the Smiths built the rock along with the house, which circles the narrow summit, rising to the peak. The lower series of halls are for public ceremony, but above is a well-appointed palace with rooms scrupulously maintained by the city burghers, used for meetings when neither King nor Queen are in residence. Words in three of the Anynae tongues are carved over the main gate to the house, all saying the same thing, "Chunombrae is the heart of the Anynae in this world." Imral translated for me, since these were languages I did not know.

Our army camped in Chunombrae's lower halls, smoke from cook-fires passing through hidden places in the intricately carved ceilings. We passed through the commotion of the soldiers settling in, noises echoing on stone walls, camp marshals running from place to place, the burghers' agents offering all that we could need in terms of firewood, supplies, the like. I dismounted when one of the grooms saw us and I handed Nixva over to her. I said good-bye with a sweet Word that he liked, for his ears only, and he whinnied and pranced away.

Kirith Kirin had claimed the highest of the rooms in the house, an apartment at the top, arches open to the sea air, closed chambers behind, with windows of colored glass. A long climb, sometimes in the open but often under arches of stone carved like slender fish. We found Kirith Kirin standing on one of the galleries gazing over the Bay of Anyn beyond the sea gates of Charnos, gray water stretching out in every direction. I stared myself, never having seen so much water, at least not with the eyes of my body. The real thing, the smell of the salt wind, the taste in the mouth, is different from conceptions of it. Imral dismissed the bodyguard and we stood alone in the salty air. Kirith Kirin said, "This city changes so slowly. It seems exactly the same to me as five hundred years ago."

"The same to me, too," Imral agreed, and I stood there for a moment, looking at both of them.

The city was a wonder to me, all brand new. I stared at the masses of buildings of every description, every color, every shape, jammed together, looming over the banks of the canals and waterways, bridges crossing here and there, a maze of a place if there was ever one, a riot of sounds and smells, but rising over that confusion the curve of the Tervan causeway that led from the gate to Chunombrae. The city center stood where the causeway traffic halted, and I watched for as long as I was allowed. We had that view of the southern city that is still my favorite, the Twar Market and the Old Market, the wharves and warehouses along the docks, and the moored ships in the harbor, waiting maybe for a wind to lift their sails.

In view of the circumstances a good deal of ceremony was being suspended; the Succession had never before taken place under force of arms and therefore the Mayor was willing to make allowances. But Kirith Kirin would have to go to the round temple, across a plaza from the main gate of Chunombrae, to meet the burghers and pray. The Anynae are lovers of prayer and pray six times a day when they can. They have come to light the lamps as we do but accompany this with the praying they prefer. Brun explained the kinds of prayer to me, that evening, when she came with the Finru company that would escort Kirith Kirin to the temple. A different style of prayer for waking, for first part of morning, for noon, for afternoon, for evening, for night. Some of the prayers are like the morning and evening songs we sing, quite simple and plain. When I asked if she were praying to YY or someone else, she merely shrugged. "If I had to choose, I would choose the Mother," she said. But I did not think that was an answer to my question.

By the request of the burghers and the Mayor, I stayed in our rooms at the top of Chunombrae, a pleasant apartment lit with many kinds of lamps. Only because Kirith Kirin insisted had I been allowed in Charnos at all. I had learned a bit of this while Kirith Kirin was dressing to go to the temple, some good clothes that had traveled with the main army's baggage train. "They're not great lovers of magicians, the Anynae. They say magic causes all our problems. And most magicians don't like to come here anyway, because of the Tervan walls."

I shrugged. "I didn't invent myself, and I don't mind missing the temple if I can stay up here and stare at the sky tonight." The red moon was already rising, a ghost in the late day. He was on the way out as I asked, "But what about the walls?"

"They interfere with magic. A trick the Tervan know."

He left and the red moon swelled, coloring the whole sky, the city below alive with light, the buildings spilling light onto the canals, the light dancing on the water, boats lit by lanterns sliding past; I could not help but gape at it all, and maybe I used better eyesight than a mortal is entitled to, in looking at it. This was not the first magic I had performed in Charnos; I had been keeping the usual eye on the south, listening for the towers, as had become my habit; and I was still wearing Fimbrel, its magic alive around me. I wouldn't have thought of it, except that the walls were supposed to hinder me, but I felt no change.

For a while I went into deep trance, to get a good look around. The top of Chunombrae is high enough to be of some use as a device. I took a long look, nothing more. I hovered in the Cloak as if I were really in the air.

To do this work I had chosen the room with the colored lamps that had been spread with Jisraegen carpets and pillows, firepots and low tables where Kirith Kirin had been reading some document from somebody. I left my body for a while, returning when there was commotion in the room. Kirith Kirin was there, along with King Evynar and Imral. They had dismissed the guard in a hurry when they found me in deep meditation.

"Jessex, what are you doing?" Kirith Kirin asked, alarm in his voice.

"Trying to see. That's all. Taking a look south."

"Here? But you can't."

"Why?"

He and Evynar were looking at each other. Drii skin darkens easily, at moments of consternation; Evynar's had done so, and Kirith Kirin was watching me in confusion. "What did you see?" he asked. "Did you have any trouble?"

"No, no trouble." I told him the Verm army was still waiting for us, that Drudaen's shadow had reasserted itself around southern Karns and across the bay in places, but that he was still hidden.

Evynar closed his eyes and sat down. "Kehan." The word for darkness in darkness, the word for the color of a winter night.

"What's wrong? Do these people have some law against my doing magic here? You should have told me."

Kirith Kirin's face had gone grim. "Don't say any more about this while we're in the city." His manner was serious and I became alarmed. He hardly seemed to see me at all. With King Evynar there, I decided it would be better not to ask any more questions. Kirith Kirin signaled that I should stay and so I sat on one of the cushions, near a firepot, closing my eyes. They conferred in easy voices, a code about armies, double-time marching, terrain, expected obstacles. They were wondering, I guessed drowsily, when Karsten would arrive.

Evynar had gone and Kirith Kirin was leaning over me. He had a sober look. "I think I calmed him down a bit, but this has upset him. And it isn't easy to upset Evynar."

"What did I do?"

"Nothing. You didn't do anything at all."

He would answer no more questions, so I asked none. After a long while passed, when we were lying together and his arm was draped around me, he said, "Remember what I told you. Do nothing that can be understood as magic." He was speaking to his court magician now, a voice that was used to being obeyed. I said I would do whatever he wanted, and I could feel the words soften him some, remind him of the sweet space between us. "You'll understand why I'm asking for this after a while, Jessex. Is it all right?"

"Yes, it's fine. I'll get some books and practice my reading. I'll be very quiet."

"Drudaen won't bother you while you're here, except maybe pay someone to try to poison you."

"He would know better, no poison he could make would reach me."

He started to answer this, but as suddenly stopped himself. "He might try anything, knowing you're in Charnos."

2

Early the next morning riders brought word to Kirith Kirin that Karsten was within four days march. They were marching under shadow, which had reasserted itself around Ivyssa and Arsk, and Karsten wrote that nothing had served to cement the determination of the Queen's soldiers or her own more than the fact of shadow, "As if the world has grown very thin," she wrote. "This is one experience I had been spared, up until now. The curse of a long life is that sooner or later nearly everything will happen to you." She went on to give some details, that the blue army was under her command, that Nemort was not building a private army for himself. Kirith Kirin seemed relieved.

He folded up the letter very quietly and looked at me. "You're not to do anything about shadow. All right? You may do the magics of vigilance but absolutely nothing else unless it's to save your own life."

No need to say yes. By now I had guessed at least part of the truth. The Tervan walls actually should have made magic impossible. Not simply difficult, but impossible. I had taken a long look at the walls and knew. But I had felt no difference. I had not speculated aloud about this. Kirith Kirin went on to something else, and I wandered to the open arches to watch the harbor, glad of the peace, the release from work.

But as it happened, the next evening, at supper by myself, I found after drinking part of a cup of wine that I had indeed been poisoned, I had drunk acht, a root extract the Svyssn make, used to kill the Husband once a decade. The Sisters had taught me to change acht in Arthen, along with many other such substances, and I made the Words in the kei space and power moved to alter the substance, to render it harmless, to take it within. Quickly, because acht works quickly, and I would have been paralyzed and dead quite suddenly otherwise. The poison was in the wine cup, which had been brought to me by one of Kirith Kirin's own people. Most of the wine still in the cup. I sent for the bodyguard and asked him to find Gaelex; everyone else was in a meeting with the burghers down in one of the ceremonial halls.

She came at once and I showed her the cup and told her I suspected the wine was poisoned. A few minutes later she came back completely pale to ask who had given me the cup. I told her I had smelled the wine and been suspicious of it, so I had not drunk any. She found that odd, I think, knowing Gaelex. The glass had been half empty.

She brought me some food, water, and wine that she herself knew to be safe, and I thanked her. After that I was alone in those stone rooms again.

Kirith Kirin arrived earlier than I expected. I was reading some poems by Ketol that Imral had told me were very fine, but the language was hard and taxed my knowledge of the formal modes of High Speech. Ketol appeared to have fallen in love a number of times and made a lot of verse about it. I was reading the one about the nightingale when Kirith Kirin came in. I put down the book. "Did Gaelex talk to you?"

His anger was visible. "Of course. She's questioning a few people. She's had to involve the burghers, which isn't good. But they staff this part of the house, the wine came from them. We'll have our own people in here from now on, after this."

"She told them I smelled the poison?"

"And that she gave the wine to a dog and the poison killed it almost instantly. One of the burghers suggested you might have put the poison in the wine yourself." He ground his jaw on. "You may imagine what I said to that." He was in fact still raging. "It will be a while before he speaks in my hearing again."

"I didn't actually smell it until I had drunk half the glass. I had to do magic to change it. But no one was here."

He washed completely white. He was near a stool and sat down on it. "Praise God."

I handed him something to drink himself, he seemed to need it. "Gaelex brought that," I said, before he could ask. "She brought the food, too. Brought it with her own hands, I mean. So it's safe."

He'd had some to drink already, beer, judging by the smell. The Charnos breweries are well-known to be the best in Aeryn, the burghers like to show off what they make. But that hardly explained the sudden flood of tenderness. He acted as though I had really come close to death, when he should know better.

There were no other incidents. The poison was traced to one of the householders in Chunombrae on evidence which nearly everyone except the burghers considered to be dubious, and the man was executed before I could question him. Gaelex talked to him, and she came away believing he might have brought the wine but he was hardly the person to afford acht, which had to be brought all the way from the farthest north country. Stolen, no doubt, since its use among the Svyssn is only for the ritual.

But Drudaen should know that acht could not act on me fast enough, that I would recognize the poison and change it. None of this made sense, unless I was right and the walls were supposed to have prevented me from making magic at all, in which case the poison would have worked and I would be dead.

That explained Kirith Kirin's reaction, too.

Soon I had something new to think about, though, when I was standing on the arched walkway high above the city. I was keeping an eye on the countryside, as Kirith Kirin had said I could do, and that day Verm troops arrived to reinforce the army hereabouts. Some of them had marched from Turis, but the bulk of them came from south, from Aerfax. That was my suspicion, and Kirith Kirin's as well. He had posted sentries on the walls, anticipating even an invasion by the sea and drilling the city militia in the closing of the sea gates, about which he knew a lot. He instructed the sentries to keep a careful eye on the Verm battalions, so we were informed right away when the army formed up suddenly and marched across the causeway, taking all the land between it and the bridge across Osar.

"The Verm believe you won't do magic from the city," Kirith Kirin said.

"Because of the Tervan walls."

He nodded, tight-lipped. "It's well known. So well known I never thought to tell you. No magician comes to Charnos because magic doesn't work here."

I blinked. *Except it works for me, and that's a bad sign.* For a moment, just a moment, I was angry at him. "I'll have to go outside. Now."

The thought made him grim. But he knew as well as I there was no choice.

He sent word for the gate to be opened on my signal. Imral escorted me out of the palace and someone brought Nixva. I was wearing Fimbrel, but kept the color plain and the texture dull, as if it were truly merely a cloak; I did magic in doing even that much, but nobody seemed to notice. We had an escort of a dozen or so, for what purpose I don't know, since I would go through the gates without any of them, even Imral. The gates were motionless as we approached, and our party halted. I gave the signal to open the gate and waited.

I turned Nixva and he walked up the causeway through the gatehouse. On the other side of the gate we stopped, and I gave the signal to close it behind me.

They saw me, the Verm did. They were formed up in battle order maybe a stade away, out of arrow-shot.

Nixva walked slowly toward them.

I made a mist around us and we vanished. Consternation rippled among the Verm, and Nixva stepped easily into their ranks. Today we would make no room for mercy; so I put away my heart for awhile and began the long incantation Dead Hand Moving, as the Verm searched this way and that, maybe feeling the breath of my breeze as I passed, and when the song was ready, I set it loose and moved my hand from place to place, and this one died, and that one, dropped to the ground, each death more, harder, more painful, the Verm groaning, something melting in their chests, a burst of pain and the flesh a puddle there, one by one collapsing, scattered through the ranks, as though I were everywhere at once. Their confusion was complete. They had served Drudaen, not opposed him, they were not prepared for me. I rode through their ranks of infantry and their mounted wings of cavalry and soon the horses were screaming in terror as their riders died on their backs. I spared the horses, not only because it is unpleasant to kill an animal but because they have a terror of killing magic, they can feel it, and their reaction would create more confusion in the lines. By the time I stayed my hand and turned to look at them, the rear ranks of Verm infantry were edging away from the bridge. They gathered their dead and wounded as best they could and began a general retreat.

I looked into the eyes of a Verm woman as she lay dying at my feet. I released the mist and let her see me, too. Taller than Imral, broad shoulders, her breasts long and slack, the center of her chest dissolved into a kind of gray paste, a light ebbing from her eyes.

At the head of the bridge with the Osar at my back I showed myself again, a burst of light to draw their eyes, stripping the mist away. This time the ones closest drew back in panic, and the panic multiplied through the formations. Their officers, a mix of Verm and gentry, managed to get them in order after a struggle. I waited at the bridge quietly.

Consternation in the skies, too, and somewhere in my enemy's mind a troubled thought was forming.

For the first time he showed himself, over Aerfax as I had expected, standing on Senecaur, and he reached to strike me with the strength of the tower, cold and sharp all through me, and I sent myself out of body in an instant, slipping rings on the fingers of my body and calming Nixva. He was on the Tower when we saw one another, him shining, white, and pure, not the image I imagined, not the monster I sometimes wished. He struck all the wards I had set from Laeredon, all the country I had learned to hold through the use of the Fimbrel cloak. In answer, the music swelled within Fimbrel, swelled and I could bend it, I could shape it, as one does with the eyestone on the High Place, so that when I defended myself he could not break me anywhere, and when I struck at him he was staggered, as though we were fighting on two towers side by side.

From the city, from Chunombrae, they saw a pillar of darkness rise from the Osar bridge, and day darkened as I drank the light in the vicinity of Charnos. This was not the pale light of shadow but the black of midnight. Kirith Kirin knew it was me, but even he had never seen anything like it. I had awakened Fimbrel and now I knew the scope of it.

Quickly Drudaen hid from me and went back to his defenses, but he was shaken, because it should have been easy for him to break me in some manner, with me on the ground and him in the air. I had no idea what he would see of the Cloak from Senecaur, what he would learn about it, so when he hid himself again I came back into the body and tamed Fimbrel onto my back. Nixva was skittish, some, and I wondered why, till I turned and saw a party of riders headed toward us from across Osar, red and blue cloaks mingled. I knew Karsten by her horse and headed toward her.

3

She thought I was riding back to Charnos, where she and her riders were headed, but I signaled her to stop the riders and drew her aside. We dismounted and she greeted me with the kind of warmth she had always shown, as though I were still that troublesome boy who tended the lamps. I told her to explain to Kirith Kirin that I needed to stay outside the walls. She asked no questions about that.

Nixva carried me below the city where the Verm army had regrouped. We scattered them farther south, this time without any more killing. I did some fireworks to keep them mindful of my presence, darkening the sky with clouds and flashing some lightning here and there, ordinary stuff. At the end of the day I held the road south and the Verm were scattered across the fens of Karns. This skirmish has been styled the Battle of Ajnur Gap by people who have the burden of naming such events. It is often cited to demonstrate the pointlessness of sending an army against a good magician.

I had enough to think about that I felt safer avoiding thought altogether, so I rode here and there on Nixva's back, then found shelter for the evening near the river bridge. I got wood and built a fire, and Nixva cropped up mouthfuls of brown grass. Before he had eaten his fill, I could detect riders coming toward us from the city. People I knew, Kirith Kirin among them.

They rode straight for my fire and before long were settling around me, starting other fires from mine, unrolling bedrolls, a few tents. Kirith Kirin dismounted and found me almost shyly, and we sat together by my fire. A night of uncertain stars unfurled. The white moon crescent hung above the bay. With him beside me I felt safer to return warmth to my heart, to restore some feeling to myself, and I let down my guard and sat with him. In the air was the scent of the dead, the Verm I had sent to Zaeyn.

While we slept I could feel my enemy brooding to the south, uncertain what to do next, his army like so many rags trying to become cloth. But one thought he hid from me, something I would want to know, closely guarded, even in his moments of doubt.

4

He woke me before dawn and took my hand and we crept away from the tent. He signaled back the bodyguard and we walked to a grove of low, twisted oaks, the park fronting someone's estate. Peaceful to stand there among those old trees, so different from anything in Arthen. To smell the sour sweat under his arm. "We have a long ride now."

"Drudaen was on Senecaur. I finally saw him."

He was searching for something, a sign. As if my face could reveal something to him. I went on, "I'm learning to fight him. I think I can get us to Aerfax. But it'll get harder from here."

"I know."

I drew his face to mine and kissed him. We walked farther, along a stone path toward a group of graves. I had never seen graves before, marked with stone slabs, some elaborate, some simple and plain. Many of the Anyn bury their dead. We walked around the edge of these, out of respect.

We said tender things that do not need to be repeated here. I have tried to write them down but it is better to keep them for myself. He had felt the strain on me in Charnos, he said, and wanted a bit of quiet. So now we would be in the country for a few days while the armies provisioned themselves. We looked at the countryside, the twisted clusters of trees along the Osar, giving way to scrub brush, low pines and swaths of marsh grass as we looked south. We stood on a rise of land, the last undulation of the Narvos ridge.

At one point he looked at me and asked, "What are you?"

"I don't know what you're asking."

"The pillar of shadow at the bridge. The day darkening so suddenly. You always forget how much of this I've seen. What kind of strength do you have?"

"Whatever I am," I said, after a while, "I do love you."

"You don't know, do you?"

It would have been impossible to answer. We stood there, turned toward Charnos now, the high walls catching the eastern light. Good to stand there, good to feel the peace. But something had changed in his hopes.

He must have felt the change in me, because he made me look at him. "I love you, too, you know. It isn't a small thing to do that, at my age."

"I don't know what it means, that you've all changed toward
me again," I said, "like the moment on Sister Mountain, do you
remember?" My heart was pounding and I let it go on, without any
magic to still it. "What does Curaeth Curaesyn say about what happens after a magician comes to Charnos?"

"Hush. Don't ask me that." Such a look of sorrow, such a
perfect ice at the center of his eyes. "There's nothing to do, my dear.
We are who we are. We're marching to Aerfax."

"I can get us there," I said.

"I know you can. He knows it, too. So now the question is, to
what lengths will he go if he's pressed?"

How far? A cold question, no answer.

We looked south. We stayed there and watched the changes
of daylight. On the horizon hung rags of gray, the edges of
shadow. Long after Vithilunen we were still standing there, as
though a sign were coming. But a sign had come, already, and
once again it was me.

CHAPTER TWENTY-ONE
KLEEIOM

1

Whatever difference that prophecy made, whoever knew kept the secret, and no one spoke about it after we left Charnos. The army marched. I lived in Fimbrel, on Nixva's back, riding ahead of the main body, in a company of mounted troops and the twice-named. A few of the Nivri rode along with us, the ones who had been in Arthen with us, though of the Finru houses there was only Brun. She had asked to join the advance troops, figuring, she said, that we would get all the fireworks. She told me this by way of a joke, though it turned out true enough.

A good horse could make the trip down the coast of Karns to Kleeiom in four days, stopping at any number of inns in the fishing villages that rose up periodically along the road, paved though not magical. The waters of the bay came lapping onto the sand, low waves, nothing like Ocean, I'm told. Now and then the water would rise and inundate the road, washing away parts of it, and some merchant from Charnos would send a crew south to repair it. There is no reason to keep the road open, no destination south of Charnos worth discussing. Except Aerfax.

We in the advance party could ride at a pace that was fairly leisurely, and we camped early in the afternoon, avoiding the villages ourselves. No one has ever told me this was due to my presence in the war party, but I expect Kirith Kirin was reluctant to have me face the Karnslanders. Often we pitched our tents in the shadow of the dunes, adapting the linings to keep out the sand. Could I call that a peaceful time? Ten days march to take the infantry from Charnos to Kleeiom, and I never slept. At night I walked the beaches in Fimbrel watching the light show in the south, below the horizon, the fireworks over Senecaur where Drudaen was spending all his time, trying to understand what device I possessed that made me into, in his vision, a walking shenesoeniis. We were, both of us, except for our vigilance, mostly quiescent in that period, though he was moving his hand toward us in other ways than magic.

Kirith Kirin got news that an army was moving down from Antelek along the western road, clearing the wreckage from the first disaster and picking up some stragglers as they went. The army had marched straight out of Cunevadrim and would not be turning back. I was with him when he was talking the news over among the Nivri, when he sent for Karsten, who was with the army, to give her fresh orders in light of the new need to protect our flank. The Verm were only a few days away by now, traveling nearly as fast as the messengers who brought us the news. "He'll send them down Kleeiom behind us," Kirith Kirin said. "Bottle us up."

The news made him nervous. I took note of the change.

At the north end of Kleeiom is a small town, Teryaehn-in-Don, Don being the name giving to the country thereabout. A lot of fishing boats put in there and a good market kept the city in the fish business year in and year out, with the bonus that a lot of shipping concerns were there, too, to tend the fleet of boats. Teryaehn was a royal town, under the rule of the crown through an appointed viceroy, and a lot of supplies for Aerfax come in through the docks. Drudaen knew we would bring the army there, garrison the town, but take our main force south toward Aerfax. He would besiege the garrison with his army and send a force down the road after us.

We moved into the town on a day in the month of Yama, the dead of winter. Kirith Kirin had requisitioned the viceroy's round-house for himself and the viceroy had moved into the inn for the night. We were two days ahead of our army, maybe six days or eight days ahead of the new Verm force following us. Kirith Kirin had sent word for our troops to move double time down the road; he had done that without my asking, and that was all that was necessary.

We quartered in the viceroy's big stone house together, in a nice feather bed, with windows opening onto the sea. Many people up north have the myth that all the rooms in a round-house are round, but I am here to tell you that is not the case. That first morning we stretched out on the sheets, me prepared for another night of lying beside him awake, listening for any sign of change on the planes, and him restive, his hair all in tangles, worrying. He threw open the windows and let the cold Yama wind pour through on us, ran under the covers and pulled me close, and we sat there with the wind rattling the lamps and shaking the tapestries. A smell of salt in the air. A good smell, Kirith Kirin said.

"How long has it been since you slept through the night?" he asked.

"Since Charnos, I guess."

He pulled my head on his shoulder. "Sleep today. We'll be all right here."

"I'm fine, I need to stay awake —"

"In case he does something. But if he does you'll wake up anyway. All right? So sleep, please. For me. Because I want you to."

So I said I would, and he sat there waiting. He could tell when I was kei and when I wasn't, so I let go of all those other places of myself, those spinning parts of me in the ether, what Commyna called the place that is not a place. I came back to the only place where I could sleep, and, in spite of the fact that I could have done without it, I was glad to close my eyes with him sitting there, the wind blowing through the room.

Dreamless. Not even the ghost of my mother visited me. We slept through the night together. Kirith Kirin got out of bed at morning but I stayed sleeping. He sat with me most of the day, let no one in the house but Imral and Evynar.

I awoke in the afternoon hearing a voice, someone I ought to know, I thought, a moment that felt more like a vision than a dream, because as it faded I saw the afternoon light through the open windows, felt the cold wind, curled under the down comforter in the rose duvet. Not my mother's voice, I had been expecting another nightmare about her; but someone else. Commyna? No, but someone like that. Kentha, maybe. I had echoes of her in the necklace, which was never far from me.

Kirith Kirin had wrapped himself in Fimbrel, which was full of afternoon light, and he was sitting by the window on a wooden chair. I pulled the duvet around my shoulders and crossed the room to sit with him, room for us both in the chair, the wind in my face. He touched me tenderly. "You look better."

I put my face close to his and rested there for a while. "You're wearing my cloak."

"Yes. I'm listening to it."

"You like it?"

He smiled. "I can see what you mean. There's a feeling of the High Place."

"Voices," I said. "The High Place is full of voices, too."

"Do you hear anything?" he asked.

Closing my eyes, lifting my head, there, yes, I could hear again, as easily as that, and I pulled the Cloak around my shoulders too. "Nothing different," I said. I could feel Drudaen moving on

Senecaur, watching me, preparing, I supposed. "We're close now. It'll be hard from here. He can try any number of tricks."

"Like an army in the mountains," Kirith Kirin said. "From the deep places under the Spur. That's what Karsten expects. And she's probably right. They'll hit us when we're close."

"But all we have to do is get as far as the gate."

"When we get there, Athryn can climb to the High Place and sing to the Rock to begin the Change. At that point, Senecaur will be of no use to Drudaen. But I have to get to the gate before Athryn can climb to the Rock."

He had said as much before but it reassured me to hear him say it again.

Kirith Kirin was looking south, into the cloudy skies that, near the horizon, became fringes of Drudaen's shadow. "I'm not afraid of his army. We're not likely to be very surprised by any kind of attack, given who we are and where we're going. No matter where they come from. He has something else in mind, he must. He has some other plan."

We sent for food and ate. Imral came later and we talked again. Peaceful. Around sundown the army showed up, first runners, then the forward riders, then lead troops, second line troops, archers, wagons, baggage, the merchant train and the supplies. Teryaehn rarely played host to so many people, an army camped on her grounds, spilling onto the road and along the dry land toward the mountains. The fish market stayed open till there was nothing left to sell and the smell of cooking fish floated over the countryside. Karsten shared our catch at our table, and we sat up late, hearing stories about the march.

About midnight I got to work, sending for my steward who kept my chests under lock and key, waking the poor woman to bring them. I got out the gems and metals I would need, true silver and smith's gold, stones as well, more than I had used so far. I took these with me in a leather pack and had one of Gaelex's people send for Nixva. I told Kirith Kirin what I was planning. He sent for the viceroy to make some dispositions concerning the countryside, that was the phrase he used.

I had Imral show me the best map we had of the Don, to get an idea where to ride. I had begun insinging and was kei; to memorize the map was not much work, and I carried it in my head with me. The north of Kleeiom is the widest part of the whole country, but that's hardly worth bragging about; a rider can make the trip in half a day from Teryaeh-in-Don to the mountains. But a stade north and the whole Karns fen opens up a hundred stades wide.

One does not lightly begin those Words, which are hard to unsay and which stain the soul forever. Nixva came up prancing with the groom trying to keep him under control. While he was coming up, I closed my eyes and gathered the cloak close about me. For what I am about to do, forgive me. I will not eat the souls that die here but will let them cross through to Zaeyn.

We were riding and I began to sing Eater of Souls, Lifebreaker, guiding Nixva toward the mountains for our first pass; we rode ithikan now, and so his speed was multiplied and we saw the land with the change on it that comes in that state. I lay a lattice of enchantment from the mountains to the sea, across the whole sweep of country, over bog and fen. I made a network of gems and metals to make a killing field, singing Great Devourer, singing We Who Depart, singing Dead Hand Moving, singing all the killing magics into these gems, setting them down in a curve leading across the road to the sea, making Bans and wards along this route, a process that took a long time, back and forth, and because I was taught to be thorough, what I made there would last ten thousand years, unless someone of my skill should come to remove it. There are still stories that my gems and metals are in the bogs of the Don.

Kirith Kirin, in the town, was speaking to the viceroy, telling him to close the road north, because nothing living would pass that way until I returned. He had sent riders north to the villages along the Karns shore to tell them the same thing. News would reach the Verm that way, and our riders would find safety in Charnos while we continued south.

We would come back this way, and I would open this deadly wall that I had built. That was my intention. I daresay Drudaen wondered what I was doing with all that commotion; I was the first to make this kind of magic, and I invented it out of necessity. We could not let the Verm take the north end of the road and keep us penned in Kleeiom. If things went badly, we had to come back this way ourselves. As long as we could get as far as Teryaehn, we would have a chance.

A chance for what? It only seemed prudent to leave ourselves a way out, and nothing else I could think of would work against thousands of Verm soldiers. I did not want them waiting for us when we returned. Why did I never stop to think I might not be making that journey back to open the gate?

2

At dawn the next day the army marched south along the narrow Kleeiom road. Many chroniclers place this day as the forty-fifth day of Yama, close to Chanii, the heart of winter. I do not believe it was so late but I have sometimes been confused about events in those days along the Kleeiom strand.

The order of a march like that one has taken a particular shape over the ages of Aryaen history, when one magician or another has accompanied the Successor, be it Prince or Princess, to the Rock of Change to receive the crown. These times of transition have not always been pleasant, even when the King and Queen were at peace. I rode ahead of the columns, not quite out of sight of them, inland, in order to scour the mountains and to buffer the soldiers from any surprise coming from that direction. Now that we were close to Drudaen, my visible presence became a comfort to the soldiers on the ground.

All day we marched under shadow. I could feel him all the time, reaching toward me with this touch or that, testing; at such a pitch we were working now, I left my body to tend itself for hours, so that no matter what the army thought it saw, I myself was distant. Thousands of us were marching and thousands more waiting at the end of the road and yet in the only place that mattered there stood only he and I.

He was unnerved that I could move so easily so close to him, that I was protected as if I were still on Laeredon, and I did my best to let him think it was the pendant I was using, Kentha's gift; I channeled everything through it to color the magic with her voice, and that kept him at bay.

From the second day, storms swept over us from the sea, pelting cold rain and driving wind. Flurries of snow along the road, in the cold coming down from Shurhala, the face of the mountains. I blunted his storms but the force that underlay them, the great movement of air at his command, I could not stop. We were an eerie sight as we moved beneath shadow, snow falling and wind blowing, rings of fire drifting up from my hand toward the clouds, multiplied as many as I was able, rings of fire drifting up into darkness, a way to mute the storm, and something like a light to guide us.

Three days into our march, Verm descended the mountains behind us to cut off our retreat. Kirith Kirin had expected this and had posted scouts to watch certain places on Shurhala. The army halted on his command, our strongest forces now moved southward, and I wheeled back to meet the Verm.

Awesome, those mountains of glossy black, rising jagged along the seacoast as far as the eye can see. A force of two thousand Verm coming around the turn. Why had he sent them, knowing what I would do? Why send so many creatures to die? To make my spirit tired, I suppose. He knew I was young.

Again I took the luxury, offered by that certain state of kei, to forget my human self altogether. To do so is a scarring thing. I had killed, but I had not yet slaughtered, and that would be my job here; to do it quickly so no more Verm would come no matter what his orders were.

The song is always the same song, always changing, a permutation possible in Wyyvisar, without the essence of the meaning ever varying; it is the part of the great irony of magic that among the easiest of all acts is the taking of life, while the hardest is the making of it. The life of a person passes like a flicker, one touches the tiiryander and the soul flies. This is how the magician dies, too, at the weakest place. I sang Soul Devourer, I rode Nixva toward them at a canter, and in a moment or so they knew they would not be protected by their master; they began to die, a simple death passing through them like a wave, and I was as cold as ice while I was riding there, until the ones at the rear broke and began to flee. Even in that state of dreadful coldness I refused to pursue them.

Verm had a reputation for fierceness and courage, strength and size. They had never faced an enemy like me before. They reacted like any mortal who sees his companions dying by the score, by the hundred, the wave of the fallen approaching. This was the end of the legend of the Verm as invincible and monstrous soldiers.

I believe I killed some twelve hundred of them before the rear ranks broke. Though I say it with no pride, I let them all pass to Tornimul: I refused to take into myself the strength of any of them. A heaviness over my heart as I rode through them, the dead Verm, the pack animals, the pets, any vermin on them, all the life blotted away.

I rode back to the head of the army, and once again the troops turned their strength to our rear. We began to march again. No more Verm came out of Shurhala.

3

Four days passed, and dawn came as a watering of darkness. We broke camp and marched forward in the haze. My head was dull from him, the harsh singing from Senecaur that had been building as we grew close. We marched along the narrow land with the waters of the Bay beside us, low waves crashing on the black sand, sometimes whipped up a bit by wind. The black mountains ahead of us fell sheer into the sea, mountains as high as the clouds, only the merest thread of road at their feet.

One more day of march to go. We made camp the night before, and though we had scarce wood we had fires that burned through the night, as many as were needed, and I walked from one to the other watching him, his voice in the sky, the stars framing him, him reaching, now, for something, I could almost see it. Making an ally, but who?

A change in the Tower. I was dreaming it. But when I woke I could feel it.

In the morning we were greeted by a Verm force on the road ahead of us, and that time I knew better than to stray far ahead of the army. We were within the range from which he could use Senecaur to make a killing wave himself, and I meant for us all to live safely for the return journey north, whenever that might be.

Shadow and mist, but for a moment the rain ended and mist lightened, and out of the soup rose the bulk of a fortress and the spire of a tower. The rain started to fall again, the veil descended, but I had seen the place with my two eyes. Something was wrong. I could no longer feel the Rock.

I had only a moment before the summit was hidden again. Imral was signaling me to come. My heart was pounding. We parleyed on the road, the twice-named and me. It had the feeling of a final meeting. We found an overhang among the rocks for shelter from the storm that continued to sheet us with its half frozen fury. One might have thought them a hopeless bunch, all wind-bedraggled and wet, until one saw their eyes.

"We form up for battle from here," Kirith Kirin spoke with calm but the wild wind whipped him, drowning his voice for a moment. "Ground strength toward Shurhala and the rear road. Jessex and more ground strength at the front, with archers in the center."

Nothing else to say, really. Kirith Kirin took me aside. He was wearing the silver mail inlaid with some of the Karnost gems, and the gems had darkened. I had never seen the mail before and thought nothing, but Kirith Kirin was looking at the jewels, his face pale. Searching then for the Tower, to see it. "Something's wrong," he said. The light was better now, the mist cleared and this time one could see the parti-colored stone that had been used to face the shenesoeniis. "That's Aerfax below, guarding the road. The ritual of the Change begins as soon as I get to that gate. But I should feel the Rock from here, and these gems should be bright."

Forlorn, the huge mass of the fortress clung wetly to the rocks, lashed by the same fury that blasted us. One could glimpse the formidable height of her walls, towers clawing the rock, upper levels where palace rooms could be seen, where Athryn Ardfalla was waiting herself at the gate of Senecaur. The road clung precariously to the mountains between us and the shelter of the house. On the nearest sweep of curve massed the Verm force, only a thousand, this time.

Karsten had completed her re-ordering of the troops. She came back to us and we all stood together. Somber. I could feel the moment near, now, when I would know what Drudaen had planned for me. Listening, hearing nothing, feeling the strength of Senecaur focused through something that was not the Rock. Wind soaked us, rain fell, and now I could do nothing to stop the bad weather, so close to his place of strength; I needed all my energy for listening and for protection.

King Evynar said, after we had the signal that the re-disposition of our soldiers was complete, "Well, I would think it were the breaking of the worlds if I didn't know better, wouldn't you, Kirith Kirin?"

"It's close enough," Kirith Kirin said, looking round at us all.

"A fine day for it, too," Karsten murmured, looking first at the storm and then at Aerfax. By the gleam in her eye one might have thought her serious.

Silence, then. Kirith Kirin had not voiced his concern, and had drawn his cloak over the mail to conceal it. We watched the storm tossed coast of Kleeiom. Aerfax, a sullen pile of stone, awaited us around a curve of that shore.

What do the immortals say to each other at moments like those? Nothing at all. Which is not to deprecate them. Their wisdom is silence. We huddled in the rain like drenched rats, they took stock of the road ahead of us, we found our horses and returned to the army on the road. Sounding trumpets, sounding, "The King is Coming," with the squadrons of infantry already deployed to guard from rear attack or mountain ambush, we marched forward.

Reaching for all the strength I had, I unfurled Fimbrel to her fullest and filled the sky with the sound of the Wyyvisar of Illyn Water, *the ladies of the lake are weaving now, see them, by the green shore.* Hailing Drudaen on all the levels of our combat, I rose out of myself and from me went out that eerie cry on Fourth Circle that begins Eater of Souls, and his Verm on the road ahead of us felt the cold brush of my hand.

What followed is generally called the Battle of Aerfax. This time armies fought, and women and men killed each other.

CHAPTER TWENTY-TWO
AERFAX

1

I had prepared as well as I could for the moment and the force of my presence appeared to surprise my enemy; the Tower recoiled and the airs around it were open to me. Suddenly the change in the Tower became clear. He had lowered the Rock out of its socket as one does to turn it or polish it. My heart pounded. I broke the storm and let some light fall through, eerie white lances falling out of an unnatural sky. Invoking the dual state, I left the confines of the body for the first time, moving over myself along the road, within and without the Cloak, holding the Bane Locket in the hand of my body and routing all that I did, my insinging, the voices of my magic on the hidden levels, all of it through the gem. Even at his most arrogant, whatever further surprise he had made for me here, he would not relish the thought I had it in my hand. But it gave me the feeling that Ellebren was close by, in a place of my mind that I could reach, and the Cloak was the same, as if a wind of Illyn were blowing around me. I made this to be true so all could feel it, even the Verm who were astonished to have a sudden breeze pour on them out of a spring when all the worlds were young.

My task was to carry us as far as the gates of Aerfax, where Kirith Kirin would be welcomed by the Rock; if I could do it, that would be the end of our journey, and we could end the war. But how could the Rock welcome him now? What was Drudaen using in its place to focus the kirilidur? Finding no opposition from the summit of Senecaur, I ruled the skies and tore open the clouds above us, I sent my voice through his Verm soldiers till their nerves shrieked with terror, and with terror alone I drove them back the way they had come, down the road to Aerfax, retreating. I burned like fire in all four circles of magic that I could fill, and in the visible world I was a maelstrom of darkness and fire, whorls of ebony and starlight. I gave myself to Fimbrel, my whole spirit, lost in magic as one can be, when one is lifted, as when music lifts a singer to sing beyond his ability.

The movement of so much force through the spirit carries with it an inherent exhilaration, and I could hardly contain a feeling of joy. I doubt I could have contained myself in that moment, and I imagine Drudaen had thought of that as well.

The Verm had their orders, they retreated. Kirith Kirin's army, moving with expected discipline and in good order, rounded the shore under clear skies and lightened rain. The Verm withdrew, and withdrew, and finally held.

At the last moment Kirith Kirin sensed a trap and adjusted more of the archers toward the rocks.

Without warning, Verm poured out of the mountain flanks, protected by a hail of arrows, trying to pin us to the road. Our own archers were ready for the charge and the infantry protecting them held against the first charge.

Far ahead, emerging from the gates of Aerfax, a white-cloaked figure cantered toward the Verm, to protect them from me. Another of Drudaen's apprentices? How many more could there be?

Above, suddenly, and not by my hand, the clouds ripped free of Senecaur's summit and the fierce light of the High Place burned over the mountains and the sea.

He had taken the Rock out of conjunction with the Tower. The great Rock that had ruled the Change through all the thirty-four cycles since Senecaur was made. To do this was to shatter the Law, to defy God. Suddenly, with the complete clarity that could only come by his permission, I could see the figure on the High Place, standing in place of the Rock, a living focus for all the energy of the Tower, and could hear the Ildaruen song with which the height was ruled.

The voice reached through me, every fiber of me, and I made some incomprehensible sound. My mother stood where the Rock should have been, straddling the silver horns of the socket, wrapped in a white cloak like all the rest, like the woman who had killed her children. He had glutted her body with his song and her eyes shone like white ice. He had saved her for this, trained her, and Ildaruen flowed from her throat, from her insinging, in waves. He had removed the Eyestone and focused the Tower through her body. Any living thing is as good a focus as a muuren stone, or even a better one, for the magic, but the creature will die after a short while, whereas the stone will last.

Mother must have had a talent for the work, she held all the levels herself but the fourth, which is enough when one is proxy. He controlled her from the fourth circle, his mind divided. Her malice

I could feel, as though she knew who I was and hated me all the more for it, and I felt the hurt race through me. Sybil my mother, alive after so many months of torment, all brought about because of me. She was the tool Drudaen would use to break me.

She was singing to confine me on the road, and I knew how to break the magic she was making, but she was my mother, I could not lift my voice.

The white figure, still riding slowly along the Kleeiom road, was coming across the closer causeway.

That was him, Drudaen Keerfax. He had invented a way to be on the ground and in the air at the same time. Why?

He had disabled the part of the Tower that ruled the Change, he had been about this work for a long time and had hidden it completely, but it had only recently been accomplished and ripples of disturbance flowed outward, beyond the fourth circle; he had taken a great chance. There could only be one reason.

From the road behind raged the battle between our army and his, and in that battle we were holding our ground. But on the road and in the skies we were beaten. Turning Nixva, my mind racing, I calculated the time left me in which to act.

Behind me, distant on the road, the wizard my enemy guessed my thought and summoned speed.

He had come to the ground for one purpose, and his first reaching toward that goal followed, ripping aside my local defenses with help from the High Place, now awake in all its strength. He could not hide his thought from me, and I understood that with the Rock out of focus, the Karnost gems would not protect Kirith Kirin and Drudaen could kill him. Drudaen sought within the ranks of the soldiers and noblefolk for the one who was his true target, and I knew in an instant he had come to do the unthinkable, the last crime left him. He wasted no time and reached, as I had guessed, for Kirith Kirin himself.

I rode through the ranks like a mad thing, searching for the Keikin. I deflected part of Drudaen's thought but my mother in the tower focused the whirling of the kirilidur on me and I was inflamed with an agony that raced through my nerves, unable to channel it elsewhere, racked. But I saw Kirith Kirin now, near the head of the mounted soldiers. When I got close I could see he was feeling the change in himself, and seemed to expect me. He waved his hand to greet me and panic forewarned me; another blow fell then, a wave of that singing in my head, a tearing of nerves, and silence. Dazed, I hardly saw. Summoning other vision, I guided Nixva through the panicked crowd.

With half my mind bent on fending off any further blow from Drudaen, I leapt down from Nixva and shouted a warning they could have heard over a thunderclap. Everyone fell back but Imral, who continued to kneel over Kirith Kirin, a moment of calm in the fighting.

He lay unmoving on the ground. Imral knelt over him, touching his neck. I felt life in him; he was not dead, though a mortal man would have been. The Karnost gems were shadowed, useless, and he would scarcely survive another wave.

The dismay that he had fallen passed through our ranks up and down the line faster than you would believe. Resistance to the Verm wavered, then stiffened with the thought that Kirith Kirin was down. Karsten came up and caught my eye and I signaled he was not dead. Imral only looked up at me when my shadow fell across him. Tears gleamed on his cheeks.

Kirith Kirin lay unmoving. His eyes were open and he was staring blankly ahead. When I touched him I could feel the enchantment at work, the Words that were fighting at this moment with his soul, seeking to tear it loose from this flesh that I loved. But he was fighting too, and would not yield. I knelt and spoke Words in his ear, as rapidly as I could make them, all my power in that, so that when my mother struck me from above again the agony penetrated every nerve, but I would not be stopped, and when Drudaen struck me with his own hand I kept speaking, singing Wyyvisar to join Kirith Kirin's soul tight to the body. I broke the killing chain but he was still away, would not open his eyes.

Karsten was with us. Only moments had passed since I dismounted. They lifted him to his feet and I stood.

For a moment, again, all was agony in my body. Already understanding what was to come, I unclasped the Fimbrel Cloak from my shoulders and, speaking to it, making it into armor to protect him, I wrapped it round his shoulders, a hood to cover his head.

Karsten gazed at me in surprise. I silenced her with a gesture. "Listen to me," I said, "we have seconds. Drudaen is on the ground, riding here to finish what he started. He's disabled the Rock on the High Place. There won't be any Change no matter whether we get to the gate or not."

They gaped at me, dazed. Even their world was changing, even they were astonished. I said, "You have to leave this place now. Go back down Kleeiom, get Kirith Kirin into Arthen as soon as you can. Keep him wrapped in the cloak till he's there." They understood me but were slow to comprehend we would not be going forward, even then.

Karsten grasped me and shook me. "Jessex, how is this happening? If he's on the ground, who's on the High Place?"

"My mother." I was already worlds away, looking into her eyes. "He kept her alive for this." I looked at Imral behind her. "Do what I tell you, we don't have any choice. I can hold Drudaen here for a while. But he's disabled the Rock, there's nothing I can do about that." Taking a ragged breath, feeling the collapse of everything. "Get him back to Arthen. Keep him alive."

Silence. In no more time than that the decision was taken. At the last second before I left them, though, I looked them in the eyes one by one. "Don't leave anyone with me, Karsten, Imral, Evynar, Pelathayn, do you hear? Not a soul. Because as soon as you start to retreat, everything I can reach hereabouts is going to die."

They blanched and nodded, grim as me. "God help you," Karsten said, and kissed my brow. "God keep you safe."

Imral was lifting Kirith Kirin to the Keikin's back.

By the time they turned again I had vanished. He had touched the thing I loved to try to kill it, the one thing in the world that might have cleared my mind at that moment. I had my wits about me now and I meant to make him pay. The last sound I remember that was familiar was Nixva's high-pitched, confused call. No, I thought, you can't help me now.

Ahead of me, along the road, the Verm were parting to let the shadow of their master pass, summoning ithikan to give him speed. I could feel him reaching for Kirith Kirin again, frustrated by the Cloak, through which he could not move his Words.

I turned to face the Verm ranks. Bare-armed on that winter day, I saw the shadow of his body and horse appear, visible only to me, a moving wind.

I held the Bane Gem in my hand. I knew he would stop for that. So I opened my mind to him, for a moment, fully and completely. Taking a breath, I swallowed the locket whole.

2

I broke ithikan around him and killed the horse beneath him, one of the Keikin's sons, and such was Drudaen's speed that the fall he took

knocked him back into his body and hurt him. Now he would pay
for the advantage he had gained: he was on the ground, and the
altered High Place answered to him through an intermediary.

But for the moment he was binding his body together, trying
to heal some of the hurts of the fall, so I could range freely. Slaughter and havoc followed me wherever I went, and I drove deep
into the mountains where the Verm assault turned to putty in so
many moments. Since I meant to lose my life, to burn it up in
magic here and now, I gave everything I had to the work of may-
hem. Verm collapsed in ruptured heaps and their horses fell on
top of them. Drudaen himself, open to me, felt the wracking of
my caress.

The gem I had swallowed settled warm into my belly, and I
began to digest it. A warm feeling spread through me.

From the Tower came my mother's voice again, unnerving, rak-
ing along my bones. In my mind's eye I could see her above the
clouds, the eerie sound of Ildaruen in my ears.

Down the road, in another part of my divided vision, my enemy Drudaen struggled to his knees.

The fall had hurt him badly in his physical body. He was moving slowly. I struck at his bodyguard, struck through his defenses at
him, laying my hand inside him for a moment, singing the first moments of Soul Eater, the song ringing plainly in his ear. He had not
been so close to the killing spell in centuries. Those nearest him fell
dead, but he was too strong for that. He hardly cared who lived or
died around him. He protected himself.

What he did care about was the jewel I had swallowed, the
enchantment presently being worked within my body, to disperse
the gem throughout my tissue, to make it so much part of me he
would never have it without taking my body apart cell by cell.

As for me, I had neither care nor sorrow, only purpose. Calling
fire out of the ground and air, seating myself before the wheel of
fire, I entered full trance and prepared to spend the tatters of my life
defending the road.

From the summit of his High Place, the monster he had made
of my mother struck at me again. I raised neither thought nor song
against her, drinking the blow into my body but continuing my work.
The warm fire of Kentha's locket spread though my flesh like a
drug, the runes and Words I had never known before, now part of
me. For a moment I felt grimly lifted in spirit. With the audacity of
the dying, I began to say Bans and set wards between me and him.

He rose up in his fourth level presence, the hurts of his body forgotten, and we struggled on the ground. I could see him now and then, moving behind a veil of mist, contesting my hold on the road, trying to reach for his High Place and finding it more difficult than it would have been, the link with my mother uneasy. My Bans held against him longer than I had dreamed they would, and it became clear he had not intended to be on the ground for very long. Now he could not return to the High Place himself for fear I would escape.

My mother moved power against me again, her voice filling me with loathing, the image of her face like a pallid flame. I felt her hand each time it passed through me but I would not defend myself against her. This cost me strength, in the end. Feeling what she had become, what had happened to her, I knew that in fact she had died a long time ago, that this was a shell, nothing more. He was reaching through her, he had found his way again, and his voice filled her, a malice that was nothing like her. She struck me this time with his force, and I fell, hurt, deeply, but at the same time in that instant of light I saw a thing I had never seen. Or rather, had glimpsed before, when I shook Yruminast.

A place between all the other places, a moment in which even the fourth circle fell away and I could see beyond.

Without warning, at the height of the storm, a horn sounded from the high walls of Aerfax. With a booming of drums and more soundings from the horn, the sea gates opened and blue bannered ships emerged.

The sight of them gladdened me, I don't know why. Even if I had not felt that instinct, Drudaen's reaction to the sudden appearance of the flotilla let me know that it must be some kind of good fortune for Kirith Kirin. Drudaen reached for lightning, for storm, for wind and water to tear the ships apart. I countered him. He reached again with no more success; without his High Place he was just another magician on the ground, and my mother was lost in the Tower magic. I saw all this clearly, as if his mind were open to me in some way it had never been before. He felt me there and panicked.

She struck me again and when she exerted herself he found her and added his strength to hers. I was down again, shaken, out of my body, and they struck me further, reaching for the place to begin to feed on me, to eat me out of myself, and in that moment I saw a place to go, between all the rest, that he could not reach.

Heaviness filled me and I knew the end of all my struggles. I saw the place and knew, now, what to do, but I had to wait for the ships to clear. I had to close the sea gates of Aerfax with a swirling wind that stirred the bay, had to shake the ground, to send a messenger to let the ones in the upper part of the house know to move down, to warn them what was coming. I sent my eidolon to Sylvis the lover of Athryn; I spoke to her across all that space, my ghost in her ear. "Get down to the bottom of the house, I'm going to destroy the Tower."

My enemy struck me again, the voice of my mother filled with his voice, and I hurt everywhere, I fell so far. All the way to the road that time, all the way to my hands and knees, in my body again. But I waited till I knew the ones in Aerfax had gotten my warning, till I saw in my eye above that the royal rooms were being emptied in a rush. The Tower struck me again and I felt my soul loosed a bit, unstrung, and could wait no longer.

Forgive me, I said. For now I had no need to be struck with pain to see into the deepest place as if with the eyes of my body: in that tiniest space of the mind I pictured the Rock of Senecaur as if it were where it should be, and I reached inside it with the hand of my body and I felt its anger, saw that inmost and smallest place inside it, and reached there and caused something to slip. Made a fire in the deepest place. I only saw it for a moment. Then I went into that place myself, to rest.

The last thing I remember, after I made the place in the rock slip, was that a white light burst out and Senecaur blew apart, and at that moment the warmth of Kentha's gem spread all through my body, my enchantment complete. I protected my body from the blast by singing a shell around the Tower in that smallest space of the mind, to contain the worst of the blast in the real world; and I knew for an instant that this was not like any magic I had ever made before. I sank into sleep, more deep and peaceful than any I had known.

In the real world, in a blast that broke the spur of the mountain, Senecaur flashed a pure white fire at the top. The tower cracked and the rock spur on which it had stood broke apart and fell into the sea, and fire rained for hours from the sky.

CHAPTER TWENTY-THREE
SENECAUR

1

I could hear the sea. Wind blew across me, and my nose was cold.

I was holding someone at arm's length, keeping him away. I had been doing that through my sleep.

I was in a room. A lot of disorder, then peace. People were fighting over me, as if I were on the ground, and then I was here.

A woman was with me. Sometimes she smoothed my brow, lay a cool cloth on me. A gentle touch. Sometimes the fingertips smoothed water over me, or sometimes clear cumbre, massaging my skin.

At other times I stood on Ellebren, or Laeredon. I felt as if I were a ghost in those places, hardly visible, but I was there. I dreamed too that I waited on Sister Mountain and two moons were full. Blood red and gleaming ivory globes hung at angles in the sky.

Memories returned to me, a fight, a shuddering of the ground. I batted them away, I preferred to listen. I could hear the sea, and I lay on stone. I slept for a long time. Intermittently I endured the touch of hands. This was my life. How long that period went on, I do not know.

One day I opened my eyes. I saw, after a long time, the stones of the ceiling.

My stone bed lay under the shallower part of a vault. I had been moved, maybe that was why I opened my eyes. Air circulated, but not from any windows. The sound of the sea came from above my head.

Even with my eyes open, sometimes I saw and sometimes I did not. Real time eluded me, a river rushing by too fast; I was afraid to step in. Sometimes a woman came into the vault where I was. Sometimes another woman came. I knew them both but I had never met them. Each woman would strip back the blankets that covered my nakedness, touch the bracelet at my wrist, pour water on her fingertips and massage it into my skin. The smallest amount of moisture conceivable. Now and then, cumbre. This is what one does to maintain the body of one who lies in ensorcelled sleep.

Sometimes the women spoke to me. They were never present
at the same time, but their voices became the same sound. "I don't
know if you can hear me," they would say, "but I'll tell you anyway.
Our ships reached the army and ferried them from Kleeiom to
Charnos. Kirith Kirin was on the first ship."

Dream time wove in and out. Sometimes I thought she was
with me but she was not speaking. This was always one of the
women but not the other. The one who would watch me sadly, as
if she had seen my face before.

"I tried to care for your mother," she said, "I tried to save her
but I was very weak."

This made me uneasy in the rest I had sought and so I would
turn away from the voice, but still it would go on, as though she
meant to draw me back. But I would not come back.

"Now there are only five hundred of us left. We're sealing up
the rest of the house. He knows where I've brought you now, little
magician. But there's nothing he can do about it, apparently. You
won't let him come close. And yet you're fast asleep."

I knew she meant Drudaen Keerfax and I understood, even in
my sleep, that he was searching for me everywhere, on all the levels
of magic. Somewhere far away, as if in the memory of some
country I had once visited, I could hear his voice. I understood also
that some part of me was protecting the people near me, in rooms
of stone. But none of this understanding meant much. I was asleep,
far away, nearly dreaming.

They came to visit me again and again, and in that way I understood much time was passing. Now the one who came and sometimes said nothing wore a veil over her face, as if she were ashamed.
But she was more apt to speak by the end, in a dry, despairing tone,
as if certain I heard nothing.

*I'll never know if you've heard me, if you know anything of what's
happened. You broke Senecaur and nearly killed him and we brought you into
what was left of Aerfax, and you have kept us safe from him all these years.
But all the rest of the world is his now. Except Arthen.*

Fragments, pieces from different times. *There are four hundred
of us left. His army is still camped outside. It does some good having you here,
I guess, since he wants you so badly... There are three hundred left now. He's
spread shadow as far north as Vyddn. He's burned Genfynnel to the ground
and torn the walls to shreds, but he can't get close to your Tower. I see
Edenna's ring glimmering on your finger in the darkness. You're fighting
somehow, aren't you? We don't know how... There are only two hundred now.*

He's bringing another army here across the bay. He's never been able to break through the end of Kleeiom, he can only come here by ship... We're sealing up the house now, we're lighting the lamps.

I remember little of it, when all's said and done. But I could feel the change in the world, like the touch of storm in the distance. Shadow was everywhere. We had lost.

The women came in together, that was how I knew it was the last visit. The oldest of them, and she was very old, told me, "There are a dozen of us left. A long time has passed. Shadow has taken hold everywhere, our people are changing, our enemy has won, if he calls a dead world a victory. I've stayed as long as I can but now I have to get back to Arthen." She spoke to me as if she had no faith that I could hear. "It will take a long time for him to find you here, even when we've gone. Stay alive and we'll come back for you."

"It's time to go, my dear," the other woman said.

"I know." She bent over me, speaking into my open eyes. "I know you're there somewhere, my silent one. You'll only have to protect yourself, now. Find your way back to us if you can. I'll tell Kirith Kirin you were alive when I left you. That's all I can do."

Then, emptiness, the ringing of the chamber, the closing of some heavy door, and the echo of waves crashing against the rock of Durudronaen.

2

Silence. I lay in darkness, far from the room and from my body, in a place where no one came. Now and then water dripped on me from the rock.

Stillness. The sleep, which Queen Athryn had troubled with her presence, deepened again.

Sometimes I heard the sea. Sometimes I heard soft singing. Mostly I heard nothing at all.

From outside, from all the places I knew to be outside, came the smell of rot and shade.

3

At first Drudaen came to me only in that realm, the non-place in which I floated. He could not see me but he knew where I must be.

He wore the porcelain face of his ancestors and he spoke my name gently, as a cousin.

I can let you out of the room, I can set you free from sleep. You could return to your body if you would serve me. He spoke in no voice, only the ribbon of thought trailing through me, and the aura of his kind benevolence. *I could always make use of someone who speaks Wyyvisar as well as you do.*

But in the depth of my sleep he brought no trouble to me. I dreamed him, as I had dreamed everything, all of time. I could see the whole curve of him from beginning to end. What he offered me, the motion of the body, was nothing.

He crooned on as if I were listening, but the sea washed over his voice, the sea engulfed him and I listened to its pulse.

When he returned the next time, his voice was harsher, and I had the feeling he was nearby. For some reason, even in the deep folds of my somnolence, this thought troubled me. He spoke again, and I could almost hear the sound. *I can let you out of the room, I can set you free from sleep. I can give you this gift willingly or I can wrench it from you by force. The choice is yours. Open and let me enter.*

In my languor a wave of trouble began to resonate. I clutched at tatters of sleep but they fled.

I can let you out of the room, willing or no; and this seemed the uttermost cruelty to me, who had wanted nothing more than to lie here, who had conceded the whole world for this peace.

He began some song then, a thin sound of ungainly Words which I had heard before. The song troubled me some and so I sang a tune to drown it out.

This went on for a while. He would change his song and so would I, when it started to trouble me. Soon this became automatic and I spared it little thought. Sleep deepened some, in spite of the nettling noise of him, who refused to go away.

I had something he wanted. I remembered it but the thought left me indifferent. He went on singing and disturbing me and now and then I wondered why it was he thought he could offer me anything. After a time I wondered who he was altogether. I had this knowledge somewhere but I could hardly be troubled to recall it. His insistence surprised me, for it seemed to me, now that I had time to think about it, that a person was really better off without wanting things very much; and here was this voice insisting on something. Insisting that I cooperate. In some work. Some scheme of his. Which involved my waking.

He tried to find me forcibly. As if he stood battering at a door. Only the sound of the door kept blending with the sea. This was really too much, I thought, for him to go on like this; the songs were bad enough but now this bullying. Still, one did not have to wake up, not entirely, not to deal with such a small problem.

I knit up my sleep again and pulled it close. I drank its warmth and nestled into it. He was close to me and tried to harm me again but his touch hardly reached me. I understood, without much caring, that I had traveled very far from him, very far from all he wanted. His thirst seemed paltry to me, when compared with my own perfect and beautiful indifference.

It seemed to me this only took a little time. How time ran for him, I could hardly say. But finally, one day, I found myself drawn away from my kingdom of silence and rest to the room again, the chamber beneath the sea. Torches had been lit and shadows danced. My body lay motionless on the slab of stone. Drudacn Keerfax was there with me.

4

He had been in the room for a long time. The effort to travel here had told on him, and now he was afraid to come closer. He harbored a fear of the place, something terrible had happened to him in the vicinity. I realized, with a slow start, that the terror was connected with me.

No one had come with him. Wrapped in a drab cloak, hooded, he wore the weariness of the lone traveler, and I wondered at this since it hardly seemed his style. In the center of that room he stood, smelling of wind and horses. Aging. He was aging.

On the slab of stone I lay. On my body I wore only an earring, a ring and a bracelet, and each of those pieces of jewelry made him wary. Light clung to my skin, which was fair and soft. I had never thought of myself as beautiful but there, from the awful distance at which I watched myself, I saw differently. Dark curves framed my fine-boned, ivory face, the full cut of lip, the flare of graceful nostril, the heavy-lashed lid. It was finally this image that held him, this enchanted youth in deepest sleep.

What had he come to do? Even in his own mind his purpose remained unclear. He had come to kill me but now that he was close he couldn't. He had come because he heard a rumor I was alive, and as long as I lived he still had something to fear. I read that thought easily. He had come a long way, and found me sleeping more deeply than his magic could reach. He also found he could not approach me with a single thought of harm in his head.

Murmuring. Beneath his breath he muttered the Words that presently guarded him. They were easy to hear and comprehend; I was surprised he considered himself defended when I could read his every thought so plainly. He moved toward me slowly—toward my body on the stone. Of me, of my disembodied presence, he had no inkling.

No malice in him. He had forgotten the thought that brought him here. He pulled back the hood and I saw how old he had become, this enemy of mine. But one could see, looking from the elder to the younger, that we shared blood. This was part of what troubled him: it was as if in seeing me he were seeing himself as a boy in the dawn of the world.

He did the strangest thing. Using the water from his flask, with the tips of his fingers he pressed the slight moisture into my cool, nearly lifeless flesh. The touch returned me, aching, to the shadow of life: I felt it even at a distance: I could not escape that much. The memory of other hands.

He performed this work and stood silently beside me. I had needed the moisture, I was far away. But he was murmuring still, ignoring my gratitude, as if the proximity of my flesh placed him in the gravest danger. Without malice he watched me. He bent to kiss my brow, and the touch of his lips on my cool skin resounded.

What a curious enemy, so tender! Some sound from far above alarmed him, and he moved away. Stones tumbling, stones falling to the ground. He had brought an army of workmen to pull down what was left of Aerfax stone by stone. He returned to the center of the chamber and stood murmuring.

He meant to bury me. He could not harm me with his hands or even with his magic, so great was his fear of what I had become. But he had thought of another way. He had come to build a tomb over me.

A sound distracted him, and finally fear took him over. At the exit he hesitated, turning to my body on the stone a last time. Babbling that nonsense that I could have taken from him with the merest touch. So I did touch him, once, in the lightest way, through the layers of his protection; I lay my fingers on the beating of his heart and said into his ear *See? I'm still here, Drudaen. Go and don't come back.*

Such was my delicacy that he almost thought he had imagined the moment. He closed the door and locked it carefully, from the outside, as if that gesture were important.

Patient, I waited, in the same room with my body if not actually inside the flesh. Presently one heard the thunder of his voice and the shaking of those ancient stones. There are stories people sailed in pleasure boats from Ivyssa to watch. Favorites of his. He pulled down the wreck of Aerfax and what remained of Senecaur. Places more ancient and holy than can be recounted, leveled stone by stone. He shook the ground, hoping to crack the foundations of Senecaur, where I slept. But he had warned me of his intentions with his ill-considered visit, when he came to kill me and found he could not keep the thought in his head. My chamber survived.

Soon he left the place; he had come to hate it anyway. Silence, and the sea again. But my sleep had been too thoroughly troubled. I began to dream of the world.

5

One day I began to sing.

I dreamed I lay over my body on the stone and sang, at first with no voice, but an ancient song, the Wyyvisar song of making, and I was suddenly in Jiiviisn Field in the sunlight and this was Vithilonyi; I danced and sang and felt the brightness of the field. True dawn resounded through my bones, and I, aching for light, basked in plenty. I sang the song and the sun rose over the horizon.

Into the field the Sisters rode, richly dressed, on fine horses; but they failed to see me, at first. It frightened me, that I could come so close to them and yet be invisible. When had I got to be made of such thin stuff?

But when I joined the song, Commyna heard me.

She stood bolt upright in the middle of the song and searched the field. I was there in front of her and she could not see. But she heard.

So did Vella and Vissyn, when she signed them. All this, and they never faltered a single note in the song; nor did I. I stood in front of them and sang, and they could hardly find me, I stood so close to death. I wept and stood in front of them and sang. Finally they found me, they watched me, and they were weeping too.

That dream ended too soon. But they saw me. They knew I was alive.

6

One day, maybe even the same one, I dreamed I stood on Ellebren High Place, and the Rock of Ellebren burned beneath my hand. Out of the Rock I called fire, and light, and many colors burned over Arthen. I had heard someone calling for me. A voice too painful to recognize. So I stood on the High Place, as much of me as I could muster, and the Rock answered me, flashed fire and burned. Once I wakened the Tower, I remembered more and more. Over the Eyestone I sat, warming my hands as if at a fire. Once I had sat there with a man, fair and clean; once I had sat there with Kirith Kirin…

That dream, once begun, never ended.

7

Voices. Or was there a torch first?

One is at the end of a long wait. The dream of a summer day. A hand has been rattling the door but it could be the wind, or rocks settling. One has been sleeping for a long time and many noises have become familiar. The careful dream of dawn on a seacoast. The fragile coloring of dawn under shadow, the ghostly glimmering of water. And a hand, rattling the cage door, the chamber door, the prison cell battered by the ocean.

The realization came to me, along with a feeling of leaden weight. This was a real noise. Someone was rattling the door. And me, I was hearing the noise. I was in the body again, and I was hearing.

A torch. The glimmering of shadow beneath the door. Haunted voices. Suddenly the ache of the body rose and warmth, real warmth, rushed into the spaces between the molecules and cells. Someone was battering the door. I am at the end of a long wait.

Torchlight slanting. The heavy door eased inward. I counted the breaths and footsteps. "Jessex," said the voice, and I knew it. Torchlight on my face. "Oh god," he said, and set the torch in a bracket over the stone where I lay.

He fell across me. The welcome weight of him sighed against my ribs. When I had seen him last he had been nearly dead. For all that time I had hardly dared endure the thought of him. Now here he was, and his hands caressed my face. I knew him by his whole being. The sleep ended. He kissed me, and I was awake.

CHAPTER TWENTY-FOUR

IVYSSA

1

We faced each other in torchlight. Even after such a long time, his face seemed a familiar and comfortable object.

Presently he asked, "Can you move? Can you walk?"

"I don't know. How long have I been here?"

He shook his head, looking to the doorway. He said, still in the soft voice, "I brought some friends."

"Who?"

Smiling, but signaling me to speak more quietly. "Not so loud. You're rather heavily guarded."

"Am I?"

He pointed upward. I had no idea how far upward he meant.

He had brought leggings and a tunic, boots in my size and good cotton underclothing. Everything felt strange on my body, and it was only when I started dressing that I realized I had been naked on the stone, except for the Laeredon ring, the bracelet he had given me, and the earring I had put on in Ellebren, before riding away to fight for Laeredon Tower. My body hardly responded to commands; he helped me to save time. He kept checking the door. Presently a slim shadow slipped through the arch and I recognized Karsten by the highlights of her hair.

Kirith Kirin said, "He's awake. He's fine."

She froze at his words. I could not see her face but I could sense her agitation. Rushing to the stone where I had lain, she touched me as if I were fine glass.

We were soon in tears. I began to understand, from the desperation of her reaction, that we had been apart a very long time. But I declined to ask again. They finished dressing me, Karsten lacing my shin-high boots when it became clear my numbed fingers could not do the trick.

I'd no memory of the corridor outside, nor of any passage to this room at all. Outside the cell lay a guardroom full of cobwebs, stairs leading upward. We bypassed these, however, and slipped down a narrow passageway which led to a small armory. When I could not move quickly enough, Kirith Kirin carried me.

A concealed doorway sprang open and we entered another narrow corridor. Karsten concealed the entrance and we moved quickly through this tunnel and into others. More distinctly sounded rushing waves against rocks over our heads.

Up a spiral stairway we climbed, Karsten ahead of us. Soon I could see daylight; it hurt my eyes and I closed them. But I smelled fresh air and heard Imral's voice. I said his name when I saw him. He lay the flat of his hand on my face.

A boat awaited us, slim and sleek, with a sail of transparent viis. Even I could tell we had emerged into the full of Aeryn winter. Cold wind bit through the layers of blanket; the sky lowered like slate. The motion of the boat disoriented me some; I had never ridden in a boat before, and I remember the thought striking me as funny. Wind filled the sail and Karsten guided us with the tiller. The west wind carried us away from the Spur, into mist.

When I looked back, what I saw shocked me. The Tower was gone, the rock spur sheered off. A pile of stones where Aerfax had stood, her only remains the sea gates that had opened, that opened now, in my memory of that long ago.

Over us, tattered and brown, the stuff of shadow. I could already feel him, Drudaen, everywhere.

Kirith Kirin told me to lie down, I was too wobbly to be standing in the boat, so I did. The smell of fish permeated even the planks of the deck, and the sharp sting of salt spray stung my nose as waves crashed against the prow. When I got tired of lying down, I huddled near the tiller wrapped in a plain brown cloak. The walk to the boat had exhausted me and I sagged to the deck, watching the swing of the sail. The others were moving grimly, silently.

We passed a dark, rocky island on the top of which stood old fortifications. That was Kmur Island, where the treasury was, or had been, and the ruins were Dernhang, a mortal palace, never meant to last forever. But the Queen had been living at Dernhang when we headed south. Now the place had fallen down, or been burned, maybe, judging from the look of it. How long ago? Suddenly I was afraid to ask.

The rocking of the boat and my body's confusion combined to make me sick to my stomach, and I lay along the deck, half soaked with spray. By then I was started to feel feverish on top of the sickness and would have thrown up but I had eaten nothing, so I heaved instead, and felt perfectly miserable.

We were a long time in the water, all day and night. They took turns sitting with me, afraid to leave me alone. We hardly talked. Fever came on me full blown, to be expected after so long a trance as had befallen me. I felt hot and sick through the night, drowsing, with the sound of their voices for company. At some point we had stopped sailing and were lying adrift.

Near dawn we began to sail again, and I saw the shape of a city emerging out of the mists on the shore.

We slipped into harbor through the commercial traffic and fishing boats. Karsten obtained us moorage from the harbormaster, as if we were local traffic, her papers in order. We were sailing into Ivyssa. All the coasts were guarded, Kirith Kirin whispered, but in Ivyssa the whole city moves on water, and one more boat would hardly be noticed.

We left the boat docked on one of the inland canals and never saw it again. We dressed in rags from the bottom of the boat, stuff I had been lying on, and we began to move through narrow streets and along dark canals and waterways. I was hot with fever and followed only part of what was happening, but the city was brown, the light thin, hardly a spot of green growing anywhere, and the people we passed seemed misshapen or discolored or sick or worse. Streets twisted, rose and fell, we crossed a canal and vanished into side streets. People were looking at us because we did not look like any of the rest of them. I put one foot in front of another, the best I could do.

Near an open-air market we waited, bits of smelly rag wrapped round our heads. Imral and Kirith Kirin had gone away. Karsten wandered with me among the wretched shoppers who crowded the place, people who had been sick a long time, who had rarely had enough to eat, people who were wounded, hurt, hardly anyone like us, whole of body. People who looked like Verm. Karsten bought a ladle of hot broth, thin stuff floating in it, and I drank that gratefully from her cup, hoping my stomach would not rebel. The merchant, who had two noses, or a nose that had divided down the middle, was glad to see a real coin, he said, and thanked her.

From the market I could see, in the distance, two high Towers soaring toward the dark undersides of clouds, one about half the height of the other. Lights flickered on one of the summits. Karsten saw me watching, drew me away. Thoem and Karomast, High Places that had stood over the Old City center for millennia. But someone had torn down Karomast, or tried.

Kirith Kirin and Imral returned with horses bought or stolen, sad wrecks of animals, wanting proper food and decent treatment. We mounted the poor animals without discussion and set off again through the streets. Overhead, now and then, I glimpsed the two slender Towers. I made no effort to reach to them in any way, but when I was looking at them, I could see the whole city as if it were beneath me, as though I were on the summit; Ivyssa had been a thriving city but now people lived only at her old center, and boats moved there as they used to, but at the fringes of the city the waterways were clogged, the bridges collapsed, the houses fallen into the rivers or canals. A city fallen to ruin at the edges. A city of a few thousand.

But even when I was out of sight of the Towers, what I saw with my own eyes told the same story. Most of Old Ivyssa and nearly all the new city was wrecked and empty. Moving through the streets were armed parties of Verm and other creatures like them, hard to recognize as human. We had wrapped our heads as best we could and sat slumped on those sorry horses, but once or twice someone in the column gave us a second look as we passed.

We reached a part of the city where hardly a soul stirred except the Verm soldiers and us, and came to a place where scarcely anyone was on the streets or waterways. We were traveling through the part of the city I had seen through the towers, a wilderness of ruins where no one lived any more. We were walking through a battlefield after the battle, an eerie wind moaning among the collapsed walls. The stones of the streets were scorched black in places as if parts of the city had burned, as if there had really been fighting here.

We found a place to sleep in one of the wrecked houses, away from the trafficked streets, and I judged by the direct heading we steered that the place had been chosen in advance. Almost as soon as we got inside I collapsed, shaking with sickness, and Kirith Kirin built a fire while Imral went after water that was fit to drink. We had to boil it, but when it was boiled and poured through a cloth it was fairly clear, and Kirith Kirin dropped a pouch into a cup of the water and gave it to me. "Unufru, for the fever."

I knew that was the right thing. He sat with me while the tea steeped. I drank it and leaned against him. He was real, his body was there, and his face, when I looked at him, seemed the same. Maybe a year or two older. But we had been apart longer than that.

I shivered until I got the tea down, my body worked with the unufru and the fever started to ease. The others were quietly getting food together, watching me, watching Kirith Kirin, who had yet to stir from my side since we got indoors.

"I've been away a long time," I said.

Imral laughed. "Away. That's one way to put it."

"We thought you were dead," Karsten said. "For years."

Kirith Kirin was not saying anything. He had an arm loosely around me and drew it tight.

"Tell me what happened."

"It was a long time ago." Imral shook his head.

"Oh, I remember it well enough," Karsten said.

We looked at each other, the four of us, and suddenly it was that day again, in front of Aerfax when we were almost at the gate, and I had found Kirith Kirin slumped beside his horse with his death working its way through him, and I stopped the killing chain of Words and put my cloak on him to keep him safe. I was there again, the memory too vivid to be distant, with Karsten wishing God to keep me safe and the high wind blowing, as if it were yesterday, or even more vivid than that, as if the whole scene were right outside the door of that ruined merchant's house.

So the story was told, and I will not attempt to narrate how we got through it. Each one told his part. They and the army had begun their retreat, Kirith Kirin burning up with a fever like the one that was now easing off in me. Karsten had stayed at the back of the column while the retreat began; she wanted to watch what was happening at Aerfax, and she saw the flash of darkness that poured out of me toward a vague point in the road that became, after a clap of fire and thunder, Drudaen and his horse, moving at incredible speed. I remembered that he was riding in the ithikan and I broke the wave of it under him. He fell into the real world at that speed and killed his horse, a royal one. That was the last she saw of me, the Verm were attacking from the mountains along the column. At first the Verm were charging in a flood and she wondered how our army would make it to the first bend of the road, but then a wave of gray passed across the mountains and the Verm there died, some of them fused to the rock; after that the retreat became orderly. But the fireworks continued at their backs, she stayed at the rear of the column the whole march, to watch.

She heard the trumpets when the Aerfax sea-gates opened and Athryn's ships came out. These were good boats with fleets of oars and trained rowers, but their sails were useless in the storm and they were afraid to come aground for a long time. They followed the army along the coast and then one of them beached and Imral took Kirith Kirin aboard it and the boat headed south as fast as it could go, toward Charnos. When the storm did calm some the rest of the boats put ashore down the road. About the time the last of the boats was pulling ashore, to the south they saw the dark sky suddenly white as noon, a fire and a blast they felt as far away as the stormy beach on which those poor boats were struggling. There was a murmur of despair from everyone and Karsten remembered that she said a prayer for me then. She guessed what had happened, that somehow the Tower had blown apart in the fighting.

Complete confusion ensued for a few days. The boats put to sea with a thousand troops in them, headed for Charnos. Karsten and Evynar marched the remaining army, about five thousand, to Teryaehn-in-Don. There they found an army of Verm encamped on the road north of the town, safely beyond the limit of my killing lattice, unable to come any farther south. The Verm had found that out at the cost of some lives, and had settled down to wait.

Karsten waited too. Pretty soon Ren Vael and Pelathayn brought the ships back, with supplies for Teryaehn. The boats took away another thousand of the army. Seeing this, the Verm were getting restive. Since the rumor had me dead, they wondered if my magic was still working, and tried to march down the road into Kleeiom again. A number of them died before they realized the killing enchantments were still functioning.

So Karsten sat in Teryaehn anxious that at any moment Drudaen would appear on the road. She left the town with the last of the soldiers. To the final moment, she said, she kept dreaming she would see me, somehow, coming out of the Don to join them. On Nixva, she said, though Nixva had gone on the earlier ships. But the story in Teryaehn was that Senecaur had blown off half the Spur and wrecked Aerfax, and that I had died in the blast.

She was glad to set sail for Charnos. But by then, shadow had taken hold over all the lands around the bay, and was spreading north. That meant Drudaen was alive. She knew that much.

By the time she got to Charnos, Kirith Kirin had been taken north by a group of picked riders on royal horses headed for Arthen. Imral was with them. The burghers of Charnos told her the prince —the King, they called him—had arrived breathing but not conscious. They got him mounted on Keikindavii and the party set out.

Karsten stayed in the city long enough to organize the army's northern march, and she managed to hold the whole force together

long enough to reach Arsk before the Queen's people broke away
and headed for their homes. She tried to tell them what was coming, she said. But as far as they were concerned, the war was over.
Her words proved true too quickly. As the Queen's officers led the
garrisons back to their old forts, their old postings, shadow followed them, and this time, when it fell on a place, it remained. She
had promised them they could find safety in Arthen, and the burghers
and the people of Charnos heard the same message from her, that
they could all come north to Arthen, she would guarantee their passage. To escape what was to come.

The Jisraegen soldiers who had been with her through it all, the
Venladrii loyal to Evynar, held together in a force of three thousand
and marched north along the river, collecting our garrisons from all
the places that had been secured for our march south.

The army quartered in Genfynnel, she said. But she had an odd
feeling about the place, because of Laeredon. The tower lights
were blazing, as if there were a great struggle going on. The people
in the city said the lights had been idle for a while now, till the army
arrived. She got suspicious, massed the troops and ordered a night
march out of the city, double time north toward Arthen, and she
recommended the city lord evacuate the rest of Genfynnel as well.

Her instincts were right. By morning Drudaen had come in person to the city, in pursuit of the army, it was thought, but he went to
Telkyii Tars and stayed. He did no violence at first, he was working at
the base of Laeredon, trying to get in, according to people from
Genfynnel who fled to Arthen a few days later. He had artisans working with him, and some of them died trying to open the base. By then
the Tower was making the most awful sounds, and the lights were so
bright that even noon was a misery, and when his magic could not
open the place, Drudaen went into a rage and rained fire on the city,
rode through the streets and broke down the houses, and brought
shadow north as far as he was standing. He called for an army to
come and waited for it, and the Verm leveled the place, burned it to
the ground, all but the Tower, which he could not touch.

They had heard this news in Inniscaudra, which the army reached
safely before the end of Yama. Imral and Mordwen Illythin tended
Kirith Kirin through those weeks, and once he was in the woodland
again, he began to return to awareness, to blink his eyes, to see the
world. At first he could hardly hold a conversation, he would ask
them if they knew how much time was passing, that was all. But
after a long time, he came to himself again.

"They told me what happened," Kirith Kirin said. "They told me where I was and how I got there. They told me they thought you were dead."

He went on when he was ready. No one spoke in the silence.

Shadow came farther north, as far south as Maugritaxa and Montajhena. In Inniscaudra, they settled down to wait.

A year passed, two. Amri the kyyvi continued to dream I was sleeping in a room and could hear the sea; she would have that dream long after she stopped serving in the shrine, until she wandered into the Arth Hills one day and was never seen again. From Arthen spies went out and risked their lives to learn what was happening under shadow, to learn the truth of what had happened at Aerfax after the army retreated. No one knew who had caused Senecaur to rupture and blow half the mountain into the sea, was it Drudaen, or was it me? No one knew whether anyone else had survived, other than Drudaen, including Athryn and her court. There were rumors of every description and no news, the whole south was in chaos, with the generals struggling to control the eastern half of the country and Drudaen sitting in Cunevadrim trying to repair himself and his High Place. When the spies came back, some of them after two years traveling, Kirith Kirin began to get a picture of the new south.

"What we found out gave us little reason to hope," he said, quietly. "We knew that, whatever happened in front of Aerfax that day, Senecaur had blown to bits and half the Spur with it. My best people got as close to the place as they could get, past his patrols in Kleeiom, and that was what they saw. Whether any of Aerfax survived, whether you survived, whether Athryn was still alive, none of us could find that out, because Drudaen had the place under guard by land and sea. But the fact that he kept the place guarded made us suspicious."

In the third year after the Battle of Aerfax, as people had begun to name it, Drudaen moved.

Verm armies marched across the south and took control of the baronies the queen's generals had set up in the absence of any other government. The Verm occupied Kmur Island and confiscated the treasury. A Verm garrison and administrators took over Ivyssa, and all commerce went through their hands. Charnos closed the Tervan gates and brought in her ships. She had stockpiles of food that would last a long time, and now and then sent out an armada to Novris to buy supplies and trade goods that the western city, also besieged by Drudaen, needed desperately. The two cities were able to hold out for a long time that way, supporting each other, but once he had the treasury he could build a fleet of his own, and he did. After that it was only a matter of time. First Novris fell to Drudaen, and then Charnos was blockaded and starved into submission and opened her gates again.

"How long did they hold out?" I asked.

"About twenty years, in the case of Charnos," Kirith Kirin answered.

I was not looking at his face. I could feel his uneasiness. That same uneasiness was opening up in me. "Go on," I said.

All that time shadow held fast, and under it the world slowly changed. As had happened in Turis, long ago, many people died outright. Of those who survived, babies who were born under shadow were twisted, grew crooked, and their parents grew crooked too, under the thin light of the new world. Everything changed. Crops grew wrong or did not grow and there was no longer enough food to send to market, and people in the cities had less and less to eat, and then nothing, and then they started going to the country to take land so they could try to raise some food and eat again. The cities emptied and people died in the countryside, murdered for land or trying to get land or simply murdered or dead of starvation.

But the strangest thing. Through the whole siege of Charnos, with all his resources turned to conquering the city, he spared the numbers to maintain a constant guard on Kleeiom and met the expense of a fleet to patrol the seas around Aerfax.

We set out to learn why, Karsten said. Imral and I went south.

They were away from Arthen for two years, and they got as far south as Novris in one direction before heading across country to the Narvos Hills, where we had marched so many years before. They followed the old road and headed south through the fens of Karns again.

No one had ever broken through my killing lattice there, north of Teryaehn Don. But Imral and Karsten landed south of the lattice and entered the don without hindrance. They wandered through the ruins of Teryaehn, flattened by order of Drudaen as soon as he regrouped after his losses at the Battle of Aerfax. Imral and Karsten moved west into Shurhala. They knew the land there as well as anyone who was patrolling it, and so were able to move farther and farther south. Close to the Spur, they tried some of the tunnels that led into the lower parts of Aerfax, but found these broken, maybe in the same explosion that shook the Spur to pieces.

So they left the tunnels and made their way along a high trail to the end of the peninsula.

They got closer than the earlier expeditions and saw that part of Aerfax had survived, the lower quarters, which were the original Tervan building, and not the upper ones, the royal part, which had tumbled into the sea when that part of the Spur broke off. So they guessed Athryn and all her folk were dead. But they watched for a while and saw that there were in fact people manning the walls of the lower house, enough in Aerfax to keep invaders at bay. So Karsten and Imral stayed and watched. Twice while they were there, a ship flying the Queen's colors raced across the bay, chased by one of Drudaen's patrols, and trumpeted to have the sea gates opened.

But if the walls of Aerfax were strong enough to keep out an army, what was strong enough to protect the survivors from Drudaen?

If ships were flying Athryn's colors, she was alive. Someone was sending or bringing supplies to her by ship. She would have loyalists in Ivyssa who could undertake work like that, and loyalists on Kmur. So they went to Ivyssa, and after some checking Imral learned that Sylvis Mnemorel herself was directing the work, moving from house to house in Ivyssa, traveling by boat at night, keeping away from people who were loyal to Drudaen now, who would have been glad for the privilege of turning her over to him.

As they described meeting with this woman whom I had never met, or at least, never met when I was conscious, it was as if I had gone into that abandoned mansion along the First Canal of Old Ivyssa with them, as if I had seen her there. She could have ridden north into Arthen at any time these last centuries, but instead had stayed in the south to oppose Drudaen to his face through most of that time, risking what life she had left. Karsten and Imral had loved her and missed her for many years, and she them, and so their meeting was joyous and full of heartache at the same time. The three had a conversation much like ours in which they shared all that had happened since they were last together. From her they learned that I was still alive, that I had been in Athryn's care since she fought to bring my body in from the Kleeiom road, and that I was the force that held Drudaen at bay there.

They were stunned, beyond belief, overjoyed again. She told them what had happened when the army left me there to hold the road, that I had done so, and that I had been beaten down again and again as they watched, she and Athryn, from the highest balcony of the royal rooms. She told them that every time I fell, the ground would shake for a while and I would get up again, and that I was driving Drudaen back toward the gates. By then Athryn had already sent out her fleet to rescue Kirith Kirin from the Kleeiom road. She had been standing at the base of Senecaur when Drudaen rode out, she had felt the blow dealt to Kirith Kirin, it had pierced her as well. She knew something dreadful would follow. Aerfax is a holy place, and what had happened, that a magician should remove the Rock in order to attack the Successor, was a matter of blasphemy beyond recount. She could feel the anger in the Rock, in the house. So when she got my warning that I was going to break Senecaur, telling her to evacuate the royal apartments and head for the rooms in the older part of Aerfax, she ordered the apartments cleared at once. She and Sylvis headed down to the Tervan part of Aerfax with the rest, and as she did she felt the ground shaking, and she and Sylvis looked at one another and wondered if the world was really breaking, if all the signs had been fulfilled to bring that moment about. Was Cunavastar waking, so far below the mountains where he has slept since he was put there, to dream the rest of time?

She saw the light, not directly but reflected in a silver bowl. A white light like the sun at noon, she said. People who looked at the light directly were blind, some for days, some forever. Sylvis was one of them but she got her vision back after a few days. A blast wave shook the ground and when Athryn looked again pieces of Senecaur were exploding into the sea and out in all directions in the air, a huge cloud rising, and the upper part of the Spur cracked and slid into the ocean as she watched. Seconds later when the explosion touched the water, huge waves churned up and would have flooded the lower part of the house except that the sea gates were closed. The Tervan house survived, as if the Smiths had known they would have to build a house to withstand this blast. The people who reached that part of house lived, though some of them were scarred by the heat and died later. The world did seem to be coming to pieces.

But something had protected the people in the house from dying outright. Athryn looked outside and saw that the Verm had all died along the road, and farther up the road, using the same spyglasses she had carried with her from the upper balcony, she saw me on the road where I had fallen the last time, not moving, lying near the gate. She saw that Drudaen had fallen too, she could see a white light on him, and him motionless on the ground, all the soldiers around him dead.

She thought I might be dead. But she thought I might as easily be alive, since something had managed to shield her people from the explosion, at least to a degree. So she rushed to the gate and, old as she was, mustered a party of two dozen out the gate to fetch me inside. She led them out herself, and they walked among the blasted land with the Verm dead or dying on the ground, some of them still struggling to stand, most beyond care. They found me, hurt, but alive, protected from the destruction I had unleashed, as they had been. She had to fight to convince the soldiers to touch me, she helped lift me herself, and they carried me into Aerfax and only barely got inside before Drudaen managed to drag himself upright again.

She looked back at him as the gates were closing. She wanted to stand where he could see.

She waited for him to follow. But it appeared he could not. She lay my body on a bier in one of the receiving halls. I was breathing very deeply, very slowly.

The rest of the day, with that storm of his slowly subsiding, from inside Aerfax she watched Drudaen, waiting. Twice he tried to come through the gate and turned aside as if racked with pain. After a while he gave up, and since none of his Verm had lived to help him, he limped away south till he found some who had survived, or at least that was what she and Sylvis supposed.

Athryn spent the next few days frantically active, sending her few remaining ships to Ivyssa and Kmur, sending letters to supporters across southern Aeryn, sending a letter that she vainly hoped would reach Kirith Kirin in Arthen. She had a certain amount of time in which she was free to act, while Drudaen was weak. She expected a Verm army to march straight down Kleeiom; only later from one of her naval commanders did she learn that the Don was blocked by my killing field, that no army would come that way. Even Drudaen had taken a ship when he went north.

She gathered enough supplies for a long wait. She would have to stay where she was for a long time, because of me. While I was alive, I must be tended by somebody. While I was alive, there was still hope. One day I might wake up. He could besiege her and blockade her but he would never be able to force his way into the Tervan house, except by magic, and she had a feeling I was fighting that. She meant to sit in Aerfax to keep me safe.

She saw it, Sylvis said, as the reason her role of folly had been assigned her, in the end. The world rested on two places. Inniscaudra, where Kirith Kirin waited. And Aerfax, where we were.

Drudaen moved quickly when he moved, flattening Teryaehn, moving an army by ship to guard the wreck of Aerfax across the broken causeway, and building a fleet of ships to patrol the peninsula by the sea.

Six hundred people were left to Athryn after the explosion that ended the real Battle of Aerfax. Two hundred had died since, some of them of sickness related to the blast, Sylvis thought, the rest in defense of the place. But no one had ever deserted. Their initial supplies held out for a long time, and while Novris and Charnos were still free, Athryn could buy food from those ports, as long as she was careful. But when those cities fell to Drudaen, she struggled to keep her people safe and fed. At present Sylvis was attending to that, but she wanted to get back to Aerfax as soon as she could. She was worried about Athryn's health. Athryn had been out of Arthen for longer than any of the Jhinuuserret. How much longer could she delay her return?

The three of them talked deep into the night, knowing they would not have another chance for a long time. Could Athryn find a way to Arthen for herself and all her people? Yes, maybe, if she sailed east to Novris and traveled through the Onge. Could she find a way to Arthen for herself, all her people, and me? My sleeping form? Would I be able to protect them on the journey as I apparently did in the fortress? They could not be certain.

These were questions they could hardly decide by themselves, and they parted saying that to one another. They would return, Sylvis to Queen Athryn and Imral and Karsten to Kirith Kirin, they would share their news. But they already knew as they parted that years would pass before they would see each other again.

"Imral and Karsten came home and told me you were alive," Kirith Kirin said, "but I already believed you were. Because the light never died on Ellebren."

There was so much more, I sat there stunned. No rescue was thought possible under shadow, while I was still alive, because there was no certainty I could keep us safe from Drudaen after I moved out of Aerfax. The safest bet was to leave me where I was, and pray that Athryn could hold on until I awoke, or until some other sign should come.

Then all parties lost touch again when Drudaen brought the war north to the Fenax. After Charnos fell to him, after a few years of quiet, he turned his attention there. At first he sent Verm armies, and quickly learned that the northerners would resist. Next he went himself. He rode up Angoroe at the head of an army, and when he did, the Ellebren lights grew fierce and bright, and so he became afraid and went back to Bruinysk. He tried again later that year, before winter, and the same thing happened.

That time he returned south, but he had thousands of Verm by then, he could send armies one at a time for as long as he liked. But finally he came himself, and Ellebren was not so bright or did not frighten him so much. He brought shadow to the Fenax, though he had a harder time holding it, since some of the old shrines had survived there, and each of those resisted his touch to a degree. He razed Cordyssa and burnt the place, killing Ren Vael and Pel Pelathayn. After that, with the Fenax under his hand, he returned south, and a long time of turmoil began. He had left Drii in peace, had not invaded the Svyssn or Tervan territories. But he had drawn those peoples into alliance with Kirith Kirin against him. Time and again the Fenax overthrew his control and he had to come back to defend his armies; each time our forces withdrew into the territories he could not reach.

"I think I can say the end. Or most of it."

"Go ahead," Kirith Kirin told me.

"As the years passed, the numbers of people in Aerfax dwindled. Drudaen never stopped watching the place, but was never able to come there himself to end the siege, something prevented him. Athryn and Sylvis refused to leave me till there were fewer than a dozen people left. I remember the last time Athryn visited my room. She had moved me to one of the deep rooms under Aerfax, where the sea would keep me moist, she said. A room in which I might stay safe from him. Or at least in which he might be afraid to find me.

"She and the last few people remaining with her fled across the bay to Ivyssa and rode north, somehow, into Arthen. The Queen was in failing health and barely made it to the Woodland in time. But she and Sylvis did make it that far." I looked at them, when I said that, and at last had a question for which I wanted an answer. "That is the way it happened, isn't it?"

Karsten seemed troubled. "Yes. They both made it. They told us you were still alive when they left. It took them two years to make the journey to Arthen. Athryn became very ill. But they did make it to safety, both of them alive. Five years ago."

"The Sisters came to Jiiviisn Field and we met them there," Kirith Kirin said. I could tell he had taken over here because this was the end of the story, for him. "They told us you had appeared to them on

Vithilonyi. They told us to come and find you, and to ask you to come back. They told us you could wake up again, if you wanted to."

"But you already knew I wanted to," I said. "Because one day you called me at Ellebren and I heard you and came there."

Shimmering in his eyes. "Yes. I thought you were in the Tower, the light changed."

"I was there," I said, "and I did come back, didn't I? When you asked."

2

That was as much as I could hear in one night, and as much as any of them wanted to relive. I had never asked the final question, I never asked while the three of us were sitting there, how long?

It was already an eternity since I woke up. We had pallets for sleeping, and I lay next to Kirith Kirin as naturally as if we had only parted yesterday. We were facing each other, and we looked at each other for a long time, eye to eye.

"Has anything changed?" he asked.

"Many things have. But this hasn't." I lay my hand on his chest, kissed him. It was warm and peaceful and I wanted nothing more. "Where are we headed?"

"Along the sea road to Novris. Then north."

"Novris?"

"We have some friends there."

I asked for no further details. Imral and Karsten had gone off to another corner to lie together. Karsten had gathered some rushes and used them to sweep a patch of floor, a place to spread the bedding, I guessed. The sound of the rushes soothed me some. Kirith Kirin lay his hand across my forehead. "No more fever. I was worried."

My body had healed fast enough, once it got unufru, that I knew magic must be in it somewhere, but I had said no Word, done nothing, felt no power move. "I'm fine."

He laughed softly in my ear. I felt more present, then. "After such a long nap."

I felt a catch in my throat. His breath on my ear made a shiver along my spine. More life came back to me, more feeling rose in me, because of him, but it was like a sob to feel it all, and I asked, "How long a nap was it?"

"Nearly a hundred years." He spoke in a simple way, as if it were nothing. His arm tightened around me and he buried his nose in my hair. He held me and helped me absorb the words. I sat there speechless as Imral spread bedding on the place where Karsten had swept. I watched their shadows. Kirith Kirin presently drew me down to sleep with him, and I did as he led me to do. He kissed me on the lips and said good-night. The echo carried me into darkness.

3

We passed east along the roads through Durme, four ragged figures astride horses that were mostly bone. I had never seen a more desolate landscape, scores of wrecked houses where not a soul stirred, the earth itself gone dull and brown, a hint of growth here and again. As we drew away from Ivyssa, hardly a tree still grew along the road. From above, through ragged clouds that extended from horizon to horizon, a thin light filtered, and one knew there was a sun somewhere, but one could see nothing of it.

We stopped for the night in the wreck of someone's farm-house, hiding the horses behind a pile of rubble that must have been a barn once. The house stood, though one wall had been smashed inward and the roof had collapsed into the rooms beneath. Inside, shards of pottery and dishes littered the hearth, and bits of wrecked furniture crowded the rooms. We used some of the furniture for kindling and lit a small fire in the fireplace. The chimney drew poorly but that hardly mattered since the smoke drifted out through gaping holes in the roof. Beyond the cloud glimmered the white moon. We drank cumbre for our supper, and ate a piece of stale bread from Imral's saddlebag. The cumbre returned old memories, riding in Arthen among these same people, clear sunlight and golden leaves.

Sipping cumbre, I felt dull and blind and realized I no longer had any sense of seeing as I had once known it. We slept a peaceful night, though there were some horsemen on the road, and Kirith Kirin stirred to listen at times. I was aware of him, even when I was asleep.

In the morning we saddled those poor horses and rode. As Kirith Kirin had predicted, we found patrols on the road, maybe searching for us even this early. Karsten guided us northeast, over some sandy hills, where we followed a sparse trail visible to their eyes but not to mine. We kept up a fair pace though we moved more slowly than we would have on the road. All day I smelled the salty wind and the acrid edge of something else, smoke the day after a fire, but this was an older smell, and pervaded the air. Maybe it was the smell of those clouds overhead, I thought. After a century of shadow, maybe that's what you get.

Riding all day, we camped in the hills, not wishing to approach any closer to the road. We drank more cumbre and ate some dried fish Imral had scavenged in Ivyssa; foul stuff, but I swallowed it. My belly was starting to cramp, now that I was awake and hungry. We tried no fire but sat in the sparse light of the white moon. We hardly talked, we were so tired from the ride, and soon unrolled our pallets and slept.

That day we came to the southern tip of the Onge Woodland, where the River Deluna flows out of the trees through the city of Novris and into Keikilla Bay. Two roads enter the city and we could see both; one brings trade east from Ivyssa and the other comes down from the north through many regions, through the Onge forest, and then into the city.

On the Ivyssa road two patrols were moving near the city, but on the northern road we saw no traffic at all. The Ivyssa road was being watched, but not the northern one. We descended out of the low hills into the edge of the forest, and Karsten found a trail there, one she had expected to find, which led us to a stone bridge across the Deluna and onto the road.

We traveled as quickly as those feeble horses could carry us, out of the Onge and within sight of the city walls. The road enters Novris over a bridge that is a marvel to see, spanning the river in two curves into the main gate of the city, which sits squarely over the river. The bridge was whole but the walls were breached in several places, and the gatehouse had been pulled down. One could see a battle had been fought here, but the memory of it was already old; young trees grew on the mounds of rubble that lay in the wall-breaches, and saplings and vine sprouted out of the bases of the walls. We merged with the thin traffic into the city and passed through the gates, leading our horses. The rags we wore blended with the rags of those we walked among in Novris, where the shape of people had not yet changed so much, and we slipped past the white-cloaked guards at the makeshift gate.

Inside, we passed through a wide plaza where many streets converged, and beyond that through a market where little or nothing was being sold, and into narrow streets that twisted this way and that, finally arriving at a hostel within sight of what was left of the

eastern wall. Karsten secured us a room and Imral led the horses to
their stalls. Kirith Kirin and I waited in the street, listening to the
echo of thin voices, the barking of a few dogs. What should have
been a busy city showed scarce signs of life.

Karsten rented us a room facing an inner courtyard, dark and
cramped, with a narrow casement window that opened inward and
a couple of beds made of packed straw. I sat on one of these and
waited. I had asked no questions, but presumed that we were to be
met here by someone. Imral returned from stabling the horses,
bringing the saddlebags, and we ate another meager meal of dried
meat and bread crusts. He had bought a skin of bad wine and
poured the stuff into the two cups we all shared. I sipped it, thinking how long it had been; thinking also, now I was one hundred
sixteen years old, or nearly, and could drink as I pleased.

"We're early," Karsten noted. "We made better time than we
planned."

Imral hovered near the door. "The city's full of troops, and
more arriving all the time."

"You think they're looking for us?" Her question went unan-
swered.

Kirith Kirin sat beside me on the narrow bed. He stroked my
hair and felt my forehead again. "You should rest. We'll be leaving
tonight."

I lay along the straw, curled at his back. If I closed my eyes I
would soon drift away. It was as if all my humanity had come back
to me, and none of the strangeness had lingered. "Who's meeting
us?" I asked.

He lay his finger to his lips. "You'll see."

Drowsiness enfolded me, I don't know how long. When I
woke, only Karsten and I remained in the room, and someone was
pounding at the door. Soldiers burst inside as I sat up, a grizzled
woman barking at Karsten in an accent I could hardly understand. I
stood from the bed and she saw me, her eyes narrowing.

Karsten lunged for me, but too late. Hands grasped me and
led me into the courtyard, where they held me while runners hurried off. I waited, hardly breathing, with Karsten pinned against
the wall by three of the soldiers. I signaled her with my eyes that
she should not struggle, and she played the part, another ragged
peasant mother afraid for what might happen to her son. After
some time, a woman rode into the courtyard astride a healthy
horse. Beyond, other soldiers had completed the search of the

hostel, and waited. The commander put herself forward and said something. But the woman on horseback had eyes only for me.

My scalp prickled when I saw her. She had power, this one, and eyed me up and down. She was reaching toward me, her lips moving, muttering Ildaruen. I was what she wanted, and for a moment she knew it. A gleam of triumph consumed her features, and she gestured that I be brought forward. I took a deep breath.

I looked into her eyes. I am not who you think, I told her, all in silence; I am not the one you want; a simple thought. I gazed at her evenly, and breathed; and suddenly her expression became downcast and she gazed sourly at the commander. "This urchin?" she spat. "You think this is the one?"

"He's the right age, my lady, and he fits the description," the soldier stammered, but when I turned to look at her, she filled with sudden doubts, as though she were seeing me for the first time.

"Look at this wretch," the mounted woman shrieked, kicking my shoulder with her stirrup. I ducked from the kick and took even breaths. "A pup not even fit for labor camps. He hasn't eaten in a month, look at these bones." She poked my side with her staff and spat at me. "I haven't ridden two days from Ivyssa to find a starveling country bastard." She gestured that I be taken away. Someone grabbed my shoulders and hurled me toward Karsten, who caught me and pulled me close. We huddled in the door to our room. The mounted woman drew up tall in the saddle. "So if that's the best you can find, we're done here, I suppose."

The commander nodded, downcast. The witch wheeled her horse and rode through the low gate, ducking her head. They headed elsewhere, and we watched as the last of their party filed out. Karsten whispered, "That was neatly done."

I had felt no power, no Wyyvisar moving through me. Something had changed.

We closed the door, with the bolt now burst loose, and waited. Karsten stayed close to the greasy window, looking out, till nearly dark. Then she gestured for me to come and we took up our packs, hurried into the street. I had no idea our journey was beginning at that moment, but we never returned to the hostel, and what became of the horses I don't know. I imagine, in a city as hungry as that one, someone ate them.

She led us toward the waterfront, I could smell the salt in the air. Kirith Kirin and Imral Ynuuvil met us at the dock and we hurried below, into a boat. We cast off from the dock and Karsten and

Kirith Kirin rowed us, dipped their slim oars silently into the black water. They picked their way among the moored boats, the hulls of the few merchantmen still in service. They rowed along the quay that leads from the city harbor into the open water of the bay, all calm, hardly a breeze stirring. Only there did anybody speak, and even then in whispers. "We were visited," Karsten said, and I could feel the attention of the others.

"When?"

"This afternoon. Hours ago."

Imral cursed quietly and Kirith Kirin asked, "Who? How many?"

"Thirty soldiers, by my count. They searched the hostel room by room."

"And?"

She sighed. "They found us. They knew Jessex and it was clear they were searching for him. They took him to wait in the courtyard and sent for the new one, Cormes. She showed up and took one look at him and suddenly lost interest and took the troops away, to continue their search, I suppose."

The name was familiar to me, but I could not place it. Was she someone still alive, from my time? "You're sure it was Cormes?" Imral asked. "You got a good look at her?"

"Oh yes. It wasn't hard to guess he would send her. She was stationed in Ivyssa, we already knew that."

"She lost interest," Kirith Kirin muttered, and I could feel him watching me. "I suppose I know what that means."

"She wasn't very skilled," I said. "But if Drudaen questions her, if he examines her, he'll know it was me."

He blew out breath, but said, "All right. He knew we were here anyway. He knows you're out of Aerfax, if he's looking this hard. So no harm done, as long as he doesn't find us."

He won't, I thought. But I said nothing.

We rowed down the coast, taking turns at the oars. With the white moon in crescent we had light; near midnight we headed for the coast again. Imral and Karsten, who were rowing, drove the boat through the gentle surf, and as we waded through shallow water to the beach, a cloaked figure stepped toward us, beckoning. I hardly glimpsed the outline of the person beneath the cloak, but I sensed it was a woman, and she led us through low dunes and sea grass, a hard passage with the sand always shifting underfoot. The smell brought back my memory of Kleeiom, those last days before I slept, walking with Kirith Kirin along the water's edge.

Another woman awaited us beyond the dunes, with fresh horses. One of these I knew by smell. He recognized me too, though he had the good sense not to whinny. I buried my face in Nixva's mane, turned to find Kirith Kirin grinning. "He's waited a long time for this," Kirith Kirin whispered, and we all mounted, all those familiar horses tossing their heads, Artefax and Kaufax, the Keikin, two other royal horses for the women who were our guides. Walking the horses through the sand, we presently came to a trail and followed it, and rode along the vestige of a trail, passing the dark shape of a house behind solid walls. We rode, and I was on Nixva's back again, and leaned over him and nearly whispered Words to him, but caught myself at the last moment.

Now we were six, and well mounted, and I had a feeling of safety from their presences, even without knowing who the guides were. We made good progress along that road, which ran, as I guessed, through Amre country, east of the city. We were headed toward the Onge forest, but not traveling along the main road.

We stopped for shelter in a round-house, abandoned but mostly intact. We lit no fire but contented ourselves with cumbre and some good cheese one of the women had brought. Spreading pallets on the cleanest patch of floor we could find, we slept a while, and rose before dawn, and saddled and mounted the horses.

I have traced our route since, and know we rode far to the east of Novris, hugging the Amre foothills in the shadows of the Barrier Mountains. Riding from the dusk of early morning into the thin light of day, we streamed over the countryside on those good horses, stopping for water at a clear stream that flowed down through the hills, eating more cheese and bread and riding on. By daylight I studied the two women who had become our companions, one dark-haired, the other with hair the color of fire; they were dressed in the same rags as we were, with tattered cloaks and worn boots, and I fancied them guides hired for the journey, or else soldiers in Kirith Kirin's service. They sat their horses with the skill of Woodland folk. I was suspicious, and could easily have known the truth then, if I had wanted. We rode, all of us, till late in the day we entered the Onge forest.

CHAPTER TWENTY-FIVE
CHALIANTHROTHE

1

We headed east along a hunting trail. I had expected we would make camp in the open woods, but we pressed forward past sunset, stopping only to water the horses at one of the creeks that descends out of Suvrin Caladur.

I felt the house before I saw it, beyond the twist of a creek, standing in a grove of trees. The outlines of the cottage loomed over us as we approached, and the women hurried forward and dismounted. We others followed, but more slowly, as one of the women struggled with a ring of keys and the other beckoned us forward. The house was neither large nor grand, but, unlike anything we had used for shelter lately, it had an aura of solidity. We entered through a door in good repair into a narrow antechamber; we carried our packs and crept into the center of the cottage, where Karsten lit an oil lamp stored in a cabinet.

We stood in a comfortable room, recently swept clean of dust and cobwebs, furnished with chairs, ottomans, cushions and thick carpets. The red-haired woman knelt by the broad stone fireplace and lit a fire; the wood had already been laid and waited only for the touch of roch in her hand. That she carried roch surprised me but I assumed one of the twice-named had given it to her. She glanced at me and smiled. She had the broad face of the people of Vyddn, a smattering of freckles across her nose. Timid, she turned quickly away. But I had time to note her beauty, the strength of her limbs, the clear milk of her skin beneath the freckles.

Kirith Kirin had stayed outside with Imral and the black-haired woman, one could hear them settling the horses. I had time to look around, noting the good hangings on the walls, the clean stone floor, the rooms that opened off this one, a small eating room and a kitchen, a narrow closet for winter gear, a study of some kind, a narrow stair; this was someone's hunting lodge, I guessed, though it had been out of use for a while. The adjoining rooms were not in such good order as the sitting room where the fire was burning. Karsten caught me snooping and said, "Curious?"

I shrugged. "A little. What is this place?"

"A summer lodge. A place we knew about, where we could be safe for a night."

When the others came inside the black-haired woman laid out food in front of the fire, real stuff like I hadn't seen since I'd wakened, fresh cheese and winter fruits, salted hams and dry breads, even a flagon of wine and Drii brandy, a feast after what we'd found for ourselves on the road. We sat down anywhere we could find a space and drank and ate, and I sighed at the comfort of the fire, the cushions, the gentleness of the room. We might have been dropped down into some peaceful time, I might almost have believed that, except for the anxiety on all their faces, the ones I knew and the ones I didn't. Hardly anyone spoke while we ate, till the wine and the fire had warmed us some. Outside the wind had picked up, one could feel the teeth of the cold through the walls. Imral remarked, "I wouldn't be surprised to see a storm tonight."

"We might get snow, so close to the mountains." The red-haired woman had a rich voice, like a low flute, that one could feel as well as hear.

"I'd be glad of that," Karsten said, "to cover our trail."

"You think we're being followed?"

"If we're not, we will be." She told the story of Cormes and the soldiers in the hostel courtyard while the red-haired woman stirred the fire. The other woman listened attentively, glancing at me once, then away.

"That would be Cormes," she agreed, when Karsten said the name. "It would make sense that he'd send her."

The red-haired woman said, "I'd wished for a better head start."

"It can't be helped." The black haired woman was watching Kirith Kirin when she said this, and he nodded agreement. Something about the tilt of her chin, the way the firelight caught the bones of her face, told me who she was. But she turned away and the moment passed; I would pretend not to know if that was what she preferred. After only a few moments in general company, she and her friend retreated to another chamber.

Kirith Kirin, Imral and Karsten sat up a while longer. I drowsed against Kirith Kirin while they talked, idle stuff, mostly, fretting about our route north, whether we would be spotted, whether the witch Cormes would follow us, whether the trails would be safe. But even then, even in that comfortable place, I felt distant from any need to speak. My anchor was Kirith Kirin, and he was all that held me in the room, at times. Without him there, I might have floated clean away.

There was only one question I wanted answered, and I asked it when their conversation had burned away to embers like the fire. "Where is Drudaen now?"

The sound of my voice must have surprised them. "I thought you were asleep, you've been so quiet," Kirith Kirin said.

"I've been listening."

He poured himself the dregs of the wine and settled beside me again. "He's camped in front of Drii with an army."

"Though he may have left there if he knows we have you awake again," Karsten said quietly.

"He knows."

2

For safety's sake we slept in the sitting room, pulling the heavy furniture aside; there were bedrooms upstairs but they would be too cold for sleeping in the winter night, and Karsten and Imral decided we should not risk another fire. They were afraid the light would be seen from the trail, since patrols might already be searching for us in this part of the Onge. I might have told them that anyone who found us here would be sorry for it, but I said nothing and let them fret. Kirith Kirin found the conversation amusing too, and looked at me. We spread our pallet in a corner where we could see the fire. We lay awake watching it a long time, wrapped in the safety of each other.

What to call my silence of those days? Was it detachment, did I truly care for no one except Kirith Kirin? Even meeting Athryn Ardfalla, as I had that night, and her lover, the redhead, Sylvis Mnemorel; even the news of Drudaen, the fact that he had Drii under siege; all this meant so little. Had I lain in sleep so long that I was condemned to numbness?

The feeling continued in the morning. We rose and everyone made a show of putting the lodge to rights, getting rid of the ashes from the fire, leaving the place as if no one had been there; and I might have spared them trouble, but I said nothing. We rode through the long day and into the night again, and took shelter in a cave for the night. The winter wind was howling. We had borrowed better clothes from the lodge and were warmly dressed, at least, but the night would be a bitter one, unless we had a fire. Sylvis was afraid to light one, there was a chance we should be seen. Karsten countered that we'd freeze unless we took the risk. They argued back and forth while Kirith Kirin watched me, and he was smiling at me without any visible change of expression, and finally, that time, I relented. "We won't be found," I said quietly, and the women stopped talking and looked at me. "We'll be safe."

Kirith Kirin had already begun to build a rock circle, and Imral gathered wood, and soon we had a fire, burning big and bold in the mouth of the cave, while Athryn laid out our meal and I spread the bedding close to the warmth.

We rode northward for several days after that, and we did encounter patrols, and other folk. The Onge forest is not like Arthen; there have always been people living in it, and there are even small villages along the road on the banks of the river, and houses and lodges in the hills. One saw wrecked cottages along the road, and everywhere one found evidence of the poverty the people endured, but these places had survived better than others had, judging from what I had seen. The forest offered some protection, being nearly as old as Arthen, and having a reputation for unfriendliness to wizard's armies. The Verm avoided forests whenever possible, and Drudaen cared little for the place, and so the Onge-folk had been spared some blows of the long war. Two nights we slept in the villages, but most often we found a hunting house away from the trails, and a cache of supplies in the houses, and I always suspected that the lodge belonged to someone in our party, or someone known to one of us, but I never asked. Some nights we slept in the open, with the wind howling down from the Caladur peaks and the hand of winter closing.

Only one patrol came anywhere near us, at the place where the River Isar runs into the Deluna, where we had to cross the main bridge. Soldiers held the bridge, a party of a hundred or more, and there was a witch with them who saw me, for a moment, till he forgot me as Cormes had forgotten me, and we passed over the bridge, following the Isar. The main road leaves the Onge there, headed west for Ibraxa and the country around the Krom Hills, but we traveled east away from the road, following old trails, where we would be hidden.

I had no notion of our destination until we had traveled nearly as far north as the forest could take us, and we reached the place called Chalianthrothe.

We had followed the Isar to its source, or at least to the place where it surfaces out of the deep mountains. To the Orloc this is a holy river; they say it runs under the mountains all the way to Zaeyn, and this, then, is one of their holy places, but was given to the Jisraegen long ago, when the Orloc left the surface for good. We rode the horses along a narrow valley which ascended at first gradually, then more steeply, and we came to a place where the Isar formed a perfect, round pool on a terrace of rock. The surface of the terrace had been polished and inlaid with cunning designs that were part writing and part picture, and the lip of the pool was carved in intricate shapes to resemble flowers and vines. From one side of the pool, framed in immense, old cedars, a series of broad, deep stone steps mounted toward another terrace. We dismounted and led the horses up, climbing alongside the craggy face of a spur of the mountain. The surface of each step had been worked by hand with more of the designs, and the faces of each step were carved in reliefs, a parade of dwarf-men on animals I had never seen before, an army passing, the faces of crowned women, a gathering of people at market, a series of panels telling a story; I had only time to glimpse it all. We arrived at the highest terrace and found ourselves facing a double gate cut into the stone. Carved into the stone were the same figures as before, but along with this script were words in archaic Jisraegen, spellings and shapes of letters I could hardly make out, though I was able to read a name, Jurel Durassa.

The gate opened when Athryn Ardfalla touched it with her hand. She gestured to us and we led the horses inside, where we found an inner courtyard, bright and full of light, where there were ample stables for the horses, and some bales of hay and fodder to feed them. Around the stables were various rooms, including what looked to be armories, and beyond, another courtyard where a fountain glittered and sang. Athryn opened a sealed door to reveal other rooms, all lit as if by daylight, when in fact we stood inside the mountain, with solid rock over our heads.

Several chambers were clustered together, each opening onto the other, separated by pillars carved out of the native rock, twisting upward in precise spiral patterns, capped by bursts of leaves and branches that were marvels of stonework; the floors of marble and granite and chalcedony and other kinds of stone I could not name. Some of the walls had been worked to a perfect polish and smoothness and others had been shaped but not finished, so that the stone presented itself rough and full of textures; the vaulted ceilings rose up in graceful domes, of mixed gold-leaf and true-silver designs, interspersed with what the eye would have sworn were skylights. The chambers were neither grand nor large, and there were not so many of them; the place had a cozy feeling, being furnished quite sparsely in the central chambers, though the outer ones had cushions and chairs and carpets. I saw a stairway in one room, carved out of the mountain rock, descending to a level beneath ours, and in the smallest chambers fireplaces nested in the walls. Wood had been laid in one of these, and packs that I guessed contained more food, but these mundane objects appeared out of place, prosaic amid the gemlike beauty of the rest. I walked from place to place and drank the beauty into myself, as though it were some kind of restorative. As though it could make me feel gratitude, and a sense of belonging. The others were making a fire in the small chamber, and settling us in for the night, and I wandered away from the noise of that, down the stairway I had seen to the level beneath.

The stairs spiraled down much farther than I had reckoned, and I passed through a library, or what had once been a library; the shelves bare. This room is important, I thought, pay attention, and it was the empty shelves I noticed most. The dust on each shelf contained outlines of books, I touched them, and I knew what the books had been. One of Jurel's libraries. The Sisters had discussed the books he studied, their links to older knowledge from the River City. Some other of these objects were as old as that, including the stone worktables that stood here, a painter's easel, some instruments used for navigating on ships. The room smelled of cedar. It had a tidy, compact feeling to it. Light entered from the ceiling, as in the upper chambers, fresh and bright, and I wanted to wander in it, to sit at the table, to lift the brass telescope. But the stairs continued downward and my curiosity drew me deeper, for something farther down was aware of me.

At the bottom of the stairway stood a door, sealed, without apparent opening, and I knew it was sealed by magic, that it had not been opened in a long time, and I knew that it would open for me if I wished. I lay my hand flat on the stone. What was beyond took shape in my head, but I refrained from opening the door.

When I turned to climb the stairs again, Kirith Kirin was there. I watched him calmly, no need to speak. His gravity, his presence, was like the tonic of the rooms above, I had only to be near it. We stood without moving.

"I've never seen a more beautiful place than this."

He assented, though he continued to watch me fixedly. "The Orloc made the house as a gift to Jurel. It's called Chalianthrothe, which means something in their language; 'little jewel,' or something like that." He gestured to the door behind me. "This is a room they made for Jurel, that no one else has ever seen."

I touched the polished stone again, and closed my eyes. "I must have known it was here. Though I can't say how or why."

"No need to say anything." He wanted to reach for me, but at the same time he was afraid; I suppose he had been afraid of me all along, and I had not seen it.

"You brought something else for me, didn't you?" I took his hand, treasuring the broad bones, the tough skin.

"Yes. It's upstairs."

"I'll need it later, when I open the door." And led him up the narrow stairs, our shoulders brushing.

3

I stayed near him through the meal that followed, out of habit, I suppose, if one can be said to have habits after a century of separation; but also because, when I felt his presence, I found it easier to concentrate on the others, to hear their voices and take an interest in their speech. We had nested by the fire on cushions and rugs, and someone had passed round wine already. Karsten handed me a cup, a pretty thing of fine glass that must have been stored somewhere in the house; it would not have traveled well. "Exploring?" she asked.

"Yes. I saw the library."

She understood what else I had seen, but we said nothing about that. "If I could live anywhere, I would choose to be here, in this place," she said.

"Have you seen any other Orloc buildings?"

"Few people could claim to have done that." She shook her head. "The story is that they made this place for Jurel because he did them a service, one time; but what it was, no one knows. The Orloc keep to themselves. Jurel kept that secret, too."

If she wanted to say more, or ask more, she refrained, and we took our places near the fire, though the rooms were warm enough that we might have done without its heat. We ate our meal in relative peace, tired from the ride. Athryn and Sylvis had put out lamps, since the daylight, or whatever light it was that filled these chambers, had begun to wane. As usual, they withdrew from the rest of us. We were keeping up the pretense that I was not curious as to who they were. This is a Jisraegen way of saving face. I ate the good food and drank the wine Karsten poured and sat with Kirith Kirin.

Imral and Karsten were waiting for me to speak. The thought came to me quite clearly as we watched the flames twist and turn, as we heard the fire sigh. They were watching me and wondering who I was, since it was clear I was no longer the child they had known so long ago. It was clear that something had changed. They had risked their lives to save me and they wondered what I had become. A feeling came to me then, a sadness, that I had no way to tell them anything, that I had no idea myself what had happened. I had only the instinct to sit there, as I had sat with them years before; I had only the need to be near Kirith Kirin; not even love for him, especially, at that moment, but the need to be near him. What good to try to talk? I knew why they had come to find me, I knew what they wanted me to do. I knew so much it had become like a whiteness in my mind.

So I said hardly anything and they waited and despaired maybe and were too polite to say anything, and after all, we had shared affection for each other once, and owed each other something in the wake of that. We sat there till the hour was late, and Karsten fell asleep on Imral's shoulder, and finally he led her off to the chamber where they had made a bed for themselves. We watched them go, and Kirith Kirin pulled me against him, and sighed.

The question persisted and grew large, who was I and what had I become? and the answer was there, too, was waiting for me to find it. We sat there for a while till we felt alone with each other. Then we stood, and found the stairway again, descending in the soft light that poured upward from the steps. Below, in the library, I showed Kirith Kirin what I had learned about the books.

He detoured to the worktable, where he opened a hidden catch and pulled open a drawer. He drew out a bundle, and I knew what that was, too, but I did not take it from him. We descended the steps to the narrow chamber in front of the door, and I felt what was beyond the door again, and Kirith Kirin stood close behind me, I could feel his breath along my neck. We stood there and breathed. If we waited the stone would open. We both knew that at the same moment. The stone panel in front of us dissolved. From the chamber beyond glittered pale light.

What does it matter what the room looked like? What carvings decorated the floor, what colors of stone lined the walls? What does it matter the shape, the vaulted ceiling, the flat expanse of the circles, what does it matter the workmanship, the beauty, of the place? What does it matter, the word, "magic"? We stepped into the room and I was flooded with joy, I knew what use it was made for, and I saw everything, and I held Kirith Kirin's hand, and we were there together as the tide of feeling washed over us. I saw the world as it was outside the walls of Chalianthrothe, I saw a long way and deeply, that the roads were broken and mostly in ruins, that the houses had been burnt or broken or worse, I saw that Genfynnel had been flattened and completely destroyed, that Cordyssa burned, that the Fenax lay barren, I saw that people died, had been dying, that the ordered life of the past had utterly ended; I saw Drii battered by Drudaen and the Verm, as if there were anything left to conquer. I saw Arthen dying, because everything around her was dying. I saw all these things in a flood, and knew them, and had known them since I wakened, and I think I was crying by then, tears of joy to be feeling so much and then tears of horror at what I felt; for I was myself again, but what a world it was to be in. The whole numb weight of Drudaen, of what he had done, fell on me, and I stood there without moving, still seeing everything, knowing what must be done to finish this, seeing ahead, and holding Kirith Kirin's hand. He was altogether inside me, we moved as if with one thought, and I would say that I loved him again except that it is such a paltry word for two people who have stood in that place. We saw the hundred years go past and we saw ourselves, two small, shivering creatures, standing in that room in Chalianthrothe. We remained there for a long time.

The bundle rested in my hand. The outer cloth, woven by the Sisters, had hidden what was inside from Drudaen, but now I opened the cloth and shook it out, the cloak the Sisters had given me, Fimbrel, my first guide. The cloth shimmered and unfolded and was not cloth at all, or a cloak; it was a smoke dissolving before my eyes, it collapsed to a point of light in my hand, and all the Words that were in it, all the afternoons on Illyn Water, flowed into my palm in a stream of light. I understood the fabric as I had only begun to do when I wore it and the light glittered and faded into my palm; and sometimes, when I open my hand, I can see that light there still. Kirith Kirin was watching me and he was no longer afraid. He closed his hand over the place where the light had been, and we watched each other, and he sighed.

"All right," he said. "So now we know how it will end."

My heart was beating hard. Finally he nodded, giving his assent.

We stood there a while longer, then we closed the stone door and climbed the stairs to find our bed. We lay together as we had been doing since I woke; I undressed him tenderly and touched him till some warmth came back to him, spilled over into me, and we were lovers again, in the wake of what we had seen in Jurel Durassa's room of three circles. The pleasure of love cut me like a knife, and the sorrow of what I knew, and the joy of living and feeling, all mixed together, and still, all in all, I moved at a great distance from the world, but understood it better, and Kirith Kirin moved beside me. We made love and slept and wakened to a fresh morning.

Far to the north, encamped before the walls of Drii, my enemy Drudaen Keerfax knew me again that night, knew even my whereabouts, as though I had lit a bonfire on the horizon to show him where I was. He had been seeking me everywhere and now he knew where I was, because I wished he should. We had begun the end game, and now we would each play out our hands.

4

We lingered in Chalianthrothe another day, while Imral and Sylvis scavenged for supplies for our northward journey, and Karsten and Kirith Kirin scouted the northern border of the Onge. I was left along with Athryn, and I understood this to be by design, though I said nothing when the horses rode away.

In the pleasant rooms Athryn avoided me awkwardly for a while, creeping about the smaller chambers, and this gave me some time to think. I knew she intended to talk to me, but was not quite ready yet, so I descended to the empty library to explore there. In that room among those ancient objects, I reflected on her face, on the feeling it gave me to be here with her, alone. When I finally returned to the upper levels she had laid out a lunch for us both, bread and cheese, and she had built a small fire to comfort us as we sat. She smiled at me in a shy way and would not look at me for very long. We ate our food in silence till we were nearly finished. "You've never asked my name," she said, and stopped there, awkwardly, without meeting my eye.

"I thought that was what you wanted," I said. "But anyway, I know who you are. And I'm very grateful for your help."

No surprise showed in her face. She gave the fire a long, sad look. "I've hardly been help to anybody, I think."

"You gave me shelter." She was puzzled, so I continued. "I don't mean today, I mean a long time ago. You kept me safe in Aerfax."

The reference pained her. Athryn Ardfalla, now queen of nothing, made a show of laying a heavy log across the flames, her muscled arms moving with a surety that was familiar to me, the same as her brother, Kirith Kirin. She looked me in the eye. "I did so much to hurt people in those days, it's almost painful to be reminded of a kindness."

"You saved my life."

She poured more water into her crystal cup, and wet her lips, and refused to look at me. "I was ashamed to leave you there."

"I remember. You stayed longer than you should have."

She was quiet for a while. "I got as far as here. These rooms. I got as far as this in six months of hiding and then collapsed."

She was asking for the acceptance that is the new beginning, as the old saying goes. That was a lot, if I looked at it one way, and not so much, if I looked at it another. Here she sat, the woman who had nearly ruined us all, who had indulged Drudaen in his wishes until it was too late to deny him his whims. Here was the queen who had led us into a war that lasted a hundred years. Here was the woman, the immortal, who had caused my family to be killed. Did the fact that she was merely human, and very sorry, make up for any of that? Did the fact that she had saved my life change any of that?

We spoke very little more, but sat in each other's company. As with Kirith Kirin, I felt no need to trade words with her when there was so much we each already knew. We sat in relative peace, and our spirits tested one another, and I understood that her heart had opened, that the sorrow she felt would never end, that she would never offer more apology than that. Maybe when I was as old as she. Maybe then. Meantime, here, the fire crackled. A smell, some strange pungent spice, drifted through the air, like clove but not quite. We had a moment of quiet together, and at the end of it I stirred as if to go, and she stopped me with a gesture. "You've made my brother come to life," she said. "Seeing you again. I'm most grateful of all for that."

I felt a sudden catch at my throat, the memory of the night before returning in a flood, and that feeling rose up in me again. Bowing my head to her, I retreated to the chamber where Kirith Kirin and I had slept.

5

The scavengers returned with supplies, and later Karsten and Kirith Kirin rode their horses through the open gate, and we sealed it again, and closed ourselves in for the night. I had a fleeting thought, watching those smooth stone gates swing closed, perfectly balanced, that we could stay here, inside Chalianthrothe, and forget all the rest, all the outside world. It was a thought that blew like a breeze through my brain, light and insubstantial, and I looked at Kirith Kirin taking off his riding boots and stretching out his toes. Maybe he had heard me thinking or maybe he felt the peace of the moment, too. "If we live through all this, we'll come back here, one of these days." He surveyed the vaulted foyer, the filigreed columns and airy dome. "I do like the place."

Inside, we took supper, and when we were done, we sat near the fire with a sense of waiting, knowing a conversation would begin, since we were here and had completed the first stage of our journey. "I suppose," Kirith Kirin said finally, "it's about time we talked."

Karsten laughed and Imral laced his fingers through her hair. I had never seen them so free with each other, Karsten leaning against his leg, taking his touch for granted. "We can't put it off any longer," Karsten said. "Which way do we ride from here?"

The question was meant for me, and I understood this; but I also understood that Kirith Kirin would answer it, and I preferred that he do so. He looked round at them all. "We ride north. To Montajhena."

"You mean to Cundruen," Karsten said, "on the way to Drii."

"I mean to Montajhena," Kirith Kirin answered.

Imral was watching me, perplexed. I understood his confusion, since it was relief for Drii that concerned him most. "Why?"

"One of the Verm armies is already heading there," Kirith Kirin answered.

"Away from Drii?"

"Yes."

Disbelief in Imral's gray eyes. Then a slow smile, as he looked at me. Karsten took his hand. Athryn poked the fire. "He sent one army down the passes, but what about the other?"

"It's marching west, across the Fenax."

"Already?"

"Yes. He's wasted no time. He's bringing all the forces he has left."

"Which way will he ride?"

"He's already ridden to Montajhena," Kirith Kirin said. "There's a place he needs there."

No one asked him how he knew so much. No one asked me why I kept silent. A moment passed, and Karsten said, "He'll be there long before we are." Here she looked at me, and here at last I did speak.

"It doesn't matter."

"You don't want to get there first?"

"No. I don't want to hurry at all."

They looked at each other in some mild surprise, which is about as far toward astonishment as the twice-named go. They had expected something more difficult, I guess, some journey or strategy that required more planning. But now we were done, and Kirith Kirin said good-night to them all, serenely, and took me to bed. We stood together in our room as the others talked quietly. I could make out no words, only the comforting sound of their voices. I had learned a new magic, called knowing no more than was necessary to do what I had to do. We took off our clothes and lay down together. That night we simply rested, content with one another, sorry at the thought that tomorrow we would leave Chalianthrothe, where we had found a new happiness.

Meanwhile, beyond that glittering house, out in the larger world, an army was indeed already moving south through Cundruen Pass, ahead of it Drudaen himself, moving on an ithikan wind down the passes. Drii, the last of all the Aeryn cities to survive the war unscathed, herself besieged these twenty years, found herself suddenly free.

CHAPTER TWENTY-SIX
MONTAJHENA

1

Rather than head directly north, across Rars and Reydon, we chose a more westerly route that would carry us toward Trenelarth Forest and the place where stood what was left of the city of Kursk. We rode at a fair pace, though without hurry. At night, as before, we camped in abandoned farmhouses or in any place that would afford us some measure of shelter. The cold winds of mid-winter fell on us, sharp and bitter, off the backs of the mountains.

I had never seen such desolation with my own eyes. Hardly a soul stirred on the landscape, and the road lay neglected and nearly deserted. Where villages had once stood there remained only blackened patches of ground, as if a hand of fire had swept them off the surface of the earth. Where a field had once grown corn or wheat, there was hardly enough brown grass to cover the ground, and above our heads stretched that strange colorless sky. Every day we rode forward in perpetual twilight through a country so bleak no one could recognize it, even among the twice-named. The sight sobered all of us, but for them it was not new. For me, it was.

Near Kursk there were more people, but anyone in the countryside who saw us riding fled from us. Some horsemen and wagoneers were on the road near the city, but they passed us sullenly, without acknowledgment, most of them having suffered the change in appearance under shadow, becoming Vermish, and we kept our heads wrapped and sought no company from anyone we met.

We entered the sad wreck of Kursk near nightfall, seeking shelter in the streets where the houses had been abandoned. We found a old roundhouse with the first floor largely intact and we settled there for the night. I climbed to what was left of the upper story and studied the city till it was too dark to see. A bit of the defensive wall had survived near where we rested, and a part of a tower, streets winding this way and that along the course where the rest of the fortifications used to run. It would not be true to say I tried to imagine what had happened here, because I already understood much about that. But there, in that present moment, I marveled at so much destruction.

We passed a peaceful night, but the next morning found the city full of Verm soldiers. We packed our bags and saddled our horses. Walking the horses through the streets without making any attempt to conceal ourselves, we gathered more and more of the Verm behind us, till, when we finally reached the bridge over the Deluna, we found it held by more of the Verm, soldiers lining both shores of the river, maybe three hundred in all. Archers fitted arrows into their bows and stretched them taut. From the body of these soldiers emerged three white-cloaked figures, one of whom I recognized as the witch from Novris, the woman named Cormes. I dismounted from Nixva and began to walk toward them. The soldiers had stopped where they were, though that was not their intention, and they were surprised at themselves. The archers dropped their bows at the same moment, and stared down at them stupidly, the bows on the ground and their arms limp, and the Verm soldiers shuddered and looked at each other and at me, and slumped to the ground, most of them, or off their horses, but they did not die. This must have surprised them, when they stopped to think about it.

The white-cloaked ones had been approaching through the moment that the Verm began to sag to the ground. A lot of noise filled my head, the commotion of their art. I might have heard the words but instead I watched them. I stopped in front of them and looked from one to the other to the next. Two men and the woman named Cormes. I stripped them clean and bare, all of their minds, till there was nothing left in them that could ever trouble anybody again. I let Cormes know who I was before she, too, fell into sleep. I let them live, I did not seek to loose the tiiryander and set their souls free of their bodies, I did not eat their souls and take their strength into myself.

The Verm watched all of this. When the three magicians were sleeping on the ground, with their riderless horses tossing their heads, I released the Verm and some of them rose up on their knees as Kirith Kirin led our party to where I stood. I mounted Nixva again and turned toward the Verm. "Let us pass," Kirith Kirin said, "and no one will be harmed." So we rode through the soldiers, some of whom made way for us, across the bridge into Trenelarth, with the Verm watching.

2

We followed the road north, somewhat sheltered from the winter wind by the forest, though we felt it when we crossed into Vyddn, cold wings spreading over us from the mountains, the promise of snow. We rode through a countryside as devastated as all those we had left behind. No one troubled us on the journey, and in fact we saw hardly a soul.

So desolate was the landscape that we had trouble finding food and had to ration our small store of dried meats, cumbre and dried fruit. We took shelter where we could find it, but in Vyddn there was hardly a building standing, and in places the road itself had been obliterated, the earth scorched and dark. We slept in groves of trees where there was dense undergrowth to break the wind; we slept in whatever walls or half-walls remained standing of a house or a barn or an inn or even a shrine. We slept in the open coiled round each other for warmth. Winter wind howled onto us, and the brackish cloud thickened and soon let fall a light, dingy snow. The touch of the stuff repelled me.

I had begun to dream I was still sleeping in Senecaur, I was lying on the rock listening to the waves when Drudaen entered. He came in mumbling those words of his, and I was irritated by the noise, but when he stood over me and took down his hood I was shocked, he had grown even older, his skin stretched thin over his skull, blue veins showing through white tissue, his eyes bloodshot; he came to me on the slab of stone and tried to rub the water in my skin but the touch repulsed me and I woke. The image of him returned when I was awake, while I was riding, the face of the sad old man, exhausted, his body nearly translucent. The darkness of his eyes, the slash of his mouth.

It was so easy now to read his thought along that part of his wave through time. What he needed, more than anything, was a way to enter Arthen again. His life was ebbing. Shadow could not sustain him, and yet he could not end it.

I remembered the real visit from Drudaen when I was sleeping in Aerfax. He had been in the room a long time before I became aware of him. He was still handsome then, not ancient like the old man of my dream. He watered my body, which was soothing. He had a sad look. He wanted me to wake up and join him. If I did not wake up, he was lost. He had come here to kill me and now he knew he could not. The thought had fled.

That was the second time I moved magic from the third circle. The first was when I destroyed Senecaur and protected myself from the blast.

3

After some days we came out of the high country into Vyddn, and rode through the hills into the foothills, following what was left of the road to the gates of Montajhena nestled beneath Thrath Mountain.

We found an army waiting on the road, many thousands of Verm encamped with slaves tending their cook fires. The Deluna tumbled over rocks in its course and gave out a perpetual roar. We made camp above the Verm on a hilltop, making no real effort to hide from them. We could see down into their camp, and beyond to the ruined stones that were once the gates to this city. Beyond, the city's wreckage lay shrouded in mist that glowed softly in the dusk, and I stared at it with the first stirring of astonishment. The hills rise up sharp around the lower city, and the upper city climbs the flank of Thrath, into a hollow formed by vast ridges of the mountain. I stared at it till the last light, sang the evening song under my breath.

Verm patrols passed us twice but the soldiers saw nothing of us. Not even our campfire gave us away. This time there was no debate about the need for it; Athryn and Karsten found rocks for a circle and Imral and Sylvis gathered wood. We slept peacefully, the six of us, with thousands of soldiers camped around us, the hills lit with the glow from the ruins of the city, a pervasive milky light. I could feel what was coming. Drudaen lay very close by, at first, and then, sometime in the night, he went up to one of the Towers and vanished. He was very afraid, he had been afraid of this journey for a long time, but he knew he would have to take it. When I woke in the morning I could no longer feel him anywhere near.

In the morning the air was clear and we could see the whole sweep of the landscape, the world rising suddenly upward, the mountain soaring out of nowhere, embracing the city on its sheer flanks. Even the wreckage of Montajhena was beautiful, stones of all colors worked in many ways, streets and lanes visible, the bases of the defensive towers and the wall, and beyond, a high, graceful arch in the side of the mountain, where the road winds through to Cundruen Pass. Beyond, farther up on the mountainside, the bases of the two towers rose up from other wreckage, Yrunvurst and Goerast, places I had seen before in what I had called the eye of the mind. The sheer, vertical landscape enthralled me, and I felt the same as in that first moment when I saw Chalianthrothe, when I realized what beautiful places there are in the world.

The others were watching it too. They gazed down mournfully at the road, the gates, the high terraces of the city, the winding streets. A cloud of grief enfolded them, not visible in any motion they made nor apparent in any word they spoke. Reflected in their eyes I could see the beauty of the city that had been destroyed.

We saddled our horses and rode them down the hillsides to face the main body of the Verm army. We were no longer hiding.

The Verm had grown canny and made no move while we approached. Maybe they had heard of the incident at the Kursk bridge and knew what might happen. We rode up to them and through them, quietly, without any fanfare, across their outermost camps, exercise yards, makeshift markets, and the Verm stood and stared at us and never lifted a hand, even the ones who thought about doing so. We rode through thousands of them and they watched, and their officers watched, and one or two of Drudaen's apprentices watched, as we found the road and the gates, threading through the broken stone. The others proceeded along the thoroughfare in the lower city, and when I caught up with them, after watching the Verm a long time, we began to climb again, along the broad flank of the mountain, through the cedars and pines, along the streets of the high city where the bones of old buildings lay bleached clean by years of weather. The Verm remained in their camps.

We climbed across the causeway to the base of Yrunvurst.

I had been brooding over Drudaen the whole morning, thoughts all unformed like a seething cloud, knowing him close, then knowing him gone. I had been thinking what he must be like now, as old as Athryn had been, or worse, and longing to return to Arthen, to the embrace of those trees. He must want that more than anything, since only that could save his life. He had won the whole world, except for that one small patch.

Five years ago he had come to the room where I could hear the sea, he had visited me there, before he pulled Aerfax down. He had tried to bring himself to kill me but he could not do it. Why not? The thought must have maddened him ever since. He must have understood, after a while, what had really happened in the room, and what I had become.

One sensed his disquiet, his weariness. The shadow he had spread over the world weighed on him, something he must maintain, something he must manage, without letup. He ruled the whole world that same way, without daring to take his eyes off it; and as time went by, in order to sustain his life, he had to eat more and more of the life around him. By now he would want to return to Arthen more than anything. As Athryn had. To be truly young again. To try to begin again. But shadow was part of his nature, now. He could never stop making it. Even if Kirith Kirin had been willing to allow him into the Woodland again.

In the base of Yrunvurst remained one room intact, invisible to most eyes, though I could see it, and my enemy could see it, and had known it was here for years. Today he had finally got the courage to go into it, a room built by his father's enemy, Jurel Durassa, and he had traveled somewhere from that room. I could almost see him, the bitter wind blowing, clouds gathering, a white figure riding through the ruined city, needing no light to see. We had grown close, he and I; and I could almost smell his sadness, his heaviness. He had come to this room searching for a way into Arthen, and he had found it, and he had gone there, I could feel the change everywhere.

I dismounted from Nixva and stood at the head of a broken stair leading down the mountainside at the base of Yrunvurst. We had been sitting there for a while, and no one had said anything. I stood near Kirith Kirin's boot, looking up at the rest of him, the Keikin blowing and stepping. "He's gone already," Kirith Kirin said.

"Yes. I think so."

"Then we're too late?"

I shook my head. "Everything is fine." I did watch him for along time. "Where will you go now?"

"To Drii," he answered. "While we can still get through the pass. Then to Inniscaudra." He touched my hand in the gentlest way, and that was how we parted.

I descended the stairs that their eyes could not see, entering the room beyond. I vanished to their sight.

CHAPTER TWENTY-SEVEN
SEUMREN

1

Drudaen had ruled the world for a hundred years only to find that the world dwindled every day while he was king of it. He had kept himself alive for a very long time through a sort of art one hardly cares to contemplate. He had come to the end of his rope. Maybe he had already known this when he visited me beneath Senecaur, maybe he already knew he had failed. Exhausted from a war that lasted so long, that destroyed the very prize he had sought, he finally understood that he would die unless he found a way to return to the Woodland.

As for the way to get there, he had known the secret of that since long before I was born. In the base of Yrunvurst is a room and from that room one can travel without moving, not to any place one wishes but only to one place, to Seumren-over-Cunuduerum, the city on the banks of the river. Jurel Durassa made the room, a way to get to Seumren to take Falamar down. A way to make certain Falamar could never hold Seumren against him. Kentha had found the room and told Drudaen about it, she had used it to travel to the River City, to study the priests' writings, the akana. Drudaen had been afraid to use the room before, had used it only a few times while he was camped in Vyddn, trying to learn the Praeven language for himself. But now that I was awake again, now that he knew I was coming, he had no choice but to go to Seumren again, and try to stand on the High Place.

In the fountain at the base of Seumren I had met Kirith Kirin. Remembering that day, a long time ago, I entered the room beneath Yrunvurst and stepped through the room onto the High Place at the top of Seumren, where the wind was blowing and clouds spread out, the same brown stuff that had covered the rest of the world for so long.

My enemy stood here. He had begun to spread shadow over the forest as soon as he arrived, not because he wanted to destroy the trees but because he had no choice, he could not stop it. But Arthen could not tolerate its presence and was already withering around us. Drudaen could feel the dying, and so could I.

He stood near the eastern edge of the tower and I walked toward him. There was no dueling between us, no strife. He turned and watched me. He stood with a slight stoop, wrapping a white cloak around his arms. I remembered him as handsome from the last time I had seen him but he had lived too long, the body had been stretched thin.

"It won't work, will it? I can't come back." He didn't need for me to tell him the answer. He sighed.

He took a last look around. We strolled along the tower, while light poured down over the tops of the trees. We came to a place where the sun reflected off a curve in the river below, and beneath us we could see the many colors and shapes of that other abandoned city. "You should have seen it when it was alive," he said.

"I can," I said.

He frowned. Drawing himself up as straight as he could, he looked me in the eye, where his lust and hunger and avarice and arrogance all suddenly yielded to a softness, a yearning for rest, and he nodded, and I said, "All right."

Overhead, as I breathed, the sky cleared again, and shadow dissolved and sunlight returned and Drudaen Keerfax watched it all. He felt shadow break apart far across the countryside north and south and he sighed with relief and sagged and shook his head. That much would be enough to kill him. Only one gesture remained. I passed my hand across my mouth and drew out the gem I had swallowed, such a long time ago, the raven impaled on the talon of God, and I handed it to him. "This is yours."

He nodded and the gem lay in his palm. He blinked at it and the light suddenly grew bright, and she was with him, for an instant, my great-great-grandmother, wrapping something around his arms. This was how Drudaen Keerfax vanished out of the world altogether, and the war was ended.

CHAPTER TWENTY-EIGHT
THENDURIL HALL

1

I stood there for a while, after he was gone. I had never known a world without the story of him. Now, in all the worlds I could see, I had no enemy.

In that city on that Tower I stood until sunset. I waited to be certain his presence had done no lasting harm. I waited for a breath of warm wind from the south; I had called it and I knew it would come. Deciding we would have an early spring that year.

I did magic on Seumren, the first in more time than a person should have to think about, and when I was done I went down. I made that place my own, walked its long stair down to the ground, emerged into the fountain court and saw it wrecked, and saw it in my minds eye as it had been in my dream, when the King arrived at the court to walk into the tower, not Kirith Kirin, for he had never reigned here. I was seeing Falamar, my ancestor, who had built this place. The last magician to reach the third circle, the last to die at the moment that he did.

To move beyond the fourth level of magic is to learn to move the force that underlies all the things we see, not the force that shapes a stone, or transforms a stone, but the force that binds a stone to be itself. Jurel had learned this level of magic and had used it to make a peaceful kingdom. His room in Chalianthrothe was a device of the third circle. Falamar had moved third level power, too, the split second before he died because he could not control it.

To move beyond the fourth level of magic is to move beyond the world of things. One rarely comes back from the journey, as I had done.

I needed only know this when I was there, on Seumren, or when I was on Ellebren, or in the room of three circles at Chalianthrothe, or the other magic places; I need not know this all the time. This was the secret the Diamysaar understood but could not teach me, the thing one must learn oneself. How never to know too much.

That night I walked out of Cunuduerum across the bridge that had first drawn me here, so long ago, so much longer ago even than it seemed. Fresh from Kinth's farm, the smell of my mother's home-made soap on my hair. I set out walking, meaning to get to Inniscaudra, step by step, the long way.

2

We met on the Illaeryn road near the three hills, when I was within half a day's walk of Inniscaudra. He was riding alone, with Nixva on a bridle following behind him, and caught me at midmorning, washing out my tunic in a creek. He had found me as surely as an arrow finds the target in the hand of a fine archer, and he was always that.

Any schoolchild can recite the words we would hear when we reached Inniscaudra, the words that are engraved on the stone seals that we placed over those doors when YY closed them this last time. *I will give you a lifetime together, and I mean the lifetime you are due, and you will have your afternoon of happiness, I promise this, and I am YY who makes all of you, so I can do what I say.*

I caught up the bridle willingly and jumped onto Nixva's back, barefoot; Kirith Kirin took off like lightning on the Keikin and we followed. I realized I had left my boots at the creek, but I figured I would come back for them sometime, or they would be there, if anyone else needed them. There would be more boots at Inniscaudra. So I rode barefoot, and Nixva tossed his head when I sat on his back again.

We rode to Immorthraegul, the flank that overlooks Durassa's Park, and in the clear noon we sat there, and he shared the food he'd brought.

She said Kirith Kirin would be King one more time, for as long as he lived, and after there would be no more King or Queen, but the world would change again.

We had the day ahead of us, now that we had found each other. We had only to cross Durassa's Park sometime before sundown, and ride up Vath Invaths to that great house that would be our home, or one of our homes, for as long as we lived. As I had learned, that might be a very long time.

Only one of the Jhinuuserret will stay behind, in my house, this one where I stand, until the end of all the worlds that I and all the others have made.

That was the first day he called me by my two names together. We were walking along the shrine path on top of Immorthraegul, and we looked across Illaeryn at the clear sky. "You never did understand what it meant, when the Sisters called you to the field that day, did you? Before we went south. Answer me, Jessex Yron."

Said with that inflection, I understood.

A mortal magician could not have lived a hundred years. Not even asleep.

She took Athryn Ardfalla, and Sylvis Mnemorel followed, by her own choice. She took Mordwen Illythin because it was his time. Ren Vael died and Pel Pelathayn died when Cordyssa was burned, so they have already gone.

She took Evynar Ydhiil, home to Zaeyn at last.

A day will come when this will be over, and all this joy will turn to sorrow, I suppose. But that day we were together, and happy, and the thing we had fought for was won. No one wanted anything of either of us, except what we wanted of each other. And I could dig my bare toes in the winter grass.

We lost the world we knew when she came. She brought us another.

We walked across the hilltop, passed the shrine, then started downward at the turn of light. We would have time to cross Durassa's Park without hurry.

AFTERWORD
Aneseveroth

This war has come to be known as the Third War of the Sorcerers, following the first between Falamar and Jurel and the second between Kentha and Drudaen. Often enough, though, it is simply called the Long War. Archival records in Ivyssan government buildings that survived indicate that at the beginning of the war the population of Aeryn was close to four million, split nearly equally along the lines of Anynae and Jisraegen, with the Verm counted among the Jisraegen, along with three hundred thousand of the people of Drii, and unknown numbers of Tervan, Svyssn and beings beyond our ken. During the war about a half million people of both races took refuge in Arthen and escaped the main force of the conflict. At no time did shadow fall on Arthen and remain. To feed these folks, crops were planted in the Woodland for the first time in ages, and in certain areas trees were felled to make fields, though nowhere near the duraelaryn. The cultivated land was returned to its forest state at the end of the war. Thus the population inside Arthen never suffered from the dreadful famines that swept the rest of the country, if not at the beginning of the war then certainly by the end of it. At the end of the three generations that the war crossed, the numbers inside Arthen increased to about six hundred thousand, most of the population growth coming from new refugees, this according to counts Kirith Kirin ordered to be taken from time to time.

Of the remaining three and a half million of the Jisraegen and Anyn peoples who never came to Arthen, by the end of the hundred years of the war, the Kellyxa and Vyddn plains could count scarcely one hundred thousand souls. A scant twenty thousand were to be counted in the north, though these numbers were increased when another twenty thousand refugees returned from the Svyssn and Tervan countries to the ruins of their family lands, their devastated towns and villages.

The numbers of the Drii dropped, too, but not as drastically, to one hundred fifty thousand. Most Drii who died were killed in the various armies, which swelled to unheard of sizes in the later stages when the Tervan and Svyssn had joined the war. At one point there were two hundred thousand troops afield in the Fenax and the north Kellyxa, and many of these died in battle against Drudaen. Worst hit of all were Drudaen's servants, the Verm, of whom merely ten thousand lived through the devastation of shadow and war.

How many people were killed in fighting and how many Drudaen killed himself in order to prolong his life is a matter over which scholars still debate in the Praevenam and the Yneset, both of which we have revived in recent years. It is a matter of concern to nearly everyone, for Drudaen touched nearly everyone with the destruction that he brought. How many members of our families will we find in Zaeyn and how many never made the crossing because he sucked their souls into himself? What has happened to his spirit since? Did he cross the Gates like anyone else? Or did Kentha meet him at that last moment because she had prepared another place for him?

I have never tried to know the answers to these questions, any of them. The why of Drudaen will always puzzle us. He was already long-lived, his magic gave him nothing more than he had already, and yet somehow the use of magic enraged him, or sickened him, or changed him, or all those things. The ones who live a long time face such possibilities, as we know from history. The sickness passes, or not. I believe it did pass with Drudaen by the end, but it was too late, he could no longer stop making the shadow that kept him alive.

Less is said of Athryn's place in the causes of the war, due to her conduct at the end of it. But when YY took her, there were not many who were sorry to see her go.

Many cities were destroyed in that war and never were rebuilt. Cordyssa vanished in the late stages of the conflict, and its ruin still sits on the mountain. Bruinysk was destroyed and never rebuilt. Genfynnel has become a park, and the only structure standing on the acropolis at the fork of the river is Laeredon Tower. Teryaehn was never resettled. Arroth was abandoned, and remained so for many years after the peace. Arsk was sacked and razed and rebuilt during the war. Kursk was left a husk but partly rebuilt afterward. Charnos and Ivyssa suffered reductions in population as people abandoned the cities for the countryside or were taken to slave camps in Antelek, where the Verm were trying frantically to farm in order to stave off starvation themselves. Teliar was abandoned during the war though people moved back there, later, and I bought Brun's house by Ithambotl the great Anyn architect for myself. Kirith Kirin and I stayed there many times while he was King.

Mordwen Illythin was too old for fighting, Kirith Kirin never allowed him to take part in any of the combat, but he kept a long account of the war that has become the standard text on all that happened after the Battle of Aerfax. By the close of the war, Mordwen had reached the end of the long life granted him, and he would have gone of his own accord into the Deeps, except he wanted to stay to see how the story came out, he said; we were saying good-bye, that last day, before YY took him with her. He gave me his books to keep, because I was the one who would be here longest.

Pel Pelathayn and Ren Vael died in the last fighting at Cordyssa, when Drudaen loosed Verm soldiers into the place and told them to do whatever they wished with the people who were left, to take whatever goods they could find, him having by then no other way to feed them or reward them, his gold worthless like everything else. The Verm killed the men and women of fighting age, raped the young ones and beat the old ones, sacked the city and burned it to the ground. Drudaen stayed back from the fighting though he saw to it that Ren and Pel were targeted and killed. So he has the deaths of those two on his head, too; but they died fighting and passed safely through the Gates, as far as we know.

My uncle Sivisal lived a long time but never married; when he died he was still serving Kirith Kirin in Arthen. He caught a cold that turned to pneumonia, not the death he would have chosen but the one he got. Since he had left no family I had none. The war proved to be the last gasp of the Clans, which were never much remembered afterward; sad to say, I suppose, since the Clans first appeared in the age of the Forty Thousand.

Brun stayed in Arthen at court until Theduril went south to fight in the Novris resistance; Brun had first met him in that city and returned there with him. She died in the early fighting and Theduril in the late. When I heard she had finally married him, though, I felt a sense of ease for her. I missed her oddly in after years.

Trysvyn died at the gates of Bruinysk when the Verm were besieging that city. She came from there, and gave her life there. Gaelex the Marshall died of old age in Inniscaudra. So too died Inryval, Thruil the groom, my old tutor Kraele, Fethyar, Unril, Idhril, Vaeyr, Kaleric, Duvettre, the clerks I knew. So died Axfel, cared for by Mordwen to the end, though Mordwen had never liked the dog.

Nemort died in the north Fenax in one of the early campaigns against the Verm. He remained loyal to Kirith Kirin to his death.

My mother's body perished in the explosion that consumed Senecaur. She herself had been dead a long time, or so I choose to believe, and it was only her body that was re-animated by Drudaen as his weapon against me, though in the end she hurt him more, that day.

I suppose it is safe to say that all those I knew would have died anyway, given that I slept for so long, except the Jhinuuserret. But one's later friends never feel quite the same.

The Law of Changes, under which Kirith Kirin and Athryn Ardfalla had exchanged the crown for thousands of years, ended when Athryn left the world. We believed that when YY came this time she would end the current age of the Jisraegen as well, but she prolonged it, for one last long afternoon of peace, she said. For she trusted Kirith Kirin to make a peace that would last a while, and so he did.

Years after peace had begun, when the work of rebuilding and restoring had been going on in earnest for a long time, we traveled to Mykinoos as Kirith Kirin had promised we would one day. He had been buying the land around my father's old farm from whoever had claim to it after the war. This had taken a while since it was a long time before such claims could all be sorted out, work he had a hand in himself. But in the end he assembled a park he named Aneseveroth, Sea of Circles, and he took me there when the new stone lodge had been finished to his satisfaction.

He had bought land right up to the Mykinoos square; the village had survived the war as a shell but was repopulated in the boom of trade that accompanied rebuilding. Kirith Kirin's current Marshal of the Ordinary Thumin had recruited settlers to return to Mykinoos along with all the legitimate claimants to the lands thereabouts who had survived. The gates of Aneseveroth were right at the center of the village, and the villagers were free to wander in the parks. Mykinoos has become a tourist site in latter days, because I was born there, and most folks think that Aneseveroth was my father's farm. The real farmhouse, the real farmyard and barns, we made into a woody garden, working together during the summers we spent in the comfortable country house he had designed by the architect of the day. An imitation of Ithambotl, as all buildings are, in my opinion, but a nice house.

But that first day, no garden had been begun; there was only the high wall Kirith Kirin had commissioned to enclose the old farm grounds, and within was more than a century of growth, a hardwood forest all matured, and the remains of the life I remembered. We walked into it alone, Imral and Karsten back at the house, our guests for the opening of the park but not for this more private journey.

I stood there and took a breath. You could still see the shape of the land if you tried, overgrown as it was. I could almost see myself running back from the fields with Axfel and Jarred, the news of my uncle's impossible visit ringing in my ears. I took a deep breath.

"You sent for me," I told him, and took his hand, warm and comfortable, in mine. "To this place. And this is where it started."

"For you," he said.

"Yes, for me."

We were quiet, wandering. Nothing to say, only a feeling of peace and completion that we could think of as something we had earned. By then we had been together a long time, and his thoughts were as comfortable to me as mine were to him.

"I can begin to think it was worth it," he said. "To feel how peaceful this night is." He meant more, of course; he meant that the crops were growing, and the Vermish changes were being wiped slowly out of people, and sunlight was falling over grass as it used to, and there were only the usual problems to deal with, like the Charnos Guild and the troublesome new navy. He meant he was happy to see a sense of the ordinary restored to Aeryn, and now that he knew the work was well begun, he could feel a sense of normalcy himself.

For me, standing there, I could agree with him, but I had nothing to add. To my family, for whom the beginning of my adventure marked the end of their lives, was our peace worth their suffering, their violent ends? One can't weigh that kind of imbalance in a scale.

We began in those years and after to celebrate Chanii, in memory of the Long War and all that we lost in it. Kirith Kirin began the ceremony quietly when he dedicated the site of Genfynnel as a perpetual park; and after that, each year, the remembrance continued there and spread to other places. People of a certain age make a pilgrimage to the Laeredon acropolis and sleep the night in the park. Kirith Kirin said we should never forget that war, and we never have, while he was with us or after. We celebrate on the darkest day of winter, knowing that the suns that shine on us will renew the year again, as we ourselves renewed our world after its longest winter.

We have left the scar of Aerfax exactly as it was when Drudaen brought the fortress down. Of all the rooms in all the buildings in all the named places of Aeryn, I have never been back to that room, nameless, where I slept. Sometimes, even now, I dream I am still there, listening to the sea, and I am trying in the dream to wake myself, because the Wizard is still outside and I have to get rid of him, before he does any more harm. Finally I do wake up, into the real night, and if I'm in Inniscaudra I go to Ellebren Tower and sit on the High Place, and if I'm in Chalianthrothe I go to the room of the three circles. I listen to the music that is all there is, and I find peace again.

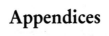

Appendices

Appendix 1:
GLOSSARY

Acht   (AHKT) A ritual poison used by the
Svyssn in the ceremonial death of the Husband.

Ae   (EYE) High; also, mountain; in some con-
texts, a people or nation

Aediamysaar   (Eye-dee-AM-i-sar) Mt. Diamysaar, the
Mount of God's Sisters, site of a device used in magic, in Arthen

Aegul   (EYE-gul) The High Stair, linking Domren
with the North Wall and the Deeps of Thenduril at Inniscaudra

Aelaren   (Eye-LAR-en) The High Walk, a stone
bridge linking Evaedren with Idren at Inniscaudra

Aerfax   (AIR-fax) The fortress on the southern
spur of the Black Spur Mountains; the High Place there is a Tower
called Senecaur, but the name Aerfax is also often used for the Tower

Aeryn   (AIR-in) The kingdom outside Arthen

Ajnur, Battle of   (AJH-nur) The Battle fought between the
Woodland Army and the Verm Army for control of and passage
through Ajnur Gap; the story is told in Kirithmar

Amataxa   (Am-a-TAX-a) A region near Cordyssa

Amri   (AM-ree) The Venladrii girl who serves
as kyyvi

An   (An) The sea

Aneseveroth   (An-e-SEH-ve-roth) The name given to
Kinth's Farm after the long war

Angoroe   (An-GOR-oh) The passage between
Arthen and the western mountains

Aniwetok   (An-i-we-TOK) The mayor of Charnos, one of the city burghers.

Anrex Valley   (AN-rex) A valley in the central Fenax where Kiril Karsten led troops who, with the aid of an army from Drii, encircled the Southern forces and massacred them.

Antelek River   (AN-te-lek) The river flowing between Lake Mur and Lake Dyvis, flowing beyond under the northern arm of Black Spur Mountains to become the Naug

Anykos   (An-EE-kos) The last month of the year

Anyn   (AN-in) The great bay in south Aeryn enclosed by the Black Spur Mountains and the Arossan Peninsula

Arossan Peninsula   (Ah-ROS-ahn) The southern peninsula which forms the eastern shore of the Bay of Anyn; the name has fallen out of use in Jessex's day since Arossa is then largely occupied by New Ivyssa and the Isar delta

Arroth   (AIR-oth) The City on Lake Mur, principal home of Kentha Nurysem; afterward, the City of the Verm, Vermhyloc

Arsk   (Arsk) A village where the southern road forks, running south to Ivyssa and east to Fort Pemuntnir

Artefax   (AR-te-fax) A daughter of the King Horse belonging to Kiril Karsten

Arth Hills   (Arth) A region in Arthen south of Nevyssan. This is the oldest country in the Woodland, the home of the Eldest Tree.

Arthen   (AR-then) The oldest of created places, a forest in the north of Aeryn.

Asfer   (ASS-fer) A type of leaf dried and used as a painkiller

Asfodel   (ASS-foh-del) A flowering grass whose purple blossoms sometimes grow so close together they form a lush carpet in hill country; the grass does not do well in hotter climates.

Athryn Ardfalla   (ATH-rin Ard-FA-la) Queen of Aeryn

Authralaren   (OUTH-ra-LA-ren) The processional walk to the Authra at Inniscaudra

Bald Hills   The hills at the northern end of
Charnosdilimur

Bremn   (BREM-neh) The fortress on Mount Bremn in Cordyssa, in which Queen Nauthren housed her garrison during the days of the Queen's Ban.

Briidoc   (BREE-dok) A region of Turis, in the
North

Brisnumen   (Bris-NOO-men) A fortress on the Fenax,
close to Drii

Bruinysk   (BROO-in-isk) A village at North Bridge, where the Queen kept many bardges and where much merchandise was shipped south from the Fenax

Brun   (Broon) Lady of Ivyssa

Calgiri   (Cal-GEE-ree) One of the two moun-
tains within the walls of Cordyssa, on which many noble folk had estates. At the top of Calgiri is the house of Ren Villex, lord of the city.

Casun   (Cass-OON) Cloak, robe without sleeves

Chaenhalii   (Khayn-ha-LEE) Literally, "long march", the name given to the march of Kirith Kirin's army from Genfynnel to Aerfax-upon-Kleeiom. The term's inclusion in the Kirithmar codifies the name. Called here An Chaenhalii, the Long March to the Sea.

Chalianthrothe   (Cha-lee-an-THROW-th) A house and lands in the Onge forest, later, part of the holdings of Jessex Yron; a gift to Jurel Durassa from the Orloc, who built it; means, 'little jewel', in the language of the Orloc.

Chanii   (Cha-NEE) Remembrance day for the Long War

Charnos   (CHAR-nos) The military harbor and city between Karns and Cuthunre Shore on the Bay of Anyn

Chasens, chasyns   (CHAY-sens) Tervan-devised columns which support tall buildings, especially well known in Inniscaudra; also used in the construction of magical structures like the Shenesoeniisae, the chasyns were reinforced with runes

Chevondraen   (CHEH-von-drain) A Venladrii settlement on the shores of Lake Dyvys

Chorval   (Chor-VAL) Lord Nivra, Nivri follower of Daerdruen, the husband of Lady Brun

Choveniiz   (Choh-ve-NEEZ) The lifetime of God, eternity; also shoveniiz, choveniis, shoveniis

Chulion   (CHOOL-yon) The stronghold of the YY-Sisters, the fortress and palace of the Diamysaar in the distant mountains

Chunombrae   (Choo-nom-BRAY) One of the Naming Fields in Arthen; a variant, Jhunombrae, was taken by the Tervan as the name for their chief city under the mountains; later, the Anynae named the citadel of Charnos the same name.

Chuvadrion   (Choo-VA-dree-on) Palace, citadel

Cilidur   (Si-li-dur) A yellow flower growing on a stalk, the blossoms close and bunched together like a fringe

Commiseth   (CO-mi-seth) Son of Dor, the neighboring farmer to Kinth's farm

Commyna   (Coe-mi-na) One of the Diamysaar

Corduban   (Cor-doo-BAN) a figure in a drinking lay

Cormes   (COR-mess) Follower of Daerdruen, acolyte in the study of Ildaruen, daughter of Dilithate

Cothryn   (CO-thrin) Son of Duris, Lord in Cordyssa

Cumbre   (COOM-bray) A Jisraegen traveling cordial that can substitute for food at need

Cunavastar   (Coo-na-VASS-tar) The first priest of YY, the first male in Arthen; a fortress on the Fenax is named for him; also the name of the House of Falamar and Drudaen

Cundruen   (Cun-DROO-en) A pass leading from Montajhena to Drii

Cunevadrim   (Coo-ne-VAH-drim) The southern palace of Daerdruen, originally built by Cunavastar, one of the oldest structures in Aeryn

Cunuduerum   (Cun-oo-DWER-oom) The Jisraegen city in Arthen, abandoned and under interdict since the fall of Falamar

Cunue   (Cuh-noo) Lake or river

Cunue Illyn   (ILL-in) The lake of the Diamysaar

Curaeth   (Coo-RAY-eth) Kiril Karsten's fief on the Fenax, taken from her by the Blue Queen at the time of the Ban on Arthen

Curaeth Curaesyn   (Coo-RAY-eth Coo-RAY-ee-sin) A prophet who wrote a book concerning the signs of the days before the Breaking of Worlds, though other events are mentioned in it as well. One of the twice-named.

Cuthru   (COO-threw) Son of None, a member of Lady Brun's entourage

Cuthunre   (Coo-THOON-ray) A valley in the South

Dagorfast   (DAG-or-fast) A village where the Fenax
road crosses River before swinging west toward Angoroe; the gold
barges were unloaded there for the overland journey to Bruinysk,
where they were loaded onto barges again for the journey south
down the Isar

Davii   (Da-VEE) King or Queen

Daviir   (DAH-veer) Successor

Deluna   (Day-LOO-na) The river that flows
down from Montajhena in Vyddn country

Denaezor   (De-NAY-zor) The name of the House
of Julassa Kyminax

Deniire   (De-NEAR) One of the three ritual lamps

Dernhang   (DURN-hang) The Palace on Kmur island

Diamysaar   (Dee-am-mee-SAR) Sisters to the YY

Dilimur   (DI-li-mur) Ridge, series of hills

Domren   (DOM-ren) The Tower of Guard, also
called the White Tower, the citadel that guards the eastern approach
to Inniscaudra

Drii   (Dree) The city of the Venladrii in the
mountains; the name is interchangeably used as the name of the
people.

Drusen   (DREW-sen) The Wife of the Svyssn, the
ruler of that country, a religious as well as political post. The Svyssn
Wife has many husbands all of whom accompany her everywhere,
and one of whom is poisoned by acht once a decade at springtime.

Dumas   (DOO-mas) A village on the North Road
where the road branches, going north to Cordyssa and east to Svyssn

Duraelaryn   (Doo-ray-LA-ren) One of the great trees
or tree-complexes that grows only in Arthen

Durassavariin   (Doo-RASS-ah-var-een) Durassa's Park, a valley between Vath Invaths, Immorthraegul and the Kellesar.

Dure   (DOO-ray) Northern, north

Duris   (Doo-RISS) A nut-bearing tree, deciduous, growing throughout Arthen and Aeryn

Durme   (Durm) The coastal flatland between New Ivyssa and Novris on Keikilla Bay.

Durud, durun   (Doo-ROOD) Black

Duruth   (Doo-ROOTH) Blood feud, blood hatred.

Duterian   (Doo-the-ree-an) Son of Maegoth, a picked warrior, sent to Jessex's farm

Duvettre   (Doo-VET-rah) Countess of Thynilex

Duvis   (Doo-vis) A small, hardy tree that grows in the upper elevations of Arthen and Aeryn.

Edenna Morthul   (E-DEN-a MOR-thul) Lady of Orelioth, Keeper of the Keys to Inniscaudra, who began Ellebren Tower and completed Laeredon, where she shut herself up and died at the end of the First War of the Sorcerors.

Elgerath   (ELL-ger-ath) A family of flowering vines. In higher altitudes, the flowers of this vine are wildly colored, while in lower altitudes only the blue varieties thrive. Also, a pale blue flower with a purple heart, prized for its sweet smell, for honey made from its pollen and for oil extracted from its abundant petals, used in soaps and cleansing oils

Ellebren   (ELL-e-bren) The High Place over Inniscaudra, the tower begun by Edenna Morthul and completed by Kentha Nurysem. One will stand on Ellebren, and only one, until the worlds are broken

Ellesotur   (El-ESS-oh-tur) The Eye-Rock of
Ellebren

Erennor Vale   (Ehrr-EN-or) The walled plateau above
Haldobran Gate where a wide meadow grows grass year round,
where the horses of Inniscaudra graze in rotation

Estobren Arches   (ESS-toh-bren) Magical entry arches on
the Falkri Stairway below Thrath Gate in the precinct of Ellebren
Tower at Inniscaudra

Evaedren   (Ev-AY-dren) The Tower of Twelve in
the Winter House

Evaenym   (Ev-AY-nim) The Twelve, those Twice-
Named who did not die from the first generation of Forty Thousand Jisraegen which YY created.

Evlaen   (Ev-LANE) daughter of Mrothe, the
doctor in Genfynnel

Evynar Ydhiil   (EV-I-nar ID-hil) The King of Drii, father of Imral Ynuuvil

Falamar Inuygen   (FA-la-mar In-WIJ-en) King of Aeryn and
Arthen, King of Cunuduerum, the Misborn

Falkri Stair   (Fall-KREE) The broad series of stairs
and ramps leading from the Under House to the Tower March and
the Domren underpass

Falthe   (FAL-theh) A ride, a trip involving a ride

Faris   (FAIR-iss) A tree like a pine

Faristae   (Fair-ISS-tay) A deciduous tree that grows
in the upper altitudes of Aeryn

Felva   (FELL-vah) Bath coat

Fenax   (FE-nax) The northern plain between
Arthen and the mountains

Fimbrel   (FIM-brel) The name of the Diamysaar
Cloak

Finru   (FIN-roo) The Lords of the Anynae

Fornbren   (FORN-bren) The Royal Palace in Ivyssa,
built by the City Burghers for Queen Athryn I.

Fortuinen   (For-TOO-in-en) The making of a Lore
Word; literally, naming and deriving

Fysyyn   (Fi-SIN) Daughter of Donneril, Jessex's
grandmother

Gaelex   (GAY-lex) Marshal of the Ordinary to
Kirith Kirin, daughter of Fioth

General Nemort   (Neh-MORT) Governor of Novris and
Nauthren's military second-in command, son of Idhrak, of Novris

Genfynnel   (Gen-FIN-el) A city down-river from
Arthen, the most northerly of the southern cities, built by the Jisraegen
after Cunuduerum.

Gnemorra   (Gneh-MOR-ah) A fortress on the Fenax
that guarded the northern end of the Angoroe

Goerast   (Ger-AST) One of the two High Places
in Montajhena; the place were Kentha died. She had taken the High
Place there from Drudaen; he used a gift she had given him to kill
her. Goerast was built by Drudaen after YY brought the Law of
Changes.

Gruesid   (GROO-sid) The language spoken by the
Svyssn

Gul   (Gull) Stairway

Haldobran Gate   (HAL-doh-bran) The Lower Gate into
Inniscaudra, where the road plunges from the Syystren Gate down
into Haldobran Gap

Halobar   (HA-low-bar) The Hall of Meeting, the
entry hall beyond the Syystren Gate, also called the Hall of Many
Partings.

Histel   (HISS-tel) Daughter of Sybil, Jessex's
sister

Hyvurgren Field   (High-VUR-gren) One of the Naming
Fields, in Raelonyii

Ibraxa   (Ib-RAX-a) The village where the Kelluxa
Road forks southeast toward Fort Pemuntnir and Ivyssa and southwest toward Novris through the Onge Forest

Ifnuelyn   (If-NEWEL-in) A powder used to start
fire.

Iire   (Eer) The eye of God ; also a stone used
for the point of a ritual lamp, the deniire

Iitana   (Ee-TAH-na) Lineage, house, family,
blood kin in the greater sense; similar to Clan, though Clan can be
used more broadly

Ildaruen   (Ill-DA-roo-en) A language of Power
derived by Cunavastar, used by him and his descendants. Unlike
Wyyvisar, Ildaruen can be taught without any limitation on the teacher

Illaeryn   (Ill-AIR-in) The high country in Arthen
around Inniscaudra

Imar   (EE-mar) The river that waters the North
Onge Forest, joining the Deluna

Imhonyy   (Im-oh-NEE) The house of Kirith Kirin,
Jurel Durassa

Immorthraegul   (Im-or-THRAY-gul) One of the hills that
borders Durassavariin, adjacent to Vath Invaths, lying southwest of
that hill

Imral Ynuuvil   (IM-ral In-OO-vil) Prince of Drii and
Chamberlain to Kirith Kirin

Inemarra   (In-ih-MAR-a) The House of Ruen Villex

Infith   (IN-fith) A sweet pitted fruit

Inniscaudra   (In-iss-COW-dra) The House that No Man Built, the house built by YY, the Diamysaar, and the Tervan in the Illaeryn region of Arthen

Inryval   (IN-ri-val) son of Thorassa, one of Gaelex's aides

Irion   (IR-ee-on) Variant of Aeryn, used in the South

Isar   (EE-sar) A river that waters Kellyxa and flows through Old Ivyssa

Isyrii   (Iss-EAR-ee) A River that branches off from Isar and flows through New Ivyssa

Ithambotl   (ITH-am-bot-l) A famous ancient archi-tect

Itheil Coorbahl   (Ith-AY-il Coor-BALL) Lover of Falamar whose death disturbs the wizard greatly; one of the Twelve Who Did Not Die, lord of Brii

Ithikan   (ITH-ih-kahn) Riding in a magician's wake, a way for a few mounted folk to travel faster

Ithlumen   (Ith-LOO-men) A fortress on the Fenax that guarded the approach to Cordyssa

Ivyssa   (Ih-VISS-a) The capitol of Aeryn since the fall of Montajhena; comprised of New Ivyssa, the Royal City, and Old Ivyssa, the oldest of the Anynae cities.

Jaka   (JA-ka) A morning beverage, a stimulant

Jarred   (JAIR-ed) Son of Kinth, Jessex's brother

Jessex   (JESS-ex) Son of Kinth

Jhinuuserret   (Jin-oo-SE-ret) The Twice-Named, also called the Evaenym, since the number of the True Jhinuuserrett is twelve

Jhunombrae   (Joo-nom-BRAY) The chief city of the
Tervan in the Mountains; the capital of what the North Fenax popu-
lace calls Smith Country

Jiivar   (Zhee-VAR) The Hall of the Eldest, a
variant name for Halobar Hall

Jiiviisn Field   (Zhee-VISN) A sacred field in Arthen
where Cunavastar built a shrine; one of the Naming Fields

Jisraegen   (JISS-ra-jen) The people of the wood, literally. The original inhabitants of Arthen, cast out of the Woodland
after the fall of Falamar Inuygen.

Julassa Kyminax   (Joo-LASS-a KI-mi-nax) The Witch of
Karns

Juneval   (Joo-ne-VAL) A crimson-flowering vine
common to every sort of climate in Aeryn and Arthen, akin to elgerath

Junwort   (JUNE-wort) A fragrant shrub that grows
in Illaeryn and West Fenax, used to make a beneficial tea

Jurel Durassa   (Joo-REL Doo-RASS-a) Lord of
Thynilex, Thaan of Montajhena, Lord of Yrunvurst

Ka   (Kah) Moon; a variety of lamp, also

Kaleric   (Ka-LE-rik) A Lord Nivri who serves
Kirith Kirin in Arthen

Karmunir Gate   (KAR-moo-near) The entrance to Illaeryn
in the Charnos Gap

Karnost   (KAR-nost) The Royal Gems, Gems of
Power

Karomast   (KAR-oh-mast) The High Place over
Zeul, which Daerdruen first wiped clean of Wyyvisar runes, then
tore partly down, a tower built by Edenna Morthul and Kentha
Nurycen

Kata sticks   (KA-ta) A percussion instrument made of
heavy round sticks, some covered with leather or lacquer to alter the
quality of sound

Kaufax   (COW-fax) a Prince of Horses, son of
Keikindavii

Kehan   (KAY-han) Winter, darkness

Kehan Kehan   The name of a hymn, "The Coming of
Winter in Darkness"

Keikin   (KEYE-kin) Male horse; the Keikin is the
short name of the King Horse

Kellesar   (Kel-ESS-ar) One of the hills that borders Durassavariin, adjacent to Vath Invath, lying southeast of that
hill

Kellyxa   (Kel-IX-a) The southern plain

Ketol   (Kay-TOL) Poet whose poems Jessex is
reading in Charnos

Khan   (Kahn) A month comprising the early and
mid part of spring; the month in which Jessex is born

Kiikin   (KEE-kin) Female horse

Kim   (Kim) darkness

Kimri   (KIM-ree) The Light in the Darkness, a
hymn

Kinth   (Kinth) Son of Daegerle, Jessex's father

Kirilidur   (Ki-RI-li-dur) The open central stone shaft
that is one of the great devices of the Wizard's Tower

Kirith Kirin   (KIR-ith KIR-in) Prince of Aeryn

Kithilunen   (Ki-thi-LOO-nen) The Evening Song

Kleeiom   (KLAY-om) The narrow strip of land
between the Blackspur Mountains and the Bay of Anyn, leading
south from the Karnish fens to Aerfax Tower.

Klyr   (Kleer) A type of white wine made in the
north Fenax, similar to though lighter than sauterne

Kmur   (Kmur) An island in the Bay of Anyn

Kor   (Kor) A type of leaf dried and used as a
promoter of healing in wounds

Krafulgur   (Kra-FUL-gur) The passage beneath
Urgiloth's Teeth, the two horned towers that guard the point where
the road twists round Urgiloth's Spur, passing beneath the Tower of
Guard and the Tower of the Twelve and along the Aegul.

Krom Hills   (Krom) Low Hills in Southeast Kellyxa,
below Trenelarth

Krysa   (KRI-sa) A river flowing from Lake
Dyvys to the Deluna River.

Kursk   (Kursk) A city on the East Kellyxa, at the
junction of the Deluna River and the Rovis River.

Kythorax   (KI-thor-ax) Lieutenant of Daerdruen, to
whom Sybil was given

Kyyvi   (KI-vee) Temple servant; literally one given
to God

Laeredon   (LAIR-eh-don) The High Place over
Genfynnel

Lake Ashmyr   The lake on the North Spur of the Black
Spur mountains, the lake which Cunevadrim overlooks, called by
many other names

Lake Dyvys   (DI-vis) The lake south of Polponitur

Lake Mur   (Mur) The lake in the center of the Barren Turis

Lake Rur   (Roor) The lake that borders Arthen and
Drii

Laren   (LA-ren) Walkway

Linvern   (LIN-vern) A deciduous tree that produces a sweet sap used to make sugar

Lise   (LEE-say) daughter of Sybil

Listrenen   (LIS-tre-nen) A region in the High North
Country near the land of the Svyysn

Lonyi   (LON-yee) Light, glow

Loris   (LOR-iss) A tall rabbit, usually three to
four feet with an ear span of another three to four feet, invariably
silver and blue in color, found in Arthen, in the mountains around
Drii and in the extreme east Fenax

Luen   (LOO-en) Bridge or crossing

Luthmar   (LOOTH-mar) No literal meaning.
The title of the epic song concerning the creation of Arthen; The
earliest extant versions of this lay date to the creation of written
language

Maleikarte   (MAH-lay-kar-the) The language of
power developed by the Jisraegen priests, usually shortened to Malei;
the Prin under the leadership of Edenna Morthul derived the language after long study, though it and the Prin were destroyed by
Falamar.

Maugritaxa   (MAW-gri-tax-a) The southern-most part
of Arthen

Menumen   (MEH-noo-men) A tree with long silver-
white leaves that flowers on the east Fenax and in the adjacent northern part of Arthen

Mikif   (MI-kif) Daughter of Sybil, sister to
Jessex.

Mikinoos   (Mi-KI-noo-us) A northern village, the
closest village to Kinth's farm

Misvaryen   (Miz-VAR-yen) The fief of Ashkenta
Nurysem in Turis, laid waste by Daerdruen Keerfax

Mithumen   (Mi-THOO-men) A kind of tree

Mithuun   (Mi-THOON) A stream in Tiisvarthyn

Mnemarra   (Neh-MA-ra) Kiikindavii, queen of
horses, mother of Nixva and Queen Nauthren's horse

Montajhena   (Mon-TA-zhe-na) The city built by the
Jhinuuserrett prior to the massacre of the Anynae

Mordwen Illythin   (MOR-dwen ILL-I-thin) the Seer in
Arthen and Lord of Ymber

Morteval   (Mor-te-VAL) A tree native to Illaeryn,
deciduous, nut-bearing, with dark brown bark and tiny leaves silver
on one side and sea-green on the other

Mur   (Mur) Earth, the mother

Murve   (Murv) A bush bearing a sweet, edible
dark blue berry; also the name for the berry; honey is made from the
pollen of the flowers from this bush

Muuren   (M-REN) A gemstone mined by the
Tervan, used to read the moment of true sunrise or sunset in the
Jisraegen lamp ritual

Naug River   (Nowg) The river flowing from the Black
Spur Mountains across Karns north of the Doreneth Fens; many
small branchings of the Naug originate in the Fens

Nevyssan Hills   (NE-vi-san) The hills lying northern of
Nevyssan's Point

Nevyssan's Point   The northernmost point of Arthen

Nira   (Ni-ra) (unstressed) Lamp

Nivri   (NIV-ree) The high born lords and ladies of the Great Houses of the Jisraegen

Nixva   (NIX-va) out of Mnemarra, a son of Keikindavii

Novris   (NOV-ris) The City at the mouth of the Deluna River, whose origin is in the Mountains east of Montajhena

Oet   (Oh-et) A coffee pot or a pot for boiling water

Onge Forest   (Onjh) The forest in Southeastern Aeryn, bordered by Kellyxa, Amre and Durme

Orelioth   (Or-EL-ee-oth) The hereditary country of Edenna Morthul

Orloc   (OR-lok) The people who live under the mountains, with whom the Jisraegen have little contact

Osar   (OH-sar) A River than branches off from Isar at Genfynnel, flowing through the western Cuthunre Valley and along the east side of Narvosdilimur before reaching the Bay of Anyn at Charnos

Pel Pelathayn   (PEL Pe-la-THAYN) The hunter and hero

Pelponitur   (Pel-PAH-ni-tur) The mountain ridges that extend into Arthen west of Drii

Pemuntnir   (Pe-MUNT-near) The fortress at the place where Osar and Osirii fork

Phyethir   (Feye-eh-thur) Literally, time on the height: the term during which a magician holds a high place; to reign, to rule over a place; the seat of power; the terrain controlled by a magician from a high place

Pirunaen   (Peer-oo-NAYN) Wizard's High Room, also called the Rensurdrun, the Room Under Tower

Pirunu (Pee-ROO-noo) Sorcerer

Prin (Prin) The collective noun (also the singular) for the priests of YY; later the college of the Prin is called the Prinama; in Jessev's time, Praeven and Praeveram.

Princess Kyvixa (Ki-VIX-a) out of Mnemarra, Mordwen's horse

Raelonyii (Ray-LON-yee) Interior light, light from within; the name for part of Arthen

Rel (Rel) Son of Moervan, Sivisal's companion

Ren (Ren) Tower

Ren Vael (Ren Vail) The Lord of Genfynnel, head of the House of Inemarra

Rensurdrun (Ren-SUR-droon) The Room Under Tower, the magician's workplace beneath the summit of any shenesoeniis

Reyn Nira (Rain Ni-ra) One of the three ritual lamps, tall and cylindrical in shape

Ri (Ree) Light

Roch (Rockhhh) The name for fire that comes from enchanted stone; there is so much of this in Aeryn that there is a widespread trade in it; roch never wears out.

Ron (Ron) Talon, claw, spur

Rovis (ROE-viss) A river watering the East Kellyxa, north of the Imar valley

Ruus (Roos) The last month of summer

Ryyn (Rin) Countryside

Senecaur (SE-ne-cowr) The Tower of Change at Aerfax is called Senecaur; the name Aerfax is also often used for this High Place

Sergil (Ser-GILL) Daughter of Vysth, also Commiseth's daughter

Seumren (SOOM-ren) The High Place over Cunuduerum

Shevis (SHE-vis) The white moon's name

Shoveniis (Show-ve-NEEZ) The mind of God, awareness

Shurhala (Shur-ha-LA) The face of the mountains, any mountain range, and Shurhala, the eastern slopes of the Black Spur Mountains, seen from Kleeiom

Sim (Sim) Son of Kinth, Jessex's oldest brother

Simishal (SI-mi-shall) The urchin in Genfynnel

Sirhae (SUR-hay) Shadowland, land under Shadow; plural Sirhaen

Sirhe (Sear-hay) Shadow

Sivisal (SI-vi-sal) Son of Veneth, uncle to Jessex

Suuren (SUR-en) Luck; the name of the ceremonial morning ride of the kyyvi

Suuren Falthe (SUR-en FAL-theh) The ceremonial morning ride of the kyyvi, taking place after dawn

Suvrin (SOO-vrin) Range of mountains; a more formal term than Ae, used always in the context of names

Suvrin Aensevere (An-e-SE-ve-re) The Encircling Mountains, the range of mountains that encircles Aeryn, generally called Caladur when referring to the northwestern ranges

Suvrin Caladur   (Ca-la-DUR) The Barrier Mountains, the range of mountains that encircles Aeryn, generally called Caladur when referring to the northeastern ranges

Suvrin Durudron   (Doo-roo-DRON) Black Spur Mountain Range; variant would be Durudronaen

Suvrin Sirhe   Mountain Shadow, a part of Arthen adjacent to Drii

Svelyra   (S-veh-LI-ra) An autumn blooming flower that grows in Arthen and on the western Fenax

Svorthis   (S-VOR-thiss) A pass leading from the Suvrin Sirhe region of Arthen to Drii

Svyssn   (S-VIS-n) A northern tribe, thought to be descended from Jurel Durassa who broke away from the Jisraegen before the coming of the Anynae

Sybil   (SI-bil) Daughter of Fysyyn, Jessex's mother

Syldivaris   (Sil-di-VAIR-iss) Daughter of Dutroya, picked warrior, sent to Jessex's farm

Sylvis Mnemorel   (Sil-VIS Ne-MOR-el) Lover of Athryn Ardfalla

Sythu   (SI-thoo) Sivisal's horse

Syystren Gate   (SIS-tren) The Upper Gate into Inniscaudra, standing at the summit of Vath Invath

Talhonesh   (Tal-hon-ESH) The Hall of Last Days, a variant name for Thenduril, the Woodland Hall in Inniscaudra

Teliar   (TEL-yar) City in Narvosdilimur

Telkyii Tars   (TEL-kyee TARS) The palace in Genfynnel

Tervan   (TUR-van) The proper name for the inhabitants of the country north of Cordyssa, known more commonly as the Smiths because of their skill in mining and metalwork

Teryaehn Don   (Ter-YAYN Don) The mouth of
Kleeiom in the north

Thaan   (Thane) Witch

Thaanarc   (THANE-arc) "The Witch of the Wood,"
the ceremonial/court title for the principal magician of Arthen; Kentha
Nurysem and Drudaen Keerfax exchanged the title under the Law
of Changes.

Theduril   (They-DOO-ril) Son of Vinisoth, Brun's
lover

Thenduril   (Then-DOO-ril) The Woodland Hall, the
main ceremonial hall of the Winter House, where the entrance to
Ydren and the Deeps is located, along with the red and blue thrones

Thoem   (Thoam) The High Place over Fornbren,
a tower built by Drudaen

Thrath   (Thrath) The spur of rock on which
Ellebren Tower stands; also, a mountain in Montajhena

Thruil   (THROO-il) Son of Koth, Kirith Kirin's
chief groom

Thuenyn   (Thyew-EN-in) a leaf used to make a
poultice for the healing of small wounds; literally "thue" blood and
"nyyn" God makes

Thule   (Thyule) The crystal fountain in the Base
Chamber of Ellebren

Thumin   (THOO-min) Marshal of the Ordinary
after the Long War

Thyathe   (Theye-ATH-eh) The lake at the foot of
Vath Invaths in Illaeryn, visible from Inniscaudra, near Durrassa's
Park

Thynilex   (THIN-ih-lex) A part of the Fenax near
the Country of the Smiths

Tiiryander   (Teer-YAN-dur) The cord which binds
the soul to the body

Tiisvarthen   (Tiss-VAR-then) Golden Arthen, a part
of Arthen where tiisloordurae, golden flowering trees, grow; alternate, Tiisvarthyn

Tirioth   (TI-ree-oth) One of the Naming Fields
in Arthen

Tornimul   (tor-ni-MUL) The Gates of the Dead, the
entrance to the lands which lead the souls of the dead under the
mountains and eventually to Zan; the Dead Gates are in the keeping
of the Orloc and only that people can find them

Trenelarth   (TREH-ne-larth) A forest in Central
Kellyxa

Trysvyyn   (TRIS-vin) A soldier in Imral's service, a
woman from Bruinysk

Turmingaz   (Tour-min-GAZ) The royal palace built
by Jurel Durassa in Montajhena, which partly survived the destruction of the city when Ashkenta died

Twar Ford   (Twar) The village at the place where the
Osar descends steeply down from the Hills of Slaughter to the plain
of Ajnur and the city of Charnos; barge traffic from upriver must
unload at Twar Ford and freight goes overland into the city

Umbriil   (UM-bril) Lady of Veriten

Umiism   (Ooo-MISS-m) The name from God, the
Second Name, the mark of the Jhinuuserret; also, the term for the
power and privileges accorded to the Jhinuuserret.; literally, 'the
mark of God in a Word.'

Unril   (UN-ril) Lady of Amataxa, a Nivri House

Untherverthen   (Oon-ther-VER-then) The sleep of Jessex under Senecaur and Aerfax; also called the hundred-year sleep;originallys, the name of a people said to live deep in the Barrier Mountains beyond the Orloc, who hibernate through the long winter in the mountains, coming to consciousness only during spring and summer

Unufru   (Ooo-NOO-froo) A root used to cure some fevers, and also used by witches in the healing of charms; used by sorcerers to cure a variety of diseases caused by magic

Urgiloth Yr   (Ur-GIL-oth) The Spur of Urgiloth, the lower of the twin summits of Vath Invath and the foundation for the Tower of Guard

Vaeyr   (Vair) Lord of Cordyssa, a Nivri Lord

Vaguath   (VAG-wath) Near-Son of Kinth; by virtue of the type of marriage; half-brother of Jessex

Vath Invaths   (VATH IN-vaths) The hill in Illaeryn raised up by YY, on which Inniscaudra was constructed

Vella   (VE-la) One of the Diamysaar

Velunen   (Ve-LOO-nen) The Morning Song

Venladrii   (Ven-LA-dree) Literally, inhabitants of
Drii

Veriten   (VER-ih-ten) A region of the Fenax

Vesnomen   (VESS-noh-men) Flowers like poppies,
in various colors

Viis   (Vees) A light, fine cloth, virtually indestructible, often used by Jisraegen tentmakers

Vilaren   (Vee-LA-ren) The abutment of wall that provides processional access to the Authra; literally, "shrine-walk"; at Inniscaudra

Vissyn   (Vi-SEEN) One of the Diamysaar

Vithilonyi   (Vi-thi-LON-yee) The Festival of Lights, celebrated at the change of season from autumn to winter

Vulnur   (VUL-nur) The Killing Rock, the place where Jisraegen criminals were executed in Arth Hill Country

Vulnusmurgul   (Vul-nuss-MUR-gul) The ridge forming the eastern border of Karns above Charnos and the Bay of Anyn, called the Ridge of Souls since the day when the Jisraegen drove the Anynae into the hills and slaughtered many thousands; also called the Hills of Slaughter, Vulnysryyaegul

Vuthloven   (Voo-THLOW-ven) Gray-barked trees with silver leaves, bearing white winter flowers.

Vuu Nira   (Voo Ni-ra) A variety of lamp made of metal strips and glass, fueled by any of a number of oils, known for its warm, rich light; most often Vuu-lamps are lit in early evening; Light from these lamps give tone and color to the flesh

Vyddn   (VID-n) The province round Montajhena, once called the Royal Province, when Montajhena was capital of Aeryn

Wyyvisar   (WIV-I-sar) The Hidden Speech, also, the Words of Power, taught to magicians by the Diamysaar

Ym   (Im) A region of Arthen adjacent to Suvrin Sirhe

Yrin   (EAR-in) Variant of Aeryn, commonly used in the extreme north, Svyssn and among the Tervan

Yron   (Ih-RON) Talon of God, claw of God, spur of God, depending on usage

Yruminast   (Ih-ROO-mi-nast) The High Place over Cunevadrim, an Ildaruen Tower which dates from the days of Falamar

Yruminax   (Ih-ROO-mi-nax) Literally, "Other Power"; the name given to the consort of YY

Yrunvurst   (Ih-ROON-vurst) The High Place in
Montajhena built by Jurel Durassa, broken when Falamar was taken
from the world; after his passing rebuilt again and finally destroyed
in the battle between Drudaen and Ashkenta

YY   (Ee) The name of God

Yydren   (EE-dren) Also spelled Idren, and in other
ways; the YY Tower in the Winter House

Zaeyn   (ZAY-een) The Country of heroes, heroes home, the land of the dead across the mountains, the golden
land; variant of Zan

Zeul   (Zyool) The Royal Palace in Ivyssa, built
by the City Lords for the King Kirith I.

Appendix 2
JISRAEGEN HISTORY

The study of Jisraegen history suffers from its length, the Jisraegen disregard for calendars (including any consistent number system for years), and the wealth of sources available. Jisraegen libraries in Montajhena and Ivyssa alone contain manuscripts in the millions. While there is a remarkable agreement among these sources as to the major events of the history, there is notable divergence as well, as the Jisraegen scholars themselves have noted. Even within the text of *Kirith Kirin* there are contradictory historical assertions by the leading voices of the narrative, particularly concerning Falamar's destruction of the Praeven and the years of war between Falamar and Jurel. The author makes no attempt to underline these inconsistencies but neither is there any attempt to conceal them. Hormling scholars have only begun serious work on the Jisraegen texts, which are physical documents and not tractable to our study. No archaeological studies of any kind have been permitted in Aeryn/Irion and it is doubtful that any such will be forthcoming. So we are left at this juncture with history as the Jisraegen assert it. The following is a general outline of the history the Jisraegen have preserved for themselves, with no attempt to address scholarly concerns or to document areas of dispute. The timeline is intended solely as an aid in the reading of the history of the Third War.

I. Creation
- A.   The great opposition coalesces and YY and Yruminax are separate
- B.   YY creates Wyyvisar and makes the first place, Arthen, and the first world, Aeryn
- C.   YY separates into Herself and the Sisters
- D.   Yruminax separates into Himself and Cunavastar

II. First Days
- A.   The Created Peoples arise in the living mountains
- B.   The Tervan build Aerfax at the southern-most tip of the mountains, on the first rock YY raised out of the sea
- C.   YY makes Illaeryn
- D.   The Sisters join her in the building of Inniscaudra
- E.   Cunavastar builds the first of the shrines that will later be known as the Elder Shrines, Hyvurgren

III. The Worlds are Made
      A.   YY makes other worlds and joins them to Aeryn
IV. The First Separation
      A.   The Sisters refuse to teach Cunavastar any of the Wyyvisar that they know
      B.   Cunavastar withdraws from Arthen and builds Cunevadrim with the help of the Other and the Orloc, who are friendly to him for a time
      C.   Cunavastar learns Ildaruen from the Other
      D.   Cunavastar builds the first stone circle on the foundation rock of what will become Yruminast
      E.   Cunavastar woos Commyna in Arthen
V. The First War
      A.   The Two Sisters make Sister Mountain
      B.   Commyna conceives a child by Cunavastar
      C.   The Two Sisters fight Cunavastar and southern Arthen dies
      D.   Commyna bears a child, Falamar
      E.   Cunavastar tries to steal the child but YY takes Falamar into the Deeps of Inniscaudra
      F.   Commyna and the Two Sisters defeat and bind Cunavastar but cannot destroy Cunevadrim
      G.   YY banishes the Sisters from Arthen and they cross the mountains to Zaeyn.
VI. The Forty Thousand
      A.   YY creates Forty Thousand humans and sets them on the hills around Inniscaudra
      B.   The Forty Thousand waken. A language has already been made for them.
      C.   They live in Inniscaudra for seven generations
      D.   Jisraegen writing is developed, Clans arise, and the Jisraegen meet the Uncreated Peoples
      E.   Early Jisraegen begin to move in nomadic groups throughout Aeryn
      F.   Of the Forty Thousand who awaken, Twelve do not die
VII. The Clans and the Evaenym
      A.   Clans arise as groups of extended family, but all persons have two Clan affiliations of equal importance, the Mother-Line and the Father-Line Clans
      B.   The first priests learn the worship of YY from the Sisters, among them Curaeth Curaesyn
      C.   Jurel Durassa leads a group of Jisraegen into the

eastern mountains at the site of a river gorge

    D.   The Twelve Who Did Not Die gradually emerge as leaders among the Jisraegen

    E.   Falamar finds his father's house, Cunevadrim, and lives there with his followers

    F.   Falamar learns Ildaruen

    G.   The Sisters teach Wyyvisar to Jurel Durassa and Edenna Morthul

VIII. Mountain and Forest

    A.   The Jisraegen settle either in the mountains or in Arthen

    B.   Jisraegen explorers reach the shore of the Bay of Anyn and explore east as far as Keikilla Bay

    C.   Jurel Durassa provides aid to the Orloc who are at war with the Untherverthen and the Orloc build Chalianthrothe

    D.   Edenna Morthul settles in Inniscaudra and becomes the first Keeper of the Keys

    E.   The Tervan complete work on Halobar, the last of the main halls to be completed

    F.   Falamar and his Clans settle along the banks of the Isar in Arthen

IX. Cities

    A.   The Praeven and Falamar organize the Clans in Arthen

    B.   Cunuduerum is founded and the Jisraegen in Arthen begin to organize a style of life that floats between the urban center and a nomadic existence in the forest

    C.   The Praeven build the first Library in Cunuduerum

    D.   Falamar and Itheil Coorbahl go south to live in Cunevadrim, dissatisfied with the Praeven's control of the city

    E.   Jurel Durassa and the Orloc build Montajhena in the mountains, intended only as a ceremonial center, though soon the mountaineers all build homes of stone in the city

X. The People of Drii

    A.   The Drii appear and ask Jurel Durassa for shelter in Montajhena

    B.   He and the Jisraegen welcome them after the long trek under the mountains

    C.   Jurel and Evynar explore Cundruen all the way to

the end

D.   Evynar and his people found a city at the end of the passes

E.   Falamar is suspicious of the friendship between the mountain Jisraegen and the Drii and returns with Itheil to Cunuduerum

XI. The Good Age

A.   The cities grow and prosper

B.   The Praeven and Edenna Morthul begin the deriving of the akana alphabet and the Maleikarte

C.   The tradition of the kyyvi begins as a result of this

D.   Jisraegen weaving and glass-working become increasingly advanced

E.   Jisraegen abandon the study of astronomy

F.   Jisraegen literature, theatre, opera and visual arts flourish in Cunuduerum, Montajhena, and Genfynnel

XII. Falamar

A.   Falamar begins to teach Ildaruen to a small set of followers

B.   Cunuduerum is dominated by his faction and, it is thought, by magic

C.   The forest Jisraegen become less nomadic and settle in or near Cunuduerum through much of the year

D.   The forest-folk become estranged from the mountain Jisraegen

E.   Edenna Morthul and the Praeven begin the construction of the first akana chant

F.   The Orloc complete work on Chalianthrothe, finishing the room of three circles

XIII. The War of the Towers

A.   Falamar enlists the Tervan to build Seumren

B.   The Praeven begin the first of the Immorthraeguls of Power

C.   Falamar uses Seumren to destroy the Praeven though Edenna and the last of the Praeven adepts manage to close and seal the Library

D.   Falamar spreads the story that the Praeven were singing the Breaking Song that will end the universe as we know it

E.   Jurel builds Yrunvurst and places the Tervan muuren-stone in the summit

F.   Edenna Morthul retires to Inniscaudra and begins work on the base of Ellebren on Thrath Rock

XIV. The Massacre in the Hills of Slaughter
      A.   In Cunevadrim, Falamar broods, hires Tervan build-
ers, begins work on Yruminast, over the foundations of Cunavastar's ritual circle
      B.   Falamar marries and fathers a child, when it was
thought that the Evaenym were barren. The child
is Drudaen, who learns his father's arts
      C.   The Anyn land on the north shore of the Bay of
Anyn at the present-day site of Charnos
      D.   Settlers from Montajhena found Ivyssa along the
river delta to the south and Cordyssa in the mountains
      E.   Itheil Coorbahl is killed in southern Aeryn by an
Anyn scout party
      F.   Falamar leads an army against the Anynae and sev-
eral thousand, or more, are massacred in the Hills
of Slaughter
      G.   Falamar enslaves the Anynae, though some thou-
sands escape to eastern Arthen, where the mountain Jisraegen give them shelter
      H.   Jurel and Falamar go to war
      I.   Charnos is founded and the Tervan build the Great
Wall to protect the Anynae from Falamar
      J.   Arroth is founded, and later Teliar and other south-
ern cities
XV. The Hundred Years War
      A.   Falamar and the largest army of Jisraegen ever
assembled besiege Montajhena
      B.   Jurel and his folk continue to be supplied from
Drii
      C.   Jurel and Falamar are matched powers of the
Fourth Level and neither can gain the advantage
for nearly a century
      D.   Jurel goes to Chalianthrothe, is absent for a long
time, and for the first time uses the room of three
circles
      E.   Jurel builds the room in Yrunvurst that allows him
to travel to Seumren instantly
      F.   Jurel drives Falamar out of Seumren
      G.   Falamar besieges Montajhena, and Jurel defeats
his army
      H.   Falamar, in fighting Jurel, understands how Jurel
is moving third-level power and does so himself

I.   The ensuing force destroys Yrunvurst Tower and kills both Falamar and Jurel

XVI.   YY intervenes

A.   A time of chaos ensues

B.   YY intervenes in the affairs of Aeryn for the sake of Arthen

C.   She gives the Law of Change and names Kirith Kirin and Athryn Ardfalla as King and Queen, their origins are not recorded

D.   When Queen Athryn I was old, she summoned Kirith Kirin and he came to Aerfax and took the Crown from her, and he became King, and she rode to Arthen and became young again, and the cycle was established

E.   Some of the Twelve who had been immortal were now taken with YY to Zaeyn and others were named

F.   The lives of the Twelve were merely prolonged and they would no longer be immortal in Aeryn

G.   The Tervan build Senecaur, the Tower of Change, over Aerfax, and place an Eyestone there attuned to the Karnost gems in the possession of Kirith Kirin and Athryn Ardfalla; the rune-work is completed by Edenna Morthul, and later Drudaen is allowed to add Ildaruen lines to the kirilidur as well

XVII.   The Rule of Law

A.   Athryn Ardfalla and Kirith Kirin reign in peaceful succession

B.   Kentha Nurysem learns Wyyvisar at Illyn Water, though this knowledge is hidden

C.   Edenna Morthul completes the building of Laeredon and begins a shenesoeniis in Ivyssa, called Karomast

D.   Settlers go to Novris and found a city there, the first jointly made by Anynae and Jisraegen

E.   Edenna Morthul retires to Laeredon when Kentha Nurysem attains the Fourth Circle of magic

F.   Kentha Nurysem takes over building of Karomast and Ellebren

G.   Drudaen builds Thoem and also begins a Tower in Arroth, but there only lays the foundation

H.   Drudaen builds Goerast and Kentha rebuilds Yrunvurst in Montajhena

XVIII. Discontent
- A.   Drudaen and Kentha become lovers in secret
- B.   They exchange gifts. Drudaen gives Kentha a sapphire he has kissed
- C.   They explore the ruins in Montajhena and Kentha shows him the room in Yrunvurst, which Edenna showed her
- D.   They go in secret to the Library of the Praeven in Cunuduerum
- E.   They part for a while
- F.   Kentha is troubled that she has taken Drudaen to the Library and withdraws to Inniscaudra
- G.   She works intently on Ellebren Tower and guards that part of Inniscaudra from Drudaen; she refuses to leave Arthen even when Kirith Kirin is King

IX. Aretaeo
- A.   In the thirty-third change, when Kirith Kirin was King, Kentha returned to Inniscaudra and Drudaen and she became lovers again
- B.   Near the time of the summons, Drudaen convinced her to return to Cunuduerum, and she did
- C.   They remain in Arthen and returned to Cunuduerum many times after the thirty-fourth Change, when Athryn Ardfalla became Queen
- D.   In some manner they conceive a child, though the Jhinuuserret were rarely able to engender or bear children
- E.   Drudaen attempts to force the secret of the Praeven magic from Kentha and she uses the Gem he has given her to read his thoughts
- F.   Drudaen attempts to kill Kentha
- G.   They contest one another to no conclusion and Kentha goes to work completing Ellebren Tower
- H.   She seals the Praeven Library and locks him out of Yrunvurst, and thus out of Cunuduerum as well
- I.   Kentha foresees the Long War
- J.   Drudaen attacks her while she is completing Ellebren Tower and Kirith Kirin and Athryn Ardfalla use the Karnost Gems together to force them to make peace
- K.   Kentha completes Ellebren Tower and makes the Bane Locket
- L.   She bears her child alone, hidden from everyone,

and gives the child to a couple who lived in Arthen to raise, hiding all this in magic

M.   Drudaen again attacks Kentha from Goerast, and uses all his strength against her, and that time the Karnost Gems cannot stop him

X. The Second War of the Sorcerors

A.   Kentha breaks Goerast Tower against Drudaen and takes it from him; this is the Second War of the Sorcerers

B.   Humiliated, he uses the gift she gave him when they were lovers and sings Great Devourer

C.   Kentha destroys Goerast and Yrunvurst both as she dies, and most of Montajhena is destroyed at the same time; Drudaen is unable to eat her soul

D.   Athryn Ardfalla, in residence at Turmengaz, sees the destruction, escapes, but is changed by it

E.   Drudaen devastates the hereditary lands that be longed to Kentha and a shadow forms over Turis and Cunevadrim

F.   Athryn quarrels with Sylvis and Sylvis withdraws to her estates in Onge

G.   Drudaen makes a way to extend life from what he learned in the Praeven Library

H.   Drudaen gathers apprentices and begins the teaching of Ildaruen openly

I.   Athryn is ill after the burning of Montajhena and Drudaen sees that her illness is partly magical, cures her

J.   They become lovers for a time, and Drudaen gains access to the Karnost Gems

K.   Athryn sends Drudaen to Kirith Kirin to tell him he is no longer needed to succeed her in Ivyssa

XI. The Long Wait

A.   Kirith Kirin bans all but his supporters from Arthen

B.   Drudaen is no longer able to enter Arthen, though he attempts to do so to get back into Cunuduerum; when he is inside the forest he can no longer breathe

C.   In a similar fashion, most people who enter Arthen either wander out again, disoriented, or vanish; and Arthen becomes known as a dangerous place

D.   Athryn purges the south of the remaining priests of the lamp-cult, and then does the same in the North

E. She builds eight new forts, three in the North, and places a perpetual series of patrols along the edge of Arthen; these prove to be ruinous expenses

F. Drudaen begins several building projects in or near Cunevadrim, and Queen Athryn pays for those, in cluding the cost of Tervan construction crews and stone from the deep mountains. Drudaen strengthens Cunevadrim and its Tower, and refortifies Arroth as well. He does further work on the Arroth Tower and abandons it again.

G. Taxes rise, trade suffers, and people become unhappy

H. A kyyvi dies of a fever, and the Seer, Mordwen Illythin, has a true dream

Appendix 3
JISRAEGEN CALENDAR

DATE	SEASON	NUMBER OF DAYS
Khan	Spring	47 days
Kemyluur	Spring	44 days
Ruus	Summer	56 days
Ranthos	Summer	45 days
Ikos	Autumn	49 days
Imante	Autumn	40 days
Ymut	Winter	62 days
Yama	Winter	71 days

The Jisraegen Calendar in use during the 34th Change was handed down from the days of the Praeven, according to the Jisraegen sources. There is no explanation for the workings of this calendar that we have learned, and the Jisraegen abandoned its use at the time of the departure of King Kirith, when Jisraegen astronomy and time-reckoning went through a series of revolutionary changes. The whole legend of the New Sky and its implications for our study of the history of Aeryn/Irion is too large to delve into in this present text, and since the age of which *Kirith Kirin* speaks belongs to the Old Sky, those debates have no bearing on the reading of this work.

The Jisraegen calendar is marked by few holidays. In the entirety of *Kirith Kirin* as it has come down to the present day, the only holiday noted is Vithilonyii, the Festival of Lights, reputed to be the anniversary of creation, in the month of Khan. Few other holidays are recorded in any source, none that are celebrated at the time of 34th Change. Chanii is later a major holiday, celebrated in Yama at the shortest day of the year, which could vary, in the Old Sky reckoning. Therefore the festival was celebrated for several days at the height of winter, the celebration ending when days began to lengthen. It may be that the uncertainty of the calendar and its changeable relationship with the observed seasons led to the paucity of holidays in the Jisraegen year. Without verifiable information concerning the nature of the Old Sky, we have no way of knowing.

It is speculated by many Hormling scientists that the lack of observable regularity in the heavens would have stunted any efforts the Jisraegen might have made toward developing science, which is one of the leading theories to explain the relatively primitive state of Aeryn civilization when we first made contact with the new continent. Others have speculated this could explain the consequent development of Jisraegen magic, which serves largely the same function in Jisraegen society as technology in ours.

Appendix 4:
High Places at the time of the 34th Change

Seumren: The oldest shenesoeniis, built by Falamar Inuygen. The central kirilidur contains a limited number of runes in Ildaruen. The main device of Seumren is the rune labyrinth on the summit, constructed all of Ildaruen writing. There is no Eyestone. Jurel Durassa made a spatial connection between Seumren and his own Tower, Yrunvurst, thus making the Tower unusable in any attack against Yrunvurst; see below. Seumren lies north of the territories to which the Hormling have access.

Yrunvurst: The first shenesoeniis to include an eyestone of muuren, a gift to Jurel from the Orloc or the Tervan, depending on who is telling the story. The kirilidur contained a few Wyyvisar runes in its original construction, but no rune lines. A Wyyvisar rune pavement spirals on the summit, notating the Ruling Dance. A room in the base of the Tower was linked by Jurel to the summit of Seumren, to allow Jurel to frustrate Falamar's use of that High Place. It is not known exactly when this took place, but the room was used during the war between the two Wizards. The Tower was destroyed during the final battle between Jurel and Falamar, that ended in the death of both. The tower was rebuilt by Kentha Nurysem with a new eyestone and a more elaborate Wyyvisar kirilidur, in imitation of Laeredon Tower, which had been completed by that time. Yrunvurst was ultimately destroyed in the battle between Kentha and Drudaen. It has since been rebuilt and may be seen today in Montajhena.

Ellebren: The base of Ellebren was begun by Edenna Morthul during the War of the Towers. She abandoned the work and completion of the Tower was taken up again by Kentha after Edenna shut herself up in Laeredon Tower. Kentha constructed Ellebren Tower after she had studied the Laeredon kirilidur and after she had completed work on rebuilding Yrunvurst in Montajhena and Karomast, the Tower in Ivyssa. She brought her experience in those works to the construction of Ellebren. The kirilidur there is made up of multiple threads of Wyyvisar runes along with lines in the Malei to which the Wyyvisar is tied, so that one Word operates both lines in harmony or dissonance. The fearsome power of Ellebren is thought to come from the duality of the kirilidur. The kirilidur borrows Edenna's innovation of crossing lines, and Kentha added lines that spiraled along the chasens as well. The eyestone, Ellesotur, is a muuren of great purity which Kirith Kirin purchased for the Tower from the Empress of the Tervan, said to be the purest stone ever found after the Ruling Rock of Senecaur. A Wyyvisar rune pavement spirals on the summit, notating the Ruling Dance. The Tower is encircled by a colonnade and three silver horns rise from the crown, these also spiraled and cross-spiraled with rune lines. The Tower was completed shortly before the beginning of the 34th Change. It may therefore be seen as one of the oldest towers, or the youngest. This Tower lies north of the territories open to the Hormling.

Yruminast: Begun nearly at the same time as Ellebren, this tower was built by Falamar over an older ritual circle Cunavastar had made, and the tower incorporates the circle intact in its lower regions, though the circle and the Tower do not function as one device. The ruling runes of the kirilidur are of Ildaruen though the earliest lines in the kirilidur were not complex. Falamar put his first eyestone into the summit of this Tower, purchasing it from the Orloc. The stone is said to be different from the muuren of the Smiths, but only one who stood there would know the difference it would make. An Ildaruen rune pavement spirals on the summit, notating the Ruling Dance. In later ages, Drudaen reworked the kirilidur with rune lines and crossing lines, like those Edenna Morthul used in her Tower constructions. Yruminast and the fortress of Cunevadrim have become tourist attractions in recent years, and Yruminast was completely deactivated as a magical device at the beginning of the Age of King Kirith.

Senecaur: The only Tower that was not constructed by a magician is Senecaur, the multi-colored Tower over Aerfax. The Tervan, who had participated in the building of all the Towers in one way or another, built this one themselves, because YY asked them to do it, at the time of the Law of Changes. The Tower was completed in under a decade, something of a record. Edenna Morthul faced the kirilidur with long rune-lines of Wyyvisar, chains of words that were often said together in making magic, making the kirilidur much more complex and useful that it had been previously, since it now provided quick access to long, involved magics. She could employ any portion of the kirilidur runes while she was on the summit, performing swift, complex magical constructions by virtue of the fact that the rune-lines need only be activated and not said. She would later refine this technique at Laeredon. Drudaen studied her technique here and added lines of Ildaruen runes to the Senecaur kirilidur, making it the only tower in which the two opposing languages of magic were mingled by design. The eyestone was a special one selected and more than likely fashioned by YY. The ceremonies of the Change all took place in Aerfax and Senecaur, the base of Senecaur being the old rock that was the first part of Aeryn to rise out of the ocean when YY made the world. The Tower was designed so that the Queen and King could stand on the High Place and partly rule the Tower through use of the Karnost gems. In this way the Queen or King could force a change of the magician who held Senecaur at the time of the Change, and this became traditional. There was no rune pavement at the summit and no Ruling Dance was functional there.

Laeredon: The fifth Tower to be completed was Laeredon, early in the Rule of Law. Of the Towers in operation at that time, Laeredon was the most powerful and versatile, due to the evolving concepts Edenna employed in the kirilidur, the laying of long rune lines in the stone veneer of the central shaft like those she had used in Senecaur; adding to that another innovation, crossing lines of runes in the opposite direction of the spiral, enabling even more complex chains of magic from the device. Her writings on kirilidur design were used after her by Kentha. The muuren stone was brought to Aeryn by Edenna herself, after a long journey into the mountains; the stone was said to have come from the Untherverthen, though there was never corroboration for the claim. A Wyyvisar rune pavement spirals on the summit, notating the Ruling Dance. Laeredon included a false fountain of crystal in its base, a device copied at Ellebren. Laeredon Tower may be seen today in north Aeryn/Irion, and marks the northern limit of the territory to which the Hormling have access.

Karomast: The Wyyvisar Tower in Ivyssa, built over the King's Palace, was begun by Edenna Morthul and completed by Kentha Nurysem. Kentha completed this work at the same time that she was reconstructing Yrunvurst in Montajhena, and made use of the knowledge she had gained from Edenna, especially of her design for the kirilidur. The eyestone came from the Tervan, a gift for services Kentha provided to the Empress. Karomast was never extensively used and, following Kentha's death, the rune shell was stripped from the kirilidur by Tervan workers Drudaen engaged, effectively rendering the Tower useless. When the Tower was torn down, in the Age of King Kirith, the eyestone was used in construction of the northern Tower, Choveniiz.

Thoem: The Ildaruen Tower over the Queen's Palace in Ivyssa, built by Drudaen during the Rule of Law. The eyestone came from the Tervan, purchased for an astronomical price. Drudaen used the Tower extensively to control Ivyssa, the Bay and the surrounding countryside. The Tower was torn down during the Age of King Kirith.

Goerast: The Ildaruen Tower in Montajhena, built by Drudaen during the Rule of Law. The eyestone of Goerast was of an inferior quality though Drudaen attempted to compensate for this through extensive use of gem-based devices in the horns and in the kirilidur. Kentha took the Tower from him through use of the Malei during their final battle, and he killed her. She managed to destroy Goerast before she died, and the blast that ensued destroyed Yrunvurst and most of Montajhena. It is possible that her death was also caused by unstable use of third-level power, available to her in the last moments of her life. Goerast was reconstructed in the Age of King Kirith and may be seen today.

Tower in Arroth: Drudaen began construction of a Tower in Arroth during the Rule of Law, but by then muuren stones of the size needed for a shenesoeniis were no longer to be found. The base of the Tower remained unfinished through the Long War. The base of this Tower still stands.

All of the Towers contained a pirunaen, some contained libraries, others contained other types of rooms, like the High Chambers in Ellebren or the Libraries of Ildaruen in Yruminast. Only the magicians who built or occupied the Towers knew the detailed contents of each.

Appendix 5
MAGIC

What is discussed here is the theory of magic as currently codified by the Hormling, who have studied Jisraegen (Erejhen, as we know them) magic without much success other than to record Jisraegen thinking on the subject.

The basic unit of magic is the Word, which exists in time and not in space. All words exist in this dimension alone, though they are spoken and written in space; and they change in this dimension alone, the essence of a word shifting as time passes. The Jisraegen infer from this that thought exists in time alone as well, and therefore consciousness is solely a function of time and occupies no space either.

A magic Word is more energetic than an ordinary word because it is a thought which is compressed into a smaller span of time and thus made more energetic. The magician accomplishes compression of thought through meditation and study.

The magician seeks to learn to create a smaller and smaller space in the mind in which thought takes place, and to compress thought into a smaller and smaller time span. Since one cannot truly conceive of a time without a space, and since it is possible that each word has a space component that is simply infinitely small, with none of its dimensions unfurled, the meditation necessary to this state begins as a visualization of placing the consciousness into a smaller and smaller space of the mind. This is the equivalent of saying that thought is occupying a smaller and smaller time due to the symmetries of magic which dictate that time is simply a dimension like all that rest, even if it underlies all the rest in terms of our perception. A meditation of this kind has the necessary side effect of slowing the passage of consciousness through time, meaning that time becomes more dense, packed with more thought.

The strength of magic is organized in a quantum fashion, with the magician learning more effective means of meditation to make the process of consciousness take up a smaller and smaller time (visualized as a smaller and smaller space in which the whole consciousness resides). The sizes of the thought-space-time, called the kei, do not exist in an infinite range but the kei is reduced from one level to the next in quantum descents. The energy of thought that results increases by exponential leaps from one level of magic to another. The smaller space-time into which a thought can be compressed produces a more energetic thought, which enables the magician at those levels to say-by-thinking Words of Power.

Eventually the magician may learn to create the minimum thought-space for all the various levels of magic, through the second. Mortal magicians have difficulty reaching any stage of power beyond the sixth; persons who have lifespans of hundreds of years may attain to the fourth level of power with due study; a different manner of training and learning is required beyond that, to reach the Third Circle. No one who is not of that circle knows what is needed to attain it, and, since most societies which are magic-based break down when powers begin to reach the Fourth Circle, relatively few powers are ever created and stabilized at the Third Circle from the ranks of either mortals or mortals with extended life. Nothing is known concerning progress beyond the Third Circle of Magic, where the only powers we know include eternal powers like the Diamysaar and Cunavastar, who are presumably powers of the second order. Eventually Irion attains to this level, and others develop over the long spans of time that are necessary for such a magician to evolve.

Powers of the first order would then be YY and the Other. Their powers are at such a level that they can never be fully stabilized into the scale of the universe but are continuously breaking apart in opposition to one another. Within the smallest conceivable time frames, however, the union of these powers, the All, is also continuously achieved and destabilized, thus preventing the collapse of the universe into disorganized magical vibrations.

SEVENTH LEVEL:

The manipulation of physical objects on the local level, objects in the macro, such as trees or rocks, whole structures, the manipulation may be, gradual or quick, depending on the level of the celebrant. Extensive use of this magic over time in a limited local area can result in a very strong structure of magical power, the greater in proportion to the size of the space, with a limiting factor that the consciousness of a seventh level practitioner cannot attain the minimum size for the higher levels of energetic magic.

SIXTH LEVEL:

The manipulation of physical objects over long distances, the use of simple focusing devices such as fire, circles of fire or stone; again limited to objects in the macro. For these purposes, a visible fire is considered an object in the macro. The beginning stages of meditation that focus on the space the mind makes, the kei

FIFTH LEVEL:

Manipulation of certain energies at the molecular level, including release of energy through chemical processes, though only over a limited area and in limited ways; these are complex processes which cannot be fully directed from the Fifth Circle. The manipulation of complex recording and focusing devices such as gemstones, precious metals, the construction of simple applications that can be effective over long distances; the art of singing without sound and the channeling of the body's energies and physical energies.

FOURTH LEVEL:

Manipulation of the physical world at the molecular level over great distances through use of hyper devices like the shenesoeniis, a massive storage device for magical applications that enables the magician to use master-words to trigger portions of the tower's script to come into play, enabling a scale of magic that can manipulate the world on a planetary scale. Mortal magicians throughout Jisraegen history have attained to this level and then were able to use either Wyyvisar, Ildaruen, or the Malei. Kentha Nurysem and Edenna Morthul were powers of this order. The Praeven College in Cunuduerum included four adepts of this circle at the height of its studies, before YY-Mother heard them sing the Great Breaking in their researches, and enabled Falamar to destroy them.

THIRD LEVEL:

Manipulation of atomic forces on the subgalactic level, release of energy from atomic forces; development and use of hyper devices like the lyri ship which travels from star to star on the ithikan, which forms the basis of the economies that permit the Hormling Conveyance. Only Jurel Durassa of mortals ever attained to this Circle of Power and stabilized into it; the only other Jisraegen ever to attain it, Falamar Inuygen, had no understanding of the force that he was unleashing and was destroyed by it

SECOND LEVEL:

Manipulation of space-time at a galactic scale. This is the level of attainment to which the Diamysaar were born, though certain aspects of these powers were limited after the women were exiled to Zaeyn. Cunavastar was a magician of this level as well. The Eseveren Gates are devices of the second circle.

FIRST LEVEL:

Manipulation of all forces at all distances, incomprehensible attainment. Capable of manipulation of the space-time fabric on the scale of the universe. The All. It is presumed that this level of power is unstable and would tend to split into two different forces continuously.

LIMITS ON MAGIC

The magician is limited in the ways and durations for which she or he may control living beings. To see through the eyes of an animal is intensive and can only be accomplished from Fourth Circle or higher. To see through the eyes of another person is only possible if the magician asserts control of the person. To directly control a living thing costs greatly in terms of concentration since once a magician asserts control of any organism, the control must be maintained or the creature will die. To take control by magic of the will of any living being is an irreversible process and the living thing does not survive it. To kill with magic, however, is very easy on every level.

GLOSSARY

APPLICATION: Any formal use of magic to achieve a specific end.

DANCE INTO SPIN: Any movement in space that is compressed in time, that is, more energetic and faster. At the higher levels of magic, this can be very great in velocity.

DANCE: Any movement in space with a patterned purpose. A movement is the equivalent of a Word.

DEVICE: Any object used in an application.

EYESTONE: Solid globes of muuren obtained from the Tervan used to focus the shenesoeniis; these must be periodically turned and polished and are equipped with mechanical devices to raise or lower them from the socket in the High Place. Seumren Tower is not equipped with an eyestone. The Tervan price for these stones was astronomical.

ILDARUEN: The language of the Other, the language of unmaking, which can be taught.

ITHIKAN: An application of magic which increases motion forward to the degree that the skill of the magician is able to do so. The ithikan is most often spoken of as a wave and requires an object already in acceleration relative to its surroundings.

KEI: The name of the mind space, the space of the small, in which the ruling languages are spoken.

KIRILIDUR: The central shaft of the Tower, an open cylinder, between the metal chasens the Tervan use to make the Tower structurally sound. In Seumren Tower the kirilidur is bare. In later Towers, spiraling threads of runes run from bottom to top or top to bottom of the Tower; the creation of these threads became very elaborate in the late Towers, and Ellebren Tower contains threads of Wyyvisar that read in harmony from lines in the Malei runes.

MALEI: The derived language made by the Praeven, for use in the chant. The language contains both scientific and magical properties; the Praeven learned to sing mathematics rather than to write it down.

PHYETHIR: The rule of a magician over a High Place; the consequent rule of the High Place over the surrounding land.

SHENESOENIIS: Also, **HIGH PLACE,** the raised stone platform inlaid with either Ildaruen or Wyyvisar runes. Raising the platform clear of the ground enables the magician to work with greater precision since the earth has a certain quality of magical interference inherent in it.

SPIN: An application of the ithikan to the moves of a dance, required in higher applications like the rune dance of encirclement required to attune a Tower to a magician.

WORD: Any packet of vibration produced within or impacting on the kei space.

WYYVISAR: The language of the One, the language of making, which cannot be taught.

Appendix 6

In undertaking this singular project, here at the fortieth anniversary of the meeting of the Hormling and Erejhen peoples, it is only right to record what impossibilities have been juggled and what compromises have occurred in the process. No translation out of the Erejhen High Tongue (for today we know the Jisraegen as the Erejhen, in the ebb and flow of the language) can hope to match the precision of thought possible in it. I have only attempted to tell the story of Jessex Yron as he wrote it down himself after King Kirith crossed the mountains, when that age of life in Aeryn-now-Irion was over. I have essayed to preserve what richness I could. The sounds of High Erejhen cannot be duplicated in our alphabet since the Erejhen hear better and differently than we do, and speak and sing over a different range, and so I have approximated what I can, and have supplied a glossary that translates the names and words into something which can be said that is acceptable. In spellings, I have attempted uses of our alphabet which allow for a look that is something like the grace of the older Jisraegen scripts, the doubling of vowels and the substitution of the "YY" and "ii" spellings for the long "e" sound, which parallels the practice in the days when "Kirith Kirin" was written some nine hundred years ago. Only the spelling of the name of God, analogous to the "YY" which I have chosen, remains unchanged today. The doubling of that particular vowel in archaic High Erejhen always denoted a divine connection to the concept being addressed.

To the author's clear intent in putting his own story into words, I can add only that any Erejhen child could tell you most of this story by heart, and that the author is the same person now called, liked the country, Irion, and who is said to be alive today in the north of that strange place, which has become our destiny. Soon after Yron wrote his book he retired to Inniscaudra and in general closed that part of Irion to strangers, so that a foreign traveler today might find a guide to take her as far north as Montajhena, which has been recovered, as the Erejhen put it, or to Bruinysk, or to the mound of what was once Genfynnel and the tower Laeredon that still stands. Further north no one ventures, or if she does, she simply wanders south again without realizing it, and that is the case as often as she cares to try.

No one in that country doubts that this tale is anything but history, a record of the Long War, no more than they doubt the living King Kirith descended to the low road and crossed through Tornimul after an age of peace. As the years pass and we know more and more about the people and the past of Irion, we come closer to grasping the reality that this may be a true history, and that magic may be real, at least in one place we know. We have all seen reason to be glad for that.

Jedda Martele

Béyoton, Year Standard 32334

Author's Bio

Jim Grimsley was born on September 21, 1955 in rural eastern North Carolina and was educated at the University of North Carolina at Chapel Hill, studying writing with Doris Betts and Max Steele. He has published nineteen short stories and essays in various quarterlies, including Ontario Review, New Orleans Review, Carolina Quarterly and Asimov's. His short fiction has been nominated for the Pushcart Prize on three occasions and the body of his work published in the *Carolina Quarterly* was nominated for a GE Outstanding Young Writer Award in 1983. Jim's story "City and Park" was listed as one of the outstanding short stories of 1982 in the Houghton Mifflin anthology *Best American Short Stories of 1982*.

Jim's first play, *The Existentialists*, was produced at ACME Theatre in May-June 1983. His second play, *The Earthlings*, was produced at 7Stages in January-February 1984. In 1986, Jim became Playwright-in-Residence at 7Stages and continues in that capacity to the present. His third full length play, *Mr. Universe*, was produced in the newly-renovated theatre in July-September 1987. The play went on to productions in New Orleans, Los Angeles and New York, where the New Federal Theatre's Off-Broadway production of the play drew praise from the New York Times.

The play won the George Oppenheimer/Newsday Playwriting Award for 1988, a prize which is given to the best new playwright being produced in the New York-Long Island area. Past winners include Harvey Fierstein, Beth Henley, Marsha Norman, James Lapine and George C. Wolfe. Judges included James Lapine and Edward Albee. *Mr. Universe* also won the Southeastern Playwriting Contest sponsored in 1986 by Southern Exposure, and an excerpt from the play was published in the summer 1986 edition. Another excerpt from the play was recently included in the actor's anthology Best Scenes of the 80s.

Jim was awarded the Bryan Family Prize for Drama by the Fellowship of Southern writers in 1993 for his distinguished body of work as a playwright. Judges for the Fellowship award were Romulus Linney and Horton Foote. Jim's full-length play, besides those mentioned, include *Math and Aftermath* (1988), *White People* (1989), *The Lizard of Tarsus (1990)* and *Belle Ives* (1991) all premiering at 7Stages in Atlanta. Jim's adaptation of *The Fall of the House of Usher* was presented at the Theatrical Outfit as part of the Atlanta theatre's Edgar Allen Poe Festival in February 1991 and his play *Man With a Gun* was produced by SAME in 1989.

In 1997, Jim's plays *The Decline and Fall of the Rest* and *The Borderland* were produced at 7Stages. A book of plays entitled Mr. Universe and Other Plays was published by Algonquin Books in 1998. Jim is currently writing a new play, *In Berlin*, for production in an upcoming season at 7Stages.

Jim's first novel *Winter Birds*, was published in the United States by Algonquin Books in the fall of 1994. The novel was first published in German translation in Germany in the spring of 1992, and was translated into French and published by Editions Métailié in 1994. *Winter Birds* won the Sue Kaufman Prize for best first novel from the American Academy of Arts and Letters and was a finalist for the PEN/Hemingway Award. In France, Winter Birds was awarded the Priz Charles Brisset.

Jim has subsequently published two novels in the United States, 1995's *Dream Boy*, winner of the American Library Association's Gay/Lesbian Literary Award and a finalist for the Lambda Literary Award, and *My Drowning*, released in January of 1997, for which he was named Georgia Author of the Year. His books are available in German, French, Spanish, Dutch, and Portuguese. His novel, Comfort and Joy, will be published in October 1999 by Algonquin Books; the novel was first published in Germany in 1993.

Jim is a 1997 winner of the Lila Wallace/Reader's Digest Writers Award, a three year writing fellowship in the amount of $105,000. Fellow winners included Ishmael Reed and Grace Paley.

His fiction has appeared in various anthologies, including Men on Men 6, Flesh and the Word 4, and Bending the Landscape: Science Fiction; his story in that collection, "Free in Asveroth," was selected for publication in *The Year's Best Science Fiction*, edited by Gardner Dozois.

Jim is represented by Peter Hagan. He has received support for his work from the Rockefeller Foundation, the Rockefeller/NEA Interdisciplinary Grant Program, the Georgia Council for the Arts, the Fulton County Arts Council and the City of Atlanta Bureau of Cultural Affairs. Jim teaches writing at Emory University in Atlanta and has been a featured reader at book events throughout the southeast, including readings at the 1994 and 1995 Southern Book Festivals in Nashville. He is a member of the Southeast Playwrights Project, PEN America, the Dramatists Guild, and Alternate ROOTS.

Come check out our
web site for details on these
Meisha Merlin authors!

http://www.MeishaMerlin.com

Kevin J. Anderson
Edo van Belkom
Janet Berliner
Storm Constantine
Diane Duane
Sylvia Engdahl
Jim Grimsley
George Guthridge
Keith Hartman
Beth Hilgartner
P. C. Hodgell
Tanya Huff
Janet Kagan
Caitlin R. Kiernan
Lee Killough
George R. R. Martin
Lee Martindale
Jack McDevitt
Sharon Lee & Steve Miller
James A. Moore
Adam Niswander
Andre Norton
Jody Lynn Nye
Selina Rosen
Kristine Kathryn Rusch
Michael Scott
S. P. Somtow
Allen Steele
Mark Tiedeman
Freda Warrington